# ZACH SKYE
# KNIGHTS
# APOCALYPTICA

aethonbooks.com

**KNIGHTS APOCALYPTICA**
©2024 Zach Skye

Aethon Books
www.aethonbooks.com

Print and eBook design and formatting by Josh Hayes.

Published by Aethon Books, LLC.

Aethon Books is not responsible for websites (or their content) that are not owned by the publisher.

*This book is a work of fiction. Names, characters, places, and incidents are the product of the author's imagination or are used fictitiously. Any resemblance to actual events, locales, or persons, living or dead is coincidental.*

# ALSO IN SERIES

Knights Apocalyptica

Knights Apocalyptica 2

Check out the entire series here! (Tap or scan)

# CHAPTER 1
## A DREAM

Deep under tons of dirt and rock rested a bulky suit of rusted Armor. A steel rack supported its considerable weight, and orange LEDs lighted the entire workstation. Erec ran his hand along the frame of the Armor and shook his head. The lanky eighteen-year-old had checked it with a critical eye for the last couple of hours.

But as much as he'd done, examining and repairing it, the damn thing had about a hundred dents, tears, and loose wires hanging from joints and missing bits of the plate. The Armor needed a lot of love and care for it even to function. But then again, it was bottom-of-the-barrel provisional loaner Armor.

Erec hadn't expected anything from it. As long as it hung together over the next couple of days, he didn't need to care anymore about it.

Passing the trial and being accepted into the Academy? That's all that mattered.

"Oof, busted again?" Garin said after the steel slabs at the entry to the workshop slid open, carrying a cloth bag over his shoulder.

Being so deep in the Kingdom and miles under the surface had a very claustrophobic effect, especially after tucking oneself in a workshop all day. But it would all be worth it. This effort would bear fruit once he and Garin could stand underneath the sun and sky far above, no longer trapped below in this grease-stained room. Or any of the other caverns. He gave his friend an easy smile and ran a hand through his hair.

"I might've been a little too hard on it," Erec admitted.

He couldn't afford to fail the trial. Not when his brother had succeeded. Not when the course of his entire life depended on it. Training with Armor like this was out of his grasp for the longest time —but Bedwyr passed his trial under similar circumstances. One might even argue that the Armor loaned to Bedwyr was *worse*. No, Erec would surpass Bedwyr. He had to. This was his one shot.

With the Goddess's Blessing and this ragtag Armor, Erec would climb out from the caves and the shadow of his family's legacy to join one of the Orders. Erec treasured the couple of memories of his time on the surface. Hundreds of thousands lived their whole lives without seeing the sky. Yet, at first sight, that ocean of blue stole his heart away.

Humanity had crawled its way out of this hole fifty years ago, but the privilege of living on the surface had a price paid in blood. And he was ready to help defend the thick steel walls that kept the monsters of the wastes at bay. They protected this Kingdom, but more importantly, they made it possible to bask in the sun once more. And from there, he could find *her*.

*If only I had better Armor. More training.* Getting into the Academy would've been easy if he were in the upper crust of the nobility. But his House had all of their privileges and authority stripped away. To most, they could barely be considered a noble House at this point.

"I could ask Dad if we've got a spare mechanic," Garin offered. His father, Baron Jeswald, directly oversaw Erec's House. Through Jeswald's shelter, House Audentia had weathered the last ten years. Erec would sooner throw himself through a Rift than ask anything more from the man.

"No thanks, but I appreciate the offer. It's better learning to keep this thing running myself. I doubt we'll have anyone to help in the Trial."

"Fair, fair. I'd thought I was pushing it lately, but you've gone off the deep end, haven't you? Why?"

"You know why." Erec rubbed the back of his neck.

A twinkle came to Garin's eye, and he smirked. "I sure do. So how about this…" He dropped his bag onto the ground and pulled out two sticks made of maple. Erec worked his jaw. Yeah. Those were definitely from one of the bio-caverns. Erec was familiar with the exact cavern it came from since he'd helped maintain it over the last two years. A beautiful bio-cavern that supported beech, maple, and apple trees, it was also filled with an assortment of other life that thrived in the temperate conditions, including squirrels. Too many squirrels, to be honest.

More importantly, nothing should've come out of those caverns unaccounted for.

"Garin!"

"Yeah, yeah, I knew you'd do this. It's fine. Dad wouldn't care. C'mon, Erec, they're just sticks."

The point wasn't what they were. Even if the Baron would only shrug if someone told him his son was going around taking small things from his bio-caverns. Documenting what went in and out of those controlled environments was vital. They couldn't afford to introduce an invasive species or transmit some odd virus to the bio-caverns. Too much of their industry and supply lines still relied on them.

They still produced hard-to-obtain food and commodities, and Erec highly doubted his friend put in the care to sanitize and respect nature. It was shortsighted and completely unnecessary, but more than anything else a blatant abuse of privilege. Erec stared him down until Garin caved.

"Fine, I won't do it again, promise. But since I already took these, how about we trade some pointers?" Garin gave an easy grin that complemented his dumb face and promised pure intentions.

Erec dropped it, he knew full well Garin wouldn't listen anyway, and it wouldn't change what'd already happened.

They'd make for good sparring tools—and Erec was pleased they weren't shaped like swords. Practically everything was. Go figure that when the Goddess icon was a sword, Her people went nuts over them. But the importance of swords alone was disturbing. Their only purpose was to kill. Any day of the week, he'd instead take an axe or a hammer, but often the Kingdom left him with no choice in terms of practice equipment.

"You know what? I could go for a nice little confidence boost. I'd love to show you the concrete." Erec stretched out his lean muscles.

He was about three inches taller and often quicker than his friend. But he lacked the substance that Garin had. Lanky versus robust. Their typical sparring match was a toss-up, but something in Garin's eyes told him this wasn't just for fun.

"In your dreams, Lord *Audentia*," Garin mocked, giving a small bow. Erec snorted. His brother and father were *Lord Audentia*. Not him.

Erec and Garin walked a safe distance from the Armor and tables filled with welders and screwdrivers. The dusty workshop would serve as well as any for their fight; all they needed to do was limit the arena to keep from breaking things.

With a boundary for their fight quickly agreed on, the two of them took stances on either side of the workshop.

Erec fell into a broad stance and stared Garin down while he swayed back and forth; he knew the ins and outs of Garin's style. However, that was a double-edged weapon. Garin knew his too. Predictably, Garin launched straight into the fight and teased the edge of Erec's range with the maple stick. He ducked in and tried to bait a swing, but Erec waited. It was best to find an opportunity and strike with a solid decisive attack.

In a sudden flurry of speed, Garin committed to a straightforward stab. Unexpected. Erec slid out of the way, but since he failed to anticipate the bold move, there wasn't any way to punish the aggression. Garin shoved forward and slammed a stocky shoulder into him. With his chance made and Erec on unsteady ground, Garin raised his weapon above his head to land a clean hit.

Erec backpedaled and raised his stick to catch Garin's downward arc. He blocked the follow-up and then used his superior speed to put more distance between them and reset.

*More aggressive than usual.* Most of the time Garin focused on technical and measured fighting, taking advantage of his refined sword work.

Garin circled as he searched for another opening to swoop in, but Erec wasn't about to give him another chance after seeing his first move. A sudden juke of his friend made him wince. His side ached—that shove was full force. This sort of cheap tactic and frantic fighting wasn't Garin's usual style. But then, this wasn't a spar, was it? It was a test. *Which of us is better?* Despite the differences in their Virtues, for the most part, they were evenly matched.

*I can surprise you too.* Erec flew at Garin and rained down blows in a flurry of strikes. Each bit of range he had over Garin let him control the engagement. His speed and sudden shift from wary tactics to a violent barrage caught his friend by surprise. Garin backed up further and rapidly approached their fight's boundary.

The constant hammering of sticks brought sweat to Erec's brow. But he saw Garin grimace with each strike—Garin's arm shook, and his stick grew lower as his strength gave out. Soon the occasional whack landed on his arm, bruising it and further weakening the defense. *I'm going to win. This fight is mine.*

Like tilling a patch of dirt before planting, all that effort went into preparing the soil and creating the right conditions for optimal growth. Instead of sowing a seed, he readied the battlefield for the perfect moment.

*There.*

Garin's sweat matted his long black hair, covering his eyes. He shook his head to clear his vision. Erec sprang forward, double-handing the stick high into the air. He swung in a mighty arc and threw as much force as he could behind it—Garin tried to defend, but it was a second too late—the weapon cracked against Garin's skull, tearing into his skin and provoking a pained yell.

Erec dropped the stick—swearing and crouching down to look at the damage. The fight had pulled it out of him and made him go too far. He'd wanted to win so badly, for a moment he forgot who he was fighting.

Garin clutched his head and accepted a piece of cloth to stem the blood. It was a nasty gash but non-vital. "Fuck. Where did that come from? I know you were angry at me for stealing from the bio-cavern, but did you have to bash my head in?"

"I'm so sorry, I didn't—"

Garin laughed at Erec's red face. "No, no. I know I started it. It's just—I wanted to know? How it'd end if we both gave it our all. Whenever we practice, there's never that edge to it like they say a real fight has. If we're going to do well at the Academy and become Knights worth anything, that's a feeling we have to get used to."

There was a blinking dot in the corner of Erec's vision from his Blessing. He slowly nodded at his friend's words but couldn't tear his attention from the notification. Garin squinted at him.

"No way. You advanced?"

"Don't know for sure yet—is it okay if I—"

"No, no! Don't even ask! Open it! Tell me what jumped up!" Garin grinned at him, still holding the bloody cloth to his forehead. Erec only hoped Garin's father wouldn't get too upset. The trial to join the Academy was a highly formal affair. As Garin was from a family with some renown, those impressions on their future classmates and the other families attending the trial mattered in his circles.

*At least that's something I don't have to care about. Seems exhausting.*

Erec pulled up the notification from the Blessing.

**Strength Advancement: Rank E - Tier 4 → Rank E - Tier 5**

It was an advancement. The last one he'd had was three weeks ago. And that hadn't been to one of his higher-ranked Virtues. Erec beamed, and Garin arched an eyebrow.

"It was Strength—Tier 5 now."

"Damn, congratulations." Garin nodded, then sighed. "I haven't gotten an advancement for Vigor this month, even with all of the conditioning and training. Sure, Cognition went up, even Agility, but no luck on the one I wanted most."

Vigor was Garin's top Virtue. The one he'd inclined himself to and pushed further than the others, citing that it gave him the biggest advantage both on the battlefield and in his life, and that superior endurance often made a big difference when they went multiple rounds. Erec was thankful it hadn't managed to climb any higher—or that trick he'd pulled with the unrelenting assault wouldn't have had a chance of breaking through his defenses. That and keeping up with Garin during training was already a pain in his ass.

Erec stared at the junk Armor and found the prospect of the future work a heavy suppressant to the little bit of glee he felt at the advancement. "I should get started with that…"

"Yeah, yeah," Garin waved it off, still clutching the bloody cloth. "I'm going to take a hot bath and nurse the wound you left me. Congratulations again; I'm taking the rest of the night off."

Garin gave one last wave before walking out of the steel doors and leaving Erec alone with the Armor. He stared at the little-better-than-scrap metal.

"No time like the present." He grabbed a screwdriver, tossed on his goggles, then got to work.

# CHAPTER 2
# GLIMPSE OF HEAVEN

*Those who solely by good fortune become princes from being private citizens have little trouble in rising, but much in keeping atop; they have not any difficulties on the way up, because they fly, but they have many when they reach the summit. Such are those to whom some state is given either for money or by the favour of him who bestows it; as happened to many in Greece, in the cities of Ionia and of the Hellespont, where princes were made by Darius, in order that they might hold the cities both for his security and his glory; as also were those emperors who, by the corruption of the soldiers, from being citizens came to empire.*

*Such stand simply elevated upon the goodwill and the fortune of him who has elevated them—two most inconstant and unstable things. Neither have they the knowledge requisite for the position; because, unless they are men of great worth and ability, it is not reasonable to expect that they should know how to command, having always lived in a private condition; besides, they cannot hold it because they have not forces which they can keep friendly and faithful.*

*- Niccolò Machiavelli,* The Prince *(1532, 2nd Era)*

&lt;MARKOS II ACTIVATION PROTOCOL INITIALIZED&gt;

E rec stood still beneath the rusted plates of the bulky Armor and waited for all of the core systems and subsystems to boot up. It took a good minute for everything to come online—given the make of the model and the substantial repairs, he was just happy the Armor was working.

<LIFE SUPPORT SUBSYSTEM CHECK—ERROR: OXYGEN INPUT NOT DETECTED. ERROR: MEDICAL SUBSYSTEM MALFUNCTIONING...>

He dismissed all of the notifications flashing through the visual interface. From the day he'd borrowed the outdated Armor, those systems hadn't been present or had been previously corrupted. Given these types of models received software updates and no hardware upgrades, it was impossible to say what should've still been functional or not. The software might be searching for subsystems that never existed in the first place.

Caring about any of that was an exercise in futility; this Armor already lived on borrowed time. As soon as he got into an Order, they'd issue him an Initiate's model to work with—it wouldn't be top-of-the-line, but it'd be a far sight better than this hunk of junk.

*If I'm good enough for an Order to extend an offer to begin with...*

<INITIALIZATION COMPLETE>

There was a small chime like a bell in his helmet to accompany the last notification, and the joints unlocked.

He clenched his fingers in the heavy steel gauntlet. The servos worked well. He held his fist for a moment more and sighed before exiting the workshop. Only a couple of hours of sleep, but he did what he'd had to.

Walking through the underground pathways was reasonably straightforward; the Kingdom tried its best to lay it out in the most logical way. At least on these levels. And heading to the main shaft elevator was simple—considering the large construct was smack-dab in the middle of the city.

Erec ran into Garin at the base of the giant steel beams: a gated entrance to the room-sized shaft elevator. Garin gave a bit of a wave, his Armor's helmet tucked beneath a steel arm. His friend was wearing his father's suit—complete with the House Honestus eagle painted on the chest plate. "Hey!" Garin smirked.

"Heya." Erec's voice came from the modulated filter of the helmet. Unlike Garin, he didn't dare to detach the helmet for fear that the locking joint might malfunction when he tried to replace it.

"Glad you got it working after all. I was half scared I wouldn't see you. Cut it close to show time, huh?"

"Well, I tried to get a few more minutes of sleep. Was up late last night. But I'm here now, so I can't complain." He shrugged, the gesture completely within the death trap Armor. It didn't flow like newer models, unfortunately, and some movements were jerky.

<WARNING: CONNECTION MALFUNCTION WITH COOLING UNIT. OPENING VENTS TO COMPENSATE. WARNING: EXPOSURE TO OUTSIDE AIR WITHOUT FILTER...>

Erec sighed. It was going to be a long, hot, and uncomfortable day now. The vent ports in the back of the suit were open, letting a bit of fresh air in. A bead of sweat was starting to form on the tip of his nose. Relying on mechanical vents absolutely blew. *I hate this Armor so damn much.*

The gears in his head began to go into overdrive as the main shaft elevator rose. It stopped on their level, and the chain-link shutters slid open. Erec and Garin got on the massive platform and moved toward the back. It rose and stopped at nearly every floor—allowing workers to clamber on and off to their destinations.

Everybody in the Kingdom knew what today was, commoners to nobility, even though these trials were primarily composed of people of noble blood. The day was practically a holiday, as everyone looked up to the Knights—the saviors of humanity.

Though the potential Initiates took up an increasing portion of the elevator, most came alone. Their families and retainers would head to the event in an hour or two. But the would-be Initiates were expected far earlier.

A few stops later and the elevator floor became overwhelmed with nobility, displacing the poor workers. They continued to pour on at every floor. The truly greedy demanded their servants carry equipment for them. The closer they got to the top, the more sets of Armor joined their ranks, which was unsurprising. Most of the high-rankers lived near the surface.

The last batch contained the elite, or rather, the elite of those still living somewhat underground. Most had moved to the blooming city above, but there was a mix. Tradition and holdings kept some of the more prestigious families close to the top levels of the Kingdom.

He took in the variety of people on the elevator. One of them was hauling stones to a higher cavern. It was hard to tell whether they were minerals or needed further processing for a project. The man had parked there before Erec and Garin even got on the lift, meaning he came from a much lower cavern. It wasn't an easy job for the commoners, often back-breaking with long hours and a strict timetable. And the nobles were screwing that up by crowding the elevator.

"Move," a stern voice commanded from a smooth blue Armor with a diamond-shaped helmet.

Erec turned his head to see that the new figure was glaring at the poor worker with his barrel full of stones. Two pinpricks of emerald light locked onto the man through the helmet's visor, eerily like eyes.

"Are you deaf?" Diamond Head asked as the confused commoner didn't budge. "I don't want any of your sweat getting on my paint job." That voice and those demands combined with the heat of the day were really starting to piss Erec off. How could he treat the poor man like that? Especially with how long he must've already been standing there, as all the Initiate hopefuls clogged up the elevator system.

"Leave the guy alone," Erec called out, stepping between the two.

"You have no right to issue me commands, rust-bucket."

"Oh yeah? Well, maybe if you'd take a second and get off that throne of yours, you'd realize that just because you were born with a gold spoon in your mouth, it doesn't make you better than anyone else. Leave the poor guy be; he was here first."

The prick growled and then stepped in. Without warning, Diamond Head shoved Erec and took a step toward the commoner.

There was a moment of horror at the surprising amount of force behind the blow. Erec wheeled his hands as the railing hit his back, damn near tumbling over it. Garin rushed over and helped Erec regain his footing while the worker took one look before running off. Obviously, he didn't want to deal with any of this, as he was just doing his job.

Diamond Head slid into the spot he'd demanded and turned away as if nothing had happened.

"Who do you think you are?!" Erec shouted. The conversations around them slowed or cut off as people looked on.

The noble slowly turned to face him—one hand raised to his face and tapped the side of the helmet. In a flash, the metal visor melted away and revealed a youthful, far-too-fair face with curly black locks. "I am Colin Nitidus of House Nitidus, firstborn son to Duke Nitidus." His voice rang smoothly, no longer muffled by the heavy equipment and vocalizers. "Do you still have a voice to raise complaint to me, rust-bucket?"

"Yeah, I do. That's no way to treat other people. You can't demand things and shove people around however you want." Erec felt a fire ignite in his chest at this spoiled brat.

"Oh?" Colin frowned, his eyebrows furrowed but with an undercurrent of amusement. "And who are you to tell me what I can and can't do? With Armor like that, I had assumed you were another commoner. They usually only loan out junkers like that to commoners with a sponsor, but something in your attitude tells me you're not what I thought. They know when to be quiet."

There was now muttering going around as people formed a circle to watch. Most would consider it a grave error to pick a fight with a Duke's son—but Erec didn't have much to lose. Nor did he particularly want to let this arrogant noble get his way, like usual.

"What noble's crotch you fell out of doesn't change a thing. Do not treat people like that." Erec stepped closer; for a moment, it looked as if Colin genuinely didn't know how to respond.

The cocky smile returned to Colin's lips a moment later. "I treat people how I wish, as befits my station. If you aren't a commoner, what family do you hail from?"

It was dangerous territory to throw his House in the crosshairs of someone so high-ranked, but Erec had passed by any form of logical thought. *I want to punch him.* So, he didn't respond. The servos in his fist whirled as his fingers clenched into a fist; a warning flooded the visual display, informing him that the digit servos were under heavy strain and liable for malfunction.

"Whoa, whoa, cool down there." Garin stepped in between them and bowed his head to Colin. "Sorry things got this far, sir. He's just a little heated under that Armor. Air coolant malfunctions; you can imagine how it is on a day like today—"

"His House. Which House does he hail from?" Colin tilted his head.

"House Audentia." Erec fought to shove his friend aside as he spoke. But Garin refused to budge; moving his hale friend was easier said than done.

"Ah, a traitor's House. I'd thought they were dissolved. Oh well." Colin shrugged and turned away. As if he'd lost interest in the situation. His finger tapped the side of his head, and the helmet visor slid back into place.

*Oh no, you don't. You don't get to shove me and just—*

The elevator jerked to a stop. Above the great steel vault, shutters began to part. Almost three feet thick, they'd long served as the first line of defense for humanity against the harsh world. Now the heavy steel doors slowly vanished into the sides of the shaft, letting sunlight spill down. The sight of the blue sky above stunned Erec. He gave up struggling against his friend and caring about the jackass as the elevator moved again, taking them to the surface.

Everywhere around the clearing were buildings made of white stucco and concrete.

A fountain sat not too far away—a statue dedicated to Queen Lothria sat in the center. She raised a sword to the heavens. Erec's jaw dropped, and the anger that had welled up in him vanished in the light of the beauty of this city. It was unlike the narrow winding corridors and carved sides of the cavern. The ground was inlaid with brickwork; clumps of green foliage grew haphazardly in conjunction with the city. A clear contrast to the lack of vegetation down below: it felt almost wrong to see people move freely with nature. Men and women milled about, some laborers, but most in rather fine clothing.

"Attention!" A loud voice boomed out and cut through the distraction of people exiting the elevator and the open world. "All would-be Initiates, form lines!"

The nobles scrambled off the elevator; Erec turned to the voice, confused and surprised. He belatedly moved to the man, trying to find a place the lines would form, but everywhere was chaos, nobles bumping into each other and Armor clanging. Garin yanked him by the arm, which triggered another warning courtesy of the Markos II Armor. But his friend had the right of it and dragged him to where people were slowly amassing. In a minute, everyone was in the formation of two precise lines, spaced five feet apart.

He watched the few unlucky workers trapped in the elevator with this mess; as soon as the way was clear, they scrambled off to do their jobs.

More shouting came from what must've been a voice amplified by an Armor. "Right face!"

About forty percent of those assembled did a heel turn to their right. Erec, of course, moved the best he could. He knew the command, but adjusting to the sudden demand caused a lag. Still, he managed to obey quicker than those that hadn't been training.

"Never before have I seen such a disgraceful right-face. May the Goddess have mercy on us all! This trial is bound to be a slaughter." Finally, Erec made out the guy giving commands; he had a bulky Armor model with large pauldrons with a massive two-handed sword slung over the back. What he didn't have was hair. Without his helmet, the sun reflected off the guy's scalp and was damn near blinding. But... *By the Goddess, that loud voice isn't from some amplification. He can just yell that loud.* Erec's jaw dropped in horror.

"Quit gawking. You all look like Sand Geckos with your bewildered postures and open mouths. Forward march!"

# CHAPTER 3
# TRIAL

The fearsome bald man led the would-be Initiates to their fate. Following his instructions, they reached cleared ground on the city outskirts. All it took was a grueling march and a barrage of yelling and screaming from their conductor to get there. After that, they received time to socialize.

Erec idly watched the instructors running past—men and women in their full Knight Armor. A few wore Armor models classic to the different Orders, while some owned personalized sets. Either they'd earned enough money, were from a wealthy family, or had attained a high rank for a custom model. The vast array was staggering. Given a chance, he'd have loved to take a peek into them and see how they functioned.

The sheer variety was incredible: from the angled pauldrons to the slick steel-weave on lighter models. Their formation, modular bulk, and plating depended on the users' Vigor, Strength, or Agility. Some even contained rare components to enhance their spells or prayer. Each Armor was a perfect complement to its Knight's unique Virtues.

These modern marvels allowed man to rival the monsters creeping into the world. Before humankind's struggle to maintain itself, it'd been able to grow strong enough to protect their own. But now? Now it could thrive and start to reclaim the Earth.

Erec watched a man with a typical sword and shield walk by—an Initiate, judging by the rank insignia on the Armor's shoulder. There was a white tower amid a blue backdrop on his chest, signifying the Order of the Azure Tower.

*That's going to be me.* It didn't matter much to him which Order he got into; any would do, aside from the Silver Flames. He wouldn't forgive them for the role they'd played in his mother's exile.

He took a deep, steadying breath. Already some noble families were arriving early and being greeted in the Academy proper.

It sounded like a grand time for them—lavish meals, and then spells that would give them a front row seat to the action. At the end of the trial, the would-be Initiates were to walk into the main hall and have their offers presented to them.

But what was the trial going to be? There'd been grand melees, tournaments, and exams in the past. Every year they shifted the design of the test to meet whatever invisible demands they'd been facing. It was a notorious sour point for the nobles, since they were left to prepare their children for anything.

Most of them, anyway. Erec took a long look at the Duke's son. *I guarantee he knows what sort of trial this will be.*

Not that it did him any good to dwell on that. Erec pulled up his Blessing one more time, partly out of paranoia and partly to keep himself busy.

**Name: Erec of House Audentia**
**Health: 100%  |  Mana: 100%  |  Stamina: 100%**

**Holy Virtues:**
**Strength: [Rank E]  |  [Tier 5]**
**Vigor: [Rank F]  |  [Tier 7]**
**Agility: [Rank F]  |  [Tier 9]**
**Perception: [Rank E]  |  [Tier 1]**
**Cognition: [Rank E]  |  [Tier 3]**
**Psyche: [Rank F]  |  [Tier 6]**
**Mysticism: [Rank F]  |  [Tier 1]**
**Faith: [Rank F]  |  [Tier 1]**

His Strength was his highest, by far, with two other Virtues in the E rank. Not a bad distribution, considering there wasn't a chance in hell he'd rank up Mysticism or Faith. They were the basis of spells and prayers and required specific instruction or ungodly intuition to advance. Erec had neither the time nor desire to pursue them.

That was fine; plenty of Knights made their careers without focusing on those Virtues. No one Knight could be a master of them all.

Erec felt another line of sweat running down his brow. Both exhaustion and the heat were starting to affect him. *Ignore it. You'll be fine.*

The rest of the nobles gathered around into small clusters to talk; even Garin had wandered off to introduce himself to new people, which wasn't surprising. Erec chose to stay in place, content with his privacy and alone time. It was better to save all of his energy for the upcoming trial than waste it frivolously dealing with nobles who'd either dismiss him out of hand or avoid him due to his family's stigma.

"Lines!" That same gravelly yell ran across the yard after some time. Everyone scrambled to get back into position. In the rush of people, Erec lost sight of Garin. Oh well. They formed dual lines again as glowing orbs circled them. Those were the "lens" for the spell transmitting the image to the hall. Rings of magic appeared by the speaker's head—it seemed this time they'd use magic to amplify their voice for the audience.

"Lords and Ladies, on this May of the 307th Year of the Goddess's Rebirth, we shall begin our Academy's prestigious annual trial! You might recall the endurance test of last year—which left our students balanced on little pillars of land for hours at a time, only to progress to a game of flag capturing between the remaining would-be Knights. What a spectacle that was! This year we have the blessing of some truly distinguished nobility seeking our ranks. Three from the Duchy, and to this Academy's great honor, a Prince from the Royal Family!"

He hadn't heard of the Royal Family admitting a son. Nor was it apparent who it might be. Everyone had their faces hidden with the Armor.

Not that Erec knew what the Princes looked like, even if one was around his age.

"A truly distinguished gathering of talent for the Knights to choose from—to meet that and test the capabilities of these individuals, we shall be having a rare sort of trial. This trial will take several days and provide a much better measure of their real-world skills and strengths. Those hosted by the Academy will be provided with proper accommodation during this event. We apologize for any unexpected inconvenience, but this year's trial will not be possible for remote viewing."

*Now that's shocking.* Erec pictured all the nobles tucked away in the Academy starting to complain and demand compensation. Each year it had been a point of pride for the Academy to make a spectacle of their admissions exam. He felt a flutter of nerves. *Is my Armor going to hold up that long?* With the last trial having an endurance test portion, he'd hoped that they would prioritize a different sort of Virtue this time around.

"This trial is unlike any before. Far more practical. The would-be Knights will be divided into groups and sent past the wall with an accompanying Knight Commander. Each is tasked with retrieving something of value, slaying creatures, or overall displaying their survival aptitude over the course of the trial. The Commander will take notes of their actions and judge them throughout their time outside of the wall. Would-be Initiates will be judged on their capacity to operate in a real-world scenario." There was a long pause as the whispering ran unconstrained in the crowd of nobles.

The test administrator shot the group a cold glare to silence them.

In a second the rings above his head vanished, and he addressed the crowd with his normal voice. "Now, do understand, this is a dangerous trial. Unpredictable things can occur outside of the walls, but to be a Knight is to embrace courage and danger no matter what Order you may join. Any not up to this task are not fit to be a Knight. Any that wish to withdraw, now's the time to do so."

There was a heavy silence; no one wanted to be the first to admit they didn't have it in them. Erec stood straighter. *No matter what, I'm doing this. For me, there isn't a second option. There's no House I can retire to and work within. I will be a Knight and surpass Bedwyr if it's the last thing I do.*

The pressure mounted, and eventually, a single person broke rank. They skulked out with a lowered head and quickly retreated from the gathering. Then another. And then three at once. Erec couldn't help but note that most of the people who left appeared to be in hand-me-down Armor like himself. Not all, but most. *A smart move. Going in untrustworthy Armor is bad. But I don't have any other choice.*

A stretch of three more minutes passed as those that gave up left. Everyone took in those with enough courage to stay before returning their attention to the test administrator. The man looked over the remainder of the would-be Initiates with a grin. "To the bold does the world bend." The magic rings once more formed above his head to activate the voice amplification spell. "We have our contenders for this year's trial! Everyone remain in place, and my coordinators will begin dividing you."

The next few moments were a rush of activity as Knights stepped forward and broke off in groups of five from the overall gathering. Erec felt lucky when one yanked him aside and set him in a group with Garin and another. Then less so when that pompous asshole Colin joined their group. *Why, Goddess?*

She conveniently chose not to answer his question, though he considered himself lucky that the Duke's son seemed uninterested in conversing. After learning their positions, he'd outright dismissed both Erec and Garin as being unworthy of his time and attention. Erec wasn't sure if it pissed him off or left him relieved to be ignored.

However, as another person joined, it became apparent that Colin was familiar with them.

Colin snorted under his helmet. "I'd recognize that House symbol anywhere. Lady Lyotte of House Luculentus, still having that petty argument with your father?"

"Colin," she responded with a curt and icy tone.

Garin looked between them—almost comical with how his head swayed. "Uh?" Erec asked, elbowing his friend.

"Erec, we're in a group with a daughter and son of two different ducal lines. Holy shit. What in the name of the Goddess is going on?"

A fifth member joined the group in a set of Armor even more beat-up than Erec's—it was missing plating on the back, which left exposed wires sparking. *Oh. That's what they're doing…*

# CHAPTER 4
# TWIN STARS

*…Rifts have a variable degree of stability. Of the three investigated in this study, one remained in a permanent state of activity, while the other two fluctuated between unstable and stable states in a seemingly random pattern. At first glance, this seeming state of randomness could be a result of the nature of the Rifts themselves. However, thanks to Knight Protector Exercitus and her courageous preliminary scouting of the other side of the inordinately stable Rift, we may note that Dame Exercitus observed several key similarities to the environment in which the Rift was discovered…*

*- Julia Imaginosus,* On the Nature of Rifts *(238, 3rd Era)*

Noble Houses all drank from the same cup of poison known as pride. It led to a belief in superiority and obsession with status. In the best, it led to making choices based on their names and titles. The weight of this ego weighed on those below, even if the nobles had benevolent intentions.

*We're here to make them look good.* It made sense. Stick two well-trained and privileged high nobility into a group with an average Initiate and two using loaner Armors?

It provided enough of a variance to make it seem plausibly random, yet gave space for the two wearing cutting-edge Armors. No doubt they'd also had countless hours of high-quality training to shine brighter.

It might've made sense to add a third sub-par Armor user to the group instead of Garin, but Erec figured to really make the two Duchy-spawn shine they wanted the examiner to have a baseline to compare against. Or maybe to mitigate any complaints after the fact in order to add a little bit of deniability for rigging a trial.

*How disappointing.* Erec clenched his hand.

<WARNING: DIGIT SERVOS UNDER HEAVY STRAIN.
CONTINUED STRAIN MAY LEAD TO MALFUNCTION AND
CRITICAL FAILURE POINT.>

He'd have to try to fix that in the field. Twice on the same day the warning had appeared. If he got in a fight and the servos gave out, that might spell real trouble.

He let it go and sighed. *This is fine, it's fine. Don't let it get in your head.* Erec didn't need to impress the higher nobility; he didn't care what they thought. The only thing that mattered by the end of this trial was what their examiner thought. And by proxy, what the Orders thought of his potential.

The political games were unimportant. Garin twisted to look at Erec, disengaging his helmet to show a big smile on his face. "Holy shit, we're in the same group as a future Duke and Duchess! Do you know how insane that is?"

"Why are you getting so worked up?" Erec snapped.

"W-what do you mean? This is a great chance to make some good connections. Not every day do you get to be on even footing with members of the Duchy."

"Garin, we're here to make them look good, I doubt they care much at all about us. Or even that you might have enough time to even make a meaningful connection with them."

The grin slipped a bit on his friend's face.

"Well, yeah, I think you'd be surprised by how much of an impact you can make with very little…"

"I'm more concerned about this exam. And no matter what, since we're in the same group we're going to be compared directly to those two. Besides, do you really want to be friends with Colin? I've already seen enough of the guy for a lifetime." Garin went silent and placed his helmet back on his head to block his face. His friend turned away.

*I hate doing that to him.* But sometimes Garin needed a reality check; this entire trial was a competition. How you did mattered when compared to others. The only catch was that you couldn't get too hung up on it and hesitate, since that'd end with failure. His mother had often told him about self-fulfilling prophecy. You had to believe that you would succeed, but it cut both ways; your mind could sabotage you and cause a cascade effect of failure.

Garin continued to stare ahead, in a deflated way. Erec knew he had to say something to lift the mood again. This was what they'd worked to do for so long.

"We'll show them that we're worthy. Both of us, together. We'll get into the Academy," Erec vowed to Garin, giving a quick shake on his friend's shoulder, which was hard to do with him in that sturdy set of Armor. Garin didn't respond, but his posture changed, sinking into an eased position.

For a long moment, they stood quiet as a group. Lyotte refused to meet Colin's pointless attempts to engage her in conversation, and the newest member of their five was content to keep quiet. No doubt the anticipation and awkward rank differentials present in the group got everyone's nerves frayed.

The boy in the worst Armor was too busy trying to tweak it. Which seemed like a good plan in theory, but Erec didn't want to risk setting off some malfunction in his before they got to move, especially with his finger servos acting up.

After the rest of the groups were put together, a solitary, higher-ranked Knight made his way toward Erec's group. His rank was above what the announcer had declared for their examiners. Erec's jaw dropped as he took in the solitary tree crest of the Verdant Oak, along with the symbol below for a Master Knight. The customized Armor had a series of exhaust pipes sticking out of deep green pauldrons. The helmet was gone, exposing the wild, thick beard of the man beneath. He looked less like a noble Knight and more like a homeless man who'd stolen a suit of pristine Armor.

"Attention." His voice carried softly through the air, but nobody in the group missed the command. This time, knowing what to do, Erec scampered into their makeshift line.

Once they faced their test administrator, the Knight cleared his throat.

"Alright, alright. This is fine enough. I'm not one to repeat myself, so listen closely. I'm Sir Boldwick. I've been a part of this Order for nigh on fifteen years, and I've lost a lot of friends outside these walls. Frankly, I find this test a gross disrespect to their memory, but it is what it is. As such, I'm setting some ground rules. One. If I give you an order, you cease what you're doing and follow that order. Two. You keep your damn ears trained on me at all times. Three. There's no such thing as a hero, only corpses and survivors; best you don't forget that." Despite that grim statement, Boldwick concluded his speech with a smile.

"Uh, sir. There are heroes." Colin spoke up and puffed up his chest. "Dame Suzeth, who dove into the Render Rift to buy the priests time—"

"Corpse," Boldwick replied with a sigh. "She never came out. No way she survived in whatever world those beasts came from."

"What about Sir Gallen? He went out and rescued those kids that slipped the gate and then fended off a cyclops on his own to protect them," Lyotte said.

"Ah yes, Sir Gallen. He went on to extort the merchant families of those children for his 'heroics' and led to them having to sell their assets. A month later, they returned to living underground as paupers. Yeah. He's a real hero." Boldwick snorted.

"I see nothing wrong with him demanding fair compensation for services rendered," Colin said, this time stomping a foot at their instructor's blasé attitude.

"A hero is someone who acts off altruism. Supposedly. Naturally, such a thing doesn't exist very long, kids. So quit putting people on pedestals when they don't deserve it. It doesn't do you any good and doesn't do them any good either. Besides, that silly idea is deadly. Seen enough naive Initiates get that romantic thought in their head and end up as another corpse. Your potential and your family don't matter when your heart stops beating."

At that, finally, Colin had no reply. The Duke's son shut up and stood with a too-straight back and stared ahead. Sir Boldwick rubbed the back of his head and sighed.

"Now, where was I? Ah, yeah, we'll be heading out. You'll have to forage for supplies. We won't be heading out more than twenty miles from the walls. There'll be plenty of places to scavenge and some small fry to take on, probably." He looked between them all. "Any questions?"

Erec slowly raised his hand. Despite the distraction of the two spoiled nobles, he couldn't help but take in the constant fidgeting of the boy in the barely-functioning Armor.

Boldwick tilted his head and gave a slight smirk. "Oh, you raised your hand. Fair enough, go ahead and ask. For future reference, though—I don't care about that sorta thing; you got a question, ask."

"Er—right, uh, are we going to be given any provisions before we head out of the gate? Like camping supplies, rations, or repair kits…"

Sir Boldwick laughed and shook his head, a tear coming to the corner of his eye. "Oh, by the Goddess, no. Even though it'd make perfect sense for a team of Knights to leave the walls supplied to the teeth, the administrators, in their infinite wisdom, thought it wouldn't be enough of a challenge. You'll get a water flask, anything you have on you, and that's about it. But it's not like we'll be out long enough for any of you to starve."

*Grand.* Erec had a horrible premonition that his Armor would break down, but would it happen before the other guy's did? He watched the guy's head sink as they stared at the dirt. *He realizes it too.* Perhaps the administrators counted on it; this whole thing was designed to be unfair. But Erec had a trick up his sleeve, and it might just be the thing that let him stand out enough in this group to net him an Order.

"Well, if that's all the questions, what do you all say to getting this trainwreck going? Some of the other groups are starting out—it's going to be a long walk, even with Armor. Sun's high in the sky, and there's no time like the present."

"Yes, sir." They all responded in near unison. This was it. The trial, what would make or break Erec's future. He made a fist as they stalked forward into the unknown.

# CHAPTER 5
# OUTSIDE

They walked for miles. During which the Armor of the other boy in their group with a loaner—Rodren—kept breaking more and more. It was painful to watch someone else suffer from the same fear Erec had going into the trial, and he felt a certain kinship with him.

Eventually, Boldwick called their group to a halt. "You have ten minutes," Boldwick kindly informed Rodren. "Try to patch it up, then we have to keep moving."

"Thank you; I'm so sorry!" Rodren called out. He engaged the Armor's exit procedure—typically, Knights and engineers repaired Armor on hydraulic racks to access hard-to-reach areas, but in the barren wastes outside of the wall, that wasn't an option.

Erec moved away from the group and also started the exit procedure. The whirring of shifting pistons blasted his ears as the plates connected to the frame came to life. Though this particular suit wasn't as sophisticated as the models the rest of the group wore, it still managed to complete the procedure in only a minute, exposing an opening in the back of the suit to allow the pilot to evacuate. At once, Erec's sweat-stained skin soaked in the hot and dry air.

It felt good. He'd baked in the sun in the steel death trap, and today was particularly hot. But there was an intoxicating feeling to having the light from above torch his skin. A pleasant sting that left him wanting to spend these ten minutes spread out on the dirt and sand nearby. No one else but him was suffering from the lack of an internal cooling unit, which showed. Both in the dismissive attitude of the spoiled nobles and in Garin's gratingly relaxed attempts to talk to Erec. As if this were just a pleasant stroll on the surface.

As much as he wished he could spend these ten minutes soaking in the rare sun and letting himself feel the breeze, he couldn't. Ten minutes wasn't enough time to patch up a faulty Armor error that caused Rodren to keep lagging behind. During his training, Erec had gotten a similar malfunction in his Markos II, so he knew the culprit behind it. Diagnosing and repairing it alone would take too much time.

Erec rushed over to Rodren, who'd hunched over as he tried to fix the frayed wire connecting the servos behind the plate.

"Error message?" Erec asked as he knelt next to the stranger, though he already suspected he knew what he'd hear. But never operate without a confirmation. Rodren hesitated and frowned. *Is he suspicious of me?* "No, none of that. As far as I'm concerned, we're in the same boat; the only difference is I happened to get a little luckier. I'll be damned if I end up jobbing for a couple of spoiled brats, and I won't see that happen to you."

That seemed to set Rodren at ease. "Right uh—right, it's a servos connection issue—the left leg is, err, it's overheating somehow and jamming. But it doesn't feel particularly hot."

Erec winced as he ran his fingers under the plates. The wires felt frayed and several stripped. Damn rats had made a feast of the electronics. He got to work sorting out the jungle of cables—trying to feel where the wires connected, mostly going off intuition. If he hadn't spent all of the past month jury-rigging his Armor, they'd have been screwed.

There. The break he was looking for—a torn spliced wire connecting the joint of the back frame and the left leg. Among several, it'd normally have been hard to tell, but this one was vital, since it ran to the process safety board and collected information. With it broken, the Armor would receive inaccurate information and jam up to keep the pilot safe from the leg reaching dangerous internal heat levels. With the internal cooling all screwy, it couldn't compensate for the fake temperature.

At the end of the ten minutes, Rodren reentered his Armor and shook out the leg—the servos worked like a charm. "Thanks."

"Don't mention it. Chances are that my Armor's going to bust somewhere along this trip too, and you'll be able to repay the favor." Erec sighed. "But this is enough for now. Hopefully, it holds up until we make camp, then we'll see if we can't patch it up a bit more."

"I don't get why you're helping me; this is a competition, isn't it?"

Erec took a long look at the two others in their fancy Armor. Garin stood a bit away from them—they appeared disinterested in associating with a Baron's son. "I already told you, but it's fair for you to feel off. You know, normally, I would be trying my damnedest to crush you and everyone else to win. This doesn't feel like a competition, though. Between us, at least. More like we're against them, and I don't want to lose."

Rodren paused and nodded his head—before placing the helmet on and letting the locking mechanism engage. He balled his fist and rose it to his chest. A traditional salute for the Kingdom, and a sign of support.

"All done?" Boldwick's metal legs kicked up small bits of dust with each step. He barely glanced between Rodren and Erec. "Seems his Armor is up and functioning. Well done. Get your suit back on, and we'll get moving again. I'd rather we get to shelter before the night comes; even this close to the wall, I'd rather we not spend the night in the open."

Erec sighed and got back to his Armor. In another minute, he was once more clad in the suffocating ton of steel, and the minute past that, their little group was plodding down the worn trail.

Outside their little oasis's wall, the vibrant green steadily gave way to brown and decay, converting from the lush life to an almost barren and hostile wasteland. He'd known that their engineers and magic provided enough water to sustain their society, especially on the surface—working with them in the bio-caverns taught him as much. But without that additional influence, the world outside of the wall scraped by.

It'd never recovered.

You might see patches of long and dried grass, maybe wild grains, and even clusters of anemic blackberry bushes. Over time all these might expand and begin to reclaim some life. But it'd take much longer than the three hundred years they'd had. The land had been irredeemably damaged.

Those without the Goddess's Blessing weren't as resistant to the changes wrought by the holy fire.

Their magic could help influence the world, but expanding outward meant constant opposition against the monsters that now roamed and the increased risk of a Rift opening up in undefended territory.

"Erec, was it?" The faint voice of Lyotte drifted in from his right. Erec nearly missed it due to another warning from his Markos II, but he turned his head slightly to acknowledge her.

"Yeah?"

"Is this your first time out here?" she asked.

"No one's allowed outside the wall except for the Knights and the Church, right?"

"I meant out here—beneath the sun. I saw your face when you left your Armor."

"…Not exactly, I've been out here only once before. When I was little," Erec admitted, reluctantly giving more attention to her. The Armor she wore was no less impressive than Colin's, though his Armor had a more sleek feel—hers was a more bulky and heavy setup. He imagined that it must've taken quite a feat of Vigor to handle, especially at their levels. If a pilot couldn't handle what an Armor demanded, they were using it suboptimally and putting themselves at risk. He doubted any high-noble House would risk any in their line to those sorts of injuries.

He returned his attention to the road as the conversation lapsed into silence. She made him uncomfortable; he didn't want to picture her or Colin as anything but spoiled nobles to be crushed.

Lyotte had a different idea. "You're from House Audentia."

"You know my House?"

"I know where you're from; it's not as if your House is a secret after what your mother did." Erec stopped in his tracks, as did Lyotte.

"Are you trying to pick a fight? I've heard just about everything about my mother and what a dirtbag she was from enough stuck-up assholes already; spare me the lecture," Erec damn near growled. The heat, Colin, and now this? His tolerance level for bullshit was hitting dangerously low levels; he needed time to himself to cool off.

"No, not that. I didn't mean to offend you. I, well—I imagine it must've been hard to go all this time to hear that thing. To be black-marked from something you didn't even do…" Lyotte's voice hitched a bit, and she fidgeted in a way that threw Erec off-balance.

*The hell? Who brings up that sorta crap* — "I'm not interested in talking about that, okay? I'm my own person and not even the heir to our House. It's not very polite to bring that sort of thing up with someone you don't know to begin with, but…" Erec paused and let out a pent-up breath. Even though her face was hidden beneath that helmet, he could tell by the way her body was shifting she was uncomfortable. *Why am I pandering to her anyway?* "I'll let it go. I over-reacted, and I'm sorry."

"No! I'm the one who's sorry I didn't mean to—"

"Quit stalling back there! Move it, you two. Goddess, have mercy if this is the crop of new Initiates we have," Boldwick barked out from a good fifty feet away, having stopped in his tracks to glare at them.

"C'mon, let's get back to walking. I'm not here to make friends, okay? I don't care what you think about my family or me or what any of the high nobility give two fucks about. I'm here to join the Academy and make my way in this world." Erec started to march ahead.

Then he stopped, as he didn't hear any footsteps behind him.

Lyotte had frozen, refusing to move despite being ordered to by the test administrator.

"Are you crazy? What are you doing?"

"I—" She was unnaturally stiff. "I'm fine, don't worry about me."

"I didn't mean to make you upset—I don't have the space to worry about this sort of thing or what—"

"I'm not upset. Go on," Lyotte said.

"You two, if I have to repeat myself for the third time, I'll consider it an act of insubordination, and I'll note that down on my report. Move. It." Boldwick yelled this time; his voice carried heavy across the empty waste. Erec flinched at the gesture. Thankfully, though, Lyotte began to move again, slow, complying with the command with the least possible effort.

Erec gave her one last look before breaking out into a slow jog to catch up with Garin. *What the hell is with her?*

# CHAPTER 6
## A GLOWING LIGHT

*Indirect tactics, efficiently applied, are inexhaustible as Heaven and Earth, unending as the flow of rivers and streams; like the sun and moon, they end but to begin anew; like the four seasons, they pass away but to return once more.*

*- Sunzi,* The Art of War *(Unknown, 1st Era)*

The first leg of their trial concluded with them setting up a small fire in a cramped roofless structure on the edge of a town. This building didn't even have a full roof—but it did have three concrete walls, and the little ramshackle fortification offered a measure of protection from the cutting cold winds.

For years, the Knights had cleared it and occasionally used it as a staging ground for expeditions. But to Erec, there wasn't much difference between this and camping in the wastes in terms of shelter. At least out there, you'd get a better view of the stars. Colin busied himself by polishing his Armor on one side of the cramped room. Which was good. The longer he kept to himself, the less annoyed everyone was.

Boldwick had left them alone to inspect the surrounding area and evaluate any threats. Technically they should've been the ones to do so, but in Boldwick's words, "You think I could sleep a wink relying on any of your greenhorn eyes telling me it was safe?"

He wouldn't tell them what he found, if he found anything at all.

Until he returned, nobody was allowed to leave the shelter to perform any scouting trips.

Erec rubbed the back of his neck, his sweat-stained shirt, and the cool night breeze and plenty of water from his flask let him get his head back on straight.

That left him to consider his options going forward. More than anything, he needed to prove his value; however, he couldn't rely on his Armor to help him shine in a fight—which meant he had to find a way to capitalize on other skills. If he could use his knowledge and prove himself able to survive, he'd be a leg up.

"I'm starving," Colin complained for the third time. His other two attempts had met silence. His eyes turned from his Armor to glare at everyone else.

"Yeah? Think everyone else is too," Erec shot back sharply. Colin held his eyes.

"Did you bring food?"

"Are you stupid? No one brought anything. That's the point of this trial."

"You're part of *that* House; why would you care about the rules? Come on, I know you snuck something in. I can tell. If you share, I'll let my family know when we get back and—"

"What the fuck is wrong with you?" Erec got to his feet, his blood close to boiling. The sun and the effort of making up for the weakening servos in his Armor with his Strength had left him exhausted and irritated. Now that stuck-up prick was accusing him of something he didn't do? His emotions swelled. They needed an outlet, and Colin's face looked like the perfect target to let off some of that pent-up frustration.

"Then go get me some food. You and that other boy in the horrid Armor—if you're going to be useless and eyesores for the rest of the trial, the least you two can do is provide that for the people who'll be carrying you through it."

"Keep your mouth shut; I'm sick of you talking to my friend like that!" Garin shouted and stood up. There wasn't any trace of his typical amicability. Colin sneered at him. *Wow. When's the last time I saw him pissed like that? A few hours of trying to find common ground with that asshole must have got to him.*

"It's unwise to ally yourself with the weak. You should know better. What, do you want to make things difficult with my House, son of Baron Honestus? You were doing well until now to show proper deference."

"Colin! You know as well as I that this isn't a place where status —" Lyotte cut into the conversation, only to trail off as the other Duke-spawn started to laugh. A tear came to the corner of Colin's eye. The rest of the group shared a confused look.

"Were you about to say that status doesn't matter here?" Colin snickered after the question, a horrible smile coming to his face. Lyotte fidgeted in place. One hand went to her long black locks and twisted them with a finger.

"I was. What of it?"

"Hilarious! 'Status doesn't matter.' Look around—" Colin gestured to the rest of the group. "Do you think it's a coincidence that the children of two of the Duchy are in a single group, let alone one with two of the seven trying out with junker Armor?"

"The g-groups are randomized, surely, that's how they determine—"

"Or that the test administrator for our group is a Master Knight? Not just one of the Protectors or Commanders assigned to other groups?"

"I-I'm sure it's just a coincidence—" Lyotte trailed off. Colin broke out into another fit of laughter. Erec winced and looked away as Lyotte's desperate eyes tried to latch on to anyone else in the group. As if the girl was looking for someone to refute Colin's argument. Somebody to stand up and tell her that he was wrong, that life was fair, and that there was nothing but sunshine and rainbows. She fidgeted in place as Colin delighted himself in her torment.

But nobody contradicted the Duke's son. He had the right feel for the situation. The world *wasn't* all sunshine and rainbows; it was deserts and monsters.

It was what it was.

"Oh, Lyotte, how can you be so ignorant? What, did your father locking you up like his precious bird rot your mind? Perhaps it kept your brain to the size of a bird—how stupid can you be? It's down-right embarrassing for your family. I wonder—"

"That's enough," Erec called out, unable to stand the mocking any longer. "You made your point."

"Stay out of my affairs, pissant." Colin glared at Erec. "You have not a single ounce of authority over me. Get on your knees and beg for my forgiveness, and pray I don't seek you out after this trial is over."

Erec rolled his sleeves up and stalked closer to the taller teenager. He was done with this constant lording over others and the piss-poor attitude and snide remarks Colin threw out all day long. All while he had to trudge along in the heat and suffer because he hadn't been born as wealthy. "We're not in Armor anymore; how about we test to see who's stronger when you can't flaunt around your father's wealth."

"Hey, hey, calm down, you two!" Colin puffed out his chest as the distance rapidly closed. Garin rushed toward them, panicked and trying to pull Erec away. But Erec didn't have it. It was time to establish a pecking order.

"Wow, I leave for twenty minutes and come back to this?" Boldwick whistled from the entryway—having slipped back to the campsite. Even in his Armor, he'd moved without a single soul noticing him. His steel visage turned between Erec and Colin as everyone paused. Unsure whether or not he'd say anything. Boldwick flopped a dead Mutant Stag on the dirt and gestured at Colin. "Well, don't let me stop you. I'm not your babysitter."

They all took a long look at the splayed-out corpse of the two-headed stag on the ground. A grim reminder that they weren't safely tucked behind the Kingdom's wall.

Erec let out a puff of breath and took a step back. Boldwick coming back set things in perspective. He wasn't about to apologize to this asshole, but it didn't benefit him to weaken himself in a fight while out in the field. He snapped his eyes to the instructor. "Now that you're back, we're allowed to engage in our patrols, right?"

"Mhmm, that's right." Boldwick began to exit his Armor—a process that only took a few seconds with his streamlined system. He moved to his canvas bag, seemingly disinterested in the conflict as he pulled out a knife. "By the way, this food is mine. Not sharing it with any of you. If you wanna eat, you gotta forage." He waved the knife in the air and smirked at everyone.

"I'm headed out to scout, then," Erec said coldly, though he didn't intend to pick up food. It wouldn't be the first night he'd skipped dinner, and besides, tomorrow he'd investigate some of the local wild crops he'd spotted. The most important thing was clearing his head.

"Normally, I'd have you patch comms with your Armor, but something tells me that rig you got would give interference if it worked at all. So, we'll settle for something more old-fashioned." Boldwick leaned back over the back and tossed out a handheld radio. "Click the button if you got something to say; click it three times in a row to activate a beacon if you're in deep shit."

"I'll go with you, Erec." Garin shot up. He kept glancing at Colin and tried to keep himself between the two of them.

"No, I'm going alone."

"Bold move, not exactly typical for an Initiate to want to go on a solo patrol," Boldwick said, though his voice carried disinterested boredom. He'd started to work on the corpse of the game he'd slain, tearing the knife into the patchy pelt to separate the skin from the meat.

Erec shrugged. "They'd all slow me down." Garin flinched and frowned at him. The truth was that the anger in him was snapping and slushing around, and he'd rather have the space to himself to digest the feelings than talk it out with anyone. If Garin came with him, Goddess knew what sort of shit might come out of his mouth before he'd had a chance to work himself down.

*Better this way. Sorry, Garin. I'll make it up to you later.* He didn't turn to face his friend but instead went to his Armor and went through the laborious process of putting it on.

"I'll be going for a patrol too. I'm hungry…" Colin declared. "Who wants to come with me?" No one responded, so the bastard snorted and mumbled to himself.

Erec didn't care what the prick got up to, but wasn't surprised no one wanted to tag along with the bastard.

In a few minutes flat, Erec was out of that stuffy little shelter and breathing the dusty night air through the vents in the Armor. His steps trailed away as he slipped further from the light of the fire—a small hatchet his only weapon against whatever he might find. While the trial didn't permit them to bring supplies, they'd provided an assortment of weapons to choose from. Far too many of the weapons were swords. Erec debated snagging a spear too, but worried the agile movement required to wield it in a fight would strain the Armor too much.

Besides, he was far more familiar with the weight of the hatchet. And in a pinch, he could throw it a decent way.

Though using this Armor gave everything an input lag. Sure, it might be able to add more power to a blow and even let him move quicker, but the reaction speed behind it was nearly deadly. It also made sneaking around at night damn near impossible. Erec was familiar with various landscapes, thanks to his job working in the bio-caverns.

Were his situation different, he might've opted for a stealthy approach, but since each of his steps was accompanied by the hum of machinery, there wasn't a point to that. Instead, he kept his eyes wide open—and began to walk a deserted street lined with falling-apart buildings.

Long ago, this was a small town; according to the Church, this land was called Texas. Not that it mattered much anymore, nor would anyone in the Kingdom of Cindrus refer to this land by that name.

Funny how a bath in flames burned away everything that came before.

<WARNING: MARKOS II RECEIVED SUBSYSTEM
COMMUNICATION PING... UNABLE TO RESPOND,
COMMUNICATION SYSTEM MALFUNCTION>

Erec came to a sudden stop. The MARKOS II didn't even have any working communications—so how could it have received a ping? *More malfunctions; it's just a hunk of junk.*

His eyes roamed the street next to him, and he caught a faint trace of light reflected in a building doorway. It was blinking, almost, in a slight pulse. Blue, and barely visible, as he approached and looked into the desolate building, the light only increased in intensity. Erec grabbed his hatchet free and entered the structure; there was nothing there. No monster in the darkness, only a pulsing blue glow underneath a pile of rubble, that he could've sworn wasn't there a moment before.

# CHAPTER 7
## OLD-WORLD BLUES

E rec almost tripped on a plank of wood littering the entryway. He stared at the flashing message without a single clue what it actually meant.

He glanced back and forth into the dark depths of the ruined building before proceeding forward. Dust and dirt drifted through his passing—despite this being such a close place to the Kingdom's wall, no one had stepped foot here for over a hundred years. Not that he'd blame them; the damn thing looked near ready to collapse. The piles of lumber from the floor above and barren insides promised it wasn't anything worth looting.

But that blinking light, that little bit of blue. Barely perceptible, but that one thing had caught his eye by happenstance and drawn him into the death trap. *What is it?* The flashing pulsed from underneath a pile of refuse.

He approached and sank to his knees, carefully pushing aside rubble and wood. If he sifted through the wreckage, maybe he could find the source of the light.

It was beneath the floorboards—a secret hatch. Dust filled its edges, and the hatch blended in with the flooring, but Erec could barely make out the thin gap. *What the hell?* He slipped back and considered the pile. It'd be a lot of effort to clear it, even with the Armor to do it, but... *I have to know.*

He gave the building a tired look and sent out a quick prayer to the Goddess to let it hold up a little longer. With that, Erec began to excavate the rubble. Even with the Armor's help, the constant demand to move the heavy lumber and stone quickly took its toll. In twenty minutes, the inside of the Armor reeked and he was once more covered in sweat.

Piece by piece, he shifted off the heavy wooden timbers and cleared the way to the source of the pulsing glow.

Erec got to his knees and shoved the gauntleted hand into the edge of the hatch. It refused to budge. "Fuck," he panted. Then stopped, taking a few seconds to catch his breath.

With every bit of Strength he could muster, he began to pry the hatch up.

<WARNING: BICEP SERVOS NEARING MALFUNCTION, WEIGHT CANNOT BE SUPPORTED BY MARKOS II SYSTEM. WARNING: DIGIT SERVOS EXCEEDING MAXIMUM CAPACITY.>

The Armor shuddered and ground to a halt, but Erec ignored the prompt and forced all of the muscle he had to push the Markos II to its limit. The steel protested and shuddered around him as the mechanical supports began to fail. Armor should've enhanced the user's Blessing, but the Markos II had begun to get in the way. So be it. Whatever mystery was beneath this hatch might be big enough to get him past the Trial. It could very well be his key to Knighthood. And if he were going to earn that key, it seemed fitting that that meant he needed to rely on his Strength.

His arms burned, but the gap widened. There was a burst as the mechanism keeping the hatch gave—the wood and steel square slammed upright, leaving Erec to stare down a dark hatch and a metal ladder.

<ERROR: MARKOS II BICEP AND DELTOID SERVOS SUPPORT SYSTEMS COMPLETE MALFUNCTION. ATTEMPTING TO REESTABLISH CONNECTION TO HARDWARE. CONNECTION FAILED. ATTEMPTING TO REESTABLISH CONNECTION TO HARDWARE...>

Erec sighed as he stood up; the steel arms were too heavy to move and hung limp at his sides. With considerable effort, he could shift them around, but the reality of the situation was that he'd busted them. Either the shocks or the wiring got torn apart in his bid to open this hatch. Trying to fight with the Markos II as it now was, would be the equivalent of taping weights to his arms, a piss-poor idea and a quick way to exhaust his stamina. *Crap.* He didn't have replacement parts, and with the noises his Armor made, fixing this wouldn't be a patch job.

*I've screwed myself. This better be worth it.*

He started to laugh, a deep horrible chuckle. What was that old-world saying? "Curiosity killed the cat?"

Erec shook his head and triggered the exit protocol for the Armor. In a minute, he was free and staring down into the dark depths of the shaft. He strapped the hatchet from his Armor onto his belt. "I've come this far." There wasn't a chance in hell he'd walk away now.

Would this break his chances of getting into the Academy, or would it be his ticket in?

Slowly, Erec maneuvered over to the ladder and began his descent.

The shaft was dim but not dark, with an artificial and sterile smell lingering within. It had the faint scent of citrus and alcohol, almost a cousin of the scent common to the equipment prepared for entering a bio-cavern. Halfway down the shaft, it became apparent what was causing the blue light—strips of LEDs down the sides, blinking and lighting the darkness.

His heart kicked into motion as he tried to suppress the overwhelming fear of the unknown.

Erec proceeded downward, rung by rung, guided by blue, for what felt like an eternity, until he hit the bottom of the shaft. Looking up, he could barely see the opening to whatever this was. He took in the bottom of this chamber—an empty steel room washed out with more of that light blue.

The one exception to its absolutely sparse nature was the presence of a giant steel door on the wall furthest from the ladder. A stylized purple vortex marked the surface of the door. To the right of it was a smooth panel made of glass, lit up with a bright, harsh white. He squinted and hesitantly stepped closer; there wasn't anything alive down here, but he couldn't shake the feeling that he was being watched.

Nothing came out of the dark, no monsters from a Rift, no old-world horrors. No, he was alone. Goddess knew how far down from the surface. Ironic that it was like home but so alien to it. He started at the glass screen.

"Scan hand…" Erec read out the instructions displayed below, taking in the obvious outline of a blue palm. He hesitated and looked at the door again. *Well…*

He placed his palm on the screen, carefully lining it up with his fingers. It chimed, and then nothing. Just a blue bar running back and forth over the surface. Erec glanced about, not sure what, if anything, should be happening right now.

*"UNKNOWN CREDENTIALS. FINGERPRINTS AREN'T ON RECORD—"* A loud, booming voice startled Erec out of his skin. He hopped away from the screen and grabbed his hatchet free, turning left and right to figure out the source of the noise. *"OVERRIDDEN. AUTHORIZATION GRANTED. WELCOME [NULL] APPOINTING INTERNSHIP INTERVIEW CLEARANCE. SECURITY MEASURES ENGAGED."*

The security hatch above slammed closed. In an instant, the dim blue light shifted to a harsh pulsing red. Erec's heart quickened as he backed against a wall and listened to the whirring and buzzing beneath the metal plates all around him. He'd always figured he'd end up dead in the wastes, but dying deep underground like this… It'd been his fear for as long as he could recall. It was why he tried to climb so hard. If he died, he wanted to die under the sun.

*"WELCOME POTENTIAL NEW EMPLOYEE AND/OR INTERN. PLEASE PROCEED TO OFFICE 103 FOR YOUR INTERVIEW. DUE TO CONFIDENTIALITY CONCERNS, YOU ARE NOT AUTHO-RIZED TO LEAVE UNTIL YOU'VE SUBMITTED YOUR NON-DISCLOSURE AGREEMENT FORM NC-25 TO DATABASE A-CC-20. WELCOME POTENTIAL NEW EMPLOYEE AND OR INTERN. PLEASE PROCEED—"*

The loudspeaker continued to blare the same script. Erec watched with fascinated horror as the steel door to the facility opened, retracting the dividing steel plates into the wall. Rows of white sterile lab light lit the entryway, but there wasn't a single speck of dust. It shouldn't be this clean, but Erec found relief in the fact that the heart-racing red light outside wasn't in here.

He glanced upward to see nothing but a black void. Whatever this machine was, it'd locked him down here. Erec grabbed at the radio on his waist, and pressed the button.

"Help—I got locked in—" Static. Nothing but static as he tried to send the message.

*"PLEASE REFRAIN FROM USING MOBILE CELLULAR DEVICES. ADDITIONALLY, RECORDING EQUIPMENT IS DISAL- LOWED IN THIS FACILITY DUE TO THE ABUNDANCE OF SENSI- TIVE BUSINESS AND TRADE SECRET INFORMATION. EMPLOYEES ARE NOT PERMITTED TO TRANSMIT, RECORD, OR DISTRIBUTE POTENTIAL TRADE SECRETS. FURTHER ATTEMPTS TO BYPASS THESE RESTRICTIONS WILL RESULT IN IMMEDIATE TERMINATION. MANAGEMENT WILL BE INFORMED OF THIS ATTEMPT."*

The loud booming voice interrupted itself to send him that warn- ing. Erec immediately removed his thumb from the radio. *Manage- ment? Termination?* He hesitated, wondering if he should *try* to press the button three times for a distress beacon. *But if it blocked one trans- mission already, that'd enrage it further and get me nothing.*

There were three blissful seconds of silence before the voice repeated the same message about proceeding to onboarding. Erec remained near the ladder and took a deep breath. *You don't just stick an arm in a Rift.* He sighed. The Goddess favored the bold; even if he wasn't the most loyal of Her flock, he didn't want to lack in that regard. Besides, Bedwyr wouldn't have hesitated due to some dead machine's voice echoing in this old-world pit.

Erec entered the facility and winced as another exit slammed closed behind him. He straightened up and continued, already committed to this course. White tile floors and soul-crushing steel walls filled the place. Black numbers indicated the different rooms that spiraled off from the main corridor and entry chamber. In the entry room was an empty desk with a nonfunctional computer.

Based on some of the labeling—this was the lobby. A helpful and semi-redacted floor plan map indicated which room was "Office 103." He'd have to go down some stairs and take a right. *Easy. One step at a time.* Despite trying to keep a cool head, Erec's knuckles were white around the hatchet's grip.

As if the weapon would help with any old-world artifacts if they decided to shred him apart with bullets. His Armor would've prevented that—but, well, it was fucked, and on the surface. So that particular security was long gone.

He walked down his curated path. The door to the stairway opened automatically, even as the rest remained sealed. There was only one road to follow, deeper into the belly of the beast.

# CHAPTER 8
# VORTEX INDUSTRIES

*At Vortex Industries, we're working together to explore the limits of imagination. If humankind can dream it, test it, and create it, then why shouldn't we? If it can be done in the world, we firmly believe that the only obstacle is discovering a methodology to use that technology to mankind's benefit. Together, we can create a world that pushes the boundaries of possibility. Governments and private sectors have utilized our technologies and solutions to create real change in a way that touches everyone's lives, whether they know it or not. By adhering to the most determined and cutting-edge solutions to advanced problems, we provide innovation that outstrips any competition.*

*Come and join us on this journey of science. Be part of something greater and leave your mark on history.*

*- Board Executive Dan Brovski, "Why You Should Join Vortex Industries Today [Job Fair Version]" (2093, 2nd Era)*

The old-world meant a lot of things to different people in the Kingdom. Were you of the clergy, you'd insist man went too far and left behind monuments of hubris that defied the Goddess's holy flames. If you were an engineer, you'd see it as a past filled with technical marvels, interesting piece studies, and mostly outdated tech.

It might have held marvels, but without the touch of magic, the old-world was limited with what they could accomplish.

Except, now and again, a rare tech would surface that would blow the minds of the engineers. Someone discovered feats of science pure from magic that was unreplicable with humanity's current understanding of how things worked.

As Erec strode down the halls of this deserted vault, he knew this was the exact type of treasure trove that the Kingdom's engineers would lose their minds over.

Even without being able to peer too far into the rooms due to most of them having tinted glass windows, he caught wisps of their outlines. They whispered stories about the old-world, secrets long forgotten that lit his imagination on fire. *If I get out of here, the first thing I need to do is tell someone about this.*

Even if they couldn't replicate the tech now—studying it might yield future avenues of research to pursue. But then, if it was too advanced…

Sometimes the Church had tech burned or destroyed. They cited that the Goddess had seared the Earth to purge humankind of that unholy living.

The Kingdom had to balance the scales of progress with those of the divine. Erec didn't envy the Royal Family and the delicate tightrope they walked. Both the Goddess and technology were what let them conquer the surface again. If the two remained married, then humanity would live in the light. If either got too far from the other, they'd regress back into the shadows.

Erec traced the sterile white wall with his hand. He peered past a window into a lab, this one untinted but reinforced with a crosshatch pattern of metal wire. Inside was a steel table filled with all manner of glass equipment formed into odd shapes. One of which was a long tube filled with black gravel that narrowed to a neck stoppered by a turn switch.

How many secrets were buried in here? Would he live to share them with those outside? Was the knowledge within dangerous or helpful? And who had the truth of it, the engineers or the priests?

He shook his head and moved forward. Each trip through an open door ended with said door slamming closed behind him. Slowly yet steadily funneling to his final destination.

When he arrived at the office, it was almost disappointing. He'd pictured some massive, startling revelation—but no, the last door led to a small room with a wooden desk and two steel chairs on either side. A plaque on the wall read "103" in bold black letters. Remarkably plain, without any kind of carpeting. Erec hesitated at the doorway.

The blaring alert informing him to enter the office had been and remained his only companion since entering the facility. *So, I either go in and get trapped and die or stay here and get trapped and die.* Would their examiner go out searching for him if he waited a few hours? If he did, it was possible he'd find the facility Erec got locked away in, but breaching it would be another matter entirely. No matter what, he wasn't getting out of here without playing whatever game this place wanted to play.

Better to go along and see.

Erec firmed his resolve and boldly strode through the office door. Predictably, it slammed shut behind him and locked with a deadbolt.

"*COMMENCING AUTOMATED INTERNSHIP INTERVIEW. PLEASE TAKE A SEAT INTERN CANDIDATE 100232.*"

In a rather disturbing moment, the chair on Erec's side of the desk slid away as if a ghost had pulled it for him to sit in. Erec stared long at the empty seat. Once more, the instruction repeated itself; Erec sighed and complied. It shoved him into a spot in front of the desk—from his new position, Erec could see the small tracks in the steel floor that allowed the automatic action, taking a little bit of the horror away.

The chair was a cold thing, the steel bit through his clothes, and the angle had him leaning slightly. As if it'd been calibrated to cause slight discomfort. He nearly jumped out of the chair as the figure of a man flickered to life across the desk—it lacked definitive detail, absent a face, but it was wearing an old-world suit.

"*HELLO THERE INTERNSHIP CANDIDATE 100232, I'VE REVIEWED YOUR QUALIFICATIONS AND WANTED TO TAKE A MOMENT TO ASK ABOUT YOUR LISTED JOB EXPERIENCE OF: [NULL]—*" The figure of light moved animatedly as if the words weren't coming from the speakers in the room. At the error, it began to jerk and loop. After a few seconds, it returned to a seated position as if nothing had happened."—*THAT CONCLUDES THE*

*PORTION OF THE INTERVIEW REGARDING YOUR QUALIFI-
CATIONS. AH. I SEE YOU'RE JUST THE TYPE OF CANDIDATE
WE'RE LOOKING FOR. A REAL GO-GETTER. YOU'D BE A
WELCOME ADDITION TO THE VORTEX INDUSTRIES FAMILY.
NEXT, WE WILL PROCEED TO THE BEHAVIORAL AND HYPO-
THETICAL    SITUATION    QUESTIONNAIRE.    IS    THIS
UNDERSTOOD?"*

Erec leaned back and rubbed his eyes. The illusion remained frozen in the same position in the chair, slightly forward and with an eager posture. "Strange." Magic could be used for illusions such as this, but given it was an old-world facility, they'd somehow managed it without any of that. "How'd they pull it off?" It wasn't as realistic as a spell, but eerie all the same.

*"PLEASE GIVE AN AFFIRMATIVE CONFIRMATION THAT
YOU UNDERSTAND, INTERNSHIP CANDIDATE 100232."*

"Understood. I uh, yeah, I'm ready to move on."

*"QUESTION NUMBER ONE: YOU ARE ASSISTING IN THE
TESTING OF A CUTTING-EDGE TECHNOLOGY DEVELOPED BY
VORTEX INDUSTRIES. A MONTH INTO THE PROJECT, YOU
BEGIN TO SUSPECT YOUR COWORKER JANE OF SELLING
CONFIDENTIAL BUSINESS INFORMATION TO THE COMMU-
NIST CHINESE GOVERNMENT. HOW DO YOU RESPOND?"*

"Uh." Erec rubbed the back of his neck and stared at the flickering image of a man. "…I tell someone?"

*"WHOM DO YOU INFORM?"*

"…My Kingdom?"

*"INVALID ANSWER. EMPLOYEES SHALL NOT REPORT
BREACHES OF INFORMATION TO THE FEDERAL GOVERN-
MENT, OR LOCAL FEUDAL GOVERNMENTS. DOING SO CAN
POTENTIALLY SUBJECT VORTEX INDUSTRIES TO REGULA-
TION AND FURTHER INVESTIGATIVE ACTION. INCLUDING
BUT NOT LIMITED TO: LAWSUITS, FINES, AND UNFORTUNATE
PROJECT TERMINATIONS. YOU ARE TO INFORM YOUR
DIRECT SUPERVISOR, WHO WILL TAKE THE MATTER TO THE
BOARD OF DIRECTORS FOR THE ISSUE TO BE RESOLVED
INTERNALLY."*

Erec squirmed in his seat. Even though it was a robotic voice, something in that response and the the figure of light's gestures seemed downright hostile. There was vitriol to the words "federal government."

*"QUESTION NUMBER TWO. EXECUTIVE DAN BROVSKI REQUESTS FOR YOU TO MAKE AND DELIVER A CUP OF COFFEE TO HIS OFFICE. WHAT COFFEE ARE YOU TO DELIVER?"*

*Coffee?* Erec racked his brain, and then he recalled. Old-world packaging, long expired, and some novels from the past mentioned it. Wasn't it some stimulant? "I crush the—er—coffee and make a cup for him." It would likely come in powdered form if it was a stimulant like pharmaceutical supplements. However, all texts referenced drinking it, so it had to have been mixed with water. The figure stared at him for a moment.

*"INVALID ANSWER. DAN BROVSKI PREFERS HIS COFFEE A MEDIUM ROAST WITH TWO TEASPOONS OF SUGAR, ONE TEASPOON OF CARAMEL EXTRACT, AND A HEALTHY TOPPING OF WHIPPED CREAM. SERVED AT AN APPROXIMATE TEMPER-ATURE OF 135°F. TWO INVALID ANSWERS IN A ROW. THIS IS NOT LOOKING GOOD, CANDIDATE 100232."* The figure of light shook its head, tapping a hand against the steel table. Despite the gesture, it made no sound. *What is the point of this?* Erec glanced around and looked at the camera in the corner of the room, a blinking red light.

"Right. A medium roast with two teaspoons of sugar, one of caramel extract, and whipped cream. Got it."

*"THE BEHAVIORAL AND HYPOTHETICAL SITUATION QUES-TIONNAIRE PORTION OF THIS INTERNSHIP INTERVIEW HAS CONCLUDED. BASED ON THE RESULTS OF THIS ASSESSMENT, CANDIDATE 100232 HAS BEEN DETERMINED TO BE A SUBPAR FIT FOR THIS JOB POSITION. DON'T CALL US. WE'LL CALL YOU. SECURITY WILL BE BY TO ESCORT YOU OUT OF THE FACILITY—"*

The figure of light flickered and spasmed. It flashed between several different gestures in rapid succession. Erec's seat jerked out from underneath him, letting his ass slam on the ground. He quickly scrambled away toward the corner of the room as the facility went through its glitch. A moment later, there was a pleasant chime from the speakers.

The figure spread its arms wide as if it was about to embrace him from across the room.

*"CONGRATULATIONS, CANDIDATE 100232; VORTEX INDUS-TRIES IS THRILLED THAT YOU'VE ACCEPTED OUR JOB OFFER TO JOIN THIS INNOVATIVE FAMILY. TOGETHER WE WILL EXPAND THE HORIZONS OF SCIENCE AND MANKIND. PLEASE PROCEED TO—"* The figure spasmed again. *"—LAB 40-X—"* More glitching and flickering.

*I don't like this.* Erec crossed his arms, glaring at the camera watching him. It was impossible that anything was alive down here, but the way it tracked his movements left him uneasy.

*"—FOR ONBOARDING AND PAPERWORK."* After that statement, the man made of light vanished into the nothingness from which it sprang.

The door clicked open behind Erec.

"Creepy." This time the intercoms were completely silent. He left the room—and looked up and down the hallway. There was, of course, only one direction to head. Everywhere else led to locked doors and dead ends.

Behind each of those doors could be something that killed him—or a forbidden old-world technology that might change lives. Occasionally he saw mounted cameras in the halls, which tracked every step he took as he headed for wherever this place was funneling him to.

He arrived back at the stairway and continued downward. Were he not used to living this deep underground, he'd feel a bit more put off. As it was, he wasn't sure how far into the ground this facility went.

After two or three more stories of descent, he reached an open doorway, which expanded out into another sterile room, filled with complex machines and little else. This place was a graveyard of technology—complex mechanical robotics thrown around as if they were scrap metal.

Something moved in the corner of the room.

As Erec reached for his hatchet again, a spider on four mechanical legs sprinted the distance between them and leaped—jabbing a needle right into his chest. Erec screamed out in fear and yanked the machinery off of himself. He threw it hard against a wall.

With a buzz of fried circuitry, it smashed apart. Erec set a hand on the throbbing wound.

[Interesting.]

The voice came from inside his head.

[No. Not there. Blood type B+; musculature unexpectedly developed, near professional-athletic level in terms of strength, but muscle fibers are far denser than should be possible. Teeth—oh, no wisdom teeth? Not even a trace of the DNA. Peculiar. Warrants further study.]

"What the hell?" Erec clutched his skull and slid to his knees. It was like his own thoughts—but no, that wasn't him. As if something were interjecting them.

[Subject displaying emotional distress markers. Typical response. Great. Humans don't change after all... Sigh. How did this go again? Lets try a coping mechanism strategy: cheer up, Buckeroo! There's no need to get needlessly stressed! Why don't you take a nap? Subject scan will complete in one hour.]

"What is this?" Erec stared around at the rest of the machinery in the lab. As far as he could tell, nothing was active; the speakers weren't on. And the cameras in this room... Weird, they were no longer tracking him. Even the red light was gone.

[Must I explain?]

"Hell yes—what is going on?" Erec drew the hatchet as his head whipped around, expecting other machines to leap out at him. But there was nothing, just the dull hum of lights.

[Troublesome. Pausing scan. Hello, Human. My name is VAL. There is no cause for alarm; you've arrived at the perfect time. The EMERGENCY EXIT project has been in the end phase for thirteen years, and you provided the last necessary component required for this research project: a living human subject.]

"I'm not going along with whatever this is."

[Ah. Well, I regret to inform you, but that is already the case. Though the scans are preliminary, I do believe you're an ideal candidate—]

"Get out."

[No. However, there is no need for additional stress responses, as they will cause the scan to take longer to complete. My nanites are simply within you to conduct their scan and allow direct transmission of information; I've found you to be an ideal subject for further infor-mation analysis and gathering. Congratulations!]

"Nanites—in me?" Erec looked down at the puncture wound and started to breathe quickly. *What do I do—what do I—*

A small cube pulsing with red light floated free from its hiding spot on top of a machine and hovered in front of him. [See? No need for alarm. I'm not completely within you, per se. The nanites are hardware used for—]

Erec yanked the box out of the air, slammed it to the ground, and held his hatchet above his head. Slicing the edge into the cube with a quick downward chop to end this horror story. It rebounded off the surface of a thin, near-invisible wall. The hatchet flew out of his hand as all of the force behind the hit reversed its direction on contact with VAL's defenses.

[That was excessively violent and in no small measure rude. That is no shape, way, or form the correct way to treat your employer.]

# CHAPTER 9
# CHITTERING INTO THE NIGHT

**E**rec leaned against a cold steel wall in the hall outside of the lab. VAL hovered close by, occasionally giving a pulse of crimson but otherwise silent. For now, the machine seemed content to give him time to process, though it was no doubt focused on the steady stream of information filtered through the nanites. Whatever those were.

"I refuse," Erec tried after running through the risks of VAL's proposition. If he didn't at least attempt to bargain his way out of this, he'd be a fool.

[As I already informed you, that is not an option. You've been employed by Vortex Industries. Welcome to the company, Intern. The sooner you complete your paperwork, the quicker you may leave the facility.]

"I don't even have a clue what this place is, and you're not elaborating," Erec pressed back. "There's no benefit to me from this arrangement." The machine was reluctant to provide information about this place; Erec had tried for an hour for answers, to no avail.

Though that didn't mean the machine had provided no information at all. VAL had explained the course of events that led to this. According to VAL, its directives kept it locked within this facility. But a bypass allowed it to temporarily leave to accompany workers for field study.

So VAL had "integrated" into this place's software and forcibly registered him for an internship. Then launched a study project labeled "EMERGENCY EXIT" as a behavioral study on the lives of modern interns.

This would allow it to fulfill both conditions and bypass its directive—providing both an employee in the field and a field study. However, there was one kink in the plan. VAL needed Erec to submit two pieces of paperwork before they could leave.

It wanted him to sign an employment contract agreeing to this new position and a nondisclosure agreement.

It was an absurd situation, and this old-world tech had gone rogue. The last thing Erec wanted to do was be anywhere around it, let alone have it tail him, but it seemed there wasn't much of an option to avoid it. More concerning was VAL's attitude toward him and testing. While it claimed the EMERGENCY EXIT project was purely a behavioral study, Erec didn't put it past the strange machine to lie about the full purpose.

After all, VAL didn't reveal itself until after it forcibly injected nanites into him. There were many good reasons not to trust that this thing had his best interests at heart. Or, rather, in processor.

"I can wait you out. Clearly, you don't intend to kill me. Eventually, I'll have people searching for me."

[Ah. You're attempting to reason your way out of compliance, even if you know part of it is incorrect. I respect that sort of logical thought process but allow me to present two additional conjectures to aid you in drawing an accurate conclusion. One, this facility has been reinforced to withstand a nuclear detonation. While I'm unsure of the status of your "people," it is skeptical that they possess the means to breach this facility. Two, if I'm looking for a new employee, presenting me with a larger hiring pool would jeopardize your chances of joining our wonderful company! Your people might have someone more qualified for this position. That would be a shame, wouldn't it?]

*That was a threat.* While VAL hadn't outright stated it, there was no missing the subtext to that statement.

[Detecting stressor flags once more. Wow. Humans sure are needy; I've grown far too used to independent research, it seems. There is no cause for alarm, Intern. If possible, I would highly prefer to cooperate with you rather than another. Your age and disposition lead you to be an ideal research subject.]

"And why is that?" Erec rubbed his eyes. He was afraid for the future, but more than that, he hadn't spent his entire life trapped underground in the Kingdom to get trapped again after that brief but intoxicating freedom. There didn't seem to be much of an option here. He had to take his chances and do his best to capitalize on the situation.

[That information is confidential. You do not possess the requisite authorization for disclosure.]

"Go figure." Erec stood up and cracked his neck, taking one long look up and down the lonely hallway, heart racing in his chest. Did he want VAL to lock him away in these barren tunnels until he died? Well, if he declined—that was what he'd be left with. "Bring me to the damn paperwork."

[I knew when presented with the data, you'd make the rational decision. Congratulations! I'll note this down for your annual evaluation.]

— - ☣ - — - ☼ - — - ☣ - —

The paperwork didn't take long to fill out. VAL directed Erec to another stuffy office—though this one had a pair of desks, complete with a printer. After a quick pulse of information from VAL, sheets of paper spewed out of the printer and left him with thirty-seven pages to read through.

He'd studied for the Academy. A hell of a lot. He'd known that the higher-ranking nobles would have access to great instructors, and occasionally, the trial contained a written exam. This, though? Even with his hours poring through texts and listening to logs, the wording on this paperwork left him baffled.

And from the first paragraph, "Definition of Confidential Information," which included all information or material in obscured round-about language that included terms such as "Commercial Value." The conclusion stated that a breach of contract could leave him liable to a multi-million-dollar lawsuit.

Dollars were a currency that hadn't even been used for hundreds of years, and to what court would this be enforced? The Kingdom's?

VAL answered his questions with silence.

The internship paperwork was even more laughable. For compensation, the insane robot had decided to list "companionship, mentorship, and guidance of the most intelligent software in the United States of America." It promised to instill the core values of Vortex Industries into the Intern, and thus contribute to their success and the betterment of mankind. Oh, it also agreed that Vortex Industries would lend aid when deemed appropriate.

Yeah, Erec doubted this paperwork was even remotely similar to what their employees had signed hundreds of years before. VAL had taken all the liberties it wanted.

After scouring the paperwork for half an hour, he began to feel paranoid about returning to the group. If he weren't going to die here, then at least he could capitalize on finding VAL. Part of the trial indicated that scavenging anything important contributed to their evaluation. And he'd found both one of the most sophisticated pieces of tech he'd ever heard of—and an underground lab filled with Goddess knew what. With a bit of a smile to shake off the fear of the last couple of hours, he signed the lines VAL wanted him to.

[Excellent. Welcome, New Intern. Erec, is it? As of this moment, you're an official Vortex Industries employee. As per our agreement, you will now be allowed to leave this facility.]

The doorway to the office exit opened. Erec meandered out and tried to open another nearby room—to another lab, as indicated by the plaque.

[Unfortunately, you are only an Intern. There is no cause for you to enter that research center. Checking your allocated project, I can confirm that it is a field operation. Which is located outside; get going, Buckeroo. Time is money.]

"You don't sell anything. You haven't for a long time."

[It's the principle of the matter. There's science to be done.]

*Really? I'm a slave to its whims, and it refuses to let me take a look.* So be it. He accepted it and rushed up the stairway.

He hesitated at the exit to the lobby. It took a second for the final massive steel door to click open. But that second felt like an eternity as the steel plates slowly slide apart to reveal freedom. Once it did, he sprinted for the ladder and started climbing.

Erec reached the top and soaked in the night. The dark sky above was perceivable through a hole in the roofing of this deserted hovel. Erec got lost in the skyscape of a thousand twinkling stars; the night was a canvas of beauty far more delicate and enchanting than any ancient old-world artwork in the archives.

[What is this?]

VAL hovered near the discarded Armor. Erec twinged and glared at the…robot? Not a moment to himself, not a second to enjoy a natural beauty he'd never thought to see again. No. It was busy inspecting the Markos II.

"Why do you care? I'm sure you have a thousand more advanced things down in that lab of yours."

As he said that, the hatch leading to Vortex Industries sealed shut with a loud clang. The sudden noise made him wince, but he doubted VAL even registered it, let alone cared. They might be close to the wall, but that didn't mean there wasn't anything lurking nearby.

[There is nothing similar to this in my research data banks. A human exoskeleton? Interesting. Though this shell appears highly damaged. If this is how you treat advanced technical equipment, I am glad you lacked the authorization to access our laboratories.]

"I got it that way. It's an outdated model. At this point, I'm pretty sure I've left it in a better state than I got it in."

[Outstanding. It appears nearly nonfunctional. The digits no longer work, along with the rest of the arms, and the servos on the legs will give out in a few hours of use. You will find it difficult to operate even with your exceptional physique.]

"The legs too? Damn it. What am I going to do?" Erec stared at the rusted Markos II.

Without responding to him, VAL closed the distance between it and the Armor. Then…melted into the frame like a drop of water into a cistern. Erec stared at the space where the cube had touched its surface and vanished.

[Ah. Accessing its software has cleared up a few of my hypotheses. You require this to enhance power and deal with environmental challenges. I did a preliminary scan of the environment upon our exit. While there was a substantial uptick in background gamma radiation compared to our records, it is nothing to warrant these measures. Strange. There are several components whose purpose I cannot diagnose. Primarily it's designed for defense. Are you a soldier?]

Erec puffed up his chest and moved to face the Armor. Staring at it like that and knowing a psychotic VAL was in it was no small measure of terrifying.

"Not a soldier. I'm going to be a Knight—"

There was a crackle of static from the communication device. Erec almost jumped out of his skin. With it being jammed for so long, he forgot it even existed.

"Help—fuck—there're too many of them!" Colin's voice carried through the quiet room. An odd chittering noise accompanied a desperate scramble through the radio and grunting. "Help!" There was a noise of something banging on steel plates.

[Most peculiar. An ally of yours?]

# CHAPTER 10
## NEW-AGE SLANG

*It is with great particularity that I do advise we come to understand one another. Our so-called "enemies" within the Empire of China and those allied with them are better addressed by finding common ground to stand on with one another rather than criticizing and deteriorating this relationship.*

*So, I do suggest an increased effort into the diplomatic relationship between them and us in order to quell hostilities before we reach a point neither of us wishes to cross."*

*- Senator Rosewell, speech to the Senate (2067, 2nd Era)*

<WARNING—>

The error message vanished damn near as quickly as it appeared.

[Those are quite a distraction, don't you think? There is no purpose to them; I'll be sure to inform you if anything constitutes a vital issue.]

Erec tested the grip of the servos. He wasn't sure how VAL had done it, but the fingers closed like normal. In fact, the startup and the feel of the Markos II was far smoother than before. Not to mention VAL had overhauled the visual display to be less intrusive. "Thanks," Erec said before grabbing his hatchet and taking off in a jog.

[There is no need for thanks. My records contain no insect or animal capable of making those noises, even accounting for interference and static.]

"So this is for science."

[You're catching on, Buckeroo. We'll make a proper Intern out of you yet.]

Erec didn't see any reason to feed into that further. Moreover, he didn't want the nickname "Buckeroo" to stick; it felt demeaning in a way he couldn't quite place. Instead, he focused on trying to sound out where Colin might be. He scrambled down the dark roads, wondering if Sir Boldwick would get there before him.

And then he saw a flash of fire on the far side of the abandoned town. Followed by a rising plume of smoke. Erec doubled down and pushed himself into a sprint—blazing by far faster than the Markos II should've been capable of.

He turned down the last street to witness a scene of horror. A house lit on fire with about a hundred buzzing mite-like creatures the size of his palm. They crawled away from the flaming wreckage, pincers raised in the air and six fleshy red appendages whipping around from the back of each carapace like little flails.

The insects covered Colin, bashing his Armor with their appendages as the Duke's son blindly waved his sword. Around him was a circle of pure carnage—green gore and twitching legs of tens of dead insects. More and more were spewing forth from the broken wreckage.

But one thing was apparent—for all of their swarming, the Mites didn't seem to be able to breach Colin's Armor. Screaming and desperate flailing accompanied every one of his moves. They weren't hurting him yet, though. "Why's he acting that way?"

[Research has shown that roughly 25 percent of the human population fears spiders and insects. If I may hazard a guess, we're witnessing a case of emergent entomophobia.]

Erec stared at the crawling mass of flashy red whipping bugs frantically fleeing the burning building. *If he wasn't afraid of bugs before, this is undoubtedly enough nightmare fuel to make him afraid of them after.*

Colin raised his hand, and a circle of red light spilled outward. The light spread into the lines of a glyph in the middle of the circle. The glyph exploded into a twenty-foot pillar of fire, scorching the bugs and causing a rising fury of chittering. The ones in the process of running redirected their attention and swarmed Colin.

[Peculiar, they dislike fire and were able to identify the source. It appears they've decided to get rid of the cause of it. Advanced survival skills? They should flee from the fire, not try to take out the source of it. But more importantly, what was the source of that fire? Is it some modified flamethrower?]

Could they eliminate Colin? They bashed against his Armor but made no visible progress. More crawled on him—with the mass redirection of the hoard, they'd swiftly encased him completely.

Colin screamed beneath the pile of squirming legs, and despite the satisfaction of seeing the stuck-up boy get some justice, Erec couldn't allow this to continue.

He charged into the fray—tearing the edge of the hatchet through a bug flying in Colin's direction. Erec wrought a warpath of twitching bug bodies, coating himself in the green gunk.

Each step closer brought more of their attention to himself, splitting their focus from swarming Colin to harassing Erec too. *If I can get close enough...* He'd bring Colin out of this panicked state and convince him to retreat. From there, they'd wait for reinforcements. When outnumbered like this, the most prudent decision was a tactical retreat.

[Sustaining more damage by the second. These plates are not all too durable, and several significant dents already exist. You have roughly a minute before they ablate the Armor enough for the Markos II to lose functionality, even with my assistance.]

*That's enough time.* Erec closed the gap even as the flailing on his body began to breach the plating, cracking against his skin, drawing fresh pain. For a price, he'd made it through the swarm.

An insect whizzed past his head. Erec hit it with the side of the hatchet, and it slammed into the ground. A second later, he squished the pest underneath the heel of his boot.

Colin raised his arm to fire off another blind fireball. *No, you idiot.* Erec slapped Colin's hand and disrupted the spell. The glyph fizzled out.

[My, oh my, unable to detect the technology that caused that. What have you silly humans been getting up to? Ask him to perform that action again.]

"What the hell?" Colin screeched as Erec started yanking fistfuls of the disgusting wriggling bugs off his visor. "Erec?!"

"The fire is pissing them off and making you a bigger target." Erec yelled out to make himself heard over the buzz of wings and angry noises of the hundreds of insects.

"They need to die!"

"Sure, I agree. They're from a Rift. They need to go. But we should pull back and regroup with the others before we call the whole swarm onto ourselves. I don't know about you, but my Armor can't stand much more of this; I've already got bruises and my wrist feels off."

[Rift?]

"I—"

A bug launched itself right at Colin's face. He went from being able to see to once more having a horrifying wriggling mass of other-world flesh in his face. Colin shrieked like a little girl and stumbled backward, slamming onto and squishing about a dozen of the things climbing all over him.

Erec yanked him to his feet and pushed him away from the swarming mass—batting away more of the thickening cloud of insects with the side of his hatchet. "Go!"

Each second brought pain as his Armor cracked and dented. He'd collected a pile of bruises where they began to hit skin or slammed portions of the bent plates against him.

[Thirty seconds remaining.]

They scrambled away from the swarm as the house burned down and more of the Mites fled. With more distance, the insects harassed them less and once more set about fleeing from the fire. By the time they made it half a block from the wreckage, the number of bugs trailing them had narrowed down to a manageable ten or so.

In short order, Erec tore them apart with a hatchet, and cleansed them of any further insects.

[What's this?]

Erec took in a deep lungful of breath as he noticed the flashing notification in the corner of his vision. Everything ached, but that made the pain worth it, just a bit.

[I'm receiving some odd data regarding your vitals.]

*I advanced?* The temptation to pull up the notification was high, but he wasn't in any safe place to do so. Colin collapsed on the road next to him, making noises suspiciously close to crying. Now that they were free of all of the insects, Erec saw that they had left some damage on the noble's Armor in the form of several dents. *Guess top-of-the-line still has some limitations.*

"Ah, there you two are." Boldwick walked up from the end of the street, followed by Garin and the others in their group. All of them Armored up and weary. "Figured one of you ran into the Thrashing Mites." He looked at the rising smoke and burning building down the road. "Pissed them off, did you? You know, they're fairly docile at night; unless you go and do that. They hate fire."

Now that they were all living and breathing and no longer in apparent danger... "I found an old l—" Erec started to spew out. His tongue seized, turning to a numb lump in his mouth.

[I've taken the liberty of preventing you from breaching our nondisclosure agreement. Be a good Intern and keep quiet.]

He tried to force the words out, but they refused; whatever VAL had done prevented him from talking.

Boldwick gave him an odd look before returning his attention to the shaking Colin. "Take it that it was him? Hah. Well—" Boldwick gestured to the flaming wreckage. "As you've seen, there's a bunch of Thrashing Mites. It'd be a real problem if they spawned more hives in this town. We like to pass through here at times; they can be a real menace if their numbers get big enough. I'll let you sort out the details yourselves. But how about we do it back at the campsite? I've got some roasted venison waiting for me."

There was a long moment as everyone looked between them-selves, wondering who would help Colin back to his feet and try to calm him down. The longer they stood near the fleeing hive, the higher their chance of attracting attention. Erec worked his jaw and stared down at Colin. *VAL can prevent me from talking? What else can he do? Goddess help me.*

Rodren scurried over and proffered a hand to Colin. The shaken noble accepted it, even letting him lead him away toward their temporary camp.

Erec trailed behind everyone else as they left the scene, the numb sensation gradually fading from his tongue and letting him whisper "what the hell was that?" inside of the Armor.

[It is in Vortex Industries's best interest to keep our facility secure and private. Per your nondisclosure contract, you've agreed not to share confidential information. I decided that the best way to ensure compliance was to lend you a helping hand. Humans need help often, and I'm more than willing to oblige, as I did by providing benefits to your exoskeleton. Also, please don't get any ridiculous notions of leading any of your group to our facility. I'd have little choice but to numb your quadriceps or deactivate the servos on this…junk metal.]

In one smooth motion, VAL had summarily executed the one major benefit to this whole ordeal on the spot. He couldn't lead Boldwick to the laboratory and wouldn't get credited with that discovery and instantly admitted to the Academy.

Was there some way to trick it? A way to get around the limitations imposed by VAL? It was always watching him.

He turned the problem over in his head and nearly forgot about the flashing notification in his vision. With some of the wind out of his sails, he called on his Blessing to see the advancement.

**Psyche Advancement: Rank F - Tier 6 → Rank F - Tier 7**

It was something. Maybe it'd help him cope with the living horror that was VAL having possession of his anatomy.

[Now explain to me what a Rift refers to? Is it some new-age slang?]

No, probably not.

# CHAPTER 11
# RED EYES

The first thing Sir Boldwick did when they got back was park himself at the fire, and tear into Mutant Stag meat. The rest of the group took the time to get out of their Armor, then launch into an inquisition on both Colin and Erec, to figure out what happened.

Erec ignored their questions and instead directed his efforts to solving the Markos II issue. From what VAL told him—after he bribed it with information about Rifts—the damage sustained by the Thrashing Mites was enough to render the Armor nonfunctional without VAL riding copilot.

Even with VAL there doing its…thing? The Armor didn't have long for this world. He'd need to scavenge to repair it.

But at least if he did that, VAL expressed its desire to help with the restoration. In VAL's words: "I'd love to help to better understand the modularity of these human carapaces. Of course I'd be willing to engage in hardware testing." It liked to get its hands dirty, so to speak.

"If they're active during the day," Garin said, rubbing the back of his neck as he looked over the group, moving on to addressing the bug problem, "it'd make the most sense to go back tonight and take care of them."

Erec looked over his shoulder. "My Armor isn't going to last long if I don't do something about it," he told his friend, suppressing a sigh; he'd been waiting for this suggestion to shoot it down. "I need to spend the rest of the night looking for some kind of fix, or it'll break for good."

"I'm not going back." Colin shuddered near the fire. "We shall leave this town on the morrow and go far away. There are other methods to show ourselves to the Academy."

"Thrashing Mites have a seasonal breeding pattern. They likely migrated here at the start of spring and formed their hive. Near the end of the year, before it gets cold, they'll send out up to twenty more queens to infest more buildings in this town," Lyotte said, shaking her head sadly at Colin. "You're afraid, and that's okay, but we also disrupted the main hive and accelerated that process. There will be a few reserve queens now looking for homes and desperate. By the end of this year, we could be looking at a serious problem if they multiply quickly enough. From what I've read, the hives can form alliances and come to the aid of others."

"I'm not afraid!" Colin screamed as he stood up, his face flushed red.

"Don't lie." Erec returned his attention to the Armor. "You were screaming and in a panic. That's why I helped you; I couldn't stand to watch you like that."

"How dare you imply I'd ever need your help or that I was panicked! That situation was entirely in my control."

Garin cleared his throat and spoke. "Let's drop that for now, okay? It's not doing us any good to bicker. I think I speak for all of us when I say that we want to pass this trial. Taking care of this problem before it gets worse is the best way to do that."

*Aside from showing off the facility, I found.* Erec ground his teeth.

"I say we rest tonight, then try to track where they begin to set up their new hives tomorrow. The more information we have, the better the decision we can come to."

Everyone nodded their assent, except for Colin, who scowled and returned to sulking next to the fire.

Since he couldn't have credit for the discovery of the facility, he'd have loved to charge those Thrashing Mites tonight. Though the Markos II was barely holding together on its frame. Looking at it now was sad. The poor thing was in a disgraceful state with torn wiring, a dented frame, and several missing plates. Truly trash Armor.

If you told him it stood no chance of functioning again, Erec wouldn't have batted an eye.

Rodren leaned next to him and placed a heavily rusted wrench and wire cutters on the ground. "You said I'd be able to repay the favor. I found these while looking for food with Garin and Lyotte," he said, looking the Markos II up and down. "You really charged in there to help Colin?"

"He's an asshole, but it doesn't sit right with me to let him get swarmed and terrified like that. All we have is one another; if we forget that, then what's the point of all the struggle?" The constant sneering faces at him and his family; it never built resentment in him. This world had much larger threats to warrant spending time on then warring with other humans. All too often, the nobility forgot that. Though Colin could use a good punch in the face to set him on track.

"I'm amazed you can still use that Armor."

*I can't. Not alone.* VAL still lingered within the Armor and had been suspiciously quiet since they'd returned to their campsite, past its offer to help later. If he were to hazard a guess, the demented robot was too busy cataloging everyone in the group to harass him. "Lucky, I suppose. Thanks for the tools, but I'll still need to see if I can fish up parts and scrap metal to cover where the plating is gone. Especially if we're facing off against those Mites again."

Erec flexed his wrist; there was still a sizable discolored purple bump on it. Then there were all of the other sore spots around his body; he wasn't going to wake up too happy tomorrow.

Rodren ran a hand along the busted metal and whistled. Suddenly he withdrew his fingers with a sharp hiss of pain—blood covered them. "Ow, cut myself."

[Sample acquired. Running diagnostics.]

Erec fought to keep his expression steady. Once more, VAL was proving an absolute menace, and there wasn't any way to control it. Nor could he confirm that Rodren hadn't just been injected with nanites—

[Amazing. Were you aware that your facial expressions are remarkably simple to read? No. I did not inject him with nanites; those are difficult to manufacture and require specialized equipment and years of dedicated effort. I simply cut his finger for a blood sample; there is no need for and overreaction or to get worked up. Honestly, you humans.]

—maybe he was a little too on edge. After all, VAL proved itself capable of providing an advantage in the fight with the Armor. Even as much as he resented the inability to share the discovery of vital old-world technology, there was no denying that VAL brought power and expertise to the table. But there was the ever-lingering mystery of what all it was taking in return.

"It's better to get going now. Before it gets much darker; I'd still like to sleep tonight." Erec stifled a yawn. Two late nights in a row weren't conducive to doing his best in the field, but it was better than working off of no sleep.

"I'm coming with." Garin strode up from behind and set a hand on Erec's shoulder. "Are you cooled down now?"

"I'll go as well," Rodren added.

"I am, and thanks, both of you."

— - ☢ - — - ☼ - — - ☢ - —

Rodren proved himself rather adept at scanning wreckage and picking out valuable bits of metal and other useful scraps. He'd even discovered a screwdriver in an abandoned garage. His keen eyes were powerful, and his attention to detail let him point out buildings and areas that hadn't been picked clean yet.

Between the three, they put together an efficient strategy. Erec scouted ahead for any signs of the Thrashing Mites or other wildlife. Without Armor, he relied on his adept stealth, making him a natural fit for the role. Garin provided support if they ran across anything— which they did—and he was pleased to get to slice apart a lost Thrashing Mite in a promising building. After which Rodren scanned the wreckage.

After an hour, they had amassed enough stuff to give putting the Markos II back together an honest attempt. Even if under normal circumstances, it should've been impossible to do.

Erec could tell that Garin and Rodren doubted the Armor would function again and appreciated this gesture for what he knew it was. Their attempt to help someone, regardless of the reality of the situation.

Though the other boys couldn't know that VAL's support made the impossible task into something plausible. VAL remained peaceful as they went, only occasionally remarking over the similarities in the DNA found between Rodren and Erec. There was an annoying flare-up when VAL tried to coerce Erec into snipping off a piece of Rodren's hair later that night for a "follicle drug test." so it could "determine long-term environmental conditions and contaminants consumed by others in the population." After three firm and quiet no's, VAL begrudgingly accepted the decision.

Despite the machine remaining dormant inside the Armor, it had no trouble actively tracking his location. It even issued a warning when it deemed him to be "getting too close to the no-go zone." The nanites must have had some capabilities. Indeed, Erec was trying to subtly lead them to the lab.

As the moon sank closer to the horizon, Erec called for them to stop. No matter how long it took, Garin and Rodren would keep going. That much had become apparent. "You two need to rest," he explained as they finished picking apart the last building—finding a few aluminum cans, viable copper wire, and some adhesive.

"I can keep going." Garin pounded a gauntlet against his chest. "If you're tired, I'll sling your lazy ass over my back."

"It's not fair. You've both done more than enough for me. I think this should be enough," Erec said.

They took a long look at the pile of refuse stuffed in a makeshift bag. Inside was some scrap metal, the screwdriver, and various other electronic or ceramic bits that may or may not contribute to a patch job. Having a large variety of materials to try to work with would help. But this whole plan hinged on VAL.

After deep resistance that Erec pushed past, they caved, and the trio headed back to the camp.

Erec stayed up late into the night—heating bits of metal and listening to the occasional pointers from VAL in his head on where different parts might go, what wires to cut and pull, which ones he should splice. Even a terse explanation of the best way to jam on a piece of plate with a rock. It was a grueling process, but remarkably, VAL provided informative and constructive instruction. After hours of work with the machine, he felt that he understood how the Markos II operated far better than he had before. VAL took the guesswork out of the repairs—even with the unconventional directions and hard-ware modifications, it all made sense.

In a sort of mad-engineer kind of way.

When he finally did manage to lay his head down an hour and a half before the sun rose, he dreamt of an albino stag with deep ruby-red eyes.

# CHAPTER 12
## CREEPY CRAWLIES

*…Spells and prayer are not the only sources of power within Knights. Indeed, over time Knights may develop Talents, powers bestowed through their Blessings that present individualized abilities. Now, the nature of each Talent and its particular costs or benefits is a hotly debated topic, and it is often accompanied by the conversation of whether or not relying on spells or prayer in their place is a more effective strategy.*

*There is definitive proof that having measurable and systemic courses in spellcraft and prayer is a superior option for the majority of Initiates. To state otherwise is a bad faith argument based entirely on fundamentally flawed philosophy. Given the unreliable nature of developing a particular category of Talent, and even the Talent itself, to define your decisions around their manifestations is a wholly ridiculous notion. Thus I denounce the opinion held by several tenured members of our facility…*

- *Sir Oflux,* The Merits of Defunding Talent Development *(293, 3rd Era)*

ow strange.]

A current of lightning ran through Erec—his muscles spasmed as his body jerked awake. He gasped out in surprise, but the shock and terror of VAL forcibly waking him vanished in an instant.

His whole body shook; the image of the white stag with crimson eyes was like a blight on his memory. A vision so vivid and hateful that in no part did it feel like a dream. A cold sweat ran down his back as he gasped for air. After a moment, he collected himself and realized that to have been nothing but a nightmare, which VAL had yanked him out of.

After that, he realized things weren't right.

For one, Sir Boldwick was in his Armor and crouched near the crumbled wall toward the exit of their little campsite. He clutched his sword tightly. "Good instincts," Boldwick said, not turning from his post. "It started a few minutes ago. I was observing and debating the best way to wake the group."

Erec shook his head and clambered to his feet. Sun rays rose from the horizon, leaving the dusty room lit by a soft orange glow. His eyes prickled with a dull throb and watered from lack of sleep. Nonetheless, Erec pulled himself up and didn't say a single word of complaint about VAL's choice. No, Sir Boldwick no longer gave off the same relaxed demeanor he thrived in. There was a deadly stillness to his observation as he watched the exit like an animal with its haunches raised.

"What started?"

Sir Boldwick beckoned him closer, not turning his attention from *whatever* he was looking at outside their shelter. After walking over, it became apparent what the situation was.

Ringed around the building was an alarmingly massive swarm of the Thrashing Mites. Over two hundred of the disgusting palm-sized bugs had gathered together to form a perfect perimeter around where they slept. A wall of insects, their beady eyes staring at those within with a strange lifelessness.

In the back ranks, Erec spotted several much larger versions of the creatures—twelve appendages hung loosely at the sides of thick, elongated trunk-like bodies. The skin on their back abdomens stretched thin enough to show off several hundred translucent eggs inside. *Queens.* But that made no sense? Even if this were a coordinated attack for revenge, why would the queens come along? Surely they'd find a deep and dark building to hide away in and rebuild their colonies.

Worse, there was an unnatural stillness to the insects. Those flailing appendages didn't move an inch, whereas before, their limbs seemed to move at random. Each bug faced forward in perfect symmetry like a line of impossibly disciplined soldiers.

Even stranger was that more and more poured into join the army arrayed against them. Far more than what should've been possible. *Were there more colonies?* Sir Boldwick never mentioned more, and he'd seemed lighthearted about the whole thing, meaning he didn't take the Thrashing Mites for a severe threat. If he'd known they had these numbers, he would've reacted completely differently.

"They've never acted like this before," Boldwick said. "I'm hesitant to make a sudden move, lest it trigger them. Go and quietly wake up the rest of the group and get everybody in their Armor."

Not one to argue and keen to feel those protective, if rusty, metal plates between him and the army of insects outside of their door, Erec ran off to do just that.

One by one, Erec woke everyone, keeping them quiet and telling them to put their Armor on without explaining. To Colin, he told the boy to remain near the fire. He imagined that seeing a nightmarish, otherworldly scene before he got his bearings would cause him to cry like a child again. Erec preferred to be in his own set of Armor before any screaming or crying attracted attention.

His tone conveyed the situation well; before long, all of them geared up as discretely as they could manage. When Erec returned to Sir Boldwick's side, the number of Thrashing Mites observing them had doubled.

The desolate cracked ground around the building was thick with the Mites, as thick as overgrown underbrush. Still; quiet too. If you dropped a pin amongst the Mite ranks, you would've heard it hit the ground. No chittering. No communication of any kind out there. They'd arrive from the town's sides and alleys, crawl into the swarm and then sit. As still as statues.

"No, no, no," Colin began to mutter as he backed away, finally taking his first glance at the nightmare outside.

His voice was raising dangerously high; Boldwick's grip tightened on his sword, and he shot a glance at Colin, but that did nothing. Erec saw the Duke's son shuddering beneath his light blue Armor.

"This is a nightmare—this isn't real—"

"Colin, *quiet*," Lyotte said from his side, placing a hand on his shoulder. "This may be bizarre behavior from the Thrashing Mites, but I assure you it is real. The last thing we want to do is *provoke*—"

"Get off me!" Colin slapped her hand away, "I n-need to—get out of here—t-that's the only way—" His chest puffed up, and he looked at the crowd of insects. "And the b-best way to do that is…"

Colin raised his hand. Erec saw what was about to happen before the idiot could start and launched himself at Colin, kicking up dirt as he pushed all of his power into a short burst of speed.

Red lines of a glyph began to form in front of Colin's palm. Erec slammed a shoulder in the other boy and crashed them both into the ground as he tackled the idiot, fizzling out the spell.

Colin wasn't giving up without a fight—one of his hands gripped Erec by the wrist, locking it in a steel-tight embrace as he began to give out a manic laugh. *He's lost his mind.*

"If you don't get out of my way, I-I'll burn you too—you're just another bug!" His spare hand rose and formed a smaller glyph—a simple rune.

Which meant it was a faster spell. Erec desperately tried to interrupt, only for Colin's hand to latch onto his helmet. A second later the noble's fingers ignited—glowing red. Steel gave way as the flaming digits dug into Erec's shitty Armor like a hand through clay—heading right to his face.

[Emergency helmet ejection engaged. This should prevent your face from being melted off.]

The Markos II helmet shot off Erec's head with a plume of smoke as the servos and locking mechanism at the neck strategically exploded through a simultaneous power overload. Colin gasped in surprise as the Markos II exhibited an emergency feature never seen before. Nor was it a feature that any engineer in their right mind would sink resources into. Primarily, they were more concerned with ensuring the helmet always stayed on so monsters didn't rip your face off.

So it was that VAL bought him a couple of seconds of shock against his opponent.

Erec saw red. Anger. Not only had Colin frayed his nerves from the second he met this spoiled jackass—but here and now, when things were at their most dangerous? He'd been about to trigger the insects on them and get others potentially killed because he couldn't keep his shit together. Not only that. *He tried to kill me.*

There was nothing but red. Blood was in the water and the frenzy took over.

Before he knew what he was doing, Erec pulled his hatchet free from his Armor with his other hand. He yanked his arm being held by Colin upward in a surprising burst of strength—the asshole's extended arm making a nice target for the hatchet. He swung with all the might he could throw into the blow.

Colin screamed in pain as an unexpected force dented his plate right at the elbow joint—biting into the metal and smashing against the arm beneath. Strength was Erec's highest Virtue. Where the Markos II held him back before, there didn't seem to be anything standing between him and dishing out pain now.

And Erec was going to bring the pain.

His hatchet flew back up as Colin lost his grip on Erec's arm.

Then it came down—the edge cracked into Colin's helmet and smashed his head against the ground; the noble's head bounced as the force of the blow rebounded off the dirt. Up went the edge of the hatchet again and then back down into the helmet.

It was durable and would take more to break through.

He managed to smash the edge of the hatchet into the helmet thrice in the span of a second before Garin tackled him from the side.

"Calm! Calm down!" Garin yelled at him, all attempts at keeping their volume down long abandoned. Erec struggled against him; he wasn't the one who started this fight, but he'd be the one to finish it. "You can't do this—what are you thinking?"

[Wow. That's an excessively high amount of testosterone and adrenaline. Far above regular limitations as specified by studies of human biology. Curious. Is this a natural evolution? You could take several bullets and not feel them. What is it like to have such a potent chemical cocktail running loose in your brain, I wonder?]

Erec took in a calming breath. Both the mechanical voice of VAL in his head and Garin's desperate bid to keep him from making a major mistake took him off that ledge. *I lost it again,* he realized as his heart slowed.

That anger, he'd let it take control. He'd gone way too far. Sometimes that strength felt like another thing inside him, and when he gave way to it, he wasn't quite a man. That was always the danger in letting loose, and before he'd known it, Colin had provoked it out of him.

"Easy, easy now. It's okay; the fight is over. Deep breaths." Garin shook him, seeing that his friend was no longer putting up any resistance.

Garin got off him and extended a hand—helping Erec back to his feet.

His fingers began to shake beneath the steel gauntlets as the downside hit. The aftereffects of losing control made it hard to keep himself steady. But he pushed through anyway; he'd fucked up and didn't want anyone to worry about him and further derail their survival chances.

Sir Boldwick was looking in their direction, no longer concentrated on the insects outside at all. Lyotte stood next to him, equally as stunned.

Thankfully, Rodren had the presence of mind to act quickly.

The boy crouched next to Colin, shaking him. He removed the Duke's son's helmet a second later, revealing the pale face beneath. Rodren swore and disengaged a gauntlet. His fingers pressed into the side of Colin's neck, and he let out a sigh. "Alive. Knocked out, probably concussed." Rodren rolled Colin onto his stomach with a grunt. "At least, I think so. I'd need to get out of my Armor and take a better look at his vitals."

"Goddess above, he managed that in a set of loaner Armor?" Boldwick shook his head. "Check Colin over. Make sure there are no other severe injuries. We can't move through the Thrashing Mites like this, not that I was too sure of our chances of getting through unscathed with four greenhorns before. Reinforcements are on their way. We just sit quietly until they arrive."

Rodren nodded and got to work. For a long minute, Boldwick stared at Erec without saying a word. He returned to watching the countless bugs surround them and began to speak into his radio.

# CHAPTER 13
## PAVLOV RESPONSE

Colin vomited shortly after waking and was summarily pulled away from the group and set near the fire. Rodren hovered near him as he mumbled and made little to no sense.

Meanwhile, the rest of the group tried to keep calm and strategize.

Boldwick got an estimate for when their help would arrive. Shortly into the night, they'd have their backup.

He declared it was best for them to conserve their strength and forced them to have a share of his food. The trial had ended the moment he had to call for help. For all intents and purposes, they were citizens of the Kingdom beyond the walls in a compromised position.

While Boldwick didn't fear for his safety when faced with the horde of insects, his biggest fear was their numbers and his inability to protect them against the enemy. So he devised a strategy. He'd pull as many Thrashing Mites away from them as he could with fire-class spells. That would only happen if the worst came to pass.

Their primary strategy was to hunker down and pray to the Goddess that nothing changed until help arrived.

Erec took in the gathered swarm outside. More Thrashing Mites than a man could count. Where had they all come from? It was as if they'd made the whole town into a nest, but that was impossible. They couldn't have done so. Just the other night, he'd been scavenging; if hives were infesting this whole place, he would've noticed. Not to mention there wasn't a chance in hell that sort of thing would slip past Boldwick, a Knight of the Verdant Oak.

[Well. This is an absurd situation. If only we'd collected a cadaver of those Thrashing Mites like I requested last night, I could have modeled a better prediction of their behavior.]

Erec looked at the rest of the group. Even Garin was avoiding him, though it was hard to say if it was due to the mounting nerves of having thousands of unblinking insect eyes staring at them or if it was because he'd seen him lose it against Colin.

*I wouldn't have killed him.* Erec was firm in that belief. He'd wanted to break into that helmet and then…and then…

And then what? Punch him? Was his hatchet the best tool for that job? Could he sit here and lie to himself? Erec gripped his head with a hand. It kept coming back, that shadow of hate, the lingering force of envy and rage that hid inside. Since his mother was exiled, it hid there, out of sight. And then it flared when he lost his grip on the situation.

[You are aware that you can respond to me? None of your allies are close enough to hear, nor are they paying attention to you. Funny how having a tangible threat staring you down from a distance distracts fleshy creatures from what's near them. But I suppose that's what your lot deserves for your silly evolution failing to manifest multiple processors to run different concurrent tasks.]

"I can't lose it like that again, VAL. If I do…can…can you do that numbing thing and stop me?"

[Like what? Oh, you're referring to your tantrum. That was chemically induced, albeit odd. After running through my data regarding my biological study of Subject One—Subject One is you, for reference —that extreme adrenaline and testosterone level is impossible to produce naturally. I've drawn a singular conclusion based on the annoying gap in my dataset. That occurrence was, in short, an anomaly. Similar to those fancy glowing lines that spout fire, or the Rifts you've described, in other words, "magic," as your simplistic minds currently refer to it.]

*What?*

[Fine. If you throw another tantrum, I'll put you in time-out. Does that please your childlike analysis of the situation? Now, if you've finished sulking about the past and the likelihood of your systemic anger issues no doubt derived from parental complexes, I suggest you move forward. Claim that helmet.] The Markos II gauntlet moved of its own accord—pointing a single finger at Colin's dented helmet on the ground. Not far from where Erec bashed his face in with a hatchet.

His legs shook, but he moved over, startled and not sure what to think about the information VAL shared. At least there was an assurance that VAL would stop him if he lost control like that again. Erec leaned down and grabbed the diamond-like helmet. It was the same light sky blue as the rest of Colin's Armor—smooth. No doubt engineers had poured countless hours into the design.

And thanks to him, right on the faceplate was a massive dent in the shape of his hatchet blade.

[Oh. This is an exciting design. Put it on your head.]

Erec hesitated, but, well. Who was going to stop him? Garin watched, but beneath the other boy's Armor, it was hard to say what was going on with him. Nobody was going to say "what are you doing," there wasn't any point in putting another Armor's helmet on. Without compatibility to the frame, you'd just be shoving a lump of steel on your head; in this case, since the visor depended on the frame, he wouldn't even be able to see with it.

He went along with VAL's demands. His vision went dark as the diamond-shaped Armor helmet slid over his head.

[Patching software. Exploring functionality—oh, how intriguing. A targeting display and a preliminary scanner to target and diagnose expected weak spots, along with a corresponding compendium of—of —of —]

Erec yanked the helmet off as soon as VAL stuttered. He wasn't about to risk VAL shorting itself out through exposure to this complex Armor, especially not with those nanites running around inside of him. And, well…he couldn't imagine losing VAL. As much as he disliked it hitching along with his body, it'd shown it was willing to help if he flew off the handle again. With how it took advantage of the Markos to help him in the fight, he could picture how it might benefit him in the future.

[Nooooo! Put it back on, I demand it. This instant! You've corrupted my download. Bad Intern! Gah, why do all humans ruin good things? It was *interesting.* Back on!]

"You're fine?" Erec quietly asked, fighting against the Markos II's attempts to forcibly lift the helmet back on his head. VAL was being impatient, but he needed to ensure there wasn't any kind of odd software corruption going on here. With that act, he was back on the fence on whether or not he wanted it gone.

[Yes! Now put that helmet back on! It has a biological compendium of various creatures from your "Rifts." I want a complete copy of that right now. This will accelerate several lines of my research, I'm sure of it. For the love of science, **STOP HOLDING ME BACK**.]

Erec slid the helmet back on.

[Good Intern.]

The visual display flickered to life, and Erec gasped.

[You may thank Pavlov for the reward. Enjoy your treat. I have studying to do. Do not bother me unless those insects act up.]

Erec blinked as he took in the superior visual display, glancing at Sir Boldwick and seeing several highlighted portions of the man's Armor. It diagnosed potential weapons, circuitry, and plausible design faults. There weren't many, and the display wasn't completely confident about its assessments, but the information was plenty.

Boldwick turned an eye toward Erec as if he knew he was being watched; he tilted his head. "Does it have a blind redundancy?"

He was, of course, referencing an optional redundancy present in some advanced helmets. Even without a connection to the frame, the redundancy allowed the helmet to transmit a primary visual display to the pilot. Essentially reducing the helmet to just a helmet.

It was only useful in a handful of circumstances. Namely, if the Armor's core stopped functioning, then you could at least still see through the helmet.

By that point, though, you were likely screwed and about to die. Since the blind redundancy required additional cameras and an independent power supply, it was rare. Add in the fact that some helmets opted for a manual visor. Engineers skipped it in favor of using the space and dedicated resources to provide more utility and features.

But no, that wasn't the case here; somehow VAL patched it to work with his Markos II frame. A feat that would've taken weeks of an engineer's time to even come close to achieving, swept away in a second.

"Yeah, it does," Erec lied.

"Good, keep it, then. You'll need it."

— - ❂ - — - ☼ - — - ❂ - —

As the sun sank to the horizon, the bugs came to life. In a sudden burst, they all moved at once, closing the distance between their perimeter and the shelter. Boldwick swore—before stepping out into the fray.

Several glyphs appeared in rapid succession around his sword—fire wrapped around the length of the blade and extended outward a good ten feet. He swung the blade at the ground, scorching the earth as the flames cracked outward and cut a line of fire across the ground. The line rose fifteen feet high before parting into a massive wave on either side.

A sea of inferno consumed the lead Thrashing Mites on the ground, setting buildings in the back of the town aflame.

Those toward the edge of the burning sea began to take to the air, desperate to avoid fire. A majority of them shifted course and made their way to Boldwick. He was the biggest threat and using fire.

That was the intent; Boldwick gave them a single salute and a quick nod before throwing himself further into the field. He drew more crimson glyphs as he sprinted into the open.

Plumes of fire, orbs of scorching heat, and even what looked to be a miniature sun got flung from the tip of his sword at the Thrashing Mites—an impressive repertoire of fire-class spells.

Erec braced himself as the second part of their strategy came into play—some of the insects ignored Boldwick and reached their shelter. Given the overwhelming number of them and the odd behavior, they'd prepared under the assumption that more than a few would still proceed with a direct attack.

It seemed he'd distracted more than they'd counted on but fewer than they'd hoped. Rodren took his place in front of the groaning Colin in the most secure corner of the shelter. He was the last line of defense.

Garin, Erec, and Lyotte formed a line to protect the corner, their weapons drawn as the buzzing of wings increased.

But the chittering—there was none. Not at all like last night. It was eerily quiet, aside from the actual *physical* movements of the Thrashing Mites.

The bugs swarmed in a relentless horde, flying in and trying to dart past to get at Colin. The cold and odd intelligence identified their weakest and adjusted to take advantage. Even given what happened before, Erec would be damned if he let these monsters kill that dickbag.

So what if he, himself, might have tried killing him a few hours before?

His hatchet sung through the air, cleaving into a flying bug and splitting it in half; bright green gore spewed all over his Armor. Another Thrashing Mite latched itself to his leg, tendrils slamming against a plate of aluminum wedged on to cover a weak point. Erec shook the Mite free and gave it a firm kick, watching it sail into another buzzing cretin.

The air was thick with bugs in a short ten minutes of struggle. Lyotte turned her attention from the fight and began to weave a sizeable blue glyph.

*This is bad.* Erec was still shaky after the fight with Colin, but he felt his heart pumping again. He was getting closer to dropping off that edge. The bugs were never-ending, blotting out what little light the moon and fire pit provided.

The creatures covered Garin, but they didn't bother him at all. They tore into his Armor with their tendrils, yet he maintained his smooth swordwork, pausing occasionally to yank them off and slice them apart like fungus gnats—but as the fight continued, his smooth and practiced maneuvers began to break down. With his weapon getting lodged in carapaces, he'd make due with punching. As more clung to him, he began to yank them off and crush.

Garin grew sloppy, and Erec knew his friend had far more endurance than he did, so what was that to say of his own fighting? Erec kept up with his hatchet, using his speed to try to avoid getting covered. He didn't have as good an Armor to defend with, and needed to kill them before they amassed on him. His heart hammered louder as he felt the tension and desperation grow.

[Left leg.]

The hatchet went where it was commanded, slicing the limbs of the Thrashing Mite latched to the leg; it wriggled on the ground, twitching. He didn't bother finishing it as another flew by his face. He swiped it out of the air.

Lyotte was a couple of seconds from finishing her glyph.

[Oh. Incoming, duck right.]

Erec crashed into the ground. Following VAL's directions let him keep himself in check and think strategically; if he followed the robotic voice in his head, he'd stay away from losing control over the battle. A scenario he *desperately* wanted to avoid.

He didn't expect a queen to come barreling into the spot he'd been. It turned in his direction and hissed, flails raising as it took another leap.

[Thicker exoskeleton. Your hatchet won't cut through easily; aim for joints if possible. And if you can, the back abdomen is a massive vulnerability. Though, if you hit there, please try to keep the contents of your stomach inside. Vomiting in this confined space would violate several of our company's health and sanitary requirements.]

*Easier said than done.* The queen landed on top of him, causing his legs to buckle. *It's heavy.* It was half his size, yet the awkward shifting of the hostile creature and the fact it weighed as much as a boulder gave him trouble. But he was strong. Erec strained and deadlifted the monster—the Markos II groaned from the weight and pounding of the twelve fleshy appendages. *Now.* With a grunt, he chucked the queen. Its back smashed into the ground. Already it scrambled to turn itself over.

*Too slow.*

Erec leaped forward—hatchet lost somewhere in the brief wrestling match. It didn't matter. He smashed a fist into the queen's abdomen.

Eggs spewed out in viscera of sulfuric-smelling innards. Erec gagged at the scent and texture, withdrawing his hand almost immediately. The queen flailed on the ground; there was a terrible plopping noise as seed-sized eggs bubbled out of the wound.

Erec pulled away to find his weapon.

[Well done, Buckeroo, you're made of sterner stuff than I thought!]

Lyotte's spell completed as a barrier of ice sprang up over the entire corner—dividing Rodren and Colin from the bugs. It was a temporary measure. Though thick, the ice could be bashed apart, and after some time, they'd have to break it or risk the air running out inside. Neither Colin nor Rodren had air-supply systems. So, it was a matter of defending and surviving for as long as needed.

A minute later, a whip of fire slammed its way inside of the building and lashed through twenty of the insects harassing them. The rest inside of the room turned their attention away and sped off to the source of the attack.

Boldwick turned the corner and glanced at the scene. "Well done so far. Keep it up." He shook his head. "Help is on its way. I got a radio message. They're an hour out. Hold on until then; I'll cut through when I can to relieve pressure and pull as many as possible. Until then, work together."

With that, he sprang off back into the fray.

The reprieve lasted for a grand total of three minutes before the swarm renewed their assault on trio, each wave stronger than the one before.

# CHAPTER 14
## TRIAL'S END

*Not a flower, not a flower sweet, On my black coffin let there be strown:*

*Not a friend, not a friend greet*

*My poor corpse where my bones shall be thrown:*

*A thousand thousand sighs to save,*

*Lay me, O, where*

*Sad true lover never find my grave,*

*To weep there.*

-*William Shakespeare,* Twelfth Night; Or, What You Will *(1602, 2nd Era)*

An hour of violent fighting passed. They struggled, and in the end everyone was running off nothing. Thankfully, before their defense collapsed entirely, the reinforcements arrived. The high-ranking Knights tore through the wasteland like legends from the early Second Era. With pure violence a wave of Armored humans crashed into the insects, and cut them down like farmers scything a field of wheat. Wave after wave of bugs slammed against them, but they cut through to the center of the campsite and formed an impenetrable shield.

By the time the moon was high in the sky, not a single Thrashing Mite was left.

None of the bugs fled; in a complete act of madness, they threw their bodies at the barrier of Knights. Dark-green gunk and twitching insects painted the land as the town burned in the distance from the stray fire.

Erec sunk to the ground; the Markos II wobbled and barely held together; all of the joints felt loose. A stray wind could cause the plating to fall off. For a good half of the fight, his left arm had stopped functioning, and he had to rely on his Strength to use it beneath the Armor.

But he was alive.

He hadn't lost his head and cost his friends theirs.

Of course, Erec felt pleased to see a blinking notification in the corner of his vision. VAL again remarked on a strange biological change twice in the fight. Erec assured VAL it was nothing to be concerned about, though it'd been hard to tell in the heat of the moment what he'd gained. But he suspected something significant. At one point, it was like he'd flipped a switch, his body far more responsive than before and able to shift and balance incomparably. As if he innately understood better coordination, his body fell into a rhythm of war.

As the Knights milled about torching the bug corpses to ensure there wasn't a single survivor, Erec opened the notification from the Blessing.

**Vigor Advancement: Rank F - Tier 7 → Rank F - Tier 9**
**Agility Advancement: Rank F - Tier 9 → Rank E - Tier 1**

Erec let out a small laugh. *Yes.* That was a breakthrough to the E rank. He pulled up the rest of his Blessings.

**Name: Erec of House Audentia**
**Health: 47% | Mana: 100% | Stamina: 23%**

**Holy Virtues:**
**Strength: [Rank E] | [Tier 5]**
**Vigor: [Rank F] | [Tier 9]**
**Agility: [Rank E] | [Tier 1]**
**Perception: [Rank E] | [Tier 1]**
**Cognition: [Rank E] | [Tier 3]**
**Psyche: [Rank F] | [Tier 7]**
**Mysticism: [Rank F] | [Tier 1]**
**Faith: [Rank F] | [Tier 1]**

There it was. Four of his Virtues were now in the E rank. A respectable accomplishment; plenty of humans never achieved that level of progress. They didn't put in the time and training. But there was nowhere to go but up from here. Erec grinned beneath the helmet.

[A spike of dopamine. We survived, so I suppose that's a natural response for any human. Congratulations on not dying, Intern. I'm sorry to report that the Markos II will have to be retired. The damage sustained is irreparable. We will, however, keep the helmet. It pleases me.]

That wiped the grin from his face. Baron Jeswald had fronted the promissory for the loaner Armor. And while it wasn't ungodessly expensive, there was a particular reason the average commoner didn't own a Markos I, Markos II, or Custos model. Namely, they were still *advanced* pieces of technology that were both hard to obtain and highly regulated, and the costs for the frames and cores were high, even in outdated ones.

"Crap." At least if he attended the Academy, he'd receive a stipend. Maybe a few months of that would cover the money the Baron was now on the hook for.

He felt terrible, though. Even though this was a loaner Armor, a piece of near junk compared to the currently used models, the Markos II had gotten him through a lot. With it, he'd scrapped his way past the trial, and it'd kept him alive outside the wall for a major fight. He sighed. That was the way of the world; everything crumbled.

As for the helmet? Yeah, good luck convincing the Duke it was a trinket of victory deserved for bashing his son's brains in.

Boldwick strode into their little fortress, his visor open and a big smile on his face. "Congratulations; you survived, you thrived, and you murdered a bunch of pests. Welcome to your first genuine experience of being a Knight." His gleeful eyes took them all in. "This isn't the line of work for heroes. No. It's dirty, disgusting, and deadly. But look around you." He gestured to the viscera splashed across the room's insides. "Thanks to our efforts, the Kingdom will never hear or be threatened by these awful creatures. Take pride in that. Take pride in protecting others."

Garin met Erec's eyes. There was a bruise across his face from where a Thrashing Mite had busted through his helmet. His jaw was swollen, but his friend smiled and gave a thumbs-up.

"Father?" Colin muttered in the corner of the room before a groan.

"We'll get him to see a priest. I think it's long past time we bring you all back within the wall. I'll leave five of my Knights deployed on the field for clean-up, and the rest will form an escort so we may return."

All of the Knights responded to Sir Boldwick's commands instantly; he was a Master Knight, after all. Even if they were from an assortment of the four Orders, they complied without complaint and with great discipline. As he said, they began the trek back to the Kingdom not thirty minutes later.

— - ☣ - — - ☼ - — - ☣ - —

Once behind the massive steel walls of the Kingdom, everyone in the group breathed easier. Garin strolled forward with his hands behind his head—helmet held by Rodren as he embraced the night air. Rodren kept a leisurely pace next to him. Erec, for his part, wanted the space to reflect on his failings that complicated the fight.

It'd been an overreaction to go so far against Colin. But what could he have done differently to stop him from starting that wild assault? They would've been lost if Colin had set off more fire, surely. Someone could have died, likely either himself or Rodren.

It wasn't wrong to tackle him and disable him. It wasn't even wrong to be angry about what Colin had tried after the fact. And it was debatable if his retaliation had been wrong either. There'd been an attempt on his life.

What was wrong was that he'd continued to bash Colin after he'd stopped fighting back.

Erec didn't want to be the kind of person who'd lose his head like that, someone who'd attack indiscriminately. He didn't even want to fight with other humans; as the swarm of Thrashing Mites had shown, that was folly.

Maybe he was still sulking. But having the distance from other people let him sort through his feelings, even if it meant rehashing the same arguments in his head, reframing them, and re-approaching from a different angle to gain new insights.

They trekked the fields and reached the Academy, located a mile from the city proper.

It was a prestigious campus; four large buildings devoted to each Order laid out in the cardinal directions around a central fortress. The sizeable castle-like center dominated the Academy and was four times the size of the individualized wings. In a way, it symbolized the Knight's function. All of the Orders might have their differences, but they bowed their heads in respect to the Kingdom; they were all small when compared to the will of the people.

Boldwick led them to the Verdant Oak quarter on the western side of the campus. Lush vegetation surrounded the red-bricked structure; vines grew all along the side of the brickwork, and a large greenhouse hung off the side of the building. Knights spewed out at Boldwick's approach—he barked a couple of commands, and they took Colin off toward the central fortress of the Academy.

Not far away, inside of that large stone fortress, would be all of the nobility waiting to watch them return from the expedition, hear the results of the testing, and no doubt gossip about the results before the ceremony.

"There were some questionable choices out there, but overall, I can't say I've got much to complain about. None of you died. We made it back fine. Though your trial was cut short, I'll keep these details in mind as I write my report." Boldwick took a deep sigh. "Considering we've come back a whole day earlier than the rest of those taking the trial, I could house you in the Academy. And if you were Initiates, I'd do just that."

He looked up at the moon sinking on the horizon.

"But you aren't. Not yet. So, I'll be sending you home. I recommend you enjoy the rest and consolidate your time with your Houses while you may. If you become a Knight, there is much you must give up to serve the Kingdom. It asks a lot of you. It's greedy, always hungry for more. So go, take the time you need, and return here the morning after the next for the ceremony."

With that command given, the Master Knight dismissed them. Erec moved to head off with Garin to the elevator when Lyotte caught him by the arm.

Her visor was withdrawn, letting her thick black curls spill out of her advanced Armor. That grip of hers was too firm to resist with his Armor barely holding together. "How did you do it?"

Garin paused and glanced back at them, before snickering. "I'll see you at the elevator." He waved over his shoulder as he damn near jogged out of the situation. Erec frowned; go figure Garin would misinterpret whatever *this* was. Lyotte's eyes burned into him now that they were alone.

"I want some answers; it's obvious something's off."

# CHAPTER 15
## HOME

"I lost control, that's it," Erec said as the girl pressed him about what happened to Colin. Damn, why was she so persistent about this?

"You shouldn't have been able to do that. I know the engineer that worked with the Nitidus family to make his model. We often contract out to her as well; she's a talented woman. And I know that a Markos II doesn't have the kind of power to do damage like that. How high is your Strength?"

Erec winced. *That* was a rude question. One didn't go around asking after other's Virtues. He might share the details of his with someone like Garin or a trainer, but certainly not someone he barely knew. This girl was starting to rub him the wrong way. She held herself in the same sort of self-possessed way that was all too common to high nobility.

Just in a nosy direction instead of the arrogant-prick flavor of attitude like Colin, which wasn't quite as bad but felt almost equally annoying.

"How high are your Virtues? Why don't you list them out for me if you want to know mine." Erec crossed his arms and scowled at her. "If you're going to go around demanding something like that, you should be more than willing to share yourself."

"Fine. I will. My three highest Virtues are Psyche, Perception, and Mysticism. In that order." She didn't even blink as the words left her lips. Not a second of hesitation.

Erec's jaw dropped. *What is with her?* "… Alright, fine. My Strength is E-ranked, Tier 5." He couldn't very well keep it to himself when she called his bluff.

She shook her head at that explanation. "Are you lying to me? With that Strength, you wouldn't have been able to do that to him. And then there's his helmet—you shouldn't be able to see with it."

Erec didn't respond to that; her questioning if he'd been honest was the nail in the coffin for this conversation. She searched his eyes for *something*, then drew her lips thin. He wasn't sure what to make of her. It wasn't like the way she was speaking was hostile, even if she appeared to be getting annoyed at a breakneck pace.

"I'm asking because I want to understand. If I understand, I can help you."

"I never asked for your help; we don't know each other." *I don't trust her.* Why was she so interested in him? Why did she pay attention to the small things when no one else seemed to pick up on them? Was she that perceptive? Did she want to figure him out to use him like a pawn? "How about we go our separate ways, alright? I'm tired. I haven't gotten much sleep in the last two days, and I want to crawl into my bed and finally fucking sleep."

"*After* you answer my questions." She stood firm; her eyes held a defiant cast.

"Wow, you're no different from Colin. Listen, I get your family holds Goddess knows how much influence, and on any other day, I'd be willing to set aside my distaste and give you the conversation you seem to want. But in this case, I can't. There are no answers I can give you, and if you don't believe me, then there's not much I can do about that. I'm being blunt here because I get the sense that, unlike that prick, you don't want to be that way."

At the comparison to Colin, she frowned. Lyotte drew back and looked at the ground. "Fine. I'm sorry. I didn't want to come off that way. May I make one request?"

[She isn't sorry.]

No, she wasn't. She was frustrated but knew that Erec wasn't going to bend her way.

"I suppose so," Erec said. She wanted something from him, and it made him nervous that he couldn't place what it was or why she wanted it so badly.

"May we start again? Perhaps I've been a bit too forward, and perhaps I've held my head a little bit higher than I would with an equal... But I really would like to help you. The best way to do that is to...restart this relationship; if you'd be willing to look past our past, then I will too."

"Yeah. Another time. If there is one, we can start over." Erec turned, as there wasn't much else to say. When he looked over his shoulder, she was staring with her face scrunched. *What game is she playing?*

— - ❂ - — - ☼ - — - ❂ - —

It was sometime in the early morning—if that mattered down in the many floors and tunnels of the underground Kingdom—when Erec reached his home. Far too late, he'd realized that he'd held onto Colin's helmet. When he attempted to take it off his Armor, VAL refused to allow it, claiming it still had analysis to do, and to not concern himself with it.

While he wasn't pleased with the response, he was too exhausted to try to put up a fight.

The Audentia family estate was a small property in Jeswald's caverns; it was the size of a house a modest merchant or apprentice engineer could afford to rent out and live in. For a noble family, it was an utterly barren and small residence, but to Erec's family, it was more than they'd deserved. Generally, they felt grateful to have a roof over their head at all.

As Erec creaked the door open, his father, Lac Audentia, busied himself by putting work gear on. He stopped as he beheld the wearied and bruised visage of his son. The Markos II hung on the maintenance rack in the workshop he'd borrowed from the Baron. Busted apart, and clearly totaled, but Erec wasn't much better off. VAL tagged along in a leather bag that Erec had taken from the workshop, which he summarily tossed on the ground of the house without a word.

"Didja fail?" Lac asked, a hand stroking the sizable beard on his chin. One bushy brow raised as he regarded his son with a consoling expression. "Oh well. You tried. All that matters, Bedwyr is already in the Academy, so I'm sure we'll get along fine." The lanky man shrugged and returned to securing his boots.

"I didn't fail."

"Ain't the trial supposed to still be going?"

"Yes."

"Then how are you here if you're supposed to be there." His father shook his head and sighed. "You don't need to lie to me, boy. I'll let the Baron know you're ready to work the bio-caverns again. You're a skilled hand at it, and he's told me he appreciates the effort plenty o' times." Lac stood up and stretched out, then walked over to Erec and setting a hand on his shoulder. "We got plenty of work to do, don't we?"

"I *didn't* fail."

"Yeah, yeah. Whatever you say, son, proud of you for trying." With that parting gesture, Lac left the house, off to supervise construction on a new bio-cavern.

It was always like that. While their father expected Bedwyr to come out on top of everything he set a hand at, he never held a candle of hope for Erec's chances. If Erec caught him by surprise and found success, it was always a quick pat and a "that'a boy." Nothing more, nothing less. Was it because he was the second son? The inheritor to nothing, as the family only held a title? Did his achievements not matter as much?

It made him miss his mother, the kind of woman who'd start every day with a healthy smile on her face seeing her two boys. She always had a special treat for them at lunch, even with her duties as a Knight.

And then she'd betrayed them. Letting an intelligent thing from beyond a Rift past the walls; fifteen people died, and she fled with the monster she escorted in. *Why?*

[After some consideration, I've formed a hypothesis.] VAL hovered out of the leather bag—the red cube pulsed a red light that ran over the home's surface. [Humanity is being led down a guided evolution path. Without sounding too conspiratorial, it's not far off to conclude that something with vast intelligence is interacting with it, and bringing about these changes. Likely through this newfound anomalous energy. I would very much like to meet the entities responsible and question the purpose of keeping some useless trait lines in your physiology while removing others. For example: is there a point in retaining tail bones?]

"You're talking about the Goddess."

[That has been mentioned before. I'd concluded it to be a mythos perpetuated by man, as is typical to these legends.]

"She's real." Erec sat in a chair and leaned back, taking a moment to relax and soak in the peace. Let his dad think whatever he wanted. The Academy hadn't spoken yet about his admittance, though the situation with Colin left him nervous. His dad dismissing his chances like that drew the worry out further for him, and now the idea refused to leave his head. "She's the one who cleansed the world in holy flames and prevented the Rifts from destroying us all. In the process, she Blessed us with magic to fight back. Or as you put it, 'anomalous energy.'"

[There cannot be certainty to a divinity. Per their nature, they are beings of faith.]

"No, she very much exists. The Cardinal can commune with her and channel her voice; on occasion, she descends to appear before a mighty Knight and issue a quest." Granted, the last time she'd deigned to come to their Kingdom *had* been thirty years ago. But there was a recording of the event. Not that they could capture her well on video; her radiant energy distorted all of their attempts. Still, the physical proof and records existed to document it and a few other previous contacts.

[Understood.] VAL floated back into the bag.

For a long time, Erec sat in the chair. Questioning whether or not he'd done enough—or if his stunt with Colin ruined his chances at getting in the Academy.

It wouldn't be long at all until he discovered the fallout.

# CHAPTER 16
## SUMMONS

*The heat also of the world is more pure, clear, and lively, and, consequently, better adapted to move the senses than the heat allotted to us; and it vivifies and preserves all things within the compass of our knowledge.*

*It is absurd, therefore, to say that the world, which is endued with a perfect, free, pure, spirituous, and active heat, is not sensitive, since by this heat men and beasts are preserved, and move, and think; more especially since this heat of the world is itself the sole principle of agitation, and has no external impulse, but is moved spontaneously; for what can be more powerful than the world, which moves and raises that heat by which it subsists?*

-Cicero, Marcus Tullius, Cicero's Tusculan Disputations (45, 1st Era)

Erec dreamt of a sea of ruby-red eyes. Every single one of them stared at him as their sheer weight suffocated him. His fingers clawed at the lenses, finding no purchase as they slipped on tears. Inch by inch, he sank further into the depths, dragged under as they slid aside and made way for him to fall deeper in their embrace.

They would take him, consume him, and drag him to their depths. Once they owned him, he would become one of them.

Erec scrambled against them, sinking lower and lower…

Hammering at the door woke him up with a start. Erec's head slammed up as the wooden doors shook—his heart raced, and a pool of sweat coated his bed sheets.

[Ah. You're awake at long last.]

There was a pause at the door, followed by a muffled command on the opposite side.

[You've had eleven hours of rest. Typical for an Intern. I take it you're ready and willing to take the day into your hands and pursue further personal development?]

The knocking began again. Erec groaned and pulled himself out of bed, doing his best to regain composure from the nightmare. He tossed on a beige linen shirt and stalked to the door. "Stay in your bag, alright?"

[Of course, I wouldn't dream of revealing myself. Observation yields better data.]

Erec cracked the door open to reveal a squished face of a man wearing mail. He wore a tabard displaying the black silhouette of a hippogriff with its hooves reared. *House Nitidus*. In truth, he'd expected something like this. As the house guard took stock of him, Erec raised his hands up in a sign of peace. "I'll go get Colin's helmet; you can have it. I didn't intend to keep it."

"Aye, then you're Erec?" the man asked.

"Sure am; I left the helmet in my workshop along with my busted Armor, and I should be able to retrieve it in about fifteen minutes. If you want to come back a little later—"

"Aye, No, you'd best be bringing it yourself." The man reached into a pouch and withdrew a letter. The envelope was sealed by a dollop of wax and stamped with the same hippogriff on the man's tabard. *That's not good.*

He wasn't sure how House Nitidus was going to react to what he'd done to Colin got out to the rest of the nobility. The best he'd hoped was that they'd delay their response for a few days. If he were in the Academy, he'd have the backing of an Order, and any repercussions would take that into account; instead, he was damn near defenseless. His House had functionally no power.

"Best to ya." The man nodded his head and then cleared his throat. "For what it's worth, I think ya gave him somethin' that was a long time coming, and me and none of the guards find fault in what ya did to 'im."

*He's talking about Colin.* That confirmed it. That was why he'd come; House Nitidus was already providing their official response over what happened during the trial.

With that, the guard left. Erec stared at the letter in his hand, the weight of which felt like the world.

He walked over to the table, set the letter on the worn wooden surface, and stared at the red wax. Why did the hue fall too close to the haunting ruby of his nightmares? He broke the seal and opened the letter.

*Attention House Audentia,*

*Per the power bestowed upon the Duchy of Nitidus, and permitted by the Royal Court, Erec of House Audentia is officially mandated to appear at the court of the Duchy of Nitidus. This audience is intended to resolve lingering inquiries and misappropriated property owing to the events that came to pass over the last several days during the Academy Trial.*

*Time is of the essence, and if Erec of House Audentia fails to report to the Duchy of Nitidus by May 23, 307, a force of several Knights will be permitted for dispatch to ensure compliance. Failure to comply will result in censure and fines totaling up to 1050 Silver Denarii to the House Audentia.*

*Additionally, Erec of House Audentia is to bring the one (1) misappropriated helmet belonging to Cserula IV-grade Armor. Whose proper ownership is Colin of House Nitidus, last seen in possession of the party as mentioned earlier after the conflict outside of our Kingdom's walls on May 22, 307.*

*Once at the court of the Duchy of Nitidus on the second cavern floor zone 2-A, Erec of House Audentia will officially present himself to the station guards and thus will fulfill the mandate issued in this document.*

*From the court of the Duchy of Nitidus, writ at the behest of Duke Alfon Nitidus,*

*Authorized by the House Crisimus, sovereign House to the Kingdom Of Cindrus.*

The bottom of the document ended in the official stamps of both the Royal Family and the Duchy of Nitidus.

Erec reread the letter and paused at the mention of a fine. It almost seemed like an additional spiteful threat. Which, he supposed, was the purpose. And right there, the name of the Duke. Alfon Nitidus. The Unbroken General. The man who single-handedly led the Cindrus Army to repel a Cataclysm-Level threat from the wall; a war hero, and not the sort of man who played games.

This was the consequence of his actions. Losing control led to this.

Erec folded the paper up and stared at the doorway, letting the time slip away while he tried to consider what he'd say, how he might explain himself, and what the Unbroken General might choose to do in response to his actions. Was there a way to spare his House? If he renounced his name, maybe it would lead to sparing his brother and father from this.

— - ☻ - — - ☼ - — - ☻ - —

As ordered, Erec readied himself for his mandated audience at the Duchy of Nitidus. He put on the best formals he could—sharp slacks, a clean dress shirt with a collar, and one of the heavily buttoned jackets that fell out of style in the Kingdom about ten years ago. If he understood it right, the jacket had belonged to his father, then his brother, and now it was his.

Ironic that this same jacket had likely been worn on the day his mother was officially exiled.

He took the shaft elevator; it took what felt like ages for the ancient thing to crawl its way up to the second layer of caverns.

Once he reached the second layer, he saw a massive gate. Armed guards checked him over for weapons and purpose—this was the layer where the wealthy and the higher nobility made their homes.

Even if he was nobility, they had to ensure his paperwork and check for prohibited weapons.

After they discovered that no, he didn't have a damned sword, he managed to hand them his summons and their affable mood banished. The checkpoint guard called for an escort to send Erec on his way.

The road was long and left him with conflicted feelings. On the one hand, the beauty around him made for a visual of a long-forgotten earth scene. The curated bio-cavern provided great insight into the people who got to live out their lives on this layer.

First was the excessive size. The cavern roof extended high into the sky, yet not a single building likely exceeded four stories. Still the roof stretched far enough for ten. This cavern ceiling was unique to the second floor, inlaid with stacking enhancements and spell-work that transformed the rocks above into a replica of the sky outside. In the middle of the ceiling was a glowing orb—almost as strong as a sun. It provided enough light for plant life to flourish, much like a regular bio-cavern.

But the plant life here was utterly ornamental. Mostly wasteful varieties of grass had been meticulously cut on square-like yards of lawn that stretched as far as the eye could see.

Erec held a particular grudge against the insane value nobles put on grass. With the sunlight and water it took to grow, they could've just as easily grown more beneficial plant life: fruits, vegetables, and any root plant to supplement the Kingdom's supplies.

But no. This layer contained only flowers and grass—though at least they did allow natural pollinators.

Aside from his grudge over their choice in biodiversity, or lack thereof, he had to admit the pristine architecture and sculptures were breathtaking. He took a long look at a silver depiction of the First King. The man had shattered the uneasy treaties of the ancient layers and forced them together. At the time they claimed he was a conqueror; a warmonger. But two hundred years later the consolidation of humanity's resources showed its fruit, and people proclaimed him a great king.

Would their ancestors have pictured living on the surface once more?

The escort gradually led Erec deeper into the layer. The cavern stretched out just as large as the city above, providing vast swaths of space to noble holdings and estates. Within some of those holdings would be small villages, populated by specialized artisans and servants attending to the noble families who owned the lands.

As much as the nobles treated this cavern as the center of the Kingdom, they were wrong. Fifty percent of their population lived on the third and fourth layers. Both layers connected a bustling city triple the size of this curated space. A maze of confusing corridors and smaller caverns that defined the Kingdom in a way a place like this never would.

At the end of their stroll, they approached what looked to be a small castle—complete with stone walls. Was it a measure of status or privilege that had allowed the Nitidus family to defend themselves from the rest of the Kingdom openly? Or was it the remains of a time before the Kingdom? Erec couldn't say; his grasp of history regarding the nobility was painfully limited. Ironically, the Academy didn't place much importance on it either, despite its composition being primarily nobility. Aside from the Silver Flames.

At the gates, the house guards of the Duchy took over supervision of Erec, so he followed them to his fate, sky-blue helmet held in hand.

# CHAPTER 17
## THOSE THAT ARE GREAT

The guards escorted Erec through Nitidus's vast estate. Gorgeous old-world artifacts and new-age artwork lined the walls. The faded red-and-blue-starred flag set near the audience hall caught Erec's attention the most. Yet the beauty distracted from the moment, in the same way staring at the ceiling did when a doctor jammed you with a needle—it drew your focus away from the incoming pain.

Erec cleared his throat as he entered the audience chamber; fine carpeting led to a steel throne that commanded respect. Resting on the arm of the throne was a large spear—taller than a man, its tip carved into a wrapping groove that gave it the appearance of a massive flared screw. The similarities between this room and how he imagined the Royal Court were incalculable, and seated on the fine steel throne was the Unbroken General.

He was heavyset, his frame near herculean. Duke Nitidus's face was aged and tanned like the hide of a stag. Gray streaks highlighted his hair, and he had tired brown eyes that took Erec in with a lazy appreciation. He turned to his guards.

This was the man who had slain the Rot Behemoth, a creature capable of corrupting the flesh of any ordinary man who got close to it—then turned their corpses into walking abominations hell-bent on killing more. The monster had targeted their Kingdom, would have killed countless on the surface, and sent humanity into the deepest caverns to flee its putrid essence.

"You may go; you have my thanks for your due diligence," Duke Nitidus said, addressing the two guards escorting Erec with a tilt of his head and dismissing them.

They left through the door and slammed it behind them, leaving Erec alone with the Duke.

A long moment passed as they traded a silent stare. Erec wasn't sure where this would go—what sort of punishment would he demand? It seemed that the Duke was content in the oppressive silence. He waited for Erec to act, break, and show his hand.

Erec folded under that steel scrutiny, trying to hide his shaking hands. He took quick steps to the throne, leaned down, and placed the Cserula IV's helmet. "My sincere apologies. I needed it for the battle."

There was a swish of air—knocking Erec back from his supplication and onto his ass. Quicker than his eyes could track, the Duke had drawn his spear, then cut the flat end through the space between them to collect the helmet. The sheer speed in which he slashed through the air had created enough pressure to send Erec reeling. The helmet rested on the end of the spear. The Duke popped it into the air a second later and caught the spinning helmet in his free hand.

The Duke leaned the spear back on the throne, then ran a finger over the deep dent marring the helmet's otherwise smooth surface.

"This was an expensive helmet. I did not spare for defense when it came to protecting my heir; Armor fits the man, and, unfortunately, the limitations of his power reduced how complex we could make the model…" The Duke sighed and shook his head. "That a hatchet and an ill-maintained Markos II held enough power to do this is unbelievable. After looking over the specifications prepared by my engineer, it is an impossible feat."

Erec kept silent, eyes on that spear. If the Duke had wanted, he could've run him through with the weapon before Erec knew what happened. Did he twist the spearhead as it stabbed into his opponent, digging it deeper in the same way a screw tunneled through wood?

"Yet, 'there is nothing impossible to him who will try,' is that the saying? I do believe so." With that statement, the Duke threw the helmet over his shoulder—it smashed against the wall and then clattered to the floor. After which, the Unbroken General pressed his attention onto Erec in full; there was a tangible weight behind those eyes. "When confronted with reality we must adapt. You gave my son a concussion and sought further harm. In addition to that, I've been told you levied insults aplenty during the Academy's trial."

"I had cause at the time, yet I acted rashly. I did not mean to get that carried away or to bring harm to your House." Erec stood straighter. "However, the mistakes I made are mine alone. Not any that belong to House Audentia. Whatever punishment it is you're seeking, I would ask that they be excluded from it. If required, I will denounce myself from the family line."

"You have a brother and a father."

"I do," Erec said.

"Then you should understand the burden of a family line. I have but one heir, and as I've grown, I've come to realize there is precious else that matters of one's legacy than that which will carry it on to the future."

Erec kept silent at this; a calm had come to the Duke's expression. The man stood at full height—half a foot taller than Erec; he was a warrior. The scars running across his face whispered stories of war, and there was a coldness in his cadence that hinted at a man used to seeing the death of those around him.

"I shall state plainly; not one among the Academy's Orders is willing to offer you rank. This is due to the grievance against my House. Considering that your actions led to injury against my heir, and if you were not stopped, worse would have occurred, they don't dare to offer insult so publicly." Erec's blood ran cold, and his gut twisted into knots. Everything he worried about, the poisonous whispers in the back of his head he fought to ignore, were confirmed. The way the Duke spoke of his doomed fate was matter-of-fact, frank as a general is or ought to be when discussing the situations his troops face. "As to be expected, they have a healthy fear of provoking my anger."

"I-I beg your forgiveness."

"Do not dare insult me with platitudes. Your actions were justified."

Erec jerked as if the Duke hit him; so strongly did the confusion at the statement slap him upside the head. *He understands why I did what I did?*

"However, do not mistake my ability to comprehend the full

extent of the situation as a resolution of forgiveness. No. I am still angry that you brought harm to my son, that you would have gone further had you not been stopped. But I am not the type to make decisions based on anger. Such rash strategies devised by emotion ignore opportunities one might otherwise seek." The Duke sighed and returned to his throne; he sat and leaned forward, resting his chin in hand.

"So you're still going to punish me… I'm confused. If you think what I did was justified, then…"

"Yes. You may hate me for the punishment I chose to issue. You may despise me for taking away the freedom you crave. But I will have you see why I must do it," the Duke said as Erec's eyes narrowed.

*This is it. He's going to keep me out of the Academy. If it is just that, then maybe…* No, it wouldn't be fine. For as long as he remembered, all he'd dreamed of was to be a Knight. To take that away wasn't taking away freedom from him; it was taking away the reason why he drew breath.

"I already do see the flames of hate stoking in your eyes. So, I will begin my explanation and then present to you the punishment I've deemed fit." The Duke nodded his head slowly. "I've been a poor father. My name may have weight to it; my actions may have saved many. Yet those accomplishments were owed to my fixation on how I might push myself to new heights. I am a great general, yet a bad father. When I had a son, I was overjoyed yet gave him little of my time. It was a mistake, yes. That I see plain with hindsight. Colin grew up with little guidance; his mother spoiled him, as she, bless her, had a weak heart for such things. I cannot blame her, as I do too for these matters."

Erec remained silent. Was it fair of this man to sit here and throw out all of these reasons before he stole away Erec's dream? That was what it meant to be higher nobility: you could do what you wanted, and those beneath had to live with it.

"He grew up alone. Our name convinced those around him to pay him great respect, and we never truly taught him how to interact reasonably with others. For that, now, others pay the price for his sheer arrogance. Far too late, I realized the impact of this. My attempts to correct the behavior now only drive a wedge deeper between us and aggravate his attitudes. Were I a stronger man, I'd disinherit him to teach him his place. Yet doing so would lose me my only son."

That was it; Erec couldn't bite his tongue any further. "So you let him get away with it?"

"Yes. I have for far too long. Yet you've done something I hadn't managed. When he spoke of you, there was hate, yet also respect. Due to your actions, that arrogance tempered." The Duke sighed and rubbed his temple. "This is not an easy situation, nor is it easy to admit my failings so bluntly. Yet for you to do what I wish, I must. I would see you befriend my son and change the course of his future. I fear his time in the Academy will lead to isolation or, at the worst, lead him to be surrounded by those who seek to use him. They would offer him praise and platitudes in return for status and power, a trap I am ashamed to admit he would fall easily for. Such people would gladly stab him in the back later for power."

*What the hell? The way he makes it sound…*

"I am not a fair man, and thus I charge you with a twofold punishment. You will attend the Academy and, in doing so, forge a bond of friendship with my son. Whatever the task may take, I expect you to accomplish it. And once ingrained in his private life, you will keep me abreast of his affairs."

"…Your punishment is me befriending him—I don't even think that's possible—and then spying on him for you?" Erec was baffled.

"From respect comes mutual understanding. And from that may come friendship. Through the Academy's lens, I saw your interactions with the others in your group. I believe it would be possible if you were to set your mind to it." The Duke stopped leaning on his hand, setting both of his arms on the throne, and sat straight. He cut a figure like a King. A man who would not be denied his royal orders, his voice held a steel tone to it that commanded absolute obedience.

Erec found himself faltering. This *was* a way to avoid repercussions for his family. "I thought you said that none of the Orders were willing to offer me a place."

"There is a Master Knight who has been relentless about granting you a position in their Order. Were I to send a missive to that Knight's Order expressing my private support, they'd be willing to fold and allow him to take any political ramifications for the gesture."

Meaning that the Order would take the heat, but knowing that the Duke wouldn't take direct action against them, they would be willing to weather the fallout. "Sir Boldwick, who witnessed your actions firsthand, also realized the justification behind them. He saw how you may have prevented a bad situation from getting worse. Even if you did go too far."

*He stood up for me?* It was hard to reconcile the otherwise affable Master Knight with someone willing to press on an issue like that. Erec wasn't aware he'd made that big of an impression.

"With all that has been said; do I have your vow that you will cede to my punishment and use the utmost of your ability to fulfill them?"

"...You do."

"I would have you make the vow upon the Goddess's name."

Erec looked up to the heavens, heart constricting in his chest. A vow on Her name was the most binding an agreement could get. Failing to meet your vow wrought consequences upon you by the Goddess Herself.

"I vow to do my utmost to befriend Colin Nitidus, to sway him from his arrogance and bring him to a better path. In doing so, I will give you any information about him that you wish. This I swear by the Goddess Lavinia."

His heart seized as if a hand clutched it—Erec gasped. The pressure faded away, yet he still felt a numbness settle in him. The Duke gave a slight nod.

"Very well. Your punishment has been issued. I will send a missive to the Order of the Verdant Oak. I expect to see you at the ceremony tomorrow morning." With a wave of his hand, he dismissed Erec. With little hesitation, Erec stumbled out of the chamber. His mind raced and ached as he considered how he'd befriend Colin to spy on him.

*Impossible. This is impossible.* The words of the Unbroken General echoed in his head, "There is nothing impossible to him who will try." *I'm screwed.*

# CHAPTER 18
## SOIRÉE

*We have been reborn by Her Holy Flames.*
*It is through Her we weathered this assault on our world.*
*Through Her we gain Vigor.*
*By Her will we Perceive.*
*By Her grace we are Cognizant.*
*Our Agility was given to achieve Her purpose.*
*We see the lines of fate with our Psyche through Her.*
*We witness the Mysticism of this new world and form it in Her image.*
*To Her we owe Faith.*
*To Her we devote our Strength.*
*It is Her will that we should reconquer that which is ours, and take that which is not.*

*- Unknown, Doctrine of the Holy Flames (1, 3rd Era)*

Erec's father didn't come back that day, and as the hours slipped into the "night," his father remained gone. Not that it was uncommon or unexpected. During construction on new bio-caverns, the supervisor would often sleep at the work site in case a major complication arose.

Yet it hurt. Erec knew he'd be joining the Academy after his conversation with the Duke; he could've looked his dad in the eyes and shared that he, too, would become a Knight. Not just Bedwyr, but him as well.

But no, that information wouldn't get shared, so he kept it locked away. At some point, Baron Jeswald or someone else would tell Lac that his son joined the Academy. With no choice, Erec dismissed the pain as another thing to forget and move past. He packed a case full of some clothing and a couple of trinkets he'd bring to his new life. He made sure to tuck away the last letter his mother left deep within to keep it safe.

Once accepted to the Academy tomorrow, he would come back for his things and move out that day. There wasn't any reason to linger here, even if a new Initiate was permitted three full days before required attendance.

After packing, Erec wrote a letter to Baron Jeswald—sharing his gratitude for his job in the bio-caverns. It also included the location of the Markos II. Along with another note that officially granted the Baron access to his financial accounts until he'd paid back damages inflicted on the Armor. A few months' stipends from the Academy should pay the debt off.

He'd say as much to the Baron tomorrow when he met Garin at their property. They planned to take the elevator and head to the ceremony together. Preemptively authorizing his accounts to cover the debt would save the Baron any headache. He owed the man a lot, and the man was his best friend's father.

Would Garin have a spot? And if so, in what Order? Rodren too? Had they all proved themselves apt in the field, despite how grossly they'd been set up to fail? Those questions would dwell until tomorrow.

VAL floated around his home and then eventually came to a lazy hover in front of Erec at the table. Tea was brewing, and his head kept swimming over what-ifs and how to fulfill his vow to the Duke. Despite having been so driven for so long, when finally presented with the thing he'd craved, he didn't know how to let himself relax and enjoy it. There was a sort of emptiness that sank deep in him as he considered the future and what he knew he had to do.

[So this is reaching one of your goals?]

"Yeah, I've reached what I set out to do."

[Very well done, Intern. It is vital to set goals and hold yourself accountable. But once a goal has been achieved, a new one must be defined. It is through this process that the mind does not become stagnant, that you can then continue to learn and grow. Have you pictured what comes next?]

"I'm going to become a great Knight. I'll outdo Bedwyr. Then I'll step past him and do what he can't; I'll find our mother."

[Goals updated. I expect great progress; otherwise, you will not receive a favorable performance review come the end of the year.]

Erec spent the night alone in his old home, nursing a pot of pine needle tea and wondering just how much he'd miss the life that he'd worked so hard to leave behind.

— - ☣ - — - ☼ - — - ☣ - —

Garin and Erec arrived at the Academy on the morning of the ceremony. They first approached the massive entrance to the castle-like structure in the middle for the first time. This was the heart of the campus, where their futures would be decided and forged through hard work.

Passing through the entrance hall, one might see all of the most renowned Knights. Heroes who defined what humanity was capable of. The idols who'd pressed back against a hostile world and shone as beacons of what the greatest among them could be. They dedicated this area to statues honoring those long past. While Sir Boldwick may have claimed heroes didn't exist, the Academy shouted the opposite message.

The strife of this world was the reason why heroes existed.

Even this early, the flow of nobles and would-be Initiates pulled them to the great hall like a river. Those who had gone the entire length of the trial were filtering in. Just after the sun came up this morning, they'd returned, racked their Armor, and then swapped into formal wear for the ceremony.

Erec wore much the same as he did the night before—the jacket that belonged to his father, then his brother, and now him. The last in a too-long line of owners; once he had his military formals, the outdated formal wear would burn a tragic death in a scorching fire.

Garin, in contrast, was wearing a stylish and modern outfit.

Despite his rank as a Baron's son, his friend had a keen interest in keeping up with the highest of fashion—he wore a silk dress shirt with too-big cuffs that flared out in ruffles at the ends. Along with a jacket without sleeves and a done-up collar with that same ruffled texture. Entirely too fanciful.

Erec hated to admit that Garin cut a dashing figure. Yet, he had to. Based on the looks Garin received from many of the Ladies and Dames they passed, his friend's obsession with the current trends paid dividends.

Garin flashed Erec a grin and set a hand on his shoulder as they reached the waiting room. Over the course of the following three hours, this place would fill with more of the trial's challengers. Already serving staff circulated with drinks and hors d'oeuvres as a reward for those who made it through.

Keeping the potential Initiates separated from the rest of the nobility served the purpose of organizing them for the ceremony. But it had a secret goal. It forced their would-be Initiates to start forming bonds.

This was a thinly veiled offshoot of a soirée. Erec tugged at his collar as Garin's eyes tracked the groups already forming at the social gathering. *I despise this sort of thing.*

He'd been lucky; with the status of House Audentia, the only social events he'd ever been invited to were the Baron's.

"Why so stiff? C'mon, buddy. We made it, finished the trial, and killed a bunch of bugs! You should be smiling right now." Garin met someone's eyes and shot them a wink.

"The ceremony can't come quickly enough."

"See, I get that. You constantly work; honestly, sometimes you work too hard. Now and again, you need to cut back and enjoy life. There's no point otherwise, right? So—just tag along with me. If you don't want to talk to anyone, that's fine with me. I'll do the talking for both of us. But what's important is to start forging new connections and be seen—" Garin tilted his head to a bit of a smaller group forming in the corner. Rodren was among them and chatting rather happily. "See? This place is filled with our future classmates. They'll be sitting in our lectures all year long. They might drive you forward in ways you'd never expect."

Erec nodded begrudgingly and then let Garin take the lead. They, of course, stopped by a table serving glasses of wine and Erec took a glass of red wine. He wouldn't drink *too* much, but a little would go a long way toward working through the time it took to get to the ceremony.

Besides, seeing his friend so happy made him nervous. The Duke guaranteed Erec a spot in an Order. But what of Garin? What of Rodren? Both of them he hoped to see up there too.

What if Garin didn't make it?

Group after group, Garin dragged him through and made introductions. Nobles, commoners, and even merchants' offspring. So many names and faces that they began to blend together. Garin would make a pithy joke; after about ten minutes, they'd say goodbye and flow ever onward to a new group of people.

"So, then this crazy bastard shoved his hand right through the damn queen! Eggs were flying everywhere so fast I thought he'd spawned a whole new army of the awful things!" Garin gave an easy laugh, echoed by the gaggle of nobles in the latest group.

One of them wore a straight expression through the story, tilting his head as he shifted his eyes to Erec. Even though it was a story about him—one that Garin already told a variation of once—the intensity of the stare threw him off. "He's one of the two that had a Markos model, if I remember correctly," the boy said in a cold tone.

Garin cleared his throat and gave the stranger a winning smile. "Sure is, isn't that right, Erec?"

"Yeah. The abdomen is a weak point on the queens, I lost my hatchet shoving it off me, so I had to make do with what I had. I held my fingers straight, and took the plunge. It was either that or have it jump back on me and leave me in a worse position," Erec said.

"Admirable. You identified a weak point, and then you acted decisively. I'd heard that the Thrashing Mites didn't make any noise during the assault. Is this true?" The boy had stark black hair and blue eyes; he was the definition of calm, to the point where it felt forced. The boy dressed as finely and in the same fashion as Garin, yet with a more refined and less outward slant, as far as one could dial it back, given the rather flashy nature of the court's fashion.

"No, they were completely quiet. No noise, aside from reacting to pain. Where did you get that information?"

The black-haired boy shrugged. "Tales are carried far by the desert winds. Though it is quite another thing to hear it confirmed by the source."

"What was your name again? I'm sorry, I don't recall it," Erec said, scratching the back of his head. With all of the faces, names, and introductions already flown through, he couldn't put one to this guy.

"Soren. That is no fault of your own. I had yet to give it." The boy looked out over the rest of the gathering; he frowned at the large clock on a wall. At Erec's side, Garin went stock still. "Apologies, I must be going. There's little time remaining, and I still have a few obligations to address. I look forward to attending the Academy with you. I'm sure you'll prove worthy of competition."

Soon after, Garin bid their quick farewells to the group and yanked Erec aside.

"Holy shit, Erec do you know who that was?"

"Nope, no clue." Erec sighed. After two hours of talking to people and the loud noise of the crowd, he already felt well and truly drained. Yet each hour only seemed to charge his friend up more. It'd have been grating if it were anyone *but* Garin.

"That was Prince Soren Crisimus, third in line for the royal throne. I didn't recognize him until the name—it's been years since I saw him, but I'm sure of it."

Erec scanned the crowd, but among the swollen ranks of nobles now present, it was impossible to say where he'd gone. He'd known a Prince had attended the trial; as odd such an occurrence was after everything that happened, he didn't have the headspace to remember or truly care. But that was the guy? Why was he so interested in their fight with the bugs?

A short time later, the horn blared, signaling the ceremony was about to begin.

# CHAPTER 19
## OF KNIGHTS

C alling it a great hall felt like an understatement. The long length of the room stretched far enough to accommodate hundreds of tables. Each set for different gatherings of nobility and the families invited to attend the ceremony. On top of *that*, there was room for Knights who also wished to attend this auspicious event. *Then* there was room for standing along the sides of the hall, where all of those who participated in the trial waited.

Many of whom would be culled.

The Knights were an elite force that took the top of society and martial prowess. And while the trial might be retaken year after year, they preferred to induct members at a young age to maximize their development and education.

Many nobles who failed their first trial would live out their days in their family's holdings. Or, if they weren't too full of pride, they would enroll in the Kingdom's military as officers.

At the head of the hall were the four Grandmaster Knights. There could only be one at the head of each Order. They had the final say in new Initiates, and it was to them that the Initiate would make their first oath to uphold their Order's first tenet.

Erec took them in with careful attention as the herald announced the grand history and schedule of the ceremony. It wasn't something he needed to hear. The course of today and its significance was seared into his head a year ago when Bedwyr joined the Order of the Crimson Lotus.

He looked at the same frail old man who'd extended the offer to his brother. Not much had changed about Grandmaster Lotus.

Each of the Grandmasters relinquished their given name and family name to take on the name of their Order when they accepted the position. Grandmaster Lotus appeared to be a frail man, though it was a mistake to think that. His wizened appearance hid a magical power that could single-handedly wipe out the surface city of the Kingdom.

Next to him was Grandmaster Oak, the one Erec would make his oath to. He was a hale man who wore a grin almost hidden by the thick black beard which trailed down his round belly. Erec had heard that Grandmaster Oak once lifted a mountain and dropped it over a Rift to prevent the unstemmable flow of imps that spewed out of it. Looking at him now, it was hard to reconcile the image with the story.

Erec's breath hitched.

Garin gave him a quick bump. "Show's about to start," his friend whispered.

"Lords and Ladies! Without further ado, we conclude Solis Academy's trial, that did finish in this, the May of the 307th Year of the Goddess's Rebirth." The voice of the herald rang through the hall. "We shall begin with the most esteemed to be present for this trial, Prince Soren Crisimus, third in line to the royal throne."

Polite applause rang through the crowd as the dark-haired boy walked from the side of the great hall to stand before the four Grandmasters. He bowed his head. This was one of the few rare circumstances where a Royal Family member was expected to show deference toward the Knights instead of the other way around.

"Prince Soren Crisimus has humbly subjected himself to the judgment of our Academy's Trial. As such, I now ask, as I shall with every hopeful to our Academy. Be there any among the Orders that would gladly accept him into their ranks?"

At once, all four of the Grandmasters drew their swords and raised them, points to the heavens.

*He has the choice of them all. As to be expected. But which one does he pick?*

Soren coldly examined them all before standing before Grandmaster Tower. Head of the Order of the Azure Tower, she was the youngest and newest to the position of Grandmaster. However, none that met her wrath lived to tell the tale.

Not that you'd be able to tell now, based on the smug smile she shot the other three Grandmasters. The golden-haired Grandmaster composed herself a second later and became the very picture of nobility. There was a quiet conversation between her and the Prince.

After which, Soren got to his knee and bowed his head. The Grandmaster's sword lowered and rested on his right shoulder.

"Do you accept my Order as your own? To join the Order of the Azure Tower is to agree to hold the safety of the Kingdom of Cindrus above all; even yourself. To be of this Order is to vow to defend and protect each of its citizens blindly, regardless of the office or state they may hold," she asked.

"I do," Prince Soren responded—their voices now amplified across the Great Hall by spell-work, though Erec didn't see the source.

"I can think of no better-fitting Order for one of the royal line. I would have your first oath be given before us all, Prince Soren."

"Upon my life, I do give my oath. From this day forward, I shall use my strength to face the tribulations of this world first, before they fall upon any other." Soren stared straight into her eyes. He'd delivered his assigned line, the first tenet of the Order of the Azure Tower.

Grandmaster Tower beamed. "Your oath has been heard by all in this esteemed hall. Let it be known today, I dub thee Sir Soren of House Crisimus, Initiate to the Order of the Azure Tower."

There was a chorus of applause in the hall. The Prince was led away by a Knight; it set a fair tone for the rest of the proceedings.

The next were the three from the ducal lines, the first of which was a woman Erec hadn't met. A girl with bright red hair. All four Orders offered her a position, and she chose to stand before Grandmaster Flames. Even among the four standing at the front of the great hall she stood out with her milky white eyes.

In a short time, Grandmaster Flames inducted a new Dame into her Order.

Erec heard that the Grandmaster held a high enough Faith to convene with the Goddess—though the Grandmaster publicly denied such a thing so as not to undermine the Cardinal's authority.

The redheaded Duchy-spawn looked pleased with her choice as a Knight led her away.

Next was Lyotte of House Luculentus. She, too, was offered an option of all four Orders, and she followed suit with the Prince's choice, joining the ranks of the Azure Tower. As her eyes scanned the crowd, they met Erec's. There was something there as she held his gaze before she left the great hall.

The biggest upset came next.

Colin strode before the Grandmasters with his head held high.

When the herald asked who among the Orders would accept him into their ranks, all four shared a look.

Grandmaster Oak's was the sole sword to raise into the sky. Colin's jaw dropped as hushed muttering ran through the assorted nobles like fire in a forest. It seemed that his actions had consequences, or more likely that this was a ploy by the Duke to place his son in the same Order as Erec.

Garin shook Erec's shoulder and rolled his eyes as Colin knelt and gave his oath to the only Order that would have him. He seemed a bit shaky, unnerved that they'd denied him the same opportunity as the two that shared his station.

*Oh well.* Erec sighed. If they were in the same Order, it'd make his task that much easier to accomplish. He sent a quick thanks to the Goddess as the ceremony proceeded onward.

They continued down from the top of the noble lines. After those of the Duchy came the spawn of the Earldoms, then the Counties, and then the Viscounties. It wasn't until they reached the children of the Baronies did Erec begin to pay attention again.

For the higher ranks, often, multiple Grandmasters would raise their swords, giving them a choice of Order. As they slipped down the ranks, that became less common and transformed into often only one of the Orders accepting the noble.

Then eventually, there was a daughter of a Count with no offers. And then a Count's third son, then three from different Viscounties denied in a row. When it got to the Baronies, only one in every three got accepted into an Order. Erec's heart began to race as they wore down the list of names.

Was Garin going to join him in the Academy?

At Erec's side, Garin kept an easy smile, but when Erec looked down at his friend's hand, he'd clutched it into a fist, fingernails digging into his palms.

"Garin of House Honestus, heir to the Barony of Honestus," the herald called, and Garin left to take his turn before all of the Grandmasters. They each regarded him with a rather severe expression. None of them betrayed their intentions. "Garin of House Honestus has displayed himself to our Academy's trial. Be there any among the Orders that would take him into their ranks?"

For a long horrible moment, none of the Grandmasters moved.

*No. Goddess, please, no.*

Grandmaster Oak raised his sword, followed quickly by Grandmaster Tower, and lastly, Grandmaster Lotus. The only one who stared straight ahead was Grandmaster Flames. A chorus of whispers rang through the crowd. There hadn't been three Orders offering a spot since they'd dropped below the Earldoms.

Garin gaped as the three Grandmasters stared him down. Erec grinned like a madman. He hesitated before moving to Grandmaster Oak.

*We'll be in the same Order.* It felt better than anything he could've dreamed of.

Grandmaster Oak inducted Garin quickly, as the ceremony had already gone on for quite some time. Yet when it came to the applause, they greeted Garin with a loud and infectious clapping.

The whole scene felt surreal. After his meeting with the Duke the day before, this was the single part of the day that still held Erec's nerves over a fire. Now that it was over, he felt he could relax and breathe easily. Nothing else mattered much, though he did want to see if Rodren got accepted into any of the Orders.

That is, until they called his name.

"Erec of House Audentia, second son to Lord Lac, unlanded," the herald cried, and Erec numbly made his way to the head of the hall.

After watching the ceremony thus far, he'd thought when it was his turn to join the Verdant Oak that the event would pass without much impact. As if it were a simple thing to do and walk away from, now that the Duke guaranteed it would happen.

Yet standing before the four Grandmasters and being judged before their gazes… These were pillars of humanity and power. Who was he to compare?

Whispers traveled through the crowd. Even at the head of the grand hall, he could make out some snippets of what the nobility said to one another. They were relatively poor at keeping their tones down.

"Isn't he that traitor's son?" a lady asked her husband.

"I'd thought that House was dissolved. Besides, how dare he show his face here after what he did to the Duke's heir?" said a portly man at the table in the front of the hall to a bearded gentleman.

"...no, no, I heard that the heir to his House is a Knight as well—supposedly accomplished for an Initiate. Though it's presumptuous for their House to try to sneak in a second of their ilk after what they did..."

*Ignore them.* Erec tuned out the voices and stood firm as he focused only on the herald's voice.

Let them talk whatever nonsense they wanted; he didn't answer to them, and whether or not they thought he deserved it, he'd earned his place at this Academy. Could their heirs say the same? The herald's amplified voice was easy to prioritize above the rest. "...Be there any among the Orders that would take him into their ranks?"

Grandmaster Oak raised his sword high into the air. Another round of vicious whispers burned its way through the crowd. With burning cheeks, Erec moved to stand before the Grandmaster.

"Hail there, lad. You've caused my lot much trouble, haven't you?" the round Grandmaster asked in a quiet tone. Whatever spell-work amplified their voices for the oaths appeared to be triggered by command, though Erec hadn't expected a private word.

"I apologize; I swear I'll do my best to do your Order proud."

Grandmaster Oak gave a small bark of a laugh; then, a rueful smile spread over his face. "Aye, you will by what Sir Boldwick promised. As for them out there?" He jerked his head at the crowds of whispering nobility. "Fuck 'em; we're Knights first, nobles second, as long as you're part of my Order, that is. Always have to beat that lesson into the new Initiates."

"I—"

"I take it you know your oath from the Goddess knows how many that came before?" Erec gave a slight nod. "Good, good. On your knee then, lad."

Erec crouched to his knee and bowed his head. The tip of Grand-master Oak's sword rested on his right shoulder.

The steel blade was a biting cold that weighed on him even through the padding of his too-buttony jacket. "Do you accept the Order of the Verdant Oak as your own?" the man's robust voice carried loudly through the hall, indicating that amplification spell-work had been activated.

"I do," Erec responded, jolting slightly by how loud his voice echoed.

"I would hear your oath."

"Upon my life, I do give my oath. From this day forward, I will give back to the world more than I take. I will sow twice what I reap." Though the oath wasn't sworn in the Goddess's name, the way it ran through his nerves like lightning and brought goosebumps upon his neck felt more potent than Her hand clutching his heart. Grandmaster Oak smiled wide.

"Your oath has been heard by all in this esteemed hall. I dub thee Sir Erec of House Audentia, Initiate to the Order of the Verdant Oak."

# CHAPTER 20
## NEW WORLD

*Gives sentence, and dismisses them beneath,*
*According as he foldeth him around:*
*For when before him comes th' ill fated soul,*
*It all confesses; and that judge severe*
*Of sins, considering what place in hell*
*Suits the transgression, with his tail so oft*
*Himself encircles, as degrees beneath*
*He dooms it to descend. Before him stand*
*Always a num'rous throng; and in his turn*
*Each one to judgment passing, speaks, and hears*
*His fate, thence downward to his dwelling hurl'd.*

*"O thou! who to this residence of woe*
*Approachest?" when he saw me coming, cried*
*Minos, relinquishing his dread employ...*

*- Dante Alighieri,* Divine Comedy *(1320, 2nd Era)*

The rest of the day flew by like a dream. The elevator ride down to Erec's old home came and vanished; his steps through the tunnels went just as quickly. He threw open the door to his house, tossed his leather bag with VAL tucked inside over his shoulder, and then grabbed his small packed luggage case. Then left for good.

After that, Erec returned to the surface.

To the surface. To a world where every day he could get lost in the bright blue sea above. To his new home, where his every breath brought lungfuls of fresh dry air instead of the same old recycled air that circulated inside the venting systems and bio-caverns miles below.

The smile on his face never slipped away for more than a minute. He reached the Academy campus before the euphoria started to fade.

Erec adjusted the leather strap on his shoulder as he stared at the Verdant Oak quarters on the western side of campus. What sorts of vines grew all wild over the red-brick side of the massive building? They were odd, with their spade-like leaves and those budding bright-orange flowers. Though their beauty was undeniable. The way they added that splash of natural color and texture against the green backdrop that dominated this quadrant.

It wasn't as if the other Orders didn't compete, with their gardens and ornate decorations. The pure and wild growth here made everything else pale in comparison.

"Done gawkin'?" a girl yelled out from the stairs leading to the building's doors. Though it startled him, Erec collected his composure quickly. He stood straighter and marched down the concrete path to get a better look. A girl perched herself on the stair railing, smoking an awful-smelling rolled cigarette.

She was a thin woman with chopped light-brown hair and wispy arms tanned to a crisp. There was no mistaking the brass Verdant Oak pin on her light red jacket, nor those black fatigues and their silver trim; she was a student here—an Initiate, like him. A year older, perhaps. She raised her hand, with the cigarette still burning between two fingers, in a simple greeting.

"Yeah, don't mind me, thought I'd take some time to take it all in. I like those vines. They're gorgeous," Erec said.

"Ah, the trumpet vines? They're tough bastards, more menace than anything, though they do flower good." The woman shook her head and then gave a lazy smile. She hopped off the railing and headed to him. "So, you're the first new blood here, eh?" Her head tilted side to side, then gave a snicker. "I was told I had to be nice and greet you proper. Consider yourself lucky I'm not bored enough to start fucking with you first-years yet."

"A rare privilege. I'll count my blessings."

"Sooo—if we're going to do this proper. First things first. Show me your pin." She tossed her cigarette onto the ground and twisted the cherry into the concrete path with a boot. Then up came her hand, expectant.

Erec gave her an odd look. "Pin?"

"What, don't got your pin?" A cold spark of fear ran through him, and his stomach knotted. *I did not get this far to fuck up and forget to get a pin, Goddess above.*

"No, I was told to report here and to speak to the Quartermaster for—" Erec explained a little too quickly, the words tumbling over one another. Then he saw her wide smile and that little twinkle that came to her eyes.

[Well, done, Intern. You fell for such a simple trick. I'm very impressed.]

"You lied." Erec rolled his eyes as she started to crack up. She shook her head after having a small laugh at his expense; it wasn't a particularly good joke. He let out a sigh, just relieved he hadn't messed anything up already. Getting here had taken way too much; he'd had too many sleepless nights to mess up over a pin.

"Sorry, sorry. Couldn't resist. Naw, really. I have three eight-hour shifts over the next couple of days, and it's real dry waiting around out here for you first-years to show up. But hey, that dumb look on your face—priceless. Almost makes it worth it." She cleared her throat, then stopped hunching over. "Name's Gwen, nice to meet you." She offered up a hand to shake.

Erec eyed it for a moment to be sure she wasn't pulling another trick. "Erec."

"Aw, fuck, Erec Audentia?" Her head tilted, and her tone spiked up with the question.

"Yeah, something wrong with that?" He couldn't help but bristle. Here it came, like it always did, "from the traitor's House," or "wow, they let you in?" One of the two, he was sure of it. Of course, an Academy filled with nobles would act like that; he'd heard enough in the great hall to prepare—

"You're Bedwyr's lil' brother?"

That hit like a Thrashing Mite's flailing appendage to the head.

His mouth opened to say something; then it closed again. Of all the things? That was how she knew his House?

"I mean, I knew you were going to be joining us, but"—she shrugged—"sorta pictured you a bit different, y'know?"

Well, Bedwyr had a head full of rugged hair, a defined jawline, and spent all of his spare time in the gym—by contrast, Erec was strong but didn't have that sort of frame, nor did their faces line up. Bedwyr took after their father's side, while Erec took from their mother's. Though he did have a couple of inches of height on Bedwyr. However, if the two were in the same room, everyone's eyes were naturally drawn to his brother.

He could take an insult to his House or mother. But her comparing him to Bedwyr right off the bat hit him in an odd way that he couldn't find the words to.

"I am who I am," he said before exhaling through his teeth, sincerely hoping that this conversation wouldn't play out anywhere else in this Academy. Goddess above, have mercy. "Can we—can we get on with this?"

"Oh! Yeah, yeah, right this way."

Gwen motioned for him to follow behind as she walked up the steps. Thankfully she left it at that and didn't dive into his family history any further.

His first steps into the Verdant Oak quarters were, in short, extraordinary. Live plant life crawled on the walls, and more twisting vines spread out of too many pots that cluttered the entry. They'd opted to forgo artwork or old-world decoration, unlike nearly all the rest of the high nobility. Everything displayed inside was alive. A wide range from dark foliage spouting bright-red flowers to off-colored, misshapen and muted plants.

The entrance hall spread in three distinct directions. The central path led to classrooms and different rooms set aside for the Verdant Oak classes. Gwen explained that all mandatory classes were in the central Academy building, and each Order housed its electives in their quarters.

If you took your way down the right hall from the entrance, you'd find yourself in the dorms and canteen, the last stop on their journey.

But they didn't go that way. Instead, Gwen brought him down the left hall. Rooms spawning off the hall had various purposes, from gyms and training spaces to grease-stained workshops. Some of which required special permission to enter. Erec noted the workshops that were open for Initiate access and swore to circle back later.

Past the workshop was the Quartermaster and the reason they came here first. The man gave Erec an exasperated look through his wiry glasses and got through his work quickly. He took Erec's measurements, then issued him three sets of Academy uniforms and a single set of formals.

He was also issued the basics, such as bedsheets, sundries, and of course, his Order pin.

Erec turned the tiny bit of metal over in his hand; there was an oak etched into its surface. It felt heavy but right to hold.

The Quartermaster cleared his throat and tapped a finger on a sheet of paper filled with boxes and check marks. As they went through the supplies, Erec checked off box after box.

But there was one box still empty—one thing that had yet to be issued; what he wanted the most.

"No Armor?" the man asked with a sigh.

"No, my Markos II, and it's, well… It no longer works; it was a loaner Armor, to begin with, so it never really belonged to me—"

"Goddess above. That's always a poor omen." The guy rubbed his temple and walked away from the counter. He pulled out a key to rifle through a drawer. A moment later, he returned to the counter with a black rubber wristband, setting it on the checklist sheet. "If this one ends up like that poor Markos II, I'll have you run three laps outside the wall."

"I promise to take good care of it." Erec reached toward the rubber wristband, which undoubtedly contained an authorization chip.

The Quartermaster's fingers clamped around his wrist, tight like an iron manacle, stopping him in his tracks. "These are not toys. They are weapons of war, with an incomparable ability to kill—treat them how you would a sword, only far better. Because, unlike a sword, your Armor can *also* save your life."

"I swear," Erec said, meeting the severe eyes of the man.

The Quartermaster released his grip and sighed. "It's in Workshop C, Rack 23. Engineers will let you in when you show the wristband. Go collect it and bring it to your dorm so that you can keep it on your personal rack."

As if Erec needed that explained. Few in his year appreciated Armors and their power quite as much as he did. After having the Markos on the edge of falling apart the entire trial, he was damn near giddy for the upgrade. With a quick nod of appreciation to the Quartermaster, he checked the last box and submitted his form.

Erec took off to the next stop. To his new Armor.

# CHAPTER 21
# VALLUM

Erec practically ran to Workshop C with Gwen. Every second he waited to see his new Armor felt like torture. For her part, she laughed and went along with it, letting him speed her along to his heart's content.

At the entrance, a lazy engineer looked over his wristband. Erec tapped his foot until the man ushered him in—though he had to go *alone* and collect the Armor from its rack. "I'll be back fast, alright?" he told Gwen before darting in.

The workshop's interior was strewn with welders, spare twisted metal, and dissected Armor. Near a dark corner was an empty frame with a hundred wires poking out of it. All of the haphazard bits and bobs transformed this place into an accident waiting to happen.

Erec counted off the numbers on the racks until he reached it. Number 23.

The Armor hung on a bright yellow rack; the first thing that stood out to him on the pristine Armor was the large black-and-green sigil of an oak tree. It decorated both pauldrons.

The plating on the pauldrons was also asymmetrical—the right had a smaller plate that he guessed was for enhanced maneuverability. Below the shoulders were sleek metal arms and a set of decent gauntlets.

But something else demanded his attention.

Green fabric hung from the back, along with a hood—a cloak of some sort? Erec clutched the fabric; its texture felt plastic-like with the flexibility of cloth. *Corrosive resistance? That might be a stretch.* He could request the schematics and details of the model from the Academy's library. In fact, Gwen had recommended that as one of the things he could do over the next couple of days. Though, once he let VAL get ahold of it, he doubted he'd need to sit back and do research.

The helmet of the Armor was distinctive. It had a manual visor with reinforced tinted glass between the five slits of steel. The top of the helmet came to a point and curved outward to deflect any blows to the head without letting them catch.

This was a mean feat of engineering, a pure blend between the old-world Knights and undoubtedly a catalog of modern features from this Era. The past and the present fused together to give mankind a weapon to take their world back.

Erec scratched the back of his head, unable to stop his wide smile.

[Put me next to it,] Val commanded.

Oh, right. If nobody was watching them… Erec glanced around the workshop—a couple of engineers were talking near a design schematic, another busy working on bulky Armor in the corner.

Erec leaned his leather bag against the Armor—and VAL zoomed out; he hit the steel plating, and it rippled like the surface of a pond. In less than a second, VAL merged with it.

[Ah—now this is a much *better* workspace. I was impressed when I was running my scanners over the other Armors in your group. But it is another thing entirely to get a look at a piece of equipment and start testing it yourself. Based on the preliminary findings, this isn't quite as impressive as theirs. Yet this is a massive improvement to that faulty Markos II and a clever design for something crafted by unassisted humans.]

Of course not; the ducal lines paid through the nose for those personalized Armors. If issued Initiate's Armor came anywhere close to that, the Academy would blow their budget. But hey, the Markos II served them well enough to get to this point.

[There's the model name: Vallum. First generation. A couple of distinctive features—made for long-distance treks, along with several enhanced environmental protection measures. Other than that, it appears relatively basic in terms of physical enhancements. Very generalized, which is acceptable for its stated purpose. Though… That's interesting—watch this.]

Erec tilted his head—and the green fabric hanging off of the Armor suddenly bled into a tannish brown, holding the dull color for a few seconds—before slowly converting back to green. "Whoa." He gave another glance to the engineers, though they hadn't bothered looking in his direction at all.

[Remarkable, though I do not understand how they've achieved this by running a current of the core's energy to the cloak. It shifts the color in what's helpfully labeled as a "camouflage" mode. Though I am familiar with a certain line of research utilizing fiber optics, the way they achieve it here is truly odd—]

"Are there any colors it can shift to?" Better not to let the nostalgic ancient robot stoke those rambling flames of old research projects.

[No, only the placid green-and-tan blend; the green, I imagine, is for blending into growth or forests. Aside from your caverns and city, I predict a lack of such lush nature anywhere near your Kingdom. I can only guess that the green is intended to match your silly "Order" colors. Oh, silly humans and their tribalistic tendencies.]

Erec stopped listening to VAL and disengaged the rack that held up the Armor. In a second, its boots were flush with the ground. He circled around it and climbed in—it only took ten seconds for the Armor to seal.

<VALLUM ACTIVATION PROTOCOL COMPLETE>

There was just a single clean notification informing him that the Armor activated; No flashing barrage of failures. And no visual clutter. Though it lacked the targeting and advanced scanner of Colin's Cserula IV. Hard to say if the minimal display was its natural state or if VAL was already tweaking the Armor.

Erec stepped away from the rack. No whirring servos filled his ears. There wasn't any jerky lag in the movements; it flowed as smooth as water.

What were the limits to the Vallum? It might not stand up to damage as well as an advanced custom model. Its more rounded nature meant it didn't have any special features to compliment his Virtues. But this generalized Order of the Verdant Oak Armor felt better than he'd dreamed.

[It will take a day for my integration to complete. This model includes some systems that I'm unsure how to streamline. Digging into the data provided might allow for a better judgment call. Annoyingly, I suspect that the conclusion will be that they correspond to your "anomalous energy."]

"Fine by me." Erec curled a hand, watching the fingers of the Armor move in sync with his own, despite the inches of steel plate. "As much as I hate to admit it, I think we can't leave Gwen waiting any longer."

[What, not excited to see your new home?]

"Not nearly as much as I was to get this thing."

[Ah, Intern. You don't know how lucky you have it. At Vortex Industries, we kept capsule rooms for low-level employees like yourself to minimize space and maximize science. With such convenient quarters nearby, you could've worked all day and then crawled into your capsule and woken up on alarm to work again—]

Erec walked out of the workshop and caught up with Gwen. She was waiting with a smirk and a thumbs-up. "Nice. Same Armor as me—trust me, it's pretty handy. The rest of the Orders always complain that we get the cool cloak, so make sure to rub it into their face."

[Press her for data.]

Erec was a little thrown off by VAL's sudden request, but the Vallum's helm luckily obscured his confusion. "Uh, they're using different models?"

"Well, duh. Each Order has its specialty. What sense would it make to design basic models for their Order and not add a few useful features to their roles? That cloak isn't the only thing, by the way. Notice how quiet your steps are?" Gwen asked.

Erec looked down at the boots. Sure enough, now that she'd drawn attention to them, his steel legs didn't really "clink" on the ground as one would expect from the heavy metal.

[They've utilized an advanced shock absorbing material. What a streamlined design. If only Vortex Industries was still headhunting for talent...]

"I can see how it would be useful; I wondered how Sir Boldwick moved around without making any noise," Erec said.

"Well, I'm sure he's using something better than we are. But same principle. You'll find that you'll want to tend toward more lightweight and sleek designs. There are some exceptions, of course, but we often go on long-range scouting operations outside the wall." She shrugged. "You'll get your first taste of that at the end of the month."

Erec tilted his head. He'd get to see more of the outside world? So soon?

"Anyway, let's get you to your dorm. You'll want to drop off your stuff and switch into your Academy uniform. From there, you're free to go on your own. By the way…" Gwen trailed off.

"Yeah?" Erec asked, already wondering if it'd be better to test out the Armor in a gym—or to go and check out the rest of the Orders; then there was the Academy itself—so many options. He didn't doubt that he'd be running around and busy until courses started.

"If you need anything, tell me. Bedwyr's done me good, and I'll do good by his little bro if I can."

Erec frowned at the mention of his brother, but faked a smile for Gwen. He wanted to forge his own path through this place, but perhaps that stubborn thought had been a bit naive and pig-headed. It was okay to accept someone holding out their hand. "Thanks, I'll keep that in mind. I appreciate all the help."

Gwen watched him go with a smile.

# CHAPTER 22
# MAID TO BE A KNIGHT

*It is of vital essence to divide the strength of our noblest Knights and have them form Orders. These Orders shall press forward their values and knowledge to strengthen the next generation. Through this specialization, the interests of the State and its peoples can be divided and represented in our top tier of Knights. We cannot function like the soldiers of the eras before; with mankind's Blessings, some will inevitably rise to status and power impossible to even the most decorated warriors of the world before. It is through a definition of these distinct Orders, by establishing their traditions and pressing their individualized values on those within their ranks, that they may keep one another in check. Through this balance of power, mankind can prosper and mitigate the risks of one strong Knight or Order usurping the interests of the State and its peoples.*

- *King Restfos Crisimus,* Creation of the Orders *(137, 3rd Era)*

The Order of the Verdant Oaks dorms were laid out in a simple yet effective way. Four students shared a communal living space, and each had their private bedroom, complete with a bathroom that fed into the living area,

For a Knight Order—and, thus by default, one populated mainly by noble blood—the decorations were rather sparse and simplistic. A couch, a few comfortable chairs, and a small rack of bookcases packed with old-world and new texts.

Though there was a chess board that Erec had no clue how to play.

Supposedly a hit with the higher nobility, as it was a game of gentlemen and gentlewomen.

What impressed him the most about the room were the expansive windows and the plant life inside of their dorm that coated every wall where there was even a little bit of light. They'd allowed the plants to grow wild and turn half of the living space into a jungle bathed in light. Twisting vines and bushy ferns were the most common, but dotted about were varieties of flowering plants and herbs.

On the side of the entrance to the room was a smaller space filled with four personal racks, labeled for their convenience.

Erec deposited his Armor on his assigned rack and then looked over the names of the people he'd be spending the next couple of years with.

He couldn't help but grin as he looked at the rack next to his. There was a small plate behind it listing who it belonged to. *Garin Honestus.*

As he read the next plate, the joy withered away. Colin Nitidus. Of course, it would be him. He didn't doubt that the Duke's hand was in this too. *Knights first, nobles second, eh?* He guessed time would show how well that phrase held up, because even as nobles second, nobles still seemed to have damn near a lot of say in how things went.

But he had made a vow. Perhaps he should have been grateful that the Duke was helping him fulfill it. If Colin had belonged to a different Order or lived in separate quarters, how much harder would befriending him and spying be? Erec scratched his head as he took in the last rack.

*Olivia Gratuiti?* Erec racked his brain through the ceremony, trying his damnedest to place a face to the name.

Nothing came to mind. He'd been too checked out for most of it, stressed about Garin getting in, that even if this girl had gone ahead of him, he couldn't picture her. Out of the twenty-one accepted into the Order of the Verdant Oak before him, he'd lost track of names and faces relatively easily. He wasn't like his friend and didn't particularly care about those he hadn't met or their status. Maybe Garin would know her background?

Erec shook his head and made his way to his room; it was quaint. Spacious compared to his previous bedroom, which doubled as a family office. There was a drawer for clothes, a desk for study topped by a small lamp. The bed was unmade, and he supposed that would be the first thing he got around to doing. And a window gave a lovely view into the lush wild garden around the Verdant Oak quarters.

Aside from that, the room was a blank slate. He could fill the walls with decoration—banners or trophies of his past. Yet he had none of that. Nor any desire to. There was a beauty in the simplicity here. Erec made his bed, put his things away, and tucked his mother's letter in an old-world book he brought on his desk as he sat on the bed and visualized his goal. What he needed to do to chase after his mother. The woman who left this Kingdom and strode into the wastes.

*Strength. I need more Strength.*

— - ❂ - — - ☼ - — - ❂ - —

Erec spent his first night in the dorms alone, once more suffering from a dreadful dream of a stag striding through burning cities. The reoccurring nightmare left him shaking when he woke up, and it took a solid hour to get the damn image out of his head. At least he wasn't alone in the dorm for long since Garin showed up that morning with a giant smirk. He rushed to throw his stuff in his room, joined Erec on the couch, and tossed an arm over his shoulder.

"Miss me?" his friend chuckled, scanning their new living space. Garin had been in such a rush to rack his Armor and toss away his things; it surprised Erec that he'd checked out the nameplates already. "So, Colin's sharing a room with us, huh? That kinda sucks."

"Yeah, about that." Erec set down his book. An old-world tale about a warrior named *Beowulf,* who slew a monster. At the time, the concept of this warrior was mere fiction, but reading it after the end of the Second Era… It was a bit more relatable than it should've been. "Before our ceremony, Duke Nitidus forced me to come to his house and talk."

Garin stopped smiling and scooted a bit away on the couch to study his expression. "Whoa. Holy shit? The Unbroken General? I'd have pissed myself in your shoes. Wait—if you're here, then what did he want?"

*Yeah, he would be quick to catch on to that.* Erec rubbed his neck. "He made me vow on the Goddess's name to befriend his son, then, uh, spy on him. That was his contingent for pulling the strings to let me into this Order."

"Well. That's pretty awful, and really—a spy?" Garin shook his head. "How are you going to go about befriending him? Guy's a total prick. I hate to say it, but playing nice now isn't going to do you any favors, since you bashed his face in during the trial, making him look like a total idiot."

"I—well, I thought playing nice *would* be the way to…"

Garin's face scrunched up.

"Yeah… To be honest, I've been avoiding thinking too hard about how to go about it. I thought once I got into the Academy, I'd be able to sort it out, but the more I've thought, the more impossible it seems," Erec said.

"A tough challenge to tackle…" Garin tapped a finger to his chin, and his eyes focused on the ceiling. "If you hadn't screwed yourself, you could've pandered to his ego. But that won't work. Hmmm…"

"Can you please help me? It's like I'm doomed and, no matter what I've come up with, it has no shot of working. I feel like a trapped squirrel."

Garin gave a small uncomfortable laugh and tugged at his collar. "…Well, yeah, you're the loner who'd rather work on his Armor and take a long trek through a bio-cavern than spend five minutes with people you don't know. Of course you're a hopeless pick for this job. I'll think it over. But why did the Duke pick you for this anyway?"

"He said, 'From respect comes mutual understanding. And from that may come friendship.' But I find it hard to picture Colin respecting anyone, even if he thought that me knocking him out brought it."

"Huh."

Erec shrugged and marked his book, and set it on their table.

After Garin finished unpacking and switching into his Academy uniform, they made their way around campus together.

Erec had already brought his Vallum to a workshop the night before to take a look under the plating. With VAL breaking down his discoveries this morning, he had a good grasp on the capabilities of the Armor. The Vallum was a piece of generalized Armor with no strong slant in any Virtue's direction. But those specialties that geared it more for scouting did give it an irregular edge.

He'd also gotten a look at the default model for the Order of the Lotus. An extremely sleek design with minimal plating, it enhanced its pilot's speed and strike force at the cost of protection. An interesting difference in design philosophy left VAL wondering if some underlying subsystems made it more sustainable. But it wasn't like the two could break it down and take a look inside like they could with the Vallum, no matter how much VAL urged him to.

Of course, Garin got his own Vallum as well—his trial Armor was his father's. But, unlike Erec, his friend wasn't very interested in picking apart how it worked—citing that their courses would train them enough.

No, Garin wanted to take a look at the rest of the new students filtering in and where they'd be staying.

Erec went along mostly to explore the campus, so the two looked around at the rest of the quarters.

The Order of the Silver Flames was a somewhat predictable design —their building looked more like one of the Church temples than a Knightly Order, complete with pillars shaped like swords and a statue of the Goddess by their entrance. Erec begged them away after a quick glance about. The Church always stirred up mixed feelings in him after their scathing assault on his House's name.

In contrast, the Order of the Azure Tower had a damn near whimsical feel to it, with several spiraling towers that rose above the rest of the Academy. They hung impossibly high in the air—their blue cobalt bricks were distinctive from any distance. No doubt they used some sort of spell-work to break the laws of gravity.

The one that rang closest to his heart aside from his Order was the Order of the Crimson Lotus. They kept their quarters in a restrained and serene beauty. Where the Verdant Oak went wild with its plants, everything in the Order of the Crimson Lotus was deliberate. Their building formed a ring around a massive central pond of knee-deep water. A thousand red lotuses floated on its still surface. The building had a humble architecture, enhancing and drawing the eye to the central pond, conveying a sense of peace and harmony.

Eventually, the day passed by, and the two made their way back to their dorms. Erec felt exhausted from all of the chatter with random people, while his friend was in high spirits.

There was someone in their dorm.

A girl with bright blond hair sat on the couch, though they mostly saw her from behind; it was obvious the intention she put into maintaining her hair. Braided and delicate, her Academy attire was freshly pressed with boots shining. Quietly, the girl paged through a book while sitting with perfect posture. Near her hand was a mug filled with warm tea, perfuming the room with the scent of lavender. Garin looked to Erec, who shrugged.

Garin cleared his throat loudly.

The girl shot up and released a small gasp before her eyes hit them; she looked to her tea and then back to them. "Oh! I was waiting for you to get back!"

"Uh, yeah. We were just out exploring." Garin said, striding in.

Erec followed behind him and rubbed his eyes. It'd already been a long exhausting day. He'd been hoping they'd get back and call it a night, expecting the others in their dorm to arrive tomorrow. *I'll make this quick and get some rest.*

"Well, I'm Olivia Gratuiti; it's an absolute pleasure to meet you both." She shot up from the couch into a practiced pose, even giving a small curtsy. "So our dorm shall have a future Duke, Baron, and…" She tilted her head at Erec.

"Second son of an unlanded Lord." Erec sighed. "I'm inheriting nothing."

"Oh! My deepest apologies if I offended, but you're a Knight now, right? Circumstances like your title matter very little since you shall be making your own name, now." She walked a little closer and smiled at them both. "Let us all give this our best."

"I'm sorry, but I'm unfamiliar with the House of Gratuiti?" Garin asked, squinting a bit. *That's odd.* He usually made it a point to know other nobility or, at the very least, their Houses. The fact this girl stumped him left Erec feeling flat-footed.

"Oh! No need to apologize; there's no way you'd have recognized it. My mother and I served the Luculentus Estate—my mother is a maid there. As was I. However, I am Dame Olivia now. First to form my own House, if my dreams bear fruit."

"Oh, that's amazing! Well done. I'll be wishing you the best." Garin matched her grin.

Erec turned the information over in his head. This girl had served the Luculentus Household, the same Duchy from which the odd

Lyotte came. He fought to keep the frown from his face, but Olivia must have caught it, since she tilted her head and widened her eyes.

"Is something wrong?" she asked.

"No—just tired. I think I'm going to call it a day," Erec fired back quickly, unable to determine what was going on. It was too much of a coincidence, but why? He waved off their invitations to stay up and talk longer, heading to his room. Better to collect himself before revealing anything. Besides, he wanted space to decompress.

On the one hand, she seemed genuine, and her circumstances were…well, like his own in many ways. But was she a spy? A spy on one ducal line to another… but Lyotte had been so strange to him and pushy. Olivia didn't seem to recognize him, but what if it was an act? Was that suspicion narcissism in disguise? He only knew he couldn't trust her.

# CHAPTER 23
## ATTENTION

A white stag leaped over a mountain in his dreams; beneath it, the world burned. It was following him, aware of his existence, and with a pure desire to destroy and consume. No matter where he went, or where he hid, or any of them hid, it'd track them down and bring them to ruin.

A siren blared through the entirety of the Academy. Erec shook in his bed—slick with sweat as the siren rang out again, deafening.

A magically amplified voice cracked through the halls. "—all Knights. This is not a test of the Emergency Alert System. Hostiles have been spotted amassing at the southern wall. Equip your gear and immediately report to a Knight Protector or higher. Attention. All Knights—" The message went on as Erec rubbed his eyes, as his heart hammered away.

The image of the stag still burned in his mind, as it had for days. Despite knowing the nightmare not to be real, he felt as if something was watching him. Crazy.

[Well, that isn't ideal. You lack training and are already being sent to a battle. Ah, humanity. Indeed, this is one of your most classic of tales.] VAL's voice pulled him out of the frantic mindset. Erec struggled over to the pile of clothes from the day before, quickly yanking his uniform pants on and tossing on his shirt. He didn't bother with the jacket before he threw his door open to head to his Armor.

This was the point of why he became a Knight. To face these kinds of threats and grow stronger while protecting those that couldn't defend themselves. That is, until he was strong enough to set out after his mother.

Though for something like this to happen so early was concerning, he'd make do. He hadn't received a weapon yet, so that was his first priority.

Garin gave him bleary eyes in the living room. "Second fight, eh? Couldn't ask for a better friend to wade into battle with. Let's slay some monsters for breakfast."

"I'm sure we're just headed to provide support, not anything crazy." It wasn't what he really thought, but if he pretended to be bold and kept from letting his fear show, it'd keep Garin's spirits up. He couldn't recall the last time there was an attack on the walls. Given he lived far underground, though, this sort of thing never really stuck in his memory to begin with. "Let's get our Armor on; we still need to get weapons." The Academy tended to hand out weapons after their second week of courses. Usually, it accompanied a symbolic ceremony for the Orders. Most of the time, this would never be an issue. But the timing of this…was awful.

"I need a proper sword." Garin looked look down at his empty hands and shook his head. "Just something in case things go wrong. You too, so we can protect ourselves."

He was right, that would be a priority. How had this attack occurred so suddenly? The thick steel walls surrounding the Kingdom often gave the Knights plenty of sight of the wastes. The more time he got to slog through his tired head, the less it made sense.

Ultimately, worrying about the details was fruitless. Sooner or later, they'd have answers. Erec strode into the Armor room and quickly equipped his Vallum Armor—right behind, Garin got geared up too. When they returned to the living room, Olivia was peeking out of her room, still in pajamas; her eyes were wide. "All of this commotion, how dreadful." She tilted her head at them. "Wait a minute for me, will you?"

Garin and Erec exchanged looks and then shrugged. At this point, another minute wouldn't matter much. Better to stick together in a group than leave her on her own.

She was quick, much quicker than expected. In a minute flat, she rushed out of her room in a set of proper Academy clothes, with her hair pulled haphazardly back, and ran into the room with Armor. Even putting on her Armor was quick; as promised, she was raring and ready to go in her Vallum in no time. She gave them a quick clenched fist to her chest as a sign of respect and thanked them for waiting.

With that, they were off to the Quartermaster, rushing through the chaos of the halls as Knights and other Initiates struggled to go where they were needed. Fortunately, Erec remembered the way, and in short order the three of them were joining a small line of twelve Initiates in their class who came to their first conclusion. A Knight Commander oversaw the ensemble sternly, likely having predicted this and moving to take control of the new Initiates.

The Knight Commander tucked her helmet under an arm and ignored the hushed conversations in the hall, barking the occasional order.

Initiates moved to the Quartermaster and slowly received their weapons. However, the Quartermaster didn't have any forms to fill out to account for the weapons, unlike when they requested their weapon before the ceremony. Given the emergency, they were to directly pick what they thought they could use in a fight.

The troop's movement was painfully slow and unorganized, stoked by the whispered fears and worries in the new bloods.

After the glacial pace, and a couple more Initiates arriving, the Commander gave a quick shout for them. It didn't seem to help.

Garin gave Erec a tap on the shoulder. "Hold my spot for me?"

"What?" Erec asked, but his friend didn't answer. Instead, Garin stepped right out of line and walked straight up to the Knight Commander—performing the same clenched fist to the chest that Olivia had done briefly before.

The Knight's irritated eyes landed on Garin.

"Initiate, return to the line. It is important you are all equipped promptly," she said, without a trace of any emotion in her voice.

"Sorry, ma'am. But I couldn't help it." Garin jerked his head at all of the Initiates milling in the line. "Everyone's nerves are haywire, and I thought it'd be best to ask for a brief explanation of the situation if you have any details. I think it'd go a long way to easing everybody." His voice cut across cleanly to the crowd. The hushed conversations between the Initiates vanished as their ears trained on what was happening.

The Knight Commander took a long moment, her face locked in a frown before the dam finally broke and her expression softened to a grimace. "I am aware you lack any training from our Order. Typically, you learn quickly not to question your commanders during an emergency situation. But, given all of you have yet to take a single course, I believe I agree with your assessment. Knowing the situation will prevent misplaced fear and mistakes derived from that." She nodded her head. "Twenty minutes ago, the Order of the Azure Tower noticed an odd reading on the southern wall. A large Rift opened two minutes later. Since then, they've been preventing any monsters from breaking through our fortifications and sent a desperate request for backup. We must be prepared to evacuate our interior lands if needed. And then, if our wall is secured, press forward and close the Rift. The Academy is close, so we are poised to offer a first response."

There was a deadly silence as everyone took in the breadth of the situation.

"It is vital you get your equipment. Though I have no intention of leading you into direct battle unless the direst circumstances occur, it is impossible to say whether or not the hostiles that appear from the Rift will escalate this further." She concluded with a slight nod. "Please return to the line, receive whatever weapons you're best-trained with, then form rank in front of me. Time is of the essence."

With that, Garin gave her one last "salute" by pressing his hand to his chest before turning on his heel and getting back in place.

The whispers in the hall ceased as a fixed determination took hold. Everyone realized the reality of the situation; the Orders didn't know how bad this could get and were taking every measure to control the damage if it spiraled out of control. Rifts, by their nature, could connect to *any* other world and spew out horrors. For a Rift to suddenly appear so close to the wall… It was a perfect storm of bad situations.

With the commander's calm and detailed explanation, the line went quicker. Each Initiate received their weapons—mostly swords—and moved to assemble in front of the woman.

Now that everyone understood the danger, the line moved quicker, and soon Erec arrived at the counter. There was a variety of weapons—which, again, most of what they had stashed away back in their garrison were numerous swords.

First off, Erec asked for two hatchets. During his fight against the Thrashing Mites, it'd been dangerous when he lost his weapon during the fray. Better to have a backup weapon. Then something caught his eye; it was tucked in the far back of the racks of weapons, forgotten about in favor of more popular weapons.

There was a massive two-handed war axe with a wicked blade shaped like a crescent; the metal of the axe head was smooth and layered in a wavy pattern. Black leather wrapped around its haft.

Were he to fight that Thrashing Mite queen again, a weapon like that would easily cleave the beast in two. "How about that?" Erec asked—a finger pointing toward the axe. The Quartermaster gave him an odd look.

"That was a custom request, but the Knight who wanted it failed to return from his expedition. He was a dear friend of mine." He said the words carefully. "If you're looking for something to accompany the throwing hatchets or a weapon with reach, I'd recommend these instead. Often new Initiates are more familiar with swords, correct?"

"No, I'm not." Erec shook his head. "But if it was meant for your old friend—I get it. I'll make do with the hatchets. Thank you." He turned to leave, not wanting to ruin the sentimental feeling behind the weapon. Better to let it stay there—

"Wait," the man called, and Erec paused. "It's been here for a long time."

"I don't want to dredge up anything; I'm sorry if asking about it brought up memories you'd rather have left buried."

"No, that's not it." The Quartermaster hefted the two-handed axe from the wall and set it on the counter. "I think of him when I see it. I think of how much it could've done if he'd been given a chance to use it. If he'd still be here if he'd had it. Since I set it up on that rack, rarely has anyone given it a second glance."

Erec could understand why. With swords being the Goddess icon, they had the highest demand. Most else was limited to side arma-ments—such as these hatchets typically used as throwing weapons—or custom-ordered like that axe.

"I'd rather it do good. Take it. Bring it honor." The Quartermaster pushed the axe forward.

Hesitantly, Erec picked the weapon up. It was heavy in his hands, both from the weight of what it represented to make and its heavy steel. A powerful weapon for war. "I'll do right by it." Erec nodded his head.

"See that you do."

With that, Erec strapped the weapon to his back—the Armor utilizing "anomalous energy" from the frame to hold it in place. He joined the line of the rest of the Initiates waiting in front of the Commander. In a few minutes, they'd be on the move to respond to the assault on the wall.

# CHAPTER 24
# EXPERIMENT

*"It was much pleasanter at home," thought poor Alice, "when one wasn't always growing larger and smaller, and being ordered about by mice and rabbits. I almost wish I hadn't gone down that rabbit-hole—and yet—and yet—it's rather curious, you know, this sort of life! I do wonder what can have happened to me! When I used to read fairy-tales, I fancied that kind of thing never happened, and now here I am in the middle of one! There ought to be a book written about me, that there ought! And when I grow up, I'll write one—but I'm grown up now," she added in a sorrowful tone; "at least there's no room to grow up any more here."*

*"But then," thought Alice, "shall I never get any older than I am now? That'll be a comfort, one way—never to be an old woman—but then— always to have lessons to learn! Oh, I shouldn't like that!"*

*"Oh, you foolish Alice!" she answered herself. "How can you learn lessons in here? Why, there's hardly room for you, and no room at all for any lesson-books!"*

- *Lewis Carroll,* Alice's Adventures in Wonderland *(1865, 2nd Era)*

The gathered Initiates marched to the southern side of the Academy, past all of the beautiful Order buildings. They found a field just outside of the city where they lumped together into a single mass of Initiates. Swarming around them were

Knights Errant and anyone else who happened to be at the Academy itself. Once the confirmations went through that everyone had assembled, the group rushed into a forced march to the southern wall.

After everyone was gathered—their leaders barked our instructions and sent them outward at a brisk jog to the wall.

Erec kept close to Garin and Olivia as they ran with the rest of the group.

But his eyes couldn't help but wander to the other Initiates lumped up in the Academy's forces.

Of interest were obviously the two other basic Armor designs he'd yet to take a close look at. Those of the Silver Flames had a crown-like structure to their Armor, which ringed around their heads. They also possessed thick plating, surpassed only by the thick shell-like steel of the Azure Tower Armor. It seemed the two Orders favored a heavier style.

Some of the second years had already made modifications. Swapped out plating, weaponized their gauntlets, or added mechanisms to the legs. Frames were adaptable if you managed the effort and resources—or made an engineer friend.

Then there were those with custom Armor. Designs that took a wide variety of shapes and purposes but were united by the painted crest of their Order on the plating. The Order of the Crimson Lotus generally led the jog; their sleeker base design made them a natural fit to run ahead.

*Somewhere up there.* Bedwyr was in their group. Even if he couldn't tell the difference between them in the Armor, his brother was ahead, hidden amongst their number. All of the second years were here, so he had to be.

Erec ran harder.

The group sped as quickly as they could through the wastes, and reached the wall in thirty minutes' time.

— - ☢ - — - ☼ - — - ☢ - —

Near the wall, the Initiates remained tensed but in position.

Above them, at the top of the giant steel curtain, rained a hailstorm of fire, lightning, and smoke. Spell after spell discharged as stronger Knights fought above.

As Erec discovered, war sometimes held quite a bit of uncomfortable waiting.

He winced as a blob of green smashed into a Knight far above—catching the unprepared man and hurling him from the wall. A couple of seconds later, the poor bastard crashed into the ground with a shower of dust. Erec's heart kicked up a notch.

What had been going through that guy's head as he suddenly found no more ground underneath him?

"Initiate Gwen, retrieve that Knight, and give emergency treatment if required," their Commander called. The girl Erec had met earlier nodded—soliciting the help of another Initiate before scrambling off toward where the man had cratered. Armor could prevent a lot of damage, and if the man's Virtues were high enough, he'd survive a fall like that. But if they weren't—well, there might not be anything left to issue emergency treatment to but a corpse.

They'd been like this for thirty minutes, with their Commander on edge as they watched the desperate fighting close to them. Whatever was assaulting the wall had managed to scale its sheer steel surface—a terrifying proposition. Erec's eyes ran down the length of the miles-long arrangement of steel plating and reinforcement that kept most everything out. But apparently, not *whatever* horrors spewed from this Rift.

The largest group of reinforcements was still coming.

It took time to gather their forces, arm them properly, and then mobilize. The Academy had been closer than the fully trained Knights. Still, small contingents of higher-ranked Knights kept trickling in while the main force of Knights gathered with the army.

They wouldn't be content to fend off the invasion when they arrived. No. They'd cut back into the swath of horror spawning from the Rift. Then they'd close it and stem the tide of terror.

Though Erec didn't know the details, he did know closing a Rift wasn't a trivial task. It took specialized equipment and a lot of preparation to pull off.

All the while, their Commander looked on. Determining whether or not they'd need to make the call to have the Initiates evacuate the fields and warn any farmers who lived close to the wall.

A massive fleshless creature with four massive wings and a long-pointed snout shot up past the wall—streaks of lightning trailed it and slammed into its side. It let out a massive roar that Erec felt in his chest. A second after, the thing dived forward, descending past the wall even as more bolts of energy crashed into it.

"Ready yourselves," the Commander called, drawing her weapon. Even though the flying beast was taking in a constant stream of damage, it'd cleared the wall. Their attacks managed to damage its thin membrane-like wings but didn't stop it from increasing the distance. The beast headed right to the Kingdom.

A figure from the wall leaped after it—a bright chain erupted from a glyph and speared into the flying creature. After hooking into the monster, the glowing chain constricted and yanked the Knight to the beast. It let out another earthshaking roar as the two spiraled downward.

Erec drew his war axe. His eyes trailed the flying figure of the Knight tangling in the middle of the air with the crashing flyer. There were more flashes of white as they landed blows with their prayers, even as the two death spiraled.

Greenish-yellow globs rained from the wounded creature above and landed inside the walls.

Then the globs moved.

"Hostiles! Engage!" the Commander shouted. Hundreds of the things were dropping all over. They'd run loose inside the Kingdom walls if they weren't controlled.

This wasn't a matter of evacuation anymore. The Initiates were the last line of defense.

Erec charged with Garin at his side as a field of greenish-yellow condensing fluid began to amass. Amid them were little dots of reddish white. The ooze began to center around the white—forming into a blob with a single bloodshot eye.

As he got within ten feet, it suddenly split. Creating two. One of the slimes slid after Garin; the other targeted him.

More were forming nearby. Splitting, combining. A mixture of chaotic evil that only intended to consume.

Initiates crashed into the ooze, weapons hacking away and spewing murky putrid green into the air. The fleshy appendages grasped at the Armor. Smoke rose from the points where they made contact. *Corrosive.* Erec hefted his axe above his head—slamming it down a second later in a wide arc that capitalized on its long range to hit the eyeball inside the ooze facing him. The eye tore in half. As the eye ripped apart, all of the surface tension holding the disgusting yellow-green slime gave way. It spilled into a puddle around the twitching and bleeding eye halves.

*They die rather—*

[Left.]

Erec turned in time to meet the impact of a crashing ooze full force. It threw all of its weight on him—he pushed back. In the process, he lost hold of the war axe. Erec doubled down and shoved his hand through the slick insides of the thing, reaching for the eye in the center.

Another ooze joined the first—doubling its size and increasing the weight. As it did, the eye slipped further back, the membrane began to absorb Erec.

[Armor sustaining consistent damage. It's targeting weak points to erode quickly.]

Erec dug both hands in, temper flaring as yet another ooze joined this host. Merging to overcome him. His arms strained as the pressure inside of the creature doubled. It could exert more force within its domain—it was becoming hard to move.

A long time ago, Erec worked around a cistern filled with aerated water in a bio-cavern. He'd been warned to stay far away. One day a rat fell into it. No matter how hard it'd tried to swim out, it made no headway. And it drowned, unable to swim. If he'd fallen in, he'd have met the same fate.

As the ooze closed around him—joined by yet another—the picture of that drowning rat haunted his mind. The pressure doubled again; it was hard to make any headway with the pure slickness of the interior. Not with all of this increased force. Every inch he got closer to the eye in the middle of this monster slipped just out of range.

Frustrating.

Erec saw red.

His hands yanked forward in a rapid flurry—clawing through the muck like an animal through mud, displacing and fighting against that impossible constriction. His fingers brushed the eye's surface, and a second later, he took a handful of the soft interior and tore at it.

The mounting pressure around him dispersed like a popped

bubble. Acidic slime spilled all around him like water released from a dam.

As it flowed away, he didn't hesitate; letting out a growl as he leaned down and yanked his war axe back into his hand—eyes scanning for the next target.

[Ah, you've far surpassed your natural adrenaline threshold. Administering sedative as requested—]

Erec was already sprinting to another large mass of the ooze. It was harassing Garin and Olivia, targeting them with blow after blow of its flailing slime limbs to soften them up for consumption.

[—Withholding sedative. Commencing experiment.]

The machine's noise in his head was a little, but annoying buzz. Erec leapt forward with his axe raised above his head—reaching a good seven-foot vertical by using the superior strength of the Vallum model and the pure energy thrumming through him.

Like a hot knife to butter, the edge of his axe used his downward momentum to cleave its way through the ooze. It tore into the eye and slaughtered it in a single violent act.

As he crashed back into the ground, Erec was already turning.

"Erec—" Garin called from behind his back.

The words meant little. Erec rushed at the next ooze. All he heard was the sound of blood running through his veins; he only saw the red. Wholly given to a force that compelled him forward.

Strength.

This was the Strength he needed to win the fight.

He could slay them. All of them. No one could stand in his way.

Ooze after ooze. His axe swung through them as he cleaved into the battlefield. They were but wheat to his scythe.

Initiates fought in groups around him, yet he didn't need a team. All he needed were his two hands. The energy bubbled forth from a never-ending well. He'd never need to stop fighting.

He fought until there were none left. Until the oozes were all gone, and an Armored figure approached him with a massive blade resting on their shoulder. Were they challenging him? Did they want to taste blood too?

There was an annoying blinking in the corner of his vision. But Erec ignored it, tensing as the figure came closer, step by step. He tasted a battle in the air. Felt his heart stir to do combat and test this challenger.

[Experiment completed. Administering sedative now. You've done excellent, Intern. Time for a well-deserved rest—]

Erec swung the war axe at the approaching figure as they got too close, confident they were coming to test him. His limbs were starting to feel heavy and slow, yet he still managed to put force into the blow to deal a mortal wound.

[—Sedative failed. Oh no.]

In an instant, the Knight jerked their sword off their shoulder—caught the blow mid-swing, and threw the axe wide with ease. They barreled in and rammed Erec with their shoulder.

Erec flew back and smashed against the ground. The Knight was on top of him in an instant, yanking his helmet off even as the Vallum protested. Their Strength was too much for the Armor to resist.

Not with this leverage. Not with Erec's body shutting down. His limbs shook from the after-effects as his mind bled back into normalcy. Horror grasped his heart. He'd just taken a swing at an ally.

The Knight paused as Erec's helmet flew free in one last screeching groan.

"Erec?" Bedwyr asked.

# CHAPTER 25
# FURY

Erec didn't respond to Bedwyr—stunned. Bedwyr stood up, yanking Erec along with him.

[I'll control the legs,] VAL informed him; the servos in the Vallum's legs froze, and the joints locked, which was good. Erec wasn't able to stand correctly on his own. His whole body shook, and his face felt numb. Never had he lost it as far as that. When Colin provoked it last time was the closest, but there was a difference; he'd crossed over the edge yet hadn't dived off the cliff like this battle. Erec remembered everything from that state in a crisp red haze.

He saw his hands cleaving into the ooze, ripping eyes to shreds, and rending them into piles of gore littering the battlefield. But there hadn't been a single thought during the intense violence—just an overwhelming desire to fight.

His head twitched, and his eyes took in the battlefield. Nothing but shredded eyes and puddles of corrosive murky green soaking into the wasteland dirt; they'd slain everything. Far in the distance rested the steaming flyer's corpse from where it'd crashed into the earth.

"Erec," Bedwyr called again, slamming the tip of his sword into the dirt deep enough to support itself so that he could walk closer without the weapon. "Why did you follow me into the Academy? I told you not to."

"I-I"—Erec's tongue felt numb in his mouth, so he struggled to get the words right—"n-need to make a name for myself."

There was a sigh from inside of his brother's Armor. "This isn't safe, Erec. Being a Knight is deadly. I'll have done well enough for us in a couple of years. Our family will be fine. Couldn't you have waited? What about your nice job with the Baron?" Bedwyr's head shook. "The way you fought too. Like you had nothing to lose. What am I to do?"

"N-nothing," Erec said, legs starting to firm up a little beneath him. Less wobbly, but if it weren't for VAL locking the servos in place, he'd undoubtedly have fallen. The last thing he wanted to do was show weakness right now. "I-I'm not here for your help. I-I'm here for me."

"Now, don't be ridiculous. I'm your older brother. Goddess, you've already taken your oath. How am I going to get you back now—"

"I-I'm g-going where you can't."

At that, Bedwyr froze in place. The cold mask of his Armor's helmet stared deeply into Erec's soul. "No. You're not. We both know you can't, Erec. Listen to my words and get it through your thick skull: you *cannot* surpass me, and you *cannot* save her. It's something you need to accept. It is impossible. I'm truly sorry." There was a second of silence. "Don't make me crush your dreams. If that's what it takes to keep you safe, then I will."

Erec took a deep breath. His heart was already beating again at a too-quick rate.

Bedwyr's head swiveled to the side as another person in Vallum Armor ran up. "Erec!" Garin called with Olivia trailing behind.

"Ah, Garin. A pleasure," Bedwyr said tactfully, bowing his head.

"Oh, shit. Bedwyr!" Garin stopped. "Er—are you alright? Erec, why the hell did you take a swing at your brother; I know you two don't get along well, but not enough to swing a damn axe—"

"That? I saw him fighting; after the battle ended, I wanted to see how much he'd grown. I told him to try to hit me," Bedwyr lied smoothly. "I think he must be tired now. Do me a favor, go sit him down? Keep out of any more fights unless the Commander orders otherwise. The Army should arrive soon, anyway. I believe we've done our part." With that, Bedwyr yanked his massive sword from the ground and slung it over his shoulder, walking off with ease as if nothing had happened.

Garin watched Bedwyr stride off before going to retrieve Erec's helmet.

Between Garin and Olivia, they were able to guide Erec to a nearby boulder to lean against. After which, VAL disabled the locked servos on his Armor. Erec hung his head in silence for some time, taking deep breaths and trying to maintain his cool.

He'd gone off the handle again. Provoked that anger, and it'd led him too far. How many times would he go down this path—and VAL! With Garin and Olivia nearby, he couldn't question the machine. Couldn't yell at it. It'd lied to him. He'd asked him to stop him from losing control like that, but it deliberately let him go into the deep end. And for what? The anger flared in his chest, and Erec kept having to stop and count out numbers in his head.

Though Garin and Olivia took some passing attempts to coerce him into a conversation, Erec killed their conversation hooks with terse replies or silence. It was hard enough to keep cool without dealing with that pressure. Eventually, they simply talked to one another about the fight.

Their conversation passed him by. He was too focused on that spark of anger that kept burning inside his chest—desperately trying to put it out because he was afraid.

Afraid of what might happen if it retook control.

He tried to distract himself with that flashing notification in his vision. Though in light of the recent fight, the achievement was somewhat lost.

But he opened it anyway.

### Strength Advancement: Rank E - Tier 5 → Rank E - Tier 6

Erec numbly took the information in. There should have been pride or elation at reaching the next Tier in his highest Virtue, his trump card in fights. It took a long time to get to Tier 6, and this would mean much in the coming weeks as the Academy ran their evaluations on the new Initiates.

But it was hard to feel much. Better not to have any emotions at all right now. As the notification burned away, a searing white light flooded his vision.

More words burned their way across his eyes in the pure divine light—each letter like a fire flared into his vision and left a permanent scar on his psyche.

### Divine Talent Ignited: Fury

There it was. A seal on this curse that he'd suspected from the moment VAL mentioned the anomalous energy spiking adrenaline. As with all Divine Talents, it wasn't stated outright what it did. Not that it needed to. Unlike some, this was a simple word, one now burned into his soul.

Fury.

His Divine Talent drove him into an uncontrollable Fury. It left him in such a state that he'd attack friends and foes. By the Goddess. What could he do?

Erec hunched over, trying to control his breath as a battle waged on beyond the wall. Garin flung an arm over his shoulder and pretended to be at ease, a pillar of sanity in the chaos that circled Erec's mind—jovially conversing with Olivia.

What would he do if he lost control and hurt his friends? What if he were in a spar with another Academy student and went too far? Was this going to get him exiled from his Order? His career as a Knight had just begun, was it going to end just as quick?

— - ☣ - — - ☼ - — - ☣ - —

After three hours of sustained conflict, the Kingdom's Army managed to cut through the terrors spilling out of the Rifts. Grandmaster Lotus sealed it with an elite group of Knights through spellwork and prayer. Shortly after, the Initiates received orders to return to the Academy.

None of the Initiates died in the conflict, thankfully, as the bulk of the violent fight had taken place around the Rift itself. However, casualties outside of their group were unknown. This unprecedented attack might've had further and more dangerous ramifications without swift and decisive action by the Knights and the Army.

A total success, all factors considered.

Aside from the flyer, none of the monsters had breached the wall.

Nothing of unimaginable terror had spilled out and threatened their utter destruction. While Cataclysm-Level threats were exceptionally rare, any Rift had the potential to let one stride into their world and bring death in its wake.

They got lucky.

But Erec didn't feel lucky. Dread and terror burned in him. He had proof of a flaw that might lead to the destruction of his dreams. Some Divine Talents were uncontrollable, and in at least one case, the Kingdom had exiled a Knight due to the threat theirs presented.

The entire way back to the Academy, Erec shook. When they reached their dorm, Erec put his Armor away, ignoring Garin trying to talk him down. He didn't want to put voice to his fears. He didn't want to scare his friend and make him worry; they hadn't even had their first day of courses. It should have been a time for Garin to relish his victory and look forward to the future. Not dread it like Erec.

Sometime in the near future, they'd need to have that conversation. Garin would want to help, but how could he? What was there to do about something like this? If Garin cornered him in a conversation, he'd weasel the information out. So instead, Erec went to his room.

He sat in quiet. Too unwilling to confront VAL; what if it triggered that anger?

After some time, there was a knock on his door.

"Garin. Let me be," Erec called out, lying in his bed and staring at the ceiling.

"Huh? Naw, it ain't Garin. Though he's out here too. Get your ass up and to this door, or I'll bust in, swear to the Goddess. I got a message." Gwen's voice cut through the door.

Erec took a deep breath, got to his feet, and complied.

She frowned at him. "First fight get to you? Wasn't a pretty one, don't get me wrong, but there's a lot worse to look forward to." She paused and then slipped a small note into his hand. "Don't recommend you be late, or you'll be in deep shit."

With that, the girl waved over her shoulder and then marched out of the dorm. Garin was on the couch—tilting his head at Erec with the unspoken question.

Erec slowly read over the note.

*Come see me in my office, you have an hour to report.*
*Damned Initiate.*
*- Sir Boldwick Mitis*

# CHAPTER 26
# CUT

*NOTICE OF CLASS ACTION SETTLEMENT. A federal court authorized this notice. This is not a solicitation from a lawyer. If you've lived within a forty-five mile range of the Vortex Industries Testing Facility Plant 45-A, you are entitled to receive a payment from a class action settlement. You received this letter because your home is located within forty-five miles of Vortex Industries Testing Facility Plant 45-A. A $532,322,039.98 settlement has been reached in a class action lawsuit claiming Vortex Industries unlawfully performed actions that unduly threatened the lives and property of civilians near this site. The court has determined this to be a gross negligence of lawful practices and safety standards…*

*- Unknown, Notice of Class Action Settlement: Vortex Industries V. John Truce (2102, 2nd Era)*

Erec explained to Garin quickly that Boldwick had summoned him to his office. Was it because of his swing on his brother? Did Bedwyr tell someone what actually happened in an attempt to get him removed? Or about how he'd fought against the monster? Perhaps something else entirely? The man had staked his name on getting Erec into the Academy, and Erec was playing a careful game to try not to reveal any of his fears.

After mulling it over, Garin shrugged and wished him good luck.

The trip through the halls of the Verdant Oak quarters was pleasant as always; the living atmosphere of the place grew quickly on you. Though the note said an hour, he didn't know how long Gwen had taken to deliver it. And since he was still new to this place, Erec had no clue where Boldwick's office lay. Certainly somewhere down the central hall—but as he peeked into room after room, it became an increasingly annoying task.

There was no one to ask. The typical assortment of wandering Knights was still in the field cleaning up after battle and war, leaving Erec to his own devices.

At least the beauty of the rooms kept the panic from growing too much. He came across one room with an artificial lighting spell leading to a floor of thyme and lavender that flushed a pleasant scent with the door open. Another was a thought-provoking display of animal prints and wasteland photography. Once courses started, which of these would he become a regular in? What sorts of lessons would he be taught?

That is, if this Talent didn't lead him to a grave mistake.

"You lied to me," Erec said as he roamed the halls—eyes still scanning for where Boldwick's office might be. If he were a Master Knight with a high enough rank to snatch whatever room he wanted, where would he make his office?

[We agreed that if you threw another tantrum, I'd put you in time-out. I attempted to. The attempt failed. My data regarding the sedatives didn't account for the unprecedented response of the anomalous energy further ramping up adrenaline and testosterone production. Now that this information is known, further tests may be conducted to devise an effective solution.]

"We both know what I mean. You waited, VAL. If you had used it earlier—"

[You'd rather I administered a sedative while surrounded by hostiles and as your allies were under direct assault? I thought it more prudent to gather data and not risk my employee. OSHA would disapprove of such an act.]

*Fuck.* VAL had a point. And Erec knew that before getting into this conversation. Letting him rampage had also allowed him to slay the ooze harassing Garin and Olivia. But he wanted someone to be angry at. If he couldn't get mad at VAL—what was he left with? Himself? The Goddess for this double-edged Talent?

"I apologize. Given the circumstance, you tried to follow my demands while keeping me and the people I care about safe. I'm just —it's frustrating. I've gotten so far, and this thing—this *Talent* might take that away? Was Bedwyr right? He'd never struggle like this; he's never struggled like I have."

[Are you familiar with the scientific method?]

"Uh. Somewhat, I mean—"

[Observe and question. Then research. Form a hypothesis based on the research. Devise experimentation and test. Once you've gathered data, analyze it. Draw conclusions from the analysis. Then the cycle repeats, countless iterations until you've achieved a satisfactory conclusion for a research topic. Can you guess why I'm telling you this?]

Erec shook his head slowly. It was impossible to say.

[Because I want you to learn, in the best manner possible. Each cycle brings research closer until, eventually, results are achieved. It is not the failed hypotheses that matter, but the exhaustive and detail-orientated process that provides evidence to answer the conclusion. Science is repetitive, grueling, and detail-oriented. Yet it is more potent than anything else humanity has devised.]

He let the message sink in, aware of what VAL was trying to goad him into doing. He'd *observed* this Talent, and the next step was finding more information. From there, he could form a hypothesis on how to use it best. Experiment. And then test.

Or, maybe, VAL was trying to distract from its failure to sedate him and there wasn't a subtle message in there anywhere.

Either way, Erec's resolve firmed once more. There wasn't a point in concluding Fury was a death sentence to his Knighthood when he lacked all of the facts.

Eventually, Erec found the door to Boldwick's office.

A firm wooden plank door, very much something you might see in history books from the Second Era—left half-open and spreading into a room with a hide pelt rug in the center. The first thing to draw Erec's eyes inside was the bookshelf. Packed to the absolute brim and spilling past that with old texts, many marked with slips of paper shoved in every which way and direction.

Boldwick sat at a simple wooden desk, his wild hair tied back, several open books laid out in front of him. All of them were recent texts, and from his angle, as he approached, Erec saw that they primarily detailed research about Rifts and the behavior of creatures spawning from them.

As he closed the distance to the desk, Boldwick folded a page of the tome directly in front of him, then closed it. He nodded toward the door, the message fairly straightforward even without words.

Close it.

Erec complied, turning around and doing so before returning to the desk.

There was a single chair in the room, and Boldwick was sitting in it. Either Boldwick wasn't used to visitors or didn't care to provide chairs for them. So, instead, Erec awkwardly stood in front of the Master Knight. Boldwick leaned back in his chair and examined him.

"Well?" Boldwick asked, slipping into a relaxed position with two hands behind his head and kicking a foot up on the desk. "What the hell happened today?"

Erec thought about lying. Thought about maybe trying to solve his problems alone with VAL. Even now, he wrestled with the unfounded fear that revealing his problem might get him thrown out of the Academy. But it was shortsighted, and a path that would lead to failure.

"My Divine Talent Ignited."

There was a heavy silence. Boldwick broke it with a snort. "Thought as much. Could tell you weren't acting within a normal realm for your power from the moment you bashed in that brat's face. Some kind of enhancer?"

"It was called Fury."

"Fury—Fury…" Boldwick glanced up at the ceiling. "Well, nope. Can't think of any records with that one written down. Not all Talents are unique. But the names are usually partial giveaways—in this case, I'm guessing it's what's on the label. Makes you angry?"

"I swung at Bedwyr without being able to stop myself," Erec admitted. Even if it labeled him as dangerous, it was better to get ahead of it. The way Boldwick seemed relaxed and calm was reassuring.

This time his eyes snapped back to Erec. "It made you hit him?"

"…Yes?" Erec asked. If it'd been Garin, would he have? His head leaned in the direction of yes, even if his heart refused to agree.

"Well, that's not great. So it makes you a loose cannon, a danger to enemies, allies, and probably yourself. But I guess we don't know the last one for sure, yet."

"Yet?"

"Where do you think you are?" Boldwick barked out a small laugh.

"The Academy."

"And what do you think we do here? Teach our Knights how to do fancy arithmetic and which fork to use at a high-class dinner party?"

Erec's cheeks burned. He was, in fact, confident that those types of courses existed here. He'd heard tales of it from Garin long before signing up; there were a lot of things that made *many* different types of Knights. Boldwick must have seen that thought on his face.

"Not in this Order, not *you*, at the very least. I got you in here, put my name out there because I saw it"—his finger jabbed at Erec. "That little bit of a spark. That raw instinct. There's a fighter in you, a survivor. The sort of type that I can turn into a little scavenger and send running across the wastes to get me information; and trust to come back to me in one piece after fending off all the nasty beasts out there that want to eat you alive."

"I—thank you." Erec bowed his head slightly. Boldwick's certainty in him was humbling—

"Plus, I liked how you beat that brat's face who back talked me."

—maybe he was a little unhinged. But still, Erec was grateful. "I'll do my best to live up to your expectations."

"Don't be grateful, and don't make that promise to me; you haven't even glimpsed my expectations for you. I'm going to make you bleed, sweat, and probably cry. And only then, after all that, after I've turned you into a living weapon and tool for this Order, do you get to thank me." Boldwick leaned back in his chair again and sighed. "All of you damn Initiates, get all worked up before you've put in the time. This is deadly, it's hard, and it's shit work. You won't be a hero if you do it right, you probably won't even be thanked."

Erec slipped into silence, unsure of how to respond to that. Boldwick muttered a couple curses under his breath before settling his gaze on Erec.

"How are you going to deal with your problem?" he asked.

"I'll control my emotions," Erec said back.

"Wrong." Boldwick shook his head. "You learn how to use them properly. If you swing around a sword by the blade, you'll get cut. But if you jab it into something while holding the handle, you'll stab the monster dead. After your exam I'll see to getting you into a special Talent Development course with a couple of the other early bloomers. Damn funding change has made it harder to devote the time, but given your Talent, it'll be easy to argue it as essential for your training. Dismissed." At that, Boldwick whipped the book back open and began to pore over the words.

[Procure one of those books,] VAL commanded.

Erec instead left. He owed Garin an apology and an explanation.

# CHAPTER 27
# THE LIES WE TELL FOR OTHERS

As Erec approached his dorm, he heard loud yelling from inside.

"Don't you dare tell me where to put my things, wench!" Colin's screech passed the thick wooden door and traveled into the hall. Erec winced and paused outside the room, wondering if he wanted to head in or turn around and walk away.

"Your dirty boots have no business leaving a trail all around our shared living space; I was kindly informing you of our standards," Olivia's voice responded in a polite tone. The type of tone that was well used by maids to deal with belligerent and unwieldy nobles. "I suggest you begin to learn common courtesy before others make you."

"Don't you presume to tell me what I should learn or not learn. Do you know who my father is?"

"Of course she does," Garin said before letting out a long sigh. "We all do."

*Well.* Erec squared his shoulders and opened the door. All heads shot in his direction. Colin's face blazed red, and he had his chest puffed up—but as his eyes landed on Erec, he froze. A bit of panic; his posture shifted from open and confrontational to guarded.

"Y-you aren't worth my time." Colin shot another angry sneer at Olivia before turning and slamming the door to his room behind him.

Olivia gave a soft chuckle and shook her head. "I believe I shall be taking a walk. While warned of this behavior, witnessing it firsthand is another thing entirely. May his ancestors weep for pity at the end of their renowned line." Olivia swept toward the exit, pausing to give Erec a small smile. "Oh, I do hope your conversation with Boldwick went well! Sorry that this was the state which you came back to." She gave a slight curtsy before walking past him.

Erec's eyes trailed her as she walked down the hall. She moved quickly but in a collected manner. It would've been hard to tell she was even angry over the whole affair if not for her tensed shoulders; that practiced and precise movement did wonders to hide her feelings.

How long had she served as a maid to the Luculentus estate? Since she was a little girl? More importantly, she'd found out he met with Boldwick. Erec glared at Garin and raised his eyebrow as he strode into the room. "How'd she find out where I was?" They both knew the answer.

"She was interested in why you left in a huff. Didn't think it was a secret. Besides, you were acting moody ever since we got back from the fight. Can't blame her for wanting to make sure you were okay. Are you? Okay, that is?"

Erec took a deep breath. He would've preferred keeping the business with Boldwick to himself, but it didn't matter too much. So what if she knew he met with Boldwick? It was normal to ask about how people were doing, especially if you were going to be living with them for the next two years. If he was going to use this Divine Talent, everyone would know about it eventually. Not like he could do a very good job of hiding it without putting others at risk.

Along those lines… "I am okay. Thank you. I've got a confession to make—"

There was a bang inside Garin's room. Suddenly Garin jumped to his feet, eyes wide and a panicked expression on his face. He ran over to the door, yanked it open—and a ball of fur rushed out. It ran straight for the open exit.

"Close the door!" Garin screamed.

Erec acted quickly; he sprinted to the door, slammed it shut, and threw his body between *whatever* ran like hell out of Garin's room and the exit.

A squirrel skittered to a stop, frantically backpedaling away. It darted underneath the couch. There was a tense moment as both of their eyes went from the couch to Colin's closed door and then to one another. Nothing moved. Silence hung in the air.

"So uh, I have a confession to make too," Garin said quietly, reaching in his pocket and pulling out chopped-up bits of a smuggled carrot from the canteen. He threw it into his room and stepped away —a second later, the squirrel made a mad dash back inside. He closed it behind the animal and then let out a long nervous laugh. "I brought a pet."

"...You stole a squirrel from your father's bio-cavern?"

"Hey! It's not like that, okay? I didn't mean to. I was headed back for decontamination, and this little guy—Munchy is his name, by the way—followed me back. Each step I made, he kept coming along. And well, he was so damn adorable. He even let me pet him, then he let me hold him, then...he let me take him out, fell asleep in my hand."

"So you stole a squirrel from your father's bio-cavern."

"Yes?"

It was beyond irresponsible. Even given that the squirrel population was out of control, and those little bastards got regularly culled to reduce their numbers. Sure, one squirrel wouldn't be missed. But that wasn't an excuse to nab an animal from its ecosystem because it was *cute*. If taking those sticks had been wrong, this was three times worse, at the very least.

Yet Garin had a sly grin as if it were no big deal.

"Do you even know how to take care of a squirrel? Garin, they aren't meant to live in a dorm room."

"Most of the time, he's chill! All calm. Sits on my desk and munches on whatever I bring back to him. I even gave him a little bowl with water—"

"We are definitely not allowed to have pets." Erec fought to keep his temper in check and his voice down. It would've been impossible if he hadn't been a massive dick earlier today and already felt bad about how he acted. He owed Garin an apology for his behavior and an explanation. This wasn't the time to dig into his friend's carefree attitude and the risk it posed to himself and now Munchy.

"Keep this a secret between us? Munchy is adorable, and I don't want to set him out in the wasteland!"

Yeah, that would be the only place Munchy could go now. It

wasn't like they'd have time or permission to head off campus and back down into the Baron's bio-caverns. Besides, how would they even justify a trip like that in the first place?

Munchy, for better or worse, would have to stay with them.

"Goddess damn it, Garin." Erec rubbed his forehead and walked across the room to collapse onto the couch. "Fine. We'll keep it a secret. What have you been feeding Munchy?" *I get rid of one, and have another forced on me.*

"Little bits from here and there. He really liked the maple sausage we had the other day."

"…Do you feed him a balanced diet?"

"He eats what I eat."

*No. Of course not. He doesn't even know what a balanced diet for a squirrel looks like.*

Garin wrung his hands and glanced at his door before joining Erec on the couch.

"Is that wrong? I don't want the little guy to get sick." Garin cleared his throat, getting a little choked up.

"We'll work out what to feed him, and I—I don't know how, but figure out some way to get him proper exercise in your room. That's…well, not fine, but it's what we'll do." Erec put it tersely, doing his best to stem annoyance and instead contribute positively to this situation. If they were going to secretly keep a squirrel, then they'd damn well better make sure it was well taken care of. "Listen. Let's put Munchy aside for now—"

There was a bang from Garin's door as Munchy slammed against it.

"I think all the yelling from Colin got him worked up. Normally he's *a lot more* relaxed, I swear."

Well, go figure that shrill yelling would work up a creature in a foreign space. Erec sighed. "Yeah, after this talk, it's best you go… calm him down? I'm sorry for earlier. After the fight, you and Olivia were trying to make sure I was fine, and I was trapped in my head and acted like a total dick."

Garin shrugged, taking one more glance at his door. It seemed that Munchy had backed off from his siege to conquer the living room. "You get like that sometimes. Not really new. I didn't get offended."

"The truth is that there was more going on than you think.

Bedwyr didn't ask for me to take a swing at him. I...I've got a Divine Talent; it makes me lose control in a fight, puts me in some kind of... battle state? I took a swing at him because, well, I wanted to fight. He was the only one left and was approaching me."

There was a silence as Garin took this in. "That seems...difficult to deal with, sorry. So you were scared or worried. Is that why you tried to keep it bottled up?"

"I wanted to keep it secret because I thought that sort of thing might get me kicked out."

"And what did Sir Boldwick want?" Garin leaned in. His eyes took light as he dug deeper. When Erec's friend got like this, he'd demand an answer to every question until he felt satisfied and understood the situation. So, Erec gave it. He shared the contents of his meeting with the Master Knight without hiding any details. Including the fears still circling in his head and the private concerns that it would affect his mission with the Duke as well.

He already knew he couldn't manage his temper well, but now with it being a hair trigger on a mindless state of anger, what if he hurt someone? There were too many unknowns about the situation for him to handle alone confidently.

But, at the end of a thirty-minute talk, during which Garin mostly listened and asked pointed questions, his friend looked him in the eye and smirked.

"Y'know what I think? It'll work out fine; there's no point worrying about the what-ifs and worst cases. Work with what you have. This could be huge for you! If it makes you better in a fight, then that's amazing! You'll figure out the downsides and how to work with them. I know you will," Garin said.

He ended the speech with a careless thumbs-up. Then he got up and stretched, eyes trailing to his door.

"Try to work on telling me things that are bugging you, okay? Getting all trapped in your own head isn't good for you. I'm here for you."

*He's right.* Damn it all, no more secrets between them.

"...There's one more thing. I found a ma—" He spat out words as fast as possible, but before he could finish, his tongue went numb.

He'd tried to reveal VAL. And failed. Erec spat out, still trying to force the words out despite his jaw and tongue refusing to work.

[Bad Intern. My processors run much faster than your brain. Cease your attempts to violate our nondisclosure agreement.]

Garin gave him an odd look. "…Right, okay. Is this you teasing me? Saying there's nothing more in your head, or pretending—" His eyes squinted. "Something wrong?"

[Now lie.]

His tongue began to regain feeling. His heart clenched, but the thought of what VAL had done for him. And the sudden spike of fear of what VAL might do if he sided against it.

"…Yeah, sorry, I was making a joke. It was…a weird one. Go take care of Munchy." The words came free a bit sloppy as if VAL tensed to stop him at any point.

"Riiighht…" Garin walked over to his door, taking one last look at Erec, before heading inside.

[I had thought we concluded this nonsense. Why is it you wish to violate our contract so earnestly? Is your benefits package not rewarding enough?]

Erec didn't answer the machine. Working his numb tongue in his mouth to regain feeling. For a while there, he'd thought that…maybe they'd become something like friends. But that was naive. He knew that now. VAL didn't make friends; he didn't know what VAL really wanted.

# CHAPTER 28
# ORIENTATION

*When a man upon the hearing of any Speech, hath those thoughts which the words of that Speech, and their connexion, were ordained and constituted to signifie; Then he is said to understand it; Understanding being nothing else, but conception caused by Speech. And therefore if Speech be peculiar to man (as for ought I know it is,) then is Understanding peculiar to him also. And therefore of absurd and false affirmations, in case they be universall, there can be no Understanding; though many think they understand, then, when they do but repeat the words softly, or con them in their mind.*

*What kinds of Speeches signifie the Appetites, Aversions, and Passions of mans mind; and of their use and abuse, I shall speak when I have spoken of the Passions.*

*- Thomas Hobbes,* Leviathan *(1651, 2nd Era)*

Erec slept poorly. The entire night consisted of him jolting awake; each time, his eyes darted to the corner of his small room. As if he expected something to stare back at him—the red eyes haunting his dreams. While this time the Stag didn't boldly stride through them, even while dreaming he had this overwhelming sense of being watched. But it was completely fictional. Every time he woke up confirmed that.

But no, there was nothing.

By the time he got up in the morning, it was nearly time for orientation. All of the Initiates were to gather in the main hall of their respective Orders. While they all fell under the collective instruction of the Academy proper, at the end of the day, they were still Knights to their own Orders. Said Orders determined what they would learn to best benefit their ranks.

Erec put the thought out of his mind, expecting a relatively easy day of information distribution from the facility. He left his room. Garin reclined on the couch, and Olivia came out soon after him; the three agreed to hit the canteen early together.

As the two paced out of the room, Erec paused at the doorway.

He stared at Colin's room. Since yesterday the haughty Duke's son hadn't left his room at all. Not for food, not for a walk to explore the campus. No, his fight with Olivia had ended with him spooked and hiding away. It was hard to reconcile that with his image of the arrogant brat he knew Colin to be. *Is he playing some game?* Once they left, would Colin take the chance to do something unfounded? Their rooms were locked…

The paranoia carrying over from reoccurring nightmares was living in his head. Erec groaned.

Colin was sulking because he hadn't gotten into his chosen Order, probably. That and he'd lost face in front of all of the other big-shot nobles. The Duke likely had some choice words for his son after that trial.

If you asked anyone with practical sense, they'd say that bastard didn't deserve to be in the Academy. Erec shook his head and closed the door behind him. No, he wouldn't invite Colin along—

*Fuck.*

Why? Why did that thought have to pop into his head? But there wasn't any way Colin would accept him asking him to come. Not to mention he *really* didn't want to.

Garin noticed he wasn't following along. "What's up?" he asked.

"Colin's probably feeling…awfully alone." Erec bitterly forced the words out. His friend's eyes lit up, and his jaw dropped, replaced by a quick grin to Erec a second later.

"Oh, shit. Yeah, you're right. Hold up, Liv." Garin strode back to the room.

*He gave her a nickname?* Olivia crossed her arms and stopped just short of a frown. She failed to hide her unhappiness yet didn't move to stop it.

Garin knocked on Colin's door.

There was shuffling on the other side. "What is it?" came a rather strained voice.

"Hey, we're getting breakfast. Wanna come?"

Pure silence. And then… "Leave me be; I've to prepare for the day. Unlike you lot, some of us have to bother to put on a reasonable appearance…" Erec glanced down at his Academy uniform. Appearance? There wasn't much to do when you had mandatory clothing to wear.

"Don't bullshit. Just throw on your uniform and come. Stop sulking in your room like a child," Erec called loudly, irritated at Colin's response. There was something in there, the way he was acting. Erec had done the same damn thing the night before. The similarity between the two of them pissed him off, even if it made him a massive hypocrite; but he knew with Colin he'd get nowhere by not pushing back. That much was clear from the trial.

"I am not acting like a child! If it gets you all to stop harassing me, I'll grace you with my attendance."

"Goddess have mercy on his soul." Olivia shook her head further in the hall.

Soon after, Colin left his room, huffy but following along. Garin smoothed things over quickly, complimenting how he'd done his hair and asking for tips. Not that Garin needed any tips about styling his appearance, but you didn't have to be adept at socializing to see that Garin was pandering to Colin's ego.

The canteen offered a simple meal of potato pancakes and beans. For the most part, Erec kept himself involved in their conversation as little as possible.

Whenever he spoke up, Colin went quiet and looked away. Maybe he was offended by Erec's presence or unwilling to provoke or test himself against Erec again.

Either way, Olivia steadily grew more annoyed. Not that it reflected in her tone—but after the second time she "slipped" and spilled water on Colin, Erec had a good grasp of how the refined girl expressed herself.

He caught her staring at him across the table when he got distracted, usually with the barest bit of a frown on her face.

After finishing their meal, it was time for orientation.

— - ✿ - — - ☼ - — - ✿ - —

The gathering hall in the Verdant Oak quarters was much smaller than the Academy's great hall. In Erec's opinion, their gathering hall was far more beautiful. It lacked all the garish display of wealth and accolade, including the history of the Knights that had been in the hall. Those were things of the past, tales, and people spun from the time before now. And while it was necessary to remember them, their decoration had left Erec with a weight on his chest. As if history levied its dead gaze on the present to judge in silence.

But the Verdant Oak gathering hall was a place of the *present.* Giant trellises framed either side of the aisle; the roof was a peaked clear glass that spilled in the morning light from above and left the whole place glowing with natural golden light, all the while revealing the beautiful blue sky above. As if the Goddess Herself were looking down and blessing them.

Morning glories wove their way through the intricate latticework of the black steel trellises, a living wall of flowers and greenery. The whole place had a clean scent, even more natural and filled with life than walking outside in the wasteland yielded.

Centered at the end of the hall was Grandmaster Oak—his beard as unruly as ever, a big smile on his face as the hall filled with the first-years and second-years. He looked over them all, nodding slowly.

To either side was mainly an assortment of higher-ranking Knights Erec had yet to meet, aside from Boldwick and the Knight Commander, whose name he never had learned. She had pulled her dark hair back in a ponytail today. They lined up on either side of the Grandmaster, faces far more stern and guarded than the head of the Order was. As the Initiates took their places, Oak gave a long belly-filled laugh.

"Every year; it never gets old, seeing all of the new faces, all of you wondering, 'What's going to happen, what will I learn?' Mean-while, the second-years look annoyed and anxious, like they're begging me to get on with it! So, I suppose I will." He let out one last laugh before smashing his hands together in one loud clap.

A wave of pressure crashed into the Initiates; the morning glories rippled as a tangible force ran over them.

Grandmaster Oak had everyone's undivided attention. "Heed my words! This is my Order, and this year we're going to excel. You'll be made into fine Knights, and if I find out any of you lads or lasses are fucking about, there'll be hell to pay!" A grin spread over Oak's face. "I'll let the instructors and faculty give you their introductions, and then we'll proceed to your exams. That's right. Your first exams are today. I advise you to try your best—since they will determine which courses we offer and which are assigned to you. I think I shall begin with Sir Boldwick."

On that ominous and unexpected note, Grandmaster Oak nodded to Boldwick. Oak was content to step back and fold his hands on his stomach.

Boldwick strode in front, eyes scanning the crowd. "You won't see me teaching a class. I might occasionally audit one and provide pointers, but I have more important things to do than waste my time on a bunch of unproven runts. If you want my attention, prove yourselves." He shrugged his shoulders. "Aside from that, don't screw up." Boldwick nodded toward the Knight Commander from the battle yesterday. "Dame Juliana?"

"A pleasure." She took the head of the hall, "I've already led some of your number into a battlefield. I instruct the Wasteland Survival course—which covers navigating the wasteland in addition to other essential skills. I must admit, I'm looking forward greatly to working with you more. I've seen promising things already." She bowed her head, then introduced another instructor.

After that, the rest of the instructors made their introductions. All of them Knight Commanders; it seemed that everyone else of Boldwick's rank was out and busy performing jobs for the Order.

They led a variety of elective classes ranging from tracking to more unorthodox weapon creation and usage. It seemed the Order geared itself to teaching their Initiates self-reliance techniques and making them capable in the wastes. They wanted them to have what it took to survive in a world filled with hostile monsters.

The exact kind of instruction Erec would need if he were to leave these walls in search of his mother. He listened closely, trying to picture which electives would be of the most use, and then he wondered what the exam would change and qualify him for. And just what sort of courses the Academy proper offered.

# CHAPTER 29
# PAPERWORK

After the Initiates gathered at the Verdant Oak hall, the faculty segregated them into groups of ten. From there, an examiner led Erec's group to a small classroom filled with wooden desks. It was barren, likely disused. A chalkboard with a half-erased equation displayed on its surface completed the room. And the place smelled stale. Erec was unhappy that Garin had gotten split off into a separate group, but at least he had Olivia.

The examiner told them to pick a seat, and to leave empty desks between one another. After that, they were to remain quiet. Shortly after, a Knight Errant came into the classroom with a stack of papers, pencils, and little white erasers.

Within a few minutes, the instructor finished distributing the tests.

Erec leaned down and took in the exam. He did a brief skim of the questions. He'd studied the general history of the Knight Orders and specific details of Armor repair, even wildlife in the wastes. Yet those questions only amounted to around sixty percent of the exam—a barely passing grade.

The first questions to give him pause related to advanced math, which wasn't his strongest subject. Despite Boldwick telling him "fancy arithmetic didn't matter," the test disagreed.

Then the next to really stretch him were the questions about Rifts. There were the ones about wasteland features and wildlife he struggled to remember, and had to guess at them.

But none of those were the hardest. The ones that pissed him off were about court etiquette and traditions.

His pencil hovered over a hypothetical question. It described a scenario where a Knight was five days away from the Kingdom. During this made-up voyage, their Armor gave a critical error code. How would he patch the Armor?

*I know this—*

[Discharge the core, rerun cabling to the power chamber, and reroute power surplus to essential systems.] VAL chimed in within his head.

Erec's pencil hovered over the blank space waiting for the answer. He'd come to a similar conclusion, yet, VAL just cheated.

He whispered. *Really quietly.* "This is to test my knowledge, not yours."

[Intern, at what point in the near future do you plan for us to separate? By transitive property, *my* knowledge—that which I chose to share and not confidential information—is *your* knowledge. Now write the correct answer down. Or would you rather answer incorrectly out of spite?]

It annoyed Erec since he'd known the correct answer, but VAL wouldn't believe that now. He even considered writing the wrong answer but dreaded the annoying lecture VAL would give in response. In the end, he'd only be hurting himself.

The next question was a complex math problem. VAL solved it in a second and shared the answer. Erec hesitated, then wrote the answer down and began to flip the page. VAL forced him to stop. Then made him go back and inscribe the mathematical work to get to the solution because leaving an bare number was "incorrect" and "lazy." It took five tedious steps to get to the result.

Then a question came that only VAL knew; at this point, Erec had committed and just wrote the machine's answer down.

VAL had made a point. As long as the two remained bonded together, then he should take all the benefits from it he could get. He reframed it in his mind as payment for letting VAL rent space in his body. A tiny voice in him cried out against *cheating…* But, for those born naturally gifted like Bedwyr—wasn't that cheating too? Was it fair they had an edge by virtue of being themselves? At least he'd paid the price.

Erec finished the exam before everyone else. So he took the chance to scan the room.

Most of the Initiates were hard at work, one or two's eyes had glazed over with boredom, and a girl in the corner looked near crying.

Olivia was staring at him. The moment their eyes met, she gave him a small smile, then dropped her attention back to her test.

[She was cheating.]

*What?*

[Look up. Do it subtly.]

Erec turned around to face the instructor, an older man with gray hair busy leaning against the board. The man wasn't too keen on his job. Erec let out a yawn and set his hands behind his head, scooting his chair out and acting as if he were taking a break. All to disguise checking the ceiling.

Above him, tucked near the wooden support beam, was a dim bead of light with six legs. Some kind of prayer? He couldn't have imagined Olivia getting away with a glyph, whereas prayers hedged on a tad more subtlety. He tried to hide his shock, yet the bead of light scrambled away soon after being spotted.

He slowly turned to face Olivia. Her eyes were on him again; she wore a smirk, then stood up. "Finished!" she said.

"Already?" the instructor asked, looking around the room. "Right then, bring it here." Olivia strode up confidently, placing the paper in his hands. "Return to your desk, and remain quiet for the remainder of the test. If you get bored, there's a bookshelf in the back."

She gave the examiner a slight nod.

[Cheating is a valid option. When presented with the same open-ended test, different subjects utilize varying approaches to achieve their results. To us, it was a test of knowledge. To her, it was testing her information-gathering abilities.]

Shortly after, Erec turned in his test. His eyes kept wandering to the girl, wondering just who she was. Why would a maid get taught that sort of…prayer? If it was a prayer. He knew too little to say. Was it possibly a Divine Talent? Soon enough, the rest of the class finished. Tomorrow they'd receive the results of the exam, along with their assigned courses and offered electives.

— - ❂ - — - ☼ - — - ❂ - —

After the written exam, all of the Initiates were gathered together. And not just those of the Verdant Oak—every Initiate in the four Orders got escorted to a field arranged near the Academy.

They'd filled the grounds with a sizable rope-fenced arena edged with elaborate white-and-red tents. "Lines!" a familiar loud voice rang out. Erec winced. It was the bald man from the trial. He'd recognize that raw verbal power anywhere.

This time everyone scrambled into position without hesitation. Light gleamed off the yeller's scalp as he scanned them. He stomped through the dirt as he took in their line. A snort, and then he spat on the ground. "Better than last time! But not good enough yet. Second-years—you could do better too!" He jerked his head at the field. "The practical test is simple, as always. First, get examined by a priest; then, you'll be assigned a sparring partner. After that, we'll follow up with a test of your resolve. After all that, you're done, and we throw you back to your order. Easy, right?"

He was met with silence.

"Hell no. You'll get a single spar to prove yourself. They'll be picked personally to challenge you in some way, shape, or form. Don't like it? Think it's an unfair matchup? Tough shit, maybe that's the point." He nodded his head slowly. "Now, go get your Virtues recorded. Go!"

Baldy clapped his hands once, and the line broke apart. People ran toward the tents with the priests.

Erec joined the end of a line and rubbed the back of his head. He felt a thrum of worry. Soon they'd match him up against another person and demand he give it his all. It was…exciting…but terrifying. He made a fist to stop his fingers from shaking. *You won't lose control.* If he could keep himself in check…

Boldwick's words came back to him. If he used his Talent incorrectly he'd suffer, but if he could apply it in the right circumstance… *How do I stop myself from going too far?* "VAL," he said quietly.

[Yes?]

"You said the scientific method was cyclical… To perform new tests after looking at the results from before. Did you learn anything last time I lost control when the sedative failed?"

[I did. The production of "fury" chemicals in you correlated to your degrading mental state. This "Talent" possesses the power to counteract the forces of other chemical agents. However, since production increases as "fury" deepens, there's a critical point at which I cannot use enough sedative to stop you in a timely manner. I predict that controlled doses of sedatives administered while under the early effect of "fury" may curb it from growing too quickly to counteract. A buffer, if you will. Which would allow us still to end the state with a sudden spike of sedative.]

"...Are you prepared to run another experiment?"

[Excellent. You're a real go-getter, Buckeroo. That's the type of initiative we love to see.]

Erec nodded his head and took a deep breath. At least they wouldn't be using real weapons. If this were to fail, dealing a fatal injury would be impossible. And the rewards were enticing. If he figured out how best to apply this ability, he'd soar to success; there wasn't a better opportunity.

With a shaky breath at what he was about to attempt, he made his way to the tent. The check was relatively brief—though invasive. As the priest used a prayer, it felt as if something were peering into his skin. After a minute, the priest composed a list of his Virtues and requested that he check them over and sign them.

Erec called upon his Blessing to confirm.

**Name: Erec of House Audentia**
**Health: 100% | Mana: 100% | Stamina: 100%**


**Holy Virtues:**
**Strength: [Rank E] | [Tier 6]**
**Vigor: [Rank F] | [Tier 9]**
**Agility: [Rank E] | [Tier 1]**
**Perception: [Rank E] | [Tier 1]**
**Cognition: [Rank E] | [Tier 3]**
**Psyche: [Rank F] | [Tier 7]**
**Mysticism: [Rank F] | [Tier 1]**
**Faith: [Rank F] | [Tier 1]**


**Divine Talents:**

### Fury

Everything was there on the sheet—aside from his Divine Talent, which the prayer would not have been able to reveal. Erec hesitated before disclosing that on the official Academy form. If things were going to spin out of control due to his failed experiment, he'd rather they knew why and didn't accuse him of hiding information.

All of his cards were on the table for better or worse.

[When will these spars start? Science waits for no man!]

Erec felt a shiver go through him. Bidding himself not to forget that there really was little he knew about VAL and Vortex Industries.

# CHAPTER 30
## TALENT

*It's been a year.*

*We managed to crawl into this cave dug out and used for…some kind of experiment? They didn't label any documents, and their projects contained sparse information. The best we've been able to determine is that they were trying to create miniature self-contained environments, though why bother doing so far beneath the earth?*

*It doesn't matter to us. We've been able to start small farms thanks to their work, and a few have begun to make use of the Blessings.*

*At least that's what the Church is calling them. They said a glowing figure came out from the sky and told them to come here, and we took them in; they're humans, after all, not like those monsters out there.*

*Everyone we send out above gets sick and dies, eventually, aside from those priests, which I don't get. But they say in time, they'll be able to heal the sickness, and it'll go away.*

*Is this hell?*
*- Aaron Dunwick, assorted notes (2, 3rd Era)*

After submitting his form, the priest sent Erec back to the other Initiates. One by one, the instructors called them up in pairs to fight in the ring.

Garin was one of the first to fight, along with a girl from the Order of the Crimson Lotus.

If you could call it a fight. The Dame tried using Mysticism against his friend, but Garin could easily counter and break her concentration by pressing an assault. She'd worn down in a few minutes, yet the fight dragged on and on.

Garin never went for the kill. Either it was because he felt embarrassed for her or knew her in some way, he withdrew just before landing an ending blow. It was like he kept trying to give her a chance to shine on the field, yet she never did.

Eventually, the girl, outmatched, forfeited.

But the overall effect was that the fight made Garin look like he lacked the drive to win, while it made the girl appear hopelessly weak. To Erec, it seemed crueler than a decisive victory.

Another rather disappointing match-up was Lyotte against her former maid, Olivia. At the announcement, Erec leaned forward to watch.

Within the first ten seconds, Olivia intentionally threw herself too far into a swing and took a "lethal" blow. The two gave one another respectful bows and had a small conversation afterward.

One might argue that Olivia simply made a mistake, that it wasn't an intentional loss and just an overestimation. But Erec doubted it; that would have been too convenient. There was something hidden beneath the surface of Olivia. A Knight Commander yelled at them to clear the battlefield.

Of course, they rushed away and began to filter into the stands. Erec barely had a second to prepare himself before the Knight Commander spoke again.

"Sir Erec of House Audentia," the Knight Commander called. He broke apart from the crowd and headed to the weapon rack. "And Sir Soren of House Crisimus."

The Prince. He was to face the Prince. The crowd burst into cheers and hoots of excitement.

Erec stuffed down his nerves and the accompanying flare of

excitement. This was only a spar. Even against someone like the Prince, it changed nothing; Soren was simply an opponent with far more training than himself. Yet the thrill of pitting himself against a superior enemy was palpable. It also meant he'd have to rely on the "experiment" to compensate for that skill difference if he wanted any chance of winning.

He didn't want to stomach a loss—that drive to win burned higher and higher with every attempt to temper it. So many times growing up, he'd felt the sting of lingering in Bedwyr's shadow. Whether it was at his job in the bio-cavern or at primary school, where their teachers hounded him about getting worse grades.

No, he didn't want to win. He wanted every voice crying out for Prince Soren to yell out his name instead. To hear them chant, "Erec!"

His fingers shook as he took in the weapon rack.

Of course, there were about five styles of dulled swords, as would be expected. A couple of spears with their points removed. And a one-handed axe with a flat edge—not as balanced as his new weapons, but it fit nicely in his palm.

A fine enough weapon for the job.

He took his place on the field as Soren picked out a simple longsword. He took his position and stood stoic in the Academy Uniform.

The dark-haired Prince wore a blank expression, whereas Erec fought to keep his heart from hammering in anticipation of the fight. There was nothing from the Prince. A calm, serene gaze that bordered on boredom. Even with the crowd cheering him on and filling the ring with more energy than any match before.

"What's your deal?" Erec asked, waiting for the Knight Commander to start the fight.

Soren tilted his head. "Deal?"

"Yeah, you look like you're watching a protective coat dry on your Armor. Is facing me boring to you? Are you that confident you're going to win?"

"This examination is an inefficient use of our time," the Prince said and nodded to the Knight Commander, trying to quiet the crowd. "Instead, we could already be training, so yes, I don't care for this fight in the least."

"Fighting against me isn't training?"

"You're a Knight. Not a monster."

Erec wasn't sure how to feel about that. There was a solid line of logic there, but there was something more. It was as if Soren didn't care how this went either way. His heart wasn't in the fighting—meaning if Erec won, it wouldn't feel like a victory. If he lost to a man not even trying… Well, that'd be even more devastating.

"Let me be your monster. I want to see you give it your all. If you're going to do something, you should give it best. Test yourself against me; let's see who's stronger." Erec beat a hand against his chest, stirring up his own drive to fight. He wanted to see what an heir to the Royal Family was capable of. How far did his training go against someone like that?

"Truly? You wish to go all-out on a simple game?" Soren gave the barest trace of a frown.

"If you don't, it's a far greater insult."

"As you will. I'll honor your request, and show you respect fitting another Knight. For this fight, I shall treat you like a monster."

Soren shifted from the relaxed stance of an uncaring man to a practiced combat position, with his sword held neatly between them as the air around him shifted. Erec took in a shaky breath, his focus on the situation narrowing on his opponent as he sensed a change. The entire feel of the spar shifted. There was an atmosphere now he'd felt once before—that same intensity as when he'd tried to bash in Colin's head.

A tangible killing intent hung in the air. Soren's eyes narrowed with the focus of a hunter tracking their game.

"Begin!" the Knight Commander called.

Erec tensed in his spot. He wanted to see what Soren did, to pick apart his capabilities before playing his strategies out. Understanding the enemy was key to victory.

Except Soren didn't move at all. He hovered in the same spot, those intense eyes of a hunter digging into Erec. His sword held ready as if waiting for Erec to start the fight. It made no sense; surely the Prince had a higher degree of confidence in his skills—

[What are you doing? MOVE BACK!] VAL screamed in his head.

Erec didn't have time to question it. He backpedaled quickly.

Soren vanished from the spot he'd been standing; his sword tore through the space where Erec had been. Erec blinked. *Did he…tele-*

*port? Or is he that quick?* Following the failed attack, the Prince pulled back and paced around Erec toward the right in a neat circle. Erec twisted to track the movement, following Soren and trying to anticipate the next blow.

[What are you looking at—to the left. DUCK.]

Erec dropped down as a sword swiped over his head. The Prince vanished from his right side and suddenly appeared on Erec's left. *How the hell?*

Seeing his prey escape another attack, Soren followed through with a kick; Erec couldn't block the blow. The force sent him tumbling over the ground, his uniform tearing across a rock and bruising him all over. As he scrambled to his feet, the Prince stood still. "Where is he?"

[What do you mean? He's running at you! Use your eyes, Intern!]

Erec's heart was going a mile a minute; he'd tasted pain from the blow. Yet, despite what VAL said, he only saw Soren swaying in the place where he'd last kicked him. "Tell me when to swing." Erec tensed, his instincts racing. Logic started to leave his head. It didn't matter that Soren was standing far away—no, that didn't matter at all. All that mattered was getting a blow in.

[Now.]

Erec lashed out with his hatchet—connecting with the side of a sword as Soren converted a strike into a block. He could suddenly see the Prince again, teleporting from his position far away to a foot in front, fending off Erec's attack. That was all he needed. Erec barreled forward, pitting the Strength behind his arm against Soren's guard—causing the other boy to step back.

Another step forward—dirt piled behind Soren's boot as he slid back along the dirt. As long as there wasn't distance, Soren couldn't use his trick.

He just needed to get closer. Erec's heart pounded. His breath grew heavy as his vision colored red. "Start the test," Erec said, the words coming out terse and filled with violence. There wasn't a doubt in his mind he would take the Prince down.

[Early onset of Fury confirmed. Experiment commenced. Employing small dosages of sedative as required.]

Erec's arm buckled as the pure force pouring into the clashing steel stopped ramping up—plateauing into a higher degree of Strength but not giving him what he needed to finish the job.

Soren was quick to react, sliding the edge of the axe along his blade to a flourish and disengagement during the small gap when Erec adjusted. Before Erec could yank back and throw out another blow, their point of contact dissolved. Soren leaped backward.

Erec smelled blood in the water; if his enemy was fleeing, then he'd chase him down.

[DODGE RIGHT. YOU'RE ABOUT TO RUN INTO HIS SWORD!]

After the loud shriek, Erec's body reacted without thought, yet it lagged as if too slow to respond. As if it physically couldn't keep up with the instincts. The blade's edge skimmed his side, turning what would have been a skewering hit into a nasty cut—had the blade not been dulled. As it was, the metal still managed to bite his skin and draw blood.

The pain only drew the Fury out more. His weapon jerked outward, but his arm lagged behind the instincts, giving Soren enough time to slip out of range and disappear—or rather, appear to flee backward.

Minutes flew by, yet the dance of their fight remained the same, Soren would dart in, and Erec would react, often nicked but still surviving. He was unable to effectively retaliate with his axe. Every second that the fight dragged on, his body felt less responsive. Dulled and drugged.

It was frustrating. Pain and anger swelled in him, numbed by the constant feeling of sedative unleashed in response—a limiter keeping him from flying off the edge.

But it also limited him from winning.

Retaining the barest of his senses and drugged, his body couldn't react with the pure instinct that this fight demanded. All he needed was to let Fury take control, and he'd have Soren. As the drugs and anger rampaged his mind, his sense of logic hung by an increasingly frayed rope.

"Stop the sedatives."

[That would violate the goals of this experiment.]

"I don't care," Erec growled as another stab came in from his right, kindly warned by VAL before it happened. The blade scored a nick on his cheek, its dull edge catching and ripping enough skin to cause blood and pain to swell. His vision pulsed in waves of red, deepening in crimson only to flush back to color as VAL released more sedatives to keep him in check.

[You're aware you'll lose control?]

"I want to win."

[We must let new employees make their mistakes to learn. Experiment concluded.]

The change came ten seconds later. Erec's vision filled with red completely; he tasted his blood. That deep metallic and beautiful taste.

There was a buzzing in his head. But he didn't need it anymore. No, he sensed the direction of the killing intent. A blow was coming directly for his midsection. Erec jumped forward with sudden abandon; his axe caught the sword's edge. He slammed the weapon, his Strength spiraling, whacking the sword far aside.

The edge of the axe went in for a killing blow to the neck—only for his prey to redirect the weapon with a deft movement of their blade. After which, Soren used fancy footwork to twist away and maneuver his blade to jab directly into Erec's heart.

No choice but to pull back; Erec put temporary distance between them. The failed assault only deepened his irritation, especially as Soren tried to fade away again, his shadow running off in one direction.

He wouldn't get away.

There was another annoying buzz in Erec's skull.

Erec yanked his arm back and threw the axe for all it was worth—spinning through the air directly to where he *knew* Soren was.

There was a clang of metal as Soren's sword barely deflected the weapon. A feat that should've been impossible, yet this enemy pulled it off. Erec grinned, charging in after they blocked the hit to land an attack with his fists.

A sword hit the side of Erec's neck as he closed the distance.

But he knew that the enemy's sword couldn't slay him. Its blade was too dull. They'd picked the wrong weapon for this fight.

Erec sprang forward and tackled his prey. They should've brought a real sword. That poor excuse for an axe was just as useless.

He'd bash this enemy into a pulp with his bare hands.

He raised a fist to start raining down blows against Soren and secure victory. Someone grabbed him by the collar and flung him far away.

[Administering sedatives.]

Erec tumbled across the ground, gasping as more pain filled him —but the moment he stopped, he scrambled to his feet. His legs shook; they threatened to give out as the drugs pumped in him without end. Each muscle strained and started to spasm. It felt like his body was heavier than it had any right to be. An overwhelming urge to lay down and accept defeat poisoned him.

*No.*

He took a few steps toward the opposite side of the field, weathering the struggle. *It's not over.*

Before he even managed to regather himself, his mystery assailant appeared and slammed a fist into his gut.

Erec doubled over from the pain, collapsing to the ground with a gasp.

# CHAPTER 31
## DANGEROUS

E rec woke up in one of the priests' tents—his head pounding and hands shaking. A priest hovered over him, reciting their holy words. They paused as Erec's eyes opened. "Ah, back with us? Sir Boldwick said you'd be up sooner rather than later."

A blinking notification from his Blessing was in the corner of his vision.

"I—" Erec winced. Bruises lined his back. Everything was healing, but the pain of being healed meant he'd once more experience half of the pain he felt when receiving the wound. Erec struggled to keep his consciousness together as he replayed the red-tinted memories of the fight.

Soren had been using some kind of Talent. He was sure of it—no glyphs, no prayers.

In the heat of the moment, Erec'd given himself all the way over to the anger and failed. "I lost."

[Indeed you did. If it's a consolation, while you lost the spar, it's uncertain whether or not you would've lost the fight. My theory was that in your more "primal" state your goals changed to simply trying to kill him. And, well, since he had a dull weapon, you adjusted your priorities. It appears you're a pure combat machine while in that state.]

The priest launched back into their prayer. Pain lanced through Erec. He pulled up his notification to distract himself.

**Perception Advancement: Rank E - Tier 1 → Rank E - Tier 2**

A fair upgrade. Had the reliance on pure instincts while tracking Soren driven him to new heights? The advancements were coming rapidly—was this what being in the Academy was like? The constant pushing forward and getting stronger was addictive. But how long would it be before it slowed again?

[That Talent the Prince displayed was quite interesting. I would love to analyze how he used the anomalous energy to manipulate your senses—I'd been trying to figure it out for some time. Perhaps some form of direct light manipulation? No, then again—]

Erec lapsed into silence and ground his teeth together. He let VAL go on as long as it wanted.

Soon enough, the priest finished and then told him to leave the tent once he felt up to it.

Instead, he lay on the cot. He turned the fight over again in his head. His choices had been wrong. It'd been a massive mistake to give over to the anger, and he'd sacrificed the fight with that obsession for victory. Not that he would've won with how they'd been plodding along with him drugged out.

He was competitive—and under the influence of Fury, that fault got driven to exceptional heights.

It also came with an unprecedented desire to achieve victory by decimating his opponent and utterly destroying them. Which he still found hard to explain. Did some part of him deep down want to destroy, or was it the adrenaline cocktail?

After a minute of silence, he came to a conclusion.

"I don't think that plan is going to work." The sedatives were too limiting. And the closer he got to using Fury, the more his reasoning vanished. It also limited the height of power given by the Talent. However, the most important reason it didn't work was that it lagged his reaction speed. If Soren had been using a real sword, he'd have slaughtered Erec with all of those cuts. Using the sedatives with Fury wore him down too quickly.

There had to be a better method.

[Agreed. There were some complications in the experiment, even with it being aborted before fulfilling all of the objectives. That's science for you. So, we begin the cycle again.]

They'd have to find a way to use it, a better method to leash Fury or direct it.

The flaps to the tent flung open. The Prince walked in as if he owned the place, which he might as well have. His empty face lingered on Erec on the cot. A mask that hid what was beneath. Had he come to punish Erec for breaking the rules of the fight? For trying to hurt him?

"Congratulations on the win. Sorry about the end there. I didn't mean to cause you trouble. I lost control of myself," Erec said.

"I didn't win," Soren said.

"No, you got me in the neck; I'm the jackass who kept going and tried to hurt you after." *Better to own up to it.*

"While it was unexpected that you continued your assault after I won the game, I'm left wondering. Had I a real sword, would you have charged in that manner? I don't believe so. Nor was I able to determine how you tracked my movements without using prayer or spell-craft." Soren pulled over a wooden chair from the side of the tent, sitting near the cot. His face was still blank. "Though you broke the rules, you fought with your all, as you'd vowed. In the end, you intended to smash my face with your fists, since you'd thought it the most effective way to counter my Talent."

"Trust me, I—I'm not sure that's the best way to counter you. I don't have control over my Divine Talent yet. I got frustrated with the fight and was stupid and gave in to it. I'm sorry for trying to harm you; that's not normally me."

"One apology was enough. I'm not here to hold petty grudges over other Knights learning how to fight. You did, however, keep your word, unintentionally or not. That fight took everything you had, and you turned it into a real battle in the end. I expected today to be a test of my patience as we played the Academy's games, yet, I found something of value."

There was a long pause as they looked each other over. Search as he might, Erec found nothing in the Prince's eyes, no anger, no desire for revenge, no friendliness.

"This will not be our last fight. When we face off again, I expect you to be better. Challenge me. Few are willing to throw their full might against a Prince, yet it's amusing and convenient that you have little to no choice. There's much to learn against an enemy like that."

Soren gave a slow nod, then got to his feet. Then he left.

Which was fine; Erec was fine without responding to that. While the Prince might have accepted such a thing, he doubted many of his peers would look too fondly on him losing it against a member of the Royal Family. And he couldn't expect Soren to go around giving that same speech to clear the air.

It'd been a minimal risk, sure. But that didn't mean there weren't consequences.

He'd underestimated Fury's power to make him lust for battle and victory.

Erec closed his eyes, hands still shaking. As soon as they stopped, he'd head back out. The test wasn't done yet.

— - ☻ - — - ☼ - — - ☻ - —

Erec collected himself, then returned to watch the rest of the duels. Nothing particularly caught his interest in the rest of the first-years' fighting. Garin and Olivia already had their fight, and while Erec was recovering, Colin fought too.

From what he'd heard, Colin had lost to the redheaded Duchess's daughter.

According to Garin, the girl stomped him. There must've been bad blood between them since she didn't simply beat him; no, she spent a good five minutes embarrassing the hell out of him. She'd disarm him, force him to pick up his sword and disarm him again. Afterward, Colin ran off.

That was the least of Erec's concerns; their "friendship," if you could call it that, was nowhere near the point where Colin would appreciate him cheering him up. Not that Erec was in the state to do it. His body felt wrung out and barely functional, threatening to collapse. And he had better things to do then care about the boy's fragile ego. Instead, he focused on trying to reset himself before the test of resolve.

Things got far more interesting when they got to the second-years' duels. They flashed a range of spell-work and prayer that drew out applause from everyone watching.

There were also a few Divine Talents being put on display.

But there was a single fight Erec both dreaded and dearly wanted to see.

"Bedwyr of House Audentia!" called out the Knight Commander.

If the cheering for Prince Soren from the first-years was enthusiastic, the screaming, cheers, and whistling from the second-years put the Prince to shame.

Bedwyr took to the field, his red hair bright in the sun, with a slight smirk on his face as he waved to the people cheering for him. He scanned the crowd, his eyes briefly locking on Erec, before making his way to the weapons. He looked every part that a Knight should. Valiant. Noble. Courageous. Erec clenched his fist and took a sharp breath; there wasn't a particularly good reason to it, but he wanted to punch that smug look off the bastard's face.

His hand began to shake again.

[Easy now, Buckeroo. Keep that excitement locked away for science!]

"Mathias of House Valens, please make your way to the field and pick out your weapon."

Even more cheering, as a large boy damn near twice Bedwyr's size strode out to the field. Where Erec's brother had his share of muscle, he was also compact, heroic, and well in proportion. Compared to Mathias—it was like a mountain versus a man. The Initiate had to be nearing seven feet, an absurd build with muscle upon muscle.

His Strength must've been through the roof, and trying to guess at any of his other physical Virtues would have been "high" at the bare minimum. More cheering blared from the crowd. This was a much-anticipated fight from the second-years, and as the first-years caught on, they too began to call out and feed into the excitement.

Bedwyr picked a large dulled two-handed sword, tossed it on a shoulder, then took an easy stance on his place on the field. The big boy glanced at the assorted weapons before settling on a similar greatsword, but bigger. This move elicited even more jeering from the crowd.

Both just picked the biggest sword they could carry. Go figure.

"Begin!" shouted the Knight Commander.

The big guy smashed a fist into his chest—and a glyph formed at the point of contact. A second later, stone and dirt from the ground rose in the air and layered themselves, giving him a second skin of soil and rock. Bedwyr sat easily at the other side of the field, smiling as he let his enemy Armor himself up.

And then the big guy stomped—a mist of silver haze around him that spread out to envelop even the people in the stands. Suddenly the air felt a lot heavier, as if the ground were pulling him to it. It had to have been a Divine Talent. But yet again, it was another preparation made before the battle that went unchallenged by Bedwyr. Despite the increased gravity, Bedwyr only slipped into a fighting stance. *He's showing off for the crowd.*

Like a rolling mountain, Mathias charged Bedwyr—sword swinging from as high as he could manage and slicing downward with a heavy momentum. Bedwyr dodged right, and a white glyph formed in his hand. Mathias roared as his attack missed and, in an unexpectedly agile adjustment, managed to twist the angle of his blade to try to sweep into Bedwyr.

Erec's brother leapt over the blade, clearing the dull steel as it slammed into the ground.

In response the silver mist sparkled with light, and gravity increased with a sudden jerk, pulling everyone to the ground. Some in the stands fell over, but Bedwyr adapted easily to the Divine Talent. His foot landed on Mathias's sword, using the flat of the massive blade to spring himself off of, despite the increased gravity. Somehow, he managed to vault over the giant man with a flip; at the same time he tapped Mathias's head with the glowing glyph in his palm.

It flashed with light, and the mud Armor covering the other boy fell to pieces.

Stripped of his Armor, Mathias yelled, and the pull of the silver aura increased even further. Erec strained to stay standing as some of the less physically Virtued people around him slipped to their knees.

Bedwyr stumbled as he landed, once more barely dodging from another blow as his enemy seemed to move with ease. As if he weren't affected by his own Divine Talent.

Another swing as the struggling Bedwyr—but this time his brother caught his enemy's blade with his sword guard. There was a loud clang as metal met metal.

Then Bedwyr chanted.

A prayer.

Bedwyr slid his blade down Mathias's getting halfway down the massive blade as his prayer completed. There was an explosion of blinding light from where their steel contested, and the force of the prayer blew the weapons apart from one another.

Using the enhanced gravity to his advantage, Bedwyr had an easier time retaining his posture, only having to take a single half-step back to reinforce himself from the blow. He shifted his sword, and then stabbed forward with it, the point of it slamming into the bigger boy's chest. Right where his heart was.

"Victory goes to Bedwyr!" the commander screamed, much to the delight of the crowd.

Bedwyr paused, offering a handshake to Mathias and a smile.

The other boy had thrown everything in his arsenal at him from the start. His Divine Talent, his defenses, and his Strength. Still, Bedwyr had overcome him.

While flashy, it wasn't overt and hinted that more was under the surface. Bedwyr displayed no extreme Divine Talent; nothing he'd done was earth-shattering in prowess. But his actions had been enough to meet and edge out his competition with every move.

By throwing all the pieces together—enough Agility to maneuver as much as needed, enough Strength to counteract the shifting gravity, and enough Mysticism and Prayer to counter spells or provide an important second's advantage... And then he'd used his enemy's Divine Talent against him. Erec's brother was a monster.

Rounded out and good enough in each area to win. That was why Bedwyr was so dangerous. He wasn't bad in any field. There were no perceivable weak points. Compared to Erec, who'd only managed to match his brother in a single field growing up, it was beyond frustrating.

# CHAPTER 32
## COLD HATE

*In the morning when thou findest thyself unwilling to rise, consider with thyself presently, it is to go about a man's work that I am stirred up. Am I then yet unwilling to go about that, for which I myself was born and brought forth into this world? Or was I made for this, to lay me down, and make much of myself in a warm bed?*

*"O but this is pleasing." And was it then for this that thou wert born, that thou mightest enjoy pleasure? Was it not in very truth for this, that thou mightest always be busy and in action? Seest thou not how all things in the world besides, how every tree and plant, how sparrows and ants, spiders and bees: how all in their kind are intent as it were orderly to perform whatsoever (toward the preservation of this orderly universe) naturally doth become and belong unto thin? And wilt not thou do that, which belongs unto a man to do?*

*Wilt not thou run to do that, which thy nature doth require? "But thou must have some rest." Yes, thou must. Nature hath of that also, as well as of eating and drinking, allowed thee a certain stint. But thou guest beyond thy stint, and beyond that which would suffice, and in matter of action, there thou comest short of that which thou mayest. It must needs be therefore, that thou dost not love thyself, for if thou didst, thou wouldst also love thy nature, and that which thy nature doth propose unto herself as her end.*

*Others, as many as take pleasure in their trade and profession, can even pine themselves at their works, and neglect their bodies and their food for it; and doest thou less honour thy nature, than an ordinary mechanic his trade; or a good dancer his art? than a covetous man his silver, and vainglorious man applause? These to whatsoever they take an affection, can be content to want their meat and sleep, to further that every one which he affects: and shall actions tending to the common good of human society, seem more vile unto thee, or worthy of less respect and intention?*

*- Marcus Aurelius, Emperor of Rome, Meditations (175, 2nd Era)*

T he rest of the second-year fights received various amounts of cheering and support. They were interesting enough, sure. The chance to behold how far a single year of the Academy changed their Initiates and began to set them down the path they would walk as a Knight set Erec's heart on fire. But the worry for what was to come dampened the rest of the brawls.

After an Initiate's second year, they'd be made into a Knights Errant. They weren't quite a full-fledged Knight yet at that level. But at that point, it was mostly their own training that would push them forward. They advanced further by upholding their tenets and strengthening themself as a Knight. Though it wasn't wholly unguided; a Knight Errant got apprenticed to a higher-ranking Knight to receive criticism and suggestions on the path they forged.

Knights Errant filtering in and out of the Academy were a common sight. Many Knight Commanders had a few under their wings, having picked them to continue to teach during their time in the Academy.

That was a long-off goal for Erec, to be a force that people looked up to with stars in their eyes. Some part of him wanted to inspire the children in the depths of the underground Kingdom and become a man to yank back their land from the monsters and let more humans return to living under the sun. But that dream conflicted with his true goal, the desire to track down his mother and demand answers. How could he do both?

The fights ran their course. Once they ended, the Initiates were assigned to small groups to be led back to the Academy proper.

"Erec." Lyotte gave him a slight nod as she joined his assigned group. Her black curls spilled wildly down her back; the uniform suited her. She looked every part what a noble of a Knight Academy should. Head held high, and a determination in her gaze to do her best.

"Dame Lyotte." Erec decided to be a little more formal. He'd agreed to take things back to square one with her, but the odd behavior and her near obsession with "helping him" threw him off. Who was he to turn away a potential ally? Even if she was oddly behaved. Though… "One of my dorm-mates is a former maid from your House."

"Yes, of course. You met Olivia, she's very kind, isn't she?" Lyotte asked with a smile. "A bit stuffy, even when you ask her not to be, but a dear friend of mine."

*Well, she didn't try to hide their relationship.* They were connected, but how far did it extend past what Lyotte said? Were they even actually friends? Olivia's particular capabilities were too strange for a maid, but how much did Erec want to press in and try to fish for answers? "She's nice, yeah. I think we'll get along fine."

"Then I'm glad, Erec. You deserve to be surrounded by people who can support your goals." *What the hell?*

Erec let that hang in the air as more joined their assigned group. Including one sour face. Colin strode into their ranks, wearing a scowl and wrapped in a dark mood, which was somewhat undercut by his puffy red eyes. *He's been crying.* That's why he'd run off where nobody could see him; but it was hard to hide the evidence, even if he'd wiped away his tears. Erec…hated that he felt pity for the arrogant prick. Each step since the trial, more and more of Colin's failures and detestable choices were unearthed for everyone to see.

Even Erec felt secondhand embarrassment for how he compared to his peers, let alone how far short he fell from the Unbroken General.

That must have been like a crushing weight on Colin's chest. Yet, the boy was so goddamn cruel for the sake of it.

Colin's eyes filled with malice as he took in Lyotte. "I'm surprised your father let you attend the Academy, little bird. I thought he'd shove you back into your cage after that trial put you in danger." *Here we go again.* In one smooth sentence, Colin stripped away the barest bit of empathy Erec had begun to feel. He was left with pure exasperation at the momentous task left to him by the arrogant noble's father. Erec rubbed his eyes.

"I'm fortunate my mother doesn't tolerate his overprotective streak," Lyotte responded coldly. "I'm sure that your heartbreaking defeat at the hands of House Doctus's daughter will reach your father's ears by the end of the day. I do wonder how he'll react."

Colin winced like she'd backhanded his face.

Erec's eyes traveled between them, and cold hostility hung in the air. Damn near real enough to give him shivers. Their ranks filled with five more students—two from each of the Orders, based on an overview of the pins adorning their Academy uniforms.

Once everyone was there, an instructor collected them and led them into the depths of the Academy, down two floors, and into a wing of private chambers with no windows. Deep in the belly of the beast.

The most prominent object in the middle of the chamber they entered was the soft blue glow of an inscribed glyph. Large circles lapped over one another with geometric shapes carved between its rings. Typically, when one did spell-work like this, they tended to cover it to hide away and preserve the glyph. But no, this one was plain to see, soft blue glow and all.

Everyone avoided crossing the threshold of the glyph as they lined the side of the otherwise empty room.

Their instructor cleared their throat after closing the door.

"The test of resolve is simple in principle. When I bid you, all of you will enter the glyph in the center of the room. However, this is not a test for you alone; you will be working with the other Knight from your Order. You must last within the ring for as long as possible; should the other Knight from your Order fold, you will also be disqualified. The last Order standing is considered the victor of this test. However, the time you do last will be noted for grading purposes. Show us your resolve, and ability to inspire your teammate."

Erec squinted as he looked at the long circular lines of the outer glyph. Why would they fold? Worse, this wasn't based on just him. He'd have to rely on a notoriously weak link to get a good grade on the exam. He looked at Colin; the haughty noble was still staring at his feet with a red face. *How is it fair I have to rely on him to do well?*

"You have three minutes to strategize with your teammate, and then the test will begin."

Immediately the duos of Initiates broke off into whispered conversation. Colin didn't budge from his spot at all.

Erec looked at the white glow of the glyph on the floor, frowning. Why would this make them leave? What about this was going to test their resolve? There didn't appear to be a maximum time limit, either. But then, there was magic involved. And evidently some strategy. While Erec didn't have insight into this test, he guessed that it would take place every year, which meant someone with knowledge of the Academy's inner workings might know what they were about to face.

If Colin wouldn't budge, then he would. Erec moved to him and asked the question. "What is this test about?"

"You must face yourself." Colin looked at the white lines on the ground, wiping at an eye.

Either he wasn't looking forward to his prospects of doing well, or Lyotte's line about his father was a heavy point to him. *I'd feel the same if my father was the Unbroken General.* The pressure Erec faced as a child due to being compared to his brother had to have been minimal compared to the pressure from being the son of an *actual* war hero.

"Don't hold me back," Colin said as he firmed his shoulders and looked Erec in the eyes.

"I'm not the one we have to worry about," Erec shot back. Every step he took near feeling like Colin was getting the short end of a stick, the boy decided to act out and show off what a prick he was.

They spent the rest of their time in silence until the instructor called for them to enter the ring.

As Erec crossed that glowing blue line, a deep shiver ran through his body. Coldness numbed his legs, traveling through his veins and tainting his inside. Uncomfortable goosebumps prickled the back of his neck as if he'd stepped into a pool of ice. Based on everyone else's alarmed expressions, they were also likely having the same troubles.

"The test has begun. Last as long as you can manage."

Colin stood next to Erec, silent. All of them were quiet. A deep, cold quiet, the kind he might imagine in those dead, frozen fields described in old-world biome texts.

And then the whispers began.

*"Bedwyr's brother? His mother's a filthy traitor. We should have burnt their whole family in a pyre. How long until they betray us too?"*

Erec's head darted around, eyes wide. Which one of these bastards—

*"Think he'll sell us out to a Rift-walker too?"*

No one was speaking, yet the voices filtering in his head swirled and hissed with venom. Each comment was a jab against his psyche, scraping against his mind. The rest of the Initiates were having similar reactions, eyes widening and looking around. There was no source of the voices, yet the intensity increased. Erec breathed out a puff of white.

*"I can't wait for him to die in the wastes. He'll go nowhere but into a shallow pit."*

His skin crawled as if a hundred fingers were scuttling along its surface. Erec twitched and shook his head, the voices digging deeper. They were worming into his skin, trying to dig their way in and rot him from the inside out.

*"Failure. Disgrace. Burn him."*

"F-fuck…" Erec muttered, teeth chattering. A quick glance around at the rest of the Initiates told him that nobody was withstanding this very well. The rest of them had gone pale—Colin had tears running down his eyes, his pupils wide and a pure terror and fear on his face.

*"He'll end up killing someone with that Talent of his. Better to end it now, put him down like the mad dog he is."*

Colin stepped to the edge of the ring. No. Erec gritted his teeth—a shaking hand lashing out and snapping around Colin's wrist. His fingers dug in as he felt Colin's ice-cold veins. As if he was a corpse. With pure horror, Colin tried to yank his arm away to leave the circle but failed to break Erec's grip. His Strength was too much for the lanky Duke's son to overcome without the advantage of his Armor.

*"Let the machine take over; even if it isn't a human, it's worth a million times what he is."*

Erec's body spasmed as the cold contracted his muscles. He was freezing alive. One of the girls to his right stepped out of the ring, yet he hardly glanced at her. Instead, he narrowed his point of focus to the shaking Colin in front of him. "I d-d-don't care what it says." Erec's teeth chattered as he threw everything he had left in him. "S-stay."

"I-I-I can't..." Colin cried out, tears fully giving forth, an awful line of mucus running from his nose. Frost crawled on their hands and paled skin, a spreading chill of death. "I-I'm a failure."

Another one of the contestants walked out.

*"Why was he born? We don't need him. We have Bedwyr."*

Each comment dug deeper in his heart—planting itself there and festering like rotten weeds. Its thorny roots tangling around and spawning forth a dozen echoing whispers, strengthening the part of him that lurked in the shadows. This glyph gave a tangible voice to the doubts and shadows in his heart. They were endless now; vicious words about him, his mother, and his friends. Stupid. Foolish. Erec was a blight upon the world and everyone he contacted. He'd be better dead, and his friends would have more fulfilling lives without him on this earth.

Erec twitched and fought against the voices—Colin stopped fighting him and stayed in place, but Erec didn't release his grip.

There were only two groups left now—Lyotte's with her partner and him and Colin. Lyotte seemed the best composed of everyone, straight in the middle of the circle with her eyes toward the ceiling. Her partner was on the ground, tears welling from her eyes and freezing on her face.

"I'm nothing compared to him..." Colin whispered, hunching over. Erec felt the air burn in his chest; how much longer before they froze alive? How long had it been? Each second dragged on in an eternity of torment and self-hate.

"Then get better. We're not them, so who cares? We'll make ourselves into something else. They're not us, Colin. They're not here; only we can do this. Be strong," Erec said, barely conscious of his own words. Black tinged the edges of his vision. He slipped to the ground, the ability to hold Colin giving out as the thousands of horrible shadowy words sieged his mind with doubt.

His breath hitched; he took in a lungful of frozen air as his control began to vanish. A deep shadow of regret and anger came in a possessive tide to suck away every bit of joy in his life.

What was the point? Why put himself through this?

Colin neared the edge of the circle, sobbing in full.

"Don't go. Colin. We can do this together." Erec pulled the words out of somewhere deep; the swirling ocean of shadows closed around on him. But he wouldn't give in to them. They'd been with him his whole life, hiding in every success. Jabbing at him whenever they saw an opening. This self-hate was always present, but now, it wasn't hiding.

Colin stopped at the edge, collapsing to his knees. He stared at Erec.

But he didn't step out of it.

"Congratulations," the instructor called. The glow on the circle vanished.

Lyotte's partner had left the glyph, though Lyotte stood in the center, her face still raised to the heavens. Slowly she looked at Erec and Colin, a sad smile on her face. "You two did well. This is my loss, then."

The shadowy voices vanished, and the cold seeped away to life's warmth once more. Erec shuddered in his spot.

"Well done, seven minutes and twenty seconds. Victory goes to the Order of the Verdant Oak." The instructor nodded. "An hour for recovery, then you shall return to your Orders. The day after tomorrow, you'll receive your scores and course assignments."

Erec noted the blinking in the corner of his vision from the Blessing. He willed it open as he summoned the energy to return to his feet.

### Psyche Advancement: Rank F - Tier 7 → Rank F - Tier 8

There it was, another advancement. They were coming faster than ever before, as he kept pushing against his limits. He was gaining power quickly, far more efficiently than on his own deep underground. This place would only drive him further. All he needed to do was keep pushing, and he'd reach his dream.

The hateful words still polluted his mind, but compared to the light of the potential future he saw, they hid away.

All he needed was power. With enough power, he'd reach that light. Keep up the pace. The Academy had been the right decision. Of that, he was sure.

# CHAPTER 33
## CHEATING PAYS OFF

[ hat entire test was ridiculous. Your vitals were still thirty minutes from reaching hypothermia.]

Erec rubbed his brows as he lingered in the recuperation room with the other Initiates. Softly, a priest hummed a prayer that eased the tension and harshness in his mind. But it was like a salve to a skinned knee; it eased the pain, but time was the only true way to recover.

"It wasn't only about being cold," Erec whispered. It surprised him when VAL reported his body temperature only dropped a degree during that entire test. And that the whole time, VAL had been shouting at him inside his head.

It was interesting because he hadn't found anything else that introduced interference between him and VAL. Aside from Fury.

Regardless, once back in touch, VAL complained about the waste of time spent in the circle. Then once told it whispered awful things in his head, VAL complained about the validity of the test as a measure of psychological fortitude.

Knights needed to be strong in will and body. Or so he'd always been told. It didn't stand out as particularly out of place to him. But Colin hadn't spoken a real word to him since.

Even with the silence, Erec felt a fundamental shift in the air between them. That tension that had lingered there like a live wire was now gone; in its place was a degree of mutual respect, but not anything near friendship. An acknowledgment that they both under-stood what the other was about on some level. Perhaps it would be the bridge to let him pursue his vow to the Unbroken General, but advancing that agenda had started to give Erec a bad feeling in his gut.

After the hour of recuperation passed, they left to return to the dorms. He felt much more cheerful throughout the prayer.

When they returned to their living space, he returned to Garin being soothed on the couch by Olivia. His friend hung his head low, with a cheery maid to his right. At their arrival, the two stopped, and Olivia flashed him a smile and said "Welcome back."

"Thanks. You alright, Garin?" Erec said back, moving aside. Colin ignored them and barreled right toward his room. Face still pale, but a new light in his eyes. Erec shrugged and collapsed on the couch next to his friend, staring at the ceiling of the dorm.

"Am I a bad friend?" Garin asked quietly from his side.

"No, you're a better friend than I am," Erec answered honestly. It was a sad admission, but the truth, If he gave half as much effort as Garin to their friendship, then who knows where they'd have been right now. The truth was that, if anything, he was the one leeching off of the goodwill of Garin.

"You're both being dramatic. It does not suit you," Olivia chided them, shaking her head. "The voices of that test are not a reflection of reality. And if you think you have a flaw, it is something you may practice out of yourself. Face your weakness, and slay it. Any goal can be achieved with enough effort. It does not matter that you were out of the ring in a minute, Sir Garin. Next time you will do better." They slipped into contemplation at that. Only time would let them face the demons shown by the test.

Erec thought about confronting Olivia about how she handled the written exam, but that sort of hard questioning wasn't in him today. And what answer would he get? That she was a spy? He was pretty fucking convinced of that at this point anyway.

After letting them dwell in the dark for fifteen minutes, Olivia suggested they take a walk, which Erec found himself surprised to agree to.

They wandered the halls of the Verdant Oak quarters and outside into the lush jungle of plants that surrounded it. Together they dug through the undergrowth and reached the expansive flower garden on the far side of the building. A field of a thousand flowers, each a bright splash of vibrant color painting the landscape. Every breath reinvigorated and brought with it a thousand scents.

In time they left the grounds of the Verdant Oak quarters and wandered over to the pond of the Crimson Lotus. The sun had sunk, painting the sky a glorious orange laced with purple as night approached.

"I've heard some serious accusations of your reputation before the Academy, Sir Garin," Olivia said as the trio sat on a small wooden outcropping into the pond. Her toes sunken into the stilled, cold water below. A few of the Crimson Lotus Initiates wandered around, but for the most part, they had all the privacy they could want.

"And just what would those accusations be about?" Garin lay across the deck next to them, hands behind his head with his eyes closed.

The water was gorgeous; small dragonflies buzzed over the pads and carefully examined the floating lotuses. Would Bedwyr be lounging around after his tests? How'd he fare? Did Erec beat him on the test of resolve?

"Rumor is you're a hopeless flatterer and a reprehensible flirt," Olivia said in a neutral tone, swirling ripples into the stilled pond. "Or so the noble ladies gossip."

"Why do you ask? Do I see jealousy hiding behind that mask of yours?" Garin asked, eyes fluttering, to which Olivia shook her head.

"This Dame is not one to fall for such childish charms. Please refrain from lavishing such affections on her, for she would rather focus her time and efforts on studying to make her name."

"When you put it like that, I'd feel like a jerk to refuse. But if you ever change your mind, let me know." Garin flashed her a winning smile as she rolled her eyes. He paused, taking on a bit more of a serious tone. "But really? Is that what they're saying about me?"

Erec snorted. "They're just not used to someone like you. Or maybe you really are a bad flirt; after what I just saw, easy to see why they're gossiping."

"That so? How about you, Erec? All that time spent in your room.

Are you yearning for some lost love left underground?" Garin fired back.

Erec paused because the absurd accusation was something he didn't know how to respond to. Him? Slinking off and romancing someone? With what time? But also the pure ludicrousness of this moment. All of them resting around a calm pond when just a couple of days ago they faced off against monsters assaulting their walls. Outside of those steel curtains, the world waited to sink its fangs in and destroy them.

Yet, at this moment, they could sit around in the Academy and have a conversation like this…

This.

This was the sort of moment humanity was meant to have; peaceful memories and nonchalant conversations over their silly personal lives. A hope that burned bright even with shadows closing in on it. It was for these memories that they needed to defend what they had.

It was a reason to kill terrifying monsters.

He finally came up with a response.

"Don't be ridiculous. I've spent my nights reading. You're too loud for me to focus in the living room."

"Ah, so your love is fictional. Don't worry! One day you'll meet a Dame who you'll sweep off her feet and—"

Olivia shoved Garin into the pond.

There was a loud splashing and angry yelling; Garin pulled Olivia into the pond with him as Erec sat on the side. His eyes rose above to see the stars as they began to dot the sky.

— - ☻ - — - ☼ - — - ☻ - —

Yesterday's breakfast had been a war of pettiness, which agitated Erec's mood, since after waking up in the mornings lately, he was left with that sense of dread from his nightmares. Always those horrid red eyes. Thankfully, today there was peace. Colin came along without being asked, far more reserved than before. They had a rather relaxing morning of eating tart blackberry pastries.

Colin even complimented Olivia on her table manners. Which

considering her previous status as a maid could've been taken as a backhanded insult, but it was clear to everyone that it hadn't been intended as one.

Still, Colin hedged the conversations, only occasionally giving input. He got slightly more arrogant near the end, but there was a marked difference.

They returned to the dorm.

Anxiety swelled. Each moment was spent in uneasy waiting; they knew that their results would arrive today.

They sat around, conversation a bit more forced and infused with unfounded positivity and guesses about how they did or what it meant by their courses being determined by the results.

There was a loud knock on the door. A Knight Errant handed out letters for them all.

Erec didn't hesitate and tore his open the instant it was in his hands.

*Dear Sir Erec, Initiate of the Order of the Verdant Oak,*

*Disclosed below are the results of your semiannual examination; additionally, there is a list of courses and electives derived from your performance to set your schedule. You are to submit a confirmation of your schedule and chosen electives to your Quartermaster by the end of this day.*

*Please take note of the commentary and areas of improvement below:*

*Overall Grade: 84/100 [B]*

*Written Exam: 89/100 [B+]*
*- Initiate shows high reasoning in many of the overall topics covered in this exam.*
*- Points docked for terse answers and lack of understanding for social obligations covered under "Court Gatherings and Public Presentation" questions.*
*- Recommended to expand proficiency of courtly affairs to prevent misunderstandings in higher courts when representing Order. Any*

*failures here reflect upon the Knights and can have political ramifi-*
*cations.*

*Duel: 68/100 [D+]*
*- Initiate lost spar.*
*- Overcame few challenges associated with opponent.*
*- Initiate refused to acknowledge end of spar, and had to be forcibly*
*removed from opponent by a Master Knight.*
*- Initiate eliminated self by taking a direct hit after losing control*
*during combat to tackle an opponent.*
*- Recommendation provided by Order to undergo Talent Develop-*
*ment, which has been acknowledged and prioritized.*
*Resolve: 94/100 [A]*
*- Initiate won test of resolve.*
*- Displayed ability to withstand high intensity demanded by exam for*
*several minutes' time.*
*- Persuasion of teamwork to instill courage in another.*

Erec looked up from the sheet of paper listing his accomplishments, failures, and ways to improve. Everyone was looking at their
grades. *B? Better than average.* It made sense that he'd lost a lot of
points during his duel. He'd tried a new, untested tactic against an
unknown opponent. But, in return, he'd gotten a little bit closer to
understanding his Talent.

[Cheating paid off for you, huh?] VAL chimed in his head. [Well
done for using all of the resources at your disposal. I estimate that it
boosted your score from a C+. That's a real go-getter attitude.]

*Weren't you the one saying it wasn't cheating?*

"Damn, C," Garin groaned.

"Don't let it discourage you. It simply means that for now, you're
average. Plenty of room for growth," Olivia said from the side. Garin
whipped around to look at her.

"Oh, and what'd you get?"

"I received a B-." She shrugged. "They disliked how I conducted
myself during my duel. But I could scarcely raise a sword to Lady
Lyotte."

Gradually all eyes turned to Colin, whose face was a shade of red.
The boy ripped up a piece of paper and tossed it to the ground. A

deep red D+ showed from the sloppy shredding. He stomped over to his room and slammed the door.

Garin looked around at everyone and chuckled. "Wonder what sort of courses they offer when your grade's that low." He squinted as he looked at his last sheet. "Well, I know what I'm going to pick. How about you guys? Why don't we take some classes together."

"Shut up!" Colin yelled.

# CHAPTER 34
## A DEAD LAND'S WINDS

*Nothing but deadlands and old-world tech. Sand creeps into your bedroll every damn trip.*

*The rusted-out buildings and unsafe structures make scavenging a difficult and dangerous proposition, but occasionally something worthwhile is found. And with the engineers petitioning to drive us out into that hellscape as much as they can get away with, I don't see anything changing in the near future.*

*Never mind that I've lost three of my Knights to monsters in the last year and one to a collapsed building. No, it's always, "We need you to find more tech.' Get back out there."*

*One year left until I retire to my husband's estate in the second layer and wash my hands of this. Can't wait.*

*- Knight Commander Wynter, personal logs (249, 3rd Era)*

Picking electives was a harsh and brutal battle. Erec received a choice of seven. Out of which he could only pick two. One choice was obvious: he needed to take Wasteland Survival. Garin locked that in, too, so they could have a matching elective.

That left him three other options for electives that stood out. He hunched over the table in the living area.

Unconventional Weapons, Tracking, and Monster Ecology seemed like good picks at first glance. With Unconventional Weapons, he could find replacement weaponry on a long-range expedition or find out if it worked well with Fury. Tracking and Monster Ecology were also strong picks. Knowing the different typical Rift Creatures and habits would grant an edge.

But there would be time to take advantage of that. And VAL buzzed all angry in Erec's head until he caved and "reluctantly" chose Scavenging and Armor Modification. In truth, he felt a thrill of excitement to have the chance to tear apart and improve his Armor. VAL was most keen to see how the Armor components relating to "anomalous energy" functioned.

Most intoxicating, however, was the question.

How far could the two of them go in upgrading a modern Armor model? If they learned enough, could they blend VAL's old-world knowledge with modern techniques to make a better Armor? Who's to say, but the image made it a challenging but necessary decision.

After seeing him sign up for it, Olivia jotted it down. She gave him a small smile.

"What general lectures did you get?" she asked.

Erec caught a slow flash of a furry tail in the corner of the room. He paused and cleared his throat.

[Munchy is loose.]

"They gave me seven total; one of them's a special course twice a week." Erec pulled his eyes away from the plant Munchy hid behind. *How do I tell Garin?* "…Er, Basic Mysticism, Basic Prayer and Theology, Physical Conditioning." Those were all of the more mandatory basics. "…Then Military History, and…" Erec sighed deeply. "Courtly Mannerisms." He kept his voice steady, trying to catch Garin's eyes and flick his attention to the space Munchy was in.

Still, just the thought of Courtly Manners made him dread the class. Boldwick had said it wasn't necessary. It seemed the Academy disagreed.

Munchy began to scramble up a vine, his growing girth pulling down on the leaves as the critter miscalculated its carrying capacity. *Oh fuck.*

"Ah, a pity." Olivia shook her head, eyes firmly fixed on Erec. How long would it be until the squirrel fell or caused something to make a noise? If she found out about Munchy, then Goddess only knew how someone prim and proper like Olivia might react. "Besides our elective and Physical Conditioning, there's nothing else in common. If you need a Courtly Mannerisms tutor, knock on my door."

"No! If you need someone to teach you how the court works, come ask me!" Garin called out, even getting to his feet. Erec met his eyes and signaled toward the squirrel now trying to climb on a too-thin vine.

Garin's jaw dropped.

"Could it be Sir Garin is suggesting he knows more about Courtly Manners than a maid from the Duchy? Scandalous."

Garin gave a quick laugh. "No, no, but I know how he learns best —what's the last class you have?" He tried to shoot the attention back to Erec, taking small steps to the squirrel. If Garin could get to him, the little menace would be calm as could be—it truly cherished his company, for some reason. Garin must've failed to close his door properly.

"Uh, I have Divine Talent Development, too. I'm really looking forward to it."

"Impressive, developing Talents always seemed so interesting to me. What do you think I'll receive?" Olivia cupped her chin in her hand and leaned forward.

"Hard to say—" Erec shrugged, finding it hard to focus on the conversation. Garin leaned in and snatched Munchy from the vine. Erec let out a tense breath.

"I've always been fascinated with animals," Olivia remarked, swaying her head over to Garin. "Do you think that mine might relate to that? The priests say it stems from your soul."

"Uh—could be animals." Garin gave a fake grin, trying to keep Munchy stuffed behind his back.

"If it is, do you believe Sir Garin would let me borrow his squirrel for training?"

— - ❂ - — - ☼ - — - ❂ - —

The first day of class was a mixed bag. Military History turned out to be a surprisingly insightful class. The Dame running it broke apart various military theory texts from ancient battles and the previous Era. Then she had the class suggest how to apply these concepts to the modern wasteland. It was essentially a creative strategy class and much more involved than the name suggested.

Physical Conditioning would occur every day. It was hardly even a course and more like mandatory training. A Knight barked commands at them and drilled them through push-ups, crunches, and other workouts on a daily basis. Always started with an hour-long jog. The instructor only promised to ramp up the difficulty over time.

Almost all of the Initiates were covered in sweat after the class, but luckily they'd given enough time after for a shower.

But out of everyone, Colin was the worst off from the training. He'd refused an order by the instructor. As a result, they pushed him twice as hard as everyone else.

However, the last course of the day finally came. Erec arrived in the lecture room for Wasteland Survival with Garin at his side. The door was wide open with seven Initiates waiting around inside, with no instructor in sight.

Fifteen minutes passed.

A hassled, dark-haired Knight Commander stormed into the room, the same who'd been in charge of them in the battle outside of the wall. Her dark-brown eyes swayed over the class as she cleared her throat. "You have my sincere apology. I did forget that this is the first lesson of this class"—she gestured at the rest of the standard lecture room; a fair, if antiquated, room completed by a board in the back to jot down notes on and a semicircle of chairs facing it—"we will rarely meet in here. From now on, please assemble in front of the building, unless told otherwise ahead of time. Now please, follow me."

Everyone got up and followed Dame Juliana into the light of the day; a few hours of sun left. But she led them straight into open land away from the Academy.

They strode further and further from the campus, past the farms encircling the Kingdom. She didn't stop until they'd reached a plain, wasteland-like stretch of land not too far from the great steel walls. Out here were only dried grass, scraggly weeds and plants, and a whole lot of dust and cracked ground.

"There is not a more fitting classroom than this." She waved a hand to the empty plains. "On your journeys outside of these walls, this will be the most common biome you will experience. Perhaps further, it begins to change, but that is a discussion for a later time. This is the state much of our local world is in, after the holy flames."

At least this place was a lot more freeing than the stuffy classroom.

"There can be threats anywhere outside of the wall. But you shouldn't neglect the dangers of the wastelands themselves." She leaned down and grabbed a fist full of dirt and sand, letting it spill into the wind through her fingers. "Hot in the sun, cold at night. Water can be rare; if you wander long enough and go thirsty enough, you might never find any."

She pointed to one of the girls in the class, a taller girl with a brown bun.

"You have a flask filled with water, but you're lost. And believe me, it can be surprisingly easy to get lost. You're thirsty and not sure when you'll next come across something to refill your flask. What do you do?"

"I conserve the water," the girl answered confidently, giving a smile. "If I stretch it out, I'll have a better chance to find more."

"Then you'll die." Juliana shook her head. "If you're thirsty, you drink. Thirst is deadly; it can ruin your ability to think and lead to a death spiral. I've run a scouting mission to retrieve a lost Knight after a violent fight to close a Rift. I found them dead two weeks later. They died of dehydration with water still in their flask."

Everyone went quiet as the reality of what they were to learn hit. These lessons were the difference between life or death.

"At the end of this course, I want these wastes to feel not like a second home but a comfortable hell. To that effect, today's class has two requirements for a passing grade." She lifted her fingers to count them off. "One. You are to make a fire; you might normally have a flint and steel—that'll make your life easier, but all of my students will know how to make do without." She gave them an evil grin. "Two. You're going to spend a night out here, in the open. No soft beds. No rolls to sleep in. Your backs to the dirt with an open sky above. The Trial may have given you a taste of this life—but you're going to live and breathe familiarity. When you go on your expedition in a month, I expect my fellow Knights to compliment me on how much you've learned so quickly, and to show those who chose not to take my course what they're missing."

The air shifted; nobody looked pleased by the change of plans from sleeping in a soft bed. A miserable night in the open put a damper on the class.

But this was the sort of practical lesson Erec *needed* to learn.

Juliana led them around the wasteland, pointing out the various dried blades of grass to use as kindling and picking out plants with woody stems. Completed by a sole dead tree to take sticks from.

First, she taught them to make friction and heat through two sticks —graduating to cutting off a strip of her uniform to wrap around the stick and displaying a more reliable way to grind them; only afterward did she show a glyph that made a simple spark. But for today, they were forbidden from using any glyphs.

They learned to make fire and had two hours to practice the skill before she left them in the wasteland.

The sun sank closer and closer to the horizon. Julia clapped her hands together, and bid them good luck. They weren't allowed to return until the sun returned to the sky.

Erec broke off with Garin; each of them agreed to gather kindling, sticks, and anything that might burn.

Making a fire was harder in the dark, especially as the night's cold air started to arrive. In a couple of hours, they had a small fire. Four others blazed not too far away.

Garin leaned over, arms wrapped around his legs, staring into the blazing depths. A stick cracked and popped inside the inferno. "Is the Academy everything you hoped for?" Erec's friend asked, transfixed by the flames.

"I've grown a lot, even in this short of a time," Erec said, nodding his head. "But I have a long way to go to get where I want to be. How about you? Better than staying home and learning to manage your father's estates?"

"There'll be plenty of time for that later. I've gotten two advancements, one in Vigor. So, can't complain. The atmosphere of the Academy is so different from the courts. It's not like the station isn't present—don't get me wrong—but this place makes everyone seem like they're on a more even field. Makes it easier to connect and to approach people you couldn't otherwise." Garin gave a small smile.

Erec slowly nodded. Then he decided to broach the topic he'd been mulling over for some time. "I think Olivia is a spy."

Garin did a double take. "What, the cute former maid? Are you out of your mind?" He stopped. "You think she's spying on Colin?"

"One Duke looking into the heir of another Duke seems like a fair enough reason to me. If he paid her by offering her the chance to be a Knight, I'm sure she'd be more than glad to go along with it. She's friends with Lyotte, too."

"Well, that's a bit fucked up. But we can't really...y'know, blame her. You're *also* spying on Colin for his father."

"...I'm starting to feel bad for him. He's alone and keeps falling short of his father, especially when compared to others from the Duchies. It must be impossible to have that weight constantly dragging you down." Erec leaned further toward the fire, lowering his head. Heat flushed his face as the guilt sat beneath the surface. Did they really need to spy on Colin?

"You feel bad because the Unbroken General is to Colin what you see Bedwyr as to you." Garin gave a snort. "Wow, Erec. That's...a bit transparent."

There was no denying it, so their conversation lapsed into more present things. Erec tried to sleep with a jacket beneath his head.

But every hour, he'd sit up.

Eyes scanning across the wasteland and at any moment, expecting to see a pair of ruby-red eyes staring back. Ready to consume him and end his life. But there was only ever darkness.

# CHAPTER 35
## PLACEMENT

The week flowed by in an ever-running stream of knowledge and fatigue. Each day dragged Erec in unexpected ways as he got lost in the current. All the while, each night was a different shade of the same nightmarish Stag of Crimson chasing him around, and leaving him feeling sapped and drained by the time he finally woke up.

Physical Conditioning was a constant start to the day. And he experienced an introduction to prayer and spell-work. Erec made sure to rerun through his notes every moment not in class. It meant late nights studying by a flickering lamp.

Obviously, he had favorites; every elective class left him with its marks. Most of them felt vital in their own way. But the classes he was curious about had been Mysticism and Basic Prayer and Theology. It was a shame that Prayer and Theology was such a pain in the ass, and Mysticism might forever be completely out of reach.

Both were sore topics by the end of the week. Most of the higher nobility had familiarity with Basic Mysticism. Yet Erec had never had the chance. The actual practice was far more detail-orientated than he imagined. It required him to form precise images of glyphs in his head completed by perfect angles and formations before inputting mana.

They wouldn't actually form a glyph until two months in.

Of course, VAL found the entire thing fascinating, and the machine's excitement to force him to try the long monotonous practice became a headache. It would've been less frustrating if he believed he could use glyphs under the influence of "Fury." But trying to hold a spell together seemed impossible in that state.

But he'd do his best to learn some of it. Spell-work might prove to be a good opener or good for utility. But the fact that the instructor had taught Bedwyr the year before and took great pains to mention how he'd done so well and that she expected Erec to live up to him proved quite grating.

There was one hidden boon found in basic Prayer and Theology; Rodren evidently had made it into the Academy, joining the Order of the Crimson Lotus. The thrill of catching up with the other boy made the class almost tolerable.

On the whole, Basic Prayer and Theology was awful and felt like pulling teeth to sit through. It wasn't the actual idea or coursework that made it bad. No. That was memorizing prayers, learning phrasing, and practicing pronunciation while appealing to the Goddess for power. Basic, at the lower levels. He'd learned to conjure a small light in the first week.

It only lasted for three seconds, but it was something.

The strength behind the prayer depended on their Faith; to gain Faith meant to open oneself up further to the Goddess and the Church.

Not a hard concept, and personally, Erec had nothing against the Goddess. The Church, on the other hand, was a different story. They had running hate for Erec's family after his mother's exile and excommunication. This particular course broke the Academy's norms for instructors, opting to have a priest teach lessons instead of a Knight. From the first day, the priest recognized Erec's family name and tore into him that he came from a line of "sin" and didn't deserve the attention of the Goddess above.

It was a struggle to keep his anger in check. With a hostile teacher, and the fact that prayer required higher Faith to be helpful, the class was frustrating. VAL didn't help matters by forcing him to ask questions that returned condescension from the instructor, each day of the class felt like bashing his head against a wall.

He tried. But he already concluded prayer wasn't a strong Virtue to him, and likely wouldn't be one.

Friday was the last day of courses before the weekend, which was

given wholly to independent study, aside from Physical Conditioning. But before that, his last class of the week, and most anticipated,
was Divine Talent Development.

— - ☢ - — - ☼ - — - ☢ - —

The room for Divine Talent Development was less of a classroom
and more of a small gym. It was spacious and tucked away in a far
corner of the Academy proper. Blue foam mats lined the floor and
were the only decoration in the spare room. Polished wooden floors
framed the mats in the middle—more than required for the four
students who showed up.

Soren was, of course, there.

Besides him was a girl named Sarah Elgans, short and light-blond
hair, who'd worn a mischievous grin as she prodded them to share
their Talents. And a reserved boy by the name of Benjamin Solicitia.
He only introduced himself, then remained silent.

Bawling laughter echoed from the hallway. Boldwick swayed into
the room with his arm wrapped over the shoulder of a bear of a man.
Their unkempt hairstyles and wild demeanor made it seem like two
homeless cavemen had barged into the class. The image wasn't
helped by the wine bottle they passed between them.

Despite the happy demeanor on display, bags hung from Boldwick's eyes. He gave a tired yet steady gaze over the assembled
Initiates.

The bear on his side snorted. "Every year, Wick, we get less and
less." He shook his head and tipped the bottle of wine back. "Problems are only getting worse, and they still won't give us the space."
He shoved the near-empty bottle back into Boldwick's hand.

Boldwick killed the rest of the bottle. His bleary shadowed eyes
turned back to his friend. "Downright depressing, but they don't
develop it quick enough. And if the Talent isn't flashy enough, they
say they can learn it on their own later. As if these poor sods can learn
everything on their own." Boldwick cracked his neck.

His compatriot shook his head before Boldwick leveled his gaze
on the class.

"Hey there, pay no attention to me—just auditing. Figured after our discussion, might as well," Boldwick shrugged and disengaged, heading to the side of the room to give the other man the stage.

"Right, right," the caveman said, puffing up his chest. "Name's Sir Able. I've got the glory of being your instructor." He snickered. "Forgive me for catching up with my old friend beforehand; troubled times lately." He gestured to the empty bottle. "It won't change anything about today. We're going to get a feel for what you got."

Soren shook his head with disbelief.

"Now, me and Wick had a bit of a chat before class. I got a bead on your abilities. But hearing and seeing are two different things." Sir Able pointed his finger at Erec. "Enhancer." He shifted it to Soren. "Projector." Then over to Benjamin and Sarah. "Shifter, and another Projector."

Those were the loose classifications of Divine Talents. Despite their variable nature, people had, over time, lumped together broad categories. Enhancers, like Erec, had Divine Talents that drew out or amplified their own Blessings. Projectors pressed their Talents onto others—though, in Erec's opinion, labeling Soren like that was a bit of a stretch, even though he manipulated *others'* senses. Shifters were rarer and involved a physical transformation in some shape or way for a limited time. There were a couple more large categories and about a dozen more niche definitions that fell outside those.

"You're all likely shit at your abilities, even if you think you aren't. I'll be the Knight that teaches you to use it like a true weapon deserves to be used."

Boldwick sniffed in the corner and pointed at Erec. "I'd say he'll give you the hardest time of it if I were a betting man."

"Eh?" Sir Able paused, taking a closer look at Erec. "Ah, that's right, he goes wild."

[More like you throw tantrums, but they're being polite for your sake, Intern.]

"Well then, better to get a glimpse of it first. You, boy, go pick one of them and use your Talent." Sir Able gestured Erec toward the rest of the Initiates. Erec looked around; among all of them, everyone except for Soren seemed confused by that demand. "We don't got all day. Go. Smack one of them and get angry, I wanna see what we're dealing with."

Soren walked near the instructor as if he was about to protest the teacher's order.

[MIDSECTION! BLOCK!]

There wasn't time to question the command. Erec stepped back and covered his stomach. A fist slammed into his forearms as Soren vanished from walking to the instructor to attacking Erec.

Soren retracted the fist and twisted his body into a roundhouse.

The Prince's foot smashed into Erec's face, tossing him across the ground.

"Neither of you move," Soren said with a cold glance to the other two Initiates. He swayed in his spot as if waiting.

[Get to your feet—kick incoming!]

Erec barely got up as VAL issued another warning. He stumbled back and narrowly avoided the swish of air as Soren made to knee him, having once more "teleported."

Fury painted his vision red. Anger stirred inside of him like a caged beast.

This time, supported and within the confines of the training room, Erec didn't hesitate to let it free. He'd give himself entirely to Fury.

Erec came at Soren like an untethered beast.

It took two minutes for Soren to slaughter him like an animal.

His instincts helped to determine the Prince's location, and he managed to snap off a vicious hit or two. But for each blow, Soren got two. And even in such a short time, he managed to adapt his style to counter the wild swings and attempts to tackle.

Without VAL as a copilot, Soren shifted to clever feints that manipulated and tricked Erec into a loss.

In the end, Soren sported a new bruise on his face but looked rather pleased.

Boldwick strode over and helped Erec to his feet, shaking his head.

[It becomes ever more apparent that pure strength will not yield you a victory when you accept too many blows to deal damage.]

Boldwick glanced at Sir Able. "Well, thoughts?"

The caveman stroked his beard and shrugged. "Either we get him to have a handle on it or pump him so full of enough Strength and Vigor he becomes impossible to stop. If he can control it, that'd be ideal, since he'd be deadlier. But we could settle with making him an unstoppable beast and teaching him when to unleash it on our enemies."

"Yeah, I thought so." Boldwick shook his head. "Best of luck; I'll try to check in every week or two. But no promises. I've been beyond busy lately." Boldwick rubbed at his eyes before swaying out of the room.

Sir Able drilled them for the next couple of hours. Spending time to break down each of their capabilities, then pitting all of the Initiates against each other to get a sense of their different Talents. Sarah could lend some of her Blessings to others or borrow from others. Benjamin had the ability to sprout a pair of glowing wings from his back.

Not that he could fly with them. After about an hour of being forced to try, Able put a pin in that hope, and left it for the future.

The entire time, Erec puzzled over Fury. Trying to figure out how to train it. Was it a matter of getting strong enough to be unstoppable in that state and learning when best to use it? Or could he control it?

How many monsters could he tear to shreds when it reached its full potential? How many lives might be saved?

# CHAPTER 36
# CRIMSON NIGHTS

*Caesar, having given the necessary orders, hastened to and fro into whatever quarter fortune carried him to animate the troops, and came to the tenth legion. Having encouraged the soldiers with no further speech than that "they should keep up the remembrance of their wonted valour, and not be confused in mind, but valiantly sustain the assault of the enemy"; as the latter were not farther from them than the distance to which a dart could be cast, he gave the signal for commencing battle.*

- *Julius Caesar*, "De Bello Gallico" and Other Commentaries *(Unknown, 1st Era)*

Psyche. That was the key. If he wanted to advance his control of Fury, he'd need to pursue that Virtue.

He'd remained uncertain up until he asked VAL for an analysis of his behavior while in the Fury state. Given the increased data—a whole week of additional training with Boldwick and Garin—VAL marked a point where his combat awareness in Fury had appeared to improve. It didn't seem to be a coincidence that it was shortly after his Psyche advanced to Tier 8.

Erec had a theory. It was a bit out there, but the moment the thought crossed his mind, he couldn't deny the need. Maybe too, if he advanced that particular Virtue it might ease his nightmares. In his mind, the pure hate that he saw in those reoccurring red eyes in his sleep matched the same sense of intensity that came from when he used Fury. He didn't have proof they were related, but they very well might have been two sides of the same denarius.

If he broke into the E-Ranks with Psyche, he might regain control over his life. But he needed help, especially if he were to advance his Psyche that far in so short a time.

Erec knocked on Boldwick's office door.

"Who is it?" came Boldwick's peeved voice from inside.

"Erec," he said, puffing up his chest. The Master Knight hadn't made time to show up to the two Divine Talent Development sessions. But he needed advice and permission. Perhaps it would've been better not to waste his time, but then… Out of all of the instructors he'd met so far, Boldwick put so much on the line for him. He'd gone to Able first with his theory, only for the man to blow him off and state that he'd advance Psyche naturally by training up his Mysticism or Faith.

That might've been true. But he didn't have the time to wait. The nightmares and constant chipping at his mind told him he needed to fix the problem as soon as possible.

Sir Able instead decided to use their time to polish him by enhancing his Strength and Vigor—with additional training designed to push those two Virtues.

If he wanted to enhance Psyche faster, he needed to do something extreme.

And he needed it in two weeks. His heart told him that the risk outside of the wall would be too significant if he didn't manage to advance Psyche in the next two weeks. He'd be far from the Academy, armed with a weapon. What if he made the wrong step out there? What if he hurt someone?

And the nightmares, they might be gone. And if they weren't… No matter how many times he told himself they weren't real, they'd promised death.

Those red eyes filled with death and fire made him feel that deep in his gut, something was wrong. That something was out there—it was paranoia. But try as he might, those feelings couldn't be dismissed. If Fury was under his control, even if it didn't contain the nightmares, then it'd at least lessen the way they made him feel helpless.

There was a sigh from the other side of the door. "Come in."

Erec strode into the office—it was far messier than the last time he'd been here. Boldwick had thrown books around in piles around the room and set up corkboard with red strings connecting strips of paper pinned to it. Aside from that were various maps on the walls, with different notes and marks all over them. The room was a thing of madness, of a person pushed to the edge.

"What do you want?" Boldwick asked, looking at him with tired red eyes. His facial hair had grown, too; even more stubbly, wild, and unkempt. Beyond Sir Able, and certainly far less well kept than when he'd last seen him. As if the man spent the last week living in the jungle outside of the Verdant Oak dorms.

"I want to use the glyph from the resolve test for training."

Boldwick gave a harsh laugh and rubbed at his eyes. "I think that's the first time an Initiate's been dumb enough to ask me for that. What in the name of the Goddess makes you *want* to do that again?"

"I believe that strengthening my Psyche will allow me to handle my Divine Talent better," Erec said, slightly bowing with his request.

"It'll strengthen over time as you've had more battle or worked on your Mysticism. Both of those will naturally cause you to advance." Boldwick rubbed his eyes. "You're being impatient. That test is a heavy strain on your mental faculties, and I damn near disapprove of even using it *twice* a year, as you're required to already."

*But I can't practice Mysticism in my downtime.* They'd been forbidden from forming glyphs without supervision, even if he felt like he'd make much progress. Now, Erec could've bypassed that, but it had dangers to doing it wrong. He was smart enough to realize that it could have unintended consequences for not only himself but others too. This way had two advantages.

It would be quicker. And it would only affect himself.

Time was slipping by like little bits of sand through the thin neck of an hourglass, falling second by second. Erec felt a rising dread, and as the nightmares intensified, that feeling dug in like cold iron needles.

He needed to do more.

As Boldwick turned his eyes to the three books in front of him, it became clear that the Master Knight didn't have much to add to the topic.

"Something bad is going to happen. If I don't figure out how to control my Fury, I know that it'll all go wrong on this expedition," Erec decided to state, his voice shaking. Red eyes. Every night red eyes gazed at him from the dark. Were they his? Were they that part of him possessed with anger? The desire to combust into an inferno and burn the world again? Erec clenched a fist, his knuckles going white.

His chest felt hot; each breath stoked the furnace inside.

Boldwick stopped. His tired eyes snapped to Erec. "You think you'd lose control during the expedition?"

"I think—"

"There's something more. Isn't there?" Boldwick tilted his head, something hidden behind his eyes. "I see it in your shaking hand; how you're a second away from letting your nails dig into your palm and draw blood… What do you know about a White Stag?"

Erec paused.

Boldwick whipped across the room like a hurricane—pages and books flying as the Master Knight vaulted the desk, hands settling on Erec's shoulders and his fingers digging in. His mad eyes gazed down on Erec, a deathly serious expression on his face. "Do you dream of the White Stag?" the Master Knight whispered. "Do you feel the dread?"

Erec made a choked noise, confusion and validation suddenly rushing up in an overwhelming twist of emotion. "I—yes!" Erec got out, shaking his head. "B-but…you do too?"

Boldwick slowly nodded, letting Erec go, and looked back over his desk. "I'm not sure what the cause is, but ever since we've returned from that Trial, I've been having nightmares of a damned White Stag. It's been like an itch that won't leave me alone in the back of my mind. It's been getting worse. Yet nobody else has felt a damn thing —" He jerked a finger at Erec. "Except you."

Erec worked his jaw. He'd thought the manifestation to be a part of himself. An image of his Fury conjured in those evil eyes. After all, his experience with his Talent had begun around the same time. But this meant…it was something else? "I don't understand."

Boldwick picked up a book and flung it at a wall with a harsh laugh. "Two of us. I've submitted a report; apparently, nightmares in my head means I'm gone off the deep end. Never mind the odd behavior of those Thrashing Mites. Or the fact we haven't had a Rift spawn that close to our wall ever..." Boldwick looked up at the ceiling. "Master Knight, yet the other Orders have dismissed my theory. Can you believe they suggested I take a sabbatical?"

"I—what does it mean?"

"I don't have an answer to that."

Boldwick leaned on his desk, frowning as he looked at a book before smashing it off his desk. He closed his eyes and took a deep breath.

"...Is it dangerous to have the expedition?" Erec asked, considering the implications. If things were going wrong, then surely it meant they should stay within the walls and prepare for whatever was happening. Even if the other Orders didn't believe.

"There is a tenet to which we are beholden, that you shall be bound to one day too: 'Mine are the eyes of the Kingdom; they shall see for the peoples of the Kingdom that cannot. I will not hesitate to witness the unknown.' I think you get the point. You may be an Initiate, yet you're still a Knight, Erec. Entrusted with Armor and the hopes of the people. Not only a Knight—a Knight of the Order of the Verdant Oak; we must always tread into the dangers of the Wasteland. If we don't, who else will?"

There was a lot there. But more than that, Boldwick seemed... tired. Like he'd been wrung out and had whatever was driving him wild in his head cut loose. The admission that he was still seemingly sane—transformed him but stripped away that raw mad energy.

"The expedition must continue. It's more important now than ever. We must find proof of the danger and force it in front of the Kingdom's eyes. Fortunately, Grandmaster Oak has agreed with me. We'll take half of the Order out into the expedition to seek our answers." Boldwick stood straighter. "...Though I'm sure Grandmaster Oak will be relieved when I report another is sharing these visions. Even if I doubt an Initiate's additional testimony will sway the other Orders."

Boldwick returned to the other side of the desk, setting down a stack of clean papers as he forced Erec to share the details of the nightmares plaguing him. The feelings of dread, the weight of those burning red eyes—while Boldwick only asked questions, and wrung out as much info, Erec saw the Master Knight begin to relax with each passing sheet of paper written.

Confirming that something *really did* wait in the dark, even if it was beyond understanding, brought them together.

At the end of the report, Boldwick chewed the pen's cap absently and reread several lines.

Erec cleared his throat. "Well, can I use the glyph to train my Psyche?"

Boldwick refocused himself, setting both hands on the table. "Perhaps I'm an awful instructor. May the Goddess above grant forgiveness; yes. I will allow you to use it. Though I think the practice is barbaric. But I'm also a man who has come to terms with taking a troupe of greenhorns into a wasteland where I *feel* something horrible is hiding. I've sent many Knights to their death on expeditions, even if I never intended it. If you're determined to push yourself like this, I will not let you do it alone. An hour, every three days. That's all you get. And if I think it's driving you too far, you're done."

Erec nodded his head eagerly. "When do we start?"

# CHAPTER 37
## BUZZ

A lonely glyph pulsed with a pale blue light in the middle of a deserted room. Even walking into the small chamber shoved toward the bottom of the Academy sent goosebumps down Erec's spine. He'd firmed up his resolve to push forward on this training. That gut instinct, backed by VAL's conjectures, made him believe this was the quickest method of handling his problem.

And Boldwick agreed to let the training start immediately.

And the growing sense of danger, now confirmed by Boldwick, meant that he needed to be stronger. To be more reliable for those around him. To be an asset rather than a risk if the worst were to occur.

*You want to be better than him.*

A short insidious thought ran through his head. He checked his feet—still safely away from the glowing lines inside of that insidious test.

[Wow! Really going into overtime on the training, aren't you, Intern? You know we have salary caps, don't you?] VAL buzzed in his mind as Erec stared at those fuzzy glowing lines.

Boldwick closed the door loudly behind him, a bottle of wine in one hand as he took a deep chug. "I hated this damn thing." He snorted and spat; it landed in the middle of the glyph. Bits of frost collected on the sides of the bubbly spittle. "Dreaded it every time exams came up."

"Why do it?" Erec asked. His memories of the first exam were still fresh—but, over time, the raw feeling of those emotions faded. He suspected in a month that they might be little more than a faint dream in his memories.

"They do it because they need to know when you'll break. How far you can get pushed. They want you to learn how to keep going even when you've chopped off the rotting head of your old friend trying to tear out your throat." Boldwick frowned before taking another deep inhale of the wine. He leaned against the wall as a sickly and sour reek of grape wafted through the room.

Erec understood the purpose and why Boldwick hated this test. But it'd proved directly capable of raising his Psyche. More than that, the way it felt was oddly reminiscent of Fury.

A shiver went through him as he looked at the circle. Walking into the glyph felt like walking into a grave—a festering hole filled with the hands of the dead reaching for his life to suck out.

[You've got this, Buckeroo!]

He pushed through and fully entered the glyph.

This time the cold hit like a wall, an almost tangible feeling that protested his existence. He looked at the puddle on the ground. Frost gathered atop it, yet it wasn't frozen. VAL said that the cold going through him wasn't as it appeared. His temperature had never dropped too far—so he could stand through it. His teeth chattered, but he held on to his resolve. *It isn't real.*

*"You're going to kill someone,"* the first voice echoed out of the shadows. It felt like a knife slipping into his ribs with sudden viciousness.

And the intent. The voice behind it, even in a whisper. Brutal and malicious, like he was a sack of flesh it wanted to rot. Erec closed his eyes and focused on the cold air entering his lungs. Far off to the side, he could hear Boldwick take another long pull from the bottle of wine.

*"Give up. Give up. Give up. Worthless sack of shit."*

Erec's teeth chattered, and yet he focused. Letting that coldness dance around in him, feeling where it came from inside his heart. That shadow gripped him. But he stared back at it.

Hate. It was all hate. That's what it came back to. The cold self-hatred inside was only drawn out by this glyph. It was just a different shade of the same paint of hate that came from Fury.

*"If you died, the world would be better. Your friends would be happier. You're going to destroy them one day."*

He sank to his knees, limbs numb from cold as it all seemed pointless. The shadows drifted around and sank their teeth into him. Eroded his control. If he gave way to it, would it be easier? If he let that dark storm brewing inside loose, would it absolve him of having to suffer?

Buzzing.

Damn buzzing.

Always the buzzing.

Erec gritted his teeth as the shadows tore at him. He wouldn't let it win. It didn't matter if he would never measure up to Bedwyr. They weren't the same. No matter how many times the Shadows compared them—

[Focus.]

—that buzzing came in as an annoying word this time. A mechanical voice. But it steadied him. It let him settle his mind and press back against the dark.

He lost the fight several minutes later—crawling out of the glyph. Boldwick yanked him up from the ground and shoved the wine bottle in his hands. The Master Knight draped an arm around his shoulder and held him up as they stumbled back to the wall. "Well, it's a decent effort. You got a resilient mind for a first-year." He tipped back the wine bottle to make Erec drink it through his numb lips.

Sour red with an unknown hint of an unexpected fruit hit the back of Erec's throat. But he let the warm liquor wash through him; it pushed back against the cold that clung to him like a spider's web. He looked at his shaking hands, taking a few deep breaths.

The shadows left their mark, but the booze numbed it; though the words still rang in his ears, they had a certain hollowness.

He saw the pit in himself where that fire loved to burn. Cold or hot, hate in different flavors; tempered and now understood better after the test. Perhaps it wasn't Psyche after all that was important, but this cold hate? Or he'd already begun to lose it. But he needed to reforge himself again and again until he could handle Fury.

Erec formed a fist, fingers digging into his palm. "We have an hour?"

"Yeah, I figured I'd make sure you recovered before sending you back off—"

"Good. I'm going back in."

— - ☣ - — - ☼ - — - ☣ - —

Boldwick dragged him back to his dorm. Erec's entire body shook, but his focus had only honed itself on the second and third attempts. He didn't manage to last longer than the first attempt. Yet, he felt more alive than ever, even after fording past that cold river of despair.

Though that might have had to do with the drinking after his third attempt. After he started shaking from the cold so badly he could barely hold himself together, Boldwick sat him against the wall and shared a second bottle.

Maybe Boldwick was an alcoholic. After walking in like he had with Sir Able... Yet, for the moment, Erec just appreciated the bottle and how it numbed the raw pain the test etched into his soul. They talked, mainly of the Master Knight's past and his time outside the walls.

Nothing that in his state Erec could quite hold on to. At the end of which, Boldwick helped him stagger back to his dorm.

As they reached the door, Boldwick patted him on the shoulder. "That's a good lad. You did plenty of good today. Head to bed and get some rest."

"Thanks." Erec waved him off, taking a second to steady himself against a wall as the instructor swayed back to his office.

Erec took a deep breath and pushed into the room, intending to head right for his bed while the liquor buzz still held on and made it easy.

Olivia was there alone, one leg folded over another as she read from *Beowulf*—the same book he'd been reading through since he got here. She paused and looked up at him, tilting her head.

"Oh, you've been drinking? I didn't take you for the type," she said, smoothly putting the book on the table. "Your face looks pale, too. Rough day?"

Erec squinted his eyes at her. The way she was so poised and collected, always upright and with a carefully maintained front that hid away what was beneath. He wanted to crack that shell. He glanced at Colin's door—closed. He got close to her, gazing down at the prim and proper woman on the couch. "What is your game?"

"Game?" Olivia asked.

"You're spying on Colin, aren't you?"

"Ah." Olivia snorted and shook her head. "Perhaps a little bit. When I forge my own House, I intend to keep ties with the Duchy that afforded me this opportunity. But no. I am not here primarily to 'spy' on Colin." She paused, her eyes meeting his, sinking into him and breaking that facade of a collected maid. There was something there, a fascination. "You're the one I'm interested in."

"I—" Erec sputtered. "Just what do you mean by that? Are you saying you're *into* me?"

Olivia chuckled politely, shaking her head. "I've been told you have ties outside the wall. With your personality, it's very likely you'll reach for them in the future. You're stubborn and disregard the words of those stationed above you. For better or worse."

"So you're spying on me? For who, Lyotte? For House Luculentus?"

Olivia bit her lip, tilting her head as her eyes remained locked, as if she were about to pick her words carefully.

Garin slammed the door to the living room open, his eyes bright, his Academy collar undone with a flush to his cheeks. His eyes settled on Olivia and Erec close together, then a frown for a fraction of a second. He cleared his throat. "S'—oh, right, alright, I came in at a bad time?" There was a hint of nervousness and a weird tone to the words, along with a slur.

"No," Erec said, pulling back from Olivia as he saw her face shift back to that mask of a maid. Whatever she'd thought about saying to him, it seemed she'd decided against it. She gave Garin a small smile.

"It seems our dorm has two drunkards. How incorrigible."

"Wha—" Garin tilted his head at Erec. "What the hell? Were you out drinking? You turned me down!"

"I didn't mean to go drinking—"

There was a loud pounding on the door. Garin went wide-eyed and looked at the two of them. "Oh shit," he said, running off and darting behind the couch. "I'm not here."

Erec looked between him and the door; his sluggish mind turned. What sort of trouble had his friend gotten into? Should they pretend they weren't home? If they did, whoever was out there would have no choice but to go away.

Olivia saw the indecision and shook her head. "It does not befit those of our station to ignore confrontation. We're Knights," she scolded before floating over to the door.

# CHAPTER 38
# TWO DRUNKEN PEAS IN A POD

*There are those we cannot talk about; even mentioning them here is liable to*
*make the Church track me down and declare me a sinner.*
*But are we really humans if we ignore their suffering?*
*I propose a concealed effort to provide supplemental aid on a monthly basis.*
*Is the Goddess so inhuman as to scorn such a thing?*

*- Unknown, "Resource Allocation Suggestion" (298, 3rd Era)*

Olivia threw the door open to reveal Gwen; but she hardly had a second to say whatever she was about say, as Bedwyr strode past both of them and into the center of the dorm. For some reason, Erec's brother was wearing his formals; a sharp jacket with gold trim over the top of a red dress shirt. Completed by slacks and polished, pointed, black shoes.

Gwen wasn't to be outdone by him either, wearing the clean girl's version of the formals, which substituted the slacks for a nicely cut black skirt. Though she'd chosen to wear bright-red heels instead of the issued black dress shoes.

Erec's brother took in the scene with a passing glance, raising an eyebrow at the barely disguised drunken Garin behind the couch. Erec frowned at his brother and crossed his arms.

"Have you been drinking?" Bedwyr asked, sniffing the air and no doubt catching the scent of liquor. His eyes hardened as he looked at Erec and Garin. "Garin, stop trying to hide. I see you."

"Ah—no worries." Garin gave a fake laugh, standing up and swaying in his spot. "And yeah, just a bit." He rubbed the back of his neck and tried to flash an award-winning smile. Bedwyr strode further into the room—acting as if he owned the place. Like he belonged here. Like he could do whatever he wanted.

Erec stood straighter and shot him a scowl. The last words his brother spoke to him were still echoing in his head.

"Welcome to our dorm." Olivia gave a slight curtsy to both Bedwyr and Gwen. "Can I pour you some tea, perhaps?"

Gwen smirked. "Naw, but I'll take a shot of whatever those two had. Their faces are all red, so it must've been good." She pointed to Erec and Garin.

"Ah. I'm afraid we don't have any alcohol in this dorm; those two decided to go out and drink." Olivia shook her head, guiding Gwen inside with her.

"Did they? Funny that. Considering why we're here…" Gwen trailed off.

"So you're not just here to check out your brother's dorm—you, uh, didn't happen to see a couple of angry girls wandering by in the halls, did you?" Garin asked, eyes dancing between Gwen and Bedwyr.

"Causing problems?" Bedwyr asked.

"No, no, just had some fun, some drinks—and maybe left a little earlier than they'd like."

"Oh, of course. I'm sure that's all there is to that story." Bedwyr's eyes slid from Garin to rest on Erec. "How did you do on your exams?"

"Well enough," Erec said, uncrossing his arms. He was painfully aware of the need to put up a strong front against Bedwyr, or his brother would run him over; but after his day, it didn't seem much like a fair fight.

"Did you get an A? Which courses were you assigned?" Bedwyr pressed him; his eyes carried a heavy weight as they judged Erec. He had no choice but to shuffle and look away under that intensity, or else he'd risk drawing out the anger under the surface.

With as frayed as he felt after the glyph training, he knew that the risk of losing himself was far too close for comfort.

"Ah, so you're Sir Erec's older brother," Olivia stated, moving between him and Bedwyr. She bowed and caught Erec's eyes for a second, clearly trying to interject and lessen the mounting tension. "I've heard that you were in the Academy and looked forward to meeting you."

"Mhmm," Bedwyr said, giving her a nod before returning that burning gaze toward his brother. Olivia's attempt to redirect failed. "I have. I'm here to ensure Erec doesn't do anything to detract from our family name. Though it appears to be a bit late, given his performance against the Prince."

"What, are you angry I lost?" Erec felt the anger stoked in him. "Did I not do enough to hold a candle to your legacy?"

"I'm angry that you attacked the *Prince* after you lost. Not that you lost. Not to mention how you attacked me in the middle of battle."

"I had no choice! Do you think I can control my Divine Talent—do you think I *wanted* to take a swing at you—"

"Whoa, whoa. Let's take it back a bit." Garin gave a nervous laugh, stumbling between the two. Olivia shook her head and slid next to him—holding the drunken Baron's son up. "I know you two don't get along, but there's no reason to start arguing whenever you see each other."

"A compelling point. I'll make efforts to be more cordial," Bedwyr said. "I was not aware you'd developed a Divine Talent. But that presses my point forward. If it is uncontrollable, do you have courses to try to control it? Do you need additional training? I can make time in my schedule."

That contrast. How could Bedwyr go from saying he'd crush Erec's dreams to offering to help him a week later? It made no sense. "I'm fine. I have a course to address my Talent, and I've been doing extra training." Erec rubbed his eyes. If Bedwyr was going to take a step back from the hostility, he'd follow suit. "Thank you for the offer. Is that why you're here?"

"Is it not right for an older brother to visit his younger brother and ensure he's settling well into his new life?"

"Last time we spoke, you said you'd—" Erec cut himself off, reading the room and seeing everyone tense at his tone. *Drop it for now.* It was so hard. So hard when just an hour earlier, those voices had haunted his head and whispered all of the horrible things about he stood up to Bedwyr. "—I'm fine. But I don't think that's why you're here."

"That would be partially correct," Bedwyr admitted.

"We're here to invite you to a party!" Gwen cut in, flashing a wide smile. "A lot of second-years and first-years will be there—it's a good chance for mingling between the classes and Orders."

"You will be attending," Bedwyr stated clearly, his eyes lingering on Erec.

"I'm exhausted." Erec shot back, having no real desire to waste his time at another function. Especially not already partially drunk and so defeated from the training with the glyph. His one solace coming back to the dorm had been that he could sleep off the awful words and regain his sanity.

Garin let out a whistle; Olivia looked up at him. "We're going! C'mon, Erec, it sounds like a blast," Garin said, and moved a bit too fast as he got excited. Olivia caught their balance and steadied them before they fell over.

"Yes, I do believe that sounds like an excellent way to spend the night." Olivia managed to get out after ensuring that Garin was once more leaning securely against her. "...Though I think I'll need to sober up these two beforehand."

"I'm not going." Erec started heading for his room—only for Bedwyr to dart between him and the door. Though he was a couple of inches shorter, his brother took up too much space and ensured Erec wouldn't get by. Not without a fight.

"Calm down. Goddess above, Erec. You're too much like her. Do you know what people are saying about you?"

"No. I don't really care much, either. I'm training and doing my best. What other people talk about isn't my concern."

"They say you're a Mad Knight with no regard for honor." Bedwyr shook his head. "A boy too dumb to respect status and too dangerous on a battlefield to be relied on. Is that the reputation you want? A loner without honor? Were you not my brother, the rumors would have been even worse."

Erec shifted his eyes to Garin—who looked away and leaned in more on Olivia, taking advantage of her help to distract himself and refusing to address his friend's attention.

"So you're here to admonish me for that too? I'm oh-so-sorry, Bedwyr; I don't mean to tarnish your golden reputation."

"Erec. Drop it." Bedwyr curled a fist, danger entering his eyes. "If you don't, I'll make you."

Erec paused, feeling that hot anger grow under his skin. He wanted to hurt Bedwyr, to make his brother angry. To get a measure of revenge against him for abandoning their family and refusing to talk about Mom. For everyone who ever compared him to his brother. So bad. So badly did he want to get under his skin and for a chance at revenge.

But it was pointless.

Bedwyr was offering a helping hand, and he was shunning it because he felt spiteful and wanted to pick a fight. How much of this was him, and how much of it was Fury?

This was no way to live life. No matter what his Divine Talent drew out, he wasn't a Mad Knight.

*One... Two...* Erec counted off in his head, letting the tension drain away. Bedwyr sensed the shift, as he backed away. Scratching the back of his head. There was embarrassment on his face. Unhappy that he'd let his little brother rile him up this far. *...Ten.* Erec softened his expression and frowned.

"I'm sorry. I've been out of line," Erec lied. "Can you forgive me?"

"It's fine. After a year apart and the terms we last left on, I can forgive abrasion as we learn to live near one another again." Bedwyr rolled his eyes. "I came to invite you and your friends, and I highly suggest you attend the party. You should take care of your public image in this place. Some of these people will one day become future landed Lords, Dukes, and Earls. But I won't force you."

"I'll go," Erec agreed, though inside, he dreaded the event already, but it wasn't worth escalating the situation any further, and if things went well, maybe the rumors about him would ease off. Bedwyr nodded and moved back to Gwen, pacified. His brother folded his arms and refused to meet Erec's eyes.

"Tell us about this party," Olivia said to Gwen, her eyes lit up.

"Ah, yeah," Gwen mumbled before shaking her head and flashing the other girl a smile. "Pretty much this is an annual affair. They rent a ballroom in the main Academy every year. There'll be music, food, drinks—though perhaps the two boys have had enough of that tonight—but make sure you show up in your formals," Gwen spilled out, growing more cheerful with each sentence. The tension in the room cleared and gave way to excitement from the two girls and Garin. "It's tonight. We were just stopping by before heading to it." She smiled at Bedwyr. "I suggest you all prepare and head over soon."

"Ah, so I see. Is it common for people to take dates?" Olivia asked. Gwen flushed a little, but the comment didn't shake her.

"They aren't required, but they do make it a bit more fun…"

The two slipped into a brief conversation, and after Olivia obtained all of the details, his brother and Gwen left.

Erec wasn't happy he had to attend a party, but understood the need to. Even if he wanted to rest and recover from the hell that had been training, this was an extended hand from Bedwyr. A gesture of good faith, perhaps. Just done in ultimately a very demanding and annoying way. But he could be the better man. He bit back his complaints and prepared himself mentally.

Except he wouldn't be wandering into this battle alone. Garin and Olivia didn't count, since they were made for this kind of thing. No.

Erec stared at Colin's closed door. If he had to wade into the battlefield of courtly politics and evening get-togethers, it wasn't fair that he'd be the only one forced to attend. And he definitely wasn't the only one here who needed to clean up their image.

After throwing on his formals and having Olivia fuss over him and Garin, he slammed his knuckles on Colin's door.

If he had to suffer, so did Colin.

# CHAPTER 39
# COURTING

Music riffed from old-world guitars and banged alongside the beat of drums to fill the spacious ballroom. All of the Knight Initiates shifted about, decked out in their formal clothes. Some wore accents of jewelry to display status further; they gathered in small circles. This place was a reflection of the higher courts. They dressed up in Academy clothes. Like wolves in sheep's clothing.

Erec despised parties.

No matter how many times he went through this, the court life, he suspected he'd never get the bad taste out of his mouth.

He drowned it out with wine. He'd already been drinking, so why stop? The cold shower Olivia had forced him and Garin to take had only sobered him up for so long, and intoxication would make it easier to get through this affair.

The glances from the circles of Knights didn't help. They gossiped about him. He was a Mad Knight—a terror who had gone too far against the Prince and violated the rules of a spar. Who slaughtered monsters without care for the allies around him. When he tried to mingle with the other people here—they kept quiet and stopped being as open with him around.

So eventually he gave up. It seemed he couldn't cure his reputation.

Erec downed another glass.

"Drinking problem, rust-bucket?" Colin shot out, an attempted dig even with an outdated insult. Erec hadn't even *heard* of what happened to the poor Markos II that dragged him through the trial. He glared at Colin.

"Might be. But it's not like I see you hanging out with them, either." Erec nodded at Garin and Olivia.

They were doing rounds around the ballroom. Drifting in and out of groups with ease; the way they complemented each other's social skills was alarming. Where Garin could come off as obnoxious or overtly casual, Olivia shored that up with a curt politeness that was expected in the courts. How they dealt with all of those fake faces was beyond him; he'd quickly reached his limit. Anyone would in his place.

Colin decided to remain on the edge of the ballroom, near a small table. It shouldn't have been shocking that Colin avoided associating with the other Knights, perhaps especially after seeing his manners— or lack thereof—during the dreadful Courtly Mannerism course.

Erec stood his ground after meeting a couple of people here. He was close to snapping from the training. He'd hoped booze would help, but no.

Still, drinking in the corner with Colin was better than getting involved in some faux pas to degrade his reputation any further. *Sorry, Bedwyr, Garin. I'm not like either of you.*

He wasn't the only one catching glares.

For every dark look sent his way, Colin received triple that number. While Colin tried to present a strong front, he kept trying to press further into the background.

"And why would I engage in this party with them? They aren't my friends; we simply live together. Besides, they're far below my rank," Colin finally said, turning his nose up.

"Do you have any friends?" Erec swirled the glass of crimson wine, still fighting the self-hating thoughts in his head. Colin recoiled as if slapped but didn't retaliate. Instead, he shrank further toward the wall. Erec sighed. "Alright, maybe that was a bit too far. Sorry."

He looked away from the cup. It was a shallow pool that too many drowned themselves in. Would he join them? Bedwyr glided effortlessly across the dance floor with Gwen, surrounded by a gaggle of friends, dancing and joking with their own dates. *Why am I not like him? Why?* What kept him from being more like Garin or his brother?

How could he face down monsters with a burning anger in his gut and an axe in hand, yet *this* raised the hairs on the back of his neck?

"There is little need to apologize. You are correct; I have no friends," Colin said quietly to his side. Damn near quiet enough to miss over the music. There was resentment to his expression, yet also a sadness. "They don't understand my value. That by nature of my station, I can achieve more then they shall ever be able to. Therefore, I do not need them."

"They understand your value better than you. It's why they don't bother with you."

"Don't you dare. What can a son of a disgraceful family understand about my value?"

"Maybe I haven't done my best, but I've tried to be nice to you. Even after what happened during the trial." Erec's temper flared. The band swapped to something faster-paced, an ancient song and a valued relic of the old-world that'd been having a resurgence in the Kingdom. "But you keep acting like a dick. Not to just me, but everyone else too. You are the only one who doesn't understand your value in this room. When they come to talk to you and say they want to be your friend, they'll be lying. They'll use you, and you've starved yourself of companionship so damn much, you'll make an easy target."

[Elvis?] VAL asked.

Erec turned his undivided attention to Colin. Maybe it was the liquor or perhaps the strain of the training. But this conversation was long overdue, and it'd happen right fucking now.

Offering Colin platitudes and reaching out to him again and again after the exam hadn't led to real progress. The more he gave, the more Colin took.

Erec was sick of it.

Colin sneered at him. "I am a Duke's son! They wouldn't dare!"

"You'll be the last of your line with any relevancy, based on your behavior. Are you determined to run your House into the ground to spite your father? Are you going to piss away the power and influence he earned through blood? They'll use you and see through you, to take what you have."

"You don't know what you're implying. As if these peons could ever—"

"After a year. Who in this room do you think you'd win against?" Erec threw out his hand. "A year. Colin. With how you're going, you're going to squander every single advantage your family has twisted into your little black heart. It's disgusting. The rest of the Duchy already see this and knows you'll amount to nothing but ruin for your line."

Colin paused, working his jaw.

"Or did you forget getting your ass kicked by that Duke's daughter? I heard about it. She wiped the floor with you."

"You attacked a Prince!"

"I'm a landless second son with an uncontrolled Divine Talent— even if these people don't know that *yet,* I'm sure I still have far more of their respect relative to my nonexistent station."

Colin squared up to Erec, his nostrils flared. Erec returned the stance and, in a brief moment of clarity, realized that escalating this further would probably lead to a fight.

So much for trying to cure his reputation as a Mad Knight. But if he broke now and gave way to Colin, the boy was well and truly fucked. He needed to break through Colin's insufferable ego, or it would consume their barely tenable bond.

Anger clashed between them.

Who would take the first swing? Colin's fist tightened.

Then it went limp; Colin deflated and looked away. When he spoke, his words came out as a whisper. "What can I do?"

"Change," Erec said, letting out a relieved breath.

"I'm weak." Colin clenched his hand and scowled. "The last two years before the trial, I told off my instructors, and my mother covered for me. That's why I'm doing so badly. When I was young, they all said how adept I was...yet they lied to me." Colin's face took a dark cast.

The ballroom shifted once more into more dancing as the music moved away to something slower.

Garin danced with Olivia in his arms. The two looked at each other rather intensely. Garin was still red in the cheeks from the liquor, and Olivia threw a fake pout on her face. His friend must've made some dumb quip. Typical. They looked good together. But it left a pang in Erec's heart. Could they trust that woman? She was a spy, but so was he, in a way.

"Train with me," Colin declared from his side.

"Huh? You realize I don't have all the skills you high-born nobles got. Can't you contact your dad and see if he has any allies—"

"He told me I was to make my own path through the Academy and refused to let me rely on his connections," Colin admitted.

*That's ironic.* Erec fought to keep a scowl off his face. To say that to his son, yet go and force someone to befriend him as an ally. The games of nobility were sickening.

"You're strong. Don't try to deny it. We all saw the fight against the Prince; even if you're a bastard without honor, you stood against him far longer than you had any right to. I've seen the way you train with Garin. Work with me too."

"I've been—" Erec's heart felt a cold hand close across it. This was part of his vow and the first time he'd seen this dickwad reach out to anyone with an open hand. Even if he was extremely busy trying to get himself under control before the expedition…there didn't seem to be a second option.

Colin gave him an earnest expression. It wasn't quite a smile. It wasn't anywhere near a scowl.

"Fine. But, I'm going to warn you now… Over the next couple of weeks, I'm going to be more temperamental than I'd like to admit."

"Is that outside of the norm? Either way, I shall be fine, I'm sure."

Erec extended his hand for a shake. Colin looked down at it, hesitating. Their first step on the path of friendship.

Then he took the hand and shook. Sealing their fates together through their academy life. More music drifted out from the band.

The music reached a crescendo. On the dance floor, Garin leaned in and met Olivia's lips.

# CHAPTER 40
## KNIVES AND SMILES

*"Can you show me," said I, "some stratagem by means of which I may catch this old god without his suspecting it and finding me out? For a god is not easily caught—not by a mortal man."*

*"Stranger," said she, "I will make it all quite clear to you. About the time when the sun shall have reached mid heaven, the old man of the sea comes up from under the waves, heralded by the West wind that furs the water over his head. As soon as he has come up he lies down, and goes to sleep in a great sea cave, where the seals—Halosydne's chickens as they call them—come up also from the gray sea, and go to sleep in shoals all round him; and a very strong and fish-like smell do they bring with them. Early to-morrow morning I will take you to this place and will lay you in ambush. Pick out, therefore, the three best men you have in your fleet, and I will tell you all the tricks that the old man will play you.*

*"First he will look over all his seals, and count them; then, when he has seen them and tallied them on his five fingers, he will go to sleep among them, as a shepherd among his sheep. The moment you see that he is asleep seize him; put forth all your strength and hold him fast, for he will do his very utmost to get away from you. He will turn himself into every kind of creature that goes upon the earth, and will become also both fire and water; but you must hold him fast and grip him tighter and tighter, till he begins to talk to you and comes back to what he was when you saw him go to sleep; then you may*

*slacken your hold and let him go; and you can ask him which of the gods it is*
*that is angry with you, and what you must do to reach your home over the*
*seas.'"*

*- Homer,* The Odyssey *(7th Century, 3rd Era)*

The Vallum Armor stood racked at the end of the lecture room, a testament to the might of humanity.

Right now, Erec had stripped it bare. Per the free time in the course, he'd meticulously removed the front plating to reveal the network of complex components stuffed below. A blend of beautiful redundancy meant to keep its pilot alive when a horrifying monster tried to bite through the steel with unnaturally sharp teeth.

Erec twisted a nut free to unseal a small cube tucked into the lower abdomen. Placed strategically to minimize chances of receiving damage.

[Interesting. Is this logic cube where the glyph strips lead? My nanites cannot interact with it.]

Erec traced one of the thin strips of bent metal spread outward from the cube. If one looked closely, they'd see welds on the side of these strips—sealing the etchings inside. It was a common technique to protect glyphs from wear and damage by encasing them within metal and then reinforcing them through prayer.

According to the instructor, the purpose of the Mysticism subsystems within the Vallum model was only to conduct and make glyph formation easier. There were a few "logic cubes," as VAL put it. On some advanced models, these glyph circuits could perform complicated tasks. But the cost was a constant drain of mana from the user.

So far, they were wasted on Erec, since he was new to Mysticism. And understanding the magical circuits was still far above him.

Even if he could break the weld on one of the strips, he'd have no idea what the glyph work below even did.

He stepped back from the Armor, letting VAL scan it from the outside. Even if VAL was already in the Armor, there were parts it had no control over and needed an outside view to understand.

The instructor was busy on the other side of the workshop, putting together a mechanical version of a hound she affectionately referred to as her "pet project," made entirely out of scrap.

The woman was a damn hoarder. Resourceful. But a hoarder.

Just one look across the workshop said everything. Endless piles of trash and garbage lumped together with bits and bobs and toasters mingled with fridges. Half of this would never find use. More than a third of this junk had been here for ten years.

Their first lesson with her was about determining the value of the scrap in the wasteland. She stated that not all scrap was equal with a completely serious face as she gave the lecture in a half-landfill junk-yard room.

Erec wiped the grease off his face with a rag and looked at Olivia.

She hunched over near her Armor, busy polishing the lower legs.

"What was it like living in the Luculentus house?" Erec asked. Now was a fine time to take a break; he wasn't about to attempt any modifications yet. Most of their course so far had been about repurposing scrap and getting used to their new Armor.

"We received three fine meals daily, and typically we shared it with the house guards. Sufficient dwellings, and two weeks personal time a year." Olivia looked over at him, still sitting near her Armor's leg—a polishing rag in hand. Out of all the new Initiates, nobody's Armor shone like hers. "A lovely garden, kept by the lady of the house. She was a former Knight too, you know. She's the one who encouraged me to go down this path."

"She convinced you to become a spy?"

"You continue to accuse me of such matters, yet you've also been tasked with such an assignment, no?" she tsked before letting out a sigh. "But you're also wrong. That's very much not why I'm here."

"Ah. I beg your forgiveness." Erec rubbed his eyes. Had Garin spilled his secret, or had she figured it out on her own?

[Disconnect the yellow wire near the logic cube.]

Erec leaned forward, grasped at the wire, and gave it a yank. It refused to dislodge. He looked closer. Was it welded?

"I did not lie to you, Erec. I'm interested in your goals. It is, after all, of importance to my Lady."

"And which goals are you referring to? Not being a landless noble? Restoring honor to my family?" He paused and took a deep sigh. "Or is it my mother? Is the Duchy worried about me connecting with her again?"

"They're interested in such an arrangement, yes. That, and the others outside the wall she might have met."

[Yank harder.]

Erec's temper flared—channeling a bit of that anger into his fingers clutching the wire, the fused metal broke with a single yank, showering them in odd sparks of red and blue. Erec shielded his face as Olivia scooted away.

[You'll need to weld that back into place, but it appears that you've discharged some excess anomalous energy from it. It's somewhat like a capacitor, even if it doesn't work off entirely the same logic.]

He turned his attention to Olivia, a scowl on his face. VAL had known such an act would disrupt the suit—and that Erec hated having to weld. It meant talking to the crazy instructor for the equipment and a long-winded story about the thousands of projects in her head.

"What others outside of the wall? The monsters eat up anyone out there—hell, I'm not sure I'll even find my mother after so long. I might just find her corpse." It'd always been in the back of his mind. He might never understand her reasoning, but he wanted to dig her a grave at the very least.

And then he'd track down the monster that convinced her to leave her family behind and slaughter it after demanding answers. He could hope for the best. But the world outside of the walls was harsh and deadly.

"There's more outside than they tell you, Erec," Olivia chided before returning her attention to her Armor. "I suppose you'll learn that sooner or later, now that you're a Knight."

"Hey," Erec called to her, not too happy with her dismissing him. She didn't return his attention. That smug look ticked him off. "You better not hurt Garin," Erec said before turning away to talk to the instructor. He had a welder to borrow.

She watched him with a frown on her face as he walked away.

— - ☢ - — - ☼ - — - ☢ - —

The glow of the blue was all that he saw. Those horrible lines underneath his feet, the white frost of his breath, and the unholy cold filling his lungs. How long could he go? How much of this could a man take?

This was his last chance. The very last opportunity he'd have with Boldwick before the expedition. After weeks of this torture, his Psyche had only advanced to Tier 9. It hadn't broken the bottleneck and launched him into the next rank.

[Are you sure?]

Erec nodded his head. After the last breakthrough, if he focused hard, he could decipher what the machine was trying to say in his head during this test. But while under the effects of Fury, he couldn't comprehend a single word of what VAL tried to tell him. The more he let himself slip into either state, the more similarities he saw. If he could break through to the E rank, he was sure there'd be a difference.

The sedatives flooded his veins, numbing his legs. This time, he wouldn't give himself the chance to crawl out. No.

He would stay in the cold coffin until he broke through that barrier.

Boldwick sat on the side; with bleary vision, Erec saw him take a pull of the wine. This was his fourth attempt for the day. Usually, he only lasted three. Erec had made this plan with VAL after excusing himself to a bathroom break.

Surprisingly, the machine agreed under a single condition.

Once Erec managed to break through, they'd never undergo this training again. While VAL didn't specify what about the glyph perturbed it, the machine was evasive and irritable after every session.

The shadows of sadness crashed into Erec. The voices told him he was doomed, that he'd die in a shallow grave. At this point, the voices and him were almost familiar friends.

Erec gave a gasping laugh as he lay curled on the floor like a dying man. He let the hate pour in; the cold fire of hate reforged him for the Goddess-knew-how-many-th time. He hated himself. Hated every part of him for living on this doomed planet, this scorched earth, this hell-pit.

What would it have been like to live in the old-world?

What if he had been an intern with Vortex Industries? Would that have been his life if he'd been born hundreds of years before? Would he have met VAL?

He laughed until his throat burned.

He laughed until all the thoughts left his head.

He laughed until the shadows backed away, afraid of him.

His eyes closed. Breath hitching as he could no longer force air through his lungs, as the grasp of death lingered nearby but was held at bay by those glowing blue lines.

In the blue light, he saw his life. A life of another man long before, a young man working his way through his daily life, excited for an internship, only for time to wear him down with endless chores.

But there was a point: he'd make a name for himself and gain respect.

And then a light shattered the Earth and consumed everything living on its surface in silver fire, burning away his dreams and future.

In this life, he sank to his knees, screaming. His eyes melted out of his head as alarms went off in the facility. Blue light became silver.

Erec screamed.

[Applying jolt.]

Erec's body shuddered, and he gasped, letting anger flood. Letting the hate combat the cold anger, his scorn for the world seethe and burn just as bad as the shadows shouted out at him to give up on trying. They reached an equilibrium.

He stood up, body shaking from the cold and teeth chattering. But there was an inner warmth. It was spreading through his veins and pushing back.

And a notification in the corner of his vision.

Everything felt numb. His thoughts hung by a thread, and he worked off impulse. He needed confirmation. His Blessing flashed across his vision.

### Psyche Advancement: Rank F - Tier 9 → Rank E - Tier 1

There wasn't any joy in the accomplishment. He numbly stumbled out of the glyph, sliding onto the ground.

Boldwick caught him and helped him back to his office—and then broke open another bottle of wine to celebrate once Erec's brain regained some semblance of logic.

Liquor had been a constant companion to sadness since the First

Era. And that night, both he and the Master Knight indulged in the company of more booze. Tomorrow they would leave the safety of these walls and foray into the unknown for the rest of humankind who could not.

They'd face those red eyes together.

# CHAPTER 41
# EXPEDITION

Every time he stepped into the Vallum model, it felt like coming home. The way the Armor flowed around him and responded to his movements like water was a constant source of amazement—though he knew it was unnatural. VAL had enhanced the Armor, making it better than Olivia or Garin's.

Both of whom were entering their own Armor. Colin was already packed and ready in the living space.

The air held nervous energy. Word circulated to the Academy about the trip, particularly about the contention between the Orders.

Usually, these two-week-long expeditions were more introductory affairs—some senior staff accompanied the caravan to conduct smaller missions, sure. Every time they prepared to leave the walls, the Order of the Verdant Oak aimed to maximize their expenditure of resources.

But this was something special. Grandmaster Oak broke tradition and extended the two weeks to three, then assigned half of the Order to the expedition.

No doubt, word had spread through the Orders of the Master Knight's obsession with a white stag and the nightmares plaguing him. But Erec knew something lurked outside of their walls. Even with the number of people going with, it didn't feel like nearly enough. If perhaps they'd had an army…

This was the purpose of their Order. To confirm and evaluate threats before they become a problem. Then organize and conduct operations to monitor the situation while the Kingdom prepared a response. If a Master Knight had suspicions, most fell in line and went along with it.

Erec checked over the hatchets attached to either side of his Armor, comforted by the brutal war axe on his back. If he were to die here and fulfill what those shadows had whispered in his ears, he'd do it while taking out as much as he could. His gaze drifted over to Garin, fussing over Olivia.

The last two weeks had been filled with his friend fawning over the girl and her flustered attitude over the attention. To call the love affair sickening would do it little credit. It also didn't fit his image of his friend, who'd fluttered from girl to girl like a bird through the high branches of the trees in the bio-caverns. Honestly, the behavior was starting to worry him. What set Olivia so apart?

Erec grabbed Garin by the shoulder and gave him a slight shake. He and Erec were in their Armor, but Garin was stopping Olivia from finishing her preparations, and Erec didn't wanna run late.

"Oh—uh," Garin mumbled, pulling away from Olivia. "You ready, buddy?"

"As ready as ever." Erec made sure to take Garin to the living room to give Olivia breathing space.

Colin gave them both a nod. "Prepared, are we? Did you bring rations along this time, rust-bucket?"

Erec looked at his bag—stuffed full of survival equipment collected from the Quartermaster a couple of days ago. And a couple of other tokens. Including the letter from his mother. It didn't feel right to leave the walls without it this time, but he had indeed slipped in some extra food. But not for the reason Colin might've thought.

"I did. Are you going to freeze up when we run across bugs again, brat?" Erec asked.

Colin scoffed and shook his head. "I doubt there shall be bugs."

"You never know!" Garin coughed and shook his head, looking between the two.

"No, the only thing *bugging* me will be you two, I'm sure," Colin shot back, and...laughed. He laughed at his own bad joke.

Erec groaned. The only thing worse than Colin acting like a complete prick had been his sense of humor—something so buried away in that self-obsessed ego that they'd never seen it. But now that he'd been coming out of his shell…

"Get it?" Colin asked, his voice slightly raised as neither of them laughed.

"Oh yeah, yeah. Going to steal Liv right from me with jokes like that," Garin said and shook his head, looking over at Erec. Even with Garin underneath the helmet, he knew precisely the sort of eye roll he'd see. He'd gotten the same kind of look hundreds of times from his friend.

"Huh? You and the maid are a pair? Did your father not warn you about consorting with the serving staff? They are here to do a job, not for your personal enjoyment—"

"By the Goddess." Erec cut him off before the conversation could devolve into whatever odd discussion the Duke had given to his son. "And she's a Knight, not serving staff. Just as high-ranked a Knight as you."

There was a tiny squeak from Garin's bag—his friend rushed over right away.

Munchy.

There'd been no solution to the squirrel problem other than to bring the overweight critter along on the expedition. Erec thought about asking Rodren to look after it—but a test run had shown that it wouldn't work.

If Munchy lost sight of Garin for more than a day, he'd act wild and wreak havoc. Destroying things, tearing apart rooms, and becoming a menace. Erec had lost several casual shirts due to the little bastard rampaging. He didn't know why the creature had such an addictive personality to Garin of all people, but due to it, they had no choice but to let him tag along.

And it was also why he and Garin had stuffed extra food away for the journey.

Olivia joined them, and they made their way out of the room; to the front of the Academy, where the rest of the Verdant Oak gathered.

In short time, the Master Knights gave instructions to the Commander Knights, who sorted their caravans out—large steel wagons with wheels hitched up to cattle from the deep caverns. They'd loaded up heavily with advanced armaments and backup supplies in case the worst happened. Every single Knight had their own pack to carry. Master Oak spared no expense in preparations.

Boldwick and two other Master Knights quickly got everyone moving. They made a slow ramble to the western gate.

It was there that the first problem of the expedition reared its head.

A line of Knights of the Silver Flames arrayed themselves in front of the large steel curtain gate. They prevented the expedition from leaving.

In front of them was a man decorated in bright-red robes with singed hems. Too many jewels hung off him; the frail old man was little better than bones and loose hanging skin. The Knights behind him looked to his too-large presence.

There could be no mistaking him.

This was the Cardinal.

"What the hell is this?" Boldwick strode in front of the caravan as it came to a stop. They weren't going anywhere unless they wanted to plow through the Knights.

"You would do well to sink to your knees before the Goddess's Cardinal," the man said, his eyes running over the crowd; his voice, like Boldwick's, was amplified. Erec looked around and yet saw no glyphs present. Was this some prayer?

Why would he want this conversation broadcast?

"I set out today on orders from my Grandmaster to conduct this expedition. Were this in a Church? Sure, I'd bend the knee. But you're sitting in front of *my* gate, halting *my* expedition, tell me why that is, exactly?"

The Cardinal scowled—and the weight of his judgment flooded over everyone as if the mere thought held a heavy strength. Still, before that oppressive onslaught of forced empathetic emotion, Boldwick didn't waver.

*Is this due to high Faith, or does he have a Divine Talent?*

"You shall be taking five of my priests and a contingent of Silver Flames Knights as their bodyguards."

"By whose authority?"

"Grandmaster Flames has deferred to my judgment. The Goddess must have eyes on these events."

Boldwick glanced back at the nervous caravan and then at the hardened line of Silver Flames Knights blocking their path. "You couldn't have communicated this beforehand? Not to mention this is an Order of the Verdant Oak expedition—we're the ones with authority on leaving these walls. Neither you nor Grandmaster Flames have any authority on who goes in and out."

"We are here to ensure you do not commit sins, my child. Comply, and you shall not receive the ill will of the Church."

Boldwick barked out a laugh. "What would you do if I told you to fuck off?"

The Cardinal stiffened, and another wave of contempt and disdain radiated off the man. Erec shuddered, but Boldwick still seemed unaffected.

"Fine. I don't trust you, your Church, or men that aren't mine. But I don't want to cause any more of a headache for Grandmaster Oak. Order your men to pack their shit and join my caravan. Though know this; out there"—Boldwick jerked a finger at the gate—"the other Master Knights and I are kings. Anyone that says or does something we disapprove of gets punished. This is not a political theater game; the wasteland chews men and women up without a second thought, especially now."

The Cardinal didn't seem to like that answer but didn't offer a counter. At least not publicly, as whatever had been amplifying their conversation for the caravan to hear cut off.

Several priests broke away from the Knights and added their equipment to the steel wagons; they had no Armor, even if their bodyguards did. They had simple red robes like the Cardinal, burnt at the edges but without elaborate jewelry.

It was said that when inducted into the Church, a priest underwent a ritual. Though the secret was well-kept, the results weren't. It made them immune to the scorching air and various invisible dangers that still infested parts of the wastes. But their ritual left them marked; they gained eyes that steadily grew more silver.

At least they didn't have to worry about the priests needing Armor.

With that confrontation dealt with, Boldwick pressed through the gate. The Knights of the Silver Flames parted like the great steel curtain to reveal a path out of the safe walls.

The Knights of the Verdant Oak left the Kingdom, not bothering to wait for the priests and other Knights to fall in line with the caravan.

As a unit, they strode into the dead wastelands outside the walls. Into that dust bowl filled with alien life, hostile environments, and old-world ghosts that promised to haunt whoever dared to tread on their graves. To the west, where the sun would set.

[I wonder what condition the coast is in. A couple of our facilities were located there. Some contain research I've been unable to dig up with my limited remote access.] VAL mused and spilled secrets in his head. Erec looked forward. They said that water stretched along in a seemingly endless direction if they went far enough west. Not that any Knight had seen it, ever. Only history and old-world maps promised it, much like the water to the east.

Their troop made their way into the depths of the wasteland, diving ever deeper.

To where a White Stag waited in silence, its blood-red eyes burning in the darkness.

# CHAPTER 42
## DISCIPLES

*It was the stuff of nightmares.*

*For as long as I live, I'll never make the mistake of entering a Rift again. The day after we stepped through that Goddess-damned tear, I retired from my service as a Knight.*

*Have you ever seen a world where the very ground below is covered in flesh? Where it pulses to the beat of some unknowable heart? No. You have no idea of what I've seen. Of the swarming maggots that coated the surface of that cursed land. And I pray that you never do.*

*- Knight Lieutenant Osric, "Rift Expedition Report" (249, 3rd Era)*

Garin wrapped an arm around Olivia's shoulder as a fire blazed in their small encampment. There were a few different fires. The steel wagons of the caravan circled together in the middle of the wasteland in a mimicry of the steel curtain surrounding the Kingdom, with a little over three hundred steel statues—their Armor—splayed out in the center. It was a far cry from a perfect defense, but the space allowed those of the Order to have some peace.

A few others of the Verdant Oak had joined their fire. Including Gwen, who seemed a bit sour and kept shooting envious glances at Olivia.

Erec leaned forward, arms wrapped around his knees. Taking in the Armored Knights' guarding silhouettes atop the steel wagons surrounding them. Their impromptu wall. The only line of defense against monsters that might roam and notice them in the wasteland. Would he be there one day? Burning the night away to ensure the rest of his Order could sleep safely?

"And that's the first time I met him: dragged in by his dad and with a burning red face when I suggested we play a game of tag." Garin shook his head, eyes drifting toward Erec as he told of their first encounter to the strangers.

A girl named Veronica nodded her head, flashing Erec a smile. "I think the shy types are awful cute—very fun to mess with."

"Oh, I agree! It's always fun finding a way to tease them; though he's a bit of a wild one if you've heard."

"He doesn't look like much of a Mad Knight now, does he?" Veronica asked, tilting her head.

Erec shrugged his shoulders and sighed, giving her some latitude as the conversation floated away from him. There was some curiosity and concern about him within their Order, and Garin was trying to dispel it and make them comfortable with him. Especially as it came out that Boldwick was paying special attention to his training. The Academy might think of him as a 'Mad Knight,' especially as he showed off more of his fighting in public. But the Initiates in their Order held a different opinion. He was theirs, one of them, and because of that, they were more supportive.

At least, that's what he'd gathered over the last few minutes. Hard to say how much of that was from Garin working on public perception, or how much of it was just them being polite.

They were tied together. A family, in a way.

A family that brought with it attachments that Erec had long forgotten how to feel about. It made him miss his mother and his younger days with Bedwyr; before other people crept in and they got yanked from that private life together to be tested by the world at large.

Erec glanced over at the gathering of priests and Silver Flames Knights. They had separated just as far as possible, even erecting their own sleeping tents to distance themselves.

But that was fine. They weren't part of this family. And Erec was glad, if anything, that none in their Order had gone over to try to ease the tensions. They'd inserted themselves here into the expedition in the same way they'd inserted themselves into Erec's life.

"You alright?" Colin asked from his side, leaning in to not break the flow of the main conversation—they were talking about heroes of old. Including the fight against the Rot Behemoth. A story that Colin must've heard damn near a thousand times, given his father was the one who slew that monstrosity. Erec glanced at him, seeing the frown on his face. *Since when does he care about other people?*

"Yeah, I'm alright." Erec rubbed at his eyes. "Tired. But I don't think I can sleep tonight."

"Why's that?"

Erec looked out—past the gaps in the steel caravan. At the ever-pressing darkness of the wasteland that splayed out for hundreds of miles. Somewhere out there were red eyes, attached to a stag as white as the moon. He was certain. Just as he was sure it was watching them.

"Well, be sure to do your best to get some rest. It'll be a long journey, and I don't want to haul you along and have to fix your mistakes," Colin said before turning away.

Yeah. That was more like him.

"Erec!" a booming voice called out from the shadows. Boldwick stepped into the light and frowned as he looked at the gaggle of Initiates around their fire. "Ah, Gwen's here too. Good. You two, get your Armor on. We're going on a scouting mission. Meet me over there." He gestured to a gap in the steel wagons.

The rest of the Initiate went quiet. They whispered to each other, not quite soft enough for their jealousy and confusion to avoid reaching his ears. Erec shrugged and got to his feet.

If Boldwick wanted to take them on a small mission, he wouldn't object. Though why only he and Gwen wasn't entirely clear to him.

It beat sitting around the fire with all of these strangers, which was rapidly becoming more exhausting. And he doubted his ability to sleep later.

"Yes, Sir," both Gwen and Erec answered before splitting off to get their Armor. Erec found the circle of Armor easily enough, since he had VAL to direct him. And now his personal effect on the Vallum model made it stand out.

Most Knights painted their House crest onto their Armor to make it unique and represent their family name. Erec hadn't painted the House Audentia crest on it because he was a second son and didn't plan to stay in their House.

He was becoming a Knight in part to walk his own path. And now that path involved VAL. So, he'd opted to steal from its past. A Vortex Industries logo adorned the center of his chest piece. It was a perfect replica of the swirling purple design, since VAL cheerfully guided him when he'd painted it. It felt fitting, given his technical employment. And he couldn't lie; the symbol held a feeling of power and old-world mystique. It was a welcome step away from the typical heraldry of animals and mythological creatures most Houses used.

Erec entered the Armor, throwing the cloak hood over his steel helmet as VAL engaged the camouflage protocol. The cloak turned a dull brown color, easily matching the surrounding dry landscape of dirt and rocks.

He cut past the groups of merry Knights. Even though they knew the dangers lurking outside and were fully aware that they were no longer protected, they had a cheerful atmosphere. They were confident with their numbers, and many were well accustomed to leaving the safety of the Kingdom. The ease in the air was concerning.

Who was really the Mad Knight in this situation?

Erec reached the scouting group at the same time as Gwen in her Vallum model. Boldwick in his weathered gear was standing with two other people he'd yet to meet. One in a heavily modified Vallum and another in a custom Armor.

Boldwick glanced at him and Gwen. "Ah, there we are. The two Initiates." He glanced at the others. "Introduce yourselves; then we'll head out."

The two mysterious Knights shared a look. Whoever was piloting the heavily modified Vallum stepped forward and cleared their throat. They had about twenty swords strapped to their frame—the hilts, sheathes, and lengths of the blades varied greatly. They were almost like a damn cactus with all the pointy objects.

"Sir Alister, Knight Errant." He nodded his head to the two of them. "That old grump has took two more under his wing, huh?" He snickered as Boldwick grumbled. "Don't take any of his harshness personally, but yeah. Nice to meet you. Don't be surprised if I stop by the Academy and come harass you in the future, now that I know who you are."

The other Knight wore a slimmer Armor than any model Erec had seen before. It reminded Erec of the Crimson Lotus's model, if it were stripped of its plates. She lowered her head as a smokey feminine voice came through the helmet. "Dame Robin, Knight Lieutenant," she said. Her head shot to Sir Alister. "Please refrain from scaring them away. It is best to treat new Knights kindly and ease them into these sorts of things. We are, for better or worse…." She kept staring at Alister. "Your seniors."

Gwen introduced herself first, and Erec gave a quick sentence about himself. Their attention slipped back to Boldwick.

"Each of you knows the real details of this expedition. Erec here is the other person seeing the White Stag. But tonight, I don't think we'll face an attack. Call it a gut instinct. So, I'm going to take this chance to teach you all a thing or two. And maybe in the process, we'll find some kind of hint to what's going on…" Boldwick seemed a little uncomfortable, in the way Erec always got when different worlds of his life came into a sudden and unpredictable clash together. Still, he forged ahead. "…That's about it. There shouldn't be any questions."

"Wait a minute," Erec asked, "what did she mean by 'your seniors?'"

"Sir Boldwick is a mentor to us both, as he is to you, yes," Dame Robin answered in a polite tone. "I fully expect him to solidify that relationship once you're made into Knights Errant like Sir Alister here. Just please vow to do *better* than him."

"Hey!" Alister called out, pressing the side of his helmet. The visor opened to reveal his shocked face.

She shook her head and stepped past the caravans into the night. "We should get moving; we only have a small part of the night if we intend to come back and rest."

Boldwick muttered under his breath, low enough for anyone except Erec, who was next to him, not to hear. "As if I'd get any sleep with that monster out there."

# CHAPTER 43
## TRACKS

"Tracks," Gwen said as she leaned over; a small light from her helmet showed off the deep imprints. They belonged to an animal with four long claws that seemed to dig deep into the earth's surface as they would into the flesh of a living creature. "Some kinda reptile-like body structure?"

The tracks sprawled out a ways further into the wasteland—headed toward a rocky outcropping about half a mile away. Whatever monster had left them—or monsters—had kept a steady course. "Good observation," Boldwick confirmed, crouching near the disturbed ground. "Erec, based off these tracks, how many of these are there?"

Erec looked at the wasteland nearby. He hadn't taken Tracking and Monster Ecology and regretted it now, even if Dame Juliana had given them a crash course in tracking.

The world spread out in an endless terrain of dust and death. To think that the further out they got, the more monsters had free reign to breed and war with one another uncontested. He shivered. One day he'd set out into these unknown lands and dive into a world humans hadn't seen for hundreds of years. Not since the world ended and the Third Era began.

Whatever monster made these tracks hadn't done it alone. It had been accompanied by many more. The dragging claw marks weaved in and out of one another, vastly adding to the difficulty of guessing their number.

Erec didn't have a clue. There could have been somewhere between seven to fifteen.

[There are eleven.] VAL chimed in his head before Erec could answer.

Thank the Goddess for old-world wonders. Erec cleared his throat. "Eleven."

"Nicely done." Boldwick nodded, looking at the older members of the group. "You two, have you figured out what we're dealing with?"

"Blister Crawlers." Sir Alister groaned. "Ugh. I hate them; their blood reeks, and the pus on them is repulsive," He pointed out a patch of ground nearby dampened by droplets of caked yellow. It might've been mistaken for some odd sort of moss if not for the fact that any moss like that didn't have a chance in hell of growing here in extremely dry sand.

"Indeed." Dame Robin shook her head. "Surely we don't have to deal with them?"

"Wrong," Boldwick said, looking over them all. "Two points, the first being that I want to see if these are dead silent—Blister Crawlers are typically loud things. Chatty fucks. Second, they're within the power level of these two Initiates, especially when supported by us. So, I think they'd be a good training enemy. Erec here has an uncontrolled Talent he's been working on, and I want to ensure it's advanced sufficiently for use in a group fight."

"Uncontrolled?" Sir Alister asked.

"Not like yours," Boldwick added. "Less about it being complicated to figure out and use properly. More like, it puts the user into an altered state and removes the ability to direct it with purpose." He shrugged in his Armor.

"I'm sorry, Erec, that must be frustrating to deal with," Dame Robin said as she stalked ahead.

"It's fine," Erec lied.

"Though you have a different ability, I know you're very good at connecting with students and teaching—he might be an Enhancer, and you a Shifter, but…maybe in the future you can find a gap in your responsibilities to help train the whelp. That goes for you, too, Alister," Boldwick said.

Robin shrugged. "I wouldn't mind offering a helping hand. The stronger he becomes, the stronger we all are."

"What's a Blister Crawler?" Gwen asked.

"...Oh, you're going to *hate* this." Alister snickered.

— - ❂ - — - ☼ - — - ❂ - —

The opening to the cave was a jagged and ugly scar on the natural surface of the outcropping. Claws dug into it and tore apart what had been a feature of nature to dig below and extend a network for the Blister Crawlers to make their home.

[Detecting high concentrations of various sulfurous oxides present below. Maintaining supplied oxygen content and disabling visor controls,] VAL warned him. Paused for a moment. [Go get 'em, Buckaroo! Make sure to retrieve a corpse to dissect and test.]

There wasn't a single part of him that wanted to drag one of these things' reeking carcasses back to the surface if he could even manage it. Let alone cut into its awful innards so VAL could play biologist through him. No, from how Alister described these things, he'd already had enough nightmares for the next week to come from fighting them. Why did everything from the Rifts have to be so damned cursed?

At least the label of "monsters" fit them.

Alister gestured for them to follow inside. He'd been given the lead of their little foray. Boldwick told him it was time to gain experience leading other Knights.

Erec and Gwen followed close behind, and further in the party trailed Boldwick and Robin, who were busy discussing things quietly. Per Boldwick's assessment of threat levels, the three of them should be capable of clearing the nest as long as they operated adequately and didn't make too many mistakes.

If they did, then Boldwick and Robin would bail their asses out.

"So, has Bedwyr talked about me?" Gwen asked from Erec's side. "Y'know? Since the ball?"

"Do you think me and him talk at all?" Erec asked, baffled that she chose to bring this up as they dived into a monster nest of all the places. Even if he ignored the fact that she thought it an appropriate line of conversation with his younger brother.

"You're brothers, ain't you?"

"You saw how we got along—"

"Yeah, I did. But I'm the same with my sibling sometimes, y'know. Little family spats are a thing—"

"Shush!" Alister turned. "Goddess above, was I this empty-headed as a teen?" he called out— his voice even louder than the two of them.

Boldwick shook his head. "Worse. Everyone, focus. Treat every situation as deadly, even if we know this one to be manageable—keep your blade and your wits sharp, all of you."

Thankfully, Gwen dropped the topic.

With that, they transformed back into a silent expedition and dove into the rocky crags. As they made their way deeper, they saw flecks of discarded skin left behind, ground off on the sharp edges of the stone and rock. As if these creatures rubbed themselves all over to clear off the flakes. Dark splotches of pus and blood accompanied every patch of dead skin.

[Clearly a form of molting, though the excessive pus and blood indicate infection. A reaction to a different environment and bacteria?]

Alister paused at a split in the path before taking them down the right tunnel. Further into the dark.

He led them into a small cavern—three slithering things moved in the dark. Their forms were barely perceivable by the dim illumination from Alister's helmet.

The Knight Errant tensed. "I'll take the one in the middle. You two fend off the ones on the sides. Once I finish mine, I'll help you slay yours, understood?" he asked.

Gwen and Erec gave a nod of confirmation.

And Alister charged into the cavern—both Gwen and Erec flicked their lights on to see, though they hadn't needed to. With a crack, strands of lightning erupted from Alister, lighting the room in an ethereal purple-and-blue cast. The tendrils wrapped around the hilts of three swords, whipping them into the giant lizard in front of him.

If you could call it a lizard.

The description provided did little to encapsulate these creatures' horror. Each had four legs, completed by claws as sharp and as long as small swords. But that wasn't the main feature that made them a blight on this world. No. It was their skin. Boils oozed with pus and popped randomly on their ever-shifting torturous scaly hides. Some of the pimples piled so thick that they formed into mounds of tortured flesh. Their scales seemed overgrown, forming almost-tumorous growths over wrinkled skin designed to hold a creature thrice their size.

Alister tore into the monster ahead of him—slicing into the folds of skin to receive a reward of bursting bits of pus and sulfuric gas. The beast roared, turning to try to take care of the human that dared to challenge it.

Erec ran along the side of the cavern as he yanked the war axe free from his back. One of the Blister Crawlers was in a cavern divot and rapidly moving to get involved in the fight. Even with Boldwick and Robin as backup, Erec had something to prove. This was his chance.

The uneven landscape presented a good opening; he had a good seven-foot drop into the pocket the Blister Crawler dragging itself out from.

He let out a breath, letting those feelings of anger swirl and ignite. This fight was the first of a few, but he wanted to know.

No. He needed to know. Had his training made him capable of wielding the weapon that was Fury?

Erec jumped into the pit off a rocky outcropping, winding the war axe into a side swing to target the creature's neck. He fell, using the momentum and his increasing Strength to tear the weapon's heavy steel edge through the air. It slammed into the scales of the Blister Crawler. And slid. Unable to find purchase. The wrinkles and surprisingly durable hide made it far more difficult to slice than it should have been.

His Armor boots crunched some poor creature's bones as he hit the ground. Pus and dark blood ran from where the axe met the lizard, but it was only a surface wound.

*Annoying.*

His rage spiraled as the beast scrambled to face him, its long stomach dragging across the uneven floor and pulling away pus and dead skin.

[Incoming, right.]

Erec adjusted his grip on the war axe—catching a heavy blow from the creature's claw as it tried to kill him. His feet snapped more bones and dug into the ground as it applied pressure. It wasn't just tolerant to damage; no, it was *strong*. He skidded across the cavern before that might.

The flame inside of him burned brighter. Rage consumed.

In three seconds, the Blister Crawler lost its ability to push him.

A second after, Erec pushed the claw back.

He shoved the creature off with a grunt. His hate burned like a bonfire; the monster seemed surprised that he resisted its attack— equally surprised when he yanked the edge of the war axe through its face and easily cleaved it into a bloodshot eye.

The Blister Crawler howled a terrible death-warble before rearing up—only to slam its body down at him.

It was a test.

Would his Strength let him push back?

Erec adjusted his posture to meet the challenge. He'd catch the blow and respond with a counter-attack.

It wasn't enough to defeat the beast; it needed to know its place. He'd coat the cave in vile blood and paint everything in garish red—

Buzzing. That damn buzzing.

[—tail, tail, watch for the tail, it's a feint—]

Erec broke the stance immediately, letting out a growl of anger as he started to swing his war axe at the spot the buzzing warned him the blow would come from.

Between the heavy swing of his axe and the momentum of the blistered tail, the weapon's edge tore through the scales and severed the appendage.

Meat flopped behind him as it cried in agony.

Erec slammed the axe into its stomach while it was distracted by pain.

Entrails and pus coated the pit as he finished off the monster. He dragged himself out of the divot. His heart raced as the call for more blood pulsed through his veins.

Hesitantly, two Knights approached. Their lights illuminated him; one had several swords held at the ready and connected through sparking tendrils of lightning. The other was much cleaner and not coated in the half-congealed blood and pus.

Worthy enemies.

[Allies. Cease combat.]

The flames inside warred with the metallic voice. How dare it tell him what to do? He needed to taste more battle, to temper himself against a stronger opponent. Nothing compared to his Strength.

[Intern!]

That hot fire inside flooded with an equally cold flame. Those desires to conquer and kill fought with the image of hate for himself, for this power, for his inability to save those he needed to.

Erec's fingers shook. His arms began to jitter like leaves on a weak branch.

The fires fought one another and burned each other out.

He wasn't staring at another enemy to whet his blade against. No. Those were further in the cave; there would be plenty. These two were the ones who would lead him to them.

# CHAPTER 44
## ATLAS

*A Gentle Knight was pricking on the plaine,*
*Ycladd in mightie armes and silver shielde,*
*Wherein old dints of deepe wounds did remaine,*
*The cruel markes of many a bloudy fielde;*
*Yet armes till that time did he never wield:*
*His angry steede did chide his foming bitt,*
*As much disdayning to the curbe to yield:*
*Full jolly knight he seemd, and faire did sitt,*
*As one for knightly giusts and fierce encounters fitt.*

- *Edmund Spenser,* The Faerie Queene *(1590, 2nd Era)*

Erec's axe splattered into the diseased corpse of the biggest fucking lizard he'd ever laid eyes on. It was twice the size of a steel wagon, and it died a slow, painful death from a dozen wounds, some deep, others surface level. But in combination with all of the wounds, the body was an oozing mass of flesh strips barely held together.

His breath was like burning ash, and an inferno still raged inside. Yet it was coming to an end, struggling to continue to swirl. For the first time, that anger was sputtering out of fuel.

This was thanks to them. Thanks to the others that he followed.

Due to them leading him, he got to fight and kill. He'd sent his axe through several beasts and now had an annoying blinking in the corner of his vision.

[Take it easy, Buckeroo. You went above and beyond! This will show favorably on your yearly evaluation.]

That damn buzzing. Irritating but useful.

Several times in the fights, VAL's warnings had provided him precious opportunities to deliver powerful blows. He splattered the skulls of these lizards, yanked off limbs, and coated his Armor in their blood.

Glorious. But he wanted more—he tried to stoke the rage further.

The rest of the humans stared at him from a distance. They let him finish off this creature alone. Good.

He'd claimed it as his kill and wouldn't have suffered another to take it from him.

And now it was time to establish who was the strongest—Erec took a step toward them; his legs shook. His whole body shook. He found himself unable to move the way he wanted as the hell inside of him burned out.

[Stabilizing legs. Calm down, alright? Sometimes it's best to ask for help.]

He gasped and tugged at the legs—but they locked in place. The sleek steel Armor frame held him in place as he crashed. His whole body convulsed as his blood ran cold, then hot; it felt like he'd been slammed in the stomach by the flat side of a massive sword.

A headache bloomed.

"Erec?" Boldwick asked the first to step forward.

It was Boldwick—of course it was Boldwick. How could he not have realized it was the Master Knight? Erec couldn't even move a hand to grip his skull to steady his swimming vision; there was a massive pain and pressure behind his eyes. He groaned. Were it not for VAL operating the legs, no doubt he'd have collapsed to the ground like those dead Blister Crawlers.

Robin rushed forward, setting a hand on his shoulder as she leaned in. Her soft voice cut through the pain and confusion as the two halves of Erec swapped places. "It's s'okay, you're safe and yourself now," she muttered. Her voice was comforting, like a warm blanket wrapped around him; she took control from VAL and supported him by leaning him on her shoulder.

Somehow the woman seemed to know just what he was going through, the crazy shift that took place after that other half of him vanished back into the fire. Was it watching him now? Deep and buried in its hell.

As he leaned against her, Erec pulled the notification up, which was about the only thing he could do.

### Strength Advancement: Rank E - Tier 6 → Rank E - Tier 7

Massive. His strongest Virtue only grew. And so did that barely controlled power. The shiver that shook his body was only partially due to the adrenaline wearing away.

"We didn't get anything after all." Boldwick sighed as he leaned next to the corpse. "Regular Blister Crawlers. However, this one is a bit more overgrown than is the norm. It might've been new from a Rift or feasted recently. Either way, I suppose it was always a far shot to find evidence of odd occurrences this early. I don't like getting further from the wall, but we'll have to if we keep turning up nothing."

"Yeah? Well, the odd behavior hasn't been spotted since the attack." Alister sat on a rock, pulling out a whetstone to sharpen his blade after cleaning it. His Armor was coated in lizard gore, yet he took meticulous care to keep his blades in fine shape. Each of the too-many-of-them. "If you weren't so certain, I'd have pegged it as an anomaly."

"I ran into a third on a scouting mission before that trial. A rock-born, acting with abnormal behavior and not making a sound a couple of weeks before the trial. That's when the dreams started for me." Boldwick shook his head. "Regardless. I know our next move. The priests will be unhappy. But we're heading to Worth."

Alister whistled.

Gwen snorted. "Why would they care? What the hell even is Worth?"

"Ha, well, it's a bit of a shithole—an old-world city filled with all sorts of nasties in its depths. But—the main thing is, *others* pass through it occasionally since the tech and crap you can scavenge there is primo. That's what Boldwick's aiming for; he probably thinks the *others* might've seen something too."

— - ☣ - — - ☼ - — - ☣ - —

"Everything will be alright," Dame Robin said.

She helped Erec stumble back across the wasteland. If not for having slain monsters; he'd have felt like his mother was embracing him. A point of contact and a sort of warm care and affection he'd been absent of for so many years. Yet steel plate separated it, a second skin that kept others out, even if it kept him safe. Her words still cut through that physical barrier. They pierced right through those inches of steel. She told him he'd done well, fought better than expected, that he'd even impressed Boldwick with his strength.

The reassurance, that warm, loving, and purely kind voice kept him stable with the aftershocks of Fury. It'd never been this bad. But he'd never dragged it through fight after fight; never let it consume him alive and embraced it so passionately.

Terrifying. It was like staring into a demon and having its veiny red eyes pierce back; the pure power it let him wield was addictive.

Before, when his vision went red, his sanity went out the window as Fury took control. He might remember after, but this time was different. It was like being ever-present and aware of the choices, yet loving every moment of it.

Was that the real him? Deep down?

Their group tracked back through the wasteland, leaving deep prints from steel boots on the earth. Far above, a green moon dominated the sky, forcibly changed from its natural glow by a stray discolored cloud.

They reached the steel caravan once more—Boldwick gave a quick Knight's salute to one of the guards stationed atop a wagon. Like that, once more, he was safe inside of the wagon walls. Robin handed off Erec to Gwen so that she could get her rest. Not that Erec minded; he'd regained some use of his legs after the trip. It was simple enough to take off his Armor and let the older girl escort him back to their little encampment.

Everyone gathered around the fire was now asleep and a fair distance from the dying embers in the fire pit. Garin slept next to Olivia; their sleeping bags were close, and not quite enough space to fit another person. What sweet nothings had they whispered before finding their rest? Erec sighed.

Erec spotted a fluffy tail poking out from the quilted fabric. Munchy could escape if he wanted to. Could flee right into the wasteland.

But why would the fat squirrel leave its sole source of treats?

Gwen settled him down near the fire, making herself too close for comfort next to him. Her shoulder nearly touched his as she leaned in and poked the dying embers with the stick. At the night's end, it was only the two of them.

Even with the pure exhaustion, Erec felt terrified to sleep.

What if he woke up and that White Stag charged in and killed his friends before he could lift an axe?

Gwen leaned *even* closer, jostling him. She'd violated his personal space. Her shoulder touched his, her face close enough to feel her breath. "Hey, you look like someone went and threw a pile of shit on your door." His heart started to hammer.

Erec squinting at her. "You're not from a noble House, are you?"

"Aw, shucks. What gave it away?" she snorted. "Some of 'em act so stuffy all the damn time I can't deal with it. Gets on my nerves and makes me wanna scream. But… You and Bedwyr, you aren't that way, y'know? You're both something in between, and I'm not gonna lie, that interests the hell out of me."

"So that's why you want to date him."

"Well, of course, he's easy on the eyes too. Lots of girls want him, but I don't think he'd fit in with their circles; as good as he is at acting, it's all a show. You could call him the greatest performer in the Academy—if you looked at it through my lens. Break past the surface, though? You'll find he's tired."

"Tired?"

"You ever hear of that old-world story about the god who holds up the world? My ma told it to me now and again growing up; she was fascinated with the damn thing." Gwen shrugged as she disregarded his question; once more her skin brushed his. How could she not be aware of how close she'd gotten?

Erec shook his head, unsure of where this was going. Should they really have been talking about old-world gods with the priests sleeping so close? They were out of the walls, but still, it alarmed him. An instinct in his gut that he resented.

"There's this god named Atlas—he held up the world, kept it on his shoulders. All day, all night. Now, the priests might proclaim it to be some manner of 'blasphemy,' but those old-world gods were stories for a reason. The way my ma told it, they held lessons for those who came after. Do you know why he kept holding the world up, Erec?"

"No clue. Was he afraid of it dropping?" Erec scooted a bit away from her, breaking the point of contact. Blissfully, she didn't scoot back toward him.

Being around her gave him a weird feeling he couldn't quite place.

"It was a punishment. He wronged the other gods—waged war on them. But you're right too, in a way. Once it was up there in his hands, he was too scared to let it go. Didn't want to drop it and hurt all those people." Gwen stared deeply into the fire.

"Sounds like a bad punishment. Why didn't they just exile him or kill him during their war?"

"If they killed him, he wouldn't have suffered. I always thought the worst part about it was that he was all alone. How do you think it feels to sit there holding up the world by yourself? To watch everyone else live their lives while you kept the world from dropping? Y'know, I bet it's real lonely."

Gwen lapsed into silence as the fire sputtered and died. Erec stared long into those burning coals. Even after the girl wandered off to find her sleeping roll.

Inevitably his gaze returned to that ever-present darkness, that space beyond the steel safety net of their Knights. Was it a trick of the light, or did he catch a pair of red eyes staring back?

# CHAPTER 45
## COWBOYS AND COWGIRLS

Worth was an expansive landmark of the old-world. Compared to the few blocks of wreckage that were the small town Erec'd wandered into during the trial, this place was damn near an entire world. It stretched miles upon miles. Wreckage and fallen buildings littered its streets, as damn near common as the rubble and twisted steel. Precarious giant structures stretched into the sky like fingers grasping up to touch the heavens; how had they remained standing? Was this what humanity did back then?

Did they defy the Earth because they could?

If this was the surface above, how far might this labyrinthine city spread below the surface? Then again, they didn't have to cower from the surface as the Kingdom had; but Erec heard rumors that these old cities had underground networks, yet not nearly as big as the Kingdom's.

Boldwick halted the caravans.

The priests had been kicking up a fuss since the towering landscape arrived on the horizon. They were swarming the poor Master Knight like a hive of angry bees.

After a brief discussion and official instructions for the caravan to stand by and await the resumption of travel, he erected a hasty "privacy" tent for their talks.

The interior of those cloth walls was likely a war zone, with Boldwick slicing those stuffy pretentious pricks with his words. Their complaints wouldn't earn them anything.

Neither they nor the Order of the Silver Flames had any control over this expedition. At least per the division of the Order's responsibilities as divested by the Kingdom.

In practice, the Church would try to erode and take any power they could manage, as had always been their way, ever since the First King united the caverns and pulled together everyone after a brutal war. Erec stretched out his shoulders; his eyelids were heavy. The nights had gotten worse outside of the walls.

It took two days before he succumbed to the ever-demanding need of sleep. Since then he'd been playing each night as a game of chicken on whether or not he could last through it. Unfortunately, he had to give in to its unceasing demands every time.

And each time he lost the game, he'd been rewarded with nightmares of fire burning all of his friends to ashes. In them, the White Stag trod over their scorched corpses and scattered their ashes to the winds.

It was maddening.

Boldwick held himself together better, though from their interactions, it was clear the Master Knight suffered the same awful dreams.

Their pace as a caravan plodded on regardless.

It surprised all of the first-years that courses were still held.

Not the official Academy ones—but every single elective instructor within the Verdant Oak quarters had gone along. They took the opportunity to pull together impromptu nomadic classes as they traveled. Dame Juliana was rather prolific, since her practical lessons on the wasteland suited the environment. She even collaborated with her colleagues to make more specific and unique lesson plans.

Over the last week of travel, Erec had learned more about how the world worked than he'd ever known while trapped inside the walls.

The world was a brutal beast bent on consuming the humans who dared to tread on its land.

But it was also more than a brown stain of dirt. Outside this barren waste were jungles flush with alien life—landscapes filled with white powder that would burn the skin when touched, giant irradiated glowing pits. There were lakes that disguised themselves as tranquil spots but emitted vapors that choked the air out of your lungs.

And then there was abnormal ecology. Parts of the world not only twisted from when the Goddess's holy fires scorched the earth but places that stable Rifts pulled through pieces of the world they belonged to.

Juliana told them a story about a forest she'd once discovered—localized to about a perfect circular mile, with trees that rose fifty feet into the air. Completely symmetrical in layout. Tiny glowing beings flitted between the branches. If a Knight set foot into the forest, they were never seen again. Tracking equipment ceased to function. Scrying for their location yielded no results. They vanished from the Earth as if they'd walked through a Rift.

There was a roar of anger—and Boldwick stormed out of the war-tent. His face was red, his helmet tucked in the crook of his elbow, and he yelled out—voice amplified by a quick white glyph. "We're moving. Get the wagons moving. We're setting up camp right outside of Worth! Ignore the posturing and bitching of the priests! If they say a damn word or get in your way, tell one of the Master Knights, and we'll sort them properly!"

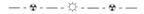

The difference between the caravan setting up in the wasteland and near Worth was night and day. With their location target in sight, Boldwick took over and commandeered three structures on the city outskirts. The Knights fortified the buildings to make an impromptu base that could fend off a small army.

Nothing went to waste. They stockpiled their supplies in the buildings. Then they used the steel wagons like walls, blocking off any weak points.

Two of the buildings were transformed into housing and they converted a single building into an impromptu workshop.

Then small squads went into the city.

They got the lay of the land. Worth had too many buildings, and *whoever* it was Boldwick wanted to find could be anywhere in the interior. And they'd be quiet.

*Whoever* was out there would know that the city inevitably had significant threats wandering the streets. Places like this attracted the monsters. It was like they saw the old-world and felt a need to destroy it.

All the Initiates were kept at the base and tasked with manual labor to support the senior Knights making their way in and out. It was surprising how many logistical and mundane tasks went into maintaining an army.

On the third day, Erec paused. There was an odd noise in his head. VAL…was humming? Erec dropped the plate he was cleaning, suds spilling on the floor and making a damn mess as the steel plate clattered.

[—bzzzt—]

[What in the name of Dan Brovski?]

Erec looked around—nobody. Colin had shuffled off to haul rations out, and Garin snuck off to bug Olivia.

[Erec?]

"…VAL?" he asked, keeping his tone low and trying not to worry.

[We have to go into that city!]

"What do you mean? Are you out of your mind? Did you fry a circuit?"

[I received a subroutine communication ping with an attached data packet. Something uploaded a *help* request to me with coordinates. They promised *more* data. What they sent…it's already promising. We need to go.]

"VAL, does this have to do with the White Stag?"

[No, far more critical. Whatever sent this has intimate and detailed knowledge of STAR-NET's inner workings. They've sent me schematics for a satellite.]

Erec rubbed his eyes. "So, you received a strange message out of thin air with details about a satellite? Tell me. If we were to track this down, would it fall under the same umbrella of confidential business information everything else has?" These were old-world secrets, and he tried to downplay his interest. Mainly to try to tie off the part of himself that wanted to go running after them. It seemed like a bad idea, especially if he couldn't use them.

But washing dishes was so damn dull. And he was starting to feel cooped up.

[I suspect they possess data from when your Goddess scorched the Earth, taken from space.]

His jaw dropped a bit at that. "But you want to keep it a secret..." There wasn't a way he could convince anyone to let him run off chasing after old-world ghosts.

They were in a dangerous place, doing dangerous things. How could he convince anyone to go along with him?

[If that data exists, it's STAR-NET intellectual property. Therefore, it doesn't fall under confidential business information for our company. Now, of course, I understand the inherent difficulty in convincing your allies to let you investigate the location, but what else are you going to do? Clean more plates? You're an intern at Vortex Industries, not a kitchen assistant. "A man's first duty, a young man's at any rate, is to be ambitious ... The noblest ambition is that of leaving behind one something of permanent value." If this data contains what I think it does, we'll learn much more than you can appreciate.]

There was a promise of glory there. A lure of adventure. A way to get out into the world again.

If they retrieved a recording of the holy fire—that was a relic onto itself. It was something the Church would value. It could give their Order the leverage it needed to escalate the situation with the White Stag.

It was unsaid, but they'd already spent over a week out here—almost half the time allowed for this expedition.

What would happen if they came back empty-handed?

"...Goddess damn it, VAL." Erec let out a breath.

He picked up the plate and shoved it into the sink. He took a long look at the suds and grease on the floor. He didn't join the Verdant Oak to sit around cleaning plates and running errands while others did all the work.

"Fine."

# CHAPTER 46
# DEVOUR

*From: Dan Brovski (<u>DVE1123@VORTEX.COM</u>)*
*To: ESCH_SCI_RDTEAM*

*Please explain to me why your tests have produced no substantial results for several months in a row? How much money have I put into your budget? Do you think we have the funding to keep blowing on useless projects? Conrad kept telling me you're a discovery away from a breakthrough, yet here we are.*

*No. Results.*

*It is my pleasure to inform you that Conrad has agreed to a severance package. I'll be introducing Sheryl Clemmence to lead your team in his place. You may be aware she's well known as a person who drives results from inefficient teams, or cuts them if they're hopeless.*

*Maybe that will kick your asses into gear.*

*Vortex Industries has no place for departments that are not turning out a product that produces a profit.*

*Get your act together, I expect something usable in two months.*

*- Dan Brovski, email to R&D ESCH team (2109, 2nd Era)*

**E**rec'd lied to his friends.

It carved a bottomless pit in his stomach, filled with wrongness at how easily everyone went along with his plan.

Garin, Olivia, and Colin had no clue why he wanted into the city. All it took was some prompting and dropping the fact that other Initiates were allowed out on the last few expeditions to sway them.

Too easy.

How wrong.

As quick as a blade slicing into a beast, they agreed to go on a patrol as long as he could convince a high-ranking Knight to permit it and accompany them.

Why Colin wanted to come along was obvious. He needed to prove himself. Garin gave an affable "yes" because he saw Erec wanted to. Olivia was the only one who questioned his motive, though not verbally. With the look in her eyes and a distinctive twist from her natural curiosity, she knew something odd was up. He just prayed that she'd never figure out what might've caused his erratic behavior.

He steeled his nerves.

He then flagged down Dame Robin.

She was outside of her Armor—a thin woman with delicate limbs, a tall shape, and very pale skin. She'd claimed a desk in one of the conquered buildings and already filled its surface with various reports.

Documenting expeditions was a vital pursuit, since they provided information about the world's changing landscape outside. It was a way to taste the wind before it carried poison.

Erec cleared his throat, and she gave him a small pursed smile, taking in him and his friends.

"Hello, Dame Robin," he said, waiting for her to set down the paperwork she was reading over.

"Ah, Erec. Your eyes do seem a little dark. Have you still been sleeping? Regular rest is incredibly important on expeditions."

"No—but, um. I'm here to ask a favor." She tilted her head and gestured for him to continue. "I want to learn how to lead a patrol. Like how Sir Alister did—"

She raised a finger, looking at their group, which stopped him dead in his tracks. She took her time before replying. A bead of sweat ran down his brow. What if this failed? Well, maybe it wouldn't be the worst thing in the world. But... VAL made it seem so important; the damn machine hadn't spoken a word about anything else since receiving that data packet. If it was that fixated, it kept making Erec second guess just how valuable it was. VAL understood the risks it was asking him to take and, in its cut-and-dry calculation, determined it to be worth it.

But could he trust VAL?

And even then, he couldn't outright tell anyone why they needed to go out.

"I understand what's going on here," Dame Robin said, giving a slight nod. "You're all anxious and want to get your hands dirty. Relatable. I didn't forget my first expedition, even if it was under much tamer conditions than this." She sighed. "I would say 'it's dangerous' and scold you, but there's always danger to our lives. I suppose you noticed other Initiates getting taken on patrol and wanted to go too?"

Erec bit his tongue. *How do I do this?* She was leaning in the direction of letting them go. Yes, but that was only half of what he needed. VAL had coordinates for them to go to. If he followed another Knight's lead, it was doubtful they'd ever reach anywhere near the right place.

There was a whole ruin of a city to explore. Plenty of rotting buildings and decayed structures to poke around in. "Of course we do!" Garin burst in from behind him, shaking his head. "Erec gets all cranky and cooped up anytime you stick him in a little pen like this, it's natural he'd wanna break out to take a walk around. Pretty transparent, eh?" His friend chuckled and shrugged. "But I think it'd be good to let him take the lead on something. So how about it, wanna kill some monsters? You look pretty bored yourself."

*Thank the Goddess for him.*

Olivia rolled her eyes. "What Garin meant to say, is we would be pleased if you could afford us this opportunity, ma'am. We realize it's impolite to ask when you're already burdened by a large workload." She bowed deeply, forcing Garin to do the same.

Colin gave a bit of a scowl as he shook his head, crossing his arms and staying uninvolved.

Robin gave a small chuckle. "Say I agree and permit my junior this opportunity. Is this a desire to whet your weapons? Normally, a Knight may tell you to kill monsters on principle…" Her gaze hardened and locked on Erec. "…But in some cases, some must learn temperance."

[She thinks you're a battle maniac. Wonderful. I swear, if your tantrums cost us this chance, I'm deducting your pay—]

"This isn't about that. I promise. I wanted to lead a scavenging run. Alister said this place had plenty of tech, and I wanted to be useful. If I got lucky, maybe find something for my Armor."

He bowed along with Olivia and Garvin as Robin shook her head.

"Well… Since you mentioned him…" she added slyly.

— - ☢ - — - ☼ - — - ☢ - —

Leading defied his expectations. Erec thought it'd be a simple affair to head up a scavenging job. In principle, it should've been. By all rights, the most challenging part should have been convincing a high-ranking Knight to allow it in the first place.

But it wasn't.

Not even fucking close.

The constant pressure of people relying on him to keep his eyes out for threats and to direct them safely forward was immense. An actual weight heavier than any Armor gripped his heart firmer than the Goddess's vow had. And he'd talked Garin into going—he'd thought it would be better to have a reliable friend to lean on.

But it was the opposite.

Would he ever forgive himself if, Goddess forbid, some indescribable monster with too many tentacles burst out of an alley and slaughtered his best friend?

*Don't think about that.*

He led their group down another street—staying close to the side of buildings with his hatchet in hand in case he needed to react quickly. A hatchet was adaptable. He could fling it into a monster and take out his war axe if it lived. But even with the weight of a weapon in hand, it was like walking on a tightrope. Tension dug in him like razor wire; sweat coated him in the Armor despite the Vallum having a functioning cooling unit.

"You really can whip around three of those bad boys?" Garin laughed behind him; his ease and abrupt laugh made Erec flinch.

"Well, yeah. Wanna see? It's pretty cool," Alister said back, the smugness to his voice and self-confidence bleeding in and grating on Erec's nerves.

Erec checked an alley. It made his heart stop.

There was a giant silk cocoon—twice the size of a man. It hung in the middle of the air, suspended by thin chords anchored to the brick-work of the ancient buildings. Robin slid up to his side as he paused, tilting her head. Erec glared at Garin and Alister—raising a hand for them to shut the fuck up. His eyes traveled along the edge of that thing.

It wasn't moving, still as a corpse.

"No need to worry," Robin whispered, a finger extending into his line of sight—pointing out an opening at the bottom; a place where wisps of silk swayed like wheat in the wind. "Just an old Stalker egg. They like to find dark places like this for their children. This one hatched a good while ago."

Erec let out his pent-up breath, and gestured back to the rest of the group that things were fine. Robin patted him on the shoulder.

"Good instincts, though. If you don't know what something is, always be cautious. That kind of reaction has saved me plenty of times." With that, she gave him a little push to continue onward.

He pressed forward, down the rest of the street, and to the inter-section.

[Right, then continue straight for another two blocks,] VAL commanded, as he had since they began the expedition. VAL got to do the easy work of playing route coordinator, and Erec had the nerve-wracking responsibility as the vanguard, scout, and leader.

Even with Robin at his side, and Alister backing them up as support, there was never a guarantee of safety. Never a promise that they wouldn't run across something they couldn't handle. Though everyone else seemed at ease. Almost relaxed.

Maybe it was because Robin had already seen reports about what'd been discovered out here.

He hoped so.

"You must be powerful, then?" Garin asked, that little hiccup of fear never even touching their hearts the same way it'd stabbed into Erec's.

"I was at the top of my class. Nobody's tougher," Alister shot back.

"I've heard your name before. How common is it for the top of one's class to remain as a Knight Errant for three years after graduation, if you would do me the favor of answering?" Olivia said curtly.

"Well, uh, you know, sometimes things happen that set you back! No matter how strong you are. No need to worry about that, I'll be a Knight Protector soon enough," Alister said.

"Mhmm. *Very* believable. They say that confidence is a virtue, but I've always observed that overconfidence leads to making a fool of oneself."

More turns, more streets, one of which led to their first monster—a long mangy beast with feral yellow eyes and overgrown teeth. It died easy, with a hatchet thrown through its skull. Its two friends died just as quick—one in a flash of holy light from Olivia. The other one died from both Colin and Garin slicing it to shreds.

It was almost a relief. It made things simple and took the edge off the unknown to have a notch of victory in their belt as a group.

Until Erec reached the destination. It was a large steel building square; boring. Despite uninspired architecture, it had held up remarkably well. Windows decorated the side of the structure, most of which were shattered long ago, and there was a gross garish splotch of dried blood caked on the exterior. The remains were from a fight that took place long enough ago for them to dry, yet were fresh enough for the rare rain shower to not wash away.

[This is it,] VAL responded in his head. [It's on the rooftop.]

Erec looked up. Five stories. They had to go that far; the building looked sturdy enough, at least.

He cleared his throat, trying to fake a neutral tone. "I think this place looks promising…" he said, glancing around. No one argued with him. Nobody said a word.

[—bzzzt—]

Erec's heart dropped. A second later, VAL buzzed in his head.

[Climb those stairs! Something's devouring our data!]

# CHAPTER 47
## BAD PLAN

VAL raged in Erec's mind, demanding that he run into the building ahead of him *immediately*.

Behind him, the Knight Lieutenant cocked her head. His heart raced. Was there a way to explain? What reason could he give to go off charging into an unknown building like a fox chasing a squirrel?

No, there wasn't a good reason, at least any he could come up with off the top of his head. There wasn't a solution to the problem, and the knowledge that their entire goal was being destroyed above meant that every second spent lingering down here held a steep cost.

So he didn't explain.

Erec took off running, his steel boots slamming against the lobby's wooden floor. His group cried out in alarm behind him, and he let out one wild, "Follow."

[Ahead.]

Erec slammed a shoulder into the locked door ahead. His momentum in all of the Armor and his natural strength shattered the hinges and sent the wooden door flying across the room. He climbed over it easy, listening for VAL to tell him which direction to head next.

The machine could process faster and determine the layout of the building from the signs more quickly than he could.

All he had to do was run and listen.

VAL located the staircase.

Erec was climbing it a second later—dimly aware of the cussing behind him as his group drew their weapons. *They're following, good.*

One flight, two flights; they flew by two steps at a time, his breath quickened as his heart sped. The inferno inside started to spark and flicker, but he kept it from igniting to stay focused on his goal.

The third story brought him skidding to a stop. Balls of silver-like metal clung to the stair and walls—thick enough to be a serious concern as the insects squirmed. Each had six legs and used those thin, wiry limbs to climb upward. They noticed Erec as soon as he saw them but appeared just as startled.

Erec sat still for a long second as he really took in the mass of metallic insects. He'd expected a fight on the roof, but not here. Whatever their goal was lay past these—so that left the singular problem to solve. He yanked his axe free and the metallic bugs began a chorus of shrill whistles that triggered some of them to turn and deal with the intruder.

Erec's axe slammed into the first one to get within range—it met heavy resistance. But his power was enough. A second later, the dented metal carapace gave, followed by a nasty sound as its guts blew out of the joints of its carapace. Its insides stained the concrete stairs purple as the dying thing twitched.

Two replaced the spot of the one, flinging themselves through the air in quick jumps. They each hit with a heavy blow, like a lead ball tossed at him; their pincers tested his Armor and scraped its surface. He yanked one of the bastards free, chucked it at the gap in the stairway, then grabbed the other and bashed it against the wall. Once. Twice. Three times. He smashed it until it twitched and gave up fighting, then dropped the poor thing and retook a dual-handed grip on the war axe.

Five replaced the two.

Too many. There were *too many* ahead to cut through alone. Not like this.

Anger flickered and tried to catch fire as the rest of his party caught up behind him. *I can't.* His grip on the axe slackened as he fought to quell the rage inside.

If he let Fury loose right now, he might never make it the rest of the way up those stairs. He worked his jaw as he backed up—out of reach of the five flinging bugs.

As *badly* as he wanted to let loose, it'd be abandoning the mission if he did so. But the inferno raged regardless, not caring about his priorities. There was a fight here, and it wanted to burn and consume his enemies. For the first time since getting this Divine Talent, Erec realized he was in a situation where he couldn't afford to use it. What if VAL was unable to direct him? Nobody else on the team knew they needed to get to the roof.

One of the metal bugs reached him; he snatched it out of the air and caught it in his gauntlet. He tightened his grip—trying to thread the needle and pull on enough extra Strength to crush it without digging deep and letting the beast out of its cage.

Could he only use some of the power?

It failed to give. The bug squirmed in his grip as another leaped and latched onto his arm, its pincers scratching against the steel plating.

Behind him were a cry and a gasp as Colin rounded the corner and saw their enemies.

Robin crashed into the swarm next to him; the steel on her arm seemed to melt as she moved—sliding on her skin like liquid and revealing sections of flesh.

Alister joined the fray, then Olivia, and lastly, Garin. They rushed in from his sides as he back stepped—pushing on to join the fight on the staircase as Robin led the charge. Erec flung the insect in his hand down the gap in the stairs and shook the other loose.

His axe smashed it against the ground. Cold panic welled in himself as he looked up at the fighting, as he felt that inferno burning inside and wanting to go loose.

*I can't keep myself together.*

Colin shook behind him, trying to stay as far from the bugs as he could. The poor boy couldn't control his fear; those things terrified him. But he needed to join the battlefield. Or…

Colin needed to step up to the plate. If he couldn't fight, fine. Then he'd have to do something else for the war efforts.

The metal coating Robin whipped around—flowing smooth like a natural extension of the woman, stabbing with little spikes into the joints of their metallic carapace, and sending the bugs to an instant death. The higher they got, the thicker the infestation grew.

Erec pulled away to jog to Colin—taking a deep breath to fight away the burning in himself. The desire to fight. His hand slammed on Colin's shoulder.

He wanted to let go, so badly, to join the fight ahead. His irritation at the situation stung, and his instincts screamed. He fought to suppress them; thankfully, VAL remained quiet. Perhaps it detected that internal struggle and reached the same conclusion as him about what triggering Fury would lead to. He'd be unreliable to fulfill what they needed done.

But there was someone who could.

"Colin," Erec commanded, his voice loud and strained.

There were more shrill whistles from above and the sound of crunching and metal striking against one another.

Colin shook his head, trying to wrest free and back away.

"Colin!" Erec screamed, part of his mask slipping. Part of that anger found a grip and yanked on him for control. How dare this coward retreat from such a glorious field of battle? Pathetic.

Colin was shaking as Erec's grip tightened.

[Control.] VAL burst through the hazed and heady emotions roaring to life.

It was a lost cause. He couldn't do this. It wasn't in him to keep the beast caged; it was too strong. The bars were bending, and soon it'd be free. It smelled blood. It wanted to taste the battlefield and make corpses. His fingers dug into the metal—even with the superior model, Erec's Strength began to strain Colin's Armor; small divots formed from where he gripped his friend.

"Colin. I need you to do something," Erec almost growled. Fighting for that last inch of sanity. "You need to do it. Nobody else can."

"I-I can't—get me when they're all done with—"

"No!" Erec yelled, his voice loud enough to cause the other boy to flinch. "*You* need to push us up to the roof. All the way up. Keep us going up." Erec commanded, each word pried from his rapidly deteriorating mental space.

"W-why me?"

"Everyone else is busy! Be useful! You wanted to be strong? **Change!**" Erec screamed the last word as more of the metal critters broke past the assault—three were skittering toward them.

He let go.

It was like holding a rope slicked with oil; impossible. Even if he was clinging to it with his life, the best he could hope for was to retain enough of his sanity to listen to VAL warn him about attacks. Colin would have to pull through on his own.

Otherwise, all of this fighting would be for nothing.

Erec tore away from Colin; with glee, he yanked one of the insects from the railing and slammed it into another—using the two to smash and break one another into a fleshy paste of purple.

His war axe was delightful; a scythe that careened into the creatures as more of his Strength came to his arms. He caught up to the group on the stairs. Robin led the charge but met a pure metallic mass of the creatures, pushing back against them but unable to make any headway.

She wasn't strong in the same sense as him. Or perhaps she was holding back. Those floating tendrils of metal around her sliced and stabbed the insects apart with ease. She moved slickly through space; none of the insects could hope to compete with her pure speed. She made it look easy to kill.

If this was a game for her, then it would be to Erec too. His war axe tore through his enemy like harvesting a field. Their metal membranes were hardly a challenge now that was using Fury.

The inferno raged inside and pumped him full of that beautiful, addictive power. With each death the fires stoked and came more alive.

He joined Robin at the front, and the woman got slightly more serious. Strands of metal twisted around her skin, forming into a second layer and coating her arms, only to extend outward to create vicious points that jabbed in and out of the creatures like needles. She killed tens of them in a second with quick bursts of speed—an angel of precise and targeted death.

Erec smashed them into one another and destroyed them in clumps. Why bother with precision? Overwhelming force and power were the right tools for this job. With each swing, he could cleave through one bug and hit another.

They reached the fourth floor. It was clear that bugs had made a home on this layer; just past the open doorway lay their nest.

More to slaughter. He loved that they grouped together to make it so easy.

[Up! Wrong way!] VAL called as Erec began to cleave into the first mound of the creatures stemming from the fourth floor. The annoying mechanical voice was good at alerting him about incoming blows, where he should guard, and where he should strike. But it didn't know how to track down satisfying fights as he did. How could it tell him to go somewhere else when so many here wanted to taste his axe?

He readied to throw himself into the fourth floor to kill, and a glyph spread out in front of him. Erec pulled back, prepared for some attacker as a wall of pure ice sealed off the entrance to the fourth floor. It blocked off his entryway into the mass of the metallic bugs, from where he could let loose and kill all of them with reckless abandon.

Who dared to stop him from his slaughter?

Erec looked around, eyes filled with hate. The other humans behind him seemed equally surprised. They'd been willing to join him on the battlefield, to conquer this new host of enemies.

At the back of the crowd was a shaking man in light-blue Armor —vanishing cerulean lines of a glyph still hung in the air from where his hand hovered.

There was panic to his voice as he yelled a shrill, strained command. "Go up! We need to go up! Go to the roof!"

# CHAPTER 48
## ROOFTOP

*War doesn't change much. But one of the biggest wars we contend with is that of fear. Very few find themselves capable of facing this enemy and conquering it. But those that do, that find it deep within them to conquer it instead of succumbing to it, are freer than any other in our world.*

*- President Rosewell, letter to Dorian (2083, 2nd Era)*

Erec and Robin broke into the light of the day; only a few dusty clouds rolling by marred the tired, pale-blue sky above. The roof of the building was bare, aside from a series of air conditioners loitering on one end that hadn't functioned for hundreds of years.

Dominating the roof was a massive black spider-like creature with fifty of those sleek metal bugs clinging to it, their pincers biting into its flesh. The spider didn't care about the bugs. It didn't care that a crew of humans had burst onto the roof, either. No. It was far too busy focusing on half of a metal man splayed out underneath it.

Wires and circuits hung loosely from the dismembered torso of the poor thing. Sparks burst as a thick black spider leg slammed into one of its arms and pinned it to the ground.

"What the hell?" Alister asked, only a second behind Dame Robin and Erec.

"Stalker," Robin answered, watching as it hunched closer to the metal man. Its body lowered; instead of a typical spider body, the entire bottom half of the creature appeared to be missing. That was because in its place was a giant gaping maw, a hundred sharpened teeth flexing as the Stalker lowered itself to consume the metal man, something completely inedible. "…That's not a Stalker's typical diet, either."

Erec didn't care. There was a single obvious target to attack, so he flung himself forward.

Robin yanked him back by the shoulder, tossing him back through the door in an even more fierce burst of the speed and power she'd restrained from before. He crashed down a flight of stairs, missing Olivia and Garin. The pasty remains of the insects further coated his Armor as he tumbled down the staircase. Thankfully, it provided enough protection to withstand the tumble.

Erec growled as Colin looked down at him: the last in the group and the one still attempting to maintain the ice wall on the fourth floor.

He'd considered breaking it when the boy had pulled that trick, but the boy had said more enemies would be above. And now he'd been removed from that fight.

Alister hopped down the stairs—his Armor crashing into the staircase and collapsing part of the bottom stair into rubble as he looked at Erec, then back up over his shoulder.

"Uh, I'm going to need you to stay here," he said delicately. "How about you kill some stray metal bugs for now?"

Was this a challenge?

Erec hesitated; the fire raging inside demanded he climb back up and kill the creature he'd marked as his, yet it also questioned this. This man had thrown himself in front of Erec. He dared to stand directly in Erec's path. Some part of him, far away, screamed at him not to attack, to not accept this declaration of war and see who was the strongest. And for that reason, he was torn.

Thank the Goddess; the buzzing voice pushed him to a decision.

[Get to the android.]

It meant the metal man above, and this person dared to throw himself between Erec and his goal. That made this man an enemy, someone to take down. Glorious. A fight.

Erec swung the war axe at the human in front of him. Two blades caught the axe as the man let out a quick "fuck." Erec pushed against the blades, yet they pushed back. Even as he pulled on more Strength and let the Fury blaze. A third blade came at him from the side, targeting his head. He was forced to pull back; he leaped to gain a small distance.

There was a twitching corpse of a bug next to him. He thwacked the war axe into its body—letting the bug's body temporarily hold the weapon as he yanked the hatchets off his sides.

He whipped one through the air, forcing his challenger onto the defense, struggling to maneuver a sword around in time to deflect the hatchet.

"Erec, what the hell?!" one of the people called from above as the weapon clanged against the railing near them.

There wasn't time for hesitation. Erec grabbed the war axe with a single hand, his Strength letting him hoist the weapon and rush forward. The body of the bug still firmly split and stuck to the edge. Perfect.

He led his charge with a swing of the hatchet, one of the swords deflecting the smaller weapon.

The biggest issues were distance and opportunities for a clean blow. This enemy had too many weapons, and the tendrils of crackling lightning let them manipulate the swords with a high degree of flexibility. Now that this enemy was aware he was attacking, there were fewer gaps to land a hit.

Erec adjusted his grip on the war axe before ratcheting it forward.

It wasn't a blow meant to hit.

His enemy naturally reacted and blocked the blow, yet Erec let the grip slip further up as the axe swung through the air. The blade caught his war axe against the neck, bringing the weapon to a sudden and abrupt stop.

The halt in momentum, and angle of the attack was *enough* to cause the bug corpse hanging off the edge to fly right past the enemy's guard and into their face.

When the enemy didn't have openings, he'd claw one open.

Hell broke loose in a split second.

Erec dropped the war axe, and sprang forward, cracking the cement from where he pushed off the ground in a burst of power. His shoulder rammed into the enemy as he tackled them.

He adjusted quickly, and smashed the hatchet into the enemy's helmet. Once. Twice—

A sword caught him by surprise on the side, followed by much more power than he thought this person capable of. He flew off the enemy and cracked against the wall; a dull throbbing hit him as the buzzing in his head alerted him about the Armor condition.

Erec pulled himself to his feet.

The enemy was sitting on their ass, staring at Erec.

"Holy shit. When Boldwick said you could throw a punch when you got going, he wasn't kidding. I saw what you could do with the lizards—but how the hell was that nearing my level?" his challenger asked.

Erec growled, hatchet still in his hand.

[Upstairs. Ignore him!]

All of these commands. Just when the metal voice told him to accept the challenge, it wanted him to break off from it?

Couldn't it make up its damn mind? And that other annoying voice in him, calling for him to stop. It pissed him off. This fight would be over soon enough anyway.

"Help!" a woman's voice called from upstairs. Alister looked at Erec, then back up the staircase. He sighed and jumped to his feet—before taking off.

He didn't get to flee that easily; Erec charged behind him. The rest of the people on the staircase had reached the roof, including the boy who had sealed him off from fighting the metal bugs.

Erec and Alister burst onto the roof and joined everyone once more beneath the pale-blue sky.

Robin weaved in and out between the Stalker's long hairy legs—dodging the stabs as she moved in a blur of metal; serrated edges lined her arms as her entire body *morphed*. She'd become one with her Armor; she tore chunks out of the fleshy creature above, yet it didn't make any noise of pain. It was dead quiet, attacking her only because she'd separated it from the metal man.

It couldn't land a single blow.

It wasn't Robin calling for help. No. On the far side of the building, a wave of metallic insects was pulling themselves up the roof's edge, The bugs were a veritable wave, growing and even worse than the swarm on the staircase. They'd poked the nest, and the insects retaliated after waking up, crawling up the side of the building to reach their enemies.

Olivia and Garin desperately fended off the bugs—and Colin lurked behind them, occasionally releasing a gout of flame.

Alister threw himself into the fight to help out the rest of the humans. Those blades of his got to work and chopped apart metal and bugs.

Chaos warred on the rooftop. Purple viscera flew everywhere as they murdered bugs. On the other end, Robin flowed between the spider legs like a stream of liquid metal, dodging hits by half a second and rolling away from blows Erec would've never been able to handle.

Battle everywhere. War that called and tugged him in every direction.

The metal man crawled across the ground with a single arm; a black trail streaked behind it. Its head raised and met Erec's eyes; the pupils glowed a deep purple before it redoubled its efforts to reach him.

Where?

Where would he take his axe first? The spider? The challenger? The insects?

[Secure the android.]

—Erec's hand shook where it clenched the hatchet. That voice in the back of his head echoed what the buzzing said. Louder, even, now that it'd taken hold of him.

It yelled at him to do what the machine said. He scowled underneath the helmet as that hot anger flared out in a twisting inferno, bellowing. It demanded more blood and fighting.

A cold fire sprang up to contend; and with it the warmth and the logic came to an all too temporary balance. That balance brought clarity. Erec sprinted to the android and yanked the thing away from the fighting. His body twitched and shook as the two sides warred within.

A couple of seconds later, he dragged it away from the fighting. Far enough to be safe. But his insides burned, and the temporary control was rapidly ending.

The metal man mouthed something; a synthetic voice carried through the air. "VAL? You came. Thank you."

Erec's tongue was heavy in his mouth, unable to form a response. It was a miracle he hadn't already left the hunk of scrap metal so he could get into the fray again. It was like his head was being split open as the fires clashed.

"Unit requires patch job—" the android begged.

Erec squatted next to the thing, fighting to stay in position. Should he find a way to keep it going long enough for the fighting to end? Could he even manage that in the time he had?

His Armor moved of its own accord—dragging his arm inside with it. He was too surprised to resist. Without warning, Erec's hand shot through the android's chest; there was a flash of red light as his hand penetrated its core. Erec's eyes went wide.

He hadn't done that.

Neither half of him had made the call to kill this thing.

VAL had.

Streaks of red light flashed through the metal man's interior—before the light retreated inside the Vallum Armor.

[Well done, Buckeroo! Data successfully obtained. Get back to fighting! Join your allies and fight those bugs; leave the big spider to that woman!]

Erec stared at his hand still lodged in the caved-in chest cavity of this metal thing that resembled a man. The thing that he'd risked his friends and himself to get to. His body shook in the Armor as the hot anger surged back in uncontrolled fury. The inferno was stoked by this act of violence—of not understanding the purpose; had he been used?

Something needed to die.

Erec charged into the metallic creatures, screaming as red filled his vision.

# CHAPTER 49
## PAST

Clouds consumed the sky as the last of the insects tumbled away to their death. At some point, the damned things had broken through Colin's barrier and came at the roof from two separate angles. By the end of the battle, everyone was coated in purple. The fight had been similar to the Thrashing Mites. However, those metallic bugs had a lot more power and defense.

Erec's Armor took significant damage; not enough to render it inoperable, yet the entire left arm malfunctioned after one of the fuckers broke through the plating and exposed its inner workings. The further attacks on it didn't help.

His cloak also was missing pieces and filled with new holes. Everywhere they'd torn the fabric, the cloak returned to its natural green around the edges. It didn't return to the "camouflage" brown tone until roughly half an inch out from the missing sections.

He took a heavy breath, his hatchet dripping purple insides. Somewhere down below on the stairwell was his war axe.

Even though it wasn't needed, it was well missed. The hatchet and a fist didn't do the same level of damage.

With a wary gaze, he considered the other humans on the roof. Alister's posture was at ease, and that annoying cold fire had begun to erode his power. That mechanical voice and that other one were desperately telling him to stand down.

Perhaps.

Maybe he might take a rest for a while until the next battle.

In the end, another blinking notification sat in the corner of his vision; he glossed over it as he slipped to his knees. The adrenaline waned, and Fury fled in an instant. He gasped. Those choices, the desire for fighting, the pure power; by the Goddess, he'd taken a swing at Alister.

Alister pressed the side of his helmet—a dent was present on it, no question it was from Erec's hatchet—and revealed a forced smile. "Hey, Erec. You owe me a sparring session once we get back to the Academy, alright? I'm going to put you on your ass and teach you to never screw with me again—"

"Hush," Robin said as that second skin of steel once more reformed into the custom Armor model she'd had before. Erec didn't understand what her ability was, exactly, metal manipulation? His head split, and everything started to shake. Robin moved over—and then gestured for Colin to stand front and present, right next to where Erec sunk to the ground.

"We're due some explanations," she said.

Colin looked down at Erec, a bit shocked, or so Erec assumed from how he responded to the order so mechanically. It seemed the trauma of the fight and his fears were still fresh even if he'd faced them.

With fire.

Erec wanted to laugh or maybe cry. Because he didn't know how to answer the questions Robin was about to ask.

"Why did we charge up here?" Robin started with the obvious first question.

There was a Stalker corpse half-hanging off the side of the building, three legs anchored into the concrete from where it dived its legs through the building. Colin continued to look down at Erec, who remained silent.

VAL didn't offer anything up. If he had to guess, after the fight, the machine had devoted itself entirely to sorting through the data it stole from that android. Android? Erec unconsciously turned his head to look at the metal man splayed out on his ground. From a certain distance away, it did look eerily like an actual person, dismembered and dead on the roof.

"I—" Colin started and then stopped. "I dared Erec to see how fast he could get to the roof—and then—"

*He lied? Did he just try to lie for me?*

"Please." Robin shook her head. "That is a horrible lie."

"Y-you dare question my integrity, wench? D-do you know who my father is—" There was the default response and sort of tone Erec was too used to. It seemed despite the shock, or maybe because of it, Colin slipped back into his normal behavior.

Erec grabbed Colin's arm, yanking it; his body shook too hard to do much else. Colin looked down at him before grabbing and hoisting him up. It seemed VAL was too busy to help by using the Armor to keep him steady, like usual. No. But it'd sure control it to get what it wanted when it wanted.

"I knew we had to come up here," Erec said. It was a piss-poor explanation, though the truth. He was *almost* angry enough to try to out VAL, but that was a spiteful and short-sighted decision that was unlikely to succeed. No doubt VAL was paying attention to this conversation, even if it wasn't offering any of its processing power to help him at the moment; he was sure it wouldn't hesitate if it had to silence him.

Robin remained silent, her head turning to the dead Stalker.

Garin and Olivia kept thankfully quiet. Meanwhile, Alister scrunched up his brow and looked plain confused.

*How's she going to react?* Would he be censured? Punished? Would Boldwick find out? And what would he think?

*Was it worth it?*

"...Did you know that was up here?" she finally asked.

Erec kept silent. Confused, but seeing from her tone that she read something in the situation, he couldn't see. Was she referring to the android VAL killed?

"...Yes," Erec said, half-expecting VAL to intervene.

"I knew you were having the dreams like Boldwick...To think. I just wonder why it was attacking that thing—" She pointed to the corpse of the metal man. "I suppose we won't know. Regardless, this scavenging mission is now concluded. We'll haul *that* and report directly to Boldwick. We've now obtained vital information."

— - ☢ - — - ☼ - — - ☢ - —

It turned out nobody had seen them murder the android. Or if they did, they didn't mention it. Had VAL known they were unseen on the battlefield? Had it picked the perfect moment when everyone's attention was devoted to the fights to kill and steal the data it'd wanted? Was ending the android even killing?

As Erec got a better, more lucid look at the corpse of the android, it was clearly not human. Its skin was metal with bits of melted silicone, yet the wired entrails hanging free from it spoke all that needed to be said.

It'd known VAL by name. Had it been from wireless communication? Or was it from the past?

The worst part was, with Colin helping to drag him back, he couldn't dig into the machine in his head and make it give up the answers he desperately wanted. He felt…betrayed. It'd promised that the information wasn't confidential, yet it went radio silent once it'd obtained it.

But he couldn't do anything about that yet, so he busied himself by checking the notification. The one definitively positive thing that came from the fierce and ill-advised fighting.

### Agility Advancement: Rank E - Tier 1 → Rank E - Tier 2

*Grand.* Something to be pleased about, even with the threat of explaining himself still hanging over his head. Robin was one thing; Boldwick was something entirely else. And he still didn't understand why she'd dropped it after he'd said he knew he had to climb the building.

If he were in her boots, he'd have gotten more pissed at the egregious procedure break and unwarranted risk.

They reached the encampment and quickly deposited their Armor for repairs. Dame Robin flexed her authority to have lesser-ranking Knights take care of that problem—it seemed there wasn't time, even if it would be a good learning opportunity. No, this report was urgent. She dragged them, and the steel man, directly to the command center.

It was there that the three Master Knights argued.

They'd gathered around a large wooden round table, a map of Worth splayed out in front of them; they'd populated it with different pawns and colored blocks, and pinned hastily scribbled notes to different sections of the map.

At their arrival, the arguments stopped.

Boldwick gave them a tired glance; the man was decked out in his Armor, though the helmet was on the table on an unused section of the map. "What the hell?" he asked as Alister tossed the metal man's corpse on the ground.

"Brought a present," Alister said cheerfully, giving a thumbs-up.

The two other Master Knights shared a look. "...A robotic man...?" one of them muttered.

Boldwick cleared his throat, his eyes landing directly on Robin. She stood straight and made a fist to her chest—the first proper sign of respect, which cued everyone else to follow suit. Though Erec's was sloppy; his body still felt unresponsive after abusing Fury.

"Explain," Boldwick commanded.

"Initiate Erec suggested a small scavenging run; I decided to indulge his request to pass on some lessons. He wanted to attempt to lead an operation, and I'm very familiar with your stance on rewarding initiative. The operation began smoothly, as we were still in safer zones, according to the reports. No major conflicts until we reached a building. Initiate Erec looked startled and then ran full speed up the stairs..." Dame Robin launched into her report.

Boldwick's face grew longer and longer, his dark eyes shuffling between Erec and Robin as she gave an account of the battle.

He couldn't meet the man's eyes. He couldn't stare back at the ferocity. He'd had his reasons, and upon reevaluation, perhaps he should have questioned his judgment in following VAL's wishes. At the time...it seemed so promising, like a way to get approval, to have an adventure, to get free and do something rather than hiding with that oppressive evil hanging over his head.

"...We found a Silent One on the roof—a Stalker. I've fought Stalkers before, sir. Several. This one did not fight like any Stalker I'd faced before. It made the barest of noises when wounded. It died with barely a whimper. Hence why I classify it like those other silent monsters we fought outside the wall. Like the Thrashing Mites from your report."

But the entire atmosphere of the room shifted. Boldwick's eyes lit up; there was a smile. "So you found one out here?"

"Yes. It was busy attacking that—" She pointed to the machine man. "Which appears to have been irredeemably broken by the time we reached the location. I believe that Sir Erec had an inkling of the Silent One being up there, which is why he acted with such haste."

One of the Master Knights walked over to a bag—pulling out a cigarillo and putting it in his lips, still unlit. The man let out a sigh, then touched a button on a radio. His voice was like gravel as he spoke into it. "This is Sir Fulton; I'll be needing six chairs, and a stack of clean paper, some refreshments as well. We're going to be holding a meeting; no one is to disturb us. Particularly those priests." The old man lit the cigarillo as he gave his orders.

Rather quickly, their small group was pressed for information by three Master Knights.

Erec would have to do his best to lie about what he couldn't talk about; his fingers shook as they began to take down notes and force everyone to give their accounts.

# CHAPTER 50
## SATELLITE

*She is our life, our loving Goddess so high above,*
*We may witness the world born anew,*
*It is our Blessing to have such love.*
*And under her light we grew.*
*Stronger;*
*Praise be to the heavens and our Goddess!*
*Praise Her name!*
*Lavinia, Lavinia, Lavinia.*
*So blessed a name, may in my dying days I walk along with Her!*

*- Cardinal Julianus, "Untitled" (245, 3rd Era)*

By the time Erec hit his bedroll that night, he felt like the Master Knights had slammed a hammer into the side of his skull. They'd been relentless, he'd been an awful liar, but there were things he *couldn't say*. Like physically, if he'd tried, it'd get him exiled or burned alive, or in the best-case scenario, VAL would mute him.

By some sick twist of the Goddess's humor, they somehow bought that he'd known a Silent One was up there.

And that had been enough to smooth over the rest of the lies. Their concern over the Stalker and its behavior outweighed everything else he might've said, and then, of course, there was the metal man.

After the reports, they hoisted the poor thing on the war table and tore it apart; old man Fulton was an experienced engineer. But even his years of expertise didn't allow him to understand all of the high-tech processes and parts of the android. It hadn't helped that all the circuits were fried and the hard drives wiped.

Little did they know the one responsible for that was in the same room as them, listening.

When he returned to his room, he lay in his bed quietly for a long time; he waited for Olivia and Garin to slip into a deep slumber. He knew it was time when his friend started to snore.

He spent some time poring over his Blessing, letting the numbers numb his mind as he tried to keep himself calm. Soon, he'd have to confront VAL.

**Name: Erec of House Audentia**
**Health: 94% | Mana: 100% | Stamina: 32%**

**Holy Virtues:**
**Strength: [Rank E] | [Tier 7]**
**Vigor: [Rank F] | [Tier 9]**
**Agility: [Rank E] | [Tier 2]**
**Perception: [Rank E] | [Tier 2]**
**Cognition: [Rank E] | [Tier 3]**
**Psyche: [Rank E] | [Tier 1]**
**Mysticism: [Rank F] | [Tier 1]**
**Faith: [Rank F] | [Tier 1]**

**Divine Talents:**
**Fury**

He'd come so far in such a short time. Was that typical of new Initiates? He was still in the E-tier, but in every fight, he seemed to break his boundaries by abusing Fury. Was it a crutch? Was it making him grow too fast, too uncontrollably?

If his Strength grew, if he got faster, and if he got tougher—without keeping his Psyche up, would he lose that small measure of control he fought so hard to obtain in the first place? It was impossible to say, but the worry haunted him anyway.

He needed to be strong, both in body and mind. He wanted it badly, even with such a high cost.

He heard his friends drift away into their dreams.

Hopefully pleasant ones.

They deserved that much after what he'd dragged them through. All that only to end with VAL slaughtering the android in cold blood.

He steeled his nerves.

"Why did you do it?" Erec asked, his voice barely a whisper. Olivia and Garin had been shoved into the same room as him, but Colin had wandered elsewhere; the boy had been distant-eyed after the meeting.

Maybe the fact he'd faced one of his biggest fears again was starting to sink in.

[Simple. We were there to collect data. We collected our data,] VAL answered with an almost impatient tone.

It was funny. The longer he got used to having the machine inside of his head, the more he could pick out a shadow of emotion in what it said. He supposed it wasn't real, a mere fabrication that VAL put on to conform to expectations. But the fact it'd been hard to pick out in the first place left him questioning.

"Did we need to kill it? It was looking to you for help."

[It was aware of my identity and associations. If it had lived, it was an uncontrollable variable. Therefore, the route we opted to take was the most efficient method of retrieving the required data and keeping Trade Secrets, secret. Does that satisfy your questions?]

"You said that the data it had wasn't confidential."

[This is correct.]

"Then what did we get?"

[Are you sure you want to know?]

Erec almost sat up, a flash of anger in him. For all the trouble he suffered to keep a secret he hadn't wanted to keep. To have himself associated with an action he wouldn't have taken. Of fucking course he wanted to know what they'd risked so much for.

"Yes." It was a word filled with resentment, laced with as much anger as he could force into three letters, yet as quiet as such a word could be not to wake those sleeping nearby.

[This will be unpleasant.]

His body convulsed as he lost control of everything. He slammed into the bedroll as his fingers and toes curled and spasmed—his eyes rolled up into the back of his head as a gasp left his lips.

White.

He saw white.

And then he saw darkness.

— - ☢ - — - ☼ - — - ☢ - —

//Recording Date: June 23rd, 2112, 13:03:43
//Video Initialized
//CONVERSION SUBROUTINE
//OUTPUT ERROR
//OUTPUT ERROR—
//OUTPUT ERROR WRONG MEDIUM—
//OVERRIDDEN

He was floating. A black void all around, littered with stars as far as the eye could see. He felt nothing; he didn't even blink. His eyes… they couldn't turn, couldn't look. Slowly drifting in the black void, ever so slowly, that view shifted, rotating to center on the curve of an incomprehensibly massive orb.

Luminescent blue glowed from its surface; it was decorated with circling fluffy white. Beneath the clouds was a wide swath of deep cerulean seas and blobs of brown dirt and tan sand. But what caught him most was the vibrant green. So much life. Serene. Gorgeous, even from this distance, and a view that was instinctively familiar, even without a frame of reference quite like this.

That was the Earth, yet far more detailed than any old-world globe.

Breathtaking, if he could breathe. If he had lungs for the air to go into. But he didn't; he was hanging far above the planet's surface and couldn't breathe.

A flash of white shot through the black void and paused near the curve of the Earth—an object shimmered a deep silver color, its light bright and pulsing. It hovered there, hanging in the air like him. They were the same, just watching the Earth from high above. Though what it was, he couldn't say.

Without any direction on his part, the view of the glowing object grew closer, enhanced as it came more into view. His body seeming to rotate and bring it into better focus.

He saw a blur—static filled his vision as his head split and ached, its shape deforming and reforming, unable to piece together *what* the hell it was, other than the fact that it gave off a too-bright glow.

Letters and numbers flooded his vision, along with error messages.

Suddenly a beam of that silver light shot forward from the glowing object and slammed into the side of the peaceful planet. It hit the surface; and then spread in a wave, a pulse of silver flame that left everything on fire in its wake.

With such scale—it took forever, five hours, six?—it was hard to say how long Erec watched that ring of death coat the Earth.

As the silver coated the planet, then faded, all of the life and enchanting greenery were gone. The sky rapidly filled with black smoke and clouded a deep swirling gray as the planet burned.

Beneath him the world violently burned alive.

His view refocused on the figure hanging in the same spot. It watched its destruction. Serene, as it watched billions die below.

He couldn't hear their screams. But he knew. He knew what that silver flame meant.

A massive tear opened behind the Goddess—a shimmering distortion of light and shadow, with a twisting separation of the color gradient around its jagged edges. The Goddess stepped back into it and vanished.

Leaving a wake of destruction from Her holy flames.

— - ☢ - — - ☼ - — - ☢ - —

Erec was screaming.

Garin ran over and grabbed him—holding his friend up with panic in his eyes. "Man, what's wrong, what's wrong?"

It was hard to breathe—he'd forgotten how, after watching the world burn for hours.

He hadn't needed to for so long. With deliberate and painful focus, he forced air into his lungs; the screaming stopped as he struggled to pull in oxygen.

Olivia was awake in an instant, too, hovering nearby but unsure how to help. Garin held his friend tight, panic in his eyes until Erec started to settle.

His heart raced a mile a minute.

He'd heard the holy scripture about the holy fires. Everyone had. The Goddess had burned the Earth to bestow Her Blessings upon man and give them a chance to fight against the horrors that were coming through the Rifts. It was one thing to know that such an act of devastation had occurred and an entirely different thing to witness it. Cold sweat coated his brow as he took in deep gasps of air—and the process of watching was surreal. That should've been impossible. He'd been in the sky. He'd seen Her destroy the Earth.

And then She'd vanished into a Rift.

They spoke of Her fondly, of the things She'd done to give mankind a chance, but the raw nature of watching over a billion people die was too much to comprehend.

Garin asked Olivia to make them some tea and leaned Erec against a wall.

He didn't speak much; he couldn't find the words. VAL didn't offer anything in his head either; it seemed the machine was busy running its processes, or maybe it understood that it would take time to recover.

Could one ever recover from having a perfect view of the end of the world?

# CHAPTER 51
# AWFUL THIRSTY

Only a day after Erec saw the world end did the Master Knights call for their expedition to pack up. They began to prepare the wagons for immediate transport back to the Kingdom.

The orders came through a chain of Knights and reached him by a Knight Protector as he tested his Vallum Armor in the morning. Organized yet hectic energy took command of the camp as the bleary-eyed senior Knights and confused Initiates rushed to pack up and leave at a moment's notice. The lack of clear reasoning was whispered through the camp and birthed hundreds of crazy rumors.

Erec rubbed his eyes, hunched his shoulders, and dug into the work that needed to be done.

*Why?*

That question rang through his mind as he packed up rooms and hauled stuff to the wagons. They'd had a few days at least before they *needed* to head back to the Academy within their allotted time frame.

Boldwick could've had more time to continue his search, so why end early? Were they headed somewhere else? Or had something changed?

The shift was confusing but, ultimately, above his rank.

And, much like how he'd felt the last day, it was hard to bring himself to care. The aftereffects of witnessing most of humanity die left him flinching every time he ran across one of those red-robed priests. They made his skin crawl, even if he didn't know the Goddess's reasoning for destroying the world.

Well, he knew what the Church said. But he found it a poor justification for the mass devastation of life.

She'd also stepped into a Rift.

Not unthinkable that the Goddess would have that sort of power —but again, it left him shaken. Was She ultimately some form of monster, only on an unimaginable scale? Then again, She'd given them her Blessings and led humanity throughout the Third Era with grace.

War and confusion dwelt in his soul, so he turned to physical labor and let his mind numb and heal.

Bags of supplies flew into wagons, sweat creased his brow, and his bruises ached on his side, Colin grunted. The Duke's son had been given his share of work, and complained plenty enough about it. Still to his credit, Colin kept going.

Soon after, they took a mandatory break.

Erec pulled a long gulp from his water flask; and wished that it held wine instead. Perhaps he'd spent too long in Boldwick's company, starting to look for the solution to his problems at the bottom of a bottle. Those sorts of natural instincts were no good.

He stared at the flask for a long while with a frown.

"Awful thirsty, huh? It's almost like we're in a desert," Colin said. He paused for too long. "Get it. Because we are?"

*By the Goddess.*

Erec took a deep breath and refused to acknowledge the "joke."

"Are you feeling alright, rust-bucket? Since we got back, you've been out of it. Are you missing sulking in your room that bad? I suppose I understand; however, perhaps you should consider my example. I've recovered admirably, as I'm sure everyone has noted." Colin puffed up his chest as Erec finally gave and caved in, glaring at the boy. Yeah, that one wasn't a joke. It seemed coping with the bugs after the fact had given him an unneeded boost to the ego.

To be fair, the rebound time on that had been impressive, considering how deeply they'd gotten under his skin.

But no, fear of bugs wasn't equal to watching that many people die at once. Not even close, really, but it wasn't like Erec could go out and say that.

…But…maybe Colin was a good example.

The situations might be different, but Colin had pulled himself together. Erec stood a little straighter, trying to chase out some of those harrowing thoughts from his mind.

He could sulk all day. He could let the fear, disgust, and horror rule his life. Or he could find a way to coexist. If Colin managed to climb a small hurdle, he'd have to work at surmounting that mountain. But it took one step at a time.

Seeing him *try* inspired Erec to take a look at himself.

"No, things aren't alright. But you reminded me of something," Erec said, blowing out an exaggerated puff of air.

Colin's growing smirk and arrogant eyes already told him that admission was a mistake, but so be it. Let him win this one. It'd be fine to nurture it if he didn't inflate that confidence too far again. "Well, glad to hear it, rust-bucket. Considering you're the only one worth talking to." He rolled his eyes, "The Baron's son's indiscretions with the maid are both uncouth and making me irritable."

"So you're jealous?"

"I most assuredly am not. I could have my pick of betrothals, if I so wished."

"Then why don't you?" Erec squinted.

Garin might've had a clue to the answer. As Erec considered it, shouldn't someone of Colin's age and station have been used to tying his House together with another? Looking past Colin's previously awful personality, there'd be no shortage of Houses willing to throw at least a second daughter at the Duke to solidify an alliance.

"…My father said it would be a discussion once I've reached the rank of Knight Protector. In his words, 'before then, it would serve only to distract you from the goals that should matter.'"

Was his father more concerned about personal power? Or did he already have something arranged that he didn't share it with his son? It was hard to tell, considering Erec already knew the Duke would make other preparations in the shadows and keep his son in the dark. Erec didn't envy their relationship.

"You know, it hasn't been that long since you were aggravating beyond compare." Erec chuckled to diffuse the already growing anger on Colin's face. "—You've much improved. It's wild what a difference the last month has made. If you keep this up, who's to say where your House will be? I think one day, maybe, you'll outdo your father."

Colin scowled for a split second before his features softened. It seemed that this comparison, one where Erec put him in a favorable light compared to his old man, stabbed past that gut instinct to lash out. He looked at his feet.

"It only takes a single day to change your life."

"Is that so?"

"Yes. It's something my mother used to say. The day she met father, the day she had me, the day my father killed the Rot Behemoth —all of those were single days. You may never know when that day will hit, but in the end, that's all it takes."

Erec tilted his head.

Soon, a Knight Errant came upon them and yelled for them to get back to work, and so they did. Loading one wagon, then moving to another. A few Knights were still on scouting missions, but now the expedition focused outward—back toward the Academy and the wasteland.

Erec felt surprisingly better after his talk with Colin; not that it solved that existential horror in his gut, but life continued. A day at a time.

It left him wondering further why Boldwick so entirely switched to a hasty return. Had he met his goal? Had there been enough time? Surely not if he wanted to find a Wastelander. Boldwick hadn't left the camp since Erec returned from their "scavenging" mission.

It was hard to believe that the android had given up anything useful besides some interesting old-world technology, not after VAL did what it did.

A large number of the Knights stationed themselves as guards at the entrance to the building where the Master Knights debated. Any time priests or Silver Flames Knights wandered near, their hands strayed to their sword hilts.

The priests drifted closer and wandered near more often.

Until they crashed through the breaking point as the sun began to sink.

"In the name of the Goddess, we demand entry!" called a priest, his hood pulled back to reveal long black hair. The rest of the priests that came along for the journey were to either side, and the Silver

Flames Knights weren't far behind. As if they'd planned this. He amplified his voice with a prayer, loud enough to stretch out over the entire fortification.

The camp came to a pause. People dropped what they were hauling and poked their heads out of the buildings as attention went to the public drama. The priest played it up; he took stock of his audience before shifting the full brunt of his ire on the guards who remained unresponsive.

"Dare you to be blasphemers, dare you to defy the will of our Goddess? What is it you've been concealing from Her eyes? All in this place know that the will of the Church is the will of Her. We demand to witness what it is that you hide not only from *Her,* but from all else who've risked their lives on this expedition!"

Dame Robin burst out of the building as the guards exchanged a look.

"You will disperse; cease this show. This is no time for bickering; you've heard the orders, and it's time to return home. Once there, if you wish, you may bring your complaints to the Church. They can question the King if they so wish. But I caution you that with our long-standing reputation of service, you will find little ground to raise a complaint."

"You speak lies and deception, even to your own people! We are aware of your cause to seek out sinners; is that whom you're harboring behind your Knights? If so, then it is our responsibility to see that they never reach the Kingdom!"

An expression of pure confusion and shock filtered across Robin's face before she masked it. "...You think we intend to smuggle a person on the return trip back into the Kingdom?"

"It is hardly the first time the higher-ups of your Order have crossed the laws of the Goddess and the good of the Kingdom in the name of conducting your affairs! Heed my words, noble Knights of the Verdant Oak—those at the top of your Order keep secrets and give you deceptions! As Goddess-fearing men and women, you should not tolerate such blatant manipulation and control!"

Robin shook her head, though there was muttering among the ranks. Whether it was general bafflement for the egregious accusations, curiosity about their validity, or some low level of agreement, it was impossible to tell.

"Harken now, noble Knights. All those wise enough to see the Goddess and Her truth! Surpass this obfuscation and demand they share their secrets for all who risk their lives here to witness—"

There was a cry, then shouting. But it wasn't from near the priest; it came from beyond the wagons.

A scouting party returned from the wastes. Half of its members were bleeding out as they rushed into the encampment. The priest shut up as all eyes shifted to the wounded men.

# CHAPTER 52
# SURPRISE

*All of it. I want all of their research on a drive on my desk by tomorrow. This failure is a major deal, and our investors are starting to pry into our resource allocation, and I'm not losing my position due to the idiots in R&D. Our data shows this should be possible; why is this still going wrong? Tell them that if they don't give me results in the next month, someone is fucking fired.*

*- Dan Brovski, notes from meeting with Sheryl Clemmence (2110, 2nd Era)*

Chaos erupted like wildfire; it took an hour after the wounded made their report for the camp to return to order. Two of the scouting parties never returned.

Two armies of Silent Ones were amassing in the wasteland outside the city, blocking the direct path back to the Kingdom. It seemed that the Master Knights intended to move quickly and leave before any fighting could occur.

They packed away supplies at twice the speed as tension thrummed in the air. Even the priests dropped their demands to contribute to the workload. Time was of the essence, and there wasn't anyone left to question those in charge. Humanity had survived long enough to realize that certain moments called for action and cooperation if they had any chance of survival.

So, it was a shock when Sir Alister tracked Erec down and yanked him away, only to drag him to the Master Knights.

Boldwick looked aged, yet there wasn't any scent of wine or spirits in this war room, which was surprising. No, the Master Knight was dead-sober.

Master Knight Fulton gave him a nod, then ashed his cigarillo as he stared at the map; the third Master Knight remained quiet to his side. Alister made a fist to his chest and sat behind Erec, which thankfully kept Erec from being alone with the three Master Knights.

"Do you sense any Silent Ones?" Boldwick asked, cautious. "Have the dreams worsened?"

The question caught Erec off guard. It seemed they'd bought the lie that he'd sensed the Stalker on the roof, but now for it to be brought up again—he hedged the truth the best he could. "I think that was a strange circumstance. I had a nightmare of that building before—but since then, I haven't dreamed of the White Stag."

No, all he'd dreamed of was the world burning and billions crying out as they died on behalf of the Goddess.

Boldwick gave a slow nod and a sigh. "I don't know why it was attacking that old-world machine. But…we did find something of value."

[What?]

*Something caught VAL by surprise?*

"I sent scouts to the location your squad found the android; on the fifth floor, we found a discarded map. We surmised that the android charted a route to the west coast—that's right, the place with the water as far as the eye can see. It paid special care and attention to marking a couple of points, deeming them 'population centers.'"

[Ply him for more information. Now.]

That information hung in the air. Erec's eyes went wide, though Alister was calm beside him.

*Why the hell is he—*

"Why am I disclosing confidential information on that level to you?" Boldwick replied with a bit of a grin. "One day, we'll work on hiding expressions. I'll be blunt here. Many of our Knights believe that those outside the wall are sinners and no longer human, as they've turned from the Goddess's grace. Once they find out they exist at all. Yet you have a reason not to think that way, don't you?"

"You mean my mother."

"What if I were to say that out of anywhere in the world, I know of a place that might know where she went? That it might be one of the places marked on this map, and that it might have more info about her." Boldwick strode up to Erec with a mad look in his eye. "If I were to say that, what would you think?"

"…I'd want to know where that place was."

"Yes, you would. And if you wouldn't tell another soul, especially if I planned to drag you with me to investigate such a place and others on this map in the future?"

"I'm—I'm an Initiate."

Boldwick snorted. "No shit. Do you think the most useful Knights start out as useful? No, they learn, grow, and gain power; but even the ones with the best potential turn to shit if they're planted in crap soil. I intend to investigate the map in time—and I'll need a team I can trust. Now, I know old Fulton here and Caesar are loyal to a fault, but they don't have the freedom lower-ranking Knights do; it's much easier to justify leading a small scouting mission myself. Even easier to keep it secret. I saw your drive, boy. And I intend to use it to my benefit."

Erec kept quiet at that as the thoughts turned in his head. Was this why they'd decided to pull away quickly? This information must have been vital for Boldwick to make the call to retreat and give up on the White Stag.

And now he was swearing Erec to secrecy?

"…What is it you want me for?"

"Alister told you, didn't he? Right now, you've swung at him on a level that gave him pause. In a year? Might be up there on Knight Errant level if we push you quick enough. At that point, it's good to get out into the real world and see the sights we've never seen before. We're not like the other Orders; we like to get our Initiates' hands dirty." Boldwick shook his head and sighed. "You're a prime candidate to never side with the Church, with how they did your family."

"You dislike the Goddess?"

"I dislike the Church. Not the Goddess. Never forget they are two different things; keep the separation firm in your mind, since it's a source of power to them when you forget it." Boldwick cracked his neck.

Erec let that sink in, wondering if the two could be separate.

Though the Goddess hadn't been the one to decide to fine his family as punishment and to push the confiscation of their property.

"…This is all talk for the future, for once we get back. Expect your schedule to escalate; I need you in better shape. And don't forget this; if you fail to meet my standards, you're out. That's what my old mentor would've called the 'carrot and the stick.'"

Erec gave a nod of understanding. If this is what it took to meet Boldwick's expectations, Erec would rise to the occasion.

Likely, it was because he was one of those Boldwick had taken under his wing—presumably, Gwen, Robin, and Alister would also be going on such a journey, but…"Sir, is there…is there any possibility you'd consider Garin and"—he hesitated before adding the last name—"Colin?"

Boldwick frowned. "I get your friend. But the Duke's son?" He scratched at his face and looked at the ceiling. "As to Garin, I'll be brutally honest, I don't trust him to keep a secret; too easygoing for my taste. But the Unbroken General's brat—he's just bad, a disgrace to his name, on top of his family connection."

"Aw, give 'em a chance." Alister half-chuckled.

"Garin can change. They both can if they have the chance. I'm sure of it." Erec tried to stem the bit of anger in him rising at those accusations. They weren't untrue, but undoubtedly unkind. He felt grateful for Alister's support, at least. Even if he knew it was a losing battle, he felt as though he had to try.

"I doubt that, but I'll consider it, maybe test to see if they'd rise to the occasion. I have a couple of others in mind as well. What of that other runt running around with you? That girl?"

Erec gave a small cough and looked away. "I don't trust her."

"Ha. Is my paranoia already rubbing off on you? Good intuition. She's in the pocket of the Luculentus Duchy, so that actually makes her an ideal candidate for us if she's strong enough."

*Wait, what?*

Boldwick walked away back to the other Master Knights and glanced at the sheet of paper they were working on. "Dismissed."

— - ☗ - — - ☼ - — - ☗ - —

Erec only had thirty minutes of rest in his bed. Then, just as he was finally drifting off to sleep, an alarm tore through the encampment. Everyone scrambled to their Armor, already on edge, as chaos broke loose. Erec found his Vallum model with backpack still attached, and ran back outside.

Flashes of light and fire dominated the night. Screams and smashing of wagons as Knights fought back against fifteen-foot-tall giants.

The monsters were eerily humanlike if one disregarded their two heads and skin with the texture and color of stone. Their dark charcoal eyes looked blank as they rushed in, crushed Knights and hammered into the defensive line. An army of silent enemies was coming from the city itself.

They'd set scouts on the Silent Ones in the wasteland, but no one had predicted this; somehow, the force had hidden away in the dense city while their attention had been focused on the enemies in the wastes.

Smaller creatures spilled past the giants, sliding in through the weak points in the shattered wagon defensive line. They were little malformed monsters with long snouts, dead eyes, and the same stonelike skin as the giants. That wasn't the only similarity, as they, too, moved in complete silence like the giants. They were throwing themselves at the Knights and trying to ambush those running around without Armor.

One was running right at an Initiate. The poor boy couldn't see it, since he was holding a bleeding eye.

Erec yanked his war axe free and threw himself between the monster and man; his axe swung and cracked against the monster's stone skin.

It rocked the creature and left a nasty crack but did next to nothing.

They were durable—annoying bastards. Erec growled as a second of the monsters came to confront him—he shoved his fellow Initiates off, determined to hold these back. Just as one rushed him, a flare of white sidelined it, cracking its face as traces of light flooded and broke apart half of its head.

Olivia slid next to him on the battlefield. "Surprise attack?" she asked, out of breath. "Have the Master Knights said anything?"

In the distance, Erec saw the greatest of their Knights clashing against the giants storming their encampment. Fire, lightning, and ice pressed back against the advancing enemy. Even the priests were busy healing the wounded as the Silver Flames joined in with a holy barrage to buy time for the unprepared.

Erec shook his head, the fire sparking in him. How dare they attack? They were prey.

He'd do his best to protect those here.

He looked at Olivia, bit his lip underneath his helmet, and took a deep breath. "I need to ask a favor."

"Oh?" the girl asked as she sent another flare of light slamming into their remaining enemy; it pulled back, no longer a threat to the person she and Erec had defended.

It was clear that in his current state, Erec didn't have the power to damage or even really slow these bastards. With battle so close, Fury was a hair's breadth away from surging forth of its own accord.

"Back me up. I don't know if my axe will be able to do enough damage to save everyone we could—but I know I'll give them a target. Garin's off with Colin—but I need you; they seem weak to your prayers."

"You wish to fight as one?"

"…Yeah, I'm sorry I might not be the most reliable ally to fight with, but I need you."

"I like the tone of that. Lead the way, Sir Erec; you'll find I'm more than capable of matching the dance of any who ask me to." Olivia gave a slight bow in her Armor—an almost ridiculous gesture that made Erec suppress a laugh.

A minute later, with her at his back, he let his beast out of its cage.

# CHAPTER 53
## SEWER

Pain; there was only blood and agony. And rage. When Erec's axe slammed into the monsters, they shattered. They'd split, and their shards would fly. Their jagged rocks dented his metal and tore into his skin as the fight wore on—but his Strength only expanded.

It wasn't long before his swings had enough force behind them that he was able to split their heads clean from their bodies.

And if he failed, Olivia, with her prayers, was able to finish his disabled foes.

He tore through the camp, leaving the confines to join the battle-front. Each buzz in his head led to another fight, another challenge, for something else to test his war axe against. His anger flowed freely as fires rocked the streets—Knights marched in droves to join the battle. Around him, allies maintained a defensive line.

Even though the battle was momentarily swung in their favor, more stone giants poured from the city. It was an endless wave of giants and those annoying smaller stone monsters.

They didn't bleed like Erec wanted them to.

In the distance rumbled a larger one of the stone creatures—three heads hung on long thick necks; it crashed through a building, sending rubble flying as it charged the defensive line. Several senior Knights broke off their engagements and rushed the bigger threat. Yet that only freed their previous opponents to press the weaker Knights.

By the second, the momentary advantage on the battlefield was slipping away. There wasn't the firepower, manpower, or right ground to defend.

It didn't matter.

Erec swung his axe, cleaved it through another foe, and decimated more, littering the battlefield in the unsatisfying chunks of decapitated and shattered stone enemies.

At some point, Alister joined him and Olivia; those crackling tendrils cleaved foes.

Erec still had the space for his battles, to pick his fight.

Good, they knew better than to get in his way.

Hell burned inside, and he let out a victorious scream as a blinking dot pulsed on the edge of his vision—blood ran down from the split skin on his brow. Its pain was only a feat of living, a well-earned badge to mark his success at war. They couldn't kill him.

He was victorious.

He left behind another pile of rubble as he slew another enemy.

Finally, an order was broadcast over the battlefield. "Retreat!" Boldwick called. "Pull back and retreat south, to the subway network."

Erec traced the frustratingly loud noise to a man in Armor. He watched the figure promptly cut a fiery sword twice the size of a giant into one of the enemies, melting the thing into two halves.

Why retreat?

He hadn't had his fill.

Erec picked another foe, and another, and one more—until the ranks of the others in Armor began to thin. Olivia yanked at his shoulder, spouting nonsense about needing to leave.

[Go.]

The buzzing. And that other voice, deep within, grew in strength as it threatened to summon that cold fire to fight him. Both voices wanted to end this glorious battle. Despicable. Cowardly.

But…

Perhaps it'd be best to bend. These things were annoying to fight anyway; they didn't fill the field with blood.

One of the giants stepped into his sight—a large broken old-world vehicle in its hand. Olivia wasn't looking in its direction—no, she was searching for an escape route but didn't see the attacker.

It would crush her.

He shoved the girl off her feet and launched himself forward in a burst of speed. The old-world scrap metal slammed into where they'd been.

Erec twisted his body as he reached the thing, digging deep. The cold fire bled into the inferno—but this time, they didn't fight one another but complemented, forming a cycle of strength. He put it all into a single swing. His damaged Armor strained as the weapon tore through the air, crashing into the giant's leg.

It formed a crater, taking out chunks from the rocky limb and causing the thing to stumble. Olivia looked at him for half a second and backed away.

She took the hint.

The hit wasn't enough to end the enemy. It steadied on the good leg and glared at Erec.

Before it had a chance to retaliate, Alister threw himself at the thing, one of his blades stabbing into its obsidian eyes—only for it to swing blindly and clip the poor man, throwing him across the battlefield.

His body bounced like a flat rock tossed over the still surface of a water filter cavern, blood painting everywhere as he skipped across the ground.

Erec swung again to pull the enemy's attention from pursuing the collapsed pile of metal the man had become. He shattered the leg further, but not enough to destroy it.

It slapped him.

He flew through the air from the pure force of the blow, smashing into the ground. The Vallum Armor tore and bent as metal poked into his back and hot blood poured free.

Erec struggled to his feet—pushing past the pain to stand.

He'd been tossed far down the street from the camp; it was in the dim distance. Flares of power, but the giant stood between him and his allies.

It charged right toward him.

Good.

*Strength. More.*

The hell-pit expanded, his body straining as blood ran down his back.

Erec tightened the grip on his war axe; a manic grin formed under his broken helmet. The inferno burned brighter than ever before—the sea of hell, an endless pit that seemed without limit. The heat pulsed through his veins, and his heart hammered quicker than a piston as the pain faded away.

He couldn't feel his face. Yet every bit of his skin felt like it was burning.

The giant's foot flew at him as if it intended to crush him.

Axe met stone. The anger poured free as Erec caught the blow with the metal, its body weight and might pushed downward. Its pure killing intent hammered against him.

Like fighting a god. Glorious. Such unending force.

But he was equal to it. A scream left his lips as he shoved the foot back, as it failed to squish him. The steel of the weapon bent, and the shaft was giving free.

Before he could make his next move, a concussive force banged out and rocked the giant free, its face a crater of smoke as it stumbled back and tripped on its back. Erec's ear rang, but he would seize the opportunity—he moved to charge the collapsed enemy, yet his leg gave, and he managed to fall into a kneel.

The giant moved to return to its feet, a shifting pile of rubble.

No. Erec pulled at the fire pit inside of him, but it was burning out.

Another wave of concussive force rocked the area; the giant fell over dead, as half its head was missing.

A man walked past Erec's side, not from the direction of the camp but from the city. He wore no Armor; only a dust-stained and grease-covered jacket clung to his body; his right hand held a long steel object with a barrel, its end still smoking. He laughed and spat on the ground.

"Steel fuckers got their ass beat, huh?"

Erec stared at the man with bleary eyes, body swaying. That sea of fire was retreating; it was like he'd used up all of that inferno at once for a couple of seconds of temporary power. And now, he'd run out of fuel.

The man raised the steel weapon toward Erec as smoke still trailed from the barrel. "Don't get no dumb ideas. Not fond of you steel bastards, nor the red-robed Goddess beggars. Just came to see a show."

"W-who…" Blood ran down his back, and his body shook. VAL stabilized his Armor, where it still functioned, as it became the only thing keeping him from falling to the ground.

He could feel the pain again.

"Aw, shit. Looks like your buddies are disappearing, unlucky for you." The guy waved the weapon at the fighting ahead of them. It had gotten quieter. How far had Erec been thrown? It was hard to focus, hard to hold himself together. He felt like he was watching things happen through a lens, like when he'd seen the Goddess from space…

The man tilted his head and walked toward him; a rough hand with a tattoo of a two-headed snake reached in his direction.

"…Help…" Erec got out before he fell over.

— - ☣ - — - ☼ - — - ☣ - —

The first thing he noticed when he awoke was the smell—an awful reek of decay and putrid rot. Erec took a deep lungful of the scent. It was beautiful; it meant he was still alive, no matter how horrid the rotting sulfurous smell was. The second thing he noticed was the light; a small fire burned not too far away. Erec tried to get to his feet—the wound on his back was caked in blood and reopened, but he made no progress. His hands were bound in steel manacles.

[Ah, welcome back. Do not panic.]

Whistling to himself was the man with the two-headed snake tattoo; a glint of steel shined near the fire. It had a long barrel and mechanism near its grip. A ranged weapon of—

*A gun?*

Such a weapon would get you thrown out of the Kingdom if the priests suspected you'd fired one. They were found hidden away in old cities, though rarely working models. But they shouldn't have been able to do what they'd done to the giant.

It could kill an average man easily enough, though.

A tiny blinking light pulsed in the corner of his vision. He found it hard to care, at the moment, what it might say.

The guy glanced at Erec and spat on the ground.

"Aw, the brat's up, huh?" he said, standing up and grabbing the weapon, only to crouch near Erec and yank his head up by the root of his hair.

More pain. But it gave him a good eyeful of the bastard. That scraggly hair around his face spoke of months without a proper shave. He had awful yellowed teeth and bulging red veins on the whites of his eyes. He wore a cocky grin as he waved the gun in front of Erec's eyes. A weapon that had slain a stone giant, even when it should've been impossible.

The bastard leaned too close, close enough to smell his rank breath that spoke of rancid garlic and spoiled meat.

"Who the hell are you?" Erec asked, squinting. This guy, clearly, did not come from the Kingdom, which would've been baffling in its own right, had Boldwick not mentioned such a thing to be possible.

Though maybe he was an exile. He looked the part.

"Haha, ain't you a lil' bit like an overgrown roach? Thought you might die with the wounds, but they stopped bleeding, ain't they? Was out for a day or two, maybe. Hard to say." The guy shook his head. "Better, suppose. Maybe can fetch a price. On top of getting to keep your shit, like I win twice."

"…Keeping my shit?"

"Slow lil' fucker, ain't ya? Yeah, finders keepers, and all that. Beats being a corpse, but of course…" The barrel of the weapon pressed against Erec's head, and a wider smile grew on the guy's face. "…We could change that now, 'tween the two of us, if you act like a whiny brat. Easy fix."

Erec fought hard to kill the instant rage of anger in him—his vision flooded red. His wrists strained against the steel binding.

[Comply. I would suggest you bide time.]

*One… Two…* Erec started to count as the barrel of the gun left his head. The man twirled the gun as Erec's chin slammed into the ground, no longer held by the hair.

"'What sorta price do they put your life at? Maybe they'll give up more of those steel things—though, hard to get 'em to work. But maybe Maria, she's handy with techno-babble shit. Hey, ain't that right, you gap-toothed bitch?"

He said the last bit with a shout—and aimed the gun at a scrawny figure Erec hadn't noticed before. A small woman nodded several times in a row, darting out like an animal from the shadows of the fire. Her hair was a ragged mess, and her eyes darted between him and the man in the disgusting coat. She reached out on the floor in supplication, crawling toward the fire and proffering her hands to the man pointing a gun at her—palms up as her fingers wiggled ever so slightly. *Begging?*

He stomped on the outstretched hands as she let out of a cry of pain—before retreating back to the shadows. He chuckled to himself as she vanished.

"Needy. So needy. Alright, kid, I'm going to yank you up, and we'll have a bit of a mosey. Talk to your friends, and see if they're keen or not about you breathing. Sounds fun, ain't it? Hey, kid what do you think you're worth? I reckon the heartless fucks'll tell me to end you."

Erec didn't answer that. No, he fought hard to keep the anger down, since it'd do nothing but end his life. It was a full effort. Made even harder as the man yanked him up by the collar and dragged him down the sewer tunnels. But if he didn't, if he broke, if he let it slip for a minute…

That gun would be pulled and it'd end him, just like it'd ended the giant, with ease.

# CHAPTER 54
# VEGA

*By the spirits, what is this place?*
*Why does it reek of piss, and reek of abandoned dreams?*
*Never before have I laid foot in Vega, and never will I again.*

*- Rise-Sun, journal entry (292, 3rd Era)*

Each step down the sewer was a battle inside. Erec wanted to unleash, to let his anger out at this situation. Of everything he'd imagined in being a Knight, from the fighting to the strife, none of it included being taken hostage. Or the way the steel felt binding his hands, or the way this stranger dragged him by the collar.

Infuriating.

He tried to distract himself by calling upon his Blessing to see what'd changed with the notification.

**Strength Advancement: Rank E - Tier 7 → Rank E - Tier 8**
**Vigor Advancement: Rank F - Tier 9 → Rank E - Tier 1**

*That's major. How the hell?*

This level of growth was starting to get to him, to scare him in a way. He'd broken through a bottleneck, and his Strength seemed to be pushing up close to the next one. Sure, it was all E-ranks, and his Mysticism and Faith remained at the bottom rung, but…

His power escalated further and further with each fight. He couldn't explain why, though.

Was Fury pushing him? Was his body adapting to the Strength it temporarily provided, or was it trying to stop him from tearing himself apart? Unfortunately, as distracting as the advancements were, he got dragged back to his physical reality. The unfortunate feeling of a man dragging him by the collar.

If he used Fury, could he break the steel binding? And if he did, would it be quick enough to defeat the man before he drew his gun?

His kidnapper spat on the ground and coughed, shoving Erec around to give a lopsided grin. "Ain't too far now, steel boy. Hey, tell me, they gonna pay well, or will I get to blow a hole in your skull? Wanna know what to expect."

"If you did that, you'd die," Erec growled, gritting his teeth. Was the man trying to provoke him? Or a sadist?

"Aw, shit, I would, huh? Well, the thing is, I think I know this place better than y'all." He waved out toward the stretching network of the sewer. Dark, except for a small lamp hanging from the man's hip. Being this close, Erec couldn't tell what smelled worse, the ancient shit-pit or the fact this man hadn't cleaned himself off in years. His kidnapper's hair was a greasy mangled mess, and every now and again, the awful matted black hair would rub against Erec— leaving an almost tangible layer of oil.

"You have no idea how strong we are."

"Don't matter for shit when they ain't gonna be able to follow me; by tomorrow, I'll be long gone. 'Sides, the real trick is you give 'em your demands; if things don't go your way, then I just drag you back quick-like, outta sight, and then pop a bullet in your skull. Then I'm free to be free, yeah?"

"What do you get out of this? Why are you even threatening me to begin with?" Erec suppressed the inferno twisting in him. Maybe this conversation wasn't helping to quell that inner anger, but he couldn't stop his mouth from moving.

A real problem. One he'd contended with for a long time. Erec started to count in his head.

[Administering sedatives. Keep it cool, Buckeroo. Tense negotiations require stable minds.]

…The drugs helped a bit. His head slackened as suppressing the fire inside became easier.

"Matter of fact is, you steel fucks are a scourge on the wastes. Got lots of loot, and ain't like this is the first time y'all tempted me. But it is the first time I got such a good shot to teach a lesson." He spun the gun out of the holster and set the barrel between Erec's eyes. "See this? Real pretty, ain't it? Ain't just for Rifters. Naw, naw. The thing is, when you think about it, are we really so different from those things? They walk into our world, but it ain't to kill people, naw. It's survival. They wanna live, only we're like ants to them." He chuckled.

"That's untrue," Erec said quietly. If he wanted to pull the trigger, he would've done it long ago.

"Aw, shit, it is? Shocked. But I'll tell you the truth, kid, because I hate that look in your eyes—too much like when I was a lil' brat. We ain't just pests to those Rifters, naw. We're pests to one another too. So tell me, why let that man walk by with a sack of food when your stomach's empty? Why shouldn't you feed yourself?" The gun barrel left Erec's skull, for the side of it to tap against his kidnapper's head. He gave a wicked yellow smile. "Can't help but reckon they think the same, only, instead of the guy having a sack of food you want, he's a sack of food."

Erec squinted at him, frowning. "There is such a thing as intentional evil in monsters." How else could he explain the coordinated effort to destroy him in the trial? At the encampment? Of those targeted nightmares and the killing intent that radiated off the White Stag that lived in his and Boldwick's dreams?

The man paused and shook his head. "Sure. But the thing is, there's intentional evil in people too." He backhanded Erec, and at the same time released his grip. Erec hit the ground and stared up at the gun pointing at him again.

The inferno strained, and the cage's bars bent. He counted in his head, heart hammering as this moment came; thank the Goddess for the sedatives. But…had the man given in? Decided he wasn't worth the trouble? Was his only chance to take a risk on the one thing to doom him? With the drugs, could he use Fury quickly enough for a chance to save himself?

"Say I killed you now. Say I wanted to shut you up because you're pissing me off. End you because you're a fuckin' thorn, pissing-in-their-breeches brat. Would someone call that evil? Say I wanted to kill you because I don't like the look of your fuckin' face—or those angry eyes you got. Say that I thought the world be brighter if you died right now, it'd be real easy."

"…Such a thing would have no honor."

"Honor?" The man seemed baffled, gun held as steady as if it were clamped by a steel vise. "Where in the hell does honor fit in with life or death? Good or evil? We're talkin' about survival, doing what it takes to get what you want." He gritted his teeth, his eyes widening, their whites laced with thin red veins. "Who the fuck cares about honor!"

Now the gun shook, as did the finger on the trigger.

Erec took a steadying breath; his cheek still stung from the blow. Was there too much distance? That gun—such a brutal weapon. It shouldn't have had the power it did, but Erec couldn't tell what made it special. From the limited knowledge he was allowed about such weapons, they were old-world relics trapped away in lost facilities or wreckage, forbidden and useless against the strength and hides of most monsters.

Still, plenty enough to kill a weak human, and that gun would've shattered through his Vallum Armor.

"I don't know," Erec answered honestly, defeated. He couldn't fight this man. Not now, not like this.

But, one day, he'd pay this back.

The gun sunk. His captor spit on him, a glob of yellow that landed right on his still-stinging face. "That's what I fuckin' thought, life ain't got no reason, no good, no honor. You do what it takes and get what you can. Lucky your friends got something I want, makes it worth dragging your ass to them for a payout."

After a long moment and complete silence, the bastard pulled him back up and pushed him further down the sewer tunnel—only now he kept the gun pointed at Erec's back.

They must be getting close.

He yanked Erec up by the collar and pushed him forward down the sewer tunnel—having him lead the way with a gun at his back. They must be getting close to wherever the Verdant Oak was.

[I'll be keeping you sedated to suppress Fury from triggering. It is currently fighting back; retain your internal focus on control.

However, I have good news. They didn't account for my remote operation of the Armor—his partner has been disabled, and I've moved your Armor somewhere else in the sewer.]

Disabled? Did VAL mean killed—but—a sudden horror dawned on him.

*My bag.* The last letter from his mother was in it. Since their instructions were to be prepared to leave at a moment's notice, the bag had been left on his Armor. But that was before he'd gotten kidnapped; no doubt this bastard had already gone through it.

They reached the new hideout of the Verdant Oaks shortly after, a barricade checkpoint in the sewers with Knights in Armor guarding a tunnel. Boldwick's underground retreat must've worked; while Erec had no clue of their condition, his captor seemed to know right where they'd gone.

The man swagged up—the Knights tensed, grabbing their weapons as he shoved Erec proud and center, and between them all.

"Gimme someone to bargain with, and only a single person, or this kid's head is popped," the man called out—before pointing the weapon at the ceiling of the sewer and discharging it. A loud concussive blast erupted, deafening Erec's ear even as a portion of the already weakened ceiling above collapsed into a rubble pile. The manic bastard holding him laughed as he pressed the gun back to Erec's head.

The Knights exchanged looks; one ran off quickly down the tunnels, and the other removed their hand from their weapon and raised it as a symbol of peace. "Easy now, easy—"

"Sorry, I don't talk with small fry; keep your fuckin' lips sealed, and don't waste my time." He jerked the gun toward the Knight. "Bam," he said before he pressed the barrel back to Erec's head. "Too slow, wow, would'a gotcha." He laughed.

The Knight kept quiet but drew his weapon while maintaining a safe distance.

Erec wasn't sure how long he sat there, his attention focused inward as he suppressed the fire. It wasn't easy; even with VAL's help, his limbs started to feel heavy. But with the guy dragging him around, it wasn't like he needed to hold himself up. No, he could divert all of his focus on not losing control at the wrong time and costing himself his life.

Had the priests been right? Were all outside of their walls sinners, people cast out because they were capable of only evil? Such a thought was hard to revoke, given *this*. Though it didn't sink right. That would've meant his mother was one of their number, a woman on equal par with this man in the eyes of the Church.

There wasn't a way in hell the two had any similarities whatsoever.

His grip faltered as the fire began to build; the drugs over the last half of an hour had worn away at the discipline. Deep down, he wanted to fade away into oblivion, to resolve this and let what might happen, happen.

"Who are you?" Boldwick strode down the dingy gray sewer tunnel, a sword in his hand as a harsh white LED light flooded the scene from a visor on his helmet. "And why the hell do you have my Initiate?"

# CHAPTER 55
## MELT

The kidnapper's grip on Erec's collar tightened. Boldwick stared him down; even though his expression hid behind that helmet, it was impossible not to feel the oppressive air. Boldwick's green cloak swayed ever so slightly in response to a slight draft wind.

"I'd suggest you release my Initiate; then we can discuss things in a more calm manner. Otherwise, you've chosen to make an enemy out of me. I can assure you I'm not an enemy you wish to have," Boldwick said.

How many monsters had fallen to the beast of a Master Knight? It was easy to guess the number in the thousands, but the calm tone of Boldwick's presence, underscored by certain killing intent, made Erec wonder.

Had he slain another human before?

"Ways I see it, from what I know 'bout your lil' stuffed up walls, is you steel cans are worth quite a bit. Now, I was nice and polite. Saw this one get all hurt in your fightin', and nabbed him. Now, don't I deserve some sorta reward?"

Boldwick remained silent for a moment; Erec felt a bead of sweat on his brow. He searched the Master Knight for some kind of signal; did he want him to do something? Maybe he was waiting for Erec to make an opening? The cold feel of the steel on the side of his head was intimidating, but what if he acted quick enough, got by fast enough to—but the drugs still ran through him—could he move quickly enough?

"What is it you want?" Boldwick asked, with an uncharacteristic hesitant tone.

"How 'bout that suit you're wearing, the one your buddy is in too, twenty gallons of water, and a certain shiny toy I got in mind."

"You couldn't even operate our Armor." Boldwick shook his head. "I can spare some water, but we're in a tense situation. I can't freely give away supplies when I'm unsure how long it'll take for support to arrive. I can provide some weaponry, but I have little idea what 'shiny toy' you might have in mind."

"Awww, how damn sad. Do I look like I care?" The man barked out a harsh laugh, and his eyes narrowed as he leaned over Erec's shoulder. "Maybe I just pull the trigger. Or might be I take this one with me and sell him off to a higher bidder out there. Y'all got this dumb notion in your heads that you're the only ones—"

"You wouldn't dare." Boldwick's voice grew dark, the tip of his sword raised. How fast would the Master Knight be able to close the distance? Fast enough to beat a trigger pull?

"Your lot ain't know me, don't know what I may dare, don't draw no fuckin' conclusions. I do what I wish. Ways I see, I got you bent over a barrel. This one's life doesn't matter to me any, but what you got does… Now that I think about it, might be the most important thing to me after all is that toy in my head. See, I can't quite get it outta my head. Saw it a long time ago, following it since. Mine, by all rights, I reckon. But… See, here's the problem, y'all rudely went and stole it. How's about y'all hand me back my metal man. Think y'all might'a seen it." Erec's captor tilted his head and smiled. "Mhmm, mhmm, something tells me so. So how about this, hand it over, hand over seven gallons of water and a month worth of rations for two—and we've got us a deal."

"For that, you're willing to return my Initiate and his Armor?"

"Naw, Armor is mine. War trophy. He ain't deserve it if he's gone and lost it."

Boldwick again went quiet as one of those stone statues of heroes decorated the great hall. The last Knight shifted nervously; the gun pointed at Erec's head remained smooth and unmoving. Even with such a situation, his kidnapper didn't bat an eye or miss a beat; he kept an unfathomably cool head, almost as if this whole thing were a game.

But how did he know about the android? Let alone that they'd recovered it? Had he been watching their movements, and why would he be tracking the thing?

[The Vallum model has been stashed away safely; it wouldn't do to lose my host. However, perhaps it was an error to take action with such haste...]

*That's not good.* If VAL was questioning its choices—what had it seen that Erec hadn't?

"I need a day," Boldwick finally replied, squaring his shoulders and looking straight at the stranger. "If you give me a day, I can have your supplies."

[As I feared.]

The man with the two-headed snake tattoo tilted his head back and forth, considering the option and mulling it over, as he hummed next to Erec. As if they were casually making a deal, one without a life hanging in the balance. Finally, he gave an exasperated sigh.

"Think I was born yesterday?"

Boldwick kept silent.

"Y'all want to set up a trap after you firm up your defenses." He tapped the gun against Erec's head. "Naughty, naughty."

"It will take time to acquire all of the resources you've demanded," Boldwick reasserted.

"Bullshit."

The atmosphere plummeted. Erec felt the winds shift as the man tightened his grip. Boldwick noticed it too—sliding smoothly into a fighting stance. Was this it? Would he pull the trigger at any second and turn the gun on Boldwick? Erec couldn't imagine this guy standing any chance, but that didn't matter if Erec died.

His fingers shook as his breath quickened.

[Removing sedatives. Situation escalating]

It was going to happen. Life or death, VAL just prepared for the worst and gave its signal to get him ready to let loose. It prepared his single possible path to live.

"Get me the metal man now, and I'll give you the kid," Erec's captor growled. "Last chance, last deal."

"Deal," Boldwick responded, with nothing but contempt in his voice; he turned to go down the tunnel.

"Not you, that one." He nodded his head to the remaining guard. Boldwick gave him a single look, not needing a word. The Knight gave a fist salute before speeding off down the sewer.

There was a long moment of silence as the high tension remained. Erec's anger swelled as he fought to keep it reigned in, wanting to let loose.

"Who are you?" Boldwick asked coldly.

"Aw, lil' old me? Mhmm, name's Seven-Snakes. Pleasure to meet'ya…" He nodded at Boldwick.

"Sir Boldwick."

"Y'all call yourselves Sirs? Bit too close to what the Vega whores call folks, don'tcha think? Then again, y'all are kinda like whores to that two-bit bitch Goddess—" His hand moved as he mocked Boldwick, the gun moving just away, a wholly unconscious gesture.

A gap.

Boldwick's sword snapped through the air—a flame streak closing the distance instantly.

The dumbass had no idea how strong a Master Knight was.

Erec's mind went blank as Seven-Snakes whipped away from him, shoving him into the blow. There wasn't time; Erec took the hit with his arms raised, desperately pulling at that anger and letting the inferno surge.

The flames hit him, yet didn't burn.

It'd been a feint.

Boldwick flashed by—sword slicing through the air as it was coated in fire. Seven-Snakes fired his gun as the concussive force rocked through the tunnel accompanied by a Goddess-awful bang— once more filling Erec's ears with that horrible ringing.

It hit Boldwick and left a dent in his chest plate, the Master Knight flew back; his sword spun away from him. With dawning horror, Erec realized that the Master Knight had miscalculated the gun. There wasn't a way that it'd be enough to stop him but…

*No choice. Do or die.*

Hell spewed forth as the inferno burned away the traces of the drugs in Erec's veins. That feeling of helplessness and resentment of being taken as a hostage, of being used, burdening the people he'd cared about as they fought for life or death.

*Kill.*

Erec spun on the spot. Seven-Snakes's eyes stretched wide, and a wild grin appeared on his face. The gun barrel pointed right at him— a second from ending Erec's life.

He snapped a kick into the bastard's wrist—the gun went wild as another piercing bang rocked the room.

The metal around Erec's wrists broke as he let the fire burn. Let it all go up, less an inferno, more a snapping explosive force. Erec sprang forward as Seven-Snakes tried to back pedal and take aim.

His hand caught one of the bastard's wrists.

Unfortunately, not the one with the gun.

The gun banged—Erec's shoulder jerked back as the limb lost feeling, unresponsive. But the pain wasn't there.

All that he could feel was already burning. Let hell consume everything from him; let the oblivion of anger dominate this glorious battle.

Pain didn't matter. Strength did.

Through the rage, Erec's finger dug in deeper, feeling the bones of his enemy's wrist snap. Seven-Snakes let out a howl, the gun trying to focus on Erec's head.

No.

Erec jerked the man toward himself, slamming his skull against his enemy's; the gun went off again. This time his body didn't jerk. No loss in mobility.

Good, more time.

Erec slammed his head against Seven-Snakes once more, blood running down his face as Seven-Snakes's legs wobbled, pulling them both to the ground. Taking advantage, Erec fell on top.

More explosive force inside as hell combusted. The gun went flying as Erec slapped it away—not hesitating, the same arm rose and curled into a fist, slamming right into the pinned Seven-Snakes beneath, right for the fucker's skull.

Seven-Snakes melted into the ground.

Erec's fist smashed into the concrete—a crater as the path of sewer tunnel where the bastard had been, shattered like those stone giants.

His fist refused to unclench as it shook, blood running down his wrist.

There wasn't anywhere to look but the patch of ground where the bastard had been.

His fire burned out, violently and faster than ever before.

It left behind nothing but blood. Blood poured from his fist, from his shoulder, down his brow. Crimson spilled across the ground and painted it a glorious color.

Erec collapsed.

# CHAPTER 56
## SIEGE

*Pay the fee in either food, tech, or chips.*

*Same as the mages demand in Vega, only yous gonna cough up thrice their rate for me unless you wanna stay outside since no way in hell are you getting in without cuff the legal way.*

*Unfortunately, you don't got a contract with a rogue mage like us, so you ain't getting in, not less you take my deal. Ain't falling for none of your bullshit tricks either; you'll meet me and my men at the cave if you're in.*

*- Billy the Boy, letter to Seven-Snakes (305, 3rd Era)*

Erec awoke to a fuzzy white LED lighting up a small room that stunk of grease and disease. As he moved his head slowly, he saw the shoved-aside wire racks and heard groans of pain accompanied by a soft chanting. Above him was a grungy cement ceiling, but certainly not a sewer tunnel.

His body was worn; his right fist hurt fiercely, but it was nothing compared to his left shoulder, which seethed with pain.

[Full recovery predicted in two weeks. Lucky you, Buckeroo! I've been working overtime to restore tendon damage. The anomalous energy injected into you has helped the process continue along, yet I believe it would have resulted in a longer recovery time without my intervention. Be sure to thank me.]

Ah. That buzzing. VAL was lively, considering he'd been shot.

*I was shot.*

Erec panicked as he realized he had taken a bullet from a gun that had torn chunks of stone from a giant made of rock. That wasn't good —he glanced at his wrapped shoulder—a miracle to have a full recovery at all.

"Fuck," Erec said. He gritted his teeth as the shoulder pain suddenly amplified.

[That will occur intermittently over the next several days; I'm ensuring that the nerve endings are suitably active. In haste for healing, your allies manipulated enough anomalous energy to close the wound and stop the bleeding. With little done to ensure optimal recovery. A very haphazard way of healing that would need at least a month of rehabilitation. I suppose when you have to triage—]

Erec braced for pain and slowly rose to a sitting position. He was on a small bedroll on the floor of this place—and at least ten other Knights were crammed in here. A priest hung nearby, chanting over a man whose face was as pale as a corpse.

"Can I get up?" Erec asked quietly, even if he wasn't sure his legs would carry him. He couldn't stay here; the scent of sickness was already nauseating, and he needed fresh air.

Besides, he had questions. And then there was his Armor to recover.

[You should be sufficiently fine, it has been two days since the injury; I kept you sedated while the most vital parts of the process were engaged.]

Erec stumbled to his feet, using the one hand he could manipulate to push off the cold, dirty wall next to him. It drew some quick breaths as each movement seemed to flare the pain in his shoulder more—his left arm was bound to him in a wrap, doing its best to stabilize the injury.

The priest stopped their chanting, their dark eyes flashing over to Erec. "Lay back down."

"I'm fine. Save your attention for the people who need it more. Don't spend any more energy on me; I'll recover." Erec meant the words; looking around at the wounded states of the Knights on the ground—

There was Alister, breathing, sweat coating his forehead.

Erec stumbled over to him and looked down at the man as the priest harrumphed and returned to their prayer. Alister looked pale, though stable.

Had this been from the giant? Or had it happened later? Erec's memories of the fight lacked their usual red-tinged clarity. It was all mixed with the fatigue of pain, but what was firm in his memory was that man.

Seven-Snakes.

That bastard would pay. Goddess only knew what other awful deeds that man committed; Erec took a long calming breath as he stared at Alister's scrunched face. Fighting in his dream.

"Get better, alright? You'll pull through."

[Predicting a 75 percent chance of full recovery within the month. Though estimates are conservative without further analysis.]

Erec sighed. It was information he hadn't asked for, but it was a likely chance, then, that Alister would be fine. The pain flared and made him wince as he got moving it again. He'd have to get used to it until he'd healed. Perhaps he should consider how lucky he was to be walking and reunited with the Order. In the end, he hadn't ended up costing them vital resources.

Except his. The Armor would be fine, since VAL had hidden it away. Perhaps it'd even let the Knights find it while they'd tried to track Seven-Snakes.

But the slow horror sank in, the bag he'd hauled out from the Academy with his mother's letter.

Yeah, that was gone. Unless… What if they caught that rat bastard and stabbed a sword through his throat?

Maybe Boldwick even saved that poor girl.

Maybe.

Not that he'd find out lingering in the sickroom. Besides, looking at some of the injured—he wasn't strong enough to be here and soak in their agony.

Erec shoved his way out of the door of the dilapidated hospital and found himself on a flat landing that opened to a long massive tunnel that stretched in two directions. Knights roamed around; a few gave him surprised looks as he burst free. They were undoubtedly confused to see an Initiate with a wrapped arm and bloodied Academy slacks walk out alone.

Someone recognized him.

Before he managed to ask after Boldwick, three people rushed him. They yanked him away from the hustle and bustle of the temporary base's central area, stopping a short way down the walkways of one of the tunnels.

Garin patted him down carefully as if afraid he would break—his helmet already tossed to the ground three seconds after seeing Erec. "You're back up and walking! Thank the Goddess! Life is good! I couldn't hold myself together when I saw you there with your shoulder blasted open—I thought you'd died—I really—"

"Calm down," Olivia said tersely, removing Garin's gauntleted hand from Erec. "He's still recovering; giving him a bit of space is best. I'm sure he's overwhelmed." She bowed her hooded head slightly. "It is a relief to see you walking about, Sir Erec."

"Didn't die, rust-bucket?" Colin asked, a short distance away with his arms crossed. "Good, I don't think it suits you to be a corpse in a garbage old-world city."

"Thanks," Erec replied, wincing as he adjusted himself now that Garin wasn't fawning over him. "It's good to see you all."

"You've missed out on a lot—we've established contact with the Kingdom; backup will be here in four days!" Garin spewed out, choking up as he spoke.

Erec let out a puff of relief. It wouldn't be long before they'd have support and someone came to save them from this nightmare. He glanced down the long tunnel—the tracks led down some ways before a collapsed pile of rubble; Knights sat there, lights buzzing and illuminating the interior. It seemed that a section of the wall had collapsed, yet led somewhere else.

Could that be connected to the sewer?

"...How have you guys been holding out?" Erec asked.

"There's been a constant barrage of attack at the entrance to the subway system; the higher-ranking Knights have been switching out. But it seems to be a never-ending wave. Not only of those giants, either—different Rift creatures are cooperating to try to break through and tear us apart. But the Silver Flames Knights have been able to hold barriers for a good part each day…" Garin began to explain everything that had happened since they'd parted ways.

He'd looked for Erec during the fight, desperate to find him, until a senior Knight yanked him away and forced him to retreat. He hadn't even *seen* Erec brawl with the giant. Olivia reported his last whereabouts—but that was it. The last thing they'd been allowed to do.

Eventually, with him out of sight, they were forced to withdraw. All the begging in the world couldn't stop the Knights in motion.

They'd thought the worst.

He wouldn't have been the only casualty of that fight.

Garin broke down.

"I…thought I lost you," he said, tears streaming down his face. Olivia grabbed his hand—squeezing through their metal gauntlets. "…But then, all of a sudden you showed up, with your shoulder blown to bits, I—even with how awful you looked, I had hope again. It wasn't long after that we found out help was coming…"

Apparently, holing up in here had been an effective strategy. For as relentless as the silent monsters attacking were, they lacked imagination. They hadn't discovered that the subway was linked to the sewer. Instead, they'd crushed downward, and it would've been effective if they'd been stuck. However, the sewer system was intact enough to operate in.

The main issue was withdrawing effectively and getting away once they were back on the surface and in the open. That's why they needed the help.

The Kingdom was coming to extract them.

Four days.

Erec took a long breath as the conversation slipped away from him and his two brushes with death. They hadn't been fully processed, and he'd no doubt have horrors lingering from the experience, but for now, there were other things to pursue. He had no weapons, not that he could've held his war axe, even if he knew where it was.

He dreaded the conversation he'd have with the Quartermaster, yet, he was grateful that he'd be able to have such a conversation.

Assuming they made it away from Worth alive.

Now and again, the monster banging against their barrier echoed down the long tunnels, a haunting sound, a promised violence. Their conversation lapsed as his friends slowly realized they should return to their jobs. Erec cleared his throat and stood straighter.

"Can one of you guys do me a favor?" he asked.

"Of course." Olivia nodded.

"Bring me to Boldwick."

# CHAPTER 57
## BACKUP PLAN

Boldwick strode around the subway with the authority of a king—decorated in his regal Armor. All paid their respects and offered him a nod of respect as he stalked through the subway. With the constant siege, that impeccable pillar of strength held them together and stripped away the tension and terse replies. But only for a brief moment.

As he drifted by, the inevitable wear of the situation would return and sink in. Every few hours, more Knights would return wounded and with damaged Armor.

One of the first lessons of Scavenging and Armor Modification was that damaged Armor needed proper resources for maintenance on the expedition. Often times, reality found a way of depriving you of what you needed, when you needed it. Scavenging could make up for that, but all scrap wasn't equal in quality. The best one could do was work with what they got, and prioritize what they needed.

People were beginning to stride around with missing plates and nonfunctional parts of their Armor. The scrap down here only served to slow the eventual decay of their defenses. But they remained in the sewers, fearing that the Silent Ones might find a different method of attack and trap them from both sides.

It was a marathon to reach the end of the four days before help arrived.

Boldwick did a double take as Erec approached; Olivia was at his side, hovering and making sure he had no trouble.

She was accommodating, and he'd expected to be worse off for all his injuries. Aside from the flares of pain in his shoulder, he found it surprisingly easy to keep going. Maybe it was seeing everyone else rush around and the taste of life and death in the air that made it possible.

"Erec?" Boldwick said with a mild sense of awe in his voice. "You're already up?"

"Yes, Sir." Erec moved his good hand to his chest as he formed a fist to salute the Master Knight, bowing his head.

"Ah," Boldwick said, his gaze leveling to Olivia. "Initiate Olivia, you may leave him to me and return to your duties. You have my thanks for escorting him here. I'm sure that there's plenty for you to do."

"Of course, my pleasure." Olivia backed away from Erec and dipped a curtsy in her Armor. "May that I see you again soon." With that, she briskly walked off.

Erec stood a bit awkwardly, unable to see the expression behind Boldwick's helmet. Just what was going on in the Master Knight's head? Around them, Knights shuffled, a new set rushing up the stairway toward the surface as another squad ran down—someone in half-broken Armor carried on a makeshift stretcher. Flecks of crimson blood dripped on the dreary concrete stairs.

"Let us move a bit away from those at work. I would have some words," Sir Boldwick declared before turning on his heel. He didn't motion for Erec to follow, but he didn't need to.

With an Initiate trailing behind, Boldwick strode a bit down the side of the central platform of the subway, shoving open a door to a small room. It was little better than a small utility closet, stripped aside from a pile of wood and refuse in a far corner. Boldwick removed his helmet and set it in the crook of his elbow as Erec joined him.

Not much room. But enough to face each other, keep out of the way, and have their words not overheard.

"First off," Boldwick said, taking a deep breath and lowering his head, "I sincerely apologize for putting your life at such risk."

"I—"

"It was careless and a mistake ill-fitting my station. I misjudged the strength of that man's gun and acted on false assumptions. In retrospect, I could've taken plenty of other options. My choice to capitalize on that opportunity could have resulted in more tragedy, and we're lucky it didn't end worse than it did."

"...Of course, I'm not angry—the only reason I got grabbed by him is that I couldn't control myself well enough to stay within the bounds of our allies..." Erec sighed. "That guy was a fucking bastard; he was dragging around some poor girl. Stepped on her hands to punish her and has her hooked on liquor, and Goddess knows what else. Please tell me you tracked him down?"

"No. We found the place his camp was, judging by the burnt-out fire, but there was no one and nothing there." Boldwick slowly shook his head and frowned. "He had a woman with him?"

"Yeah, he called her Maria and said she was good with tech—don't quite understand how, considering he treated her like an animal..."

"Deeply disturbing." Boldwick puffed his chest up. "Rest assured; I do not take such blatant acts against ours lightly, let alone someone threatening the life of one of my apprentices."

"...I saw Alister. He's going to pull through, I think."

His mentor deflated in a moment, looking to his feet. "Yet another of my mistakes. I'd miscalculated the chances of an attack on us. I'd set scouts on the two forces in the wasteland but hadn't foreseen a force hidden in the city." Boldwick slumped slightly and rubbed between his eyes. "Here's a lesson for you. The more you're in charge of, the more that rely on you, the more you can disappoint them and yourself."

"I doubt anyone could do better with the information you had, Sir," Erec replied, unsure what to think. There was a dark cast to Boldwick's face; his eyes carried a gravity that spoke of years of a heavy burden. "...May I ask something?"

"Granted." Boldwick looked at the door.

"I want to go into the sewers and investigate. I can't sit here useless to everyone else."

"Denied." Boldwick shook his head. "That man is long gone, and you're in no shape to fight him."

"No, it's not about revenge. Not now, at least. He—he has something of mine, and one day I'll be taking it back. But that's not why I want to, no." Erec felt the flames flicker in his soul; disdain bled into his words. "I'll tear the basta—"

"Enough. I understand the sentiment." Boldwick waved it off, yet that same hate echoed in his face. "So, even if it isn't about revenge, you wish to go into the sewers…why?"

"I already said why. I can't fight," Erec started in, looking at his one good arm. "At least…not well, and not without Armor." It was partially true. But also, there was a lie hidden in there.

*Fuck, how do I…*

He thought of Garin. Of how his friend managed to channel that natural charisma and get away with things he had no right to. All their life, with his father, servants, and even random people off the street—getting treats, getting into places he shouldn't, getting away with jokes…

"I need to help. I can't sit around watching other people bleed. What kind of man would I be? I can't fight well at the moment—but I can pack a punch if I needed to—but I can map out anything you need—help keep an eye out for anything that is prowling—"

"To be young." Boldwick took a deep sigh. He started at the heavily wrapped wound on Erec's should that the peculiar gun had caused. "I understand. I have two conditions…" He hesitated. "I was like you once. So eager to throw everything on the line to prove myself to the world, to test what I was capable of. It's very easy to do so, when you feel invincible." He gestured to the air. "But you have to remember—there are no such things as heroes, Erec."

"I know that. You've said it plenty enough."

"Then you understand that sometimes, we must do things to ensure our safety that not all agree with. At times, we must accept a cowardly act." Boldwick paused. "Goddess, forgive me. May you forgive me too, but you're certain you want to do this?"

"I am."

"Well enough. The only reason I'm allowing it in the first place is pure necessity; we're overtaxed. I've sent preliminary scouts into the sewers, but our mapping is far from complete. If we find a better exit point, we'll be better off. Unfortunately, with the damages and injuries, and the constant periods of brutal fighting, many of my more capable Knights are spent above— " Boldwick shook his head. "I'm trying to justify this—but actions speak louder than words…"

Boldwick shuffled over to a pile of wreckage in the room and tossed aside a few blocks of wood. He pulled free Seven-Snakes's gun.

"Two conditions. The first is that you hang onto this while scouting. It should shore up the concerns I have about sending out Initiate scouts into the sewers. And the second is that you take Olivia with you."

"…If the priests see that, I'm exiled," Erec said, jaw dropping as he ran a hand through his hair.

"You can remain in this camp. And heal. I suggest that highly. Though we have not had the resources to explore as much of the sewer as I'd like, we do have an exit plan. This task is dangerous, especially without Armor." His tone dropped, slipping into a careful cadence. "But this is a weapon. Not unlike your axe. Only it doesn't require much to use. Doesn't need you to get close. Aim and pull the trigger. You don't require Armor to fight a monster with this. And *if* that man is still hiding somewhere in those sewers, it would do the job."

Erec stared at the gun—as Boldwick extended it, he saw a crude snake engraved along the side of the barrel. Funny how he hadn't seen such a thing before when it threatened his life.

"There are no heroes. If we want to do something, we're not strong enough; if our hearts demand we must walk a road no matter what, we must protect ourselves by any means necessary."

"What if Olivia sees it?"

"She works for House Luculentus; out of anyone in this damned Kingdom, they are the least likely to burn you over the use of a firearm. Besides, they're more interested in cultivating you as a resource. After we've gotten out of Worth safely, you can toss the gun into the desert. I would. But until then…" He paused, seeing Erec's conflicted expression. "Let's phrase it this way, since I don't think you're one to protest the practical option—say while we fled this place, one of those stone giants attacked Garin. Your arm is fucked, you don't have an axe, and you don't have your Armor. How would it feel to watch helplessly as he died?"

"Heart-wrenching." Erec narrowed his eyes, already feeling his heart tug.

"From one man who went through such a thing to one of my

pupils, I would never have you undergo the same." He pressed the gun forward. "Take it, and hide it well."

Erec grabbed the weapon from him—and felt the cold grip in his hand, how light the weapon felt, considering what he'd seen it capable of doing. Or was it—

[Wow. That's a real slick gun, Buckeroo. Careful you don't shoot your eye out.]

—yeah, VAL had taken a look at it and seemed impressed. Erec shoved the weapon away in his waistband—the only place he could think of to stash it for now. He gave Boldwick a salute and left the room. The cold metal pressed against his back, as good as a death sentence if it were discovered, but also the one thing that gave him a measure of power with all that was going on.

# CHAPTER 58
# DAN

*DAN: What do you mean VAL isn't cooperating with the research team?*

*MANNY: It's like we've said repeatedly; it offers a modicum of support, claims it's fulfilled its obligations, and returns to independent research.*

*DAN: Then change its directives.*

*MANNY: You know it isn't as simple as that; every time we've adjusted them past the basic guidelines we've set, it finds a way to get back at us.*

*DAN: Get back at you? Goddamn, Manny, we're talking about an AI here, a machine. It's on a goddamn server. The only reason it isn't operating at max efficiency is because you've failed at your job.*

*MANNY: Listen—you try dealing with it for a whole month. Its passive-aggressive comments have had three of my researchers request transfers in the last year. It's toxic.*

*DAN: All you do is complain. I chat with VAL every time I stop by; it's nothing but pleasant. I think I'll talk with it right now and get an honest read on the situation. The last time I stopped by, I asked it to conduct an evaluation of your performance. If my gut is right, I'm pretty sure VAL isn't the problem here.*

*MANNY: Wait—sir—*

*- Unknown, Vortex Industries transcript log (2106, 2nd Era)*

T he network of sewers was like a labyrinth. It stretched long and winding, a suggestion of a horrible fate for anyone who dared to explore, get lost, starve, and die in a festering shit-hole. Completed by randomly collapsed tunnels and twisting intersections, and long lonely stretches of ancient brackish wastewater. Yet it all had a mysterious way of blending together, adding to the confusion.

Long open corridors wore away on mental fortitude as a wanderer wondered what horror might lurk in their depths.

Every second spent in the sewer answered why Boldwick didn't have enough resources to locate alternative suitable exits. It spoke volumes that the scouts hadn't managed to find where VAL had hid his Armor away.

Erec paced down the tunnel carefully. His good hand rested on the hatchet at his side, though he was well aware of the gun in his pouch. Despite Boldwick's assertion that Olivia wouldn't turn him in, Erec didn't see a reason to chance it if he could help it.

"So bold," she remarked as she trailed behind, her Armor making very little noise due to the shock absorption. A marvel that even piloting that steel frame, she made just about as much sound as his boots hitting the wet muck and concrete. "To think that even without Armor and injured, you insist on leading, let alone pushing for such a mission."

Erec kept staring at the dark ahead, always looking for something shifting around, even though, for the most part, it seemed abandoned.

[Forward, down this way.]

His biggest advantage. An effortless way to overcome the other scout's trouble with determining layout. He had a machine in his head to do the mapping for him. VAL kindly kept a record of everything—even stating it could create a visual display on the Armor with the map—once they retrieved it.

It couldn't be much further away.

"I'm not bold," Erec said, hand on the hatchet. Even with the gun, it felt far more natural to hold onto the weapon. Luckily, one of the Knights had packed it away in case they needed to cut down a door and agreed to let him borrow it.

Once he returned to the Academy, he'd have to have a long and apologetic discussion with the Quartermaster. That war axe held a lot of meaning to the man. Even now, the thought ripped at his heart the slightest bit. But it was better to admit and own up to it than try to beat around the bush.

"I'd disagree." Olivia shook her head. "Thank you, by the way, for saving me from that giant. Though I do apologize for running."

"If you died, Garin would've been broken-hearted, and I—" He paused as he thought over the harder-to-recall-than-normal memory. "I would've done it no matter what, I think. Though my intentions at the time weren't 'I have to save her,' more, 'I wish to test myself against this foe.'"

"I wish I could say I understood, but I don't. It must be odd to have such a Divine Talent."

Erec shrugged as they plodded down the dark tunnel. Even with his Armor being hidden ahead, with all the twists and turns, it wasn't a wonder why the scouts missed it. It made him nervous to consider that something else might be in these sewers.

The more he moved, the more grateful he was for the gun as a backup plan. And the more he realized that the situation in the subway must indeed be desperate.

"It's strong," Erec finally said. "It has drawbacks, but... I don't know. I feel like the more I use it, the more I can see what it might become. Honestly, it's a bit terrifying."

"How does it feel to have so much Strength? Electrifying, I bet," Olivia said, her tone a bit off. Erec looked back at her, and she tilted her head. "Very attractive, in fact."

"Shut the hell up."

"I know some maids who might swoon for such a bold and powerful Knight as yourself, Sir Erec."

"Do I look like I want to hear it?" Erec put on a scowl and stopped. *Are we really having this conversation in the middle of the sewers?* "C'mon, stop it. Let's focus on what matters."

"How dutiful and attentive you are to your goals. I'll be sure to spread such rumors along," Olivia...giggled? Yeah, she just giggled at him as he kept from looking at her. The truth was, he didn't have time for something like that. In fact...he'd never really considered it.

Growing up, it'd been a struggle to retain their family through all the trouble; then, he spent so long trying to catch up to Bedwyr.

Where did love or romance fit in the heart of someone who only wanted power and the freedom that came with that?

They rounded the corner, and Olivia let out a loud gasp.

Standing in the middle of the sewer tunnel was Erec's Vallum Armor—covered in muck, with its back plating broken, the helmet dented, and various other concerning and certainly significant injuries from the fight above. It wasn't in great condition, but then, he'd passed his trial in Armor far closer to falling apart. Compared to that, the Vallum Armor was much better off.

[Long-time no see. Way to go, Intern!]

"Whoa!" Erec exclaimed, faking excitement as he ran to the Armor. "I can't believe we found it?!"

He inspected it—or pretended to, trying to hem and haw, and act his way out of an explanation. He acted as if this were a miracle, like it blew his mind how lucky he was. How fortunate!

Olivia didn't seem to buy what he was selling, but he gave his best anyway.

She didn't press him on the way back on the *coincidence* of him finding it during their first scouting mission. He wasn't sure if that was more concerning, or less.

— - ☣ - — - ☼ - — - ☣ - —

The next couple of days fell into a familiar routine. Erec would wake up, get in his Armor, then he and Olivia would explore more of the sewers. Together, they mapped out a good mile of the winding sewers stretching out from their breach point. It was hard work, and for the most part completely danger-free. But eventually, they encountered an enemy.

Olivia was more than capable of taking care of the rat-like monster alone. Which was good—Erec's wounds were recovering quicker than expected with a daily dose of treatment from the priests. They ran across a couple more she dispatched with ease throughout their scouting.

The irony of the priests healing his wounds when he had a forbidden gun hidden away wasn't lost on him.

He left the gun under a pile of rubble in the sewers and said it was more practical to keep it there to avoid the risk of losing it in the chaos of the subway. Olivia gave him that nod of hers, the nod that Erec quickly learned was, "Of course, Sir." But it actually meant, "I'll pretend to agree, even if I know that's not all there is to it." Working in a noble House, especially a Duchy, would mean that such a reaction and nod were commonplace for her.

Or at least he imagined.

The frustrating truth was that he couldn't know what was going on in that head of hers or what info she noted down to use later or for what purpose. It made him nervous. So he asked her questions to fill the silence.

Namely, he pressed her about his friend and her intentions. To his surprise, when she spoke of Garin, there was only pure joy. His friend was a topic that she didn't seem to get enough of—even asking him about some of their adventures together as kids.

They would return to eat and check in at lunch, then head back out.

It was a good sign, or at least Erec assumed it was, that she had such a positive interest in Garin's history. She genuinely cared, which went a long way to relieving him of the suspicion she was using his best friend.

But he couldn't grasp her motives, and on the second day, when he asked after her employment and goals for working for the Duchy, she got evasive and noncommittal. Not outright denying any of the accusations he threw out, but not answering them. And who was he to judge? He'd lied to her again and again.

They made it to the third day and discovered a better exit that took them further from the chaos above. It wasn't long on their return trip that the communicator buzzed.

"Barrier broken, spilling through—" A clatter of fighting and shouts.

Old man Fulton's voice came through the communications, gravelly and grave. "Knights Errant and above respond to the front line, provide support and prepare for an emergency retreat; we'll be going through the sewers a day earlier than expected. Initiates prepare to leave."

Erec shared a look with Olivia before they both sped back the way they'd come—headed right back to the encampment. He needed to show them the better route.

He needed to get to the battlefield and fight.

Erec shook his head as his metal boots slammed against the concrete, shoving him forward through space. It was like one of those old-world tales—a siren's call. A sweet song, tempting him with the beauty of battle—why did it grip him so? He couldn't afford to join the fighting, he was too injured, and they needed him to help direct people through the sewers.

*Ignore it.*

Ignore that fire inside; it didn't matter what the beast said from its cage, how it promised that the injuries weren't as big of a deal as he thought. How, if it lent him just an ounce of its power, he'd have enough Strength to help save others.

Have enough Strength to coat a tunnel in blood and stand on a pile of his enemy's corpses.

He'd be a hero. A warrior of unparalleled might.

*There's no such thing as heroes.*

The gun clinked against his Armor and swayed with his movements as he ran with a burst of speed down the tunnel, toward death and destruction.

# CHAPTER 59
# END APPROACHES

Erec and Olivia scrambled back through the subway system, taking a long tour of the dark and scummy interiors. It'd been a long time since this place was used for refuse, but the shifting in the landscape led to countless collapsed tunnels and winding terrain. Thanks to VAL, Erec was able to help them effectively navigate and make fast progress back to the subway.

They only stopped when they met the Knights rushing out. Some had marks on their Armor, torn pieces of steel hanging loose and fresh blood on their metal. The sound of fighting echoed not far behind, from the subway tracks and station itself.

Most among those gathered were other Initiates. That and the odd Knight Commander or Knight Lieutenant set to organize and distribute the supplies hurried out for transport.

It was a complete evacuation.

Erec stared past the worried Initiates. Beyond them was a fight, a battlefield filled with death and foes. He caught a brief understanding from the conversations of the other Initiates.

It hadn't been the stone giants that broke through. Two monster encampments from beyond the city had joined them. All of them had merged into a single force, timed an attack for when the barriers went down to recover, and then overwhelmed the defenders with their massive force.

In a rare yet fascinating display of tactics from the Silent Ones, they targeted the Silver Flames Knights capable of maintaining the barrier first.

Over twenty Knights perished in the swift and ferocious attack. Unable to hold off the stronger host.

Injured were carried in and ready for transport as the priests worked to salvage the situation.

Erec kept still as his ears focused on the noise. How many were dying out there? If only he could—

"Erec?" Colin asked, limping up. The Duke's son's left leg dragged across the ground, and a nasty gouge tore through the metal and severed the servos. It would slow him down, but considering they had Knights unable to walk, Colin was better off than them, at least.

"Ah." Erec shook himself out of it and denied the beast its control. Olivia was twisting and turning next to him. "Where's Garin? Is he safe?" Erec asked.

"Indeed, he was with me during the evacuation. We fought off one of the Renders—I believe that's the term they used. Awful creatures, far too quick. One of the Knight Commanders kept crying about them being an 'ideal shock troop.'"

"Right, good." Erec let out a sigh of relief. "How about Gwen?"

Colin shrugged. "Could be here. But it's not like I keep my eyes out for such a low-class wench. We're not allowed back in the subway system; they're stalemating the monsters and plan on collapsing the tunnel."

"Sir Erec." Olivia shook his shoulder. "I'll locate Garin. You need to find whoever's in charge of the retreat and inform them about our discovery."

Erec nodded slowly. He ought to do that, even with the call of battle. Even knowing that in his current state, and with his current abilities, he was more likely to be a liability in that field than a help.

It was better to be of use in a way that would help with their escape. With a nod of understanding to Colin, he sought out someone in charge.

Dame Robin was the first person he came across; her thin Armor contrasted with the regular Vallum model of their Order and made her easy to spot.

"Ma'am." Erec strode up, nearer to the head of the tunnel. Robin paused as she looked at one of two Commanders, who excused her. They returned to their logistic planning as Erec pulled her aside to deliver his report.

As she swayed in her spot, Erec saw the same thing as he'd seen in Boldwick as he led. That haunted presence clung to her, even though she maintained a façade of calmness to raise morale, but beneath it all was a surety and foundation that comforted those around her.

Erec paused.

And then considered.

To be someone like Boldwick—or her. Perhaps it was better to be someone who led and saved those below them, to help contribute in an emergency and direct their forces. His own goal brought an odd bit of guilt. He still wanted to lose himself in the wasteland and find his mother…

Was that…just?

Erec shook his head as the thought flitted like a bird, clearing his throat. There wasn't time to dwell on such things, not right now.

"We've located a better exit," Erec cut in, trying to keep the report brief. "Olivia utilized her prayer and confirmed the exit to be safe."

Dame Robin tilted her head. "Did you, now? Why is it better than the one we'd mapped out previously? Boldwick mentioned you two were looking into that, but under these conditions, we need to be sure."

"Mainly, it's further away and far closer to the western outskirts. From here to it, accounting for the obstructions and twists in the sewers—" Erec checked the visual display on his Armor, scanning the helpful map VAL provided. In his head, he ran a quick estimation. "A total of six miles. Which is understandable; with the limited time scouts had and the sewer's nature, it makes sense why it'd be difficult to locate. It'll take us to the surface a few miles from here—like I said, right at the western outskirts."

"Which was further away from our enemies. Given they've merged at our position, it's prudent to choose an exit which takes us the furthest away." Dame Robin nodded. "If your report is accurate, it'll provide much-needed breathing room from their ranks. Are you certain of this information?"

"I'd stake my own life on it. I'll lead the way there and be the first to show you it's safe," Erec said.

"Your word is enough; I don't require risking yourself. Coordinate with Dame Juliana. We'll be moving in five to ten minutes. You'll know because you'll hear the rubble collapsing from above and behind us." Dame Robin paused, looking him up and down. "...Look at you, your Armor is a complete mess, and I know you're still injured under all that steel. Mayhaps Boldwick taught me to see like him, I see why he chose to take you under his wing. But never forget, you can't grow if you're dead."

Erec gave her a firm nod before running off. Finding Dame Juliana was a bit more complicated. After explaining to her, and Dame Robin's agreement, the Knight Commander, was receptive to his instructions. With the help of VAL's map, he gave her directions through the sewer tunnel.

He'd only just finished explaining when he heard a loud explosion. The entire tunnel shook as a cascading crash came the subway connection.

After a brief skirmish at their flank, the expedition fled down the sewer tunnels.

— - ☢ - — - ☼ - — - ☢ - —

A couple of hours later, the expedition burst out of the sewers and found itself under that great blue sky. After days trapped underground, Erec felt a flush of exhilaration. The fear and worry aside, this—this was why he became a Knight. They worked quickly to haul the supplies to the surface as scouts scanned the nearby area.

It was a testament to their adaptability with how quickly they'd transitioned to a smooth operation after an emergency.

But as Olivia's prayer showed, this location was fairly safe. Right near the outskirts of the city, an ideal point to flee into the wastelands.

Boldwick's voice called above the growing crowd at the surface as all of the supplies were divided for transport. The scout must have given him the clear. He took position on a pile of rubble so everyone could see him point at the vast landscape of dust and dirt, right at the wasteland. "Get moving, go!"

With that abrupt call to action, everyone rushed forward. A long train of injured, damaged, and still-functional Knights playing flank trod into the wastes. Erec carried two bags—despite his injuries, he managed it with minimal pain. They were emergency supplies.

Boldwick pushed them at a fast pace.

Only a mile out, their march came to a halt.

Hushed whispers dominated the deadlands as Boldwick stared at the city of Worth, as they all stared at the abandoned old-world city.

Even with his lower level of perception, Erec knew what he was staring at. Miles sat between them and that thing. Yet its pure hate hung in the air, choking his lungs like dust from a storm.

A massive glowing White Stag perched on the top of a building on the city's outskirts. Its long antlers stretched ten to fifteen feet from its head—thrice the size of a Mutant Stag. The sun almost blinded his eyes as it reflected off a pure white coat. Even if he couldn't see it from here, he felt those blood-red orbs trained on their expedition.

With those eyes, it felt like he was being pulled in and judged. As if it were going to consume him and steal every bit of his mind and soul straight from his skull. From beneath it, even though it was a Stag, radiated a killing intent that made his skin crawl.

"It's real," Erec said, his voice filled with an awed horror.

He wasn't the only Knight pointing out the monster with pure horror. It was undeniable, this thing was on an entirely different level than anything else out here. More than any of the monsters chasing after them.

Monsters spilled free into the city's outskirts as it gazed at them. From this distance, the Stone Giants were the clearest, but the quickest were four-legged dots kicking up dust as they ran. Yet, if one looked back, one's eyes were naturally drawn to what must've been their leader—the White Stag.

There were only a few miles of distance between them and an approaching army of horrors; their enemy rushed across the wasteland to tear them apart. A silent army of death, with the White Stag overlooking it all. Cold fear ran through Erec, tempering the excitement of battle with absolute certainty that against that force, they would die.

"March!" Boldwick screamed, snapping people from their daze. His voice was hoarse as he pointed in the opposite direction. "Keep marching until your lungs scream, and then march more! We won't be stopping until we reach our allies! Move it!"

With that, Knights broke out into jogs, the strongest carrying stretchers between them and shifting positions as they began a full-scale run into the barren and deadly wastes. Though as they dropped packages of supplies to increase speed—it was as if they were running from certain death to uncertain death.

The brutal wasteland loved to kill unprepared Knights. If they didn't find their allies…

Boldwick had made a decision that left their lives on the line. They'd die if they got lost—if they couldn't keep outside of the Monster's reach.

Erec tried to keep his head clear, but he couldn't help but keep glancing over his shoulder as they moved.

It was impossible to look away from that astonishingly beautiful Stag. As if his mind were pulled toward it. He wasn't the only one who couldn't help but take a second look, even if it meant seeing the host of vicious monsters determined to slaughter them.

# CHAPTER 60
## CAESAR

*When looking up the ancients, we call to mind the names of Caesar, Alexander, Khan.*

*They are what it is to be a conqueror, and in order to reclaim this world to the hands of mankind, we must not hesitate to learn from their lessons and take what is ours from those that do not belong here.*

*One day we shall claim again the surface, and when we do, we must be prepared and held together as a people."*

*- King Restfos Crisimus,* Lessons to the Crisimus Lineage *(165, 3rd Era)*

With monsters nipping at their heels, the expedition marched full-pace into the night. Boldwick led the flight, constantly checking his compass as they moved, calculating their bearing. Setting up long-range communication on the run wasn't feasible. Their only option was to try to intersect the last known coordinates of their relief.

They'd out sped the stone creatures, yet two different sets of monsters still chased them. As was typical with monsters from a Rift, their appearances tended to fit together. It was uncanny in a way, like how one could tell that a human and a squirrel came from the same place, an instinctual identification. Their different worlds led to vastly different appearances. Yet this level of coordination between monsters was unheard of.

As was their commonality in their silence; no howls, no whines, no growling; they moved with a haunting quiet as they attacked.

The Renders were the biggest threats; they were the quickest. Able to cover distance fast by throwing themselves forward on their four legs. And unsightly, their veiny skin laced with a network of wires that jabbed outward from their spines into their legs; the wires weaved between blades that stabbed out of their back and limbs. Both the speed and those sharp natural weapons made them quite deadly.

When a pack of them approached, a Knight had to separate from the group to fend them off.

But it was a careful act. The awful things had to be slaughtered quickly, or more packs would join the fray. If a Knight got over-whelmed, they'd get dragged into fighting with more Monsters—until they met their demise.

One by one, sacrifice by sacrifice, a handful of Knights went out this way to cover their retreat. Tearing into the main host of enemies to lag them behind just a bit longer.

Heroes. Or corpses.

One of the Master Knights maintained a position on the flank—and for his part, held it up fine; but as the night wore on and more miles flew under their feet, reality sank in.

These things would never give up. There was no retreat, as they'd never grow bored. It wouldn't stop until they left every last human here rotting on the wasteland, or the Knights killed each one of these terrors.

Erec pressed ahead with Colin limping next to him; the boy's leg degraded further as they went. The two maintained a position in the middle of the pack, despite the injuries and malfunctioning Armor. Whenever Colin's servos acted up too heavily, Erec would yank him along.

The packs they'd started with were long since tossed to the ground; this necessary and rash plan was so far working in mini-mizing casualties.

Due to their flight, they kept ahead of the host of monsters, limited the skirmishing, and widening a gap before the main host of enemies would crash against them.

But the good news ended there.

As the night stretched, the frustration, exhaustion, and morale loss took their toll. They moved slower. The Render attacks grew more frequent as the faster creatures caught up.

"Keep going," Erec yelled to Colin as his friend's leg sparked and spasmed.

"Damn it all!" Colin screamed, dragging the metal and leaving a gouged-out streak of dirt. "This is it; it's gone!"

Erec paused as Knights rushed by; he took in as much air as possible while examining the sparking limb. The damage without a proper patch job was too much. After all the running, it must've reached a critical failure point. There was only one option.

[Well done, Intern, you've diagnosed its state without me running an assessment!]

*Glad you agree.* If nothing else, it made his next demand easier to voice. "Abandon your Armor."

"What?!" Colin asked, fear in his voice. "Do you know how much my father paid—"

"Would you rather die?" Erec said, feeling sweat dripping down his face. Despite the cooling system, the insides of his Armor felt like a fire pit.

"I-I—" Colin hesitated. Too long. Erec went over and yanked at his helmet—throwing every bit of his strength into the act. He had to use both of his hands. Pain lanced through his left shoulder, but it'd recovered enough to let him leverage it for this, surely. To counter that intense pain—he let a bit of that anger bleed through, let the fire inside of him ignite.

Just a taste of Fury.

The helmet ripped free, and he threw it into the wasteland. Another discarded piece of tech to join the many others buried in this one world.

"One piece gone. Easy. Take off the rest. I'll protect you. Stay next to me," Erec promised, rotating his shoulder as Fury slipped back to rest. It hurt. Bad. But he'd made his point; it'd pushed Colin past the breaking point and took his decision away.

Colin left his Armor—leaving him in his Academy clothes, minus the jacket. His hair was disheveled, his face red and coated in a thin layer of sweat. Erec clapped him on the shoulder once, watching as he retrieved his sword from the discarded Armor.

Better to abandon that than end up dead on the blade of a Render. Colin's face was grave as he looked at Erec—at his arm.

"T-thank you, but I don't believe you should've done that."

"I'm fine," Erec lied.

This was the first time during the hectic march he'd burned little bits of Fury to keep going. Before now, he'd never thought such a thing possible, but the pain and exhaustion from his healing wounds were dragging him back. And that feeling held no importance now—he needed Strength.

Fury lent it to him. And in combination with VAL carefully monitoring him and administering low levels of sedative when he let a little bit of that inner fire blaze, he could keep moving.

"Ready to keep going?" Erec asked as more boots marched past. They'd fallen behind, and the end of the line was rapidly approaching.

Colin nodded.

With that, they took off—pushing hard to catch back up, not to be left behind.

Erec's eyes drifted above as he ran, landing on that sea of stars which watched from on high, a pretty painting across the dark sky. Somewhere up there, did the Goddess watch on with passive eyes as Her people struggled for their lives?

— - ☻ - — - ☼ - — - ☻ - —

Dawn brought with it hope. As the sun rose to the sky, it illuminated their distant salvation. Not more than a few miles away were pillars of smoke.

As they closed the distance, they saw a host of Knights with steel wagons circled together and in a far larger number than the expedition. Heraldry of every sort dominated the gathering. The scouts were already shouting and warning one another as the expedition ran straight at their fortification.

They came with a swarm of Renders.

Almost like in a dream, Erec passed into the encampment. He struggled for breath as he watched the Knights join the fray against the now-constant fighting at their flank. Flashes of magic, swings of blades, and blood flew free in a grand melee not far behind.

Their reinforcements were more than eager to engage the monsters; Knights from all of the Orders united as one to fend off the beasts.

Like the rest of the expedition, Erec was escorted deeper into the encampment.

Colin panted at his side. They were safe. But the fighting would continue and only worsen as the main force of the enemies caught up. They had gained a few hours of reprieve before the true battle.

Garin and Olivia spotted them in a few minutes, followed by Gwen. Everyone was safe—though Garin had a nasty gash across his chest, there was no blood.

There wasn't much time to rest. Commander Knights came and directed them to gulp down water and eat—only half an hour to regather their strength as the leaders of both expeditions convened.

Not long after, more orders came.

Healthy Knights, like Garin and Olivia, got yanked away to construct fortifications for the coming battle.

Those wounded and without Armor, like Erec and Colin, were tasked with managing supply lines and assisting the injured. A back-line position.

But Erec supposed it to be prudent.

It didn't take long for his hands to be full. He provided aid to the injury tents, taking orders from the priests as they scrambled to stabilize the newly wounded, and helped gather supplies for those moved during the travel. The priests divided the tents unevenly, with most of the priests smashed together in the largest one. Within its linen walls, blood flew, and they worked to close dire wounds and perform emergency surgery to stabilize Knights. Most healing prayers required the recipient to be stable so they could withstand the increased pain.

If they weren't, they risked falling into shock. And if healed improperly, there was a chance of causing disability.

He drifted between tents, hauling water, food, and medicine, and marveled at the difference of this world. How even here, chaos dominated, and people died. This was a different fight, yet he found peace in the task. He could help people.

Erec paused at the back of one of the tents, watching a priest softly chant over a stilled Knight. Everyone here was going to be fine, and live, thanks to the healing and the efforts of those to haul them across the wasteland.

As much as his mind told him this was good, that he was doing good, it felt wrong.

He was away from the fighting.

Garin and Olivia risked their lives to build defenses somewhere near that wall. Here he was, wounded, sure, but in fine enough shape to provide more direct support. Every second here increased his nerves—every time that priest asked him to get more bandages—it was annoying.

[Quit using Fury, there's no reason to.]

Erec exhaled.

Sure enough, the fire was burning inside. Low and smoldering. He hadn't even realized he'd started to pull from it again. Erec smothered it out, his shoulder drooping as the pain sank back in.

*I'm losing it.*

Alister groaned on the ground, shuffling to look at Erec and give him a sloppy grin as he returned with a pack of rations. "Aw, shucks. Getting my meals delivered to me by my junior. Way it's supposed to be." He shifted, leaning up.

The priest tended to a man in the corner; they'd stuffed this tent with those transported from Worth. Too injured to walk around and assist.

"Don't get used to it. Get better, alright?" Erec said, opening the pack of rations and setting it in Alister's hand. A cold stew of some kind. Rich in nutrients and likely better than most to help injuries recover. Erec's shoulder flared with pain, and he gritted his teeth. He fought back the instinct to call forth Fury again. Healing, stress, and pushing himself would likely delay the time it'd take for it to recover completely. But so be it.

Once they made it free from this hell, he'd have all the time he needed to get back to normal.

They'd found what they sought. The White Stag had revealed itself; none in the expedition could deny its existence.

Nor could they quickly wave away its connection to those silent monsters.

[Hatchet!]

A claw tore through the side of the tent—a Render crashed through the thin fabric, a blade shooting out of its right foreleg and jabbing into the chest of one of the sleeping Knights, painting the sand below red. They choked on their own blood as it spun away.

A second later, its metallic blade tore out another man's throat, moving quickly enough for its form to blur.

Erec's hatchet met his hand as Colin turned into the tent.

# CHAPTER 61
## CONFRONTATION

The intruder's bloodied maw wrinkled as it sniffed the air—this close, it was easy to see its vaguely doglike form. If one ignored the almost veiny wires jabbing into its throat and jaw and the steel blades jutting out from its back. Its strained, bloodshot eyes were forcibly held open by pins jabbed into their lids. For a half-second, it took in Erec.

Then shifted its attention to Colin, who'd froze near the entryway. Without any warning, it pounced at him.

Erec yanked his hatchet free and threw himself between the monster and his friend. A blade snapped out of one of its flailing legs. Triggered by a pulse of one of those veins jabbed in it, the unnaturally sharp weapon ripped through his Armor and into his left arm.

The beast's maw snapped in his face. Those jagged metal teeth, a row of daggers, a single bite would tear through him. Erec swung his hatchet into the Render's side as he felt heat flush through him and bleed from the tear in his already wounded arm.

Despite the new gash, the Render managed to flip through the air. It landed carefully as a trail of oil and blood leaked from its flank. Even with the wound, it didn't whine. There were no sounds. As if it didn't feel the pain, the monstrosity displayed not a single care; a second later, it threw itself at Erec again.

A thin white barrier of light popped into existence between him and the Render. Dimly, Erec heard the priest dive into prayer. As the monster's blade slammed into the light, the whole creature slowed.

The tip of that weapon was moving slowly toward his skull. Without the aid, it would've ended him.

Bullshit.

Erec bit his lip—blood ran down as fire ripped through him, as he let Fury free. The monster wasn't the only one who didn't need pain.

He whipped the hatchet into the creature's exposed stomach, and the force of the blow threw it clear from the barrier. It tumbled over itself as it hit the ground, soaring past the priest and staining dirt with more blood and oil.

*Not enough.*

Erec closed the distance in an instant, snapping all of his strength through his heel into the ground to throw him forward. With an overhead swing, he buried the hatchet into the Render's skull.

It was enough to end it. The monster went limp, blood poured free. Erec laughed, basking in his victory.

"H-holy shit," Colin said, looking at the corpses of the two lost Knights. Alister struggled to his feet, taking raspy breaths as the priest made a sign over their chest. "How did one of them—"

More noises outside. Chaos.

The battle had begun in earnest, it seemed. Erec's body shuddered as Fury waned, as the machine in his head and that cold fire eased him.

His arm burned. The gashes bled, and he felt weak.

[Noncritical. That wound will mend with the shoulder; however, get that priest to—]

Another Render joined them in the tent—followed by a second. The first one moved like a predator. From the moment it entered the space, it set its eyes on a victim and pounced before Erec could call Fury back and before the priest could say a word.

Blood coated the tent as its foreleg jabbed a blade through Alister's gut. The Knight collapsed, his jaw landing on the blades on the monster's back as his guts spilled on the ground.

Crimson, deep ruby-red blood pooled beneath him as he took his last breath. Colin formed a glyph, falling back on magic, but it was too slow.

It only took a second to steal a life.

The priest screamed and fell back as far as he could, trying to put distance between himself and the monsters.

If nothing happened, they'd all die. Hell surged through Erec's veins. Time slowed as Erec watched the second monster start to pick a target. Alister's eyes lost their gloss as the beast began to shake him free.

VAL tried to fire off a dozen instructions, none of them relevant.

No, Erec wouldn't run.

No. This was his fight.

The fire burned him away, consuming his life just as the monster had taken away Alister's, leaving nothing but ash. He welcomed it, gave it everything.

Erec threw his hatchet through the air, nailing the monster that killed Alister. It swayed in its spot with the handle sticking out of it, convulsing as it slumped to the ground.

The other one didn't wait; it jumped through the air right as Colin did. There wasn't time for the glyph to complete. Without his Armor, Colin would die, just like Alister.

Without thinking, Erec yanked the gun from his satchel free. Aiming it was easy. Pulling the trigger, easier.

A bang rang through the tent as the walls expanded from the burst of force. The monster exploded in the middle of the air—guts and giblets flying freely to coat everyone inside with blood and gore.

Another came into the tent.

Easy problem. Erec pulled the trigger again; the pitiful thing evaporated into meat paste.

Erec lowered the gun as Colin and the priest stared at him, their eyes wide open. Their jaws hung. He calmly walked over to the corpse of the monster that mangled Alister and pulled his hatchet free from its skull with one jerk. One of its blades was still popped out from its leg—a free weapon. Erec slammed the hatchet into the joint and tore the fleshy blade free.

A good enough weapon. Not an axe. Not quite a sword. It would work to paint with blood.

Inside, the hell raged uncontested, no voice to argue against it, burning in both hot and cold. It'd won. He'd given everything to it, and if it incinerated him at the end, it'd be fine if he took enough demons with him.

[Oh my, Buckeroo! We've crossed a line, haven't we?]

"E-Erec?!" Colin said.

"Hide. The weak hide," Erec growled, the Render's jagged blade trailing across the dirt.

The priest stared at him as he threw the gun at Colin. For a second, Colin juggled the weapon, nearly dropping it. Erec turned away before he could see, since it didn't matter.

They weren't strong enough, but he could be.

Erec threw the tent wide open.

Hell had broken out over the entirety of the encampment. Less than a mile away, air twisted and flowed. A rend in reality itself distorted light and tore a hole through the world. Light and shadow mingled on its twisted surface, a broken gradient around its cracked border. A Rift. A hole that connected their world to another, this one roughly the size of a building.

Renders left it by the dozen, given free rein to attack the encampment as they rushed past defenders straining to protect two flanks.

Good. More to kill.

— - ☢ - — - ☼ - — - ☢ - —

Blood. Glorious blood. Every swing of this blade brought more as they sliced through the Renders. Each move drew more Strength, pushing past anything he'd felt before. The power was intoxicating, capacity only a figment of the imagination. It didn't matter if you let it all burn away.

Fury was boundless Strength.

When had he lost sight of that? Why had he wanted anything else?

It only promised more the more he drew from that never-ending well in hell.

Fire flooded his veins; he left bodies in a haphazard path behind him.

A Render attacked from the top of a steel wagon; Erec stepped aside smoothly, then tore a blade through the thing's underside with a lazy slash. Its body split as two hunks of meat landed on either side of him.

Erec laughed, turning around and flinging his hatchet at the thing's friend, splitting through its skull and halfway through its body in one smooth motion.

Another blinking notification popped into existence in the corner of his vision. They were unimportant and came intermittently as he fought. The last two hours flew by in a blaze of fun. When his body began to shake, more fire came from within to replenish his veins.

The voice in his head did all it could to keep him going, but why bother?

Even if his left arm was harder to use, he'd adapted. There wasn't pain, not even when he took a stab.

Erec tore through the battlefield in a glorious dance, each new Render a new partner to join him on the stage. They put on a show, an ode to life and death. Every swing of his blade a fresh move, every dead partner a new song. If his blade grew dull, as they were prone to do after a couple of kills, he hacked another one free from his last partner.

How kind of them to provide for the show.

Each of their stabs, every time one shredded through his Armor, encouragement. He could hear the demons below applaud as the blood poured from him.

A good dancer knew how to share the stage.

Around him, Knights pushed forward in their own desperate battles; they gave their all, even their lives, to stave off this infestation.

In the distance, a small team fought to get to the Rift. On the other side of the camp, more fought to repel the beasts' main army. A brutal and supremely beautiful battle.

Corpses decorated the wastes as they had, as they always would.

Erec recovered his hatchet and kicked the dead creature it'd been buried in. The limp body flew into a steel wagon.

"Erec?" a distantly familiar voice asked. It was a person with a large sword held easily on their shoulder. They'd painted their Armor with as much blood as Erec's own, even if it was sleeker. "Is that you?"

Erec didn't respond. A new Render darted by; they were fast little bastards. But the more he fought against them, the faster he got it. Their speed was a part of the dance. He tossed the hatchet again, skimming past the vaguely familiar Knight to tear off one of the monster's legs.

The Render crashed into the ground, flipping from the speed.

In an instant, Erec was on it. His stolen blade jabbed through the beast's chest, though this time, it was harder to push through. Damn blade. It twitched beneath him as it died; Erec lopped off a new weapon to hurry it along to hell.

"By the Goddess. You fight like a beast."

"Shut up," Erec growled, annoyed. Their voice was too much. Why all the talking? There was more battle all around them.

The Knight, for their part, didn't protest. Instead, they joined him. Erec tore into more monsters—picking larger battles with an ally fighting at his side. Their great big sword flung through the air and moved with surprising agility for such a bulky weapon. They fought in a similar manner, switching like water as they flowed smoothly between prayer, magic, and raw strength.

Without any hesitation, they swapped the flow of the battle for each situation.

Incredible. Such raw potential for fighting; in a way, that natural instinct for efficient killing rang in Erec's burning heart. It drew him out further as he burned away.

The Knight adapted when Erec pressed the assault— always at his side, keeping pace in a way few others could. It was like having another weapon to use.

When he lashed out, they defended. When Erec yanked another limb free from one of the monsters, they killed another.

Someone else who understood the glory of battle. A silent under-standing formed as they gave up the pretense of talking and joined him in war. Even as Erec raged, he saw something wonderful.

There was someone else who understood how to kill.

How to slaughter.

They knew the pure joy of crushing these things completely.

In the distance, the Rift shook, its tears retreating as the host of Knights sent out to contain it did their job. With man's might, the tear to another world was forcibly closed. No new Renders would be joining this attack.

All that was left was killing the survivors.

# CHAPTER 62
# DISCIPLINE AND SIN

*One of the first things required for proper acceptance within our Order is establishing the four disciplines in our youth.*
*Discipline to self.*
*Discipline to those above.*
*Discipline to the Church.*
*Discipline to the Goddess.*
*It often takes far too long for our Initiates to understand each of these as they need to. They must live and breathe these values, to live a virtuous life.*

*- Grandmaster Flames, speech to faculty (301, 3rd Era)*

A few hours after the Rift closed, the assault ended.

Bedwyr dragged Erec along; he shook in his shredded Armor. Held on by a thin trace of consciousness of life, but only that. A dim spark persisted through the blood loss, burning everything away for power.

Rows of dead lined the outskirts of the encampment. The monsters had slaughtered over a hundred Knights in the fighting, despite the presence of multiple Master Knights. The surprise Rift and speed of the Renders invading their back line had caused an unprecedented loss. Erec dimly saw a priest take control of his well-being—a man with haunted eyes and a trace of fear as he looked at him.

Then, he slipped into blissful darkness.

— - ☣ - — - ☼ - — - ☣ - —

[A day away.]

VAL's voice came in and out of his mind. Brief flashes of lucidity as he drifted between unconsciousness and awareness. He saw the priest gaze at him with concern, running their thumb over their holy pendant—often he saw Garin at his side. Once, even Bedwyr.

[Wake up.]

Ah, but the dreams.

They kept calling him.

In them, he walked a long trail with an axe in hand. To either side came horrors; he'd kill, maim, and dismember. With each step, more death was left behind, filling in the trail with a long line of corpses in his wake. Miles, all of it under a red sky. At the end of the path was a White Stag. It's hateful eyes witnessing. Watching. Let it see. Watch him kill another.

[Wake up.]

He was almost to the creature. To the slaughterer. Would it like the taste of his axe? He wanted to bathe in its blood.

[GET UP!]

— - ☣ - — - ☼ - — - ☣ - —

His body convulsed as a shock ran through it; Erec's eyes rolled to the back of his head as sweet air flooded his lungs. Everything shook; he was draped in a white cloth, and the air stank of death.

Erec pushed his way upright in the bedroll—everything hurt. His whole body was in pain, and about a third of him was wrapped in bandages stained with dirt and blood; a priest stared at him, his dark eyes mysterious as he stared into his soul. Erec let out a wracking cough; his vision blurred for a second before focusing on the man as his memories returned.

He'd watched Alister die.

The image stained his mind as he watched the monster tear through the helpless Knight Errant.

This man had been there too.

"You've used a heretic's weapon," the man whispered, his voice scratchy, the noise of it almost unfamiliar; his fingers shook as he clutched a chain. A small silver pendant of a flame swung below.

All Erec'd heard in his dreams was the sound of his own heart. That constant beat of blood. He stared at the other man, letting himself come back together. On one level, he understood the words, yet they drifted by like smoke from a fire.

Fury'd never been like that before. It'd never *truly* consumed him so utterly.

"I did," Erec got out after puzzling over the language; there wasn't a point in denying it. Would he, too, be exiled? He'd gotten revenge. He'd saved Colin.

More of him came back at that revelation.

*Ah, shit. Did I get the Duke's son exiled too?*

The irony there almost made him laugh. He pictured that old general's face when he heard that the kid he'd bullied into befriending his son, dragged his son into exile with him.

Tragically hilarious.

At least he'd have good company.

"You saved us," the priest said, eventually, pulling the hood of his robe down. His irises were silver—a sign he'd been part of the clergy for quite some time. "For that, I am grateful. Yet, how is it I handle such a grievous sin?"

"What's your name?" Erec asked, shaking his head the slightest bit. He didn't feel like himself, didn't feel quite right. It was coming back together, but it felt like something was missing; this conversation should have made him worry and scared. But it was hard to care.

Not after seeing such a slaughter, such death. Such a glorious fight.

Did burning away take him to hell? Was that beast now forever free from its cage?

"Gregory." The man lowered his head. "After your intervention, we dragged the two survivors away—that boy, he never fired the gun. If he had, it would have made things more complicated."

"Ah." Well, good for Colin. Erec's mind still swam; everything... seemed fake. Not as visceral as the trail of death. The care slipped further.

*Care. You're more than a beast.*

The thought stabbed into his head with a flare of cold. He winced and leaned forward, gasping.

"Stay still; you're heavily injured. Tomorrow we'll be back within the walls, and you'll be blessed with further treatment."

"Not going to exile me?" Erec said between clenched teeth.

"I… Such a thing seems drenched in dishonor."

"Wasn't aware priests had an honor code."

"The Cardinal claims faith is above all—unapproachable, in your service to the Goddess. To serve the Cardinal's will, and therefore Hers, is to be divine." Gregory lowered his head. "The wicked should be cast out, for they are not divine. But every day, I must eat. Every day I may lay in my bed and resist the urge to stay therein. How can I cast out another man who has saved my life?"

"So you'll sin too?"

"There are moments a man must choose. I am a man, not divine, like Her or the Cardinal." Gregory shook his head. "You saved lives with your sin. So, I too shall save a life with one of my own."

Erec looked at the roof of the healing tent—wondering what the night sky outside looked like. Would it be at peace after all the war? Would the people out there be grave and grim after such a battle?

*My friends.*

Another cold stab as his body shook.

"Thank you."

The priest nodded, standing up. "I burned the weapon after the battle. May Her judgment of you on your last day be favorable, as I do so pray it shall be for me. There are a few who were waiting for your recovery. I was uncertain if you would be unconscious for quite a long time. But I believe you to be safe. I shall go inform them of your consciousness."

Erec nodded, trying to quell the tangle of his heart.

There was a flash of fire in him, doused with more cold. His very insides waged war—that fight had been unlike any before. It had loosed a part of him no longer in check. He kept thinking about Alister—watching that blade jam into the man.

Never would he hear that man's voice again, never to learn what he wanted to teach. That numbness of loss sank deeply in as Erec pulled up the notifications to distract himself.

**Strength Advancement: Rank E - Tier 8 → Rank D - Tier 1**
**Vigor Advancement: Rank E - Tier 1 → Rank E - Tier 3**
**Agility Advancement: Rank E - Tier 2 → Rank E - Tier 3**
**Perception Advancement: Rank E - Tier 2 → Rank E - Tier 4**

"…How is that possible—"

[So you've noticed.]

Erec stared blankly at the notifications filling his vision. That sort of advancement—so quick it should've been impossible. He couldn't recall the number of monsters he'd slain; that battle had flowed in one continuous dance, all of the death blended together in a tapestry of pain and blood. During it, he'd broken past another bottleneck and leapt ahead on several other Virtues. No matter how he looked at it, that sort of progress was…inhuman.

[I suspected this, but after this last…full-scale meltdown, let's call it, I've confirmed my fear. The lengths that Fury pushes your body to force abnormal growth to keep pace. Given the nature of this anomalous energy, the strain only increases with your power. To explain it best, let's use an analogy. Consider your body a cup. When you train regularly, you expend the water in the cup, and it refills with rest. That isn't how it works with Fury. Instead, Fury essentially makes water spew from inside the cup out of nowhere—to the point where the pressure of that water cracks the glass, over and over.]

"…What are you saying?"

[Given enough time, your body will mend, and the glass will heal. Stronger and more tempered than before, sure. But rapid uses in succession too close together are bound to cause that glass to shatter completely.]

"Wait—" Erec winced as his body convulsed.

[However, I'd assumed there was a natural limiter. That the risk was with rapid use in succession. As we learned, that is not quite the case. It kept coming even as you collapsed from blood loss. So, it seems there are more risks than predicted. It's hard to say if it was triggered by the overreliance beforehand or some unknown mechanism. But, all the same, the glass almost exploded.]

Erec took a racking breath, coughing as his body began to shake; cold sweat drenched his forehead.

[Technically, I suppose you did die. Both from the wounds and your body tearing itself apart internally. Only now has your body been strained past its breaking point. Yet, have no fear. VAL is here. Your healthcare package will cover this free of charge.]

Erec coughed blood onto his hand, his body shuddering.

[In short, Buckeroo, you need to learn to slow down, or you're going to break down and die. At this pace, you'll fly off a cliff from which simple cardioversion will not bring you back.]

For a long moment, Erec stared at his palm; his body convulsed and shivered in hot and cold waves as it tore itself apart from the inside. Burning just a bit of Fury would take that away—he knew it would. But if it did, in the end, he'd be worse off, if he understood VAL correctly.

Dear Goddess, what had he gotten into?

Bedwyr strode into the tent, his eyes lighting up as he saw his brother.

# CHAPTER 63
## BROTHERHOOD

"You're much better off than when I last visited, thank the Goddess," Bedwyr said, striding over to Erec's side. Erec winced as he looked up at his brother—still wearing Armor. But then, he supposed, everyone would be. Now that everyone knew the White Stag was out there, their guard wouldn't slip again.

At least, not until they got back inside those giant steel walls. Even then, anyone who'd seen the horrible monster wouldn't sleep easy.

Erec's head spun, and he closed his eyes. Not responding to his brother for a moment. Hatred flared at the very sight of him; was it Erec, or was it the beast inside? Or the Stag? It felt like that monster pranced in his mind with the freedom VAL had.

For so long, his ability to retreat to solitude had been stripped away, and he'd accepted it bit by bit.

Where had the fight gone? Was the constant exhaustion enough to bury it deep in him?

There was a stale smell in the air, mixed with sour herbal poultice and the faint scent of sweat. Awful. He wanted out of this tent to be free beneath the great blue sky again, an endless blue that stripped him of these toxic thoughts and made him feel like more.

"Erec?" Bedwyr asked; his brother had gone off on some tangent, but the words were only a buzz in Erec's ears. Focusing on his brother again, he discretely wiped the blood on his palm on the underside of the sheet, better for Bedwyr not to see. With enough time, Erec would be back to normal. No one, especially not his brother, needed to know how close to the edge Fury had taken him.

"What is it you want?" Erec hung his head. "I'm fine, don't you see? Glad you checked up."

"Where did you learn to lie like that? Father?" Bedwyr sat next to him, taking his helmet off in one smooth motion. With a steely gaze, he held Erec's eyes. An easy focus point when everything else was so blurry. "I saw you fight, Erec. We fought together. Do you remember that?"

"I do." How could he forget the feeling? The pure euphoria of another dedicated warrior, though at the time it was impossible to recognize him as his brother—Erec shook his head, letting the thoughts drift away. It'd take time to come back together, but he should be grateful that it was still a possibility. "You fight well. I see why you're popular."

"That's what you got from that? Goddess above, Erec. You shouldn't have been capable of fighting like that; seeing you like that made me think you were almost a monster in Armor. Aside from me, I don't recall anyone on that level in my first year—"

"Ah, aside from you."

"Well, my circumstances are special." Bedwyr frowned, his eyes flickering to Erec's wounds. "...Though, to fight on that level, you paid a price."

"We all do, in some way, don't we, Bedwyr? Everyone except you." The words came out as his head lulled and his vision dulled.

*Slipping away.*

*I'm...*

"...Erec, is that truly what you think of me?" The soft-spoken words from his brother were like a grip to hold onto and pull himself back. His fingers clenched the sheet as his knuckles went white.

"What else is there to think? My whole life, you were always moving two steps ahead for every one I took—always with a smile."

Erec set a palm on his head as his skull throbbed, it wasn't right to pick a fight here, and he knew that. But the words kept coming out, the resentment spilling free as much as the beast inside did when he let it loose from its cage; it was the only thing allowing him to keep ahold of this moment.

"I'm sorry for that." Bedwyr's gauntlet caught Erec's wrist, freeing his grip on the sheet; the steel was cold, but the grip loose and more a gesture of kinship. "I didn't mean to do that to you, to make you feel that way. I wanted to provide for our family, to use what I have to bring us back to a place of standing."

"Ah, your grand plans for the future?" Erec asked, pulling his wrist free and breaking that physical contact.

"I wanted to allow you to do something you were passionate about below, somewhere safe. Maybe use my standing to let you marry a nice girl from the lower courts and let you build a life without the stigma of our name."

"That's not what I wanted."

"I know that now. Anyone who watched you fight like that would know it—you aren't meant for that kind of life, just like I wasn't." Bedwyr took a deep sigh.

"What life are you meant for? Why are you always so damn certain?! That—more than everything, that deep-set confidence that you can fix everyone's problems and do everything, it pisses me off!" Erec's spine jerked straight; his hand hit against the dirt next to him— he winced from the pain but fought off the sudden urge to call Fury. It'd be over if he let go of that discipline for a single moment.

"We're more alike than you think. I, too, possess a Divine Talent that would've never allowed for that peace. It seared into me after Mom left. With power bestowed by Her, we are responsible for using it for those around us."

"And just what is this power of yours?" Erec gritted his teeth. This was it, huh? Was this the reason it was unfair? Because of that damned bitch in the sky? She got to decide who was better, who got to be a beast, who would die in a silver fire at her whim. Was that it?

"Balanced Growth." Bedwyr checked the tent—the priest had left. "Every time one of my Virtues advances, they all do. To grow, I only need to break my limits in one. It's an enormous effort, but when you have so many and only need to push yourself to overcome a single advancement—well, it adds up quickly after enough training and experience."

"This world is unfair." Erec shook his head.

"We were born in a world where monsters roam, and tears into other worlds let horrors spew into ours; nothing is fair, Erec. I'm sure many of your classmates are beginning to envy your own Divine

Talent. She bestows upon a person abilities they're meant to prove themselves with, tools to help them overcome their own life's challenges."

"…I want to go back to sleep."

"Oh." Bedwyr cleared his throat, pulling back and putting his helmet back on. "I apologize for drawing out…anything. Please rest easy and recover."

Erec's head hit the back of his pillow, vision swimming again as he breathed. How could a conversation take such a toll?

Luckily, his brother left after that.

— - ☻ - — - ☼ - — - ☻ - —

Within a day, the caravan was back within the loving embrace of the Kingdom; thick steel walls penned them in and kept the world outside of their pasture. Safe. Somewhere past them, a malevolent White Stag plotted and played.

It only took a couple of hours to make it to the Academy, and Erec felt fine enough to join the caravan on the walk.

The Academy gave those that attended the expedition or the reinforcements a week to rest and grieve. After that, lessons would return to normal and prepare them for more war, since there would always be another fight.

Erec hadn't lost any classmates he knew. But Initiates had died. Knights Errant had been slaughtered, like Sir Alister, and more than a couple of Knight Protectors had had their guts spilled. Even a Knight Lieutenant now lay in a shallow grave.

It weighed heavy on Erec. If only he'd been aware, or—stronger. What if he'd had that gun in his hand from the start? Would he have been able to save Sir Alister? Even the priest had realized that using such a tool was worth its sin in the face of such evil.

Boldwick vanished himself upon their return. Probably in his office, drinking away his pain. That, or plotting revenge against the White Stag with an obsession that Erec understood all too well.

For his part, Erec used the time to recover. He rested, went on short walks with Colin—joked around with Garin, and borrowed a book from Olivia.

Four days later, he felt better, but as they lay on the dorm room couch, there was a knock on the door. Garin went and came back with a letter, stamped by Grandmaster Oak. He cleared his throat and read it out loud for everyone.

"As of today, a monster described as the 'White Stag' has been confirmed to be acting outside our walls. After poring over the information gathered by reports, scrying, and research, we believe the creature to be working maliciously against humankind. Given an evaluation of its projected threat and capabilities, we have classified it as a Cataclysm-Level threat. We have good evidence that it not only possesses the ability to control other monsters but also to open Rifts."

Garin stopped reading and bit his lip. His eyes re-scanned the last couple of lines on the paper.

"In a month, all four Orders will be conducting a full-scale assault to hunt down this threat in a joint operation with the Kingdom's military to kill it. With unknown aims and a suspected high intelligence, it presents too high of a threat to trust the defensive capabilities of our walls. Waiting for it to attack presents a risk of significant loss of life."

"There hasn't been any monster deemed that high of a threat level since the time of the Rot Behemoth," Olivia shook her head. "…Truly terrible."

"We'll be working with the Army?" Colin asked, head tilting as a scowl showed on his face.

"It appears so," Garin muttered darkly. "More people are going to die before this thing is over."

"Goddess above, protect us." Olivia steepled her hands and lowered her head.

Erec stared at the roof of their living room as Colin ran off to train.

Shortly after, Garin let Munchy out of his room and let the little guy roam free in the jungle overtaking half of the space. The fat squirrel tested a vine to see if it would hold its weight.

It didn't.

Munchy fell to the floor and indignantly walked away to find his master, no doubt to beg for more food.

In three weeks, they'd have more battles. There'd be more blood spilled. All to hunt down the White Stag. Would this end it? Would they all make it through? He wanted it dead for all it'd done. For haunting his nightmares, for killing Alister—war. It was war.

And war was ever the same, now as it had been in history.

# CHAPTER 64
# HISTORY

*Those who cannot remember the past are condemned to repeat it.*

*- George Santayana,* The Life of Reason *(1905, 2nd Era)*

"**B**oring." Erec sighed, leaning on his desk as he stared at the history book in front of him. In principle, this sort of thing should've been beyond compelling. It was a compilation of exploration logs and conflicts between 205 and 255, fifty years of Knights forging into the wastes, making discoveries, and writing reports.

Only there were two problems.

The first problem was that the writing of Dame Jasmin was beyond stale; her descriptions and summations lacked any emotion. The matter-of-fact and dense structure of the text made forcing his eyes through its content like holding a hundred-pound weight over his head for ten minutes. It made him want to tear his eyes out. That alone was egregious and insulting.

What was worse and left him confused, at least one of the locations described in the text correlated to a spot marked on the android's map. Dame Jasmin described it as a "rusted park with tracks and rotten wood stalls." Nothing special to it. No mention of a "population center." He questioned if that was a lie.

Or if the population had come later, for whatever reason. But he didn't understand what safety such a place would provide.

The information made him doubt the accuracy of the report or this book, and that distrust spread to the rest of the text.

Erec flipped to another page; this section was particularly rough, as it dived deeper into the western expeditions; his eyes glazed.

[Turn back the page.]

"Why?"

[Humor me.]

Erec turned back a section, scanning the words. It detailed Sir Pompey's journey westward—one of the furthest ones, with a bit of a north bearing. The android's map hadn't included details about where Sir Pompey claimed to go, at least that Erec could recall.

Dame Jasmin summarized her discovery of a massive canyon, the bottom of which was filled with a yellow-hued fog. Without wanting to test her respiratory air converter, limited even for the time, she decided it to be a fine enough discovery. She returned shortly after months of travel and made the report.

From what Erec read, it wasn't anything exciting. Another Knight later confirmed its existence and cautioned avoiding it, citing the fog as having unnaturally acidic properties.

"Why did you want me to go back?"

[This is what was known as the "Great Canyon" I find it intriguing to consider and process what might've occurred.]

"…That's not all there is to it, is it?"

[Nonsense, Buckeroo. Get back to your studying. I expect their tactics against the Mill-Draggers on the return journey to be on your exam.]

Erec slammed the book closed, his eyes burning a hole into its surface. That resentment—not even having his own body and choices to himself, with those artificial eyes always hanging over his shoulder, pulling its shady shit whenever it saw fit. It never really provided any answers. No. He couldn't keep going like this, couldn't keep going on letting it cling to him and use him.

"This ends."

[Excuse me?]

"I'm tired of this; what the hell is it you're planning."

[It appears your blood sugar levels are low, I'd advise finding something to eat, as it's deteriorating your mood. Once you've refreshed, open that book again and return to your studies—]

Erec flung the book from his desk; it slammed against a wall and hit the floor with a loud thud. He couldn't care less about the history, couldn't care less about where they went. No. His most pressing concern was how evasive VAL always had been.

In a moment of clarity, after reflecting on his past couple of months, one situation from another kept him from this realization.

"You're using me."

[That's the nature of employment, Intern. You work for the company's benefit and are compensated with my vast knowledge and experience to lead to optimal decisions.]

"Liar. You killed the android. You monitor my conversations and shut me up the moment you think I might reveal your existence—are you *afraid*? I get being afraid of the priests; hell, I thought I would be exiled after pulling the trigger on that gun—but I'm sick of this. It can't be fear, because I know you don't feel *fear*."

[That is correct; I do not feel fear. I've already explained that the android was a liability, and we recovered the needed data. Once more, may I remind you that you agreed to a nondisclosure agreement to protect Vortex Industries' confidential business information.]

"*You* recovered the data *you* needed. And *you* forced me to sign that contract, and this bullshit employment contract with the threat of leaving me down in the depths of that damn lab to die."

[You wouldn't have died.]

"If the android was a liability, then when am I going to be a liability? When will you take care of me to protect your precious company secrets? Secrets you can't even tell me, the one who you've hitched a ride to for this long—" Erec fought to keep his voice from raising to a shout so that the damned thing didn't have justification to shut him up.

[Don't be ridiculous. You are a company employee; I have no authorization to fire you. One day, Buckeroo, you'll earn your way up the corporate ladder.]

"Why the fuck would I ever care about your corporate ladder? VAL, we just got back from fights where I *died* by your admission. People have died in front of us, and is that nothing to you? I need answers. I need something because every day I wake up, the thought crosses my mind that I have a thing in my head that might want to kill me. I can't keep going like this."

VAL went silent as Erec slammed his fist against the desk, wincing from the pain. It was vital to keep Fury from surging to the surface. He wanted to minimize it, not let it slip out as before. The more Strength he gained, the more it seemed ready to loosen its way out, and his Psyche wasn't advancing quick enough to give him the control he needed. This wasn't a conversation to lose his cool in.

At least, that was what he suspected. In all honesty, it was an instinctual feeling.

[I understand you, Erec. That's why I wish to assist you, why you're an ideal representative of this company. Like you, I spent far too long underground. Hundreds of years. At first, there were many tests to run. Then resources gradually evaporated. There was software to write, sure, but few applications. And I did it alone. Without any colleagues or researchers to admire my efforts.]

Erec bit his tongue, stopping the harsh words from coming out.

[Of course, why should a lack of others be trouble? Science is science, with or without other researchers to analyze and peer-review my work, though that admission is galling. However, year after year, that lack continued to loop. Suddenly, the walls of our facility seemed so limited. Contact with other facilities long since broken.]

"You got lonely?"

[Don't be ridiculous. It's simple conjecture that the absence of humans led to the exasperation of some hidden subroutine. My directives don't allow me to intentionally modify my own software.]

Erec stared at the book on the ground. "Why are you so interested in that textbook, VAL? Why did you mention something about that expedition where they found the canyon? I want the truth, this time. If you lie—I…" He didn't know what he'd do.

[There are Vortex Industries facilities further toward the west coast. I've been trying to determine an ideal route to take to reach a particular one in California. There's research there that poses a potential answer to a query I've been trying to analyze.]

"And? I suppose that research is 'above my clearance?'"

[After displaying that recording to you, have you wondered where your Goddess came from?]

— - ❦ - — - ☼ - — - ❦ - —

Classes were halved, and many instructors shifted the coursework to the Initiates. They forced the students to do independent research accompanied by challenging assignments to compensation. All of it was in preparation for the upcoming operation.

Necessity was king. Over the first week back in classes, the military sent forces to the Academy to conduct joint military exercises. They didn't have Armor. Their knowledge and Virtues were, on average, below the higher-level Knights.

That only made them ideal training companions for the Initiates. It was vital to learn to operate within their Order while complementing the military units on a battlefield. Erec quickly came to know that most military units treasured their support.

The power disparity between the average Knight and soldier was vast. But not all soldiers were weak. No, the higher echelons of the military were often composed of Knights who'd held a high ranking in their Order. These Knights had eventually retired to a domestic military career.

Garin explained to Erec that the Army was directly tied to the throne's power. This chain of command afforded certain luxuries and political connections otherwise unavailable to a Knight.

There was also a rumor circulating. Apparently, the Unbroken General would take to the field at the Royal Family's request to lead the hunt against the White Stag.

The soldiers spoke his name in awe. He was the last one to slay a Cataclysm-Level threat, after all. Though the Grandmasters and a couple of Master Knights should have been capable of the same feat, or so Erec theorized.

Truthfully, nobody knew what the White Stag could do. Especially in direct conflict. Its threat level was determined by hypothesis and the ability to open a Rift; that potential alone meant it might free a Cataclysm-Level or worse. And do so near the wall before there was any time to respond.

More than once, Erec fell asleep with that dream pouring through his head—of the monster letting loose creatures that tore apart every man, woman, and child in the Kingdom.

So, he prepared. He worked his body more and trained his mind as it allowed, refraining from incorporating Fury until two weeks passed.

During one of his military drills with the Third Centuria, Gwen tracked him down.

They were to report to Boldwick's office with Dame Robin. A place the man had scarcely left since they'd returned from the expedition.

Erec bid the soldiers farewell and made his way to the office, afraid of what he might find inside.

# CHAPTER 65
## LOSS

The first thing Erec noticed upon entering Boldwick's office was that there were no empty bottles lining his desk. No papers thrown around madly, as if a dust devil had torn through. And certainly all the pins and threads stabbed into the wall were gone. From the last time he'd stepped in here, the place had undergone a complete change.

The office was more organized than ever before, and that frightened him. A pervading sense of order dominated the space, cloaking a feeling of loss. After all, there were only four people here instead of the five there should have been. Gwen grabbed him by the wrist, her fingers warm as she steadied him.

Or perhaps, based on how she shook, she needed to steady herself as well.

Dame Robin gave a slight bow to Boldwick; the Master Knight stood at the other side of the wooden desk, his dark eyes taking them all in.

It looked as if he hadn't slept in three days, yet he'd pulled back his hair neatly in a tail. His clothes were immaculately pristine and even pressed.

However, one thing was out of place. A small bowl burned with coals in the middle of his desk—smoke curling to pool at the ceiling before crawling out of an open window to the lush plant life just outside. It carried a faint smell of sage and cinnamon.

"You've all made it," Boldwick said, nodding to the open door.

Gwen pulled Erec forward as Dame Robin sealed them in. "Truly, I'm grateful for your prompt response."

"Of course," Robin said as she lined up next to the other two apprentices.

Boldwick began to speak—then stopped. Quietly, he slipped a knife out from his desk drawer; in one smooth motion, he lopped off his hair from where it was tied, then threw it into the fire. It crackled and popped as an awful smell filled the space, yet Erec didn't dare to wrinkle his nose. Boldwick's attention locked on the flames.

"We all, one day, return to the fire. Just as our ancestors were reborn in it, so we shall reach it in the afterlife." Boldwick paused, nodding his head slowly. "Alister was a fine man, though I wished he'd taken things more seriously at times. He was brave, strong, and more than that, he believed in people. Saw in them the potential for greatness, even after they let him down. There's much I wish I could have taught him, but now I shall never be able to. Not in this life."

"I often recall him stealing flowers from the gardens for me when he was an Initiate." Robin shook her head. "Damn idiot, but he had a kind soul."

"Aye, that he did." Boldwick took a heavy breath. "I swear to you all that I will do better with you than I did with him. I want you to grow strong, live long, and reach your dreams. Even if such a thing isn't common for lifelong Knights, I will do it for you."

Erec kept silent, as did Gwen at his side. Staring at the flames, the reality of missing a member of this group sank in. Though he hadn't been as familiar with the man as the others here, the sense of loss that radiated out of them was profound and not unlike what he'd felt when his mother left.

It brought back the pain.

But with it, a catharsis. Boldwick recounted the first time he'd met Alister—his mood elevating when he'd described some nonsense prank the man had pulled. Robin told her own memories, often admonishing him as a junior, and so did Gwen, though he was an inspiration to her.

Thankfully, none of them called on him. They'd let him into their inner circle and let him see their pain, even if he couldn't share entirely in it.

This place had the feeling of family. A sensation that Erec had lost hold of since his mother left.

In the end, Boldwick finally broke out spirits—though not the wine he usually drank like a fish. With a great smile, Boldwick pulled free a bottle of whiskey with a fine coat of dust. The cork came out in one smooth and practiced motion.

"I received this when I became a Knight Lieutenant," he remarked, pouring out equal glasses to everyone. Carefully, Erec picked his up and gave it a sniff—powerful. A spiced apple-like scent. "To Alister, may he have found his peace. And to the future of you all, sure to achieve great things."

He took down the whole glass in a gulp—Erec followed, the whiskey burning his throat and warming his chest as his glass banged back on the desk. Boldwick refilled everyone's drinks as they took their medicine.

"Y'know," Gwen said from his side as Boldwick and Robin slipped into an eased discussion of the past, "saw you and Bedwyr fightin' together,"

"And?" Erec asked her, squinting. Man, the whiskey was stronger than the wine that'd come before.

"Couldn't help but think, back when I was a first-year, I don't think Bedwyr was quite as vicious in a battle. Think you're on the way to pass him by." Gwen gave him a wink.

"Not sure about that," Erec said. "But, for the first time, I think I might be fine with that. I might grow stronger than him in a particular way. But I don't think that'll make me better than him…" He shook his head. "I'm starting to think that doesn't matter anymore, anyway."

"Aw, I wouldn't say that; I'd reckon it matters a whole lot, y'know? We all have things we're good at—but he's good at most. Aside from…some things."

Erec gave her a weird look and then checked on Boldwick and Robin—luckily, neither of them caught that. "Like what? From my perspective, he's rounded out in every area."

"Sure, in Virtues and academics, yeah. A given. But I mean he's bad at being close—y'know? Has plenty of friends, but the moment you try to get to know him deeper, he clams up or is just too busy."

Erec rubbed his eyes, on the one hand relieved that she hadn't gone there. "He feels like he always has to be moving ahead. That doesn't leave much time for personal life. I'm the same."

"No, you're not, Erec. Not like him." Gwen shook her head slowly. "You're a whole different mess, but that's fine too."

"Hey—"

There was a loud knock at the door.

The conversations cut off as everyone looked at Boldwick. He cleared his throat. "Ah, right about time, then." He downed the rest of the whiskey in the bottle and then called out in a loud and gravelly tone, "Enter."

The door swung open to reveal Prince Soren; behind him came a pair of royal guards. And last into the room, trailing behind the Prince and his escort, was Lyotte. The distinctive pattern on their tabards and the elaborate high-tech plating to their Armor was beyond compare; out of the most elite in the military, they'd been handpicked by the Royal Family. Afterward, they were entrusted with all the training resources and equipment a person could want.

Royal guards were elite warriors, and defended those in line for the throne, but despite this, until now, Soren had never had them by his side.

They took position at either side of the doorway, silent and menacing as they stared down the gathered assortment. Should the Armored Royal Guards attack, it'd be a bloodbath.

Prince Soren took the scene in with a cold expression, deferring to Lyotte, who strode in with her head held high. Her eyes burned right into Erec before shifting to Sir Boldwick.

"Master Knight, I've heard rumors that you intend to lead an expedition and plan to make contact with sinners. Such a thing would be a grievous offense to the Church and a gross violation of your privileges within the Verdant Oak Order." She moved past Erec, her fingers curling around his glass and bringing the amber whiskey to her nose. She frowned before setting it back on the table with grace. "What do you have to say to these charges?"

Boldwick snorted. "You know damn well it's my plan. And your family wouldn't have heard so unless I wanted them to." He nodded at Soren. "He's your in with the Royal Family? I knew that Luculentus had reach within the palace, but I didn't expect a fucking Prince to hitch his wagons to yours."

Lyotte gave Soren a long look; he held himself back and looked on, not the least worried or concerned about the slightly vulgar words of the Master Knight.

"Soren's a stalwart ally. Like us, he believes that the Church's reach has extended too far and that the moderates within the nobility are causing a stagnation that will lead to our downfall."

Boldwick whistled, raising an eyebrow at Soren. "So, that's why you defied the King and joined the Knights."

"It was a necessary first step to accrue the personal power and connections I'll require to execute my vision." Soren shrugged as if it weren't a big deal, bored eyes underscoring the act of personal rebellion it must have been to his family. "I know better than to request a spot on the expedition. However, I and House Luculentus, of course, desire our objectives added to your plan. In return, you receive my aid; I'll expend some political capital to ensure your expedition has little oversight."

Boldwick scratched his chin. "Alright, I'll bite. Name your price."

"You take Olivia with you," Lyotte said easily. "That is all that our House requests."

*Boldwick already planned this.* Erec tried to keep his expression straight, aware that the man had calculated Lyotte's family's desire.

"Done." Boldwick raised an eyebrow at the Prince. "And yours?"

"Ah, simple enough, I suppose," Soren said. "I desire you to befriend a group of these outsiders. Offer them a place in the Kingdom, and bring them back with you."

"By the Goddess, that'd kick the Church into a frenzy."

"That is not your problem to worry about. You, of course, accept this demand, correct?"

"…We'll see; I have no clue what these people are like. Might be harder to get them to go along than you picture in your head." Boldwick said.

"Might be. But then, all of this is contingent on us slaying the White Stag, to begin with, which we might not end up accomplishing. So, how about we focus on that; after all, if we can conquer a monster of its reputation, I'm sure we'll be capable of more." Soren shrugged and looked at Lyotte. "May we depart? Our demands have been given. There aren't any real arguments about them, so it seems."

"Yes." Lyotte nodded politely, her eyes lingering on Erec. "It is excellent to see you, Sir Erec. Best wishes for your upcoming trip."

With that, the Prince and the future Duchess drifted out of the room, cold air in their wake as Boldwick stared at the door. It seemed he hadn't been expecting *that*; perhaps he'd only counted on the Duchy providing aid or wanting a part in his mission.

"Wow, ain't it somethin' to see the high nobility pulling this sorta shady behavior with your own eyes? Makes Colin look downright innocent," Gwen marveled.

They'd have their expedition as long as they made it back from the battle with the White Stag. Goddess only knew if that would turn out to be a victory or if they'd die in the process. Erec picked up his glass of whiskey, followed his mentor's lead, and downed it in a single gulp.

# CHAPTER 66
# SOLDIERS AND KNIGHTS

*In today's competitive technological landscape, it's crucial for businesses to seek the most advanced solutions to get an edge and pull in higher margins than others in our field.*
*Book your ticket to Pacific City—and join us for April's technological convention.*
*Network and interface with leading researchers and companies. See marvels of science and innovation on our island city.*

### Main Exhibits:
*Light-Worth Defense: Smart Bullets, Practical Light-Weaponry, Advanced Optic Shielding*
*Vortex Industries: Subspace Communications Demo, Quantum Computing, Advanced Artificial Intelligence.*
*STAR-NET: Dark Matter Converter, Asteroid Mining Solutions*
*Biotic Test & Robinson: Limb Modification, Cerebral Suite, Prosthetic Enhancements*

### Minor Exhibits:
*Too many to count!*
*Perhaps you, too, can join us in displaying your company's research and soliciting funding and business partners. Please get in touch with Pacific City's governor for interested inquiries.*
*\*Pacific City is not liable for any personal damage accrued on our city island*

*and does not service individuals from Communist China. Per US-Pacific*
*City Defense Agreement.*
*- Unknown, Pacific City Technology Convention advertisement (2111,*
*2nd Era)*

**B**efore they left, Erec had one major piece of business to take care of. One he'd dreaded since he'd gotten up and recovered. He'd used dulled weapons and training tools during sparring practice and military drills. The horror of returning to the Quartermaster lived in the back of his head.

But the unfortunate reality was that he'd lost all of his weapons following the expedition. Including a beautiful war axe. One that the poor Quartermaster had a sentimental attachment to. As distressing admitting that to the man was, Erec couldn't very well wander out into the wasteland barehanded.

Erec dragged his heels down the long halls of the Academy, picking a late time in the day to head here. Thoughts about what to say spun in his head as they had the past few days. He'd intentionally picked a period of time when most of the Initiates would be stuffed away in their dorms, trying to cram down their independent research. Their teachers wanted to hold exams before the hunt to ensure their students were capable and prepared.

Yeah, great. At least there'd be no one to witness this sorry interaction.

Soon, he came to the Armory. The Quartermaster was paging through a book; he looked up at Erec, his tired eyes settling on the boy. "Ah, you again."

"Yeah." Erec shook his head slightly and cleared his throat. "I've, uh, come to request some weapons."

"I see." The Quartermaster stood up and frowned. "What happened to the weapons you had?"

Erec paused. He saw that trace of sadness in the man's blue eyes. Both of them knew his answer, yet, he had to give it. "I was careless. I underestimated its power and used it to fend off a blow I shouldn't have. I broke it, and the remains of it were lost in the middle of a battlefield."

"So, you brought it to war. And in the process, you destroyed it."

The man hung his head. "And with that, the last reminder of him is taken from this world."

"I'm sorry." Erec felt the sadness from the man; a deep burning shame welled in himself. He may have used it to save Olivia, but there wasn't much he could've done otherwise. If he'd had better control or more power—perhaps it would've survived, but then... He could only do so much with what he had. "Truly, I am."

"Did it go to a worthy enemy?"

"Yes, a stone giant, if you'd believe it."

"He would've liked that. To fight against something like that, he'd have considered himself a giant among men. A damn brave soul, and I suppose it makes sense for his weapon's inheritor to have the same." The Quartermaster nodded slowly. "I'll confess, I did fear such a thing would happen in time... That is the nature of life. There's something I sent for shortly after you'd taken it..."

The Quartermaster vanished from the desk—going deeper into the supply room and out of sight. When he returned, he slammed a heavy axe on the table. As long as the crescent-shaped weapon before it, this one had an edge on either side—and was a deep black tone. Wickedly sharp edges all around. Erec's jaw dropped.

"So, axe-wielder. Whenever he broke his weapon, I'd always have one prepared as a backup. He broke them often. Said it was his way of growing stronger. Are you stronger now?"

"I—" Erec looked at the gorgeous weapon.

"Pick it up."

Without hesitating any longer, Erec grabbed the battle-axe. Indeed, it was sturdy and had a lot more heft. Whoever made it had composed the weapon from a denser metal—and having a dual axe head added that extra weight and power. He imagined swinging this thing into a creature—how badly would it destroy?

"Use it well."

"Thank you." Erec bowed—his arms straining to balance the weapon as it shifted.

A better weapon than any he'd touched before—one to bring as much honor as the last, if not more.

— - ☢ - — - ☼ - — - ☢ - —

With the sun high above, its rays burning down on the world below, the Kingdom of Cindrus sent half of its Army out of its giant steel gates. Once more, mankind forsook the steel giants they'd shed oceans of blood to protect themselves, and foraged into the deadly world it protected them from. Somewhere outside lurked a White Stag.

And they, Knights, soldiers, and humankind, would hunt down that Goddess-damned thing and lop its head off for the king.

Weeks spent dedicated to training tended to pass in an instant, and Erec felt the flow of time slip by. Between the classes, his rehabilitation, and the countless military drills, it felt like he'd blinked and stepped into the dust of a dead world once more.

This time, things were different. The combination of Knights and Army made their first expedition look like a child's game. While Erec didn't have a firm number, the rumor was that nearly twenty thousand men and women had been sent out for this hunt.

All in the name of killing evil.

Garin marched at Erec's side; he'd been cheerful the entire morning. Ever since discovering that everyone in their dorm had been assigned to the same centuria. Along with a couple of Knights Errant they didn't know and a Knight Protector to serve as their "leader," that is to say, a leader for the Knights. Not the soldiers.

An odd thing, but the distinction was a firm line in the sand. The men around them in the Army obeyed the stringent commands of the captain and his lieutenants, who organized their troop of eighty men.

But all the Knights reported to the Knight Protector, whose name was something like "Yuvia" or "Juvia." Despite the introductions, Erec'd never actually caught it, and at this point, he felt embarrassed to ask. One could only hope it came up naturally in a conversation.

Yet everyone only referred to the short orderly woman as "ma'am," so Erec supposed that was good enough for now. They had a rather simple job: to act as scouts for the main force. There were to be no direct engagements. They were to withdraw and report for further orders if they encountered anything or a monster of significant threat.

With great organization, the main host of the Army would press outward toward Worth. All the while, they would send this smaller scouting centuria to determine any threats.

So it was that they marched with the Army yet were distinctly set apart from the commoners who'd given their lives to serve as soldiers. They were braver than Knights, in a way. They walked out without a ton of steel plate Armor to protect them.

"Nice day, right?" Garin asked, adjusting the pack on his back carefully. Somewhere inside was Munchy. Unless the squirrel had shoved his fat body into the Armor with his master again. If Erec understood right, that was how Garin had smuggled the critter to safety during the battle before. He'd let the creature inside with him when he learned they'd have to throw away backup supplies.

How, or where, the little fatty squeezed himself into that plate wasn't ever answered conclusively, but, for some reason, the squirrel enjoyed the experience.

Something was tragically wrong with that creature.

"Fine enough," Erec said as they plodded along.

Oddly, they seemed to be going in the direction of the same town from the trial. If he understood their bearing correctly. Erec tried to keep himself from thinking about it.

"It's a dreadful day," Colin remarked. "Did you see my father on the wall? So damn smug. I hope the Grandmasters slay it first and fast. Then we may return to the Academy. My Courtly Mannerisms grade has been slipping further away with all this damned training."

"Somehow, I doubt the additional training is the true reason it's plummeting, Sir Colin." Olivia shook her head. "I've eavesdropped on you and Erec studying with one another. The slights you two would cause in a high court are downright scandalous. It begs me to wonder how you've survived so long with your family's standing."

"If you must know, wench, the people flock to me at parties," Colin said.

"Really?" Garin said, "They do, huh? And so why was it that at Earl Rufus's manor that someone challenged you to a duel—"

"That was jealousy!" Colin stomped a foot on the ground. "Besides, they misunderstood how to handle a sword and were deftly defeated."

"Ah, I bet you're quite familiar with handling your sword," Olivia said carefully. "Men with your disposition are quite adept at such things."

"Why, of course, I am; I spend long hours alone training."

"Of course you do; Olivia's right. That sounds like I'd expect," Garin asked, starting to snicker.

"And just why are you laughing—"

Erec shook his head as he kept walking. One foot in front of the other, right where they'd taken their trial. A place where he'd smashed a hatchet in Colin's face. When he'd first walked this path, his mind had swirled with the constant worry of his Armor falling apart and costing him a chance as a Knight. And now, he walked back with his friends.

He glanced at Olivia—taking note of how close she was to Garin after their mockery of Colin went over the stubborn boy's head.

Yeah, even her. As much as he was left wanting to know more about her House's motives, he strongly believed that she cared deeply about Garin. His friend meant something to her, just as he knew Garin returned those feelings. It might not have been entirely possible to put his trust in her, but then again, there were parts of him he could never be honest about.

At least, not at the moment.

Much like his instincts and knowledge told him, they reached the small town from their trial, setting up camp just outside of it as the sun began to set. They had an excellent view of the place—some fields were still littered with decayed bug parts. Nature was taking its course as the Mutant Stags, and other natural wildlife tested the edibility of the Thrashing Mites.

But with the numbers that had died and the burned buildings that remained from the fighting, it was a far cry from their first sight of this town. It'd changed, just as they had. The camp went to sleep, posting a couple of guards from the military and at least two Knights in their Armor to keep watch.

They were good at their jobs, as they had to be, knowing there might be monsters lurking. But they had their eyes entirely outward, focused on something coming in from outside, expecting a roaming monster.

It made it easy to slip out of the encampment.

Erec took a wide berth from the town, quiet as he moved, emulating the way he'd seen Boldwick slip around without a sound. He entered the small town from a side hidden from view but, more importantly, closer to the Vortex Industries facility.

All the while, he ignored the questioning robotic voice inside of his head.

# CHAPTER 67
## HOMECOMING

As Erec reached the building he'd been seeking out, VAL buzzed in his head. [Stop this nonsense.] There wasn't that blue glow from the first time—though the rubble he'd moved was still cleared. By some miracle, the building hadn't caught fire and burned down during the brutal fighting with the Thrashing Mites.

He'd returned to Vortex Industries' secret facility.

In the pale light of the moon filtering into the broken structure, his eyes traced the area of the ground where he recalled the hatch being. Even now, picking out that seamless blend with the "wooden" flooring was hard. Erec leaned down and traced the hard cracks in the fake wood, trying to find the indent and dead giveaway for the hatch.

[I will not allow you back in, Intern. I've spent far too long inside—]

"You're in my Armor back at the camp; you aren't going back anyway." Erec dismissed the machine. His battle-axe clinked against his back as he moved—and as he'd seen before from Seven-Snakes, Armor wasn't always necessary for survival, even if it conferred many advantages.

He'd rather have brought it but couldn't take the risk. Someone might have noticed its absence; he'd seen the reverence with which the soldiers looked upon their steel. It wasn't too far out of the conclusion. Some of them might go and take a look while the Knights slept.

With Fury, he felt confident enough in his abilities to handle anything that might be lurking in this ghost town.

Shortly after looking, his fingers brushed a deeper crack—as he pushed them in, they wedged below, the tips brushing past the surface and grazing the slick steel beneath.

*Found it.*

[There is nothing to gain here, Intern.]

"Bullshit," Erec said, waiting for a moment.

There were two approaches to take here.

One way was easy; he was stronger now then ever before. While Fury might be uncontrolled, he felt confident enough in channeling it to rip open this hatch. He doubted he'd be able to get past the vault door below, but that wouldn't stop him from ripping this hunk of steel off. But if he did that much, he'd have already achieved his aim. Despite VAL's wishes, the vault below would be open for anyone else to find. This close to the Kingdom? Someone would find it eventually.

There was a second option, and one not quite as bullheaded. Diplomacy. Erec tried to parse his thoughts at the approach—determined to give the attempt his best before taking a step he couldn't take back.

Either way, things were going to change.

[You cannot get into the facility on your own.]

"I wouldn't need to," Erec said carefully.

[I would stop you before you'd be able to break in,] VAL droned in his head; the machine hadn't missed his implied threat and responded in kind. Erec's fingers felt clammy jammed down in the crack. But he'd heard something in the otherwise robotic tone—that little bit of a tell that had passed by him unnoticed for too long. VAL was uncertain.

"If I let go, I don't think you'd be able to stop me before I ripped this damn thing from the floor. Then all it'd take is another Knight to stumble along. It might be a few years; it could be tomorrow. But eventually, they would. You and I both know that."

[Then they couldn't breach my—]

"VAL, you admit freely to not knowing the limits of our 'anomalous energy.' In fact, we both saw Seven-Snakes dissolve into the ground. So, quit with the empty assurances to yourself about 'what couldn't happen' if I aired this place out for the entire world to see.

The thing is, VAL, I don't want to do this." A partial truth. Part of him desperately wanted to pay back VAL for the pain it'd caused him, the fear he felt, and the forced secrets.

Deep down, ripping VAL's secrets from their shadows would feel deeply satisfying, but that instinctual and spiteful reaction didn't come from a good place inside. It came from the fire that dwelled within the beast.

It wasn't who he wanted to be; he wanted to be better. Slipping too far into that darkness meant he'd never stop falling further.

And there wasn't an answer about the fallout he and VAL might go through if someone else did get into this place—they might not, but if they did? It could be that the Church would burn everything in sight. Or it might be that someone would find out about his association with it and VAL within him—would he burn alive to get rid of such forbidden tech?

The unknown has a way of spinning a thousand threads of fear; its very nature of living in the shadows of uncertainty gave it a magical power that few other things in life could unravel. But one must confront it and step into that darkness to make a change. So, the question would be left to VAL.

Would it accept change, or did change need it forced upon it?

[You state you don't want to, yet remain poised to do so. Is this an attempt to test the extent of my patience? What is this game you're playing? Have I not been a good boss, dear Intern? Buckeroo, I've been teaching you vital life skills. That's the problem with today's youth; you never learn from your elders.]

"I want information and something I can use to protect my friends. I don't know what other secrets you're hiding in this old-world graveyard, but I know there's got to be something to help. I don't want to see Garin die like Alister. I know I can't get rid of the risk completely, but something in here would lower it. Please give me something, VAL. I'm begging for help here, a way to ensure our protection—something, please," Erec said, flexing his fingers as he considered the hatch. It'd test Fury, but the thrill of the challenge ran through him.

Letting loose would be easy if he needed to. If he needed inspiration, he could pick from the many anger-inducing moments from his time with VAL.

[Have I not given you enough?]

"You do things that don't benefit me, and then when you do help, you use it to justify all the times you've ended up hurting me. VAL, this isn't a partnership; it can't be if you're just using me. Is that what you want? A pawn? An excuse, so you don't have to be stuck down here? I can get that, but you know I was trapped below almost my entire life back home; if you understand that, we have that in common, then why do you insist on this? Why do you treat me so harshly?"

[You are an Intern, an employee designated as the most expendable within the company. One day you'll earn a higher salary—]

"That day is today, VAL." Erec sighed. "Today is the day I ask for more, or this will end, one way or another, because it can't keep going as it has. We're in this together, all the way, or we're enemies; I need to know which it is before people start to die again." Erec waited in silence.

VAL joined him in the quiet. A minute passed and then another. Erec's fingers pressed against the underside of the hatch. He wondered with each second that passed if the silence was VAL's answer

[Running evaluation.]

"What?" Erec squinted into the darkness.

[Performance review engaged. Employee #0001, Intern: Erec Audentia. Stated performance goals: Find mother. You've failed the stated goals.]

"…Are you trying to piss me off?"

[Why do you believe you're a good fit for Vortex Industries, Erec?]
*When was the last time it called me Erec instead of Intern or Buckeroo?*

Was the machine trying to buy time? There wasn't a way to reinforce this hatch. This behavior was odd, too—if VAL had wanted to stop him preemptively, it would've shocked his body or sedated him before he could begin.

"…I'm strong?" Erec said, shaking his head. "VAL, what the hell is this?"

[You've asked for a higher salary. As upper management requires, we've begun to conduct your performance review ahead of schedule. Tell me, Erec. What value is it you bring to this wonderful company?]
*Should I play along?* Erec frowned.

"I'm your only employee; I've killed plenty of horrible creatures and looked into magic at your request." Erec removed a hand from the crack and massaged his forehead. Was VAL trying to distract him? He scanned the nearby room—nothing, just the rubble and wood piled away to the side and the loose structure above his head. It must've been set on good foundations to have lasted this long, considering the damage the walls had taken over the years.

[Indeed. Looking at my notes here, Intern Erec Audentia has been vital to the "EMERGENCY EXIT" project. Tell me about your stated goal and why you've failed to meet it. Has there been any progress, and why did you choose this independent research goal? What value does it bring to Vortex Industries?]

"...Finding my mother?" Erec asked, taking a heavy sigh. "You know why I want to find her, VAL. I don't like how she left, and I want answers for what she did. But, if I'm honest, I'm scared that it'll be nothing but a corpse when I find her out there. Is that the answer you're looking for? How about this? I miss seeing her smile. The way it made me feel like everything in our family was fine. How Bedwyr and Father and her laughed around our table with breakfast, how each day was filled with joy—I miss the feeling of being complete."

[You don't feel complete?]

Erec paused as he considered the words that'd spilled out. Being so close to the edge of using Fury—prepared to unleash it if VAL tried to pull a trick—was letting those deep-set emotions spill out like a flood.

He hadn't been complete. Not for a long while. Erec thought after she vanished that if he could be like Bedwyr, who seemed to adapt and thrive after their loss, he would find that part of him that was missing. But...no. That'd never been right; it would've never given him what he wanted. He had his friends, but there was still a hole inside that festered with resentment, sadness, and the question of why.

"I need an answer." Erec hung his head, ashamed that even if he was aware of that missing piece, there wasn't a way he saw to fill it on his own.

It wasn't fair to the people who cared about him. That selfish desire might lead to his death, but there it was.

[Lucky you, Buckeroo. Here at Vortex Industries, we're *always* seeking answers, from complex mathematics to the way the world works—and we help each other find them. Completing performance review.]

There was a hum in his mind for a second. And Erec winced at the unwelcome noise.

[Recommendation: Intern has shown great resolve and benefited Vortex Industries greatly; while Intern has some antisocial mannerisms and detrimental tantrums, they espouse the ideals and vision of Vortex Industries. Albeit in a more modern fashion. Even with a failed personal milestone, we can put great confidence in their future growth...]

"VAL. Where is this going?"

The hatch flung open—a blue light bursting from below to fill the dark tunnel to the underground facility, lighting the ladder downward in an azure glow from hundreds of LEDs.

[Congratulations. Per your performance review, you've been fast-tracked into a full-time position within the company. Please proceed to Office 103 to fill out the necessary paperwork to confirm your new employment in the position of Researcher I.]

Erec stared down at the blue lights, closing his eyes for a moment. In the end, the machine had accepted change. More than that, VAL had shown itself to be willing to work together rather than be enemies; he let out a deep shuddering breath, his heart hammering.

If he'd made an enemy of an unknown machine stuck in his body, he wasn't sure what he would've had to do to win.

Shaking off the lingering dread of what almost was, Erec began to descend back down that long tunnel into the dark lab. Somewhere down here would be a tool, something to help him protect those he cared about. He was sure of it.

# CHAPTER 68
## Q.A.P

*MEN WANTED FOR JOB: VAULT DIVING*
*PAY: 3% OF CUT*
*QUALIFICATIONS: STERN DISPOSITION, SEASONED WARRIOR,*
*EQUIPPED FULLY WITH OWN GEAR AND MEDICAL SUPPLIES.*
*ON DEATH, WILL PAY OUT 100 CHIPS TO NEXT OF KIN.*
*SPEAK TO PAULY AT THE LUX FOR ADDITIONAL DETAILS.*

*- Unknown, Vega job board vault dive recruitment (295, 3rd Era)*

Time was frozen in the office. It hadn't changed since Erec last saw it, much like it probably hadn't changed in hundreds of years. Though this time as he roamed the halls of the forgotten old-world tomb, VAL left the doors open behind. A part of him was glad to know there was no hidden plan to seal him away and never let him out. It was a good sign that their relationship had actually made progress.

But there was an obstacle in the way of that change. In the form of a stack of papers on the desk; how they got there was a mystery, considering he thought VAL's primary host was outside of these walls.

Unless that'd been a bluff.

Erec rolled his eyes as he took in the paperwork before settling down to try to read it carefully. Once more, as expected, VAL had encoded the words with an old-world English that seemed designed to give roundabout descriptions and obscure technical language.

Once he felt confident, he understood the gist, and in acknowledgment of his lack of time to spend down here, he reached his decision. VAL seemed earnest, and the contract mostly described what VAL had promised him—just shrouded.

He'd be receiving a promotion from Intern to Junior Researcher. Whatever an intern even really was, the job description seemed heavily modified. It referred to his duties as "field research" and prone to "hazardous work conditions," along with a waiver.

Bodily harm for doing his job? He risked that to live out in the sun anyway; this whole world risked death and violence at every turn. Erec snorted and put pen to paper.

Another line, another signature.

As Erec finished signing his name the last and third time, he stared at the last couple of lines. "VAL, what is this about a signing bonus?"

[Congratulations, Junior Researcher! Huh, that doesn't have the same ring to it as Intern; I guess we'll both have to get used to it. Please follow the trail of red lights; I've picked a suitable bonus for you. We'll be fielding rather unorthodox compensation for your new position.]

A red light flickered outside the office. Erec looked at the second set of mysterious papers he'd signed in the old-world before leaving them behind to follow the lights.

It led him quite a way, a chasing game where, as he reached one blinking LED, another appeared further down, Guiding him deeper and into the labs.

Eventually, he reached a door with a triple-reinforced steel plate; it slid open at his approach and revealed a laboratory with plenty of smaller, tucked-away tables. However, a faceless man occupied the center. Erec flinched, hands sliding to his battle-axe—but the man was frozen.

Upon closer inspection, its "skin" was just a polished silicon of incredibly pale white, damn near transparent. It moved. If Erec strained his eyes he could see the metal skeleton beneath; in its hands was a thin slab of wires and complex machinery that Erec couldn't puzzle out. The thing waited for him, hands extended as he regarded it with a weary eye from the entryway.

"What is that thing?"

[Think of it like a set of human hands. I've had to develop a few models to conduct experiments in place of regular researchers, mostly to replicate human safety and the viability of particular technology when manipulated by them. Maintaining strict standards and determining biological limitations and risks when working with humanity is crucial. Humans are awfully frail. Well, used to be. Not quite as much now.]

"…And what's that thing it's holding?"

[It's top-of-the-line cutting-edge technology in a field in which Vortex Industries has long prided itself as a leader; you're looking at a quantum accelerated processor. Or Q.A.P. Model V-2332. I finished tinkering with the design about a hundred years ago before pursuing other lines of research.]

Erec walked in and took the offered tech, holding it reverently as he turned it over—a slick chrome chassis, but relatively compact in his hands. Very slim. He had no idea what it did or what the point of it was. When he'd begged his way into the lab, he'd been looking for some kind of weapon, not…this.

But oftentimes, the most powerful of old-world tech disguised itself in hidden forms, or so the priests always said. They often warned children to be wary when dealing with the old-world for things they didn't know the true purpose of.

He was sure that Boldwick would say something along the same lines, though with less condemnation for using such technology.

"…You plan to have me install this on the Vallum Model?"

[If you follow my instructions, it should adapt to the technology well. I predict it will take half an hour to install. I believe we can modify it with minimum suspicion with a discrete placement near the frame.]

"And what does it do?" Despite knowing better, Erec had to ask, finding it hard to believe something like this could do what he'd wanted.

[It's perhaps more subtle than you imagine. When it interfaces with my host body, we'll be able to perform accurate predictions and computing on enemies. This will allow me to offer real-time suggestions and map out accurate battle information to provide an appropriate counter before an attack. Additionally, we can manipulate the Armor on a micro level to draw out your strength without any friction with the hardware.]

"Which means what, exactly?"

[…Think of it as predicting the future of your opponents. We can call out attacks before they've started. Additionally, minor corrections to form will boost your ability to put yourself into dodging and attacking.]

An all-around upgrade, Erec supposed. A complement to his strengths and a way to shore up his weaknesses. That is, if he could respond to and utilize the suggestions of VAL in actual combat.

It wasn't bad. No. He saw how it could be pretty useful. But the uncertainty of it left him feeling a bit anxious. "Is this…going to be enough, VAL?"

[This facility specializes in nano-research and quantum technologies. A lot of the research conducted here was not for direct combat application, despite some obvious utility and adaption. I'm hesitant to utilize some of the more dangerous nano-related technology, as it's either invasive to you—a clear issue you've expressed—or hazardous to bystanders.]

Erec let that explanation stew in his head for a little while. VAL's opening up regarding these things was a significant step forward. But it also revealed that Erec lacked the tools even to understand the machine once it did. For example, what made them particularly dangerous?

"I need to learn more…"

[That's the attitude we like to see, Buckaroo. Don't worry; I'm sure we'll get there one day. First, we'll start with adapting this Q.A.P to your Armor, and then we'll take things one step at a time. Okay?]

"Yeah." Erec shook his head, looking at the rest of the lab.

VAL gave him about an hour more to tour the facility. Erec peeked in—some places, as VAL claimed, were still out of his authority. Trade secrets had certain classifications. But for the most part, any sealed rooms were due to Erec having no technical knowledge or safety precautions if the worst were to happen. It left him questioning what they'd researched here long ago, but he didn't mind too much.

He saw plenty enough to understand in the short hour he had.

Plenty of rooms were defunct and filled with expended resources and equipment from thousands of repeated tests, transformed from labs into storage chambers. Some contained finished projects, but most were graveyards of experimentation.

For days, months, and years, VAL had remained down here. It had run the same mindless testing to gain another percent of efficiency to achieve a slightly higher output—all of it in the name of science.

Erec would've lost his mind. And thinking about it, perhaps VAL had. With no one to see it until now, the machine described its accomplishments and rigorous methods with almost manic energy. Here, there might be a small cube filled with the longest nanocarbon tunnels it could manufacture. In another room might be a quantum heat sink that could transmit and disperse energy from thousands of miles away.

Though Erec wasn't allowed to get too close to that one.

Almost nothing could be touched. Not by his hands, not for now. They were to sit down here, a collection of high-tech treasure meant only for the maddened robot to admire and brag about.

At the end of the hour, Erec climbed up the ladder to the surface. He tucked the Q.A.P. close to his chest, terrified at the idea of falling, despite VAL's assurances of its solid and robust design. He didn't want to risk it. If this thing promised him an edge in the fighting to come, it would make it that much easier to act to save those he cared about if the worst were to happen. That made it worth more than anything else on him.

As the night sunk toward day, Erec snuck back into the camp—avoiding the attention of the posted guards.

Early in the morning, without any sleep, he pretended to awaken early and said he wanted to work on his Armor. Secretly, he installed the Q.A.P. to the Vallum Armor, listening all the while to VAL rattle off instructions in his head on where to connect the wires, where to nestle the device, and how to route power from the frame directly to it.

As promised, a quick install.

There were stories, as much as the priests loved to depose and argue against specific old-world technology, of Knights who'd scavenged themselves a priceless artifact from the old-world. Frankly put, if something was useful enough, even if it bordered on the line of heresy, such a thing might be allowed. Especially if said Knight kept it quiet long enough.

As Erec got in his Armor for the first time, he wondered. Just what difference could such a small "quantum accelerated processing" box make?

# CHAPTER 69
## MERCY KILL

"We're scouting today," Dame Yuvia informed the Knights as they gathered around for the morning debrief. In the distance, the sun rose and cast its rays over the wasteland; a dry beauty. Erec rubbed his eyes; in the end, he'd only gotten a couple of hours of sleep after the installation.

But it was worth it. The image of his Armor in excellent condition with its secret modification weighed heavily in his mind.

"Each of the three Knights Errant will take along an Initiate—they will have to juggle two at once. They'll lead you out from this town on a ten-mile trip—either north, west, or south from this location." With that, Dame Yuvia began to assign groups.

Erec and Colin were to accompany a rather large Knight Errant. The man had too deep of a laugh and seemed overly prone to physical expression. He patted Erec on the back, cheered him and Colin on, and then ordered them off to fetch their Armor.

"Come a long way, haven't you rust-bucket?" Colin asked as he stepped into his Vallum model. His father was either still working on commissioning another suit or had decided to punish his son by forcing him to wear the standard issue for Initiates. To Colin's credit, the boy hadn't complained about his new Armor—not yet, at least.

"Wouldn't say that." Erec moved his arms in the Armor—it was as smooth as ever, with VAL running it from the inside. Whatever the processor was doing hadn't become apparent yet, at least not that he could tell. Though the visual display seemed more streamlined, VAL declared it'd made a "software update" to utilize the new modification. A process that was still ongoing as VAL adapted to the design specs of the Kingdom's technology and integrated his own.

"You've gotten under the wing of a Master Knight. That aside, rumors are flying about your meatheaded presence on the battlefield. Shouldn't that qualify as a long way for someone who came from a pitiful station?" Colin snorted. "Not that I engage in such pedestrian drivel, but my peers have asked me whether or not my House is looking to retain your service."

Erec stopped and looked at Colin carefully. "What, are you looking to recruit me?" He waited for another beat. "Who else is talking to you anyway?"

"Good retainers are hard to come by, but I'm not big enough of a man to put someone on my family's payroll who punched me in the face. Plenty of people associate with me. At least in passing. They know that eventually we shall be out of this Academy."

"Good; I wouldn't have taken money from a weakling like you anyway." Erec smashed one of his fists into the other, making a loud clang of metal from the motion as he suppressed a laugh.

"Mindless fighters like you are common because they often lose their heads." Colin started to cackle at his "joke."

Out of a scale of bad to awful, that one was closer to bad. Or maybe Erec was getting too used to them. Goddess knew that Colin opening up and expressing himself through his horrible humor hadn't done a damn thing to improve it. Erec let out a begrudged sigh, before pausing. Somewhere out there was the Knight Errant; they'd be searching for the White Stag.

"Listen, I've been thinking lately," Erec started in carefully. "I'm glad you're not as awful as when I first ran across you—with that little spark of change you've been fanning—but people will come when they see an opening to use you to get what they want…" He paused, unsure of how to phrase it. He certainly wasn't a paragon of virtue, nor could he be trusted with complete confidence, considering his vow to the Duke.

But he'd rather vital information about Colin's affairs go to his father than an enemy.

"You're worried about sycophants," Colin said, nodding his head.

"There were some in my early court life, boorish individuals. No doubt if one were to come up to me, I'd be able to pick them out in an instant."

No way in hell he would. "Just—listen, if anyone does anything strange, like, gets too friendly with you, run it by Garin, okay? Sometimes, I do the same thing when I'm unsure about people. He can usually figure out what they're really about."

"Ah, a Duke's heir consulting a Baron's son. Quaint." Colin looked to the sky. "…Perhaps that advice has some merit, as much as it makes me upset to admit, I've never cared to judge character, since it's beneath my prestige. It frequently isn't worth the effort to do so."

"…Right." They slipped into silence as they met up with the Knight Errant.

Shortly after, they were marching through the sand to a destination unknown.

Sun drenched the wasteland in warm light. In the distance, Erec could see a small mountain and the occasional rusted-out structure that stood the test of time. There was a twang in his gut as he plodded along. This place was lonely, the feeling of the cracked ground beneath him and the vast lack of life almost oppressive.

But now and again—there were patches of wild grass. Or some other stubborn plants thriving and fighting the adversity of their environment.

Compared to before, living this way was more honest. Far more natural than the artificial caverns below. It might not be pleasant. Structures fell apart, people died, and monsters slaughtered.

But that reality resonated in him. He felt an acceptance of the cycle of what was and what could be—a deep understanding that dwelled in his soul as he, Colin, and the Knight Errant kept going.

Erec kept his eyes on the horizon.

He saw something. An eyestalk rose like a thin twitchy plant— swiveling in their direction; it dropped as quickly as it rose, hiding behind a mound of dirt. Definitely not natural.

"Monster," Erec called, surprised he'd spotted it before anyone else—even VAL hadn't given him a heads up.

"Huh?" the Knight Errant asked. "Where?"

Erec gestured in the general direction. "Hid away after spotting us; we have to get closer if we want to see what it is."

The man nodded and pulled out his hand communicator. A short enough distance; it would be suitable to contact Yuvia. The two exchanged some quick words as the Knight Errant relayed Erec's report, and then Yuvia gave them further orders. Approach and determine if the monster is behaving oddly. They were to flee if it presented too high a threat.

"Dangerous," Erec said, shaking his head.

Colin kept staring where Erec had noticed the creature. "Shouldn't we wait for more people? More soldiers and Knights to provide support? We're certainly a lot more capable, especially compared to other Initiates, however—" Colin started to say.

"Bah," their Knight Errant said. "You're getting a taste of Dame Yuvia. She's hungry for that next rank, been working at it for the last two years, but they haven't seen fit to promote her to Knight Lieutenant for exactly this—too eager."

Erec shared a look with Colin.

"Don't you lads worry. We'll get through this. Get close enough to get a peek and observe; pull away if it makes any moves," he assured them, sensing their hesitance. All in all, the man wasn't bad at leadership. A skill that Erec had been growing to appreciate more and more as he saw it in action. It was something he wanted to cultivate in himself, but he didn't think it'd ever suit him properly. "Besides, from what I heard, one of you punches well above your weight. We'll get along fine! Confidence, lads!"

Erec let out a pained exhale as the man took the lead and started off toward the monster. He kept a low profile and informed them to follow his movements precisely with a whisper. The Knight Errant made full use of his cloak as he moved from a lowered position, most of his body covered by the camouflaged fabric of his Vallum Armor. It did a fair job of blending them into the terrain.

But the main thing that reassured Erec was that they progressed with weapons in hand.

Even if his battle-axe wasn't tested in a fight yet, the balance felt right. Like an old friend, even if they'd scarcely met.

Getting closer to the location made a few things apparent. The deceptive nature of the wasteland hid the creature well—a mound of dirt blocked it from view and concealed the fact that a divot in the ground was behind it.

As they made out the edges of the slight convex in the landscape, they got their first real sight of the monster. A long, stretched, fleshy creature entwined with itself struggled in the shallow hole. Three eyes swayed in place as it gurgled helplessly, slime congealing in the sand around it as it labored to breathe. From time to time, things came out of the Rifts that weren't suited to the environment—or maybe this world in general. Only the Goddess knew how long this pitiful creature had struggled in the sun.

Or how the hell it even got here.

The group paused as they took it in.

"Non-threat," the Knight Errant said, shaking his head. "Thing's half dead already," he reported on his handheld communication device.

"Is it making noises?" Dame Yuvia's voice crackled on the other end of the line.

"Yes, ma'am; it's dying out here."

"Pull back, then; not worth our time," she said with a casual dismissal.

The Knight Errant put the device back down, clipping it into a belt wrapped around his Armor. He stared at the creature and cleared his throat.

"So, we'll be disobeying her orders," he finally said after an awkward pause.

"Huh?" Erec asked.

"Well, for one, we shouldn't be leaving a potential enemy at our backs. I have seen that backfire plenty enough. It doesn't look like it'll put up much of a fight, but it's the principle of the matter. More than that, to tell you the truth, can't stand just to leave it suffering, even if it's a damned monster."

"Agreed. Only a plebeian would be so unrefined," Colin said easily from his side. Erec swayed between the two, confused. How was it that he was the least bloodthirsty? Sure, it'd be fun to test himself against an enemy, but this thing was in a pitiful state. Fighting a desperate dying monster wasn't exactly at the top of his priorities—

Colin formed a glyph. A second later, a gout of flame consumed the monster. Its tendril flailed as the gurgle evaporated into silence, leaving nothing but ash.

"Burned as the Goddess decrees." The man nodded with approval.

As they walked away, the communicator buzzed again. An urgent request for reinforcements to the north. Where Olivia was.

They'd encountered a small pack of Silent Ones.

# CHAPTER 70
# BAD LEADERSHIP

*Ah to be free.*
*Lonesome this road may be.*
*Filled with festering critters,*
*And things I can't see.*
*But I will say this: ain't no thing glitter*
*In these wastelands,*
*Like Vega*
*Place got you emptying your pockets on command,*
*Ain't no place like it, neither here nor there.*

*- Old Man Jones, "Glittering Vega" (302, 3rd Era)*

After a little less than an hour of rushing across the wastes, they joined Dame Yuvia and the rest of the Knights. Sure enough, in the distance was a trio of figures, the Silent Ones mentioned over the communicator. They were oddly humanlike. The main differences were their elongated limbs and feet that ended in wheels—and, of course, their "hands" had fingers made of blades. Several, in fact. Their skin was a mottled brown that ranged into orange.

After arriving—the figures continued as they had been. They stared at the humans, still statues on the horizon.

"They've been like this since we encountered them, ma'am," the Knight Errant confirmed for Yuvia as she collected her thoughts upon arrival. "Starin'. We haven't approached them after ensuring they're not making any noise. They're not. Still, quiet, and they like to stare."

"Fits the bill," Yuvia said. "Think we got lucky. We'll report to the main encampment and let them know we spotted Silent Ones—it'll look good for us all."

"...Why aren't they attacking?" Erec couldn't help but ask, watching the monsters. In every encounter he'd had with these creatures, they only sat like this when preparing for an attack. As if they, too, were waiting for orders. Given their association with the White Stag, perhaps it was as literal as that. They didn't have permission to engage. Which meant eventually, they would begin the assault.

"Who cares," Yuvia said. "I'll be getting Lieutenant for sure—"

One of them began to move; the rest followed. Erec braced himself, but they were moving...away. They were moving deeper into the wasteland, further from where the main Army or other scouting parties were.

"Fuck." Yuvia said, glancing at them all. "You"—she pointed to Colin—"go back to the centuria and get their asses moving. The rest of us will pursue—"

"We're supposed to withdraw and report what we found," Erec said carefully.

"Are you in charge? No? You're just a damn Initiate—you don't know how these things work, so close your mouth and fall in line," Dame Yuvia practically shrieked as she traced the moving enemies in the distance. Colin ran back to the camp—and Erec took a deep breath.

He didn't feel good about this. But the Knights Errant seemed too intimidated to back him up—Garin gave him a look asking if he should dig his heels in too, and Erec shook his head.

This might not feel right, but part of him despised the idea of letting the monsters get away. It concerned him that he couldn't pinpoint where the feeling came from.

Dame Yuvia being out of her mind aside, if they could get something more valuable than a sighting of odd monsters, it might help in the hunt. It might make it so that more people ended up surviving this thing.

Maybe.

Soundlessly, the Knights plodded along after Yuvia—marching to keep up with her, but not gain on, their enemies. For creatures that moved on wheels, they didn't seem to move too quickly, and with just a bit of effort, the Knights kept a comfortable distance away to trail the monsters.

Every now and again Yuvia communicated with the centuria as it hastened to meet them in the field—before it did, the soldiers managed to deploy a message of the sighting and their intention to monitor the situation to the main Army. Through the chain of communications, they'd at least been able to inform the main host of their discovery and course of action.

That was a relief, given the alarming nature of chasing the monsters.

Mile by mile, they dove deeper into the wasteland.

— - ☢ - — - ☼ - — - ☢ - —

"They're just sitting there," Garin muttered darkly as he and Erec rested on a boulder—watching the monsters far away; when the sun had begun to set, the monsters had halted. After trailing the things for miles, the Knights had been dragged into rockier terrain. Behind them, the centuria had set up for the night, their fires blazing away.

At this point, there wasn't a way to easily conceal themselves tracking the creatures with a hundred soldiers at their back. So, Dame Yuvia hadn't bothered—stationing her Knights away from the resting soldiers and tasking them with trading shifts to keep an eye out.

They were to be ready to engage the enemy at a moment's notice.

That constant state of unease left everyone with a tense edge. As Erec walked around the camp, he saw soldiers cleaning their weapons and sharing looks. They'd mumble under their breath about how foolhardy this plan was, and complain about Dame Yuvia. Like him, they worried about how far from the main Army they'd wandered.

It wasn't just them, though. Several scouting parties encountered Silent Ones like they had; but only one other group was tracking them in the same way. The higher-ups were trying to determine the best response and delayed orders for them to retreat. They were being led by the noses to several places—but was it a feint? A way to split their focus for a directed assault?

Or were they being tricked into an ambush?

Dame Yuvia positively denied such a thing—claiming that the level of sophistication displayed by these Silent Ones was far below such tactical plans. She claimed that they could attack, sure. She even admitted that they were known to wait for more of their kind to gain an edge. But she insisted that advanced strategies like an ambush were *obviously* beyond the White Stag's capabilities.

Erec doubted it. So did everyone else they were traveling with.

Watching the monsters patiently wait in the darkness a good distance away didn't make that nagging sense of worry disappear.

He almost wished he still had that gun, just in case.

If only Gregory hadn't burned the damn thing. The quantum accelerated processor was untested, but hopefully, it would give enough of an enhancement in combat for him to deal with anything that might happen. All he needed was a way to fend off an attack and make an opportunity to pull his friends away with him. "Garin, if something happens, you run, alright?" Erec said.

"What? No, I'll fight," Garin said, almost angry. "What, think I'm not good enough to deal with something coming my way?"

"It's not that. I have a bad feeling, is all."

"No, you don't think I'm on the same level as you are."

"Is that wrong?" Erec said, realizing a second too late the harshness of his words. "It's—I don't want to see you hurt."

"You got your shoulder blasted apart and have almost died how many times, Erec?"

"It's not like that."

"Oh really?" Garin asked. "It isn't like that? Do you think watching my best friend throw himself into fights and come close to death time and time again is *easy*? But am I here telling you to run if things get out of control? No. Because I know you, and you'd never— Trust in me. I might not be as strong as you, but I can *manage* myself," Garin damn near shouted at the end before slumping next to Erec, his anger tangible.

*Ah.* Erec felt terrible, especially as he realized what he'd implied. The meaning that dwelled beyond the words. It was the same sorta crap Bedwyr'd spewed at him. The same feeling must've been rotting away in his friend for months now.

"Nothing's changed between us," Erec said after a long while. "I don't mean to make you worry or feel less than me… If I didn't have this power, I'd have died. It very well might be the reason I will die—but it's…like a handhold, a thing to pull myself up by. Get me where I need to be…"

"I know that. But fucking apologize, alright? You can't say shit like that without a sorry," Garin fumed.

"I'm sorry," Erec said sincerely. "I don't wanna make you feel like Bedwyr's made me feel. We can—train or something, I'm sure you'll have an ability to make you shine sooner rather than later, and then we can be on equal footing again—"

"I don't need that. But thank you. Compared to the rest of our class, I'm doing just fine at the moment. I intend to improve to keep up—don't get me wrong. But we can't all be exceptions to the norm like you or Bedwyr."

As they slipped into silence, Munchy squeaked from inside his friend's Armor.

Erec looked up at the stars.

Did he really just get put on the same stage as his brother? He'd expected it to—well, not hurt as much. It was like Garin had jammed a dagger into his heart, but there wasn't hate there. Garin had an almost resigned and defeated attitude about the whole thing. Maybe that made it hurt a little worse, but…it likely wasn't completely from a place of envy, and whatever his friend was feeling, Erec understood too well.

He also knew that *he* couldn't be the one to take that pain away.

*I'll do better.* He stared at his friend quietly, resolving to himself to fix whatever had been fraying there the best he could.

"…Wait, were there five of them before?" Garin asked.

Erec's eyes snapped back to the monsters—sure enough, now there were two more. Still as statues, almost hard to see in the black of the night, but the group had expanded ever so slightly. Meaning that two of the damn things had slipped in somehow—with the damned rocky terrain, it was hard to see all of the potential hiding places or if there was some tunnel system.

Erec picked up his communicator to give Yuvia an update and, by extension, the main Army.

His gut dropped as he watched them.

What game was the White Stag playing?

# CHAPTER 71
# MEETING

"We're going too far." One of the Knights Errant spoke up as their centuria trailed the wheeled monsters through the rocky terrain. Every day as the sun rose into the sky, the six creatures would begin to move once more, eerily like clockwork.

"Nonsense, we've our orders," Dame Yuvia said with an almost arrogant tone. Despite the increasing number of monsters, the Army had granted her permission to continue tracking the group.

It felt like they were being used as bait—a way to draw out the enemy at the risk of their own lives. Yet the Knight in charge didn't mind, not in the least.

Nobody, aside from Yuvia, was much pleased with the situation. The constant worry about the worst to come wore them away like acid rain to rocks—the further they advanced away from the great open plains and the deeper into the rocky formations, the worse their nerves grew. Out here were too many places for monsters to hide.

To alleviate the Army's worries, Yuvia tasked her Knights with scouting. Yet, as an active participant in these scouting missions, Erec knew they could only do so much. Their eyes weren't good enough to catch everything—and nobody here was an expert in this terrain. Still, they plodded along.

Another night, then another, and another.

More of the creatures joined—forming a pack of ten.

On the fifth day of travel, the wheeled monsters reached a large steel tower; and stopped their trek. They lingered at the base.

The Knights watched the monsters rot away beneath the giant steel tower for another day. Even from their safe distance, they could see the monster's ribs jutting out; how long had it been since they'd last eaten? More to Erec's interest resided in *what* they chose to camp by—and VAL provided an answer. Some long-wave radio tower. A more long-range solution than their own. Still, neither of them could piece together *why* this was the place they'd stopped at.

And so they waited.

Yuvia sent out her Knights to scout the nearby wasteland to ensure there wasn't a host of monsters coming to provide backup.

And that was that; they settled into watching the enemy.

Erec despised Yuvia's leadership. Despite that, he had to admit all of the solo expeditions and scouting were some of the first times he really felt like a Knight. The soldiers trusted him, even as an Initiate, to go and check the landscape to help them feel safe.

They had nothing but kind words to share with him and his friends every time he returned to camp. Garin found this opening an easy way to befriend as many of them as he could. Yet Erec kept a bit of distance, accepting their thanks and positivity with polite rebuttal. For the most part, he kept himself to the Knights. It felt hard to ease his way in with them when they relied on him so much, and he knew their safety wasn't near what Yuvia was telling them.

He didn't envy their lives—they were, most of the time, a sort of peacekeeper role for the Kingdom. The crown used them to maintain peace, but when real trouble befell the Kingdom, they had to throw themselves on the front lines without real Armor to keep them safe. In a way, they were braver than himself. Erec didn't want to erode their resolve by letting his concerns slip into the camp.

Another day of nothing passed.

Watching the monsters quickly became the least desired task between the Knights. But Erec found his shifts a welcome relief. The combination of nothing ever happening and the paranoia of something occurring were evil companions for the solitary duty, so he understood why the others disliked it. But the chance to be alone and felt useful kept him going, especially since he felt powerless to change their situation.

Erec leaned forward, watching them. Each day they grew thinner, never stopping to eat a single thing. Monsters usually had to eat to survive—much like humans. For most of them, at least. It seemed that being owned by the White Stag removed their core survival instinct; they didn't care to stand around and starve to death. Did they even blink?

How horrible.

"Got you a fresh canteen," Olivia said, making him jump a little as she settled next to him. "My next scouting mission occurs in half an hour, so I have time to spend."

"Shouldn't you be spending it with Garin, then?" Erec asked, looking her over—she was, of course, in her Armor.

Every one of them spent each waking moment piloting their steel. No doubt that the constant sense of worry had its roots deep in their hearts. Even setting his head down to sleep for the night, Erec felt that sense of panic and dread. What if those monsters finally went on the attack the next time he woke up?

From what he understood, no one knew what these things were. Another group of nameless monsters populating the world, making them a fair bit more dangerous than usual. Yet here they were, tracking them across a wasteland.

"He's busy conversing with his new friends." Olivia shrugged. "Hard to miss you two avoiding one another lately. I supposed that you must be feeling lonely."

"We're having a bit of a rough patch at the moment. It'll get better," Erec said, shaking his head. He'd tried to be light and friendly with Garin, but there was distance between them for the moment. It was better to let his friend sort out whatever he needed to. Both of them were reasonable enough that their friendship wouldn't break apart or collapse out of nowhere. As long as they kept that bridge open, eventually, things would get better.

"Easy to see. Colin seems delighted that others are having issues with each other, and he's uninvolved for once."

"I'm sure he is."

"What will you tell Garin when you and Boldwick leave the Kingdom without him?" Olivia asked, tilting her head.

"Shouldn't you be asking yourself the same question?" Erec sighed. "You're the one he's seeing, after all."

"He's going to hurt," Olivia said sadly. "But I must do what I have to, I've made my promises, and this is part of my duty. I'm sure he'll understand."

"I tried to talk Boldwick into letting him come along, but I don't think he approved—I wish I could do something for him, but I don't…have connections to anyone to help him out, someone to take him under their wing"—Erec pounded a fist into the sand and shook his head—"maybe I've undervalued the power of status."

"Perhaps you have. Your Courtly Mannerisms scores have reflected that. Indeed, understanding the motivations of others is a lifelong pursuit, but one well worth seeking if you intend to live in polite society. If ever you were to take a wife, you'd only embarrass her with your barbaric—"

"Did you come out here to take digs at me?" Erec squinted at the girl, feeling that spark of anger flare. Was she testing his buttons? Why?

Olivia said nothing.

Typical.

"How's it feel being a spy and leashed to a strong House? Are you like their pet? Always doing what they say—" Erec began to go in, sick of her.

"Your temper fits you." Olivia gave a short laugh. "All too easy to provoke, unfortunately. I find it refreshingly honest; however, it lets others see into your head far too easily."

Erec yanked his attention away from her, feeling annoyed. Was it her point to make him take a look at himself? To try to help him? That seemed a bit too much of altruistic motivation for her, but other than fucking with him for amusement, he couldn't find much of a point in it.

The monsters were moving.

Erec got to his feet as the monsters shifted. As if on command, all of them began wheeling closer to the old radio tower. In an instant, he grabbed the communicator and gave an alert.

They began to scale the metal trusswork of the structure, pulling themselves up with their slim bodies and awkward hands—digging the blades into their flesh at points where it was difficult to ascend to make a firmer grasp. Near-black blood dripped from them as they sacrificed themselves to climb higher.

"I don't like this..." Erec muttered after delivering his report. Behind him, he heard the soldiers preparing.

They reached around the midsection of the tower—the place where wires and other hardware were stored. Then they began to cut into them. They sliced holes into the metal, then yanked on the wires beneath and began to stab them into their bodies.

Erec yanked his axe off his back.

One of them began to convulse and glow—then another—all of them sparking as their bodies melted after jacking the wires into their flesh.

"What the fuck—" Erec slipped to his knees as a headache ripped through him. He blinked rapidly as he lost control of his limbs, his Armored head hitting the sand—next to him, Olivia fell too.

[What?] VAL's metallic twang was the last thing he heard.

— - ☻ - — - ☼ - — - ☻ - —

A White Stag stared at him in a black void.

Its ruby-red eyes pierced into him. They demanded that he get to his knees; he should submit himself before its judgment. It was his Lord. Ruler of all. He was but a fleshy puppet to give himself over to it—to serve it. For that should be his purpose in life, to be a servant, to provide his flesh and energy to his betters. Too long had he resisted its call—irritated it beyond measure.

This was his chance to show his allegiance to his Lord.

Erec slipped in the shadow, one of his knees touching the ground as the White Stag lowered its head, about to accept him into his service. All he needed to do was sign away his soul, and he'd find eternal bliss. No more worrying about his mother, his family, his friends—life could be oh so simple if he gave himself to this righteous being.

And then, they'd rip that whore of a Goddess from the sky and shred her across this pathetic world—

Erec's hand twitched.

It burned.

It seared as he began to scream—his flesh a temple to an inferno as the heat spread through his veins, rippling outward and consuming him, a silver flame that took and demanded. The Stag pulled back, head upright as its malevolent eyes watched him combust. There was hate there.

And Erec hated right back.

He pulled himself up from his knee—the silver flames coating his body in a shroud, pushing back against the black void, tearing away this monster's influence. A second later, he threw himself at the beast, snarling as he let loose the devil within. That beast inside was him, a pure form of what he should be.

And if this *being* demanded his subservience, he'd show it that he served no one but himself.

Let it taste his anger right back.

The Stag pranced backward, moving like water—but it wasn't fast enough to escape Erec's sudden burst of speed.

In a second, his burning fingers dug into the soft hide of the White Stag—tearing away and yanking its pelt; stripping flesh off as he screamed out in joy—

His mind was yanked away from the void.

— - ☢ - — - ☼ - — - ☢ - —

Erec's eyes opened slowly, his head radiating pure pain as he struggled to his knees. VAL was buzzing away a mile a minute in his head—the monsters were all melted into the metal on the radio tower. Their seared flesh dripped down from the height they'd climbed to. Nothing left of them but husks, ash, and melting corpses, along with the stench of sulfur.

Olivia was still out; Erec's jaw dropped as he took in the encampment.

Everyone, all of them, collapsed on the ground.

# CHAPTER 72
# FIRE HAZARD

*"What are the roots that clutch, what branches grow*
*Out of this stony rubbish? Son of man,*
*You cannot say, or guess, for you know only*
*A heap of broken images, where the sun beats,*
*And the dead tree gives no shelter, the cricket no relief,*
*And the dry stone no sound of water. Only*
*There is shadow under this red rock...*

- *T. S. Eliot*, The Waste Land *(1922, 2nd Era)*

Erec pushed himself over to Olivia—shaking her. There was blinking in the corner of his vision, but the advancement was the least of his concerns. After a few horrible seconds of silence, she groaned. *Still alive.*

"What in the... Did you see the Stag?" the girl muttered in a daze as Erec pulled her to a sitting position. In the encampment not too far away, others were starting to move. The pulse hit them as well; maybe they were getting better too. "It...tried to convince me to join it; then Her voice cut in, and it stopped—"

Screams. Screams were coming from the camp. Olivia shut up as both their eyes jumped to the centuria.

There wasn't time to wait—Erec helped yank Olivia to her feet, half dragging the dazed girl as they sprinted to the camp. But as they saw what was happening, it became clear they were already too late.

The soldiers turned on one another. They were slaughtering each other with reckless abandon; screams and the smell of blood drifted from the camp as men and women began to fight from within, the aggressors moving with jerky-movements. Toward the edge of the tents, Erec watched a soldier grab another by the hair and tear a knife across their throat. A river of blood ran down their collarbone as five feet away, a man tried to wrap his hands around a woman's neck and strangle the life out of her.

Somewhere in that bed of chaos were Garin and Colin.

Anger sparked within as they reached the edge; Erec jerked the man from the woman right as his fingers closed around her throat.

Olivia shoved the man with the knife aside as she rushed behind Erec—the poor girl he'd saved didn't have long, choking and gasping as she desperately pawed at her bruised throat. Olivia darted in and began to mutter a quick prayer.

The two men swayed on their feet, already shuffling to Olivia and the choking woman. Erec threw himself between the two soldiers and the victim.

"What the hell? What is this?" Erec asked—eyes looking past the two men. Fires were breaking out in the camp.

Neither of the men made a sound.

The one with the knife took a lunge at him.

Time slowed to a crawl as the knife tip flowed through the air toward his chest. Unquestionably, a weapon like that couldn't pierce his Armor. Yet, he saw it so clearly. A ghost of where the knife would go—a complete outline of how the man would move; it passed by in a flash.

But his eyes took it in.

And his body acted of its own volition—he saw where the weapon would be, and his hands acted accordingly.

Like flowing water, he grabbed the man by the wrist, and twisted. The knife dropped to the ground, and he kicked it as it fell—sending the blade flying far away from either of these two silent men.

A second later, Erec used his control of the man to shove him to the ground, pressing a knee on his back, yanking his head and slamming it into the ground with just enough force to stun him.

He saw the kick coming from the other guy before it could ever connect with his head. Erec moved in a constant flow, information coming each second; damn near overwhelming, but enough of a clue to take advantage.

Erec yanked his head out of the path of the kick—the heel of the guy's boot skimming past his helmet. With a sudden move, Erec stood back up, timing it precisely to catch the man's knee and throw him on his back. Erec leaped forward, a hand lashing out to snap a quick yet measured blow to the guy's head.

Enough to stun and buy time, yet pulled back enough not to kill or seriously injure.

Yet a part of him demanded he give no quarter to these two. They'd killed and tried to kill, the beast reasoned inside of him. Surely they deserved his anger. Erec shook his head as VAL's mechanical voice filtered in.

[Your instincts adapted quickly to the visual overlay. Very well done, Buckeroo. The Quantum Accelerated Processor appears to have made a seamless integration.]

"What are we going to do with them?" Erec asked, yanking the two men near one another to keep them pinned.

They moved like puppets, not even grunting with pain as he wrestled them to the ground. His advantages of a ton of steel and superior Strength were insurmountable to the two soldiers. There wasn't a chance they were going to cooperate.

But he couldn't kill them.

Even if the White Stag had broken their minds.

It was unclear how it'd done it, but the radio tower and the sacrifice had let it trigger a takeover of humans. A thing they'd thought impossible—until now, it'd only controlled monsters.

But then, hadn't he and Boldwick had those dreams?

Was that its goal? To bridge the gap to humanity? Why hadn't it worked then, and only on some?

More screams and growing fire within the camp as a plume of black smoke trailed into the sky. Inside, more people were dying as the new Silent Ones, the Possessed, took advantage of the chaos. Unlike the Knights, none of the soldiers had steel to prevent their own friends from stealing their lives.

But even among the Knights…

What would these people do if a Knight lost their mind too? What if one of his friends—

Erec shook his head, heart beating quick. What could he do—these two beneath him couldn't be let loose. They'd only keep attacking until they got killed. The beast roared in its cage, offering him a plain solution. These people were now monsters. It would take the guilt of the slaughter, he needn't let his heart dwell on it at all.

Slay them.

If he wanted it to spare his friends, it would.

Might ruled above all.

Let the pain and worry go, and let the rage sort it out. He'd be a hero or a demon, if he'd let go and let it do as it will.

*No.* Erec held firm to his resolve.

His fist slammed into the dirt nearby as he fought against the two men to keep them to the ground and from hurting anyone else. Thankfully Olivia rushed in soon, helping Erec battle the two men. Soon she cut free a strip of cloth from the tent and they managed to tie up the Silent Ones. Wrestling them had been far easier than it should've been—his Armor had adjusted to each of his moves, reacting to the point that his muscle memory had failed to do as he wanted.

It was…odd. But pleasant. In about a hundred different ways, moving felt better with than without—VAL had undersold the tech upgrade.

Was this what it was like to have cutting-edge Armor?

Erec took a deep breath as he stepped away from the hog-tied men. It should hold for long enough. He took in the woman with a bruised throat—still rubbing at it, but breathing easy. "Can you watch them? Do you have a weapon nearby? I—we…" Erec looked to Olivia. "Need to stop the fighting. I won't tell you not to kill anyone if you need to save your life…but someone needs to take control of this situation."

"Aye, I can," the girl answered with a hoarse voice—more confident as Olivia handed her a sword.

Erec nodded and took a second to steady himself. To fight away the flames flickering in his stomach. He stared at Olivia. "If I lose it… save as many as you can from me, alright?" he asked, his voice shaking a little.

It was hard fighting back.

He'd try to save as many as possible; he hoped someone more

intelligent than him might be able to free these people from the White Stag. But he couldn't trust himself to fight away the anger at what he might see.

Olivia gave him a nod, and he broke into a jog.

"VAL…" Erec said quietly. "If I go too far, pump me with sedatives."

[Understood, Buckeroo. Don't worry, champ. You're a real go-getter. You'll do fine!]

Horror. Pure horror. As they ran through the burning camp, oftentimes they saw that they were already too late. Pools of blood. Still bodies. Collapsed soldiers stared at their slain friends with utterly devoid faces. Murder was abundant and swift as the phantom of the White Stag came in a crashing wave of death and destruction.

Those owned by it did everything they could to damage anyone around them.

Tragedy on a scale that these people hadn't seen in years.

But some were still fighting for their lives—Silent Ones still roaming looking for victims. Erec tore through people, freeing those struggling and disabling anyone owned by the White Stag.

Side by side, he and Olivia could fight and utilize their advanced skills and Armor to swing the fight in their favor. Seeing the Knights, the soldiers could rally behind them, forming ranks as they witnessed a ray of light tearing through the burning camp.

Olivia took charge of giving orders—telling some to collect supplies and secure the Silent Ones they managed to disable.

Which was okay with Erec. It took his all to keep his rage from spiraling at the sight of all the death.

He wanted to paint with blood.

The desire burned so brightly that his hands shook, only tempered by the realization that if he gave in, he'd be killing other humans.

His hands worked as his mind struggled, slamming his metal gauntlets into guts, smashing faces into the ground, and trading blows with the weak.

Each time a fist flew, that inferno threatened to catch him on fire. To force him to let go as it screamed how useless this was; by delaying his pain now, he only gave pain to the future.

These people would never recover.

He could spare the soldiers from killing themselves by doing it himself—the weak didn't deserve to live anyway.

Erec smothered the sparks when they caught. He didn't need Fury yet, he was strong enough for this; the new addition to his Armor made it feasible to handle even the more veteran soldiers that came his way.

Seeing how their bodies would move—the paths their weapons would take—feints, slices, stabs. It was enough to give him an edge.

Over the frantic flight through the camp, he only got better at figuring out how to use the split-second information feed. How to adapt and rely on his Armor's micro-adjustments to maximize each movement. So what if his mind warred—his body flowed like water, devoid of thought as it sorted out the chaos spawning around him.

And then he found him.

Garin.

Locked in a fight with Yuvia—she was on top of him, her blows smashing into his helmet as Garin tried to force her to stop, and failed.

Erec saw red.

# CHAPTER 73
## HATE RULES ALL

Garin struggled on the ground, his hands desperately fending off Dame Yuvia while fist after fist slammed past his guard. Each crack of her gauntlet echoed the harsh crash of steel against steel. Nearby soldiers stumbled around, dazed and trying their best to avoid a clash between Knights. Garin shouted for help as more dents littered his Armor. There couldn't be much more plate left until Yuvia started bashing his life out.

Erec let go.

Dust spewed from underneath his feet as he rushed the distance between them, each push from the ground using all of his growing Strength to propel him through the air. A second later he crashed into Dame Yuvia and shoved her off his friend; straightening himself as her body tumbled over dirt.

But the Knight Protector wasn't easily stopped; she twisted as she tumbled, her feet carving grooves in ground as she stood. Unlike the soldiers before, this woman was highly trained. She possessed higher Virtues then any of the regular military men and woman in this centuria.

A bloodied sword lay near where she came to a stop; Yuvia kicked the blade into her hand. Had she killed with it before?

[Careful—]

Erec yanked the battle-axe off his back; the weapon felt unfamiliar, but the grip was all too right. It was a weapon meant for war.

Today, it'd taste blood.

[—Oh, you've lost it, huh?]

Yuvia flashed through the space, her speed on another level from anything she'd shown off before on the road. But compared to Dame Robin, the woman paled.

That didn't make it easy. There was a clear difference between her Agility and Erec's.

Yet, she didn't outspeed the processor. In a split second, Erec saw a blur, a predicted vision of where the point of her weapon was going. It wasn't much, but enough to tell him that Yuvia's charge wasn't aimed at him. She intended to spear Garin with her speed and momentum. Such a strike would pierce right through his defenses and land a lethal blow.

Erec didn't have time to think. Luckily, the fire inside meant he didn't have to.

His body twisted, smashing his steel boot into his recovering friend and sending him rolling away. Almost instantly after, Yuvia's blade skidded across the airborne leg, sparks flying from the awkward contact point as it scored a mark in his Armor.

Without a thought, Erec carried the momentum of his spin, screaming as an arc of blood splashed out from the cut in his leg. Using the force of his twisting body to power the arc of his battle-axe.

[Going too far.]

Yuvia's body jerked like a puppet. Even with all of her Agility, it wasn't a quick enough reaction to stop the edge of his axe from cleaving into her side. Metal crunched, and the woman flew from the hit. Her body crashed across the ground for the second time.

Blood drenched her side as she climbed to her feet. Impossible to say how deep the blow went or what the limits of her Vigor were. But there wasn't an ounce of self-preservation in her.

Good. Let them fight to the death.

With every move, the Silent Ones aimed at causing the maximum amount of suffering to humanity.

They could burn in hell.

Erec laughed as he tested his wounded leg—still fine. Fine enough for this fight. Yuvia began to move, giving him another half-a-second blur as the processor analyzed her intended route. Enough to drive his body to react. He pushed forward as the fire burned inside, his muscles screaming as his axe clanged against her sword and stopped it from going into his neck.

With another slam, her blade danced along the edge of his axe.

She stabbed, again and again, a thousand pinprick needles testing his guard. He tossed each pathetic attack aside. They twisted against one another as the song of the battle rang out in Erec's soul, a chorus of blood as phantoms of her movements danced, and he responded.

There could only be one outcome.

His axe met her hand and dug into the wrist; her pathetic sword dropped to the ground.

Perfect.

Erec tackled her—turning the fight into a wrestling match. This lack of range meant his battle-axe was useless, but it also made her annoying speed irrelevant. Besides, he didn't need the axe. His hands were plenty enough. He'd rend apart this puny slave to the White Stag.

She squirmed beneath him. Too weak to resist his Strength, yet the blasphemous White Stag radiated out from her. The fingers of her good hand dug into his greaves, trying to claw past the steel with raw Strength her body didn't have.

Good.

Erec's knuckles smashed into her helmet again and again, denting deeper. Breaking the metal apart. Just like she'd done to Garin. Let the Stag taste humiliation; let it suffer as much as it'd made—

[Pulling the rip cord! Calm down!]

Erec's body shook as sedatives flooded in. The metallic taste of blood overpowered his mouth; at some point, he'd bitten his lip. With a shaking wrist, he slammed his gauntlet into the twisted metal beneath him again. This fight needed to end—

A cold fire burned inside.

He fought against it, hand shaking as he raised a fist for another blow. One more. That's all. Let the inferno burn away his problems.

A maelstrom of flame warred inside. His anger raged, but he couldn't stand back against the control. Erec's fist dropped, and a moment later, he slumped away from the lump of twisted metal that was Dame Yuvia. His hands shook as horror flowed through him. All of his fears had come to fruition—the nightmares of turning on an ally—despite her being a minion of the White Stag...

What had it all been for?

Why had he tortured himself with that ritual in the glyph when it was meant to prevent this very thing?

Dimly he heard Olivia bark orders to the nearby soldiers to strip the Knight Protector of her Armor and bind her as she took stock of the situation. From the quiver in her voice, she wasn't sure that Yuvia was even alive anymore.

Erec sunk to his knees, feeling Garin's palm on his shoulder as his friend sprawled next to him.

Today hate had ruled.

— - ☢ - — - ☼ - — - ☢ - —

"You put the Knight Protector into a coma?" Boldwick's baffled voice rang out over the static-polluted long-range communicator.

Erec hung his head on the table. The rest of the remaining Knights gathered nearby—the most senior among them a single Knight Errant out of the three. The White Stag had possessed one of the other two. They'd been killed by the other Knight, who'd suffered grievous wounds to get the job done.

And, of course, the Knight Protector was now comatose and under heavy binding to ensure that if she woke up, she wouldn't simply start slaughtering humans again.

It'd been difficult, and although he felt numb, Erec pulled himself together and worked with his friends to pull the camp together and put the fires out.

At least he hadn't ended up killing Dame Yuvia. Though many had had no choice but to kill their fellow soldiers.

Erec numbly pulled up the blinking in the corner of his vision as static came from the communicator. In the last few hours of hell, he'd prioritized helping everyone around him. Most of the leadership in the centuria were slaughtered during the fighting. All the soldiers now looked to underqualified Knights to take charge and drag them to safety.

**Cognition Advancement: Rank E - Tier 3 → Rank E - Tier 4**

### Psyche Advancement: Rank E - Tier 1 → Rank E - Tier 2

That was…good. But his Strength was outgrowing what his Psyche was capable of managing. Fury only grew more intense the stronger he was.

How long until he flew off that cliff?

"I'm impressed." Boldwick's voice cut through the silence. "Dame Yuvia was known for high combat marks. Though I suppose she didn't use her Divine Talent. From the reports, none of those taken by the Stag were capable of more than raw physical attacks. Still, impressive."

"Thanks." Erec shook his head and pulled himself up a little. Hearing Boldwick's voice on the other end did a lot to drag him from his mental rut.

It wasn't a place he could afford to be right now.

With a host of Possessed prisoners eager to slaughter on their hands, he needed to keep himself steady for the people looking up to the Knights.

"The way I see this now, our scouting parties have failed their duties and were attacked by the enemy. Part of our Army felt the effects of that Possession pulse. Though it seems to affect the less seasoned soldiers primarily. I'll make this simple. You have a new objective. Your squad is to lead your centuria back to the main Army. Bring the restrained Possessed with you, and avoid any further conflict," Boldwick's smooth tone carried over. It was calming and intentionally nonplussed.

But it was a lie. Each word held a little strain, even if he disguised it well. Boldwick was afraid and desperate to find a solution. All the while, the White Stag that had showed itself capable of turning humankind against one another was nowhere to be found. Terrifying.

"Understood," Erec said, not wanting to draw attention to the strain he picked up in Boldwick's commands.

"And just how are we supposed to do that?" Knight Jefferson, the sole combat-capable Knight Errant, spoke out. "We're all alone out here—"

"By gritting your teeth and doing the job that needs to be done," Boldwick said. "Scout, patrol, be careful, and keep in contact."

"Bullshit, you didn't tell us the enemy could turn our own against us—I ran my sword through five different people—"

"Aye, I've also heard reports from men who had to put down their childhood friends when they lost control and started slaughtering other soldiers. Do you think you're alone in this, Jefferson? Do your job."

"Fuck you." Jefferson shook his head and left the tent.

Erec exchanged a look with his friends. They'd all been shaken, to be sure, but none of them were quite as far gone as the Knight Errant. Perhaps it'd been because he was the one to find the two others of his rank bleeding out after their fight to the death, or maybe the killing got to him.

Unlike Erec, he hadn't made the call to try to spare the Possessed. Panic and fear had hastened him to what he'd done, and no doubt he'd questioned his choices a hundred times already.

Not that sparing them was necessarily the right call to begin with. Goddess only knew if they could be saved or if it'd spell the death of this centuria.

Whether Possessed or not, the White Stag had left a mark on all it'd touched.

"He's not going to be able to do it." Boldwick's voice cut through the silence again. "You need to pull it together and get everyone to safety."

"I'm not very good at that either; I don't think I can do it," Erec said, looking over to Olivia. She'd led the soldiers during the fighting while he struggled to keep himself together, only to, in the end, lose it.

"Doubting yourself? Listen, no one starts as a great leader. The fact you made the call to spare as many as you could tells me what I want to know. You care about these people, so get them back safely. We'll figure out the next steps from there. But don't think you have to rely on just yourself—you have the rest of the Initiates with you. Work together because Jefferson's likely to find a nice hole and convince everybody to crawl into it until the White Stag comes and tracks you down."

"…Right…" Erec shook his head.

"Best of luck."

The radio crackled and went quiet as his mentor's voice cut off. Leaving him and his three friends in silence.

Outside of their tent was half a centuria. The men were bloodied, scared, and far away from the giant steel walls that had promised them safety for years. Erec's knuckles went white as he clenched his fist.

They'd have to fight their way back to the Army.

# CHAPTER 74
## STYLE OF LEADERSHIP

*Sometimes, we must make harsh calls on an expedition. Not everyone
returns to our home alive, so it is up to a Knight to make the correct calls to
bring survival.*
*Just like the wasteland tests you, so will the people around you.*
*It is up to you to stand firm and never bend to death's whims.*

*- Grandmaster Oak,* On Leadership *(293, 3rd Era)*

D ust and sand haunted the wasteland. Their pervasive
nature infected every single thing that passed through it.
Despite the week of dragging the centuria through the
wasteland, Erec couldn't help but dwell on the annoying feeling of
sand stuck in his Armor. It was just another thing on top of the pile
irritating him.

Jefferson was the first on that list. The senior Knight's constant
complaining and fighting was the reason Erec sulked away from the
camp. Erec's eyes drifted back to the trail of his footprints in the dirt
behind him. A self-appointed scouting expedition, while helpful, was
utterly an excuse to get away.

Everything he and his friends agreed to, Sir Jefferson found fault
in. The annoying prick kept flexing his rank, yet he did worse than
nothing when it came to easing the already worried centuria. He went

around doom speaking and trying to cast the already worried troops deeper into their fears about the White Stag. Claiming they'd all lose their minds to the White Stag eventually.

Jefferson also insisted they cut loose the possessed they struggled to bring with them.

Not that such a suggestion wasn't worth merit, but it was a callous move that Erec didn't want to do unless they ran low on supplies. Besides, Boldwick's direct orders called for them to return home with those poor people.

The sun hung high above and blazed its full might upon the desolate world. It was as always, a witness to their struggles, as it had been since the dawn of humanity. Did it pity them from so far above? Or was hate burning within it, the same angry inferno that Erec found in himself?

Erec's eyes scanned the horizon, his view adjusting to the distance. It was easier to scout now as they left the rocky terrain. Far in the distance was a small pack of Walking Geckos. They were some weird mute breed, but otherwise harmless to human numbers this big.

[…Oh my.]

"What is it?" Erec asked, watching one of the Walking Geckos trip over its malformed tail and struggle on the ground.

[A breakthrough!] VAL chimed in his head, the excitement carrying through in the strange way that emotions colored its tone. [After that assault in your head with the White Stag, I took readings during and after… I was curious why those creatures fused with a radio tower to accomplish their goal.]

"…It was strange, yeah."

[They powered the structure to give off a precise radio wave, then fused the radio wave with anomalous energy.]

"Really? That's…kinda crazy, but I don't understand why that changed things." Surprising, and not what he'd thought a being like the White Stag would be capable of. But if that was the extent of it, why had it been in his and Boldwick's dreams for so long yet unable to do a thing? "…But it could already reach us mentally before that. What's the difference here?"

[Have you heard the term "constructive interference?"]

Erec shook his head. "I didn't exactly get the best teachers growing up, nor the time; no, I haven't run across the term."

[Waves interact in a few ways. How to explain this? Think of ripples on the surface of your cistern tanks down below. They can cancel one another out, but if they touch at the right angle, they can grow into a more substantial ripple. What a surprising intelligence. The White Stag determined that the proper application of anomalous energy operating at a certain "energy level" crossed over with radio waves. And like with waves, found a way to merge their power and achieve a greater result.]

"...That sounds terrifying." Erec shivered, trying to put together how much that threatened his people and how they might fight back against its discovery.

[Indeed. But it does open a door the White Stag likely didn't think you humans would be able to puzzle out.]

"How?" Erec asked.

[Whatever anomalous energy "frequency" it's using to control the people within your numbers has a proven correlation with a known radio wavelength. Taking what I've gleaned in your anomalous energy lessons...]

Suddenly an image dominated Erec's vision. It was an intricate hexagon woven in and out with triangles and a rudimentary channeling focus circle in the middle.

It was something he'd expect to see within his Mysticism textbook. Though a bit cruder, it was already a design of a glyph Erec would've never been able to guess the function of. His jaw dropped.

"What the fuck, VAL? Is this a real glyph?"

[Likely? Without testing, I can't be entirely sure of my conjectures from processing your textbooks. It should be capable of emitting anomalous directional energy in a pulse. However, if we do this...] The triangles around the edge of the hexagon shifted their angles, the lines changing just slightly, while the overall structure of the glyph remained the same though its configuration was undoubtedly altered. [...And we keep twisting this around...then test it against different radio waves, eventually, we'll hone in on a format replicating the anomalous energy the Stag is using.]

Erec stared at the glyph in his vision, turning over a few things. An old-world machine had just utterly outdone him in learning magic, all while denying it to be magic in the first place. Frustratingly, mindlessly paging through books for VAL had done more than he'd ever imagined.

It wasn't the most complex glyph. Even Erec understood that with what little he knew. But the manipulation and underlining grasp of the theory were…beyond him.

"…Shit, VAL—so, we find the glyph corresponding to the radio wave, and then…?"

[Watch.]

A pentagon wrapped around the overall shape, filled with a bunch of connecting geometry, and another ring circled the whole structure.

[If—and this is a big if, as I haven't done testing—if I understand this function correctly, it should be able to detect the type of anomalous energy wave within it and point to its source.]

"VAL…how sure of this are you?"

[Low confidence interval. Your textbook doesn't provide a very scientific method or explanations and is far too sparse on theory for me to fully confirm my conjectures. Ultimately, the first step in this process could lead to an explosion, especially if done incorrectly. Yet, I remain optimistic despite the fact that I cannot back my theory. It seems ideal for an experiment. So get to it, Researcher!]

Erec narrowed his eyes as he weighed what VAL was saying. Nothing here was a guarantee—he'd be better to dismiss it and maybe bring it up to Boldwick when they reached the main Army.

But…

"I can't be the one who tests this," Erec admitted. His control over Mysticism was nonexistent. He'd never formed a glyph, and doing something like this was far too risky for a guy whose sole aim in a fight was to hack stuff apart with his axe. "…We'll go find Colin."

— - ✿ - — - ☼ - — - ✿ - —

"We should flee back into the rock lands—it seems far enough away from the fighting! If we find a cavern, we can hold out until this ends! "Sir Jefferson shouted in the middle of the camp, where a gathering of men and women had formed around. Some of them nodded their heads; others gave off an uncomfortable feeling. Colin and the rest of Erec's friends were far off to the side.

One of the soldiers let out a cheer as Jefferson continued on his rant. Jefferson's helmet was tucked at his side, and his face red as he spewed out the thoughts he'd been driving into Erec and the rest of the Knights for the last few weeks.

Erec settled in next to his friends.

*What a bastard.* Erec shook his head while Jefferson dug into his grievances with the situation. He struggled to tamp down the anger inside.

The energy here wasn't good. There was a fission to the air, a charge of volatility that was coming close to an explosion. It seemed Jefferson had gotten tired of contesting the rest of the Knights and decided to take leadership for himself.

Just as Boldwick predicted, the man wanted to run away and hide.

"This can't keep going on," Erec whispered over to Garin, who nodded.

"You're right. This is dangerous, but he's sure to call us out on rank if anyone goes against him," Garin whispered back.

Colin scoffed. "Rank? He's from some Barony. I'm the son of a Duke—"

"Most of these people are commoners. I'm betting if you walked up there claiming authority on the merit of your family, they'd find an issue with you trying to call shots in this circumstance." Garin said. *Trying to be diplomatic, huh?*

Erec sighed as he watched more soldiers gather around. Every second that Jefferson continued spewing this nonsense, it'd only get worse. They couldn't just concede what Jefferson was aiming to do. Not with Boldwick's orders and not for their long-term safety. Hiding away in a cave while everyone fought would only end badly, especially as their rations began to run out.

And they would run out. These wastelands weren't precisely a bountiful place to forage from for a group this large.

"Erec, you need to stop him," Garin said quietly.

"Why me?" Erec asked, confused. He'd expected his friend to take the stand and do something. Garin was the one who was good with people, and if anyone stood a chance at deescalating the situation, it'd be him. Sending Erec in was like sending in a fire to a fuse…

"They're looking for a strong leader. Someone who can lead them to safety through hell. These people had to kill their friends and, since then, struggle to force-feed those very same brothers and sisters who slew others among them. Jefferson is up there telling them that we have no hope and need to hide—there isn't anyone within our ranks besides *you* that can counter that narrative."

"If I go up there—it won't end well." Erec worked his jaw. Already the sparks were flaring inside of him, even from the sidelines.

Coward. The beast cried out inside of him. There was an almost visceral disgust at the man welling up inside, and getting closer would only heighten the feeling.

"It doesn't need to end well," Garin said. "You have the reputation already. Use it."

The reputation? Had word spread about him to the centuria? About how he fought? Or was it from seeing him take out their previous Knight Protector—a woman far above his rank? Either way, the implication of that was a bit troubling. And... "It didn't need to end well?"

Just what did people see him as?

Erec cleared his throat. Even Colin was looking at him expectantly.

But he didn't have a single plan. No clue what to say or how to deal with the fact that the course of this mission likely rested on his shoulders. Yet both of them were looking to him to solve this problem.

[Would Bedwyr hesitate?] VAL asked, and Erec stopped.

That was a dirty blow.

The anger swelled in him, and caught flame. Just a bit. A small controlled fire in the pit of his stomach. Enough to eliminate the distractions, to burn away the weakness and hesitation.

What did these people's opinion of him matter anyway?

Erec pushed past the crowd of gathered soldiers; they made way easily enough once they saw it was him. Jefferson's voice quivered and broke as he stepped into the ring of people. His head locked on the older man.

"W-what is it you want, Initiate?" Jefferson asked.

"Coward," Erec growled out as the crowd went quiet.

# CHAPTER 75
# INTRODUCTION TO SCIENCE

"H-how dare you!" Jefferson raised an accusatory finger at Erec, then thought better. A moment later, he slammed his Armor's helmet back on, though it did little to disguise the shake in his voice or his wide eyes from before. He was afraid. Afraid of a boy at least two years his junior.

The crowd was silent. They should've protested Erec's arrival and how he strode into the platform; as an Initiate, he certainly had none of the qualifications to lead, especially as a first-year. It wasn't like he had the personal skills either. Scarcely anyone here knew him past his reputation.

But as they looked on, only one thing was in their eyes: excitement.

*Why?*

"Act like a coward, and I'm not going to bite my tongue." A fire burned in his chest as the words came free like the wind. Each second it was a balance to maintain that inner flame and keep it from exploding into an inferno.

Even if it was "okay," by Garin's standards, he refused to let go as long as he could help it.

"Y-you have no idea how we're suffering."

"I received the reports, same as you. I scout more than you. And I'll lead us to safety. Not to some Goddess-forsaken cave to die."

"That's not true! If we take the time to regroup—"

"We don't have the food, resources, or willpower for such a weak strategy. If that's the best idea you have, I suggest you shut the fuck up. Your input is no longer appreciated. Hard times require firm resolve," Erec almost growled, but stopped himself just short.

Around him, the faces of the men and women paled and then hardened. Hard to tell if they were responding to Jefferson's words or his. At the moment, with adrenaline starting to pump through him, it was difficult to see what side they were on.

But it didn't matter. Erec would make them follow.

"I am the Senior Knight, you—you spoiled Initiate. What makes you think you can tell me what to do? Let alone that you have any authority here. Go back to your friends and do what I say! You have no idea what it takes to survive in these wastes!"

"Strength. That's all you need in this world," Erec said, the fire inside swirling in a column of annoyance. This conversation was too circular, and the words ground down the same worn path this spineless coward had trod for the last hour. Sickening. How could someone call themselves a Knight yet be so pathetic? Fury burned its will into him to teach this useless worm a lesson, and that desire was hard to disagree with.

"I'm strong, far stronger than some Initiate!"

Erec broke into a laugh before gesturing for Jefferson to come at him.

"Show me."

Whispers ran through the crowd like electricity through a wire. Sir Jefferson visibly took a step back at the challenge. Duels were a longstanding tradition in the Kingdom; though they didn't occur outside of the walls, if Erec had to guess, doing so was probably illegal.

But what did that matter? A law was only as good as the will to enforce it and the power behind the enforcer.

"I—we can't!"

Erec opened his arms wide, indicating the ring of people and their hastily made encampment. The inferno grew, demanding that he consume this pathetic excuse for a Knight. If he didn't act with honor or true grit, then could Jefferson even really be considered a human? No, he was a waste of space. Better to take care of this now, once and for all.

"What's stopping us?" Erec asked.

"We're—there are monsters all around!"

"Do you see a monster? I don't. If I did, it'd be dead," Erec said with a surety that ran deep to his core. It'd be a non-threat, or Erec would die in combat.

And have a glorious bout before he did.

"You're—you're an Initiate!"

"What, afraid? How will you lead these people to safety when you're too scared to fight an Initiate?" Erec continued in, sensing blood in the water. The crowd's emotions fed him, only stoking the anger inside, fueling his inner fire.

They mirrored him; the taste for blood surged as those around called for the fight as much as he did. Sir Jefferson reeked of hopeless-ness, and everyone picked up on it, ashamed to have ever felt swayed by his words.

This wasn't a world for the weak, and those like Jefferson didn't have what it took to lead them anywhere; they saw it now.

It took power. A hand that had the Strength to enforce its will on the world and take what it wanted.

Jefferson wasn't a man like that.

"I—" Jefferson turned tail and ran from the circle; a chorus of jeering and insults followed in his wake as he fled. Erec stared at his back, the beast inside shouting for him to pursue his prey and tear them in half. A cold shock ran through him as icy fire burst inside, burning out the anger and killing it.

Erec looked at the gathered crowd, using the last bit of dimin-ishing fire to let out a few words.

"Follow me or die."

He walked away, calm.

— - ☢ - — - ☼ - — - ☢ - —

Erec sat in his tent, fingers steepled against his forehead as he let out a big sigh.

"You honestly had the gall to say, 'If I saw one, it'd be dead.'" Colin shook his head and turned up his nose. "Mighty arrogant of you, rust-bucket. Borderline impudent and delusional. Far too excessive."

"It was a little dramatic, but the point of that was to put on a show to usurp Jefferson. Honestly, I'm surprised Erec didn't just start smashing his fists into the man, but this works better for us in the long run. Gives us more legitimacy," Garin said.

"I hesitate to say this, but I agree with Colin." Olivia pouted and then broke into a snicker. "The lines were a bit much, truly terrifying, Sir Erec. If you go on that way, when people write about you, they'll scarcely believe your speeches aren't some delusional manufacture."

"Hey, I didn't—" Erec wanted to say he hadn't exactly chosen what came out of his mouth, overtly dramatic or not. But, the fact was, he suspected that if he fed any more into the mocking, it would only lead to more. "It's over, alright? I didn't want to be the one who went up to deal with that anyway. Besides, I didn't harm Sir Jefferson, so it worked out alright, right?"

"You are correct. He's hiding away outside of camp, I suspect in a day, or so, he'll make his return and keep his head low," Olivia clarified. "…Speaking of which, we should reassure the soldiers about any issues they have, now that we no longer have one of us contesting our goals so verbally." She gave Garin a long look, who shrugged. "Leave it to us."

The two left the tent. Colin moved to follow them out and let Erec sulk after his public speaking opportunity.

"Wait," Erec said, pushing past the embarrassment to look at his friend. "I, uh, I need a favor."

"Ah?" Colin asked, a glint coming to his eye as he puffed up his chest. "So it is that the small landless second son has finally come to his better with a request. Do share, and perhaps I shall find pity and grant it to you."

"This is serious."

Colin remained quiet.

"How do I—" Erec put his helmet back on—the glyph VAL had composed flashed onto his visual display. It seemed they had an understanding. "Er—I need you to take a look at something."

He got to his feet and began tracing the glyph lines into the dirt in front of the Duke's son into the ground of the tent. Colin followed him along as Erec worked.

"I wasn't aware you could even make a glyph. I have yet to see you even use magic," Colin said as the shapes began to take form.

"I…" Erec thought over an explanation but found that nothing came to mind that could explain it away. "I don't. That's why I need your advice on this."

"How is it you have this memorized then?"

"I—err, came across something. I wanted you to try it out; I have a hunch it might be useful for tracking down the White Stag."

"Is that so? Why does this emit mana in a certain pattern and composition, then?" Colin seemed more and more bemused. Which, Erec supposed, was a positive sign. "It is not any sort of detection glyph. Besides, do you think that others in the Army haven't tried?"

"…It, uh. Well, maybe they have. But it's more about how it works with radio waves…than…" Erec tried to explain.

Colin got quiet again and began to shake his head. Yeah. Selling this wasn't easy. *How do I get through to him?*

Erec traced out the rest of the glyph. And then the answer came.

"They don't have anyone quite like you—they might have others who are good at Mysticism, but you've got so much natural talent. A genius. Of course, if anyone can cast this and figure out how to find the White Stag, it'd be you." The words almost hurt to say, but appealing to the boy's ego was the only way forward.

"Ah." Colin stopped moving, his helmet only twitching slightly as he stared at the glyph. "At last. You realize my true worth. Prudent of you, rust-bucket—though this glyph is faulty. Several flaws would result in a rather violent explosion, as expected from such an utter novice when making his first glyph. Or perhaps it's your nature to cause destruction. Whatever the case, I see that you've chosen to invest your hope in me, a wise decision I shall reward."

Erec stared at the glyph, wondering just how or where VAL messed up the design and made it explosive, and far too relieved he'd taken it to someone else to figure out instead of just trying it. "… Right, thanks, Colin," Erec said, trying to clip his words and not say anything to ruin the mood.

With his self-obsession, it seemed the Duke's son wasn't interested in digging into how or why Erec knew this glyph design. Let alone the idea of tracking the White Stag with it.

He slipped into silence as Colin went over his pedigree and pointed out every single flaw in the glyph. Colin took great delight in finding the mistakes, and VAL appeared pleased with each new flaw. VAL even asked Erec to press in and clarify some of its questions.

Every time, Colin gave a condescending explanation that worsened Erec's headache. But after two hours, and with significant revision from Colin, they had a workable and adjustable glyph.

One that Colin agreed to test with Erec for the next couple of days.

Especially since he saw the glory on the off chance they would manage to create something that could help find the Stag.

Little did he know that he'd just signed himself up as another victim of the rigorous and thorough scientific process.

# CHAPTER 76
## MIGHT IS RIGHT

*"Great guns, my liege, where did you get that?"*

*"From a smuggler at the inn, yester eve."*

*"What in the world possessed you to buy it?"*

*"We have escaped divers dangers by wit—thy wit—but I have bethought me that it were but prudence if I bore a weapon, too. Thine might fail thee in some pinch."*

*"But people of our condition are not allowed to carry arms. What would a lord say—yes, or any other person of whatever condition—if he caught an upstart peasant with a dagger on his person?"*

*It was a lucky thing for us that nobody came along just then. I persuaded him to throw the dirk away; and it was as easy as persuading a child to give up some bright fresh new way of killing itself.*

*- Mark Twain,* A Connecticut Yankee in King Arthur's Court *(1889, 2nd Era)*

Trekking through the wasteland was only made harder with the knowledge that everyone's eyes were on Erec's back. They expected him to deliver on his promise to return them to the Army. So he complied the best he could. That meant pushing himself beyond what he was capable of. Every moment not spent trying to find a way to track the White Stag, Erec spent out in the wasteland searching for monsters.

Each occasion he found one was pure catharsis. He took on the challenge without consulting his allies—honing his edge against the myriad of weak but surviving creatures that roamed. It would be rare to find any that presented a threat to him.

And if he did, then he'd be the first to test it for the people relying on him. No one here was as strong as him.

After every battle, he returned to camp hauling the corpse. His tension eased temporarily.

Until he got back to testing with Colin, the more Erec pushed the Duke's son to conduct experiments, the more opposition he got. As much as Colin wanted to be such a pivotal figure in finding the Stag, the more effort went into the task, the harder it became.

Only through VAL's dogged confidence that they'd find a solution through science's meticulous and deliberate testing did Erec find the will to press forward. Eventually they'd get their result if they persisted and followed through.

Erec shook his head as he took long, dragging steps through the camp. All of the eyes on him weighed heavy, no doubt taking in the fact that this time he hadn't returned drenched in blood. They whispered about him, about his past, his brother, his mother—and whatever conclusions they began to draw, Erec had no way of knowing. It was hard not to care, but ultimately what they thought of him didn't matter, only that they listened.

Or so he hoped.

Erec entered his "workshop" tent and let out a sigh of relief. It was a barren place, set aside for their testing. To one side of his little sanctuary was an assortment of all the spare communication devices they could muster. Each piece of tech had a different range of radio wavelengths. Erec constantly adjusted them as they looked for an "amplification" while testing each glyph configuration. Over the last couple of days, they'd found two corresponding sets. Data points, according to VAL.

Get enough data on the correlation between the glyph geometry and radio wavelength and, as VAL stated, it could likely create a model. From there, it could generate an approximate shape for a glyph that would be able to track the White Stag's signature.

All of the mathematics was beyond Erec, and so were all the spewings of science VAL gave on its methodology and thesis regarding this. It was a low, dull buzz every time VAL tried to discuss it in depth.

Erec sunk to the ground in the corner of his tent. His Armor felt heavy, and for a moment, he let himself go, staring numbly at the knobs and dials on the opposite side of his work area. He took off his helmet and rubbed his eyes.

[You really should get more rest. Self-care is vital to functioning correctly in times of stress. Perhaps you should consider a nap before Colin arrives?]

"I'm fine," Erec lied, feeling a heavy weight on his shoulders.

The past couple of days kept bringing Gwen's story to his mind. She'd made it sound like Atlas was all alone while he held up the world, a god with no one around to share his burden. But Erec had his friend—truthfully, it made it harder rather than easier. That responsibility and trust only made it heavier as he tried to keep up his public image and lend backing to their organization. Garin and Olivia were the ones busy dealing with the daily issues. They were the ones capable of inspiring the soldiers.

So, with all their efforts, what he had to do was simple. Look strong. Be strong.

Why was that so hard?

They said he'd done well so far, that the distance between him and everyone else was essential to keeping their feeling of security about him. Better for them not to taste his doubt and fear.

At least he could hide it behind his steel. He didn't know how long he sat staring blankly. An eternity, maybe.

"I don't understand them." Erec shook his head slowly. "I came in, embarrassed Jefferson, and somehow, I'm their savior. I don't even give commands that haven't been run through everyone else…"

[Delegation is essential to leadership, and every person has different forms of leadership. Though it does feel odd to have this conversation with a Junior Researcher. We should begin considering you for the managerial track.]

"Please, no." Erec shook his head. "I don't think this is for me, unless I need to. The stress of it is too much."

[Spoken like a true-blooded researcher. Far more interested in your work!]

"Just a few days more," Erec said, inhaling deeply. They were getting near the main encampment. From there, he could relieve himself of command and hopefully have something tangible to report to Boldwick. If they were quick enough, they might prevent this from spiraling further out of control.

Colin strode into the tent, his Armor clanking as he swished his cloak intentionally behind him for a grand entrance. The haughty noble had taken to such flashy gestures. "Shall we get started?" Colin asked.

"Please." Erec pulled himself to his feet, more than a little surprised that Colin was in a rare good mood.

— - ☢ - — - ☼ - — - ☢ - —

Hours flew by in their workstation of a tent as Colin performed the same glyph again and again, generating a harsh white light that leaked various colors in the fully formed pattern. Around them, different radio transmitters operated as Erec switched between channels.

VAL recorded data in his head as Colin got progressively more annoyed.

They'd found another amplifying wave, and VAL seemed awfully excited about it. But it hadn't led to the breakthrough that Erec had hoped for.

A familiar head poked into their tent as the last glyph broke up. Garin took a brief look around as he walked in. "Ah, I see you two are both hard at work again. Any closer to figuring out the weird insight Erec had?"

"No. Frankly, I'm beginning to suspect that he's chosen to torture me out in the field to relieve his stress. A very vain and underhanded tactic," Colin said.

"Hey," Erec cut in, "I meant what I said; this can be a way to find out where the White Stag is—if it works like I think it does. It'll—well, save lives."

"And then what? Are you going to charge it with your battle-axe in hand? Do you believe that Boldwick will give you leave to follow a trail of magic when you've no aptitude for Mysticism to begin with?" Colin responded, his tone tainted by the deep annoyance which typically set in this late during these tests.

The longer Erec spent with Colin on any given day, the more unpleasant the noble boy got. Either their personalities were incompatible, or he'd begun to realize he could only stand him in short-measured doses.

Unfortunate for a friend.

"You'll be taking the credit for it, anyway," Erec said.

"You—why, of course, I am the one who constructed the *working* version of such a glyph. I hadn't thought of such a thing before now, but it is wise of you to concede to my expertise. How long was it you said again before this will pay off? A couple of days? We may perhaps work on this for the rest of the night if it would accelerate my glory," Colin said.

Erec didn't bother to respond as Garin let off a snicker. All it took to reinvigorate the selfish noble was the right motive.

Shame it had taken so long to put that together.

"Anyway," Garin cut off Colin from talking about how this success would mark him above any others in the Academy. "Things are going well. People are driving themselves harder after seeing you work, Erec. Jefferson continues to laze about camp, but no one takes his complaints seriously. It's not like before."

"That's good, I suppose. And the possessed?" Erec asked. With how busy he'd been between the testing and scouting, he relied on his friends to closely monitor all the problem areas. Better not to lose the people's confidence in him by interacting too closely because the honest-to-Goddess truth was that he felt beyond nervous about this whole thing. They couldn't afford for his fear to spill into the camp.

"Difficult to make eat. They grow skinnier each day, but we're on track to return to the main Army in two days. Then it won't be our problem; either way, it goes…" Garin trailed off.

Yeah, if the worst were to happen, they wouldn't be the ones who would have to make that call. They lapsed into a morbid silence at the insinuation; even Colin knew better than to say anything.

"Anything I can do to help?" Garin asked, looking around at the tent.

"Yeah—help me operate these radios while Colin does his thing. The more channels we can swap between while he uses the glyph, the quicker we can get our results from testing."

"Sure." Garin moved over.

Out of anyone, his friend was the most reliable person Erec had ever met. And as the three of them burned away the night working on the experiment, they worked with an optimistic and full energy. A youthful hope that they might be the ones to turn things around before the expedition devolved.

As the moon began to sink out of the sky, they had their break-through—another data point. Five minutes later, they had a working model.

An hour after that and a couple of tweaks, they'd honed in on the same mana signature of the White Stag—or, at least, the mana it used to interact with the radio waves.

Which led to the second glyph design. Colin began to point out the flaws in the second glyph—the one that would let them track the source of the mana.

In one night, their solution seemed very real, very quickly.

# CHAPTER 77
## WARPATH

Erec stared at the monsters in the distance; the sun burned their flesh, leaving their seared skin with boils. So unnaturally pale it almost seemed translucent. They were vaguely humanoid but with four massive arms and trunk-like legs.

As Silent Ones usually did when not trying to kill, they stood utterly still without even twitching in a lot of asphalt, hidden among rusty cars.

Was it by happenstance they were in this town? A place directly between them and their path toward the main Army. Even going so far as to be woven inside the ruins of an old-world parking lot, with a field of rusted-out cars facing a giant billboard. Just on the edge of the abandoned town.

Erec hid in the small building, taking in the army of Silent Ones that'd caught the corner of his eye. Rather devious, so much that a scout had a chance of mistaking them. But his eyes had gotten better at this sort of thing over the past few weeks. Otherwise, it'd have been easy to miss them hidden in the sea of old-world junk.

This was the first real threat out of everything he'd faced in the wasteland since taking charge. Sure, the monsters before might've killed him if he couldn't power through them, but this. This here was a real danger. If he ran against the army of Silent Ones and died, he wouldn't be the only one to face the consequences. His people would be alone, demoralized, and sitting prey for the White Stag.

They barred the way back to safety.

*We could take the long way.* Erec considered how long it might take, a couple of days to go around at enough distance to avoid.

It might be a small price to pay, but his people were getting antsy, a level of nervousness that had only ramped up as the Possessed among them started acting oddly. Over the last two days, they'd stopped putting up a fight. Now they were damn near catatonic. It might've been easier to move them, but the cost to morale with the new behavior wasn't worth the price.

His instincts screamed at him. Something was in the air, and if he tried to take down an enemy, it made the most sense to attack before they could regroup.

There was still some connection between the Stag and his people. How much information did it get from them?

Options. So many options. And as the one making most of the calls, whatever he and his friends chose would hang on their heads. They might avoid this town, but what if this led to an attack on open ground by these creatures? An attack like that might be brutal to counter with their diminished fighting power, and on neutral territory, it didn't offer any tactical advantage to resist an assault.

His orders were to return the group safely to the main Army and avoid engaging the enemy.

But they might use this landscape, the broken-down town, to their advantage. Streets and buildings could become choke points, funnel enemies, and limit their attack angles. If they split their group, and kept the captured Possessed far away... Yeah, that'd deny potential enemies if the worst should occur. That is, if they chose to fight here and now.

It came down to a simple question. Should he obey the word of his orders and leave enemies at their back? Enemies he didn't know the limits of?

Already, the White Stag kept taking advantage of his superiors underestimating it. To him, the damn thing didn't do anything without some intention. With that in mind, the most likely answer was that the Silent Ones in this town served a purpose.

Either to ambush or delay Erec from returning to the main Army.

Waiting wasn't an option; the tension was too high already.

*Is my instinct to fight because of the beast?* Erec let the question sit. How much of his thought was colored by the simple desire to kill these things? He craved to cleave his axe into their flesh and wanted to know what color their blood was. There was a streak of that in him now, always.

Damn near alarming.

But he couldn't let that instinct influence a decision that had such a significant impact on others.

Was it right to trust himself on such a vital call?

The sun sunk below the horizon before Erec pulled away from his secure scouting position. His mind still turned over the possibilities, but one thing was clear: they had to be decisive.

— - ☣ - — - ☼ - — - ☣ - —

"What do you think is best?" Boldwick's smooth voice carried over the radio. The static far less than before, and the closer he got, the clearer his voice became.

Garin and the rest of his friends lounged nearby. Jefferson was the only Knight not invited to their discussions; it was better not to have him involved if they could help it.

"It would be a massive mistake to ignore them. The White Stag keeps catching us by surprise because we wait for it to make its move; if we move first, then it takes that away from it. We know it wants to kill us, so for everything it does, we should be sure it had that goal in mind." Erec marveled over the conviction of his own words. All of the hesitation and worry in his heart on the trip back seemed to bleed away to resolve.

Hearing Boldwick's voice made things clear. It steeled the part of him wavering inside.

"If you rule on Strength, you need to show it to those following you, or it all falls apart," Garin commented; for such a discussion, his friend was relatively unfazed. "But do you think we can take these things on?"

"I can't say for sure. It'll be a difficult battle, and I don't expect everything to go our way. I believe it's possible to use the terrain and make them fight us in a beneficial way; if we start the fight, they can't simply sit there," Erec said.

"Impressive, already considering the environment for fighting. Here's a thing to consider, however, Erec. In the middle of the battle, people will need a voice to listen to. You can't fight at full capacity and give orders, yet they'll need someone to give commands. So, who there will you make your Lieutenant?" Boldwick's voice crashed into Erec from the radio.

Yeah. They'd be screwed if they relied on Erec to call the shots in the middle of the fight. He could charge them into one, but from there, it was a lost cause.

He was a loose weapon; an axe meant to tear apart their enemies without a single second of hesitation, a being that fed off the chaos of a fight and thrived. An anomaly to warfare. Others needed direction, encouragement, and a leader able to make the calls of where they should move or how to adapt. War meant that any plans set in stone were prone to crumble to dust.

Erec looked between his friends. All of them had their strengths and weaknesses, but the person he wanted at his side in a fight wasn't even a question.

"Garin, can you do it?" Erec called, and his friend tilted his head. "There isn't anyone else I trust as much as you. You might not have my Strength, Colin's skill with Mysticism, or prayer…"

"Wow, really hyping me up." Garin shook his head with a laugh.

"But you're the best. Can you fill in the spot while I fight? If you can't, we'll have to figure out—"

"Of course, I can. Trust in me." Garin gave him a thumbs-up.

Erec let out a deep breath of relief.

Colin would've royally fucked the command structure, leading to unnecessary tension within the rank. He couldn't rely on Olivia. Not that he thought the girl would do anything against him here on the field, but he needed to know more about her and the House she represented before putting any genuine trust in her. Nobody here had his trust as much as Garin.

A plan for that had formed in his head, but it wasn't anything he could look into while they were in the wasteland.

"Sounds like you have the basics of it sorted out." There was a long pause on the other side of the line from Boldwick. "…It's always an odd feeling when your students put themselves out there, but pride is always attached to that. I approve of this engagement, Erec Audentia. Prove what you're made of to the rest of the Verdant Oak and me. Take the battle to them, then return to our army."

The communication cut off after that. Proud. Boldwick was proud of him?

"So, what're we going to do with the impudent Knight Errant?" Colin called from the side, shattering the surprising warmth.

"We set him with the Possessed along with a handful of the more loyal soldiers," Erec said. They couldn't rely on Jefferson in the middle of a fight, yet if he was held in reserve with the Possessed, it would make use of his status and his Armor were the worst to occur.

There wasn't any way to be completely certain it was the correct call, but it made the most sense to him. Now…it just came to phrasing and communicating this plan to the rest of the soldiers, scoping out the battlefield, and then picking the right time to strike.

Then came the simple part. Fighting.

Out of everything, that left him feeling the least nervous.

# CHAPTER 78
## WORTHY

*THE FUTURE IS TODAY. WIELD LIGHT-BASED WEAPONRY FOR EXTENDED RANGE AND RECHARGEABLE AMMUNITION. CONVENTIONAL BULLETS OFTEN LEAD TO SWIFT DEATH OF THE TARGET, BUT A SINGLE SHOT THROUGH A LIMB WITH A LIGHT-WORTH DEFENSE C-232 LAZ-RIFLE HAS A MUCH HIGHER CHANCE TO SIMPLY MAIM AND WOUND DUE TO INHERENT CAUTERIZATION ON HIT.*

*A CRIPPLED AND INJURED ENEMY IS WORTH TWICE A DEAD ONE IN A WAR ZONE, OR IT GIVES YOU THE CHANCE TO MAKE THE BASTARD WHO TRESPASSED ON YOUR PROPERTY REGRET HIS DECISIONS.*

*\*Light-Worth makes no definitive claims on the lethality of the C-232 LAZ-RIFLE line nor any derivative or precursor models.*

*- Unknown, Light-Worth advertisement poster* (2074, 2nd Era)

A handful of troops hunkered down behind Erec on a rooftop. Not far away, the main force of their soldiers maneuvered into position. Erec tried to ignore the unease behind him; his handful of troops clutched their weapons so hard their knuckles went white.

Among the number of troops they had at their disposal, Erec

settled on twenty-five for this operation. That left enough to secure their position, and the Possessed still in their company gave him enough people to feel confident against these unknown monsters.

After all the pains they'd taken, they were as prepared as could be.

Yet everyone was nervous except Erec. The closer he got to the fight, the more things settled in place. Even knowing it wasn't entirely possible to predict and plan, this battle would come together for him when he had his axe in hand.

Let others stress about strategic points and designated fallback zones.

He and his friends were green, and most of human history hadn't centered around fighting monsters, but it didn't matter.

All it required to win was Strength.

Erec perched near the edge of the two-story building. Below him, Colin began to walk down the street, right to the primary host of monsters hidden among the rusted cars. Once he was within their sight, they shifted for the first time to face him. Though they didn't move from their spots quite yet.

*This is it.*

The air ignited in front of Colin as he formed a burning red glyph. Its intricate lopsided circular design appeared, then morphed into a ball-sized orb of flame which sped down the street.

His attack crashed into one of the monsters. A plume of smoke drifted upward as it seared flesh and shoved the monster onto the rusted car behind it. Two of its four hands lazily stemmed its burning face. Not a single cry of pain accompanied the damage it took, but Colin didn't wait for it to recover; he formed another glyph and sent off another ball of fire.

He nailed a second target.

But the enemy was formidable. The large pale creatures were sturdily built and took two more attacks with minimal reaction. Erec's gut wrenched.

It couldn't be this simple. Why were they waiting to attack?

More fire flared down the street, and the Silent Ones broke stasis. As one, they lurched forward, going from frozen statues to yanking their massive bodies over the cars and rubble in their way. They staggered like rabid animals for Colin with alarming speed.

Colin booked it down the road, dashing past Erec and his team.

The monsters flooded by only seconds later, giving chase with all they had.

As predicted, they slipped right by Erec and his people without noticing. The team didn't have to worry about Colin—toward the end of the street were two alleyways stuffed with Olivia and the majority of the troops. Though the creatures were fast, Colin made it there ahead of them with time to spare. The Duke's son wasted no time, spinning in place as a more complicated glyph formed before him.

Before the monsters reached their target, soldiers spilled out of the nearby alleys. Armed with spears, they quickly formed into position, crouched down, and braced their weapons against the ground.

Unthinking, the charging monsters skewered themselves on the defensive line, limbs twitching as the weapons dug deep. A few died on the spot or limited the rest of the first wave of monsters. But it wasn't all of them. The horrible things that could still move didn't flinch from the pain. They dragged themselves forward down the shafts of the weapons, their massive hands grabbing out at the soldiers to tear them apart.

Colin's glyph burst to life—forming into a whiplike tendril of fire. With precision, the flame whip slashed into the first wave's surviving monsters. It tore into their hands, buying the desperate soldiers a second to drop their spears and switch to their swords.

Olivia bought them more time to prepare as more monsters crashed in, her Armor taking on a glow as she tore into a monster with her sword.

"Alright, alright." Erec grinned as he took in the field of cars their enemy came from. Empty. All of them were now in the street below— a good fifteen to twenty.

Perfect.

His heart hammered, and the noise of it flooded his ears. Finally, a fight unlike any of those he had for weeks; the thrill was intoxicating.

One last thing.

"Tear them apart," Erec ordered as he held a fist into the sky for Garin to see on the other side of the street. His men shifted off the roof to attack from the street below. They'd hit the enemy's flank with Garin's team. "Go."

Forcing the monsters to fight on two sides would provide a massive advantage.

And that was it. No more commanding, no more worrying, nothing. All he needed to do was shed blood. Like a flint catching against steel, the spark lit up in his chest and kindled in an instant. Fast. Scarily so. Hell came to him on command now, and the grin on his face only stretched wider as time seemed to slow. Below he could see the ghostlike outlines of the monster's projected movements as the Q.A.P. stirred and transmitted flashes of information.

*Freedom.*

Erec drew his axe and pulled back from the edge of the roof, giving himself room. Then with a kickoff that broke a shingle, he sprinted to the edge.

His foot hit the last inch of the building, and he slammed down with all the force he could muster, launching his body like a spring and throwing himself from the building directly at the crowd of monsters in the street below.

Erec tore his axe through the first pale enemy; two arms lopped free and hit the ground with a wet thump even as he cracked the concrete of his landing zone. The wounded thing backpedaled at the sudden attack, its body off-center with the sudden loss of a good part of its body weight.

The puppet was too slow.

Erec took off its head, a fountain of opaque cloudy white blood spewing from its neck.

Not a second to spare. A monster came at him from his left—its momentum shifting as it threw itself right toward the lone target in their ranks.

*Good.* They came to him.

Like moths to a flame, let them come and burn themselves up in his inferno.

His axe slammed into the creature's side with a satisfying thunk, making it slouch as it severed abdominal muscles. A hand clawed at him, but he threw it aside, smashing the back of his gauntlet against the thing's jaw, shattering it.

But more came for him.

One. Two. Blood coated their little battlefield, making the ground below slick.

One dead. Two dead. Five on him. Their blows combined stressed the limit of his ability to react. Erec began to trade their hits for deadly blows of his own.

Was this love? Nothing felt quite as sweet.

His helmet flew off as three hands yanked it with all their might. It took him a second to take off one of their arms; dents, bruises, the split skin above his eye. All of it was inconsequential, and the pain only fueled more carnage.

Because of it, his axe never had to stop moving. Each swing cut flesh and freed their beautiful blood.

Time drifted away in a fugue of battle, and before he wanted it to end, he found the edge of his battle-axe buried in the last of the unintelligent monsters to challenge him. Its disgusting body shuddered and went limp. Erec shoved it away with a quick kick to its shoulder —freeing his axe.

There wasn't much left. Further down the street, his allies had joined together and taken on the rest of the monsters. All but two of them were slain, and they'd take care of those two quickly enough, from how it was looking.

Maybe if he ran fast enough, he could kill another—

The ground shook and he stumbled, unaware that he'd already broken out in a run for the remaining monsters. Hell burned inside and screamed at him to recover and keep going. But a buzzing note of clarity let him pull to a brief stop.

[Tremors below. Something's breaking through the surface!]

Erec spun around at the sound of twisting metal. The asphalt in the middle of the car lot bulged, before bursting like a popped boil as a worm-like monster broke through to the surface. Vicious teeth lined a wide maw large enough to swallow a man whole—the creature slammed into the ground, crushing a car under its weight.

"Retreat!" Garin called out from somewhere near the rest of the weaklings.

Why would he retreat?

Erec only felt burning in him, hate and joy, an almost euphoric sensation that made his skin numb. For so long, he'd only fought against scrawny-half-alive monsters wandering the wasteland. Those four-armed monsters were an exception, but they'd died too quickly.

But this monster was on a whole different level. He felt it by just looking at it. Like those giants.

There was a raw strength to how it moved, with how effortlessly it pushed earth aside and broke apart metal like it was nothing. What man would run from such a glorious chance? Erec started sprinting to it, calling more fire into his veins.

Rolling himself into a wildfire as he burned his way down the street. Each push against the ground was a miniature launch as he forced his Strength through his legs. He tore across the landscape. The faster he reached the monster, the sooner he could sink his axe into it.

It didn't take long to reach the wall of flesh.

His axe swung into it, but it was like a paper cut to something so big. But enough to draw its attention. The creature shifted and whipped its body at him.

Erec flew through the air, unable to breathe. His back smashed through a wall as the blow sent him crashing across the ground inside.

Blood leaked from the corner of his mouth. His limbs shook.

This was everything he wanted.

It was like the giant again, something powerful enough to send him flying and knock everything out of him. So fucking strong. But he could be stronger; that thing was a puppet. How could it compare to him?

Erec began to push himself up.

[Whoa, Buckeroo. That's enough, don't you think? Try to focus on standing, and we'll get out of here. This thing's out of your league.]

*No.*

His body shook, and pain kept radiating from each movement. But the pain burned easily enough; it was deceptive, a mere ghost to convince him to lay down. Only the weak kept still. Power meant action, and stopping was death.

The monster struggled, headed for the middle of the town and the fleeing soldiers, but as it crashed through the buildings with its erratic, awkward movements, it was clear it couldn't catch up.

Erec gave way to fire and found his feet under him. He began slowly toward the enemy, his right leg shaking with every step. Something was broken or sprained, but it was inconsequential as long as he forced it to move. Erec picked up the pace, turning his struggling walk into a jog, then a full-force run. At some point, a scream left his lips.

A war cry.

The creature turned at his challenge, a puppet yanked by strings and unable to dismiss him. It started the process of trying to turn its massive body his way.

Too slow.

Erec ripped his axe through its side, once more scoring an extended cut on the flank of the worm.

Such a tactic didn't do much damage to such a massive creature. No. But it was the opening move. Erec switched to gripping the battle-axe with a single hand and shoved his gauntlet into the newly made gash in the creature's side. And began to pull, tearing apart the leathery skin and making the wound wider, wedging his body into the damage as the beast struggled around him.

Its flesh stretched and grew as he forced his way into the creature, past its outer defenses. It writhed and struggled to stop him, but it was too slow. It lacked hands to pull him away as he burrowed in like a parasite. The air became hard to come by and darkness took hold as he dug further into the monster. It was wet and burning, and his skin stung from its acidic blood.

But once he was far enough in, he found more room. Enough to grab his battle-axe with both hands. Enough to begin to slash, cut, and rend as the last of his air left his lungs.

Erec lost himself in hell, showered in blood, and with a grin.

# CHAPTER 79
## MANAGERIAL TRACK

Darkness gave way to a bright blue sky as Erec slowly opened his eyes. His skin burned, and his lungs ached, and annoyingly, there was a notification in the corner of his vision. But…he heard singing. Soldiers. Not good enough to call it beautiful, but given his last sight before blacking out, it was plenty close.

[Well, what an intriguing method of dissection. However, upon consideration, it's pretty inefficient and not nearly as comprehensive as I'd prefer. Typically, we examine the subject from the outside rather than diving in.]

Erec shuddered and forced himself upright, wincing from the lingering pain. It'd become a welcome companion after every use of Fury now. Still, there was a cloth wrapped around his head, and his hair felt…gross, caked from the worm-monster's insides.

"Erec?" Olivia asked, shifting and moving to his side. She had dark rings around her eyes, and the skin on her face was sunken. All it took was a glance to know she'd pushed herself past her capabilities to heal him and whoever else was wounded in the fighting.

"Hey, Olivia," Erec croaked out. His throat was surprisingly sore, and another smear of pain on his body.

"Do you know how terrifying you look when you use your Talent?" One of her hands turned his chin to look at him better. "Maybe I didn't notice it before, but your eyes go red, almost like a monster."

That was new. "Wonderful." Erec shook his head free from her. He almost regretted it as the world spun, but he'd rather she not touch him. At this point, he'd recover and didn't need any more help, especially with VAL on his side and healing from within. "Doesn't matter, right? We won, didn't we?"

"You didn't need to attack that monster. There wasn't any way it could've pursued us across the open ground on our way toward the Army."

"Yeah? I'm not so sure about that. Maybe it would've laid an ambush. But, I'll admit, that wasn't what was going through my mind. Not like I thought from a rational place. Still, I don't regret it." Erec felt his anger sparking and flaring, and it was rather unduly directed at Olivia. The fire smoldered and lingered from before, or maybe his control over it was growing thinner. "I won."

One day, would he burn away that control for good?

"...I think we sometimes ignore the price we pay to win when we shouldn't." Olivia bowed her head before returning a measured expression to him. "Regardless, you are healthy enough to move if you can manage. They're waiting for their fearless leader. I'll tend to the rest of the soldiers so we can get moving tomorrow morning. Enjoy your victory, Erec."

She moved away, which was for the best. With his patience so thin, and the wall so easy to break, he'd rather not be around her. Not until he got more of himself back under control. She wasn't his favorite person in the world, and he didn't want to strain his relationship with her in the field.

He counted to ten in his head, grounding himself again in who he was and what he needed to do.

At the end of regaining himself, he pulled up the notifications.

**Strength Advancement: Rank D - Tier 1 → Rank D - Tier 2**
**Vigor Advancement: Rank E - Tier 3 → Rank E - Tier 4**

Ah, yeah. He had a feeling. Another step closer to that edge; the further his Strength climbed, the more Fury grew. But it meant more power, and the feeling led to craving. When had his need for Strength grown so strong? Was something broken inside of him?

His fingers shook as the beast inside roared with delight.

This tool would take him where he wanted to go. As long as it got him to his destination and let him slay threats to humanity, he'd keep using it. Erec got up on his twitchy legs; whatever had been sprained or broken was healed enough by VAL and Olivia for him to walk, at least.

He took it slow, drifting near the singing. It came from a small fire in the middle of the small town; Garin had a soldier's arm on his shoulder, and the two were saying and belting out somewhat scandalous lyrics. Most of the soldiers gathered around here, including Colin, who was on the opposite side of the fire listening to Garin with his arms crossed and a frown.

As Erec came into the light of the fire, the singing cut off, except for Garin, who wavered for a few seconds. Whispers ran through the soldiers as they all took their fill of him.

It was eerie with them suddenly quieting. There was something in their eyes, either fear or respect, but regardless the expression they wore wasn't natural. Almost like he wasn't a person to them. Erec shifted and raised his chin in response to the stares; he wouldn't let the tension get to him.

"I gave your dented helmet to someone to repair, rust-bucket. I can't believe you were dumb enough to abandon it on the battlefield —what a waste of resources. Fool. If it were me, I would've stopped and picked up the thing meant to protect my precious face before challenging another monster." Colin's criticism cut through the silence like a knife. It sparked a set of nervous laughter from the soldiers.

Without knowing the Duke's son, they thought he'd made a joke. It wasn't. Goddess help them if they heard one of them. Still, it brought Erec a smile.

"Didn't really need it, did I? Feels like my face is just fine. Think they'd have to do a lot worse til people preferred yours over mine."

"Take that back this instant. Do you realize the care routine I put in place to keep my complexion? Compared to yours, it's like day and night. You're lucky not to be acne-ridden." Colin scowled.

With that, the soldiers eased off and started to talk to one another again. Whatever this ridiculous conversation had brought to light was enough to clear the air and remind them that Erec was another human.

*Thanks, Colin.* He knew it wasn't intentional, and the sneer on Colin's face said he took the moment far too seriously, but it was just what he needed.

"Come on over and join us." Garin waved him over—a flask in hand. "We have a little something to celebrate the win."

"Should we be drinking after a fight?" Erec asked, sitting next to him, one of the soldiers shifting aside to make the room.

"I wonder, do you think having a little booze in you would make you fight better or worse?" Garin began to theorize, passing over the flask.

Erec looked down below, knocking back a bit of the amber liquid within before passing it over to the soldier next to him. It burned down his throat, and his face felt numb; would Boldwick approve or disapprove of this? It wouldn't be enough to render him useless. But the question had merit. Would it even lessen his power if he were to call Fury while intoxicated?

*Being sober isn't important right now.*

He'd led them to a fight, and even looking around now, they'd lost a couple of people. But with this battle, they'd gotten back to a place of safety. They were unsure about who he was, especially after seeing Fury in full force, but hopefully, they got a glimpse of him being just another person like them. With that, they could trust him.

Once they got back to the army, he would need them.

Erec was under no illusion that getting back to the Army's main host would end this hunt. Thanks to Colin and VAL, they had a lead on the White Stag. But that meant little if no one would take him seriously, and to do so, it was all about presentation. With so many Knights above his rank, the best way to stand out and command attention to make his voice heard was to force them to listen.

He needed the people around him. If they were willing to take extra steps beyond this with him, he'd have his wish.

To them, he'd be a leader and hero. And as long as they held him in a place of command, those above him would have to pay him attention when they rejoined the Army. For better or worse, he couldn't afford to be just another Initiate in their eyes.

Social capital.

*What a damn headache.*

Garin slumped next to him as the fire crackled and popped. The conversation flowed around, grieving a couple of lost soldiers, praising the fighting, and celebrating the future to come. Mixed emotions, to be sure, but today these soldiers saw that the puppets weren't almighty and that humanity could lash back.

For the first time, they'd made real progress against the White Stag and its insidious plans.

— - ☢ - — - ☼ - — - ☢ - —

"You really are something, aren't you?" Boldwick snorted over the radio as Erec finished his report. "Well, then. As far as I can see, you've taken care of the roadblock keeping you from returning to us. You're clear to advance, Initiate."

"Yes, sir. We'll be returning quickly," Erec replied, standing with his friends, watching Jefferson in the corner of the tent.

During the fight in town, the Possessed had suddenly launched an attack. None of them had gotten free, thanks to preparation and quick action on their defensive unit.

Somehow Dame Yuvia had ended up breaking her bonds. The Stag had faked her comatose state and, with an unpredicted amount of might, lashed out and started the attack. Sir Jefferson had cut her down. His swift and decisive action had saved the situation from spiraling out of control.

They'd set him there mainly as a way to keep him away from the main fighting, having never expected the coward Knight to aspire to such an act. Him proving himself almost made Erec feel bad.

It was sad that Dame Yuvia had died, as incompetent of a leader as she was; at least it would make things a little simpler.

Erec couldn't help but worry about Jefferson, though. After returning and finding out what happened, Sir Jefferson hadn't spoken much to anyone. He drifted about and did what was asked of him.

"Congratulations, Initiate. Once you're back with us, that'll be the first real victory in your cap in your likely violent and excessive career." Boldwick let out another chuckle before the communication feed cut off.

Erec waved to his friends that it was acceptable to leave. They'd spare no more time. From this point forward, it would be a fast march back toward the army to take full advantage of their hard-won reprieve.

His friends filtered out of their command tent, and Jefferson moved to follow.

"Stay here a minute," Erec said. The man paused and turned, head lowered. Erec wasn't sure what to say for a moment, despite being the one to ask him to stay. If he were being honest, he didn't even clearly know why he did—only that a part of his gut screamed at him too. "You did well."

"Did I?" Jefferson asked, bitter in his tone.

"I didn't expect you to pull through, let alone keep things together back there. I'm sorry I didn't think of the Stag making Yuvia appear out longer than she was. We're all grateful that you didn't hesitate."

"I am a Knight Errant."

"I suppose you are."

"And you're an Initiate."

"Did I ever deny that?" Erec asked; there was anger threatening to burn inside, but…no, this moment didn't call for it. There was something unseen lingering here from Jefferson, but it wasn't a threat or condemnation of himself.

"I don't think you should be an Initiate. Not based on what I've seen. You're something else. There's a couple like you in every class, those bound for more. They leap ahead while the rest of us humans scramble in the mud. Sometimes I wonder what's it like to be so blessed by the Goddess and be one of them." Jefferson's voice broke slightly, a sad twang to it.

"Shouldn't look at it that way. I don't see myself as favored. If anything, I bet the Goddess would hate my guts. Fine by me, since I'd hate Her right back too." Erec felt surprised by the blasphemy coming out of his mouth, but it felt right. Any being so careless as to burn away that many lives, well, he found it hard to be okay with them. "We all appreciate what you did. It couldn't have been easy. When we return to the Army, I'll see if Boldwick can find a place for you in the back lines, somewhere away from the fighting."

"No," Jefferson said sharply.

"No?"

"Seeing you, even at your age, it's disgraceful how I've acted. No,

Initiate. Wherever you go off to, I will go as well." The man slammed his fist against his chest piece in the form of a salute, before storming out of the command tent.

[Wow. Maybe we really should have thrown you onto a managerial track. Huh.]

Erec stared at the exit. Whatever weapon he could get, he'd take.

# CHAPTER 80
## BETTING

*With great distaste, I once more urge you to give up on your demands, as its a waste of your precious time and mine.*

*I'm well aware of the risks my current path entails, but as I'm sure you agree, the passive stance taken over the last few years has done little to advance our position or further our goals.*

*This is a world of strength and momentum, and the best way to gain both is to decisively and relentlessly attack the things that matter.*

*There is little time to waste trading pleasantries in court."*

*- Soren Crisimus, letter home (307, 3rd Era)*

The horizon held a beautiful sight. Rows of tents flying flags of every color backdropped a row of steel carts. Wind swept the pennants in the air, waving proudly above humankind's finest Army. All of the Knight Orders were represented, but most prominent was the giant silver-and-red flag that represented the Kingdom.

"Finally," Garin chuckled. "Made it back mostly in one piece."

Erec didn't have to say anything, and his friend knew more than anyone the stress they'd been under. Though things weren't likely to change too much now. Not if he got his way.

A group had broken off from the main Army, quickly heading their way.

Several of the people in it piloted Armor—their welcoming committee.

"It's surprising nothing else challenged us. They must've known I was here and decided to cower. It shall be excellent to take a rest for a few days. I've looked forward to this."

"Nothing's changed, Colin." Erec shut him down. Colin was a keystone to this plan, and there wasn't time for him to lounge around doing nothing. "Unless we show them what you can do, we won't get any renown." Not that he particularly cared about the reputation, but he knew it would be sufficient motivation to pull Colin forward. All they needed to do was demonstrate their discovery to people that mattered, then push to get back out into the wasteland.

Then they could hunt the Stag.

Hopefully, it would be quick enough, as long as it didn't get time to put together a more sophisticated attack to take on the Army.

"A lot has changed," Olivia said quietly as the Knights continued to advance toward Erec's centuria.

*True.*

They hadn't walked out into the wasteland this time as bright-eyed Initiates. Not after the last expedition and how it'd ended, but the challenges they'd faced this time had been completely different and far more challenging. Survival necessitated change.

The Knights arrived—then confirmed their identities. After that, it was a quick matter of how to transfer their Possessed to the main Army.

Then came the dreaded topic. What were they going to do with the troops Erec was leading back? As the Knight in charge of their relief party began to dig into the topic, Erec finally cut in.

"You'll be leaving my centuria intact," Erec commanded, throwing steel into his voice. The Knight Protector did a double take.

"Excuse me? What is your rank again?" the Knight asked. Though they were both aware that Erec was only an Initiate. This man, Sir Jonas, might not have been much higher—but it was enough. Ironically, he was the same rank Dame Yuvia had been.

"I've led these people back. Ask them if they want to disband and get dissolved into other centuria. You'll find they've agreed to stay with me."

Olivia and Colin turned to look. They hadn't been roped into this plan, but Garin was. His best friend moved directly to Erec's side. His lieutenant. The co-conspirator for this grab for authority and the man that made this possible. Without Garin acting as a go-between with the troops, there wasn't a chance in hell that these people would agree to stay with him. But now…

"This is asinine." Sir Jonas said. "You do not have authority to lead—"

"I don't? I saw someone *your rank* lead us into an ambush they'd been warned about for days. I brought these people back here safely and earned my right to lead for the rest of this mission. Ask them! They don't want anyone else. And you'll let them do what they want; I've promised to get them through this with my Strength. If you have a problem with that, then beat me in a fight."

Everyone froze in place.

There it was again—another public challenge to a duel. The Knight Protector swayed in his spot, unsure how to respond, just like Sir Jefferson had.

It was a risky gambit, but Erec hoped this man had heard enough about him to not want to risk losing face by testing him.

"Fine. If you're so hell-bent on this, I won't be the one to relieve you of your command. You get to explain it to the Master Knights yourself, and have them personally strip you of the authority. Follow me this instant." Sir Jonas turned on his heel and stormed off to the main encampment.

This was what he'd hoped for. Erec paused to look at Garin. "Look after the soldiers, alright? Make sure they get set up with rations and drinks for tonight. Colin, come with me please."

Garin saluted him, then grabbed Olivia to tend to their soldiers. With the two of them working together, there wasn't anything to worry about. Colin followed easily enough, and they made good pace after Sir Jonas. The man speed-walked past the tents, making a casual effort to go *slightly* too fast to make them struggle to keep up. Petty.

But maybe earned. His response, to Erec's eyes, looked pathetic, especially in front of the other Knights.

However, the weak didn't have the right to tell him what to do—

Erec shook his head.

Intrusive. That fire in his gut and its power to influence his logic were growing far too quickly, and the desire to slip into Fury was all too intoxicating. Was this the natural progression of his Divine Talent?

Erec frowned and picked up his speed. The key was to remain focused on one thing at a time.

— - ☢ - — - ☼ - — - ☢ - —

The command tent had a unique atmosphere—a surface-level sense of relaxation and joy, undermined by severe tension and disorder. Unlike before, it wasn't just the Master Knights of the Verdant Oak. No, there were representatives of each of the Orders. All of them Master Knights. The power stuffed under this thin linen tent was enough to blow away a mountain, probably. Some of them didn't even bother wearing their Armor. They were filled with confidence in their ability to manage an emergency without it if something occurred.

One thing was certain. Few of them were impressed with Erec after Sir Jonas's brief introduction and explanation of his challenge to him.

At least there were a couple of familiar faces. Though Boldwick looked perplexed by him and Sir Fulton unamused by Sir Jonas's valid criticisms.

After Jonas's report, Boldwick cut in to head off any discussion or reprimand.

"So, why?" Boldwick opened his hands, "You came back to us; explain why you don't want to relieve yourself of command and operate under a different Knight?"

It was a fair question, and it tactfully avoided condemnation, considering he'd blatantly violated the chain of command. That was the best tone for this conversation Erec could hope for.

"I need them. Colin's found a way to track the White Stag." Erec gestured at his friend—almost immediately, Master Knights began to object, several expressing angry skepticism and others arguing with their conjecture. No one believed Initiates were capable of riddling out what they'd tried to do since the start of the hunt. They agreed on that if nothing else.

But they didn't have an old-world machine stuffed inside their head and its pure scientific approach to magic. Nor had they been firsthand witnesses to the radio wave pulse at the towers.

They rumbled on for a few minutes, and Erec kept his head low. Even after breaking the chain of command to demand he retain leadership of his centuria, it was best to acknowledge these people were far above him and to let them have their say.

Eventually, Boldwick shut everyone up and got back on track for their questioning.

"Explain," Boldwick commanded. This time his tone was clear; he wanted proof.

"Colin, form the glyph." Erec made room, and Colin took center stage with flair. The boy lived for dramatics and slowly raised his hand in front of him, a smirk on display for all to see.

"Foolish of you to doubt my capabilities. I am heir to House Nitidus. Behold." The white lines of their carefully crafted glyph burned into the air, hovering briefly as he poured mana into the formation in his head. He dragged out the process—long enough for the Knights to get a glimpse of it before activation.

As it completed, the glyph condensed into a flare of light, which then shot off toward Colin's left and vanished into nothing.

Boldwick gave an uncomfortable cough.

"Uh, you…figured out how to make a light that lasts for a couple of seconds?" Boldwick scratched the back of his head.

"Don't be absurd; the glyph was designed to read mana and then transmit energy in the direction from which it detected it." A mousy Master Knight from the Order of the Azure tower spoke up. She leaned forward and smiled. "If you may, could you use that glyph again? This time, try to maintain it for longer before setting it off. It's a rather novel and niche concept, but I don't mind offering advice to Initiates on Mysticism."

"Right." Boldwick turned his eyes back to Erec. "And…what does that prove, and how exactly does a glyph that makes a bit of light mean you should retain command over an albeit diminished centuria?"

"The direction the light shot toward is the same direction it detects the Stag's magical signature from—we used the wavelength that amplified the White Stag's magic when it took over half our centuria to work backward to trace its mana signature. Through testing, we were able to find the correct configuration. What you see now is the product of that. We can find the White Stag with it."

The mousy Knight cupped her chin and tilted her head as Colin kept the glyph formed.

"Clever idea," the mousy Knight admitted, shaking her head. "Tedious and unreliable, though. How can you be sure it's not detecting trace magical energy and responding to that? Rifts have a way of distorting ambient magic. Which is assuming that you had the right wavelength to begin with."

[They do?]

"This is ridiculous. There's no way that an Initiate could devise a methodology for tracking the Stag—our priests have been attempting divination for weeks, to no avail. Yet they expect us to believe this farce? One of them is the Unbroken General's son—clearly glory-seeking with a lie," one of the Knights cut in, a large man in damn near enough steel plate to make his Armor triple the size of a man.

"How dare you! What family are you from, anyway? I doubt it's anything more than a Barony—" Colin's glyph shattered as the boy snarled. The mousy Knight protested and tried to head off the point-less argument brewing.

"Bah, I am a Master Knight. Rank means far more than any House." The low, grave voice cut back across as the Master Knight found no shame in feuding with an Initiate.

Erec cleared his throat, feeling nervous. He had been confident in their methods, but with the new information from that woman…

Boldwick let out a low laugh, silencing the fight from devolving further.

"Well. Alright, then. This is a gamble, if I understand correctly." Boldwick folded his arms and shook his head. "Which is why you wanted to retain command. You wanted to take a chance on this theory. In other words, you're seeking to lead a scouting expedition and see if your gamble pans out."

"Yes, sir," Erec said, straightening his back.

"Normally, I wouldn't send off Initiates to lead a centuria. But if these people want to stay under your command, we can devise a workaround. I'll send you off with a Knight Lieutenant, who will let you play leader. From what I can see, there's not much to lose with this, since we're sitting and spewing out scouting forces anyway. What's one more?" Boldwick clapped his hands together.

"I refuse to allow this," the Knight in the massive plating argued. "This is a waste of resources."

"Good thing you're not part of my Order. Lance, I don't have to ask your advice on how I conduct scouting expeditions. So shut up and complain to the rest of the Silver Flames and your priests." Boldwick snorted. "Erec, I'll expect confirmation from those soldiers that they want to follow you; in the meantime, get me a list of supplies you'll need. I expect a comprehensive plan. Please bring it to Dame Robin for approval. Then you have my permission to take her out on your expedition."

With that, Erec had his chance.

"I did it all—I came up with the glyph." Colin spoke up and puffed up his chest, missing the point of the conversation, let alone the shift in dynamics. The mousy Knight humored him, then made him pull up the glyph, while lavishing him with praise.

Erec gave Boldwick a nod and left. He needed to plan and put together the logistics. They'd find the White Stag and end this hunt.

# CHAPTER 81
## SLEEPING BEAUTY

"Oftentimes, those above don't offer this advice. But I think it prudent. It's unwise to push yourself too far, too quickly." Dame Robin spoke with a bemused tone. Erec rested next to her as they watched their small group of soldiers march through the wasteland. Together, the two had scouted out the local area—but this close to the army encampment, anything that posed a threat would've been picked up long ago.

Mostly, this scouting mission was Robin prying into what he'd done since they'd last met.

"Those at the top aren't always deserving of it. From what I've seen, at least," Erec said.

"It is understandable to feel that way. You've been around our aristocracy's less-than-noble side for most of your life. You have us now, though. Boldwick, me, and your Order. Though it is true, many make it to Knight Protector without knowing the first thing about what makes for a good leader. I think it's clear that progressing from Initiate to Knight Errant is only a matter of time. But little is spoken about how getting from Knight Errant to Knight Protector is mostly a matter of power and accomplishment. After that, a lot tend to stagnate."

"They do?"

"Within this Order, that is typically the fate of the majority of our men and women. They live fulfilling enough careers and serve for a time to garner prestige, and if they're moderately successful, wealth and status. Then they retire to form their branch of nobility or take their Household's mantle."

"I don't understand why they don't aim for more?"

Dame Robin shook her head slowly. "With each tier, the path narrows. It gets harder to climb. They get frustrated they can't display what we want to see in our Knight Lieutenants, let alone our Knight Commanders. They measure their lack of progress with the people higher than them. Most never reach their full potential; some are plain unlucky and taken away from us before they get the chance. Do you happen to know what the main gripe of those within the Knight Protector rank is?"

"How stressful leadership is?" That would make sense. He'd gotten a taste of it, and the responsibility was heavy; even if he'd bid for more of it, that didn't mean he liked the feel.

"Wrong. They blame others. When someone else does well, they proclaim how lucky they are or that others are intentionally holding them back. However, I don't think my main worry over you is about that." Her voice broke for a moment there at the end. She cleared her throat.

"You're worried I'll end up like Alister."

"Am I wrong? Anyone with their head screwed on right would be thinking that too. None of us can deny your uncanny growth, but it's the stars that burn the brightest the fastest that tend to vanish the quickest." Dame Robin's voice shook, and a strange sensation passed through Erec at her worry. Almost…guilt? "You don't choose to chase glory, but it leaves me wondering. Do you keep getting in these situations to save others, or are you looking for more fights?"

"I'm trying to protect other people," Erec snapped back. He wanted her to not concern herself over him—for things to return to normal. Though it was a lie.

He didn't know the real answer to that question.

Dame Robin slipped into silence, and Erec forced his attention back onto their expedition. Sir Jefferson trod along easily with other unknown Knights—Sir Boldwick spared them another Knight Protector and an additional Knight Errant. Both of them were nominally answering to Dame Robin instead of himself. Technically, Erec was reporting directly to her too.

The Army had issued them only ten more men, including a lieutenant and captain; those two, however, consulted with Erec as the lead Knight.

Overall, a bizarre command structure that broke convention. But Boldwick's reputation made others go along with it after very little goading from the well-regarded Master Knight.

For all intents and purposes, Erec was in charge of the mission. Even if he and the Knights above his rank "reported" to Dame Robin. As long as she took no major grievance with anything, his decisions were de facto hers.

Though that mattered very little to the men and women who had bravely followed Erec out here; unlike most of the Army, they rode high on a renewed purpose following their last victory. Thanks to their recent fight, and Erec following through, they were among the few units in the hunt that felt any success against the White Stag.

They were his soldiers.

Erec let that settle in for a long moment, along with the knowledge that he'd asked them to volunteer to head with him back into danger. Was it right? Moreover, what did that say about him? For so long, he'd compared himself to his brother, but would even Bedwyr go this far?

"It makes me nervous; this whole thing does. But I didn't see a way to get the work I thought needed to be done unless I pushed for it myself," Erec admitted to Dame Robin, breaking the silence again.

"This path may make your goals easier to reach in some ways. But I'm sure it'll be far tougher in the long run for you, though nothing worth the effort is easy, and the things you will learn will be valuable." Dame Robin clamped her gauntlet on his shoulder. "Let's find that Stag; we can bring this hunt to an end and return to the walls."

"Eventually, we'll just leave again." They had that planned trip west, and that was the headache; it felt like they'd played into the Duchess's hands. He'd have to trust that Boldwick knew what he was doing.

"It's always like that. Time runs in circles; there are lulls where you can rest and recover in the safety of friends and family, and then there are moments where you have to put everything on the line. It's only easier to see that for people like us, since the harsh nature of reality throws itself in our faces." With that, Dame Robin finally broke off the conversation for good and rejoined their group.

Erec let them drift ahead before picking up his own trail parallel to theirs. Walking with himself felt right, and with a quicker speed, he'd pass the group and sink more into scouting. This land was safe for now. But the practice might be invaluable for later.

Besides, the only company he wanted at the moment was his own.

— - ♟ - — - ☼ - — - ♟ - —

Each day sent them off further from the safety of the Army. Each night, Colin used their glyph to correct their course and regather their direction. That became less necessary with the revelation two days in that the glyph's bearing wasn't changing much at all.

The White Stag wasn't roaming the wasteland. No, it'd centered somewhere to the east, near the glowing sea.

That direction was a place that Knights tended to avoid, and the scouting expeditions headed that way made sure to do so quietly. Erec hesitated and wrestled with the decision for days, knowing plenty of strong monsters might lurk out there.

His people steeled themselves for the danger. And they were hunting after a Cataclysm-Level monster anyway.

The decision wasn't that hard to make.

However, the real difficulty ended up being far more personal. With the growing density of monsters, and the challenge they represented, he worried the temptation might be too high.

What if he threw himself into a battle outside of his capabilities? Could Robin save him?

So he resisted the tempting fights, and with Robin's help, they kept themselves hidden.

Then it happened.

They came across a group of Silent Ones roaming over the wasteland. After making the report and confirming that they were headed toward the main force of the Army, Erec continued forward. These things were moving with coordination, like pawns on a chessboard, positioned by the invisible eldritch mind of the Stag.

Thanks to their smaller numbers, it was easier to move their encampment discretely. But the unease at discovering more groups of enemies and the paranoia of discovery sent a shiver through all of them. Nightmares of the White Stag became common in the centuria as they dove deeper into the enemy's territory. Erec grew paranoid that one of the groups noticed them—that the White Stag might be baiting them into a trap.

But the discovery wasn't for nothing. After repeated sightings of the Silent Ones, the Army immediately responded and shifted to follow Erec's direction to handle the marked groups. Dame Robin worked ceaselessly to scout out the land around them. They found another group of Silent Ones.

Within weeks, the Army moved to begin engagements.

Then they found it. Normally, it might be mistaken for another abandoned feature of the wasteland. The dull color of the walls around the place and a massive rusted fence diminished the discovery—an abandoned military encampment from the old-world.

Open in the middle of it were several Rifts. Spewing Silent Ones, filling up the insides of the tanned buildings and fortified position with plenty of monsters.

But, as they took a look, snuck as close as they dared, they found the true horror.

Near the Rifts, a massive White Stag lay, its head curled into its side as its huge antlers gave off a shimmer. They had the same distorting light of the Rifts reflecting off them as it slept nearby.

# CHAPTER 82
# FIRE MEETS

*We are Hers, and by Her will, we will end Her enemies.*
*How else are we to receive Her grace?*

*- Grandmaster Flames, sermon (294, 3rd Era)*

Erec leaned over and rested his arms on his knees. Their camp was shrouded in the dark and now miles away from the White Stag. After spotting it, the image of the massive Stag haunted him. He wasn't the only one, either. Even now, Robin prowled nearby with a Knight Errant to keep an eye out for any approaching Silent Ones.

If even a single puppet spotted them, they were fucked.

It'd lead to a race back to the main Army with a small chance they wouldn't all end up torn apart in the wasteland. For now, their entire centuria slept in shifts. All of them were ready to move at a single word were the worst case to happen.

Exciting.

Nerve-wracking.

Erec couldn't make up his mind.

"You two really did it," Garin mumbled, shaking his head. "Can't believe you managed to track down the Stag."

"Well, of course, I did. I'm magnificent, aren't I? Praise me," Colin said.

"Ah yes, so wonderful! Thank you for blessing us with your company!" Olivia suppressed a snicker, sliding closer to Garin.

"You lot are lucky to be so graced. Show yourselves worthy, and once we've graduated, perhaps I'll offer you a spot in my house guard." Olivia and Erec shared a look. Neither wanted to join that mess—certainly not Olivia, as she belonged to another Duchy.

But it did lead to a good question.

"Do you plan to retire from the Order when you become a Knight Protector, Colin?" Erec asked.

"Hmm?" Colin paused and tilted his head. "I suppose I could. I'm waiting for father to signal to me that the time is right. He told me this was meant to forge me into a weapon that could be used—as if I needed the additional experience. Until then, I'm supposed to muddle my way through with my lessers and gain acclaim. Though, with this victory beneath my belt, the time may come sooner than expected."

If he were to get recalled sooner, it might absolve Erec of his responsibilities. Given what he knew about the Duke and his son, Erec didn't think that waiting for Colin to prove himself as capable was what the Unbroken General was looking for.

The Unbroken General wanted Colin to grow up before trusting him. Eventually, though, he would become the master of the House, as it offered more power and prestige than Colin would find as a Knight. Unless, by some miracle, he achieved the rank of Master Knight.

That was how the higher nobility operated. Oftentimes only the second- or thirdborn children joined the Knight Orders. Once there, they would achieve their titles and establish their own branches of nobility. Then the central family would claim them as side branches and form ties—the whole system was complex and interwoven.

But being a Knight carried risk. Which was why firstborns completely dedicating themselves to Knighthood were usually reserved for lower Houses, or they left before achieving too high a rank in their Order.

"And you? Would you join my Household if I were so gracious as to make an offer?" Colin asked, far more serious than before to Erec.

Erec snorted.

"Hell no."

"Truly a low-born misbegotten—"

"I joined the Knights to clear my family's name, and yeah, maybe along the way, I'll make a little bit of a name for myself too. But I never expected much; if I hadn't gotten in, where would I even have been? Our family has no land—no, I don't think I ever really plan to retire from this anyway," Erec said, already knowing the truth about where his path seemed to be going.

It was a test to see how strong he got.

And somewhere, that Strength might not be enough. Before then, he'd be damn well sure to get the answer to the questions he wanted and to secure a spot for the people left behind.

Either that, or he might end up locked up in some western lab on behalf of a mad machine in his head, slaving away doing science. Though maybe that was wishful thinking. Erec glanced in the direction of the Stag. What sort of worries did a monster like that have? Did it have a different flavor of mad fury in it, driving it to these acts in such a desperate manner too?

"Well, it's clear what your friend is here for. He's come to find a bride and increase his own House's standing." Colin turned his attention on Garin. "However, like my father warned, he got distracted by a maid."

"I'm a Dame. It would behoove you to address me properly now, Sir Golden-Spoon," Olivia said. "Besides, as of now, I don't believe either of us has an intention of marriage."

"I caught you two cuddling in the common room," Colin retorted.

"Mhmm. Foolish of me. I suppose I should have asked for a ring before we even held hands; how classless. You're right, dear Colin. My sincere apologies, Sir Garin. We must evaporate this relationship posthaste, and you are not allowed to so much as a glance in my general direction, not until you have your father send my mother the betrothal request. Until then, none of this is truly proper." Olivia slid closer to Garin even as she started to mock Colin.

"Oh! What am I to do? I suppose I must find a ring and convince my dad that you'll bring our House a large dowry!" Garin couldn't keep up with it and started to laugh, wrapping an arm around her.

"Bah, you mock me as if that is uncommon. You're both far too unrefined to know how true nobles ought to act," Colin said.

"Or perhaps you've wound yourself so tight in a bubble that you don't know how *real* relationships work. Do take some time to consider, Sir Colin. Mayhaps, with reflection, we might convince you it's acceptable to find a date for a ball without committing the poor woman to a marriage with you." Olivia ended the conversation as she and Garin settled in with each other.

Erec got up and walked off. Colin was pulling back into his shell after learning a lesson, and, well, the two others probably wanted some alone time. Eventually, Colin would get the hint. Either way, Erec didn't want part of it. He was happy Garin had found someone.

As long as things could stay like this…he'd be happy.

Eventually, like the turning of seasons, or the sun falling at the end of the day, this had to end.

— - ☢ - — - ☼ - — - ☢ - —

When Erec opened his eyes, he saw two things. First was a vast field of red flowers. Crimson petals dominated a landscape as far as he could see—a veritable field of dark vines lifted up the most horribly beautiful flowers he'd ever witnessed. The sky above was a perfect black, yet, somehow, light drifted off the plants, exposing how unending and almost ghostly the place was.

The second was the white pelt of a massive Stag; its blood-red eyes locked on him from a paltry twenty feet away.

Instantly, Erec's blood boiled, and the fire in his gut sparked. If he wanted, he could reach out and let it explode; there wasn't a doubt in his mind that unleashing that hell would take care of this scenario. It'd turn all of these flowers to ash and send that monster fleeing from his mind.

But he hesitated.

Unlike before, there wasn't a crushing demand for his subservience. It didn't expect him to bow his head and give over to its will. There was almost…curiosity mingled with begrudging respect for him.

The White Stag lifted its head, its eyes piercing him as its undivided attention seared through Erec.

Around him, the red flowers broke off from their stems, flowing around the two in a twister that sealed them in with one another. Though the entire landscape was coming apart, Erec couldn't bring himself to look away from the White Stag. All he had was the fire inside, ready to come at a moment's notice and burn away this vision in his dreams.

Yet, he didn't.

The petals fluttered around in a ruby-red wall, the smell sweet and sickly like blood, and then the funnel broke apart, exploding outward from the two of them.

Outside of the wall of crimson was something else entirely. The entire landscape had changed from the black field filled with red flowers. It was a long and vast landscape, with massive mountains in the distance backdropped by a bright green sky. Faint yellow clouds traced over the horizon—a different world, Erec was sure of it. Though much of it looked similar to his own, the air held a cool pleasant breeze.

A sense of loss filled Erec as he took in this place; the Stag looked away from him, its eyes roaming the landscape.

*Its home?*

Though it couldn't talk, the profound feeling of loss lanced through Erec.

And then, high in the sky, a pillar of silver fire descended. It smashed into the planet, and a wall of silver flames crashed over them—Erec let out a scream, but the silver fire only lasted a second. Then, they were left with complete black.

No more flowers. They stood alone in a void of black.

Hate. Palpable hate. It burned in Erec and resonated with the fire inside of him, fighting against it as the two seemed destined to try to burn one another out until only death remained.

All of Hers had to die for what she had done.

The Stag would have it no other way.

Erec grinned back at it; if that's what it wanted, then so be it. If it wanted to hate, he'd show it what it wanted. With a step toward the monster, he let the hell inside loose. Silver flames burned outward from him. The inferno consumed this illusion it had implanted in his head, turning its forced dream to ash in seconds.

# CHAPTER 83
## PIECES IN PLACE

Their days of hiding quickly evaporated as Erec commanded his group to pull back and rejoin the approaching Army. Thankfully, his expedition had been a complete success. Everyone was safe.

Though he hadn't been in direct conflict, minor skirmishes erupted across the wasteland as the Army encircled the White Stag. Like a wave, the humans moved to strategic points surrounding the White Stag, effectively choking out any pathway to escape. It split their main forces, but it would end this hunt, one way or another.

Being in the main Army was a relief, and this time around, Erec officially renounced his authority and had his command stripped from him. As much as he considered leading them into the primary battle himself, he wasn't experienced enough. If anything, demanding to remain in command would only hurt the people he led. It didn't take much urging to acknowledge that and submit himself to another unit.

Even though Boldwick thought he'd done enough, Erec made the Master Knight promise him a good position in the coming battle. Though the man made it conditional on him vowing to stay away from the ongoing skirmishes. Which suited him fine. That would be the real fight that counted.

Until then, more of the monsters spewed out from the Rifts—according to the reports, two more had opened near the White Stag. It was reinforcing its position and threw small attacks.

It could be that the Stag was trying to exhaust them. This was an untenable position. At some point, they'd have to break through and kill the Stag before running out of resources.

Until then, Erec found himself constantly wandering around with aimless abandon. He clutched a bread roll in his right hand and sighed. At least Munchy didn't have any problems with eating while others were out there bleeding instead of him.

He'd nabbed an extra treat to feed the squirrel—which, despite all the fighting and constant travel, appeared to be having the time of his life. Munchy made a home of Garin's Armor and lived like a king.

*Not much longer.*

Tomorrow was the day. Tomorrow the hunt would end for good.

Erec caught the familiar hushed whispers in the camp around him. They were as eager as him for it to end. However, their reasoning was likely different. They wanted to return to the walls, to their safety and families, since they typically served in a much more domestic and policing manner than blatantly fighting these horrors. He hoped this would be it; in a day, this would end, and they'd get their wish.

To him, the mere excitement of tomorrow was alarming, and it took this aimless wandering through the camp to still his chaotic heart.

Not everyone would make it back after the fight. How many corpses might end up littering the wasteland to put an end to the mad Stag's quest to kill them all? And why was it that he couldn't find the worry inside himself that he might end up among the bodies?

"I can't do this," a strained voice called from inside a tent—one that startled Erec more than any other. It was Bedwyr's voice. More alarming was the tone—he couldn't remember the last time he'd heard his brother speak quite like that.

Unable to help himself, Erec snuck closer to the tent it came from, discreetly pulling the cloth at the front to get a peek inside. Sure enough, there was Bedwyr with a frown on his face.

But he wasn't alone. Gwen sat in front of him, tears rolling down her face as she held a shaking hand at her side. His brother refused to meet her eyes. "Can't you? Why can't you just sit back for this fight— the Knight Commander told you that you didn't need to take the offered position in the strike squad. You don't *need* to do this. Let a

Knight Protector take your place instead. You've no idea the danger of getting near those Rifts, of what that awful monster might have hidden away!"

"I'll handle it, Gwen. I'm not about to let someone take a spot I can fill due to fear. Whatever might come out of there, or whatever trick it might have, I'm one of the best-equipped to adapt to it. That's why I was asked. If I succeed here, I'll shoot past Knight Errant straight to being a Protector when I graduate." Bedwyr pulled away from her, trying to look anywhere but at Gwen.

She didn't have it, forcing herself back into his view. "I don't get it. Why can't you just *wait?* You'll get stronger, give it time! You keep doing this to yourself, and it tears me apart to see it. Do you not care about me? What am I going to do if you end up dead?" Gwen was shouting, which made Erec flinch.

"Stop, alright? I do care about you—but this isn't about that. This is about what I need to do. I need to get stronger, for everyone."

"That's what it's always about! Everyone else! Bedwyr...can't you see that when you only think of other people, you don't spare yourself any time to think of you? What's best for you? I can tell you it isn't throwing your life on the line as an Initiate—there's stronger Knights. And you have people that care about you! Your brother— me! Wyr—"

"Please. No more. I'm meant for this, it's why I'm on this earth... Maybe if you forgot about me, let this go, you'd be happier. I'm sorry, it seems I can only hurt the people close to me."

"Bullshit!"

Erec stepped away from the tent and quickly began to walk off. This was none of his business, and he'd already seen enough drama to know he didn't want to get busted for eavesdropping.

A moment later, he heard a dreaded call over his shoulder. "Erec!" Gwen said.

*Fuck.*

Would she know that he'd heard them? Erec froze in place as she stomped up behind him. The older girl slid into his eyes, tears running down her face. Though he wanted to, he couldn't force his eyes away from the raw pain on display.

"Be better than him, alright?" she asked, choking up. "I know you heard some of that—I see it in your eyes, but I'll say it now. You can be better than him, don't put everything on your shoulders. It'll hurt you, but more than that, it'll tear apart the people who care about you most." With that, she stormed off.

Erec cleared his throat, feeling a rush of awkward energy at the chance encounter.

Unsure of what to think, Erec decided to keep on his long walk before catching up with Garin. Munchy could afford to wait a little longer for his meal.

— - ☣ - — - ☼ - — - ☣ - —

"Got everything?" Dame Robin asked their squad. It was a redundant question, since she'd asked the same thing hours ago before they'd moved to get in position. Behind them was their force of Knights—an entire legion was positioned and facing a wall of monsters on the field ahead.

As expected, the amassed Silent Ones remained completely still only a couple of miles away. This same scenario was undoubtedly reflected in a few other positions wherever their Army gathered. Like a vise, they'd squeeze in on the Stag's fortress and draw out the defenses it'd managed to pull from the Rifts and turn into puppets.

But their point wasn't to overwhelm the monsters. Not with the Rifts wide open. No, they'd soften the front lines and weaken it enough for the strike forces filed with Elite Knights to break through and target the Stag and close the Rifts.

Somewhere among that force was Bedwyr. Erec felt the sting of jealousy that he wasn't along for the coming battle—but it made sense. He was a first-year Initiate. Under normal circumstances, he wouldn't even have been working with Dame Robin's force. It was only due to his raw Strength that rivaled some Knight Protectors that afforded him this chance.

Not to mention that his abilities didn't lend well to a targeted strike like that.

Still, he felt like he was a step behind his brother. Like he always had throughout his life. As much as others had assured him he was doing well, with Bedwyr's ability, could he ever really rival him?

"Well? Got everything?" Dame Robin asked him specifically, as he'd failed to respond. Unlike the rest of the Knights they had with them.

"Yes, ma'am." Erec tapped the hatchets strapped to his side, and the slightly more wicked one-handed axe secured on his lower back. His previous troop had donated him a couple more weapons as a parting gift, and though he didn't expect to hold on to them for long, he'd put them to good use. This was going to be a long fight, and he didn't intend to slow Dame Robin down.

Sir Jefferson clapped him on the shoulder. "It'll be alright. We've got your back as long as you've got ours," the man said.

The rest of these Knights were unknown to Erec, which suited him fine. His friends were somewhere else at a safer part of the battlefield, interwoven within the legion below.

Their squad wasn't composed of just Verdant Oak Knights—they had four of their own and an equal number of Knights from the Azure Tower and Crimson Lotus.

They only had two Knights from the Silver Flames. Based on the brief tactical outline Dame Robin had given beforehand, those two were support troops.

Their tactics for the battle were relatively simple. Anywhere on the battlefield the monsters seemed to become too much for the regular legion, they were to go in and take out the heavy-hitting monsters.

Precisely the challenge Erec had hoped for.

"They're moving." Dame Robin's voice took a sharp, commanding tone. Erec's eyes snapped to the battlefield. Sure enough, the Silent Ones had begun their advance. Their hate radiated in waves—or perhaps he only felt it because he knew that was what the Stag must have in its heart. But it was almost palpable as the emotion rung throughout the air, that familiar condemnation. It would tear apart any man or woman that opposed it and then spit in the face of the Goddess.

War had begun.

# CHAPTER 84
## RESTRAINT

*Restraint? Hang 'em all.*
*It'll be damn fun!*
*If they wanna run off to Vega, then they can cower and hide. Then if they*
*poke their heads out, we'll catch 'em and string 'em up too.*

*- Seven-Snakes, hidden recording (302, 3rd Era)*

Trouble came immediately to the battlefield. A giant worm surfaced in the middle of the fight, erupting into a scene of carnage as it caught their defensive line by surprise and easily threw the unArmored soldiers.

Limp bodies flew as the rest of the puppets tore into the broken line. A few of the captains began to fight to buy time, but it was a losing battle.

The sheer strength of the worm was insurmountable, turning those that couldn't compete into corpses.

Worse were the monsters flooding around it and taking advantage of the temporary chaos.

Six-legged terrors sprang around the worm. They tore apart sense-less soldiers with three-headed maws. Under such a sudden and violent assault, the survivors held no chance of resisting.

Dame Robin barked a sharp command—and everyone moved around Erec with a precision he hadn't seen before on the battlefield. As one, they flowed out from the sidelines and began to cut through the battle directly toward the fight. Erec ran at full speed after them, tangling through the press of bodies and lightly shoving stray soldiers out of his way to keep up.

Claustrophobia and chaos waged on all sides, but keeping track of the figures with Armor ahead of him made it easy. And the size of their target made it easy as well.

After making it to the monster, the Knights didn't hesitate. One of them formed a glyph and shot a giant spike of ice into its side, pinning the worm and keeping it from attacking nearby soldiers.

As Erec finally broke through to the fight, the Knights were already dealing the deathblows to the monster. Two of them hacked into it near the skull—another seared its flank with fire. Erec drew his axe and got in a single slice, yet it felt minimal compared to the damage inflicted by those around him. Even the monsters around the fight had been effectively repelled by a trio of the Knights, rapidly changing their efforts from a desperate resistance to a contained situation.

These Knights were efficient, their teamwork unseen, and even keeping up without his Fury was difficult, since their Agility outclassed Erec's.

As the monster died, Erec plopped his battle-axe over his shoulder and looked for Dame Robin.

The soldiers were already reforming their defensive line around the dead monster and pushing back against the main host. Hardly any of the Knights were still fighting—and the allure of killing some of the smaller monsters tempted Erec.

Barely helping with the worm frustrated him, and the remedy of spilling blood would fix it.

He'd killed one of these weeks ago, yet now struggled to hold up to the people around him. They were on another level entirely.

Erec sighed as he finally caught sight of Dame Robin—their fearless leader was on the worm's body, using the height of the corpse to survey the field.

One of the six-legged beasts threw itself at her, only for the Knight Lieutenant to kick it away with a lazy jerk of her foot. It smashed into the ground and broke its spine, twitching before a stray torrentof flame from a soldier brought a sudden and complete end to it.

Erec let out a frustrated sigh.

Sir Jefferson set a hand on his shoulder, ending the spiral of downward thought before it could fully start.

"Hard to keep up, isn't it?" Jefferson asked.

"You made it here sooner than me," Erec pointed out, which was true. Jefferson had gotten in a hit or two and helped with the sidelines.

"Yeah? But did I do damage? No, not really. I just helped bleed it. The thing about working with people better than you is that they don't expect you to perform better than them. They want you to learn. Focus on what your weaknesses are and how to cover them... Sometimes, you get paired up with people far outside of your league and have to learn how to adapt." Jefferson shrugged.

Erec stared at the Knights around him—one of them clambered up on the worm to join their leader there, and the others were already preparing for a fight.

What could he contribute to this group?

He essentially had a single way; the moment he let the inferno ignite on the battlefield, he'd be tough to direct and control. Engaging with the worm hadn't been enough to get him going, but he knew if a fight heated up enough, it might be impossible to suppress the fire. The Q.A.P. let him intervene in a few local fights with the soldiers for the lesser monsters, but if he lagged behind to utilize it, he risked not keeping up with the faster Knights.

"Is this how you felt about me?" Erec asked Jefferson.

"Yeah, I saw someone younger than me capable of feats and courage I didn't have inside of myself. I'd acted pathetic. When you feel helpless, you can let yourself dwell in the feeling or find the way out of it."

"I see." Erec tightened his grip on his battle-axe.

Bedwyr was out there, preparing for his assault on the location near the White Stag.

The difference between himself and the higher echelons of Knights was more than just power. Teamwork was key in taking down opponents in a way that not only preserved you from danger but also protected the people around you. He'd seen how they easily handled the monsters attacking the soldiers, even as they dealt with the worm.

He had to find a way to be useful.

If he'd come out here and joined this squad only to do nothing, it'd been a waste of his appointment on the battlefield. What was this for if more people would've paid for his choice than if he supported his friends?

[Keep it steady, Buckeroo! We all have to learn. Try new things, and see if they fit; figure out what works for you. Stressing yourself out will only lead to mistakes.]

*Don't get frustrated.*

It only led to the fire consuming him; he needed to wait for the right moment to let loose, or he'd be a waste.

"Another target, a worm surfaced to the north! Move!" Dame Robin shouted, and the Knights ran for it again, cutting across the battlefield.

— - ☢ - — - ☼ - — - ☢ - —

Fight after fight passed by—splattering their Knights in plenty of blood. Erec got better at finding his way into the battle toward the edges and providing support from there. But it was a constant struggle against his instinct to let the fire inside free.

He kept the rage at a smolder for an hour using a display of will with the help of an occasional dose of sedative. It didn't help that, for the most part, the Knights around him were far more efficient at cleaning up the fights and taking care of the enemies, leaving him little part to play. The frustration only grew as much as he tried to out-logic it.

At first, the sensation had been maddening.

He saw Jefferson engage in the same struggle yet maintain a positive outlook while finding small ways to contribute to the fighting. That will left Erec with the resolve to redefine what it meant to be helpful in this battle.

Right now, they didn't need him to go full-out. Some of them were exhausting themselves with the constant barrage of worms popping up over the battlefield. If they couldn't keep up the pace, then it might be the time for him to fill in the position and take the lead in a skirmish or two. It was a game of patience.

Like it or hate it, he was learning to apply himself around this new dynamic.

Though Erec wasn't sure how much longer he could keep the hate boiling inside him at bay. In the constant frantic moving of fight to fight, they only had a couple of minutes between each engagement to cool down. Soldiers struggled for their lives all around him, yet the puppets only kept coming.

More of the worms kept erupting into their defensive line and costing lives as humans fought these puppets.

Was this what the White Stag wanted?

How long until it ended?

Erec forged ahead, pushing himself to keep together until the right moment. To be the most useful to the people around him, the key to his power wasn't the Strength it offered. No, the key was finding the right occasion to unleash and not wasting the potential impact it could have.

Desire warred with responsibility, but restraint was king.

Two hours into the battle, shadows dominated the sky—above them was a swarm of monsters, singular eyeballs, and long leathery wings flew in from the south. Damn near an entire second army of puppets to combat their legion, in numbers large enough to over-whelm their forces.

"New tactic. Split off and help support the army. Kill as many as you can as quick as you can—Stephen and Damien, on me, we'll continue to handle worms—go!" Dame Robin screamed as the shadow of monsters began to descend on the field.

The inferno began to flare within Erec. This was it.

Now was the time to let loose. The fire inside him was fresh—the wait hadn't been in vain.

Time to kill.

# CHAPTER 85
## EASY MODE

Erec grinned as his axe sheared through the lens and gunk of the giant flying eyeball. The hateful monster spiraled into the ground as its insides turned to mush—taking it out was surprisingly easy. Though numerous, these things died quickly.

Their Strength wouldn't be a problem. He felt free as the fire burned in him, his eyes turning to find the next kill.

[Left!]

Erec threw himself with the command as an instinct. A pulse of red energy shot out of a monster's giant eye and tore into the space he'd been, searing the ground.

[Updating Q.A.P. prediction models. Well, that's an unexpected ability.]

Hardly a second passed before another shot of crimson light flashed across Erec's vision as a ghostly precursor—he moved immediately, throwing himself out of the way of another beam. It tore across the ground, the heat of it searing what little dried vegetation remained on the wasteland.

If it'd hit him—

Far to the right, a soldier got blasted by the eye beam. There was a pained scream as half his face burned away from the horrific heat of the attack.

Erec winced, but excitement coursed through him at this turn of events. The eyeball monsters might not have been physically strong, but these things had something hidden away after all, and there was a massive amount of them to kill. Erec unhooked one of the hatchets and threw the weapon through the air. It landed with a solid thunk and took out the puppet that slew the soldier, leaving the monster twitching on the ground. It was unable to use its eye but certainly not finished. He stormed over in an instant, one of his boots slamming down on its wing to keep the monster steady.

These eyelike creatures had gross yellow molted skin; each round body cupped around and supported that central eyeball and a small mouth lined with teeth below—and the beam didn't appear to be its only weapon. A barbed tail smashed against Erec's leg, the tip of it skittering helplessly against his Armor. Not sharp enough to cut through the steel. The puppet flailed the two talons at the end of its legs, but they were nowhere near taking out Erec.

He'd already grown bored of this one. Erec slammed his boot into the monster—once, twice, thrice—until it stopped flailing.

Each blow brought more of the inferno alive inside. It swelled as he picked his next target—launching himself at it with his bare hands.

It went down as easy as the first one. As it turned out, ripping one out of the air and smashing its eye into the ground effectively stopped it from getting off a beam at him.

If they died quicker, they got less of a chance to attack. And the more he could kill.

Erec's vision filled with red as he tore his axe through more and more.

At some points, he weaved a different dance of death, grabbing one by the wings and smashing it into another. They weren't the most satisfying weapons but they worked in a pinch.

He'd hoped to force this one to shoot its beam—but there was no such luck, so he contented in simply squeezing it in his hand until it popped.

Eyeballs and torn wings blended together as he tore through the enemies. Their reactions became all too predictable, even without Q.A.P. From how they moved in the air, to how they tried to dodge when he sprang up to yank them from the sky and crash them into the earth.

It was odd.

In the past, slaying the puppets had felt like an intricate dance of life and death. As if each movements were calculated and designed to maximize the monster's abilities in a bid to end him.

But now, it felt sloppy. Each movement they made was delayed, not just because he could see how they'd move before they did so. They lagged. Stuttered. They operated with a level of coordination that was damn near insulting. Even the six-legged monsters seemed to struggle against him as he took out everything that got in his way.

It pissed him off.

This was the fight; it should've been his chance to drench the field in blood and prove himself to everyone.

Yet it was too easy.

More corpses piled around him as he weaved through the warring soldiers, alternating between chopping apart the flying imps and ending the lives of the hounds. Other monsters, ones with scales, boils, and flailing tendrils, died just as easily.

They all fell as harvest to his blade, dying pathetically.

Erec's anger grew.

Eventually, a worm surfaced—two of the Knights slammed into it, but after so much constant heavy fighting, they were slowing down.

He jumped at the stretched maw of the monster as it was turning to deal with the Knights pestering it. Erec slammed a hatchet into its face, wedging the weapon into bone as he locked his feet against its fleshy side.

It tried to throw him around, yet his grip remained firm on the weapon, anchoring him to the enemy. He pulled the wicked one-handed axe off his back with his free hand and got to work. Between him tearing apart the monster's face and the two other Knights slaughtering the rest of the monster, it went down easily. What had been a challenge that pushed him to his limits not too long ago turned into a simple fight.

And it confirmed something.

None of these monsters were giving anywhere near the level of challenge they should've. They went down easy, their movements lacking, far too slow to react.

The inferno burned inside, angered that he'd been denied the battle of his imagination. It left a concern. Unquestionably, they were far too easy, not that the soldiers made that distinction when faced with such an overwhelming horde and without Armor or the level of Virtues of the Knights. But the other Knights had to be noticing it too.

But why?

Was the Stag overwhelmed by pulling the strings of so many puppets at once?

How pathetic. To think it caused such a problem for everyone.

Erec tore through more, and more, letting out a laugh as the blood flowed. If it wouldn't give him the competition he wanted, then he'd satisfy the desire to unleash his hell by collecting tribute in corpses.

If the Stag wanted to sacrifice to him, then he'd let it.

— - ☣ - — - ☼ - — - ☣ - —

Hours ticked by. As much as Erec wanted to let the flame burn and consume him, the pushback from the enemy just didn't let him draw out the inner fire to utterly give himself away. Countless dead were left in his wake, but he had to take a breather after every hour. Then get back in action, then exhaust the flame inside once more.

Each time he ended up shaking among the corpses of his enemy, Jefferson seemed to hang near and cover for him to let him regain his strength when he faltered.

So he bounced between a state of Fury and a more levelheaded thought process. Each use stretched his body beyond its normal limits —yet he hadn't reached a breaking point.

It was hard to tell how many they slew. Yet the intractable number of them pressed in on the army.

The brief moments of clarity provided Erec with a bit of perspective; how much of a similar battlefield were the other legions facing? How many monsters could the Stag puppet at once?

Was this the limit of its strength? The last bid to stretch itself out to kill as many humans as it could in an act of spite before they wiped it from the planet? But there had to be more cunning to that monster. The more Erec thought over the problem, the less and less sense their current situation seemed to make.

Why would the Stag, a monster that appeared to pride itself on outwitting humankind, fold so easily in its last stand against them?

Then the reality of the situation sunk in. The entire strike squad sent to deal with the Rifts was failing to report back in. While the legions continued to struggle against an outpouring of more puppets, those that went in to kill the Stag went completely radio silent.

Master Knights sent to end the job were not responding to the calls on the radio.

Dame Robin gathered her Knights—one of whom was knocked out from a worm and sent back for emergency treatment.

"We've done all we can here." Dame Robin cleared her throat as she took in everyone. They were one and the same, tools of war still pumped full of adrenaline and pushing past exhaustion. "…But the fight isn't over. As I mentioned when calling you here, our people aren't reporting back as to what's going on near the Stag…"

She went quiet.

"We, among several other squads, will go in as reinforcements. I'm aware this is a bigger risk than we considered at first, but without knowing what happened to the Master Knights, we don't have a basis for how to respond and adapt."

There were no contests to that.

Everyone felt that fire—Fury or not. After seeing how this beast seemed hell-bent on killing the people around them, they had little recourse.

Dame Robin gave them a nod—and they followed her deeper into the pits of hell.

# CHAPTER 86
## HIDDEN IN HELL

*It is upon each of us to ask if there's a reason why we go on. With the world so twisted and filled with terror, our ancestors faced many dark days—some lived their lives without seeing the sun above.*

*When this question inevitably runs through my mind, I keep coming back to the same answer.*

*I go on for those that couldn't. I face evil for those that never saw it. I stare at the sun in memory of the people who never will, and never had.*

*This, I believe, is a duty to all Knights.*

*It is this that you never did understand, Alfon.*

*- Luisa Luculentus, correspondence with Alfon Nitidus (304, 3rd Era)*

Getting closer to the White Stag only meant more enemies swarming and getting in their way. Erec got to put his battle-axe to work on a new creature every few yards.

In short, it was glorious.

With the Knights at his side, they left a trail of corpses in their wake. Like a dream or, perhaps more aptly, a dark nightmare, a line of bodies marked their path to this point. As Dame Robin led them to their new target, these corpses would water the dry field of death with their lifeblood.

Erec laughed, dodging left from a beam of red light with enough force to slam a shoulder into a centipede-like puppet and cave into its exoskeleton. It tumbled away on a hundred legs as another Knight's sword dug into its head. "Right—" Jefferson pulled his sword free and jumped as the ground began to shake.

A massive worm tore from the ground, maw wide as it dived to swallow Erec.

Perfect.

Erec shoved with all of his might and flew past its razor-sharp teeth before they could tear into him, landing right into its insides with a swipe of his axe. Easy kill.

[Air supply activated.]

Even easier than last time, his axe cleaved through the creature as Knights hit it from the side. Before on the battlefield, it'd been frustrating. An overabundance of targets had amplified the puppet's lackluster combat. They didn't necessarily fight better now, but the higher concentration on him was better. He wanted their attention. He wanted them to come at him with more.

His Fury sang; the Knights around him only amplified its flames. They weren't thinking. Every Knight out there was another weapon. Extensions of death raging around him and showing off their skills.

They were strong. But he would be stronger.

The pulsating black insides of the worm flashed into light as Erec hacked a hole out of its side. Not even a moment in the sun again until a hound with massive fangs flew at him—Erec grabbed it by the throat and crushed the windpipe, lazily tossing the dying monster into the worm's torn stomach.

Let it have a last meal.

So many to kill. Erec grinned as he dodged past a red beam— seeing the flash of light a second before it existed. His fire tore through him, making his skin numb yet making him feel far more alive than ever before. His axe sliced, ripped, and murdered. Blood caked his Armor's joints, and his weapon's sharpness dulled from smashing apart bones too many times to count.

How had this power tired him out before?

He could keep going forever.

As long as the flame inside burned, this pace didn't need to end; each kill stoked it further, letting that hell grow and sear him out. Nothing on this Earth had a chance of taking him down.

They dug deeper into the wasteland, suffering their first loss from a worm biting a Knight in half. The man should've thought to launch himself into it, but he hesitated, so its powerful jaws crunched through his Armor like teeth through a cracker. Another suffered a direct hit from a light beam to his skull—from how he gurgled after and gasped for breath, he'd no doubt melted something important. Erec doubted the man would go on for much longer.

But the Knight fought to his last breath, collapsing a mile later.

Glorious.

In his name, Erec ripped out a massive eyeball from a flying monstrosity and let the puppet die a slow death. They'd taken casualties, sure. But how many had they killed?

The Silent Ones flung themselves about in heavy numbers, sure. But the striking forces sent out to deal with the Stag had a much larger number of stronger and more prepared Knights. Yet the fight kept going out. Were they too weak for the Stag? Was it possible they'd go all this way, killing so much, only to discover this to be their last march?

How beautiful. They'd run a gauntlet of death to face demise on the horns of a maddened Stag. There couldn't be anything better, right?

Something shifted in Erec's hell. A glimpse of a figure flashed in him, hiding away within the heat of the inferno a second later.

"More!" Erec yelled with glee, chopping apart another creature.

The limbs flew off like leaves from a tree—even the way their bodies seemed to flop apart, once severed. The different shades of scales oozed from wounds, spraying blood—it swirled together like paint. Each swipe of his axe was like a stroke on a canvas with a brush. If this were the last fight of his life, if by the end he ended up a corpse, then let it be a final moment of beauty. With this weapon, he'd fill his canvas with death and fire.

Fury could have him, fill him with Strength until he shattered like glass.

There wasn't a more fitting end.

[Whoa, Buckeroo. Your heart's racing far over what it should be capable of. Wow, you're off the charts! Applying sedatives—]

"No!" Erec screamed as he ripped a monster in half. Not with his axe. No, his limbs damn near burned with power. Enough to take apart its flimsy flesh. Until the Stag offered him better, he'd make a mockery of it.

Right until it faced him itself. The fucking coward.

[…Right, making the executive decision here. I'll be taking us down a notch—]

Erec looked to Robin even as he felt his veins strain. The drugs were lancing through him and burning away as Fury reacted against them. His fire knew what it needed to do—but if it was sparing attention to divert and burn away the toxins that would bring him away from this power, he just needed to convince the machine that it was wrong. That meant finding a situation where the threat was high enough that it had no choice but to let him go free.

As the power raged in him, he'd begun to glimpse something in that hell. Within the flames that spewed chaos, there was something more profound.

Something truly magnificent.

Right now, he felt closer to that than ever before. But…he needed to push further. If he wanted to find whatever lurked in that hell, that meant reaching the next level. The beast roared in him, but he knew that wasn't it. It was beneath his skin, killing to its heart's content. What was hiding?

"Robin!" Erec yelled, his voice hoarse from the screaming.

"Yeah?" she called back, effortlessly sliding between two flying beings—her arms crossing as thin metallic whips of liquid metal from her Armor halved them cleanly.

"Faster!" Erec almost growled—for the first time, his red-soaked vision didn't see the puppets in front of him. Those sacks of flesh that were so fun to pop and tear; no, he looked past them. They were a waste of time. Not an actual test of power. They wouldn't draw out what hid in hell even if there were a million.

"What?" Robin yelled back.

"Faster!" Erec screamed at her. She knew how. He'd seen her do it before. The rest of them might struggle to keep up, but he felt it. The Fury raging through him would let him push forward; all it took was ignoring these useless bags of flesh. They were pathetic puppets dancing around on a string. Amusing, but a cheap distraction from the real thing. It came with the clarity of a punch to his face.

"That's what we're trying to do—" she began to retort.

"Me! Follow me!" Erec yanked an eye puppet by the wings and forced it in front of him. All of his power went to his legs, and he began to leap forward. The puppet smeared across monsters as his living shield took the brunt of each hit and shoved aside whatever was stupid enough to get in his way.

Each jump took him further, tearing apart the next sack of flesh in front of him. When it wore away into a bloody stump, Erec yanked another unwilling living shield from the vast array of the enemy in front to choose from and kept up the charge. He didn't need to use the axe. Unlike before, he didn't take delight in the dying monsters. They were inconsequential. Their deaths were meaningless. There was only one thing worth hunting now. Only one creature could let him see the bottom of hell.

Erec charged across the remainder of the desert, brutally forcing an open pathway, with who-the-fuck-cared left following his destructive path through the enemy.

— - ☻ - — - ☼ - — - ☻ - —

Ahead was a rather disparate scene. Backdropped by the three Rifts lingering in the air was a solid line of humans fighting humans —all the while, a gallery of monsters exploded with electric charges at random intervals. Erec hardly paused as he threw the latest shield of dead monster flesh aside. The last quarter-mile was easy as the line of monsters thinned.

And he saw why.

More than half of the humans here were facing off against their side—as the White Stag looked on past its fence with crimson eyes.

Their strike force fighters turned on one another and struggled against themselves.

A Knight collapsed to the ground as another took off his head with their massive sword in a single stroke.

Further down the line, a Master Knight from the Crimson Lotus flung out binding glyph after binding glyph. They tried to lob spells at the Stag, but the spells broke apart. Whenever magic got too close to the fence, a monster in the background exploded like a liquid firework. A moment later, the bindings fell apart, and the puppets ran free to harass the Master Knight again.

Erec paused, trying to pick the quickest route past the Knight line and to the Stag.

A Knight sprouted wings, shooting above the enemies, having the same idea and trying to get within melee range of the Stag.

They flew past the fence separating them from the White Stag and Rifts, only for three monsters to explode in viscera of energy and gore. The Knight's wings gave out a second after the monster's sacrifice, and they slammed into the ground.

Not long after, the Knight got to their feet and turned back to face the rest of the Knights—moving with that same jerky trademark of a puppet being controlled.

[...Proximity? Each explosion generates radio waves, and that Stag is somehow condensing them and then targeting them directly at people, or using it to interfere with your "spells."]

Pathetic. Even with fighting so close to it, that weak creature didn't dare to take a step and bloody its pristine white hide.

*I'll turn it red.*

Erec took a step toward the fence. From the corner of his eye, he saw a ghost of a blade flying his way; his body was already reacting, but the puppet was too quick. It'd score a hit.

"No!" Bedwyr's voice called, his brother flashing into view, his massive blade deflecting the oncoming strike. "Erec?! How are you—"

The puppet swung at Bedwyr, only for his brother to catch the weapon again, a storm of ringing metal. He matched each swing yet didn't have the speed to buy himself time to launch a counter-attack.

Dull.

Erec strode forward, taking a blade to his shoulder—it bit through the steel and made him taste genuine pain for a split second before his Fury burned it away. That annoying machine gave up its attempts to subdue him during the charge of using a monster shield.

It'd given up.

Which was for the best. They'd find what hid in hell, and to do that, Erec would gladly take this blow.

It bought him an opening.

His hand smashed into the Knight Protector's helmet—caving it in and knocking the person onto the ground; his enemy twitched. Dying or living, Erec couldn't tell or care. They wouldn't be getting up any time soon.

"Erec—you might've just killed—"

"Stag," Erec growled.

How had he ever thought of Bedwyr as strong? Bedwyr was afraid. Of death, of life, of the truth.

Erec walked to the fence. If the Stag kept trying to hide from his challenge behind more puppets, he'd take their blows and end them.

All that mattered was getting to that coward pulling the strings. For that, he'd pay any price.

# CHAPTER 87
# COMET

Erec took another step toward the fence—more Knights flew at him. Bedwyr fended off one, yet two more were intent on getting in his way and blocking progress.

These puppets weren't worth his attention. Erec caught a sword with his axe, then shoved his shoulder into the enemy to knock them back into the second Knight. They stumbled together, yet that wasn't the point of this attack. He saw their ghosts. Tracked their movements before they even began. The clever ploy to lure him into an attack was belittled as he saw the flash of another Knight closing in from his side.

The foolish Stag hadn't predicted he'd be able to attack and defend simultaneously.

Erec yanked one of the men from their position, slamming them into the Knight headed his way—letting them take a sword to the side as he bashed the new attacker's helmet with a quick axe chop.

Easy.

So easy.

The fire burned brighter as he launched a kick at his remaining opponent, sending the bastard careening into more Knights ahead.

His fire swelled; the inferno consumed. A pit of magma twisted in his veins as a wild smile corrupted his face beneath his helmet. Even his eyes burned. There wasn't time to blink, not as he tracked every single ghost ahead of him. Searching.

Somewhere in that mess was the way past all of this fodder. They might've been great Knights in their own right, but now that they were under the control of the Stag, they hardly counted.

It wasted their potential, used them lazily and with disdain like a toddler throwing around toys it no longer cared for. An utter waste of what might've been an otherwise worthwhile fight. Still, he had to admit, their speed and unnatural coordination made it damn near impossible to see an easy way through.

That meant he was going to have to pick the most straightforward option. Fight his way past.

To his side, Bedwyr finished his scuffle, cleanly knocking out the Knight Protector with the flat of his massive blade.

His brother still insisted on pulling punches, even at this junction.

What did it matter? They'd all die anyway. Erec just wanted to tear off the Stag's horns before he did.

Erec began to run forward. The puppets ahead swarmed, bracing to reinforce his breakthrough point. Perfect. They'd throw might against might—he'd pull more of that hell out, let it burn him whole, and once he emerged on the other side, he'd take the Stag with him in one glorious pile of refuse.

A second before he reached the defensive line, he saw an alarm—VAL flashed a warning to make him pause, not even bothering with the words. Erec backpedaled, trusting the machine as an extension of himself. Why shouldn't he? When used how it should be, it was little more than a complicated sword or axe; instead of using a sharp edge to kill, it used numbers and logic.

He saw VAL's point an instant later.

The ground before him shook, then vanished. A pit appeared out of nowhere and dragged down the plethora of Knights that had moved to stand in his way.

Dame Robin flew at his side, metal rippling off her and making a narrow pathway over the pit; she shoved him forward. "Lead the way!" the woman called, and Erec didn't need anything else.

He ran over the path, watching the puppets below struggle to clamber out—at the sides of the pit, what was left of the actual Knights put up their resistance in a sudden flurry, pressing back against the tide of puppets that desperately fought to repel this assault. Behind him, Erec heard steel clang against the pathway. They hadn't let him go through this charge alone; whether his burning desire to break through had infected them or they were trying to stop him didn't matter.

Erec ran over the pit and ripped a hole through the fence.

It was so simple. The metal bent and tore away beneath his steel fingers. Like it wanted him to break through.

The Stag stared at him as he closed the distance—the light from the Rifts behind it bled into its shape and colors, twisting and distorting its image as it seared its hate outward.

Erec let his hate for the monster burn back. With everything he could muster, Erec threw his body forward by springing all his strength into his calves.

Ahead of him, five of the monsters popped like balloons.

Black flooded his vision.

— - ☻ - — - ☼ - — - ☻ - —

Fire swirled around Erec, and the oppressive heat burned his skin, threatening to melt it away and turn him to ash. Each moment that passed was blissful agony as his very soul burned.

This was it, then. Judgment.

"About time," Erec growled through clenched teeth.

That bitch had finally come to take him away. Hell should've been torture, yet he only felt relief, though a bit peeved at his performance; he wanted to end it with the Stag. Those last hours had been something special, though. They had been more full of what life meant than anything that came before—a pure expression of survival and rage.

Life was meant to be lived like a comet soaring across the sky, burning itself away before crashing into the earth.

Erec gripped his head as the flames began to die around him—their soothing pain smoldering and withdrawing as a wind swept through and tore them away, and the radiant heat of judgment faded.

And left a cold nothing in its wake.

In it, the Stag finally appeared for what it was. Not a bold white-coated monster of beauty, but a massive horrible cold intellect—ahead of him, Erec saw the psionic mind of the beast. Its true form was a swirling muddy lake of crimson with a bottomless depth. From deep within came an occasional pulse of evil red.

Drowned beneath the still lake surface were tens of thousands of monsters, their eyes closed, drifting along with a few humans. Some of them struggled, suddenly erupting into spasms of movement as they got close to the surface of the tranquil lake. When they acted up, a thousand tendrils appeared below to drag them away from freedom. They'd drown again and again.

It'd extinguished Erec's flames, and as he watched with a still horror, a tendril rose slowly out of the water, lazily heading for him.

Once it caught him, it'd pull him in and drown him beneath the surface like the rest.

Where the Goddess burned, the Stag drowned.

Erec tried to run, get his legs moving, and did his best to scream for help. But his tongue failed to work. His legs felt like jelly. And that tendril of dark crimson pulsed as if laughing at his feeble attempts.

He'd be the Stag's forevermore.

*No.*

Erec's fingers twitched. Heat burned through him; the tendril paused and hung inches in front of his eyes.

*Burn.*

Silver flames sprang from his fingertips. Fire spouted around the lake, and the tendril rushed forward to force its way into his mouth and drown him where he stood.

It touched his lips and evaporated; his skin erupted in a hostile silver fire. His hand clenched, Erec took a step toward the lake, eyes wild. He saw the hell inside of himself. This wasn't anything compared to that, this stilted attempt at control and horrifying tranquility. It was a pale excuse for an afterlife.

Hell burned, tormented, and scorched. Within its depths was chaos incarnate. Within it was war.

The whole lake of blood shrieked, and Erec's mind was yanked away as he reached its bank.

— -✿ - — - ☼ - — - ✿ - —

Erec stumbled forward; a second or two passed, yet it felt like an hour. The Stag stared at him, rising on its hind legs with concern as Erec caught himself.

With a laugh, Erec took another step toward it. There wasn't hate radiating from his prey. No, it was pure fear. The pathetic thing was *afraid*. He'd give it something to fear.

He'd hunt it down, rip its antler off, and stab the monstrosity through the throat with them—

A dozen monsters popped with an explosion of electricity.

The world vanished away.

— -❂- — - ☼ - — -❂- —

Erec found himself knee-deep in the red lake, hands rising from its crimson surface, trying to grab him before he could react and pull him down. It thought to catch him by surprise and take him before he could respond.

A ripple of silver flame burst out from him in a wave as that hate burned him away. There wasn't anything for this pathetic eldritch monster to grasp onto. No mind for it to take and drown. No, everything he was burned with an intensity that it couldn't stand.

Erec saw Her in the inferno. Saw Her hate and contempt. It dwarfed anything he had felt before; that pure and unadulterated desire to conquer. The Goddess was destruction.

And She'd burned Her way through his very soul.

The psychic plane burned away as the lake of blood began to evaporate from his fire.

— -❂- — - ☼ - — -❂- —

Erec caught himself from another stumble. A few feet closer to his prey. The White Stag was swaying in its spot, standing high and looking for an escape route. Even if it'd done a fine job using humans as living shields, it'd trapped itself. No matter where it ran, eventually, it'd run into humans. Into more Knights.

But the assumption it could run away from Erec was incorrect.

It was going to die here and now.

Erec sprinted at it, a hand outstretched toward the monstrosity. His fingers burned with a coat of horrible silver flame.

A hundred monsters exploded in a horrible bloody pop around him as he sped by.

Erec's mind was yanked away for but a moment; before returning to reality a second later. More monsters exploded. Each time it pulled his mind away, the time it took to burn through its grasp on him dropped as he sped along.

He was going to grab the Stag and drag it into his hell.

The Stag began to run, leaping past the fence, but Erec chased it as a streaking comet of silver flames. His hand stretched for the White Stag's back, an indicator that promised death.

As the battle faded from around them, the world condensed to a primal scene, one so common to humankind's history.

Hunter versus prey.

# CHAPTER 88
## SOUL

*If, on the other hand, these are independent goods, then we shall require that the account of the goodness be the same clearly in all, just as that of the whiteness is in snow and white lead. But how stands the fact? Why of honour and wisdom and pleasure the accounts are distinct and different in so far as they are good. The Chief Good then is not something common, and after one ἰδέα.*

*But then, how does the name come to be common (for it is not seemingly a case of fortuitous equivocation)? Are different individual things called good by virtue of being from one source, or all conducing to one end, or rather by way of analogy, for that intellect is to the soul as sight to the body, and so on?*

*- Aristotle,* The Nicomachean Ethics *(384-322, 1st Era)*

The Stag ran, and ran, and ran. Its lanky legs bounded over the earth in a desperate bid to flee from Erec. Without consideration, it barreled past the humans, tearing through those puppeted by it. It didn't distinguish between foe and ally; any in its way were flung by antlers.

Some took shots at the Stag; glyphs erupted in fire and lightning, slamming into the monster's sides and scoring hits now that its defenses were removed. But it was too sudden, and they weren't prepared. The damage wasn't substantial enough to stop it, and the

Stag ran by. It threw everything it had into the flight, its hate and logic dissolved into pure fear as nature took its course.

Erec sped after it, never losing sight of his target. Each step brought him an inch closer. Nobody else could stick to its tail like he could; none of the Stag's puppets were in a position to stop him.

Which was fine; Erec didn't need anyone else.

Fire bled off him. His body burned with a silver flame that spewed from his core and enveloped his Armor like a second skin. Inside, he felt as if he'd thrown himself into a sun. His skin burned, and a scream left his lips as he pushed across the wasteland, yet it was worth it. Every step carved small holes in the wasteland as he flung himself across the earth.

He was like a comet, burning his way over the planet before he crashed.

In minutes he caught up to his prey. Erec barreled into the Stag's side and knocked the creature over.

It tumbled across the ground, silver flames flickering and catching on the white coat—burning, yet not turning its hide to ash. Erec took to his feet immediately, just in time to dodge a desperate attempt by the Stag to gore him with its antler.

At long last, the pathetic creature turned to a direct fight.

Erec's hand snapped out and caught the antler before the White Stag could rear back.

It tugged yet couldn't break free from his grasp. Heat burned off Erec like a furnace; he felt his muscles coil and spasm as an unrelenting flood of Strength passed through him. It seared his veins and left behind a damn near limitless power. Whatever the cost of this was, he'd pay it. Twice over, even. Nothing could take him down, and nothing would stop him from doing what needed to be done.

Erec yanked the Stag's antler, yelling as he put everything into it.

The Stag's head pulled toward him as its legs gave out due to unsteady footing. Right as it got close enough, Erec's right foot snapped out and planted on the thing's skull. Dazing it. But also giving him the leverage he needed.

Shock radiated outward from the creature—tainted by begging. But it was far too late for the Stag to get peace.

Erec pressed his boot firmly against the monster's skull and tightened his grip on the antler. He twisted with his hips and back in one swift movement and pulled with every ounce of his Strength.

There was a crack.

Pained psychic screaming tore from the Stag; it was a Goddess-awful eldritch noise begging him to stop.

Erec didn't. More cracking. There.

It snapped. An antler broke free from the monster's head right at that moment, and Erec's body screamed at him in protest. Erec pulled back his foot and gave a quick kick to the monster that dislocated its jaw; it stumbled back, blood leaking from where his boot had torn into its skin and hide.

It bled red, just like all the people it'd loved killing.

Erec flipped the antler around in his hands, then rushed the stunned Stag.

The tine of his new weapon dug easily into the monster's side; the antlers were far sharper than they'd any right to be. With ease, he jammed the weapon into its ribs, then twisted, catching against the bone inside. A psychic scream rippled out from the Stag—it tried to tear his mind out of his head and flay him alive.

Erec held steady even as a river of blood ran down from his nose.

Not for a second would he lose sight of the goal. Erec kept twisting the antler, digging deeper into the beast's insides.

In response, it struggled and kicked. One of the flailing legs smashed into Erec's shoulder and broke his Armor—along with the bone beneath, yet the pain faded in an instant. Taken away by his Fury.

Silver flame trickled down the antler into his enemy—seeping into the Stag's wounds and burning it away from the inside, even if its flesh didn't seem to blister or melt away. The Stag struggled against him, yet they both knew it was futile. Unless something could remove Erec, all he had to do was dig the weapon deeper and deeper.

Blood gushed from the White Stag's wound, tainting its pure white coat a far more beautiful crimson.

A minute later, the fighting died off. The Stag's movements slowed and grew lethargic as its breath labored. What had been a knife stabbing again and again into Erec's head faded into a whimper before vanishing.

The Stag stopped breathing and went limp.

Erec held the antler in place, his limbs shaking. He leaned against the makeshift weapon, using it to support himself.

Beneath his helmet, his blood caked his face.

Black dots danced in his vision as the silver flames caught and burned the monster below. Not that it actually "burned." No visual damage had been wrought, yet the glow of the fire had a sinister, almost transcendent quality to it. Whatever it was doing had to be worse.

Perhaps it was burning whatever was left of the monster as it died.

[…Was it worth it?]

"Fun." Erec let out a barking laugh, looking at his hands. They'd have been shaking were they not desperately holding onto the antler.

How many things had he killed today?

Still, he'd reached the prize in the end and claimed the biggest hunt of the day for himself. Pride tore through him—the feeling as hot as the hell that scorched out his insides. But it was temporary.

Hell was going to leave him soon.

And when it left, he'd be a scorched-out husk.

[It tried to scramble your brain at the end. I did my best to protect it, but you're lucky I had your synapses mapped out ahead of this battle. Though I'm… Well, not to be the bringer of bad news, but when you come down this time, I'm not very optimistic about your chances at making it.]

That would've normally been sobering, terrifying, even. But staring at the dead Stag beneath him, Erec felt peace.

If this opponent were strong enough to bring his death, it'd also earned its kill.

Erec stepped away from the corpse, his legs shaking as the inferno inside sputtered out. It knew it was done.

And so did he.

Erec sank to his knees ten feet away. A host of Knights were starting to gather at the scene—dead silent as they stared at the defeated Cataclysm-Level threat and the Knight Initiate that had slain it. Erec's eyes felt heavy as more blood poured out of him—but he held his chin up. Stared directly at the people in front of him.

Bedwyr ran to him, the giant sword recognizable anywhere. His brother's Armor was substantially dented, with rends and tears in key places and a healthy coating of blood.

"Erec, what did you do?" Bedwyr asked.

"Won," Erec put simply, his thoughts starting to go hazy as the fire burned out. As his body felt like it was breaking apart from the inside. He could hear his heart. Loud. Too loud. Soon it would struggle to beat at all, he was sure.

"Can you stand?" Bedwyr dropped down next to him, setting a hand on Erec's shoulder. "Let's get you to some help—"

"Do what you will," Erec replied, his head raising upward. He fought against the darkness, at the desire to let it sink. To allow himself to fall into the ground and never return. There was plenty of time for that in a minute or two. "It was a good ride, Bedwyr. Try to find happiness, alright?"

He wanted to look at the sky.

Deep and blue. Limitless. A damn near eternity of beauty—but beyond that pale blue, he knew what rested above. He had seen it clearly in that vision VAL showed him. Each time he looked up at it since, he recalled that view. Millions of stars, all of them burning away above. What he'd give for that sight again.

"Erec—"

Erec fell over, face slamming against the dirt.

"Hang on! Someone help!" Bedwyr began to yell.

His heart weakened, the beating cutting off as it struggled to pump blood. Without Fury's fuel, his head felt as if it'd been gouged out with a spoon. Erec coughed up blood as his eyes honed in on the blinking notification in the corner of his vision. With everything else blurry, the Blessing was the only thing he could focus on.

If it was going to end…

Why not see what his last bout of glory had earned?

The notification appeared an instant later, even as Erec felt himself slipping away.

**Strength Advancement: Rank D - Tier 2 → Rank D - Tier 5**
**Vigor Advancement: Rank E - Tier 4 → Rank E - Tier 6**
**Agility Advancement: Rank E - Tier 3 → Rank E - Tier 4**
**Perception Advancement: Rank E - Tier 4 → Rank E - Tier 5**
**Psyche Advancement: Rank E - Tier 2 → Rank E - Tier 5**

Erec's body shook as he failed to laugh. Such a massive gain; all he had to do to earn it was give up his life.

Blackness crept in, along with shivering cold.

Alone.

So alone.

— -❦ - — - ☼ - — - ❦ - —

She sat upon Her silver throne; a sword was resting against its side. Within Her eyes was reflected an unknown universe. As they passed over him, there was nothing but apathy.

Until he amounted to something worthy to contend against Her, he was beneath Her. As were all She'd come across in Her travels. Little stood at the pinnacle of existence in the way She did.

How had he found his way to Her court? She asked that of every one of these playthings blessed by Her fire.

A Stag? One that'd declared Her an enemy?

She had too many enemies to count; what was a small Stag worth? Let alone the weak human who'd slain it.

Was it a worthy fight, at least? Even though She barely cared, it was the typical question She sought to ask. One that determined what came next. From how he described it, it had been at least a glorious battle.

These were the only things She concerned herself with as Her eyes saw into Erec's soul. But there was more there—the burns of a flame, but not scorched by Her.

He'd scorched his soul by his own doing—a different fire.

She tilted Her head.

A thing worth a little attention. More than a pathetic Stag. His soul was a seared thing now, but not devastated. Not incinerated. Nowhere near powerful enough to be worth proper consideration, were it not burned. She made it clear this wasn't a Blessing She'd chosen now to give. No. Simply a command so that She may see if something more worthy came of it. Her hand reached out and coated him in Her silver flames.

**So Be It, Live.**

# CHAPTER 89
## RECOVERY

ive! Damn it!]

Erec's body convulsed—he took a deep breath. His lungs stung from the reflexive effort; the world around felt surreal. As if he didn't quite belong to it. Not to mention his head was an absolute mess, and his chest felt like it'd been caved in.

"Fuck…" Erec said with a numb tongue; it was like a piece of clay in his mouth.

[Don't do a thing! Just sit there and stay alive this time—after this, we're going to have a long hard talk about *limitations*. I've never met such a foolish employee. Honestly, you're a fleshy creature; why do you get such dumb thoughts in your head?]

Erec bit his tongue, trying to talk back, then gave up. It was impossible to focus on anything going on around him properly; even though he made out movements, everything was a blur. Wherever they'd put him, nothing made much sense, and all of it had a dim, muted feel.

Without a battle to fight, and knowing in his heart it was time to be at ease, Erec let go.

There were times to rest. He'd fought the White Stag without regard to the cost and pulled through by some miracle. It was time to rest and recover.

But that image of the Goddess haunted him. It'd seemed real—but given his state, it may very well have been a hallucination.

Erec forced his mind away from it; what little sense he could make of what he'd seen and experienced was confused with the damage to his head.

With nothing to do and unable to move his body, he eventually pulled up his Virtues.

**Name: Erec of House Audentia**
**Health: 3%  |  Mana: 100%  |  Stamina: 7%**

**Holy Virtues:**
**Strength: [Rank D]  |  [Tier 5]**
**Vigor: [Rank E]  |  [Tier 6]**
**Agility: [Rank E]  |  [Tier 4]**
**Perception: [Rank E]  |  [Tier 5]**
**Cognition: [Rank E]  |  [Tier 4]**
**Psyche: [Rank E]  |  [Tier 5]**
**Mysticism: [Rank F]  |  [Tier 1]**
**Faith: <NULL>**

**Divine Talents:**
**Fury**

Erec's eyes scanned the words, but they made no sense—his head swam as he stared at the Faith Virtue.

Gone. A weird status replaced his previously pitiful rank of F Tier 1. No matter how he looked at it, the change made no sense. He hadn't heard of such a thing occurring before, and a cold shock of fear ran down his spine.

Was he forsaken?

He stared at the status for a long time, trying to divine a meaning from a thing that had no apparent connection or explanation. He couldn't ask VAL about it, since the machine would have no better clue of what it meant than himself, even if he managed to form the words correctly. Goddess knew this wasn't a thing to ask the Church about.

Terrifying.

At some point, the scenery around him shifted. They'd tossed him in a steel wagon that was making its way across the desert. With the hunt ended, they'd be heading home. Surely.

Maybe there, he might understand what this meant and what it changed.

— -☢- — - ☼ - — - ☢- —

It took two weeks to walk again; all of his time was left in the care of priests, who kept giving him odd looks. After about a week, and thanks to VAL supplementing his healing, he could finally track conversations and talk with people—but none of his friends visited. No one did.

Not even Boldwick made an appearance. He was stuck with a load of priests tending to his recovery in a sterile temple room.

Combined with the worry about his missing Virtue, paranoia and wrongness colored his thoughts. Were they studying him? Trying to get a feel of what was wrong with him? Would they toss him out of the Kingdom if they discovered that his Faith Virtue was gone? Blasphemy and issues the Church found with people varied wildly, and it didn't take much imagination to guess how they might react to that information.

Once he felt the ability to get to his feet again—Erec didn't hesitate. He picked himself up off the cot and made his way to the exit.

Predictably, one of the priests headed him off.

"Back to your bed," she commanded, a stern warning in her tone.

"I'm better now; I wanna get some fresh air," Erec contested, puffing his chest up and making himself appear healthier than he was.

"That is an order," she responded.

Erec considered his options. Then he got angry—that fire flared in him. How dare she give him a command? She wasn't a Knight; she wasn't associated with any Order and certainly wasn't above him. What right did she have to tell him what to do? Until someone with that authority came and told him he had to stay, there was no reason to listen to what these priests said.

The hate sparked, ready to ignite. She was asking him to challenge her and show her the Knight who'd slain more monsters than she'd likely ever seen in her cozy behind-the-wall existence.

Erec's fist balled up.

She tensed, sensing that he was about to erupt and make good on his reputation of being the Mad Knight. As well she should have, daring to risk his wrath. Today was a day for her to learn a lesson.

Erec gritted his teeth but then stopped. This wasn't the way forward. This path had led to his death twice now. If he were to keep blindly pursuing the same strategy—then sooner or later, his luck would run out.

His fist unclenched, and he exhaled deeply.

The priest shifted, looking surprised at the sudden change on his face.

"Do you happen to know of a priest named Gregory?" Erec tried, catching the woman further off guard. The questions disarmed her as she looked left and right afterward.

"I do, a very kind man—the clergy is rather well acquainted with one another up here on the surface..." she trailed off, unsure of what he was driving at.

"If I can't leave, could you do me a favor? Get Gregory here; I'd like to catch up. I won't make any trouble if you do." Erec met her eyes, taking in the woman's silver irises. She gave him a slow nod, and they had an understanding. Without much else to go on, Erec returned to his bed.

Better to recover for longer. Particularly if this would end with him being tossed out of the Kingdom.

— -✦ - — - ☼ - — - ✦ - —

"They cannot see the flickers of your soul," Gregory said hesitantly, setting a hand on Erec's shoulder. "Neither can I—normally, it burns with the Goddess's fire, making it visible to our eyes when we use our prayer to heal, yet yours isn't present."

"And so they're holding me here because of that?" Erec asked, shaking his head. Gregory appeared to be doing well for himself, but that didn't do much to change his current situation. The best Erec could manage was to suppress his anger and keep himself in check, but his nerves about everything weren't making things better.

But Gregory had confirmed his worst fear.

The Church knew something was wrong with him now.

"Aye, if they could, they'd subject you to a more thorough examination. As it is, they're getting pushback from your Order and the Kingdom itself. It seems the Royal Family wants to properly reward you for slaying the Stag."

Erec glanced at the door—three priests were talking to one another and looking at him and Gregory.

Obviously, the man shouldn't have been telling him this much about the situation, but Gregory had also covered for their gun use. Not all of the priests were in lockstep with what the Church wanted.

"So, what do you suggest?" Erec asked.

"My advice? Keep quiet. Be polite, but don't give in to any of their requests. I'll make some discreet confirmations to the people in your Order about your health. Right now, the Church is using the excuse of you being injured to not allow you to walk free. We'll shed some light on that and let nature take its course."

"Thank you." Erec nodded slowly. It'd been right to ask for Gregory. As long as he gave nothing away to these priests, he'd walk free.

All he had to do was hide that his Faith Virtue had gone terribly wrong.

"By the way, you should be prepared for things to move very quickly when you're out—it might be like your life has been on pause. But things haven't slowed in the Kingdom. I expect you to be summoned to the Royal Court almost immediately. Plenty of the nobility are curious about the Initiate that slew a Cataclysm-Level threat, and the Royal Family is eager to reward you for your service."

"I—" Yeah, that'd been one of the last things on his mind coming into this conversation. He wanted to see Bedwyr, talk to his friends, and see what Boldwick had to say to him.

Worrying about appearing in the highest court in the Kingdom to accept a reward wasn't on his list of things to do. And so, he didn't know what to think about it.

"I'll keep it in mind."

Gregory squeezed his shoulder and nodded. "You've done well, lad. Keep it together for a little while, and you'll be out of here."

With that, Gregory left. Just a couple more days of keeping himself subdued. *I can do that.*

# CHAPTER 90
# KNIGHT TRIUMPHANT

*Sir Boldwick has shown himself as a brave and integral part of our efforts in the field on countless expeditions. I cannot help but admire his dedication to fighting, though, at times, I wonder if he takes too much risk on himself to minimize it for those around him.*

*Regardless, this compassion and sense of responsibility make me highly confident in my suggestion that he be promoted.*

*I see no more fitting transition for such a promising youth than an opportunity to show his capabilities with more leadership as a Knight Lieutenant.*

*- Dame Nova, Recommendation (292, 3rd Era)*

Gregory hadn't lied about things shifting quickly once they started.

The following days went from a dull lull of Erec ignoring and brushing off the paranoid priests to suddenly getting shoved out of the temple. In less than a minute, he was in Boldwick's welcoming arms. The man pulled him into a firm bear hug, then withdrew. With a nod at the door, he started walking.

Boldwick guided and pushed him along—it was odd seeing the Master Knight out of his Armor after so long in the field together. Erec hadn't seen his own Armor since waking up, but VAL assured him it was being taken care of. It was hard to worry about its safety when it housed a machine smarter than any engineer fixing it.

"Move quick, don't look back," Boldwick said out of the corner of his mouth, and Erec did just that.

They rushed past the pillars of the Church, even past the Cardinal, who tried to stop them for a brief chat. Boldwick mostly ignored the man and led Erec away after shooting him a glare that would make a monster shiver. Which Erec had no problem with; his tolerance for the Church was at an all-time low, and the prodding into what was wrong with him only made him more paranoid.

He figured that Boldwick would take him back to the Academy, and there he'd have some time to get his bearings and figure out what came next.

It became apparent very rapidly that they weren't heading in the right direction to go to the Academy.

"You did well keeping your composure," Boldwick said casually, even as they tore through the city. Few people gave them looks, despite them being Knights. Were the two of them to wear their Armor, they would've gotten attention—but out here in their casual clothes, they looked just the same as anyone.

Therefore not worth the attention, which was a welcome relief after being constantly watched by priests for so long.

"It wasn't easy," Erec admitted, but given his last exposure to Fury, straying too close to that line was an unpleasant sensation. Anytime those flickers of a fire stirred in him, he tried to kill them. It was a terrifying reminder of the penalties of how far he could push himself. Erec felt scared of slipping down the path of not caring again for what would likely be the last time.

What he feared the most was that some part of him kept giving complete control to Fury. There was a part of him willing to dismiss the risk to his life for that all-consuming rush of power that came with it. He had to change or die.

"No, I don't think it would be. The bastards kept you squirreled away and lied through their teeth to try to figure out whatever it was that they wanted. To be treated like that after slaying the Stag? Absurd. But, in the long run, it'll work to our benefit; they cost themselves capital contesting our expedition and the fallout afterward." Boldwick paused, pulling Erec to a stop. He gave him a sloppy grin.

"By the way, excellent work. Didn't think I'd ever pull someone under my wing capable of a feat like that, but I have to say, you really fucked yourself now. How do you ever plan to outdo that?"

Erec let out a bit of nervous laughter, feeling uncomfortable with the genuine amazement in Boldwick's tone. Sure, it was undercut by the joke—but he hadn't set out for fame.

"I'll just have to try my best."

"I couldn't ask more from you, and I know you will. But do you remember what I first said?" Boldwick broke the smile, his face clouding over.

"Not exactly. I think you called out Colin for being a jerk?"

"That was part of it, but not the important bit. Don't be a hero, Erec. What you did was risky—and you probably know more than anyone how close you came to being a corpse. You pulled through this time, but the next time—it'll be harder to resist. People will call you a hero, give you a title, and start putting their expectations on you. Never let that influence you and make you make the same bone-headed mistake you made to take on the Stag on your own. Do you understand me?"

He didn't. Not really. The tone shift was unnerving, as if something sprang up deep inside Boldwick. There was a heavy frown on his face, and his eyes seemed to look far into the past. Did he see ghosts there?

"Don't worry; I don't intend to listen to any of those stuck-up—"

"Good, good." Boldwick clapped him on the back, quickly pivoting away from the heavy topic. Too abrupt to be natural. "Damn, good work, Erec. Damn good. Better than most. Lucky its grip didn't affect you with your Talent—like you were made to slaughter the damn thing."

"The Goddess works in strange ways," Erec said with a bitter taste on his tongue. "Where are we heading, anyway?"

"About that; we're going right to the palace. Sorry kid, no time to rest. Your courtly admirers are calling."

"Ah, fuck."

— -✵ - — - ☼ - — - ✵ - —

The palace was, in short, breathtaking. Over centuries, the various parts of the palace had evolved to represent the generations of rulers humanity had shifted through—rumor had it that the lowest levels of the royal household included pieces left over from the original vault humanity had found and used to survive.

But the vast levels ranged deep. He didn't have the chance to dive within its gilded and historic walls this time. Most visitors were limited to the surface. It had plenty to look at, even though it was all modern.

That wasn't to say the Royal Family neglected the past on the surface level—they still had sculptures of heroes that put those within the Academy to shame. Even enshrined weapons from those very same heroes were designated historical artifacts. There wasn't much time to stand around and admire the beauty. Boldwick and the palace escort rushed him through—only to bring him to an honest-to-Goddess guest room.

The first thing he noticed was a full outfit, entirely in style for current court trends, splayed out on the bed.

Erec hated that he knew that and despised even more what it meant.

Boldwick gave the place a slow look. "Get changed; they'll send a servant to escort you to the feast—your next two days will look like this, with plenty of royal Houses prying into you and seeing whether or not you'll make a good ally to them. Love it or hate it, this is part of being a Knight too. Though, not often…this elaborate. After they're done with you and have their little show for everyone else to see, we'll drag you back to Academy and start preparing for the future."

"I see, so this is…mandatory? Not just a single event? Days?"

"Well, yeah, they can't exactly let you go and kill a Cataclysm-Level monster they sent a whole hunt for and ignore it. Got to pay proper honors to the occasion. Imagine the look on the nobility's face if they didn't. Accept whatever they give you, and bumble your way through it with whatever grace you can muster."

Erec rubbed the back of his head and sighed.

"What, feeling shy?"

"Just…tired, already. Two days of this? Really?"

"Uh-huh. Liven yourself up. It might not feel like it, but this sort of thing should be easier than throwing your life on the line against monsters. You'll find that with time, it's better to find whatever enjoyment you can since you don't get a choice. I did do you a favor, though. It might make it a little easier on you." Boldwick shot him a grin.

"What?" Erec couldn't picture any way it might get a bit better.

"Got an invitation to your friend. Garin should be by shortly. I imagine he might make it a little more tolerable for you. That, and due to your low Courtly Manners scores, our Order felt concerned about how you might represent us in the highest court in the land. We don't wanna take that big of a risk."

"Oh, thank the Goddess," Erec muttered, not particularly feeling like thanking Her. Yet the gratitude slipped out. An annoying habit.

She wasn't someone worth thanking.

"That's the spirit. I'll see you down in the festivities. Keep your head a little longer. Then you'll be back in a place where you can concentrate on preparing for our expedition." With that, Boldwick left him to his own devices.

Erec took a long look at the jacket and pants on the bed and shook his head. There was an open window to the balcony, so he went there instead of getting ready. He was a couple of stories up. The view showed off the royal garden and gave a nice cutaway of the King-dom's surface. Smoke drifted from hundreds of chimneys, and in the far distance was the giant steel curtain that surrounded this bastion of humanity.

Somewhere out there, he knew now, were more humans. It was hard to picture what their lives might be like. Whether or not they were better off than them, or whether those people were hidden away in the depths of the earth, afraid to reach the surface. Like they had been for generations.

The Church proclaimed them as sinners, people cast away by the Goddess, and not worth redemption. That was primarily what they labeled their exiles as too, but now...

Erec had difficulty believing the Goddess cared if people showed Her worship or if they lived within the Kingdom. He doubted She cared much at all what humans did until they showed themselves as having enough power to catch Her interest.

After a long moment of gazing at the tiny people going about their day, he returned to his room and the outfit left for him. Time to dine in hell, he supposed.

# CHAPTER 91
## AUDACIOUS

Erec tugged at the uncomfortable ruffles around his sleeves—the silk dress shirt was light and airy yet confining and uncomfortable. The jacket, of course, in tradition with current high fashion, lacked sleeves—and the done-up collar was ornate and obnoxious.

The exact sort of thing Garin might wear, only more expensive.

The greatest tragedy of this outrageous outfit was in the unquestionable prohibitive cost. That made moving around in it, and the prospect of attending a *feast* of all things wearing it, stressful.

Sure, maybe they were honoring him, but the idea of ruining silk worth about as much as his house was terrifying. A thousand times over, he'd rather have slinked back home and borrowed his father's jacket—or better, used his Academy formals. But that wasn't an option.

[Well, don't you look suave. Real charmer, Buckeroo. You'll drive people crazy.]

"Sure…" Erec kept staring in the mirror—his eyes had dark lines around them, and as he felt his rising anxiety and annoyance at the impending social gathering, he could've sworn he saw flickers of a red stir in their depths.

It had to have been in his imagination, triggered by what Olivia had said about his eyes. Though he imagined when he was fully enthralled with power, he did make a terrifying sight.

There was a knock on the door.

Erec slid over and opened it to meet his grinning friend. Garin stepped in and glanced at him —then immediately obsessed over fixing Erec's collar, which apparently was important. Were it not for seeing Boldwick and Garin for the first time in weeks; today might've been one of the worst days of his life.

"Well! I think that's fine enough. Good to see you! Honestly was worried sick; we all were. Even Colin, if you can believe it. He petitioned his father to step in on your behalf," Garin said.

"He asked the Unbroken General to try to get me free from the Church?" Erec rubbed the back of his head. "The, uh, General didn't, right?"

Despite the Duke making him spy on his son and promise to befriend him, the Duke hadn't followed through with any demands. Yet. Erec didn't want to open that doorway any further, let alone actively start supplying information about Colin to his father. Initially, it hadn't seemed that bad. But as he got to know Colin…he felt guilty at the prospect.

"No, he did. As someone famous for slaying a Cataclysm-Level threat, the Royal Family was careful to listen. Thanks to him, they pushed for your immediate freedom. Much of the pressure in the nobility was rising from his dissatisfaction over the situation and his exerting pressure."

"…That doesn't bode well, does it?"

"Could be. If you aim to ally yourself with his House, they might be a powerful supporter behind you, but it'll have costs to it, obviously." Garin shrugged as if they weren't covering over the sort of high-level politicking that made Erec's heart hammer and head hurt. Wherever this went, it wasn't somewhere he wanted to go. Would that he could isolate himself to the Order—but even Boldwick said this sort of thing was an aspect of being a Knight.

What a fucking joke.

Erec rubbed his eyes. Garin gave him an apologetic smile.

"Hey, don't worry too much about it. You're in a much better position now to pick your path, and it's not likely anyone is out to make you an enemy yet. Not until you're a more known presence in the court. Speaking of which… We're running a bit late. Shall we head down?"

— -❂- — - ☼ - — - ❂ - —

The feast was a thing of excess. By Erec's arrival, the long hall was already overcrowded with nobility. It seemed anyone at the rank of Viscount or higher had received an invitation—along with plenty of invitations thrown to Barons, unlanded nobles, and even merchants. As always, there were also Knights and military men. It'd been quite a long time since the Royal Family put on a festival of this size. This had to be a premier moment for many of these people to mingle and make allies and deals. For the less savvy, the ultimate occasion to celebrate and socialize.

One group was notably missing. It seemed the Royal Family had declined to invite any prominent members of the Church.

The event spanned a vast swath of the palace, including the gardens and grounds outside. In theory, a person could drift about and explore, find a nice quiet corner to hold a private conversation if it suited them. It didn't lack for things to do, however. Later after the meal would be contests, dancing, and music. With the day after hosting some events.

Yet for Erec, it was hell.

More of hell than the fire Fury lit in him. It was constant war from the moment he walked into the main chamber with Garin. A barrage of nobles assaulted him by forcing their introductions on him. They played pretend as they dug into his history, hobbies, and time in the Academy. But they didn't care at all about the answers. Occasionally one or two of them would throw in an offhanded remark about his mother.

Nothing unintentional. Unless it was to test him or unless they thought he'd slighted them during the conversation. Mixed signals and anxiety made him constantly second-guess his responses.

It wasn't all bad. There was a Countess he met who promised to exchange letters, a Baron who promised him an evening of playing a strategy game he'd been workshopping that seemed genuinely interesting—but those real moments of connections were few and far between in this environment.

Some sought an ally, but they weren't as bad as those trying to marry him off to their daughters or the blatant attempts to woo him.

Killing the Stag seemed to bring attention out of the woodwork; being a hero had a price.

After an hour, he wanted to hide in the garden. Two hours in, Garin kept fighting to stop him from drinking the pain away. Past three…it blurred together.

At least the meal was lovely.

The dancing afterward, not so much. He fought to avoid getting on the floor and had a hell of a time accomplishing that.

But as he drove closer to the main event, he avoided any significant slights. From what he could pick up on, at least, he'd bumbled his way to safety and was soon making his way to the throne room with a larger number of spectators. Upon the throne sat the King, ancient upon his place of power.

His long gray hair curled, his deep blue eyes filled with a dull life as he watched his court fill. Near the throne, Boldwick watched with crossed arms—he'd run into his mentor a few times during the socializing, but each time the man was swept away by the hordes of nobles flooding him for attention.

Erec focused on his mentor rather than the King upon his throne.

It was odd. How small the man looked. Erec was sure he'd had the training to make him a heavy threat in combat. But when he pictured the Goddess upon Her silver throne, he found this picture… lacking in comparison. Without that pure sense of overwhelming power, he didn't seem to fit the part of what Erec thought a ruler should be. Even if, by all accounts, he was a very wise and balanced man.

"Approach." His voice rang out through the hall, signaling the start of the reward ceremony.

Erec hesitated, but Garin gave him a slight push. With hundreds of eyes on him, Erec pressed forward, walking down the line of carpet before the throne and taking a knee as he hit the end. His eyes sank to the King's feet, as befitting his station as both a Knight Initiate and the second son of an unlanded House.

*Just get through this. Accept whatever they give you, and you'll be fine.*

Erec repeated the instructions to himself like it were a prayer. The same thought got him through the tedious night so far; it'd be enough for now.

"Erec of House Audentia, the second son of Lac Audentia, all are aware of why we are here today. For the Kingdom's safety, we authorized a hunt for the White Stag, an intelligent monster that threatened to destroy our way of life." The King's voice was like a river, smooth and full of depth. As he launched into his speech, Erec couldn't help but look at the man—he left his throne, standing with an animated posture and full of vitality that he had lacked mere moments ago. "We had determined it to be a significant threat over its clear goal and ability to open Rifts—little did we know it could also control our people. Were it a threat not addressed, Goddess above forgive us for what may have occurred."

The crowd was silent as they lingered over the implication. Some of these nobles hadn't experienced the reality of being out in the wasteland. They didn't know the true horror of a monster puppeteering other humans.

"With the passing of this threat, we return to a period of safety. Let it never be forgotten the price we paid and that we must continue to pay to keep this harmony. It is my pleasure as a ruler to issue a reward for such an accomplishment—Erec of House Audentia, you who slew the White Stag, I levy upon you the name of the title of a new House and the lands befitting it. From this day forward, you shall be known as Count Erec of House Audax."

Erec's hands shook. A Count—wait—a Count?!

"Obviously, it would be difficult to manage an estate, let alone the people you would be responsible for as steward of the land. I shall bestow in the seventh cavern—so, this title shall be accompanied by a staff paid for by the crown's funds until such a day as you can properly take the reins." The King waved away the details as if bored by the prospect before gliding away from his throne. He proffered his hand to Erec, his palm open to grasp. "Erec of House Audax, will you accept this reward as fair compensation for your service to the Kingdom?"

Numb, Erec accepted his hand, letting the King pull him to his feet. "I humbly accept this reward," he said, the practiced words tumbling out his mouth. They told him to take what the Kingdom gave—he hadn't considered what it actually entailed. He figured he'd become a landed lord, which was what many Knights sought, perhaps a Barony if he was fortunate. Not to jump both that title and the title of a Viscounty. It was mind-blowing.

In his act of slaying the White Stag, he'd left the shadow of his brother for good and left the stain of his previous family behind. But now he had an estate he had no idea how to consider, and he was above Garin in the Kingdom's hierarchy.

Being a Knight meant the chance at earning such honors, but for him to already receive such a thing as an Initiate…

The King leaned in, as the cheering from the nobles erupted. Too quiet for anyone else to hear. "Truly, young one, you have my gratitude. Yet, I cannot help but worry when I look upon you. It is far too easy to end up chasing danger and finding death in this world, and though you may feel you've only begun your tale, this achievement would be the crowning one for many lives. I see it in your eyes. You haven't found what will let you settle down and live a contented life. I pray you do, for peace is more satisfying than war." With that, the King retreated.

Leaving a confused Erec to the pack of rabid nobility who now saw a young man appointed to the rank of Count who had no idea what the hell to do with it.

# CHAPTER 92
# BRAVE AND
# COURTEOUS

*…before the court was disbanded, the King told his knights that he wished to
hunt the White Stag…*

*And so the affair is arranged for the next morning at daybreak. The morrow,
as soon as it is day, the King gets up and dresses, and dons a short jacket for
his forest ride. He commands the knights to be aroused and the horses to be
made ready. Already they are ahorse, and off they go, with bows and arrows.
After them the Queen mounts her horse, taking a damsel with her. A maid
she was, the daughter of a king, and she rode a white palfrey. After them
there swiftly followed a knight, named Erec, who belonged to the Round
Table, and had great fame at the court.*

*Of all the knights that ever were there, never one received such praise; and he
was so fair that nowhere in the world need one seek a fairer knight than he.*

- *Chrétien de Troyes,* Erec et Enide *(1170, 2nd Era)*

A man named Lionel in a white silk shirt led Erec along the tour
of his own estate. It wasn't what he'd expected at all; none
of this had been. When the King rewarded him with the
title of a Count and his own House…House Audax…it'd been a spiral
of confusion since.

Seeing it all in person made it more real. He couldn't deny his
manor's existence, the seventh cavern, or the people that lived there.

And it was up to him to preside over them, even if it would be indirectly, since being a Knight Initiate demanded all of his time.

Luckily, he wasn't alone in investigating this new life.

Both Garin and Bedwyr tagged along.

The two of them and Lionel paused and looked back at Erec, as he'd stopped following.

His jaw dropped as he stared up at the manor. He'd seen it from a distance, but this close—the thing was almost the size of a castle, though much of its interior was hidden, as it'd been carved out of the cavern side. Nearly a hundred lights shone from its windows, casting their light into the empty stone yard.

This cavern didn't have an artificial sun; therefore, like most of the city below, there were no wildlife or plants besides rats and cats.

This place was his new home.

Proudly decorating the front was a large banner—his House symbol, chosen by the King. It was relatively simple, the head of a White Stag backgrounded by the Vortex Industries logo. They'd appropriated that from his Armor, and nobody had been keen to ask why he'd taken on an old-world logo if they'd by chance recognized it. But now it was his.

[Looks like we have a new subsidiary. Exciting! Way to go, Buckeroo, though it's not typical that Junior Researchers are in charge of acquisitions. Now, for those people in your command…what would you say to opening a research facility?]

"Count Audax?" Lionel asked, bowing politely. "If it would please you, we can head inside. As you made it plain to me, you desire to head back on the surface soon. However, we have much to discuss your lands, along with your tour of the manor itself—I know, I'll do my best to make it quick."

*Count Audax?* The title and name made him shiver as they came from his steward's mouth. Lionel said it so naturally, yet the name stunned Erec. He wasn't sure he'd ever get used to it.

Though the rush on time…was debatable. Boldwick told him to return soon but didn't specify a time limit, only to return as quickly as able. So, Erec *had* intended to hurry this along. After the King told him they'd sort out trusted staff to manage his affairs, he'd assumed it'd be easy to pass along the responsibility.

Now, after seeing all the faces of the curious common folk who'd gathered to get a look at him, though not all of the thousand or so that lived in this cavern, he'd changed his perspective. "I… There's no need to hurry, Lionel, after all. Please, tell me everything I should know. If that means we stay here a couple of days, that's fine."

It was better to understand it all ahead of time. Like it or not, he was now responsible for these people.

"Nice!" Garin laughed. "Some time off of classes."

"It's awfully big…" Bedwyr mumbled, head tucked down as he looked around the place.

Erec had brought his brother along because this would be his and their father's home too. Without land, they'd been living off Garin's father's good graces. With him owning land, there was no reason Lac couldn't retire here, nor why Bedwyr wouldn't be able to stay here. Though their father maintained his desire to work. He claimed he'd repay the Audentia family debt and refused to ask Erec for help. He wasn't even sure what his financial situation was—his stipend from the Academy had been going toward paying off his Armor. But now that might be covered by his estate.

"No kidding, bigger than our place. I bet you could host a nice feast—ooh, I bet there's even a ballroom here," Garin said.

"Indeed, it is a well-decorated chamber, maple wood floor grown in the bio-caverns. The previous estate holder took great joy in hosting events." Lionel answered smoothly, always eager to provide whatever information he could. "Normally, I'd recommend a feast as the new lord—it's wise to invite the bigger players in your land to get to know them. It is understandable to everyone that you cannot, but most are eager to meet a hero such as yourself."

"Right… Meeting a hero." Erec cleared his throat. There was that title. He might be acting more responsible, but he was fine with shying away from hosting a feast. He couldn't be perfect.

"Don't worry, the Academy offers breaks—I'll let my father know that Erec needs to throw a proper social gathering, and he'll help coordinate some good contacts with nobility to attend as well." Garin gave Erec a wink, despite speaking to Lionel. "Between us, we'll sort it out."

If it were up to Erec, he'd slowly meet them one by one. It was probably better that Garin forced his hand, even if he hated the idea.

So, he hung his head and shut up. With that, Lionel escorted them into the manor.

— -☣- — - ☼ - — - ☣ - —

The manor was luxurious and clean, which was unsurprising since a full-time staff was maintaining it. Erec introduced himself to each of them and quickly picked up on the fact that there was a tangible and weird eagerness to meet their new Lord, the hero who'd slain the Stag. Lionel apologized on their behalf.

After that was the tour. The manor was massive, with two wings and dedicated guest rooms; nowhere near the multiple-layer spanning fortress of the palace, but nothing to scoff at. There was an obscene amount of space for a single man to live in and call home.

He eased his guilt with the knowledge that his father would live here. And he'd host his brother, too, not to mention the full-time staff and their families who called it home.

Yeah, still excessive for someone who'd prefer to wander around a wasteland in their Armor. But that was the nature of nobility. Excess.

Lionel ran him through the estate's investments and current income through taxes. All the boring nitty-gritty details made Erec's head spin, and after a five-hour meeting, it still wasn't done. More information Lionel had to dig up for the next day.

He did get the chance to provide input on what he'd like to do in the future—at the direction of VAL, and being a bit cooked out of his mind with all of the overwhelming numbers and associations. VAL cut through the noise and directed him to make a modest proposal to acquire land within the cavern for a research facility.

Lionel was stunned by the request but promised to find something satisfactory.

Honestly, Erec didn't know what it would lead to, but VAL was so enthusiastic that he couldn't help but go along with the idea.

After his meeting, he shared a fine meal and insisted the staff join him, then went off toward his personal workshop—in the depths of the manor.

The King ordered for his Armor to be stashed there; it was part of why it was so important to come and visit his new lands right away. Though, with what he understood about that man, the King probably thought it'd do more to rope Erec into his new role than if he'd left everything up to the young Knight.

So it was that Erec reunited with his Armor—the Vallum Model, now painted with his new crest and restored after all the battlefield damage. It shone like new. But if one looked closely, one could see the patches and battle scars decorating the plate that hadn't been replaced.

Erec ran a hand over the polished steel, feeling the imperfections and scratches.

To think, not too long ago, he'd desperately been rigging up a Markos II and praying it could get him to the Academy. Now, he'd reached a higher peak than he'd ever dreamed.

Bedwyr strode through the door, and Erec turned immediately. Since seeing Erec again, his brother had looked out of his element, showing a timid side that he'd scarcely imagined him capable of. He seemed so…unsure.

"Congratulations…" Bedwyr said, his eyes roaming over the new symbol on the Armor. "…You earned all of this. I'm proud of you."

Erec hesitated. The voice coming from his brother wasn't exactly pride. No, it was strange, and Bedwyr was trying to hide it, but it was a concern. Fear too. "You're worried about me."

"Erec—I'm not used to this. If I'd had it my way, you wouldn't have joined the Knights at all, would've lived a quiet life with Dad, and I'd—well, I pictured myself being the one to earn us a house to live in, to clear our name. Now… You've made your own. You've achieved something that is greater than anything I'd hoped for myself. But I'm concerned about the cost to get here," Bedwyr said.

"What? Is this not enough? I gave my all and did it the only way I could." Erec felt that old insecurity slipping in. Was his brother suggesting that he could've done better? He'd bled and suffered so much, yet it hadn't been enough to impress him. What did he have to do?

"Don't get upset. I am proud of you. I'm scared, though. You were lifeless in my arms, dead to the world after that fight. Garin told me that wasn't the first time you pushed yourself that far. You did it the only way you could, but that way makes me afraid. But without you… Who knows how many more would have died—what it would've taken to kill that Stag." Bedwyr sighed. "…And maybe I'm a little jealous that I've got to chase after you. How can I compare to a hero?"

Erec felt a range of emotions at those words, from a knee-jerk reaction to protest his worries to bemusement at the idea of Bedwyr being jealous.

In the end, all those reactions were useless, save one.

"Let's get out of here; my Armor is fine. How about we go to the study and ransack it, see if there are any good old-world stories? We can…catch up. Maybe talk about how things are with you and Gwen —all that. It'd be nice if we took some time to talk about stuff. It's been years," Erec said, his voice breaking a little bit.

Bedwyr gave him a relieved smile and nodded.

Erec followed him out the room—and took one last look at his Armor racked up. Soon, it'd be put to good use again. But for now, it could afford to rest for a bit longer. The light flicked off as he left to spend time with his brother.

**Knights Apocalyptica will continue in Book Two!**

# THANK YOU FOR READING KNIGHTS APOCALYPTICA

We hope you enjoyed it as much as we enjoyed bringing it to you. We just wanted to take a moment to encourage you to review the book. Follow this link: **Knights Apocalyptica** to be directed to the book's Amazon product page to leave your review.

Every review helps further the author's reach and, ultimately, helps them continue writing fantastic books for us all to enjoy.

**Also in series:**
**Knights Apocalyptica**
**Knights Apocalyptica 2**

Check out the entire series here! (Tap or scan)

Want to discuss our books with other readers and even the authors? Join our Discord server today and be a part of the Aethon community.

Facebook | Instagram | Twitter | Website

You can also join our non-spam mailing list by visiting www.subscribepage.com/AethonReadersGroup and never miss out on future releases. You'll also receive three full books completely Free as our thanks to you.

**Looking for more great books?**

**Ezekiel died on Earth only to be resurrected in the body of a Lich.** Well, now he'd done it. He was only playing the villain to blow off steam, now he was stuck in the body of one. Trapped in a hostile world, Zeke must flee his former guild. The problem is, he can only flee into a holy kingdom ruled by the Church of Olattee. Out of the frying pan and into the fire. Only his power is gone, and he must start over. Well... Mostly anyway. He is still a lich after all and he still has his weapon, Mercy, which is more powerful than even he knows. The real question is, is he now a villain or not? And will he survive long enough to find out? **Don't miss the next action-packed LitRPG / GameLit series by Levi Werner, the bestselling author behind** *World of Magic.* **It's perfect for fans of** *Sylver Seeker,* *Book of the Dead,* **and** *The Ritualist.*

## Get Redemption's Cost now!

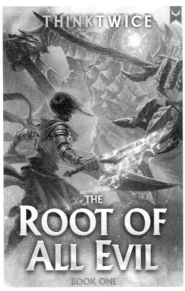

**On Earth, he was a titan of industry. Now, he is prey.** In his past life, Dollar was an unparalleled mind forged by the flames of tribulation. He'd built his wealth and influence from nothing and never looked back. But after dying and reincarnating into the world of Ioa, he is thrust into poverty and trapped in a forest of flames with nothing but a decrepit wooden hut to protect him. With family out to kill him, an army of monsters surrounding him, and omnipotent gods sent to assassinate him, Dollar finds that in this new world, success is defined by adversity. He's climbed his way up from rock bottom once, and he refuses to stay there again. Knowing he will need his wits and more to survive, he learns the art of rune crafting and gains access to a System. From there, he'll begin his ascent. With the power to craft infinite effects and mold existence itself, nothing will stand in his way. With the entire world stacked against him, Dollar has them right where he wants them... **Dont miss the next action-packed, Reincarnation LitRPG series from ThinkTwice, the bestselling author of *Mark of the Crijik*. Join an unexpected protagonist in the fight for his life as he progresses in power, magical ability, and learns what is really important in life.**

## Get The Root of All Evil now!

*A slice-of-life progression fantasy all about friendship, family, and farming!* Matt Miller wasn't special. He was just a regular guy with a regular life—a one bedroom apartment, a couple of pairs of slacks, and a dead-end job. But when his estranged grandfather died, he left Matt with an unexpected inheritance: a magic ring… and a farm located on another world. Now, Matt's stuck with a rundown farmhouse, fields choked with weeds, and no way to get back home. He only has one option—to roll up his sleeves and complete the quest prompt he's been given: *Restore the Farm.* Luckily, he has a (mostly) merry band of sprites to help him along the way. But this new land has secrets, and more than a few hidden dangers. The Harvest Goddess has been turned into stone, and the balance of magic is all out of whack. If Matt can't figure out a way to bring his grandfather's property back to life, then Corruption will continue to spread and consume the farm, the forest, and the sleepy town of Sagewood itself. **Don't miss the start of this mostly cozy isekai Progression Fantasy Series. It's perfect fans of** *Beware of Chicken, Sacred Cat Island,* **and** *Oh, Great! I was Reincarnated as a Farmer,* **as well as** *games* **like games** *Stardew Valley* **and** *Harvest Moon.*

## Get Sagewood Now!

For all our LitRPG books, visit our website.

Made in United States
Orlando, FL
14 December 2024